THE
VALLEY
OF
DECISION

BOOKS BY MARCIA DAVENPORT

———

THE VALLEY OF DECISION

OF LENA GEYER

MOZART

CHARLES SCRIBNER'S SONS

THE
VALLEY
OF
DECISION

by

MARCIA DAVENPORT

New York

CHARLES SCRIBNER'S SONS

1945

To MR R. W.

If, as mine is, thy life a slumber be,
Seeme, when thou read'st these lines, to dreame of me,
Never did Morpheus nor his brother weare
Shapes so like those Shapes, whom they would appeare,
As this my letter is like me, for it
Hath my name, words, hand, feet, heart, minde, and wit;
It is my deed of gift of mee to thee,
It is my Will, my selfe the Legacie.
So thy retyrings I love, yea envie,
Bred in thee by a wife melancholy,
That I rejoyce, that unto where thou art,
Though I stay here, I can thus send my heart. . . .

                                    JOHN DONNE, 1633

Proclaim ye this among the nations; prepare war; stir up the mighty men; let all the men of war draw near; let them come up. Beat your plowshares into swords and your pruning-hooks into spears: let the weak say, I am strong. Haste ye, and come, all ye nations round about, and gather yourselves together. . . .

Multitudes, multitudes in the valley of decision! for the day of Jehovah is near in the valley of decision.

JOEL, iii. 9, 10, 11, 14

CHAPTER I

[*1873*]

AT NINE O'CLOCK on the morning of September nineteenth, in the year 1873, a young girl walked slowly up Western Avenue, in Allegheny City, across the river from Pittsburgh. The street lay west of the district to which old residents referred by its earlier name of the Second Bank. Dressed plainly in gray cloth, the girl carried in one hand a small canvas valise, and in the other a slip of white paper. She looked carefully at the house number on each gatepost. The wide street had been cut through elevated land. On either side the mansions stood far back and raised above the pavement, each approached by a carefully tended path ending in a short flight of steps descending the grassy embankment to the street. Large oak and elm trees shaded the handsome avenue and the wide lawns which surrounded the houses. The air was hazy with smoke and with the powdery dust from falling leaves, but the sun shone warmly; summer was barely past.

The girl paused at a pair of wrought-iron gateposts.

"This wud be it," she said aloud.

She looked up the gravel path to the wide front steps of the brick house. That was not the entrance she should use. A man in overalls was raking up leaves from the lawn and carefully picking them out of the round flower-beds planted with stiff cannas and scarlet sage. On either side of the path, near the house, there was an ornamental iron urn on a filigree pedestal, filled with striped and mottled leaves and trailing English ivy. Mary Rafferty still hesitated at the gate. Presently the man picked up his filled wheelbarrow and trundled it away to the side driveway, which Mary had not noticed until now. That must be where she should go. The driveway turned in from the avenue and ran past the side of the house to a stable far back in the yard. Mary stepped along this gravel drive, followed it round to the right, and passed inside a service yard, where she found the kitchen door. She pulled the wrought-iron knob, and listened, holding her breath while a bell jangled loudly inside. The door was opened by a stout, gray-haired woman in a striped gray calico dress and a large checked apron. Her hair was skewered to the top of her head with thick metal pins.

"Good mornin'," said Mary timidly. "Wud this be Mrs. Scott's house?"

"It wud," the cook replied, putting her heavy hands on her hips and eyeing Mary critically, "and ye wud be the new 'tweenmaid, wud ye not?"

Mary nodded, swallowing.

"Come in," said the cook, "and set yer grip on the landin' there. Mrs. Scott will be wantin' to see ye at once."

She shut the door behind Mary and led the way through the stone passage into the kitchen. This was a basement room, built beneath the house on land which sloped away to form, far at the back of the property, one

3

of the river-bound precipices indigenous to Pittsburgh. Mary's eyes travelled eagerly about the large room, resting with awe on a towering copper boiler gleaming red, and resplendent in an intricacy of pipes. This adjoined the great coal range, recessed in the chimney-piece; but on its other side there was another range, the like of which Mary had never seen before. This had ovens stilted up on top of it, and a surface made of open ironwork, and a row of small handles across its front. A gas range! Mary gaped at it. And she looked wonderingly at the gray iron sink with its longnecked faucets for both hot and cold water.

"Wait here, if ye please," said the cook, and crossing the room she lifted from a hook on the wall an object which looked like a short piece of garden hose and to Mary's astonishment began to shout into it.

"Delia!" she cried. "Delia! Will ye be tellin' the Madam the new girl is here? Shud she come up?"

Mary heard a rattle far away in the garden hose, then Cook turned to her and said, "Mrs. Scott will see ye in the back parlor. Ye go up here and Delia'll meet ye at the top o' the stair. Delia's the waitress."

Mary's heart beat hard as she climbed the dark back stairway to the pantry. She was not quite sixteen. Today she was wearing her first long skirt, of stiff gray alpaca, which she lifted awkwardly over the insteps of her buttoned boots, and dragged in a bunch behind her up the steps. She had not yet learned to convert skilfully her long red braids into the high twist on top of her head. She had laughed at herself, a strong girl, because her arms grew tired before her hair was done. But she did not feel like laughing now. She felt frightened. Her stiff new corsets dug into her sides. Her throat throbbed with fright and suspense. If she pleased Mrs. Scott, and stayed in this house, tonight would be the first that she had ever spent away from her father's roof.

Delia met her in the pantry, a pleasant-faced Irish girl dressed in a striped morning uniform of blue and white calico with a high, starched collar, a white apron, and a ruffled cap. She smiled encouragingly when she saw Mary's white face.

"Don't take on, dear," she whispered. "She's a nice lady, far nicer than most. Ye've only to mind what she tells ye. She's in here."

Delia opened a door and paused respectfully. "The new maid to see you, Ma'm."

Clarissa Scott was watering her plants in the bay window. Against the light her figure was tall and solid. Unable to see her face, Mary advanced timidly.

Mrs. Scott put down her watering-can and turned. "Come here," she said. She seated herself in a rocking-chair, and indicated that Mary was to stand before her. Mary folded her hands in their gray cotton gloves, and stood quietly while her employer scrutinized her. Her pulse pounded, and she hoped Mrs. Scott could not see that she was trembling.

But, "you must not be frightened, Mary," was what she was told. "You have never been away from home, have you?"

"No, Ma'm."

Mary raised her eyes and let them meet Clarissa Scott's calm blue ones.

She looked at her mistress's wide brow, as smooth as her own, with the ash-blonde hair drawn back from it revealing strength and gentleness in the youthful face. Mrs. Scott was smiling a little, ready to put the timid girl at her ease. She was struck by the child's eyes, dark gray, intense, and singularly bright, set deep beneath the high forehead, so deep that the nose, at its bridge, was unusually thin and fine. Its aquiline modelling was a clear cameo line. The girl's mouth was wide, with its thin lips—colorless just now from apprehension—pressed tight together. A mass of pale red hair sprang strongly from her white forehead, crisp and curly. The high collar of her gray dress was edged with a freshly laundered white cambric fold, which followed the line of her throat, sloping downward beneath her ears to a point where it was fastened with an onyx brooch in the shape of a cross. A plain black straw bonnet trimmed with gray ribbon was tied over the mass of shining hair, and fixed under the pointed chin with a neat bow.

Clarissa Scott realized suddenly that by her scrutiny she was creating anxiety which she had wished to avoid. She began to speak quietly.

"Now, Mary," she said. "I know that you have not had much experience at this sort of work. But you know how to clean, of course?"

"Yes, Ma'm." The thin, pale lips trembled.

"And make beds. Naturally I will show you exactly how I wish things to be done. Can you sew and iron?"

"Yes, Ma'm. The nuns taught me sewin'."

"Good. Now these will be your duties. You are to be chambermaid, taking care of all the bedrooms. You are to help me and Miss Elizabeth to dress, and you are to press our dresses and keep our wardrobes in order. Also you are to help Delia in the pantry with the dishes, and help her serve at table when we have guests. Do you think you can learn to do all that properly, if Delia and I teach you?"

"I'll try, Ma'm."

"Good. Now Delia will show you to your room. You and Delia share a room. Of course—" she stopped. It might be a mistake to think so, but an admonition to keep her own room neat and clean would not be needed by this girl. "Of course I have uniforms for you. Delia will give you what we have on hand and if they do not fit, you can alter them. Blue and white striped for morning and black for afternoon. Put on one of the dresses now, and then come downstairs and Delia will go through the bedrooms with you. Oh—and just a moment, Mary. Did Miss Peterson explain about the wages to you? And your days off?"

"Yes, Ma'm."

"Seven dollars a week; and every other Sunday off. You may leave as soon as the dinner dishes are done. You are Catholic, are you not, Mary?"

"Yes, Ma'm."

"You will have time off to go to church on Sunday mornings."

In later years Mary's memory of that first day in the Scott home was to remain clear in each minute detail. She remembered her pleasure, on being taken up to the third floor, at the large square room which she was to share with Delia. There were four windows, on two sides of the room, with freshly starched curtains. There was a flowered carpet on the floor, paper with bunches of pale blue roses and pink lilacs on the walls; the woodwork had a light varnish, easy to keep clean; and the furniture was ample—two large mahogany bureaus (displaced from family bedrooms downstairs by the massive marble-topped walnut that had come into fashion), a wardrobe, a centre table with a coal-oil student lamp on it and a chair on either side. At opposite ends of the room were two narrow iron beds, and near each a washstand fitted with a white china bowl and ewer. Mary had never had so much space and privacy before.

She stood in the middle of this pleasant room, staring at the narrow white bed which was to be hers, and at the clean starched dress laid out on it, and began slowly to untie her bonnet. Her fingers fumbled a little with the bonnet-strings; her hands were still trembling. Dear God, she said silently to herself, dear God, it ain't possible. It ain't true I'm really here. It must be three whole years now that she had been dreaming and planning and longing for this moment. Here in this spotless, quiet room she stood and thought with deliberate finality, as if for the last time, about the cramped and gloomy place that had been her home. She thought about the dirt, the greasy, cindery soot, the miasmic foggy pall that hung over the waterside, the clangor of the freight and ore cars that roared and screeched a stone's throw from the door. She thought about the endless, hopeless battle with dirt and squalor, compared with which the work in this house would be sheer delight.

She unpacked her few belongings and put them away in the bureau drawers—her underwear, made out of remnants bought with hoarded pennies, her three pairs of black woven stockings, her six plain handkerchiefs, her thin flannel nightgowns with tight-cuffed long sleeves and high necks, which she had made under the supervision of the nuns at the parochial school. These simple things were the garments of the world that she had left behind—her crippled father, her brother James, her sisters Kate and Bridget. Kate was old enough now to keep house for the others. Mary loved them all very much, and she would never forsake them. And yet, even as a small child, she had been a stranger to the Flat. She had never accepted as part of her life the ramshackle hovels, the barren cinder-crusted ground, the clotheslines flapping with stained, darned underdrawers and workshirts. Sometimes when she heard her own voice speaking the crude brogue of her parents she knew that there was a different way to speak. And she was not content.

She had no knowledge of the imagined world beyond the bounds of the Flat, only an instinct that it existed. To her it was as if the Scott family clothed this instinct in flesh and blood. She felt that men like Mr. Scott were strong and reliable, the creators of security and permanence. Ladies like Mrs. Scott were lovely and gentle and serene. Such men and women together with their children, enclosed in the framework of their quiet, beautifully ordered homes, personified everything desirable and admirable, everything for which this child had blindly hungered.

Though she was awed by the size and by what she thought the grandeur of the Scott house, and though she was confused by some of the unfamiliar intricacies of its routine, she was too happy to remain frightened for very long. And she was too excited to feel tired, in spite of following Delia about from morning until night, learning a hundred things she had never known before. She was so busy that first day that there was hardly time to ask questions about the members of the family whom she had not yet seen. She knew that there were five children. Delia assured her they would all be at dinner, all except the nine-year-old twins who were too young, and who still had nursery meals with their governess.

But after supper in the kitchen, with Joel the gardener and McCready the coachman joining Cook and the girls for thick barley broth, oat cakes, cottage cheese, scones with butter and jam, and quantities of strong green tea, Delia and Mary went up to set the table for dinner. There were to be guests tonight. Mary found herself burning with impatient curiosity for the moment when she would see all the Scotts together. Setting the table for their dinner was, she thought, a very intimate introduction to them.

While the girls were at work in the dark, panelled dining-room, Mary marvelling at the rich, heavy linen, the massive silver, the Waterford tumblers heavy as rocks, they heard the front door open and close with an authoritative thud. Delia glanced at the pantry clock.

"That's the master," she said, a little breathless. Though she had worked here for nearly seven years, she had never outgrown the sensation of awe, amounting almost to a fleeting fear, which William Scott's presence roused in servants and subordinates. The house, once he had entered, was a different place. One was on one's mettle.

"You go, Mary," Delia said quickly. "Ye'd like to see him. Take his hat and stick and hang 'em up."

Mary's feet lagged in a momentary panic as she opened the hall door. Delia gave her a kindly shove. "Go on. He's expectin' me."

"Good evening, Delia," said a heavy bass voice. A bearded giant was towering over Mary's head, handing her a square-crowned derby hat and a knotty walking-stick with a gold head.

"Gud—gud evenin', sor." Her hands trembled as she took the hat and stick. William Scott looked down at her. He seemed the tallest and heaviest man she had ever seen. A gold watch-chain as thick as her finger crossed his high-buttoned braided black vest. Mary moistened her dry lips and looked up at him timidly. There was a scowl on his forehead. He looked stern, and troubled as well. Could he be annoyed because Delia had not been there to meet him? There was no telling; he was halfway upstairs already, his steps heavily measured. Mary went back to the pantry and whispered, "Wud he be cross, do ye think, Delia? He's got a look on him!"

"He's been lookin' that way for a week or more. He don't notice us the while we do the work proper. Here, fix them salt-cellars next."

William Scott was entering his dressing-room upstairs, abstracted and frowning, and barely noticing his wife's greeting from the bedroom doorway. When she questioned him he answered only, "My dear, Jay Cooke and Company were suspended from the New York Stock Exchange today; this will have extremely serious consequences."

"Is it likely to be—to—?"

"To affect us? Very much so, Clarissa." He was putting his massive gold studs into a clean lawn shirt, and his wife noticed his fumbling impatience. She had seldom seen him unnerved.

"Give it to me," she said, taking the shirt. "I wonder, William—will we feel it immediately?"

He smiled faintly. "Not this evening, at any rate. But you had better be prepared for a good deal of bad news, Clarissa."

"What do you mean?"

"The signs point," he said, "to a general panic. Banks are closing at the rate of two and three a day. Business has stopped dead. Security markets are chaotic. It will mean shutting down the mill."

"*William!* You can't mean that!"

"What else? I can't make rails if the roads are bankrupt. I expect Gaylord is going to give me unwelcome news tonight." William Scott scowled. He was in no mood for guests. "We may be a considerable time in the study after dinner. You must entertain the ladies by yourself."

"Yes, William. Goodness, I suppose I wouldn't have done it if I'd known all this, but I engaged a new housemaid today, a little Irish girl. I wonder if that was wise."

"You knew no reason not to engage her," William Scott said. Even the grave worries on his mind did not precede the sense of justice which shaped his whole existence. He was silent while Clarissa finished inserting his shirtstuds. Though she knew it to be hopeless, she thought she might distract his attention from the troubled world that she did not very well understand. She said, still chatting about the new maid, "She's a nice girl, William. Her father worked in the mill years ago, when Father Scott was with us. His name is Rafferty—Pat Rafferty."

"Oh—Rafferty—yes—"

"She has such character. You could almost say beauty," Clarissa said, tying her husband's tie. "She's been keeping house for her father and the younger children ever since the mother died four years ago. Apparently the father cannot work any more. He must have been injured in the war. There—" She gave the tie a pat. "We should go down now. I believe I hear the bell."

"I am ready, Clarissa."

CHAPTER II

[*1873—Continued*]

As the family filed into the dining-room from the parlor, Delia and Mary stood at either end of the table, behind the master's and the mistress's chairs. The girls had set the table for eleven and even Delia did not know who all the occupants would be. Mrs. Scott entered the room on the arm of Mr. Laurence Waterbury Gaylord, of Boston, who was passing through Pittsburgh at the end of a transcontinental tour with his wife and his daughter, Julia, both of whom were here with him this evening. In addition the Richard Kanes were present—the well-known Pittsburgh banker, his wife, and his daughter Louise. They were old family friends, almost as familiar to Delia as the Scotts themselves.

After placing the dowdy but distinguished Mrs. Gaylord at his right, William Scott took his seat in his usual deliberate manner. He sent a commanding glance around the table, bent his head, folded his hands, and asked the blessing in a flat, rather hard voice which twanged its R's slightly and pronounced each word with emphasis. Then he turned to the duty of conversing with his guests while Delia took the cover off the tureen before Mrs. Scott. The girls handed the steaming plates of mock turtle soup as the hostess ladled it out. "Always to the left, Mary," Delia whispered once.

Mary was giving such close and anxious attention to her new work that she hardly dared raise her eyes to look at the people about the table. She had to watch Delia closely for each cue as plates were changed, courses brought in, and the bewildering variety of food, all in handsome silver dishes and platters, came up on the dumbwaiter from the kitchen. But even with all that to think about she could not keep her mind off the Scotts themselves. They were so striking. The stern and bearded master at the head of the table, the gracious mistress at the foot, the startling differences among their three children whom she saw now for the first time. In accordance with family custom, the young people were grouped in the centre of the table with their elders at either end. And all of them provided striking contrasts. Young Miss Gaylord, Mary thought, was what you would call refined, and she spoke with a strange, liquid accent that Mary had never heard before. Louise Kane, on the other hand, a Pittsburgh girl, had no such worldly poise. She was very pretty, with small, soft contours; but she sat nervously forward on the edge of her chair, nibbling her food in quick birdlike pecks and constantly turning her curly brown head. She was watching everybody with a curious sort of intensity, though her round brown eyes were fixed oftenest on her father. She had to lean forward to see him, and when he spoke she followed his words with exaggerated attention.

But Mary was much more interested in the Scotts than in their guests. Their daughter Elizabeth did not compare very favorably with the other two girls. She had sandy hair and rather a narrow face, and during most of dinner she sat with her eyes on her plate in a moody way. But the two Scott sons were enjoying themselves. William junior had a rather arrogant manner. The eldest son of the house, it was his duty to entertain the languid Miss Gaylord, and apparently he found the duty a pleasure. Mary thought he could not hold a candle to Mister Paul. Mister Paul was not talking much, even to Louise Kane, who sat beside him. He was big and hulking; he still kept some of the lumbering traits of boyhood. Delia said he was seventeen. It was plain that he was interested entirely in the conversation of the men, to which he listened intently. He ignored his brother and the fine airs of Julia Gaylord. Mary understood that.

The imperious Mr. Gaylord had been telling Mrs. Scott and Richard

Kane some of his impressions of the West. But he waved his slender hand as if to dismiss that wilderness, so far as civilized travel was concerned.

"I would never recommend such a trip for pleasure," he said. "Since I had to go for other reasons I thought it might be instructive for my daughter to go along. But I am sure she prefers our summer trips abroad."

"I think she was so fortunate to see so much of this country," Clarissa Scott said mildly. "I have always wanted to see the Rocky Mountains and California."

"Oh—magnificent. Quite. The scenery is superb. But—" Gaylord indicated with his eyebrows that no cultivated person could have any other reason for travelling West. Of course his real reason, as his hosts knew, had not been "scenery" at all. He was one of the largest Eastern holders of railroad securities. Since the end of the war eight years before, all American railroads had been in a frenzy of expansion, and large stockholders and directors like Gaylord had found it increasingly important to see their investments at first hand. This would include too a better knowledge of Pittsburgh and its ironmasters, on whom the new construction programs so directly depended.

Mrs. Gaylord was also talking about the Western trip.

"It would have been dreadful," she said, "if it had not been for Mr. Huntington. We spent a week in his private car."

"Most interesting," Julia Gaylord added. "Quite like a palace on wheels."

"But vulgar," Mrs. Gaylord hastened to add. "Those railroad men! Why, do you know, some of them—"

Mary did not hear what Mrs. Gaylord had seen some of them do because she had to help Delia change the plates. And from then on she was too busy to listen to the talk.

At the foot of the table Clarissa Scott knew that Richard Kane on her left was profoundly troubled. His wife Sophia was one of Clarissa's closest friends, and had whispered on her arrival that Richard had been up all last night at the bank and had not left his office all day. He would not have come here this evening if William Scott had not particularly asked him to meet Gaylord. The women were not very clear about the nature of the matters that were worrying their husbands, but they did know that New York had been stunned this week by a wave of bank failures, and that this would have something to do with the business their husbands would discuss after dinner. Clarissa tried now to distract her guests, to draw them into joint conversation. She caused Kane to reminisce about the stockade at Fort Fayette, which his grandfather had commanded through the Indian fights after the Revolution, and which should be interesting, she thought, to a Bostonian whose opinion of a man depended on his family's place in the nation's history.

The young people had heard these stories often before and Mary saw Elizabeth exchange a bored glance with Paul behind Louise's head. But Louise, who knew each detail down to the last feather on the last savage's headdress, was leaning forward listening raptly to her father. Mary stole a curious glance at Mrs. Kane. She wondered whether this family lived entirely as a worshipful audience for its head. But Mrs. Kane was not looking at her husband; she was listening to something Laurence Gaylord had just remarked to her, and she was gazing thoughtfully across the table at Paul.

These people seemed to put so much attention on talking, Mary thought. She had never seen a fine family at dinner. Mealtimes in her experience were a business of seeing that children were washed, plates and cups filled, bread sliced, and the kettle kept hot for the dishwashing afterwards. James and Dad and the neighbors never talked at meals. They applied themselves strictly to feeding and usually did not say a word until, satisfied, they were ready to tilt back from the table and light their pipes. But people like the Scotts and their friends talked all the way through their dinner, seeming hardly to notice what they were eating. Mr. Scott carved the roast, a huge leg of mutton resting in a wreath of parsley, but once that was finished he too seemed to lose interest in the food. Delia shook her head when Mary asked if all such people had no appetites.

"Himself's a big eater, usual," Delia said. "But they're all troubled in their heads tonight. That wan"—she motioned toward Kane with her chin—"he comes here often, but sure I never seen him that black-lookin'. He ain't eatin' at all."

Mary saw that the talk was an effort for Mrs. Scott, and that she was relieved to sit back, after she had served the blanc-mange with raspberry-jam sauce, and Delia had passed the tiered cake plate with choices of Sarah's two masterpieces, Devil's Food and Angel Food. The moment to withdraw had almost come; Mrs. Scott had given the order for the gentlemen's coffee to be taken to Mr. Scott's study, where it would be consumed with the cigars that were never lighted elsewhere in the house. She caught Mrs. Gaylord's eye and was about to rise from the table when Delia came in quickly from the pantry and bent over her shoulder. Clarissa turned to Kane.

"Your coachman is in the pantry and says he has an urgent message for you," she told him quietly. He rose and bowed, apologizing.

His wife blanched as the pantry door swung shut behind him and Mary heard a stifled gasp from Louise and saw her turn suddenly to Paul, with that odd, rapt look in her brown eyes. The boy looked uncomfortable; he too was staring at the pantry door, and his mother was hesitating about leaving the table. But while they sat there, as if in a tableau, Richard Kane hurried back into the dining-room, his lips pressed together. His wife's hand, holding a handkerchief, went to her lips and Louise slid suddenly from her chair and ran to him and clutched his arm with both hands, gazing up at his face. He put his arm around her but did not look down at her. He was speaking to the Scotts.

"I know you will forgive me. William, I must be so rude as to take you from your guests for a moment. Unfortunately, I am called away on a most urgent matter."

All rose from the table and moved in a group to the drawing-room, while Kane and Scott disappeared into the small study at the end of the hall. They were not long. Before Mrs. Gaylord and Mrs. Kane were settled in tufted satin chairs, the two men returned, Scott now as grim as his friend. Mrs. Kane rose and went to her husband. "Richard," she murmured.

"Daddy," they heard, in a whimper from Louise. Her mother tried to restrain her but the child would not stay away from Kane. She was clinging to his arm again as she had done in the dining-room.

"I must go down to the bank at once," he said to Clarissa. His fingers were opening and closing on his daughter's shoulder. Mary and Delia were shutting the dining-room doors across the hall. "Saints!" Delia whispered, staring. "Somethin' awful's happened, sure."

Clarissa Scott sensed that Kane was uncomfortable with the young people present. She turned to Elizabeth and asked her to take Miss Gaylord and the others to the upstairs sitting-room. They filed out, Clarissa indicating to Louise that she should go with them. But Louise shook her head violently, clinging to her father's arm, her eyes round with fear. Her curls bobbed. Kane said, "Thank you, Clarissa, but I am going to leave Louise and Sophia at home on my way to the bank." He walked to the door with Louise, his wife following in a dazed way. He turned in the doorway and said stiffly, "I regret most deeply that we have not given you a better welcome in Pittsburgh, Mr. Gaylord, but I have asked my old friend William Scott to explain and apologize for me. Good night." He bowed and escorted his family quickly from the room.

There was a silence. Gaylord cleared his throat. Scott stood by the hearth, his hands clenched behind his massive back. The two women waited uneasily.

Presently William Scott raised his head.

"This is a very bad thing," he said slowly. Gaylord and the two women did not speak. They were waiting for him to tell them whatever he could. He was a taciturn man and it was difficult for him to look up and say, "I am afraid Richard's bank will not open tomorrow."

A low gasp circled the room. Clarissa's eyes filled with tears. Mrs. Gaylord looked at her husband. Gaylord drew himself up and pulled nervously at his sideburns. William Scott stood with his legs apart, his head bent, his heavy hands clenched behind his back.

"Can nothing be done?" Gaylord asked after a long silence.

Scott shook his head. "They have had the entire force working for the past forty-eight hours. Richard would not have been here tonight, except that I especially asked him to come to meet you. It is quite hopeless. They would be unable to meet their withdrawals tomorrow morning. Actually they were unable after noon today, but they were helped by other banks. Richard believed they might weather it."

"And now?"

"The Cooke failure this afternoon."

Both men had forgotten the presence of the women.

"How badly is he involved personally?"

"Oh, entirely. He has already given over every penny of his own and his family's to meeting the bank's obligations. That is all swept away already. I have never seen a man more unnerved."

"Poor Sophia," Clarissa Scott choked.

There was another long, trying silence. Gaylord broke it.

"That was your bank, of course, Mr. Scott."

"One of them. We had a cash account there, rather small."

"How extraordinarily fortunate!"

"It is, I feel almost ashamed to say so. It was a providential judgment that I decided not to undertake any new financing with them six months ago. I was considering the installation of a Bessemer converter at that time."

"You have not done that yet, I gather—"

Scott looked up. "Not for the time being. Installing a Bessemer is such a big undertaking that I decided to wait and see how some of my competitors did with theirs. Carnegie and McCandless are building one now out at Braddock's Field."

Gaylord raised his eyebrows. "Rather a bad time to be branching out."

"I'm not so sure. If they weather this panic and begin producing Bessemer rails on the scale they'd planned, I won't try to compete with them at all. I shall stop making rails altogether."

Gaylord was surprised. From what he knew of William Scott it was not like him to concede defeat in any kind of competition. More probably Scott had some alternative of his own. He nodded when Gaylord suggested this.

"I could not compete with the steel rail production proposed for this Edgar Thomson works," he said slowly. But he added, "They cannot compete with me if I concentrate on special alloys for tools and farm machinery, that kind of thing. Nobody," he said slowly, "is opening up that field much."

Gaylord found himself unexpectedly interested. He had thought of the Scott Iron Works solely as a producer of rails. That was why he was here tonight. If Scott was enterprising enough to look about for a whole new field, uncrowded, unexplored, he was worth some serious attention. Nevertheless Gaylord sought to appear casual. "To what extent," he asked, "would you feel like pushing such an idea in the present situation?"

William Scott looked at the floor. He knew he was talking more than he meant to, and more than was his habit. But the shock of Kane's catastrophe had unnerved him, too. There was no action he could take, and deprived of his normal outlet of prompt action he permitted himself the unusual recourse of talk.

"I'm not going to do any experimenting or expanding now," he said. "If things get bad enough I may even shut down. Until that happens I'll keep right on making pig iron." He glanced away, with the remote thoughtful look in his cold gray eyes that memories of his father always brought. "Our Henrietta blast furnace is no banker's pawn, I am glad to say. My father built her in the first year of the war. She is thirty feet lower than that seventy-five foot Lucy of Carnegie's but her forty-five feet is paid for—in cash. We can be profoundly thankful for that tonight," he added soberly.

"I must say I am impressed by your judgment," Gaylord said after a pause.

"I have been following my father's policies, on the whole. This business is in a state of flux, Mr. Gaylord. New inventions and processes follow one another with amazing speed. My father built his first forge here in Allegheny in 1837, barely thirty-five years ago. He would not recognize the iron business today, and he has only been dead seven years."

"I wonder what he would think of Carnegie?"

"He would be profoundly suspicious of him," Scott answered stiffly.

"His financial ways are certainly not conservative. But perhaps he is a genius, Mr. Scott. Some think so."

"Perhaps he is. I could not say. His methods appear piratical to me. Tom Miller is a friend of mine. With such a man in the business I cannot do better than continue my father's policies, especially in respect to finance."

Both men were by now so absorbed in their conversation that they had withdrawn to a corner of the room, leaving their wives by the fireplace. They accepted coffee from the tray that Mary passed them, and drank it absently.

Scott said thoughtfully, "No snowball of speculation like that of the past two years could keep on rolling indefinitely. Expansion and overproduction have been unreasonable. I have warned Kane repeatedly, and urged him in the strongest terms to reduce his loans. He could not see with me, nor could any of the other bankers in town. Indeed, they tried their best to induce me to go along in the swim; they wanted me to hurry and get in my Bessemer before anybody else could start; they showered me with offers of money." He paused, meeting Gaylord's questioning look.

"As a matter of fact," he concluded, "I took just the opposite course."

Gaylord smiled shrewdly. "Pulled in your horns, eh?"

"Why yes. I have been reducing my balances, quite gradually, in all four of our banks, for the past fifteen months."

Scott closed his lips firmly then, as if to indicate that he had said all he cared to. But Gaylord was fascinated; he kept his sharp blue eyes fixed on his host's face and asked his next question in a manner so admiring that Scott could not help but answer.

"What," asked Gaylord softly, "did you do with your money?"

"Put it in government fives," answered Scott gruffly.

"So that your position right now is entirely liquid."

"You could say so. Of course we have our coke interest out at Connellsville."

"Ah. That too."

"Oh yes. I bought in on David Rogers' ovens last year. Coke is essential to the modern blast furnace. Rogers can keep on producing it against our future requirements right through this crisis. I shall probably for a time, however, bank the Henrietta. It will be expensive, but I am not going to carry a payroll and over-produce during a panic."

They finished their coffee, exchanging a meaningful look over the rims of the cups.

Gaylord said, "When you are ready to reconsider that question of a

Bessemer, Mr. Scott, I should be very glad of the opportunity to talk to you further about this. Will you let me know?"

Scott's stern, bearded face reacted to some unspoken thought with a slight twitching of his thin lips.

"I expect so," he murmured. "Now I think we really should join the deserted ladies."

At this signal, Clarissa rang for Delia and told her to request the young people to come downstairs. The conversation became general; in spite of her heavy heart, for she had been thinking constantly of Sophia Kane and the catastrophe that had struck her, Clarissa moved over to the square ebony piano and opened it.

"I think we might all enjoy a little music," she said. "Miss Julia, I am told that you sing charmingly. Will you favor us?"

Miss Gaylord consented, and with much settling of her ruffled pink balerno skirts, was made comfortable on the horsehair piano stool. William junior solicitously adjusted the candles on the music rack, and stood by, gallantly erect, to turn the pages. Miss Julia looked up at him archly.

"But I did not bring any music," she reminded him in her clear voice.

He flushed with embarrassment and then laughed, too heartily. "Stupid of me, wasn't it!" He shifted from one foot to the other. In the end of the room, where they sat close together on the window seat, Paul looked at Elizabeth and snickered. She glared at him.

"I will sing from memory," said Miss Julia. "Would you suggest a particular song, Mama?"

Mrs. Gaylord turned to her host, who had seated himself, after a surreptitious glance at the ormolu mantel clock, at her side. She smiled in a certain way, a little gracious and a little condescending.

"I think our host might enjoy one of your Scottish ballads, dear. Am I right, Mr. Scott?"

"Oh quite," he answered. He had not heard a word she said. "By all means."

So with William standing, useless in respect to page turning, but gallantly attentive at her side, Julia Gaylord raised her small pink hands to the keyboard and accompanied her own thin soprano through "Bonnie Sweet Bessie." Both Papas sat uprightly attentive, in the clearest of efforts to be appreciative, and both Mamas smiled tenderly as they contemplated the tableau.

Out in the hall, as they passed through it on their way upstairs to turn down the beds, Delia nudged Mary in the ribs.

A sharp ring roused her. Mary started up, wide awake and clutching the covers. For a moment she sat upright in the dark, straining to understand where she was, why Bridget was not curled up warm and knobby-kneed beside her. She had a sense of space about her, an unnatural feeling of space and height. Then she realized with a shock where she was. She crept out of bed and tiptoed on her bare feet to the centre table where the alarm clock stood. She peered at it in the dim gray light. Half past three. She rubbed her eyes. Why was she awake? She slipped out to the hall and down the dark stairs, feeling her way. Just as she got to the second floor landing the gas in the front hall flared up and she stood at the top of the stairs, realizing that Mr. Scott had reached the door ahead of her.

In his nightshirt he was opening the front door and letting in a breathless young man whom he appeared to recognize. The two stood in the vestibule, the messenger pale and panicky, William Scott listening with an intent frown to what the boy was saying. Finally the boy took an envelope from his pocket and handed it to Mr. Scott and, shaking his head in answer to some further question, left the house. Mr. Scott stood in the front hall reading the note. Mary could see his great chunks of hands trembling as they clutched the paper. She was quite unconscious of any thought of spying on her employer. Clearly some dreadful emergency had brought the messenger to the house. She realized in a moment that there was nothing she could do and she went back to bed.

William Scott had a foreboding of the news before the bank messenger told him. Richard Kane had shot and killed himself in his office, sitting over the books. The clerks who heard the shot rushed in to find the body slumped over this note addressed to William Scott, with the added direction: "To be delivered immediately."

William took the scrawled paper upstairs and handed it to his wife to read while he hurried, stone-faced, into his clothes.

"I know this is the depth of cowardice," his old friend had written, "but I cannot stay to face disgrace. My dying request is that you do what you can for Sophia and my beloved child, Louise. Give them your protection. You may be able to salvage something for them. If not, I am helpless. Forgive me. Richard."

Clarissa knew better than to break down and give way to her feelings now. For a brief, stunned interval she stood in the centre of the gaslit bedroom saying dully, "It can't be true. He couldn't. . . . Richard. . . ." Her husband's hurried motions reminded her that there was much to do. She began to dress quickly. She would go to the Kane house to help Sophia while William took charge at the bank.

"Poor Sophia," she choked, drawing on her clothes. "What *will* she do, William? And that child—she'll never get over this shock."

"Richard was unbalanced," Scott said sternly.

"Louise—" said Clarissa, in a strange way. "Louise—do you know, I always felt she loved her father too much—"

"Are you ready?" William was putting his ponderous possessions back into the pockets from which he had neatly removed them on going to bed. "There's McCready." They heard the carriage wheels at the side door. Mary, lying tensely awake up on the third floor, heard them descending the stairs, leaving the house, and slamming the carriage door as the horse clopped quickly away.

Clarissa tried not to cry in the carriage. She said, "What a frightful thing for poor Sophia! What on earth is she to do?"

William Scott did not answer. He was sitting with a heavy frown, his arms folded firmly. Clarissa knew what he was thinking. She knew the answer to her own questions. She knew that her husband would take the responsibility for the Kanes. But she knew too that his stern morality looked upon Kane's act as weakness; that William would scrupulously fulfill the dead man's responsibilities to his family in a perpetual spirit of silent judgment. Her husband was a just but not a compassionate man.

CHAPTER III

[*1873–1874*]

TEATIME WAS THE PLEASANTEST part of the day, and Clarissa Scott always gathered her family around her at that hour. Paul and Elizabeth, home from school in the late afternoon, usually joined her. Mrs. Kane was often there with young Louise, and other close friends came too. Then there were the twins, Edgar and Constance. They would come from play, faces washed and hair brushed, and pretend at least to be on their good behavior. Clarissa had a rule that nothing unpleasant was to be brought up at teatime. Miss Deacon reported on the twins' inexhaustible wickednesses in the morning.

On warm Indian-summer afternoons like this one in late October, Clarissa liked to have tea in the summerhouse. She was very proud of her garden. In spite of the soot from the mills down by the river, the wide lawns were green and beautiful from constant watering and mowing. On the highest part of the Scott land, before it sloped away to the river precipice, the octagonal summerhouse with its spired cupola and ornamental iron screening was a cool and charming spot. Clematis, trumpet-vine, and Virginia creeper were trained to form a thick curtain about it. Inside were rustic chairs and settees and a bark-covered table. As late in the fall as the weather stayed pleasant Clarissa could be found here each afternoon; and when it grew cold she moved to the back parlor.

Delia carried the big flowered black teatray down from the side porch, and Mary followed with the tiered muffin-stand. On it were three fancy openwork china plates; one of bread-and-butter, one of seed and ginger cookies, and one of chocolate layer cake. Clarissa poured the tea and Mary handed the cups around. The twins sat side by side on one of the settees, their green eyes round with anticipation as they stared at the cakes. Mary handed them each a cup of weak cambric tea and then came back to them with the muffin-stand. Constance's hand shot out and seized a slice of cake, but Edgar hesitated over the cookies, pushing two or three aside until he saw the one he wanted.

"That ain't polite," Mary whispered. "Yer mother told ye yesterday."

Edgar looked sidelong as he bit round the edge of the cookie. "Excuse me," he mumbled. "Don't tell her."

His mother, chatting with her neighbor Mrs. McKelvie, appeared not to notice what was going on. Indeed, for the moment she was more absorbed in Louise Kane than in her own children. Louise sat sadly on a low stool close to Aunt Clarissa's knee. Her mother was at home today with a headache and she had walked over alone. She managed to make herself a tragic figure. The big Kane house on Ridge Avenue was being sold because they could not afford to live in it any more, and Louise contrived to remind people of all this whenever they looked at her. Their new home, which William Scott himself had rented for them, was a modest clapboard house just around the corner in Bidwell Street, where Clarissa Scott could look after them. Just at this moment Clarissa was wishing that her own child Elizabeth could be more intimate with Louise. They were in the same class at school, and they had done the same things together all their lives. But this did not make them friends. Sometimes Clarissa felt herself on the point of exasperation with Elizabeth; only recently she had said, "Why can't you be nicer to Louise, Lizzie? Sometimes you almost make a face when she comes around."

"She's so—I don't know, Mama. Sort of silly and giggly. She used to be, I mean. Since Uncle Dick died she just sits and looks tragic in those black clothes of hers. That's worse."

"You'd hardly expect her to giggle now! I think you're unkind to her."

"I'm sorry. But don't you see what I mean? If she didn't have that way of staring with her eyes—"

Clarissa looked thoughtful. She was very fond of Louise. The child was warmer and gentler and prettier than her own daughter. Elizabeth was brusque and her manners reflected her flat, angular looks and mousy coloring. Yet she was twice as good a student as Louise, and though she struggled against dancing-school and the pretty clothes Clarissa wanted her to wear, she got the highest marks in her class. Clarissa laughed when she looked at her other daughter, sitting with her legs dangling from the settee, the tassels on her buttoned boots swinging, licking chocolate icing from her fingers with a quick pink tongue. Constance had a cascade of bushy, brilliant red curls. Everything about her was as conspicuous and flamboyant as her extraordinary hair. Her voice was shrill and excited, her glittering green eyes danced and darted, it was almost impossible for her to sit still. She infected her twin with all her electricity. Though the little boy's hair was sandy blond, he was otherwise a replica of his sister. Both of them, even when on their best teatime behavior, seemed alert for the next possibility of mischief that should come their way. The Scott twins were known in the backyards and nurseries of Western Avenue as holy terrors and limbs of the devil. They were usually out of Miss Deacon's control and into everything in their own and the neighbors' homes where their busy hands and feet could wreak havoc. It was not safe to leave a pot of glue or ink, a pair of scissors or hedge-shears, or a box of matches where a twin could get at it. But just now they were completely demure.

Paul came up the summerhouse steps, flinging his cap and strap of books aside. He kissed his mother, greeted the girls, placed a mock right hook on Edgar's jaw, and tweaked one of Constance's fiery curls. He swallowed a whole piece of bread and butter at a gulp and doubled up his big body on the top step, balancing a cup of tea. Louise smiled wanly when he spoke to her.

Mary, coming down from the house with a fresh jug of hot water, thought what a pretty picture they all made. This was exactly the sort of scene she had so often and so longingly painted in her imagination. This was the way fine and kindly people lived; this was the sort of thing they did. Mrs. Scott's inclusion of Louise and her mother into the family circle was just what one would expect. It was a pity, Mary thought, that Louise did not fit in a little better. Perhaps she would lose some of those wide-eyed, breathless ways of hers when she got over grieving for her father. Everyone was so gentle and careful with her now; that was only natural. Mary doubted if Paul liked to have some of those sorrowful glances turned on him, but she knew he was sorry for Louise; she had heard him say so; and anyone could see that he tried to be extra kind to offset Elizabeth's brusqueness. He was enough like his mother so that one knew he would do that.

Clarissa said, "Thank you, Mary," as she set the jug down on the table and looked the tray over to see if anything more was needed. Mary bobbed her head in a quick unconscious gesture. Clarissa had noticed that from the girl's first day in the house. It was a way of saying, "You're welcome, Ma'm" when words were unnecessary. Mary moved very lightly; her hands when she worked were neat and precise. Clarissa saw that Mary would never place a thing crookedly or leave a dish or a piece of silver askew. Clarissa said, "Children, it's time to go now. Run along with Mary."

The twins slid off their settee like a pair of wound-up dolls. They had sat still just as long as they could endure. They whizzed past Paul on the top step and tumbled down to the grass. Mary followed them. Edgar was lying in wait behind the vines. As she walked past him he grabbed the bow of her apron and twitched it. She caught the white apron as it fell, while Edgar and Constance whooped delightedly. They broke into a run, waggling their fingers at Mary. Miss Deacon, or any other maid, would have scolded them. But Mary picked up the front of her black skirt and ran after them, laughing, up the long slope of the lawn. Clarissa watched. When Mary caught the twins she gave them each a smart smack on the rump, then squatted down and put an arm around each of them. Their heads came together to hear what she was, evidently, whispering. Clarissa, turning back to Elizabeth and Louise in the summerhouse realized suddenly that Mary was the same age as these girls. What a difference there was, she thought.

The marriage of William junior to Julia Gaylord took place the following June. The family's first romance provided plenty of table conversation in the Scott kitchen. Mary felt a little uncomfortable about the freedom with which Cook and Delia discussed every aspect of the match. But she knew that by their lights they were devoted to the family and particularly to Mrs. Scott; and their verdicts on the haughty Gaylords were both pungent and just. Delia had taken a canny dislike to Julia

Gaylord. She called her derisively the Duchess of Boston and mimicked her high treble drawl.

"This *ghawstly* smoke," trilled Delia, with her mouth full of Monday's boiled dinner. "Deah William, I cawn't think how I shall ever enduah it!" She took a gulp of tea. "Endure it, indade! I'm thinkin' she'll endure the money from where the smoke comes from, aisy enough!"

Mary was speechless with delight when Mrs. Scott told her one morning that she was going to take her to Boston for the wedding. There would be much entertaining, many gowns and wraps to press. And the plan was to travel to Boston both by railroad and steamboat, and stay at a hotel!

"Oh, Ma'm," Mary blurted, her eyes watering from excitement. "Are ye sure ye want me? Not Delia?"

The departure was an unforgettable event. William junior was already in Boston. The family party consisted of Mr. and Mrs. Scott, Paul and Elizabeth, Constance and Edgar with Miss Deacon, and Mary entrusted with the luggage keys and Mrs. Scott's best faille silk dolman, too fine to be crushed in a portmanteau.

The twins, dressed alike in sailor-fashion, except for Constance's full calf-length skirt and Edgar's tight breeches, wore new buttoned black boots and round black porkpie hats perched on the fronts of their heads, with two streamers fluttering behind. Elizabeth's travelling dress of blue mohair, heavily piped with white braid ("Elizabeth, be sure to keep your elbows close to your sides and don't touch anything in the cars") was completed by a straw bonnet wreathed with daisies, and a short jacket of figured chintz. Mister Paul made a fine picture, Mary thought; so fair and tall, with his new straw boater and his yellow gloves. He seemed a man of the world to Mary; he had been through this several times before, had seen both New York and the seashore, and had even spent a night in one of the new sleeping-cars where you actually took off your clothes and went to bed.

But this time it had been decided not to take the sleeping-cars, on account of the twins. They would behave better in the day train, everybody felt sure of that. Miss Deacon was armed with books and games and her severest expression. She had no doubt of the ordeal ahead of her. The train was hot and close, the red plush seats prickly and grimy with cinders. Outside the early morning sun shone hotly, promising a trying day, and Clarissa boarded the train with a discouraged expression.

"Children, have you all got your drinking cups?" she asked. "Now I want you all to be on your very best behavior. Elizabeth, you might do some of that dark-blue tatting; it won't show the dirt. Paul, have you a book to read? And children," she bent severely toward Edgar and Constance, standing side by side in the aisle, their green eyes round and glittering with excitement, "you are both to sit quietly in those places with Miss Deacon"—she pointed to a corner where a seat-back had been turned over to make two seats face—"and you are to be *quiet*. No squabbling or noise, do you understand?" They nodded, waiting for her to finish; then made a swift break for their corner and flung themselves on the seats with whoops of delight. Clarissa bit her lips. Mary leaned over her shoulder.

"Don't worry about 'em, Ma'm," she said. "I'll help Miss Deacon keep 'em quiet. I'm used to childer."

Clarissa gave her a grateful look.

"Thank you, Mary. Now if you'll just give me my little balsam cushion, it's in the top of that satchel there, and the pair of cotton gloves, and the eyeshade—that's right." She handed Mary her jacket to hang up. "You might just put Miss Elizabeth's bonnet into the bandbox—those daisies, you know—where is Mr. Scott?"

Paul looked up from his book, with which he was already settled.

"He's gone to the smoking-car, Mama."

"Oh dear. *Do* you think the conductor will find him when he comes for our tickets?"

Elizabeth sighed. "I don't see how he could help it, Mama. Look at us."

The train snorted out of the station and through the dingy yards, then rounded a bend with a scream of its whistle. An answering scream burst from Edgar and Constance. They were kneeling on their seats with their noses pressed to the sooty windows.

"Look," Constance shouted. "Look, everybody. There's our mill! See, there's the Henrietta down there."

"That's not the Henrietta," Edgar yelled scornfully. "Just like a girl! *There's* the Henrietta, way back there."

" 'Tisn't!"

" 'Tis so!"

" 'Tisn't!"

" 'Tis! Sissy, what do you know about it?"

"Sissy yourself! Sissy, sissy, Edgar's a sissy! Doesn't know a chimney when he sees one!"

"Aw shut up!"

"*Edgar!*" Clarissa was out of her place, scattering cushion, book, and handkerchief. Mary stepped to her side.

"Let 'em alone for a minute, Ma'm. They're that excited. If they work it off now we'll keep 'em nice and quiet later."

She went over and sat down beside Miss Deacon, whose freezing look she calmly disregarded.

"Wud ye be knowin' what they do down there, when the Henrietta blasts?" she asked in a sociable tone.

Edgar looked around at her with scorn.

" 'Course I know. Besides *you* don't have to tell me. You're nothing but a servant."

Mary gasped. She waited for the governess to reprove him, but no reproach came. In fact, she saw Miss Deacon's lips twitching in barely dissembled malice. Mrs. Scott had not heard.

"Go ahead and tell us," Constance said. "He doesn't know anything, he might as well learn."

Miss Deacon opened a book officiously.

"Children," she began, "I shall start with the chapter where the—"

"We don't want you to read to us," Edgar said. "We're sick of that story. We'll read to ourselves if we want to."

"We'll read when we want to," Constance echoed. "I want to hear about the Henrietta, Mary."

"Aw, she don't know anything," Edgar shouted. "I want to play dominoes, Mama," he roared, "where are the dominoes?"

"Edgar, will you be quiet! I shall have your father punish you if you make another sound. Constance, stop that squabbling. I have a bad headache." Clarissa leaned back in her place.

Edgar flung himself down on the seat, drubbing his heels on the plush bench opposite. Paul turned his head and caught Mary's eye. He came sauntering over.

"Mary, shall I take him out in the vestibule and thrash him?" he asked.

Edgar looked up in alarm.

"Why yes, Mister Paul, why do you not?" answered Mary, with a wink. Paul made as if to roll up his sleeves. A screech burst from Edgar.

"Really!" Miss Deacon jerked her head and glared at Paul and Mary. "I do think, Master Paul, if you will just leave my charges to me, and Mary goes off where she *belongs*," she said pointedly, "we will have a pleasanter journey."

"You mean old thing!" Constance cried. "Leave her alone. I want her here. Stay here, Mary," Edgar saw suddenly the advantages of that idea.

"Yes, stay here," he shouted. "Stay here and let *her* go away." He pointed at his governess. "She's ugly and she smells."

Holy Saints, Mary thought. They really are devils. I wonder where they get it.

Both children pinned her on the seat between them and began to clamor for a story. Mary plunged in, eager to fix their attention before they could think of a fresh outbreak. Miss Deacon sat stiffly scowling, turning the pages of a book. Nearly two hours went by. William Scott returned from the smoking-car and paused to stare at his two youngest, intent and silent, listening to Mary's low voice recounting an Irish tale of pixies in the bogs.

He went over and seated himself by his wife.

"Clarissa," he murmured, "would you mind telling me why you don't dismiss that useless ramrod over there and leave those children to Mary?"

"Why, she's only a few years older than they are, William. And besides, I need her myself."

They lunched at Harrisburg, in the depot restaurant, on gritty ham sandwiches, tepid bitter tea, and limp slabs of dried-apple pie. They sat in a row at an unappetizing long table, first William Scott, then Paul and Elizabeth, then Clarissa, then Edgar and Constance, with Miss Deacon between to keep them apart, and finally Mary. Clarissa poked disgustedly at the greasy thing on her plate, and drank her tea gingerly, trying to keep the chipped crockery mug from touching her lips. She waved aside the buzzing flies with shudders of repulsion.

"Really," she sighed, "I can't think what possessed me not to bring our lunch along, the way we used to."

Elizabeth flushed. "Oh, Mama," she said, "*please* don't bring that up again! You don't want us to look like a lot of—*immigrants,* do you?"

William Scott looked severely at his daughter.

"Your grandfather passed through this very town as an immigrant, Elizabeth," he said, "and so did the forebears of all your friends. Plain fare was good enough for them. I wish I had some right now."

He pushed aside his uneaten food and stood up.

"We will go back to the cars as soon as you are ready," he said.

It was very late when they arrived at Jersey City. The twins, crumpled and dishevelled, had long since given up the struggle and fallen asleep. Elizabeth, passing up the aisle, looked at them as if she had never seen them before. But Paul paused, helped to wake them up, and took Edgar in charge as they descended from the train.

Mary could have groaned with relief. This had been the longest, most tiring day she ever remembered; its novelty and excitement were counteracted by the dirt, in which she felt as if she had been mortared. The heat plastered her clothes to her body, and made her gray alpaca dress itch and sting under the arms and across the shoulders where it fitted tightly. Her face, which she could not manage to wipe often enough, burned scarlet. Her crisp red hair hung limply about her forehead. As she collected her mistress's belongings she breathed a prayer of relief, and the change of air as they descended from the car was delicious even though it was the rank, smoky air of the terminal. William Scott marshalled his party with orders to follow him and stay in line; then he led off down the ramp to the ferry.

The water sucked and slapped against the squat sides of the boat. It made an exciting noise, one not unfamiliar to a girl born along the waterside; but this was different, the challenging voice of a strange place. Mary stood by herself at the bow, drinking in the damp night air as the boat churned through the river. She overheard Mr. Scott, pointing out to his children the landmarks of New York as they loomed up in the dark. But she was too tired to listen. She was glad to stand there, luxuriating in the cool wind; she even felt chilly enough to draw her light shawl around her shoulders. She breathed deeply, unconsciously in rhythm with the throb of the paddle-wheels.

"It's great, isn't it?" she heard in a quiet tone at her elbow.

Paul was standing there, holding his hat in his hand, the wind ruffling his blond hair. Mary studied his face, turned in profile as he gazed forward toward the shore of New York. His lips were parted, and for all his manly poise, Mary realized that this experience of travel was quite as exciting to his seventeen years as to her sixteen. In a couple of years journeys would become so frequent in his life as to lose all their novelty; he would be going East to college. But Mary could not imagine a future for herself when travel would seem any less wonderful than now.

"Oh, yes," she breathed, answering Paul. "Indade it is!"

He smiled at her and they stood eagerly watching the panorama as the boat approached its slip.

The night before the wedding there was a large dinner at the Gaylord house on Beacon Street. Clarissa Scott thoughtfully offered Mary's help to Mrs. Gaylord, knowing that the party would require much extra service. Mary was assigned to the large front bedroom where the ladies were to lay off their wraps. She had seen something of Pittsburgh society when the Scotts gave dinner parties, but Pittsburgh people were nothing like these in Boston. Pittsburgh ladies usually smiled a pleasant good-evening as they handed her their shawls and dolmans, and greeted one another with a friendliness that these Boston women apparently did not feel. At least, Mary thought, they do not act as if they did. Many of them had pursed, critical expressions and some exchanged clear signs of silent disapprobation. Mary heard the explanation while two of the ladies stood before the mirror smoothing their hair.

"I really can't understand why the Gaylords consented to it," said one. "Have you ever heard of these people before, Georgiana?"

"Certainly not, Serena. Nobody has ever heard of anyone in Pittsburgh."

Mary drew back stiffly into the corner by the window.

"I think it a most unsuitable match. There is no reason whatever for Laurence Gaylord to permit Julia to marry a—a—"

"—a nobody," said her friend. "I hear these people have spread themselves all over the Parker House like a circus troupe. I think it disgusting."

"At least *she* might have some breeding. I understand she is a Haynes from Baltimore."

"It must be the husband, my dear. Why, he was a *mill-worker*. Have you noticed his *hands?*"

Mary was trembling with temper. She coiled her hands into tight fists and squeezed her lips together, checking the impulse to step up to these women and give them a piece of her mind. That mind, so youthful and ingenuous, had snapped into a sudden realization of her feeling for the Scotts.

A third woman appeared and let Mary take the shawl from her shoulders. She seemed to understand quite well what the two ladies at the mirror had been saying and she joined the conversation with, "Of course, Laurence Gaylord would never have consented to this if it had not been for that steel mill in which he has invested."

Raised eyebrows and marked attention made it clear that she had some information which her friends did not yet possess.

"Why yes," she said. "Grafton told me Laurence says this Scott person has the most promising business of its kind in the country and Laurence has bought a share in it."

Mary could not help wondering why on earth Mr. Scott would have made such a blunder. She wished she dared go to him and repeat this talk she was hearing.

"Naturally, then," said the woman called Serena, "Laurence would want his interests looked after. A son-in-law—" she turned from the mirror with a shrug.

"But that poor child," said Georgiana with a shudder. *"Pittsburgh!"*

"Pittsburgh!" Mary muttered behind stiff lips as the ladies swept from the room. "Pittsburgh's a lot too good for the likes o' you!"

The wedding next day impressed the various members of the family according to their ages and tastes. Clarissa was amused by her husband's stony disapproval of the elaborate ceremony in Trinity Church, and of the reception at the Gaylord house, where champagne was handed about in profusion. Not only the men, but the women raised glasses to toast the bride. This was too much for the stern, Presbyterian William Scott, an elder of the First Church of Allegheny, grandson of a Highland dominie, and a rigid teetotaler who had all his life imposed his rules on his family. The Boston ladies did not get a chance to snub him; he remained aloof from all the proceedings. And the men of Boston knew better than to dismiss him heedlessly. They stood about, sipping punch, champagne, and Madeira, and scrutinizing the sombre bearded giant with marked curiosity and interest. All of them had heard of Laurence Gaylord's amazing investment in the iron works owned by this outlandish man.

The bride and groom stood in the bay window of the parlor, in a bower of palms and white flowers, with Julia's bridesmaids fluttering and twittering as the guests went down the line. The ushers were all Princeton classmates of William's except Paul, who looked as uncomfortable as he felt in borrowed finery. There had been a dinner-table argument at home about this question of ordering formal afternoon clothes and a Prince Albert coat for Paul. William junior had insisted on it; Paul had refused to wear the clothes if they were made for him.

"But you've got to have them some time," Clarissa had said, coaxing. "You'll certainly never outgrow them if they're made now." Paul, at seventeen, was much taller and heavier than his brother.

"I don't want 'em," Paul said. "I hate monkey-clothes."

Now as he moved through the crowd, hot and uncomfortable in the makeshifts he had been prevailed on to wear, he caught sight of Mary crossing the stair-hall on an errand. He winked at her and made a desperate gesture at his throat encased in a wall of starched Piccadilly collar. The Gaylord waitress, a formidable biddy, observed this and tossed her head with a sniff. Mary burst into a giggle and disappeared, while Paul stood wistfully watching a waiter pass champagne.

"Gee, that looks nice and cool," he said to nobody in particular. He wondered what would happen if he tried some. He did not like to deceive his father who had that morning stipulated that, wedding or no wedding, no Scott was to touch a drop of alcohol. Paul knew that Bill had been drinking away from home for a long time. He stood alone watching the crowd surge through the stuffy rooms, the women barely concealing their mingled curiosity and condescension as they shook hands with his father and mother.

"Aw bosh," he said suddenly, half aloud. He stepped back into the dark embrasure under the stairs and as the next waiter passed with a tray of glasses full of champagne, Paul helped himself to one and turned his back and drank it.

CHAPTER IV

[1874]

A FEW WEEKS LATER, on a burning July Sunday, Mary picked her way across the rutted and littered yards, skirting the rusty tracks where the ore cars lurched, screeching, up and down with their loads of material for the iron works on both sides of the Flat along the riverside. She crossed the cindery patch in front of her father's door. Her sisters were watching for her at the window. The door flew open before she reached it, and she was smothered in hugs and kisses. She hurried over to her father.

Patrick Rafferty sat out his life in a crude wheelchair which James had devised out of his mother's old rocker and three iron wheels he had made at the mill. Patrick's useless legs hung limp, resting on a wooden footpiece. They had been crushed by cannonshot at Gettysburg. He had dragged out the years since then in idleness, eking out an existence from a tiny government pension and the earnings of James and Mary. Each kept only enough for pocket-money and supposedly brought the rest to Patrick. James, Mary thought, did this with the worst possible grace. He was sitting there today, moodily scowling over the kitchen table.

He had been talking to Patrick before Mary came in. She had heard his voice from outside, but when she entered he pursed his lips together and hunched himself over the saucer of tea he was drinking. Mary, with Bridget and Kathleen clinging to her sides, greeted him gaily, pretending not to notice his surliness. He grunted at her.

"And how is it with ye today?" she kissed her father. "Sure, and it's glad I am to see ye."

"Ye're a fair sight for sore eyes yerself," he answered. He jerked his chin at James as if to indicate a warning. Mary nodded absently, her eyes busy examining the untidy room. She decided to begin by baking today; bannocks would go quick, and she had both flour and butter in the string sack she was carrying.

She never came empty-handed. She would barely have laid off her bonnet and shawl before she'd be stirring up a batch of soda-bread to eat with the gooseberry jam that Sarah, at Mrs. Scott's direction, had given her to take home. Or she would stare in pretended disapproval at Bridget's tousled black head, and have both child and head in the kitchen tub as quickly as she could heat up a kettle of water.

She had not seen James for several weeks. He was seldom at home when she came; he was usually out at some union meeting. Today she thought she would make him a real treat.

"Lave off with that stale tea, James," she said, "and I'll be makin' ye some fresh soon as ever I get my apron on. And I'll have a nice bite to go with it, too."

"I want no bite from that hell ye come from," he growled. Mary started, and the little girls gasped. Patrick clenched the arms of his chair.

"James Rafferty," Mary said in a low tone, "what do ye mean? Have ye no decency, talking filth afore yer little sisters!" She went over and bent close to his face. "Are ye in drink?"

"I am not."

"Then sure ye've lost yer mind. What call have ye to be swearin' and callin' of bad names to the best people in the world?"

"There ye go, ye sentimental blatherin' fool," James said. "A man wud think ye're after believin' in fairies, with yer innocence and yer 'best people in the wurrld.' Have ye not heard what yer best people are up to now, that are so grand with their charity gifts of jam and butter?" He twisted his mouth almost as if to spit.

Mary stood quietly by the table, her hands clenched under her clean apron.

"James, if ye're tellin' me ye're up to more trouble-makin' in the mill, I won't hear of it. What good are ye to a fair employer, for all yer bein' so smart at the pickin' rods? Why are ye forever hangin' round with Joe Bishop and thim?"

"Joe Bishop and the rest of us will see yer grand Mr. Scott kneelin' to th' Amalgamated," James said, "and t'won't be many months more, neither." He pronounced the word Amalgamated with the accent on the fourth syllable, and rolled the name sonorously on his tongue. "Wud ye but listen awhile to me, Mary, and forget yer eternal play-actin' and yer fine fancy manners, ye'd hear somethin' t'wud really open yer eyes, instead o' the blather around that dinner table ye ought to be too proud to wait on."

"Oh, I ought, ought I? And p'raps ye'll tell me why I haven't as much right to an honest livin' as yerself? Was it you bought Katie her winter's coat? Or took Bridget to the doctor whin her eyes were sore? And if I don't bring home money to Dad and the childer, will ye ever be able to save enough to wed with Annie McGlone? Too proud indade!"

She turned on her heel and went over to dishpan, taking the children with her. "Come now, girls," she said quietly, "We'll red up. Bridget, you take the dishclout there."

James got up and leaned against the wall. He stared at Mary, rubbing his long jaw for a moment, then he started to speak.

"Mary," he said. "I wouldn't have ye take offense at what I tell ye. I talk too strong, maybe, but ye know I'm earnest. I'm that grateful fer yer help. And Dad too. Ye'll believe that, will ye not?"

"I'd rather not talk about it," Mary said shortly. "I want no thanks for doin' me natural duty. I like to do it. But it fair makes me boil to hear yer treacherous talk against the Scotts, what's good to me and has been to our whole family ever since Dad started to work for th' old gentleman. I'll not believe the things ye say. What wrong has Mr. Scott done ye?

He even kept ye workin' last fall, tendin' the Henrietta when he had 'er banked and could o' laid ye off."

"He did that. But I'll say this, he had no choice. Don't ye understand, Mary, the trouble's not wi' the wages and the job, though they're none too fair and square. The trouble's the way these owners has cleaved together to keep the union from gettin' any power in the mills. 'Tis the same in every wan, and now with new plants goin' up on every hand, we've got to get closed shops—closed shops, do ye hear?"

"I hear. What is it ye want, anyhow? Is it work or is it trouble? Those of us as does our work proper and minds our business don't need to go on strike and let our folks be starvin'."

James sighed. He was baffled by Mary's blind attachment to the Scotts and by what he thought her infantile refusal to believe anything but good of William Scott. This question of the union and the dream of making the Amalgamated strong enough to dictate a closed shop to every iron and steel mill in the district was the passion of James' life. He was comparatively indifferent to the prospect of marrying Annie McGlone. He would marry her when he got around to it; but Mary knew that the sums he kept after contributing to Dad's support went not into savings for his wedding, but into the Amalgamated's treasury.

Mary could not believe that William Scott, to her a pillar of justice and dignity, could be any such ruthless despot as her brother pictured. She often heard Mr. Scott and his friends talk of their anxiety about the Amalgamated's growing agitation. Mr. Scott had worked in the mill all his life, starting as a cinder-monkey when he was fifteen, and to this day he could put his hand to anything any employee could do. How could he help but see things fairly?

"I'm tellin' ye," James was saying from his place against the wall, "ye need to have yer eyes opened, Mary. Ye're a smart girl. Why wudn't yer master be kind and lordly at home? What cause has he to be else? But did ye know, maybe, that only two days ago he sat the entire afternoon in his office drawin' up a yellow-dog contract he means to hand us on the furrst o' August?"

"What's a yellow-dog contract?"

" 'Tis time ye asked a reasonin' question. A yellow-dog contract is a rotten paper they try to force us to sign, sayin' we'll never belong to no union the while we work in that mill where we are. I'd a' said it wud only be thim new Carnegie crowd wud do such a thing, but here's yer saint of a William Scott doin' it, and for less reason."

"And how do ye know he has less reason? Scott's is a small mill, small enough for himself to know every man and boy in it. Why wudn't he be better able to judge what's good fer 'em than some union what only wants to use 'em to its own ends?"

"Mary!" James shook his fists despairingly. "Are ye but a child? Is it a child ye'd always remain? Cannot ye see the union's ends are ours? Do ye think steelmakin' is a parochial school—with all the good obedient childer doin' what they're told by the wise howly fathers? Will ye not be a woman grown, for the love of God?"

"Ye'll do better to talk about the love of God when ye do nothin' to bring starvation down on helpless women and childer," Mary snapped.

" 'Tis a waste of time to talk wid ye," James said, relapsing into his lowering mood. "Ye're a traitor to yer class and yer birth. Ye come o' workin' people, ye work as a servant yerself, and ye've got yer head turned on a lot o' luxury and fancy manners. Ye fair make me sick. A man can't believe in his own flesh and blood."

Mary turned slowly towards him from the dishpan. Her face was flushed and her thin lips were white, as if all the color had gone from them into her forehead where the reddened skin blended into the vibrant hair.

"James Rafferty," she said slowly, "when talk turns to traitors in this house, watch yer own bitter blasphemous tongue before ye dare to turn on another body. Ye don't know the meanin' of loyalty to flesh and blood. 'Tis only an idee will hold ye—and a rude, cruel, dangerous idee it is. Get along now about yer crazy business and leave me visit with Dad and the girls. Ye ain't seen Annie fer two weeks, she told me so a-cryin' out there on the steps awhile ago."

James muttered angrily between his closed lips, flung his cap on his head, and shouldered his way out. Patrick watched him go, shaking his white head wearily.

"Ah, Mary," he said, "and can ye two not make peace? I fair misunderstand why ye're always quarrelin'. James is a good boy, and a fine hand with the rods. A rare true worker."

"Sure, and that's the very trouble, Dad. He is a good lad. But he's poisoned by all them wild wans what's got him in the thick o' this union mess. He's bad misled, he is."

"Mary, he ain't led nor misled, my girl. He's doin' the leadin'. Ye don't see James important like he is. He's a big man among thim others. He's that close to Joe Bishop." The old man held up two crooked fingers, pressed close together.

"Och," cried Mary impatiently, "and ye'd have me believe Joe Bishop is a leader to be proud of? That devil, leadin' dacent boys astray?"

"Bishop's head o' the Amalgamated," said the old man, "and James is organizer fer Scott's and all the other mills outside o' Carnegie's. He's trusted, James is."

"Not by me," said Mary bitterly. "He's got ye full o' poison, too. If Mr. Scott was a bad man, or a mean man, or a fool of a man, I might maybe understand. But this I will never understand. Sure, I can't see the right in me own brother. It makes me that miserable, it does. Come now, Dad, drink yer tea and then I'll give ye a nice wash and rub yer back. Come here, Bridget, and tell me yer catechism, Father Reilly's that mispleased with ye. He says ye'll never be ready for confirmation at all. Why won't ye be a good girl and behave yerself proper? Can't ye keep her to her duty, Kate?"

Bridget had appeared until this moment to be a homely and ordinary child, busy with helping Mary and pathetically glad to have her at home for the day. She had stayed close to Mary's skirts during the disagreement with James, looking from one to the other of her elders with round, puzzled eyes. But now, with attention focussed on her, she turned suddenly furious, much as James was wont to do, and glared at both her sisters in an ugly, defiant way.

"She's that wild, Mary," whined Kathleen. "She won't pay me no mind, nor Dad neither. She's a wild wan for runnin' in the streets all the while. She won't come home from bein' out with thim Flat hussies till I fair threaten her with the p'lice, she won't."

"Ah, Bridget." Mary put her arm around the child's shoulders and tried to draw her into her lap.

"Lea' me alone!" screamed the girl. She made an ugly face.

Mary looked at her closely. "Is it sick ye are, Bridget?"

"Nah. Only sick o' talk. Y'all talk too much."

Mary sighed. This sort of thing went on every time she saw Bridget. And yet the girl could be sweeter and more affectionate than anyone in the family. Mary worried constantly about her. If she could only take Bridget out of this atmosphere, get her away from the dirty, sniggling little girls who roamed the alleys of the Flat in gangs, or held whispered conclaves in the shadows of the back sheds. Mary longed to put Bridget in a convent, and she resolved now to do this no matter how great the cost might be. For it must be a proper boarding school, no ordinary refuge for street children. Sometimes Mary wondered if she had really done right to leave home and devote herself to another family when her own needed her so badly.

As she walked back to the Scotts' after sundown she kept on worrying about Bridget. There must be some way of looking after her better than this. Next week Mrs. Scott was taking Elizabeth and Louise Kane and the twins and Mary to the Jersey shore for a month. Miss Deacon would have her vacation during part of this time, and Mary was to look after the twins. She thought uneasily now how much worse Bridget needed such a holiday than any of the Scott children. She hated the thought of leaving her here in the dirt and the heat, among the Flat riffraff. She decided she had better talk to the nuns about Bridget and see if she could not get her into a convent before she went away. When Mary was thinking hard she had a way of carrying her head on one side, and as she always walked very quickly and lightly, she looked like a small bird skimming up the steep hill, away from the dingy Flat to the wide sweep of Western Avenue.

CHAPTER V

[*1874*]

FOR TWO SUMMERS Paul had worked in the mill during his school vacations. On hot August mornings, while his mother and the other children were away, he and his father had their six o'clock breakfast alone together. The dining-room was cool and fresh. Delia opened the windows early before the house was screened and shuttered against the blazing mid-morning sun. By half past six father and son were on their way to the mill, striding in step down the broad avenue, and through the tangle of narrower streets that led to the river.

Their way lay steeply downward; down Western Avenue, down after a turn on Beaver Avenue, and down the roaring alley that ran parallel to, though fifty feet above, the shoreline of the Ohio River. The Scott Iron Works sprawled below them on their left, facing a tangle of railroad tracks.

To the unknowing eye the mill seemed only a formless maze of corrugated iron sheds, some roofless and open to the brassy sky, some dark and mysterious in their walls and roofs of blackened metal. A fearful shattering noise roared up from the rolling mill at the east end of the meandering string of buildings, and at the far western end there was teeming activity, centring around piles of different sorts of masonry brick and blocks, plunging teams, shouting drivers and laborers, and the ear-splitting hisses of a dinkey-engine which was hitched to a flat loaded with castings. Here the Bessemer converter over which William Scott had ruminated and hesitated so long was under construction. Paul watched his father's gray eyes combing the scene for evidences of progress since yesterday. Then the Old Man's glance went back, almost as if for reassurance, to the row of stacks blackening the summer sky with their eructations. These were the old puddling furnaces which antedated everything else in the mill. They were the core of the Scott Iron Works. Every innovation, every modern departure, would always strike in the Old Man's heart a questioning note of reproach. His father's great blast furnace, however, was his deepest pride and joy. Her dun-colored chimney, blackened at the mouth, towered above and dominated the whole panorama. Her cast-house and domes, her busy skip-hoist, and the sweating men shovelling in material always made him feel at ease.

The mill sprawled between a hodgepodge of railroad tracks along its northern length and the swirling, lead-colored Ohio on its southern side. Ore, coke, and limestone came down the river on barges almost directly into the furnaces. Finished pigs, bars, and rods were shipped away by rail straight from the landward side of the mill. These tracks lay in a gully down at river-level, but the street along which the Scotts were walking was much higher, the edge of the original precipice that had bordered the Ohio at this point. Access to the mill from the street was had by a footbridge and a steep flight of steps descending straight into the main office entrance. The bridge spanned the whole width of the gully, and beneath it the freight engines and cars and flats crashed and clattered day and night. Paul and his father strode across the bridge now and descended to the mill. The Henrietta bulked over their heads, cast-house and hoist huge against the sky. Her stack was smoking. Paul looked up at it, gauging the progress of the heat by the texture of the smoke and its color and density.

"Half an hour," he said to his father. He was boyishly proud of his lore.

The older man nodded. He followed every day of Paul's apprenticeship with fascinated interest and pride, which he was at some pains to hide. Paul was working now as a puddler's helper on C furnace, having been promoted from cinder-boy. His mother still protested that this was a brutal way to treat a boy in his summer holidays, but William had merely said, "I started working for my father at the mill three years earlier than Paul has. It will not hurt him, Clarissa, it will be the making of him." And since William junior had so far been a bitter disappointment to his father in his distaste for hard and dirty work, and his indifference to ironmaking, Clarissa did not dare to interfere in her husband's plans for Paul. Paul loved the mill the way his father did. All his life he had begged and teased to be taken down there. He had long since learned to know all the puddlers and department bosses by name. Everybody new that his father was planning to put Paul straight through the mill from the bottom to the top, so that by the time he finished college and came to work for good, he would have had first-hand experience in every department.

William Scott was only fifty-two years old, but he had been so long a fixture of the mill that he antedated everybody in it except his father's bookkeeper, Richard MacTavish. Scott was always called the Old Man. He was gratified by the sense of dynasty and paternalism that the title emphasized. And by the same token he was outraged by the increasing union activity in the mill, which appeared to him vicious defiance of his rightful authority. He was entirely aware of the activities of Mary's brother, James Rafferty. His awareness even included memories of James' father, old Pat, who had also been a trouble-maker in his way. The Old Man resented trouble of this kind, which seemed to him unworthy of ironmasters.

On the same ground he could not help resenting his own eldest son. Nobody but Paul ever called William junior "Bill"; the nickname seemed too rough-and-ready for such a smooth and cool young man. William junior detested ironmaking. The only place for him was the office, and that was where his father had put him, to learn the finances of the business from MacTavish. But the Old Man was embittered about it. Sometimes the mere sight of William, elegant and smoothly brushed, sitting over the ledgers, sent him into a rage. The past weeks had been worse than usual. William had recently returned from his honeymoon and was at small pains to hide the fact that he preferred the delights of White Sulphur Springs to this burning, sooty prison. The Old Man found him seated on a high stool in snowy shirtsleeves, looking bored.

"Good morning, Father," William said.

"Good morning, William. Morning, Mac."

"Guid day, Boss." The old Scotsman on his stool, with a green eye-shade across his gnarled features, did not look up from his work. He was running his forefinger down a long list of figures and checking them against a sheaf of items bound in a blue folder. He was shaking his white head slowly and muttering under his breath. Scott senior shoved his hands into his pockets and stood watching him with a look of benign amusement.

"Too much money, Mac?"

" 'Tis a muckle o' money ye've gi'en yer word on. I dinna like the look o't."

This was not the first such comment about the Old Man's rash decision to expand. "An' unco soon after yon panic nae a year ago. Yer Daddie wudna done sae crazy thing."

"This was the only time to do it," the Old Man said gruffly. "Would you want me to wait until everybody else has grabbed all this new Bessemer business? I mean to be in on the ground."

"Four hunnerd ninety thoosan' dollars! Tae build a muckle mudpie! An' half o't borried to boot. Ye'll live to rue it, mark my words."

William Scott stood staring at MacTavish. For the first time in all his life he could trace, if he dared, the flicker of a gnawing doubt. He had been making crucial decisions for more than thirty years of daily association with old Mac, and this was the first time his judgment had ever been questioned. If MacTavish, instead of being stubborn and crabbed from age and habit should just chance to be right about this . . . the Old Man stuck out his bearded chin and growled, "I know what I'm doing. I didn't *borrow* a quarter of a million from Gaylord. I sold him that share of the business. You do your job around here and I'll do mine."

MacTavish was still shaking his head and muttering. "Yer Daddie wudna done it," he said in his teeth. "Yer Daddie hoordet his ain siller to build yon Henrietta. Ye sud hae done the same."

William junior bent his head self-consciously over his ledger. Nobody else in the world would dare to talk to his father like this. Such insolence from any other subordinate would have evoked an instant explosion. But MacTavish was a privileged character in some way that William could not understand. His father merely gave a gruff chuckle and said, "Well, it's all in the family, Mac. You be my watchdog."

"An' Willie maun luke out for his guidfather," old Mac cackled sourly.

"Willie" turned a dull red and bit his lip. There had been some satisfaction in sitting by and watching MacTavish aiming barbs at his father, but he could not stand being teased himself. He knew very well that nobody in the mill took him seriously. In his mind the mere matter of seniority should have commanded respect for him as the Old Man's eldest son. He did not understand the fraternity of ironmasters, the mutual respect in which every man from boss down to youngest puddler's 'prentice held one another. To the Old Man that was the basis of a man's right to be considered a man. It was the foundation of his life, to be on the job at the stroke of seven every day; to be on hand when the Henrietta gave up her glowing stint; to know every man in the mill by nature as well as by name and face; to walk as easily and surely between flaming streams of molten iron as across the bare board floor of his grimy office. Bookkeeping and the financial details of the business were suited to spare hours, to the slack periods between chargings, to evenings or noontimes; but a man, an ironmaster, did not spend his life sitting at a desk, keeping his hands clean and reading foremen's reports of operations. Nor did he spend his life in luxury, travel, and show, like that conscienceless Carnegie who saw the world of iron and steel only as a rich land waiting to be plundered; who made decisions thousands of miles distant from where they would be carried out, and who profited so vastly by these decisions, though their piratical injustice was enough to shake any man's belief in a higher law. Doubtless William junior liked to dream of himself in such a rôle, his father thought. He would eventually have to smash these dreams for good and all, and give that lazy, affected youth the choice of getting down to business or getting out.

In his inmost heart the Old Man was able to face this possibility without flinching; and he knew the reason for that was Paul. Sometimes in the dead of night during the past anxious winter, when he had lain awake pondering the problems of adjustment to the swift reaction after the panic, he had followed his imagination down the dim corridors of the future. And there, always, in his own place, in his own father's place, he would see the big blond bulk and absorbed devotion of his second son. Once it occurred to old William, in a kind of eye-opening shock, that if this were to be the pattern of the future he might have been unwise in placing such a weight as he had in the hands of Gaylord. At the time he had sold him the share it had seemed the wisest possible course. It had been the quickest way, too, of getting into production of Bessemer steel for machines, tools, and specialties while Carnegie was preparing to swallow up the rail business.

Well, William Scott thought, as he started towards the casthouse to watch the Henrietta tapped, there were plenty of years ahead in which to work this out. He still had time. His father had worked twelve hours and more every day of his sixty-nine years, and had solved greater problems during the Civil War than anything with which William was faced today. He did not like labor agitation. His thoughts returned once more to Rafferty, whom he had recently promoted to keeper on the blast furnace. This was the dangerous and responsible job of tapping the iron, and no man in the mill was better qualified for it. But the Old Man knew that Rafferty was the spearhead of the Amalgamated's agitation among the men. He would take watching and the firmest handling.

The Old Man tramped down the long dark shed past the double row of puddling furnaces, five to a side, with the line of sandmoulds for hundred-pound pigs in the centre. At C furnace he saw Paul, his face scarlet, streaming, and streaked with soot, swinging a shovel as he helped the boss puddler, Tim Callahan, line the furnace with ore. The heat in the shed was almost beyond endurance, but the men working there were all used to it. Paul was swinging away at his work, naked from the waist up, his back running with sweat, and his blue denim pants soaked along the thighs. He did not see his father as he passed, but Callahan caught the Old Man's eye and gestured with his thumb at Paul and winked heavily.

CHAPTER VI

[*1875*]

THE PARTY was in full swing. It was the largest party the Scotts had ever given. Paul was graduating from preparatory school at the head of his class, and his mother felt the occasion warranted the utmost festivity.

The whole house was brilliantly lighted. Strings of Japanese lanterns were festooned from tree to tree across the lawn, and a three-piece orchestra played for dancing in the front parlor. The music echoed through the ground floor, where all the double doors were thrown open to make a continuous sweep of the spacious rooms. All the heavy winter draperies had been taken down, and the carpets were replaced with slippery straw matting. Through both parlors and the wide centre hall, young men in light summer flannels and girls in ruffled mulls and dimities waltzed and polkaed and laughed and bantered with one another. Every girl carried her dance-program dangling by a silk cord from her wrist.

Paul was dancing with a very pretty girl named Kitty Wheelwright. She was tall and slender, with a froth of yellow curls and twinkling blue eyes. She was, in fact, generally thought the prettiest girl in Allegheny and she was accustomed to being told so. She loved dancing with Paul. He was graceful in spite of his height and weight, and he danced well, and above all, she liked the way other girls followed them with their eyes; especially Louise Kane. Anybody would think Louise thought she owned Paul, the way she was always watching him. Paul was even used to being teased about it. He shrugged off the remarks like a dog shaking water from its coat. He did that now, when Kitty said something about Louise.

"Shucks," he said. "You girls are always making up stuff like that. Lou's—why, she's just one of the family."

"You mean she wants to be."

"We have to—oh you know, Father sort of looks after them. Since Uncle Dick died."

Kitty made a mocking face. She had heard her mother say that Mrs. Scott and Mrs. Kane had set their hearts on Paul's marrying Louise some day, and she felt sorry for him. It would be fun to cut Louise out. She flicked her eyelashes and raised her beautiful blue eyes to gaze at Paul. She thought him the best-looking boy she knew. She liked his wide forehead, his large blue eyes beneath broadly arched brows, his short, straight nose. His chin was square, slightly cleft, and his blond hair was parted in the centre and smoothly brushed down. They danced in silence for awhile; then Paul said suddenly, "Gee, you're pretty, Kitty."

He liked the quick color in her cheeks and the soft pressure of her hand. It was fun to have some girl beside Louise seem interested in him. He decided he would let Louise shift for herself a little more after this. All this time since her father died he had just gone along helping his mother try to make the Kanes forget their tragedy. They should be able to stand on their own feet by now, he decided.

Delia, going through the front hall with fresh lemonade, saw Paul and Kitty and duly reported, with her unfailing volubility, in the pantry.

"He's got the belle o' the ball," she said triumphantly. She did not like Louise. "That'll lairn that cow-eyed gazelle not to moon over him."

"Don't be takin' all that so serious," Mary said, arranging sandwiches on a lace-paper doily. "They're only kids, the lot o' them."

"Ye're wan to talk!" Delia snorted. "Kids!"

At every young people's party there were always a few girls who clung together in a shy, giggling group and kept away the boys. Elizabeth would not mingle even with them. She loathed dancing; she detested boys; and before this party she had done her best to dampen Paul's spirits by sniffing, "Whoever heard of giving a party for a boy? Nobody but Mama would think of it!"

"Oh, Liz," he had answered impatiently, "can't you be human for once? You know very well the party's not for me. It's for all of us. If you won't make an effort to be decent to anybody, don't blame Mama if she tries. Don't you ever want any friends?"

"Not your kind of friends!" Elizabeth retorted. "Frivolous idiots! 'Would you care to honor me with this Schottische?' " she mimicked in a squeaky voice. " 'Miss Elizabeth!' Oh, I'd rather be upstairs in the attic with a book."

"It's a pity you won't be. You can't even let anybody else have a good time."

"Don't worry, Lord Chesterfield," she jeered, "I'll keep out of your way. Be sure and pay attention to that ninny, Louise."

"Oh shucks!"

The evening was too perfect for anyone to spoil. Clarissa stole a moment to stroll out to her garden. The air was warm, the sky clear. The starlight peppered the vast black arc of the sky, only to be obliterated at intervals by the swift, rushing red blaze of some distant furnace. Though she had travelled in the highest mountains of Europe, and had seen the Atlantic in all its boundlessness on glorious summer nights, Clarissa Scott sometimes felt, standing in her own garden and gazing at the black and scarlet drama of Pittsburgh's spaces, that nowhere on earth did the sky seem to possess so potent a vastness, nowhere did it arch itself over a wilder and grander panorama than here, where man had joined with nature to create a more unbelievable spectacle than any she had known. Its quality varied with the seasons. It took on the fantasy of spring, the gloom of autumn, the hot breathlessness of summer, the fiery contrast to winter's grim cold. By day the view spreading in the distance from the Scott garden was a cluttered and ugly prospect, jagged with stacks and bulky with the crude sheds of mills and foundries, dirtied with the eternal pall of smoke. But by night the dark covered these prosaic and ugly sights, and seemed to widen the peculiarly vast sky. Those were the qualities of this fierce and strange city to which she had come full of doubts and misgivings. She wondered now, standing there in the garden that she had made and which she loved, how she had ever become reconciled to a place so crude and ugly, to noises and sights that shocked the cultivated ear and eye, to the eternal dirt and soot that made life one constant struggle to keep clean. In twenty-five years she had grown utterly into the texture of this surging, turbulent place. Her old home in Baltimore seemed like a cocoon, some silken retreat in which she had slept until her red-whiskered husband had lifted her out of it and whirled her off to this maelstrom. She sometimes felt surprise about it still.

"It's a great sight, isn't it, Mama?" Paul had come up beside her and stood, his arm in hers, gazing out across the Flat and down at the flaming sheds by the river bank.

"I'm glad you feel that, Paul," she answered. "I think one has to, to give one's life to ironmaking."

"Yes," Paul said slowly. "But——"

His mother glanced at him quickly. Now it struck her that it was rather odd of Paul to leave the party where he was having such a good time and come out here to look at the view with his mother.

"You have something on your mind," she said.

He nodded, his face very thoughtful.

"It's something I've wanted to talk to Father about," he said. "For a long time. About my plans."

His mother waited. He waved his hand towards the panorama before them.

"It's about that," he said. "It's not going to stay just that way. I—well, I've been thinking about what I ought to be getting ready to do."

"I thought your plans were all made. Your father——"

"Father's ideas are fine, as far as they go. But he doesn't think of the iron business as a science. A new invention, like our Bessemer, is a mountain for him to swallow. And they keep inventing new things in steel before they've really learned how to use the ones they've got. There are some men——" he stopped, and bent down to pluck a blade of grass to chew.

"I think Father would be interested to hear what you think about all this, Paul." Clarissa spoke thoughtfully.

"Well, yes, he might. But you see—he doesn't like some of—of these people. Like—well, Captain Bill Jones out at Edgar Thomson." Clarissa understood now. Anybody connected with Carnegie was anathema to her husband. "Captain Jones," Paul said reluctantly, as if some disloyalty were involved, "is the greatest steelmaking genius in the world."

His eyes gleamed, and Clarissa found his young face inspired. She realized that she was the recipient of her boy's most guarded confidences. He had been afraid to take them to his father.

"Do you know Captain Jones, Paul?"

The boy nodded slowly. "I don't think Father'd be—well—pleased," he said uneasily. "But I've always heard so much about him. And when they tried out his new mixer this year—it's the most important development in steelmaking. Even more than the Bessemer. Well, I just had to meet him. So—I did."

"How?"

"I asked Roger Hull in school to introduce me. His father worked at Cambria with Captain Jones. So we went there one Sunday afternoon."

"And was he all you expected?"

"Even more. He's a great man, Mama, a really great man. Of course he knew who I was. He knew Grandfather well and he spoke about Father, too. He said it's a pity more iron men don't know their business the way our family does."

"I hope he is a sincere man, Paul."

"Oh, he couldn't be anything else. You just know he's all right. He talked to us about the future of steel, and showed us a lot of his drawings and formulas. And he gave me some advice, too."

Clarissa saw now that Paul had come to her in this mood and at this moment because he wanted the reassurance of telling her his plans before broaching them to his father. She could not have dreamed that he had been influenced by her husband's outstanding rival, the competitor who had already driven him from railmaking. It was not only from Paul that she had heard of the steelmaking genius of William R. Jones; her husband had said, "That blustering absentee millionaire"—(Carnegie)— "doesn't deserve a superintendent like Jones. He's too good for him."

"Captain Jones told me," Paul said, "that the future of steel will be shaped in the laboratory. He says that uses will develop for steel that nobody even dreams of today. He says they will make alloy steels with metals that haven't even got names yet. The whole future of our business, he says, will depend on metallurgy." Paul looked at his mother. "He says that's what I ought to study."

Clarissa nodded. Paul's voice was warm with enthusiasm. He said, "Captain Jones told me it's up to me to learn how to make these new steels. Especially for our business, we'll be making the very products that Edgar Thomson and Carnegie are too big to bother with. He advised me," Paul said, coming hurriedly to the point, "instead of going to Princeton like Bill, to go where I could major in chemistry and metallurgy. And then when I go into the mill—you see?"

"That's wonderful, dear." Clarissa did not want to show too much pride in Paul's judgment and initiative. That was not the Scott way. "Did Captain Jones tell you where to get such training?"

"Yes, he said either at the Massachusetts Institute of Technology or the Sheffield Scientific School at Yale. But I've decided already, Mama. I want to go to Sheff. I've had enough of Boston." Clarissa knew he was thinking of Bill and of his father-in-law's unwelcome intrusion into the Scott mill. "The only thing that bothers me is, I hate to take this up with Father."

"But Paul, why in the world? Father will be very happy and proud. Nothing could please him more than your making decisions like this. It's wonderful to know how much you care about the mill and what plans you have for it."

"Well, that's good. Only I wish you'd tell him, just the same. I kind of dread to. Tell him Sheff's only three years, too. I'll be in the mill a whole year sooner. Only—I guess you'd better not mention Captain Jones, Mama." He spoke uneasily.

So that had been Paul's trouble. He was shrewd enough to know that his father would resent any obligation to Captain Jones, even for something so purely friendly as good advice to his son. Clarissa laughed and squeezed Paul's arm and said, "I'll tell Father. You go along back to the party. And Paul, dear—" she hesitated.

"I know," Paul said quickly. "I ought to dance with Louise. All right, Mama, I'll be nice."

Re-entering the house, Clarissa came upon William junior bending solicitously over Julia, who was seated on the drawing-room sofa. Clarissa paused somewhat sadly to watch her eldest son. She was glad to see him taking such care of Julia. Yet she deplored the marriage. The little drama of this scene was quite apparent to her. She knew that Julia had at first refused to come to this party so soon (six weeks) after the birth of her son, William third; and she had only given in at the end because William had urged her so strongly. Clarissa could see that Julia was making a martyr of herself, and something of a fool of William. Clarissa wished she could help him.

As a matter of fact—and Clarissa could guess this too—Julia's real trouble was her bitter resentment at her father-in-law for making it impossible for her to go home to Boston to have her baby. She had conceived a plan of going there—with her husband, of course—six weeks before the child was expected; and she had planned to recuperate for several months afterward at her family's place at Marblehead. Goaded by her prodding and pleading, William had been rash enough to propose this to his father. The Old Man had merely stared at him and answered, finally, "If you have taken leave of your senses, you can take leave of me too. You haven't earned a fortnight's vacation, much less several months."

"But Julia," William had said unhappily, "Julia can't travel alone to Boston in her condition, and it would be quite unthinkable for us to be separated at a—er—at this time."

"Who said you'd be separated?" his father asked impatiently. "Your wife's place is where you are, where your duty is. Do you think your mother went trailing off to Baltimore or Kamchatka every time she bore a child? She had her children where she had contracted to have them—in her husband's house, where they belonged. Go and tell that to your wife. Tell her what her duty is, and if she declines to perform it, order her to. Boston. Bah!"

Julia was never to forgive her father-in-law. From then on the sole aim of her existence was to get out of Pittsburgh. She pressed her parents about it, she nagged William. But William knew that while his father was alive he had no choice except to do as the Old Man said. "Otherwise," he had told Julia, "we wouldn't have any money." Even Julia's parents told her that until William could leave the mill with no loss of prestige or income, she must stick it out in Pittsburgh. At home they spoke of their son-in-law picturesquely as a pioneer on the industrial frontier.

Clarissa stood watching them. William had brought his wife a cool fruit cup from the big punch-bowl in the hall which she refused with something like a shudder, though the room was warm. William drank the punch himself, with patent scorn of its innocence. Not the least of William's tears where his father was concerned was the possibility that the Old Man would discover his emancipated habits.

He did not see his mother's troubled expression as she watched Clarissa knew that Julia was a perfectly strong, able-bodied girl, consid erably heavier of bone and muscle than herself, who had actually gone through the experience of childbirth with no disturbance to her health at all, and whose bearing now was the pose of a spoiled and ungenerous nature. She knew the indifference, and to some degree the contempt, in which Julia was held by every member of the family, and the scornful nickname of Duchess that the servants had given her. She knew her own inability to do anything to improve the situation, and she was troubled by her sense of failure. Her husband, coming across the room to her, read her thoughts in her face.

"Why worry about it, my dear?" he said.

They stood side by side, watching the young people waltzing to a new piece by Johann Strauss the Younger. Only because of his wife had William Scott unbent in recent years to permit dancing in his house.

After the waltz came the Virginia Reel. This was the climax of every dancing party, and the young men usually kept their reel partners for the supper that followed directly afterward. Elizabeth was so determined to avoid the hateful possibility of having to take supper with a boy that she slipped off upstairs just before her father's friend, Angus McGowan (to whom, because of his booming voice and jolly, sociable manner, the duty usually fell) took his place by the musicians and called out "Choose your partners!"

Paul had succumbed to a twinge of remorse and asked Louise to save the reel for him. After all, it was the least he could do to please his mother when she had been so grand. But originally he had intended to take Kitty Wheelwright in to supper, and he knew she expected him to ask her. She must have parried several more attractive offers while waiting for Paul, because now her partner was Georgie Cottrell, who was a head shorter than she, and red-faced and fat and an awful dancer. All the girls thought him the last resort. Gee, Paul thought, Kitty must be furious. Her face was very pink and she held her chin defiantly; but she managed, too, to smile conspicuously at Georgie.

Louise was bridling with delight and pride as Paul led her to her place. The young people were lining up in two rows facing the length of the hall, clapping their hands in rhythm as the musicians struck up *Turkey in the Straw*. Everybody loved the reel. The old-fashioned dance was dearer to the tastes of the Pittsburghers than the more elegant polkas, waltzes, and schottisches that Julia considered the only dances fit for ladies and gentle men. The reel she thought a rough, boorish thing to which only clouts would descend (quite overlooking its ancient tenure in the aristocratic South). She watched it disdainfully from her sofa across the hall. Even William Scott, her cold, detestable father-in-law, at the head of the line, was tapping his gaitered foot on the matting and clapping his heavy scarred hands with as much gusto as a boy.

Louise was a beautiful dancer, Paul could not deny that; and she was sparkling with the thrill of winning Paul back from that bold Kitty Wheelwright. There was a fluttering giggle in her voice as she spun through the figures, and nothing less than triumph in her brown eyes. As the last couple, hands clasped, cheeks flushed, panting and laughing, sashayed down the center, Clarissa motioned Paul to lead Louise, with her cheeks scarlet and her curls flying, into the dining-room. The whole party trooped in after them.

"Och, *begor*!" Paul heard a squeal as he entered the room with Louise on his arm. He was just in time to see the last of the amazing sight of Delia and Mary, down by the pantry door, holding up their black skirts in their hands and vigorously performing the Irish jig to the music of the reel. They swished through the pantry door with gasps and giggles. Paul followed them out there. They were panting and blushing furiously, smoothing their hair and settling their aprons and trying to compose themselves before coming back to serve supper.

"*Mister Paul!*" Delia choked. "Och, away wid ye, please!"

"Why?" he asked. "This is fun. Don't stop. Come here, Louise." He reached through the door and drew her out to the pantry. "Go on, jig some more. The music's still playing."

But Delia shook her head violently, and Mary was blushing so furiously that Paul felt sorry for her. There were tears in her eyes and she swallowed clumsily. She felt guilty of a dreadful breach of manners, and would have given anything to have undone the embarrassment of having Mister Paul and his young lady come on her at such a moment. She hung her head and tried to compose herself. She was afraid she would burst out crying.

"Why, what's the matter?" Paul insisted. "You oughtn't to mind, girls. This is a party. Come on, you can't stop in the middle of the jig, we want to do it too. You'll have to teach us."

"No, no," said Delia, having had time to recover her poise and anxious to give Mary the same chance. "Have ye forgot where ye are, Mister Paul? It's all the guests are in the dinin'-room now, waitin' for their supper, and we've our work to do. Go on now, there's a dear, and leave us be."

"All right," he said reluctantly. "But will you do the Irish jig for me some day soon? Promise?"

"Sure," the two girls chorused. "Sure we will. Go on, now."

So he returned to the dining-room, to help see that everyone was served. The girls were seated in chairs grouped about the room, while their partners circled the long table spread with all the favorite delicacies. There were bowls of chicken and potato salad, platters of moist pink ham and cold sliced roast meats, piles of dainty cucumber, cress, and cream cheese sandwiches, tiny tartlets of Sarah's airiest pastry, spicy crisp pickles and relishes, trembling jellies, piping-hot buttered yeast rolls, and a proud mountain of a bristling white coconut cake. Finally there was strawberry ice cream, that very far from commonplace treat even to these young people on the verge of adult dignity. It was, as Louise with shining eyes and eager affection said to Clarissa, "a lovely, lovely party."

Paul thought so too. For, when the last guest had gone, and he was starting out the side door to help Joel snuff out the paper lanterns, his father came up and dropped his heavy hand affectionately on Paul's shoulder. Looking into the Old Man's face Paul knew that his mother had already spoken to him. Neither of them knew exactly what to say. "Your mother," said old William at last, "has just told me—"

"And it's—all right, Father?" Paul asked.

William Scott nodded slowly, studying the boy's intent young face.

"It is," he said. "I had hoped for such a son, and I am proud to know that I have one."

Their hands clasped hard for a moment. William Scott turned into the house and Paul went outside, lifting his head with a motion of joy and purpose. At this moment it did not seem as if anything in the world would ever be difficult or uncertain. He had a sense of clear sight into the future, a perfect, solid knowledge of what he wanted to do. It was as real to him as the familiar but stunning panorama spread out in the darkness beyond the crest of his father's land. He stood there for a moment, recapturing the mood in which he had talked with his mother. Then he heard a homely sound behind him on the kitchen steps; the clink of dishes. The maids were sitting there relaxing after their hard day's work. They were eating the ice cream that Sarah had saved for them.

"Don't forget you're going to teach me that Irish jig, Mary," Paul called over his shoulder as he walked away to take down the lanterns.

A soft laugh in the darkness was the only answer.

CHAPTER VII

[Spring 1877]

CLARISSA COULD NOT get used to having all the boys away. She liked her family to be at home all together. Now with William married and gone, and Paul at Yale, and Edgar at Lawrenceville, the house seemed very queer with only the girls at home. Clarissa had not wanted to send Edgar away to boarding school. Neither William nor Paul had gone. But the twins had grown so wild in the past year, especially when they were together. They alternated between violent, sometimes bloody quarrels, and equally violent demonstrations of affection and partisanship. Their father had decided that Edgar must go. "That boy cannot be left in charge of women. He needs a firm hand all the time," William Scott told his wife.

So Clarissa had to be content with letters from Edgar and from Paul. She made a great to-do about their letters, reading them aloud at the breakfast table, and sending the news from one absent son to the other. She regarded all their doings as matters of the utmost importance. When Paul wrote that he had made the Varsity crew, after stroking the Sheffield crew the previous year, Clarissa glowed with pride.

"Isn't that splendid?" she said to Elizabeth. This particular letter had come in the afternoon mail and Clarissa could not wait until evening to share it with the family. She took it for granted that Lizzie would be as eager for news of Paul as she was herself. Clarissa read the letter aloud, even though Lizzie was writing something at her desk and could not really be paying much attention.

"There was a big crowd of men out for the tryouts," she read from Paul's letter, "and I didn't really think I had much of a chance. They don't notice us much over at Sheff, you know. They leave us pretty much to ourselves, which suits us all right. Most of the chaps at Ac seem pretty young to us. But my club seems to feel good about my making the crew. Two of my friends are on the Regatta Ball committee. The ball comes at the end of Class Week. Tell Lizzie if she decides to come East with you for the races and everything, we'll see she has a good time."

"Wouldn't you like that, dear?" Clarissa asked.

Elizabeth looked up from her desk and said, "Oh—I don't know, Mama. It seems sort of—silly."

"Why, I don't think so," Clarissa said. "I should think you'd love to go to that ball, with all Paul's friends to look out for you."

"Well—we'll see."

Clarissa looked hard at her daughter. She still at times could not help comparing her with Louise Kane, so pretty and eager and fun-loving. Louise would be overjoyed if she were to be asked to the Regatta Ball at Yale. Clarissa wondered whether Paul was going to invite her, and whether Louise would be going East with her for Class Week, whether Elizabeth went or not. Clarissa stood up.

"I'm going over to Julia's for tea," she said, drawing her watch out of her belt and looking at it. "Don't you want to walk over with me?"

"I don't think so, thank you, Mama. I want to finish up this work so I can take it to the parish house in the morning."

Clarissa said, "Very well, dear, I'll be back in an hour," and went out.

Elizabeth went on writing until she was startled by a commotion in the hall. She laid down her pen with a frown and put her head out of her door. Constance was standing at the foot of the third-floor stairs shouting to Mary who was up in the sewing-room.

"Mary!" she yelled. "Aren't you ready yet?"

Mary's face appeared over the banister. "Sh! Haven't I told ye not to yell like that? Ye sound like a harpy!"

"Well, when are we going?"

"Soon as I get them patterns out. Now ye be patient."

Constance sighed, went to her room, and slammed the door shut behind her. Almost immediately it opened and Elizabeth stood on the threshold, a furrow between her eyebrows. Constance stared at her. Lizzie was so plain and angular and earnest, full of purpose and good works. She was deeply interested in the foreign missions work at the First Presbyterian Church and since finishing school had been spending most of her time at the missionary office. She wore a puce-colored dress with a buttoned basque unflattering to her bony figure, and she looked nearer thirty than the nineteen she actually was. She said irritably, "Haven't you been asked not to scream at people? Nobody can think with you in the house."

Constance was standing before her mirror, twisting the masses of her gleaming hair this way and that, piling it high, bunching it low, studying the lines of her throat, her chin, and the curves of her small pink ears. Her hair was an extraordinary color, a gold-red so vivid that it shone almost like burnished brass, and it grew in a profusion of tumbling curls that positively irritated Elizabeth by their dramatization of a personality already much too conspicuous. Elizabeth could not understand why Constance had to be this way; why her eyes, instead of being merely eyes, must be two restless, darting emeralds—yes, they were actually green, and who ever heard of bright green eyes!—set in slanting lines in her triangular face in a way that only heathen eyes ought to lie. Everything about Constance had that different, that disturbing, foreign quality. The rest of the family all had the solid good looks and manners that well-bred people ought to have. Why must Constance be a freak?

She stuck out her tongue at Elizabeth in the mirror. Her sister caught her breath and said, "I'm going to tell Mama about that."

"Go ahead," said Constance, practising a new expression. She was holding her eyes very wide open with a sophisticated stare of surprise. Mary came in, bonneted and shawled, and said, "Get yer things on. I'm ready now."

"Hooray!" Constance seized a bandbox from the wardrobe shelf, flung the cover in one direction, two or three bonnets in another, and began to tie on the one she wanted to wear, carefully fluffing her brilliant curls to frame her face. She was completely absorbed in what she was doing.

Elizabeth regarded these manifestations with something akin to disgust. She could not understand how any sister of hers, even in the silliest part of her 'teens, could care so passionately about the angle of a curl on her cheek, about the half inch more or less that would give the perfect finish to a hemline. Constance finished her prinking and turned to leave the room.

"Now ye'll pick up all them things ye strewed about," Mary said dryly.

"I won't! I'll do it when I get home."

Mary said, "We ain't goin' till ye pick up this room."

"You mean thing!"

"Just as ye say," Mary said. "But if ye want to get to Boggses ye'll hurry and do what ye're told first."

Constance's red mouth set in a hard bow and she began sullenly to pick up the bonnets and ribbons she had scattered around the room. Elizabeth turned away with a sour smile. She thought it unsuitable for her mother to give Mary so much authority over Constance, but it pleased her to see Constance forced to obey.

She went back to her room where Constance's racket had interrupted her in the report she was writing for the mission office. She stood at the window a moment, watching Constance and Mary emerge from the side door and start up the street. Constance walked with short, prancing steps, her small feet dancing in and out of the folds of her skirt. Mary, who always moved quickly, had to hurry nonetheless to keep up with her. They were on their way to Boggs and Buhl's dry-goods store to select material for a new dress for Constance. They would come home with a length of serge, merino, or bombazine, braid or buttons for trimmings, gimp and skirt-binding, sateen for lining, and even, as Constance's young figure had begun to fill out to subtle curves, whalebone and buckram for shaping the fashionable stiff basques. They would spend absorbing hours in the big attic sewing-room, crawling around on their hands and knees with their mouths full of pins, while they worked out the intricacies of cutting by patterns from Godey's (Constance would hear of no others) and putting in untold yards of careful bastings, only to rip them out a day later.

It occurred to Elizabeth at the window that she had never been allowed at fourteen to choose the material for her own dresses and go shopping without her mother. Maybe that was only because she had never cared about clothes anyway. She stared absently at the two figures disappearing up the street and with a sudden jerk turned back to her desk. She did not really care a rap what that silly Constance did; and if anyone had suggested that Elizabeth could be envious of her sister, she would not have known what he was talking about.

CHAPTER VIII

[*July 1878*]

NOW THAT HE had graduated from college and taken his permanent place in the mill, Paul often noticed the difference from the six summers when he had worked there. Some of the men had changed in their attitudes towards him. When he was a youngster they had all bantered and joked with him, and in their thick brogue carefully explained the jobs they had been told to teach him, and self-consciously watched their cursing when he was around. He knew, too, that when he had been working at something dangerous, there was always some trusted old hand keeping an eye on him.

But now that he had authority, and a whole section of a shed made into a laboratory where he worked out formulas that were Greek to the oldtimers, many of them kept their distance. Some of them thought his formulas and experiments a lot of blather. Others treated him with respect because they knew he could wield a shovel and raveller with the best of them. None of them realized the importance of what he was doing. Hard alloy steels were still so new in the United States that the mills producing them had to import European metallurgists to develop their formulas. Paul intended that Scott's should produce new specialty steels superior to anything being made either in the United States or in Germany or England. And he meant to perfect them himself. He told his father so, walking down to the mill in the early mornings, bristling with energy and enthusiasm.

"But," he said one day after he had spent weeks making up his mind to do so, "we can't work out most of these alloy formulas with the equipment we've got, Father."

This was a daring thing to say and Paul had expected his father to protest or disagree gruffly. He should have known the Old Man better. Old William merely looked thiughtful and pulled at his beard. The Bessemer had not in any way come up to expectations and who should know that better than the Old Man?

"I wish we hadn't built that thing," he said. They were approaching the mill now and he stared gloomily at the egg-shaped dome and huge bulk of the smoking converter. "I was wrong about it."

"It seemed the right idea at the time."

The Old Man was unlocking the door of his office. He always carried the key on his ponderous watchchain. "My mistake lay in thinking we needed a Bessemer to make our kind of steel," he said. "The only thing I can say for myself is that we never tried to compete in rails, Bessemer or no Bessemer. Edgar Thomson would have ruined us if we had." The Old Man's eyes turned stony and Paul knew what he was thinking. The investment in the Bessemer had hardly paid for itself. At times the mill had lost money on its steel blooms and billets, and the profit-and-loss account had only been evened out by the business in pig-iron. In view of this it always irked the Old Man to think that he had sold an interest in the business to Gaylord—that he had let in an outsider—for the very purpose of building the Bessemer.

Paul said now, watching to see his father's reaction, "It might sound kind of rash to you, Father, but my idea, if you wanted to act on it, would cost us some more money at first."

It was time for the day's first rounds and the Old Man would normally be on his way through the mill. He looked at his watch. Paul regretted having brought this up now. He ought to have waited until they were walking home at night. But his father stood thinking. Presently he looked up and said, "Well, what is it? Do you want to build an open-hearth?"

Paul smiled. He loved the Old Man for broaching the thing himself. Maybe he would not want somebody else to get the credit for the first mention of a new idea. His stubbornness was as much a part of him as his gruff speech. But underneath he was proving to be surprisingly openminded.

"Is that it?" he asked Paul again.

"Sure, that's exactly the idea. You've followed these new processes closely enough to see why we need one, Father. If we had an open-hearth we could put out formulas with any specific content of different materials. We could make special carbon and tungsten and chrome and manganese alloys that nobody in the United States has tried yet. Gosh—we'd have the market to ourselves."

The Old Man was looking pretty pleased with the idea. Paul went away and left him alone to think it over.

Down in the casthouse of the blast furnace they were closing the taphole with fresh clay and loam. A cast had just been run off and the dark cavern was a hell of raw heat and suffocating sulphur fumes as Paul stepped in. The breakers were at work shovelling sand over the moulded pigs in the casting-floor. Paul could scarcely see the sweating, hairy, half-naked giants through the curtain of hissing steam that boiled up from the floor as the hardening pigs were sprayed with water. Jim Rafferty and his two helpers were ramming the taphole from which they had just cleaned the last of the slag. Paul stood aside, watching them man the mud-gun which forced the wet clay into the hole. Jim did not do much of the work himself but directed the others. He had the responsibility for timing and tapping the furnace, a big job that he had earned through years of skilled work and judgment at the puddling furnaces. Before going on the blast furnace he had been as expert at ravelling iron as any puddler in the district. He was a master at judging by sight alone the instant when a charge of boiling molten iron and cinder was ready to be ravelled into balls and tapped off into the sand-moulds. And his handling of the rod—the long raveller that was plunged into the hell's brew to prepare the liquid fire for pouring—was so perfect a coordination of skill and instinct that even the Old Man himself would pause in sheer admiration to watch Rafferty at the climactic point of a heat.

When the taphole was closed Paul stepped over and asked Jim if he could come down to the laboratory within the next hour or two. It would be four hours at least before Jim had to start preparing for the next cast. He opened his mouth and said something but Paul could not hear because the words were drowned out in an ear-splitting clangor which suddenly shook the casthouse. The breakers had started smashing the hardened pigs from the moulds, wielding sledges and bars in tremendous swinging blows. Paul motioned to Jim and they walked out to the yard. It was not much quieter here; the rattle and crash of the skip-hoist, the piercing hisses of steam-engines and the grinding roar of the limestone crusher pounded their eardrums.

Jim only said, "I ain't sure I can get away." He scowled.

"I wanted to talk about this new furnace we're thinking of trying. An open-hearth."

"One of them college idees, no doubt."

Paul laughed uncomfortably. "Well—it's a new way they've been trying out. It's not just a theory—they've got one at Midvale. I kind of thought—"

Jim kicked at the cinders underfoot with a thick-soled boot.

"I wanted to show you some of the stuff down in the lab," Paul continued. "About the results you can get from the open-hearth process. And—" he started to turn away, knowing instinctively that this was the way to handle Jim, "we thought you were the likely man to put in charge of the thing if we do build it."

He did not look at Rafferty to see whether the hard dark mask of his face would reveal any pride or interest in this recognition. He looked at some schedules in his notebook.

Jim said, "I got a new snapper in there I got to keep my eye on. I can't come right away."

"I'll be down there between nine and ten," Paul said, walking away.

Paul knew that the real reason for Rafferty's sullen suspicion of him was bitterness over the union question. For five years past the gulf between the Old Man and the Amalgamated members in the mill had been steadily widening. It was Jim's unquestioned mastery of his craft, and his knowledge of his own excellence that gave him his fearless and violent impetus to organize labor in the mill, and which also commanded the Old Man's respect to the extent of tolerating Jim's agitation. William Scott regarded an, ironmaster more highly than anything on earth, and there was none finer than Jim.

But their relations were never better than an armed truce. Rafferty thought the Old Man a despot. Scott was excessively secretive about his real methods of dealing with organized labor, and very vociferous in unspecific denunciations of it. No person could verify the existence of spies —they were called scabs—and blacklists in the Scott mill. Yet every man who worked there knew that in some devious form they must exist. Rafferty's furious assertion to Mary, years ago, that William Scott intended to force a yellow-dog contract on every man and boy in the mill was not a suspicion. It was a fact, obtained and verified in some manner that James would never reveal; he too had his informants. The contract had never been signed, and both sides had threatened violence.

Paul made his way slowly into this tense situation. With the unprejudiced optimism of youth he supposed that sincere open-mindedness and some kind of working, practical confidence would solve the impasse between his father and Rafferty. He tried to discuss the union question with the Old Man but he was abruptly rebuffed. "You have enough to do without butting into that," his father said. "Between your turns on the floor, and that soup-kitchen of yours you have no time for management problems. I am still here and while I am, I'll attend to those matters."

There was nothing to do about the Old Man, then. But something might come of a better understanding with Jim Rafferty. The proposed new open-hearth would be the best chance for talking to him and working with him as much as possible.

So on a cold, stormy Sunday afternoon in February, Paul knocked at the door of the Rafferty shack. He had the blueprints for the open-hearth rolled up under his arm. He had never been down here before, and he was a little doubtful about this idea of talking to Jim at home, but it seemed worth trying. He found Jim hunched in his characteristic position at the kitchen table. The small stove was roaring red-hot, and old Patrick was sniffling beside it in his wheelchair, wrapped in a soiled quilt.

"Good afternoon," said Paul, removing his hat. "I dropped in to see if you had a spare minute, Jim. I'm stuck on these plans."

Jim looked up frowning. "Well?" he said roughly. "And what's ridin' ye? Don't ye keep yer work to weekdays like the rest o' us?"

"Well—sometimes. Only I've been trying to push this thing through and I thought if I could clear up this point here—" he began, somewhat too hurriedly, to unroll the plans on the table—"I could go ahead and work at home this evening."

Jim shrugged. It was so unnatural to see Paul Scott here that he could not react with ease to his presence, even though he seemed to have the best of reasons for coming. Besides, it was union principle that all matters concerning work must be discussed in the mill, during working hours. Jim considered this visit an infringement of his free time, although he had done nothing all day but sit brooding in this room.

"It's about these spouts," Paul was saying, ignoring Jim's scowls. "If we're going to tap from the other side of the furnace, we'll want to carry this channel through here—" he was tracing with his pencil—"and connect it there. But can we do that without interfering with charging?"

Jim bent over the plans and followed the line of Paul's pencil. He leaned forward so stiffly as to appear to be doing it against his will, but he did lean forward and put his horny black forefinger on Paul's line. "Nah," he said. "Ye'd have to start there—" and he began to work on the problem from his practical knowledge of tapping. Paul felt pleased. This was the kind of interest he wanted. Secretly Rafferty was tremendously proud of being chosen boss on the new experimental furnace. "But he'd rather die than admit it," Paul thought.

In a short time both were absorbed in the plans. Patrick dozed in his chair, the stove sizzled and puffed, the coal-oil lamp spluttered, and outside icy particles of snow whirled against the window panes with pattering noises. Paul, intent on his discussion, was nevertheless conscious of having finally broken through the wall of Jim's militant unfriendliness. Not even to himself would he confess that any part of his visit had been a ruse. But when Jim, in the absorption of their talk, called him Paul, he felt that he had at last made progress.

And then the door flew open. Mary stood on the threshold, her face scarlet from the cold, framed in a black velvet bonnet with an edging of sealskin. Beneath the dark fur her hair gleamed vividly. She held a small sealskin muff close to her chin, and wore a short cape of the fur around her shoulders. The outfit had been a Christmas present from Clarissa Scott, made over from Elizabeth's old sealskin dolman, and worn by Mary with tremendous pride. Her first finery, and she was to treasure it for years.

"Bless me soul!" she cried. "Ye got a visitor!" She hurried in and shut the flimsy door behind her. "Welcome it is to ye, Mister Paul," she said, as she kissed her father and carefully laid her muff on a high shelf. "James, ye didn't tell me we'd be havin' company to celebrate me day off."

James grunted. This development was something he had not thought of, and he neither understood nor approved the look of it. It was all wrong. "We ain't got company," he said. "Ye ain't, anyway. Mr. Scott came in to talk business with me, that's all." He spoke with finality, plainly dismissing Paul and anxious for him to leave. But Mary did not pick up this hint.

"Still an' all," she said, "Mister Paul's here, whatever it was brought him, and ye're not leavin' without yer tea now, Mister Paul. With the kettle boilin' and so cold out too—ye must have yer tea."

While she talked she moved quickly about the littered kitchen, picking up things that had been flung about all during the week, putting them away in drawers and cupboards, setting cups and spoons on the oilcloth table. "Funny yer mother told me to bring down a batch of honey buns today," she said, taking them from her bag and arranging them on a plate. "She'd laugh if she knew ye was to eat 'em here, the way ye're fond on 'em."

Paul laughed too. "Honey buns! Great! And I'm starved." He reached over and helped himself to one. He pushed the plate across to Jim. "Good!" he said with his mouth full. "Specialty of the restaurant. Try one."

James had retreated into his black sulk like a turtle into its shell. The weekly gift of food from the Scott house infuriated him as always. The incongruous situation of Paul eating this food in these circumstances, and urging him to eat it, with Mary standing there smiling and chatting, natural as ever, drove some spike of feeling deep into his chest until he winced with bitterness. What was this, what was Mary up to? James's head swam with uncertainty and bewildered resentment. He could not tell whether he saw Mary as Paul's servant, as his own sister, or as some stranger dressed up in fine clothes and play-acting the part of a hostess with airs that she certainly hadn't learned here where she was born and belonged. And this 'Mister Paul' business! It irritated James unbearably, driving home Mary's inferior status in a way which, he thought, should have offended her, and instead seemed to suit her very well.

He pushed back his chair with a jerk.

"I ain't hungry," he mumbled.

Paul found his position extremely difficult. "Oh, come on," he said. "I want to ask you one more question and then we'll all drink tea." He drew James back into his chair, while Mary shoved her father's wheelchair close to the table.

"Ye've not seen Mister Paul for a long time, have ye, Dad?" she cried. She always spoke extra loud and clearly to Patrick, supposing that his age and injuries must make him deaf, which was not really the case. The old man shook his head.

"Not for near twenty year," he said, supping his tea loudly from a saucer. "I saw ye last when yer grandfather brought ye down to B furnace when I was bilin' there. That was afore the war."

"Let's see—it must have been about fifty-nine or sixty. Why, I wasn't more than four! I remember Grandfather taking me down to the mill. We had to climb down the embankment on those rickety wooden stairs, and up the other side. He carried me part of the way."

Patrick nodded and smiled. He chewed his bun with his toothless gums. "That's right," he said. "That was afore th' Ould Man built the bridge over the railway gulley. 'Twas all right gettin' to the mill from the river side, but a domn plague a-climbin' them ould wooden stairs."

"And we had to wait for the tracks to be cleared before we could cross them. I kind of remember I got pretty dirty. I had a white dress on."

"A dress!" James exclaimed in spite of himself. "A boy—in a dress?"

"Yes. I guess it didn't turn me into a girl, but I certainly did wear a dress, or at least a kind of jumper. I had pants underneath it, though. And later I had to wear a kilt, Sundays and holidays. Grandfather made all of us boys wear kilts."

"Lot o' nonsense," James muttered.

Paul looked up quickly from his tea to study the man's dark, brooding face. James sat in his characteristic hunched position, his head sunken between his shoulders and his eyes fixed on the pattern of the oilcloth table cover. Clearly he was troubled by something far more profound than contempt for starched jumpers and clan plaids. Paul had a dual sense of knowing, and of not wanting to know, what this was. He tried to draw Mary and her father into talk again, but Mary was not impervious to James either. Her expression as she looked at her brother was resentful. Had she been alone with him she would have "straightened him out," as she now thought to herself, with a few vigorous strokes of her energetic tongue. Like Paul, Mary knew against her will what James was thinking. She hated the kind of mind that gave rise to bitter, twisted ideas; and almost as if looking to him for relief, she turned to Paul.

"Me brother's an odd one," she said nervously. "He'll talk to ye fair enough about some things, but he don't like small talk, do ye, James?"

"Och, Mary, let me be!" James stood up and reached behind him for his cap hanging on a peg. "Since ye've learned what ye came for," he said rudely to Paul, "ye'll not mind if I'll be on me way." He tramped to the door, flung it open into a rush of icy wind, and slammed it behind him as he stepped outside.

Paul turned to Mary in dismay.

"Oh, Mister Paul," she said. Her face was red and she kept her eyes on the table, blinking them rapidly. "Oh, please, Mister Paul. Don't be too angry with him, for all he's bad and rude like that. He's a queer lad. Sure and I don't know what call he's got to be makin' a fool o' me!" she added bitterly.

"Why, I'm not angry, Mary. I know Jim pretty well. He's always surly about something or other. He just didn't want me to be here, that's all. Maybe I'd better go," Paul said lamely.

"Oh, no," Mary answered in a dull tone. "Don't be hurryin'."

"Well, I think I'd better. After all—Jim did remind me that I'd finished what I came for." He smiled, making some effort to do so, and gave old Patrick his hand. "Good-bye, Pat. Maybe you'll get down to see our new open-hearth when she starts. She'll be a beauty."

Mary walked to the door with Paul. "I feel that bad," she said in a low voice.

Paul paused and looked at her. Her thin face was suffused with unusual color and her gray eyes were large with tears. Paul knew, looking at her, that those tears would spill over the moment the door closed behind him. He kept his eyes closely on her face, studying as if for the first time the delicate white skin, the pulsating blue vein in the temple, the striking line of brilliant hair at the forehead, the chaste thin lips. He had an impulse to take her hands, red and chapped and, he saw, bluish with cold, and chafe them together in his to warm them. But the impulse was gone as quickly as it had come, before she could have noticed. He wanted then to walk straight out of the house, nodding a casual good-bye to her as he had made his everyday greetings for years past. But he stood still at the door, looking down at her. Mary's face grew redder as the moment lengthened. Presently she raised her head. She did it as if with great effort. And Paul felt that every line of her face, every quiver of her features, the muffled tone of her voice, belonged to a woman he had never seen before, and yet whom he had known always. He did not conceal everything of this from her. Mary saw discovery, amazement, bewilderment in his face. In the same moment she saw herself as if in a mirror, the girl standing with him at her father's door. And she saw too in the tall man with the square cleft chin, the fair hair and the intent eyes, a person at once a stranger and the most familiar of all people. She moved her lips but he did not hear a word. Both were quiet, for a very brief minute. Then Mary turned away.

"Good night, Mister Paul," she said. "I am sorry about my brother."

He walked away, kicking rubbish out of his path and climbing over the haphazard tracks of the Flat. His head felt light, curiously detached from his body; the sensation was unpleasant. He felt as if nothing he might touch were real. There was surprise in the contact of his feet with the cobbles. He had a sense of profound unreality, coupled somehow with concrete discovery. Nothing that he had seen or felt seemed so much to emphasize this as the last words he had heard at the door of that shack. Mary had spoken to him totally without her brogue.

CHAPTER IX

[1879]

THE WALK to the mill was bitterly cold on winter mornings like this lowering Monday. It was still dark when Paul and his father left the house. Wrapped in their heavy greatcoats they kept their heads down against the wind and their hats pulled forward to protect their eyes from cinders.

Today was a particularly bad one for walking. The air was bitter, the sky an ugly dark gray streaked with black smoke from the riverside mills. Yesterday's sleet lay in frozen patches on the cobbles and brick sidewalks, treacherous spots which Paul hated to see his father tread. William Scott had been stubborn in refusing to consider driving to the mill, even after a pneumonia two years ago, the only illness of his life. "I've walked to work since I was sixteen, and I'll walk until I die," he said. "What's more, you'll walk, Paul, so long as you're running things with me. Let others do the driving." By "others," Paul knew, he meant his son William.

While he was going over the day's schedules in his private office, the Old Man heard his two sons together in the adjacent outer office, a big, dreary barren room overlooking the freight-yard where outgoing flats were loaded. He walked through the door and heard Paul saying, "I can't stop to talk now, Bill. I've got to get over to the new shed, they're waiting for me. Can't you take that up this afternoon?"

William junior adjusted his starched white cuffs and looked contemptuously at Paul. Paul had changed his street suit for a dirty blue denim shirt and a pair of canvas overalls. On his feet were heavy boots with massive soles over an inch thick; he wore these when he needed to walk on hot cinder. He was pulling on hand-leathers also. He and Jim Rafferty were going to draw a sample of molten Bessemer steel which they were to test for comparison with the projected new open-hearth formula. William junior looked at his brother with hostility, while the Old Man in the doorway eyed them both.

"Very well," William said in his drawling way. "But I shan't be here after four. You'd better make it before then."

"And why won't you be here after four?" old William asked. "Four o'clock is not quitting time that I know of."

"No, but I'm leaving early today. Father Gaylord is staying with us and he is taking the six o'clock to Chicago. He asked me to be home in time to see him before he leaves."

Paul gave his father an expressive look. He hesitated a moment, reluctant to waste any more time, but also, old William saw, anxious to convey something about his brother. He stopped at the doorway. "If I don't see you before four, Bill, it can wait till another day. The questions you want to ask me about the new job have nothing to do with Mr. Gaylord, *so far as I know.*" He spoke with slow emphasis, deliberately bringing the full meaning of his remarks to his father's notice. Then he walked away. His grotesque boots clattered loudly down the stone-floored passageway.

Old William seated himself in a chair, leaving his eldest son standing awkwardly before him. "Well, William," he said, "what is the meaning of this argument?"

"There is no argument so far as I am concerned," William said, stiffening.

"It sounded that way," his father said. "What did you want to see Paul about?"

"I wanted to talk to him." William did his best to let his father feel his resentment at this inquisition. "About business," he added.

"About business, eh? That's fine. Did you have some suggestion to make about business?"

"Well—not exactly—"

"Some questions you wanted to ask, maybe."

"Yes—a question."

"Maybe I could answer it." The Old Man looked shrewdly at the tense face of his son. "I know quite a bit about this mill."

William did not know what to make of this irony. He had never seen his father act quite this way. He took a deep breath. "Frankly," he said, "I wanted to ask about the—the new open-hearth."

The Old Man dragged his heavy fingers down his beard. "And why this sudden interest in the open-hearth?"

"Well. Father Gaylord—"

"Ah," said William Scott, settling back amiably in his chair, "I thought so."

"He has a right to know, Father."

"Right?"

"He has an interest in the business. He's a partner."

This fact was a very unpleasant one for the Old Man to face, and young William knew it. His father sat with one heavy fist clenched on his knee. Presently he leaned forward. His gray eyes began to glitter: "William," he said, "these are hard things for a man to judge within his own family. I have tried to be just, but I don't know whether I am just in this matter. I can only tell you—" he spoke slower, thinking—"without rancor, what my decision is. Laurence Gaylord does not own this business and does not run it. I do. Therefore I tell you that he will know what he is told twice a year in my reports, and nothing else whatsoever. Nor are you entitled, as my appointee in the bookkeeping department, to give him any information that I do not authorize." The Old Man paused and took a deep breath. He wanted to say more. He wanted to say that he would like to tear out the Bessemer, as if it were a special equity of Gaylord's, and fling it in his face. But he only said abruptly, "That is my decision."

William junior chewed his lower lip. His face began to lose its cool, expressionless composure. He knew that his father-in-law would press him tonight for information, and that he would look like a fool for being so ignorant about the business and about the new installation. This made him angry. "You treat me like a half-wit," he blurted, suddenly losing his control. "I've been kicked around this place for eight years." He paused. "I won't stand it any longer!" he shouted.

Normally the Old Man would have flayed him in anger at this. But he kept silent. William had never seen him so calm. "Go on," old William said. "What do you propose to do about it?"

"I want my rights."

"Just what do you consider those rights to be?" The Old Man folded his hands over his waistcoat and leaned back as if to invite a long discussion. William was baffled by this question too. He felt turgid with the desire to say something sharp and clear and forceful, to make some concrete demand to which his father must accede. But when he opened his mouth he only said, "I want to be respected around here. I want some recognition."

Old William looked at him narrowly and almost as if with pity.

"William," he said, "it seems those things you're asking for are what I can't give. Nobody can hand them to a man. They follow automatically after he's done something to earn them. They come by themselves—if you do your job and do it better than anybody else. I can't make an iron man out of you."

"Like Paul!"

"Yes, like Paul. I didn't make Paul, William. I didn't give him any special privileges. He thought out what he wanted to do and he's doing it. He's a brilliant steel man, whether you like it or not. Of course they respect him around here. It has nothing to do with his being my son. Your failure has nothing to do with your being my son, either!"

"My failure! And you talk of justice!"

The Old Man rose, his shoulders heavy as if he were carrying a burden. He faced his son squarely. "Yes, William," he said, "I talk of justice.

There is a justice in heaven which perhaps you are not old enough to understand. I pray to God that He permit you to see it before you die." He shook his scarred forefinger slowly. "You have not pleased me, William. You have not taken part in our affairs. You have not given an honest day's work. You are lazy. You care nothing for the iron business. You have put on airs. You serve spirits at your table. You have married a woman who thinks herself better than we are. Sometimes I feel you think the same of yourself." He paused, glowering majestically. "When you speak of justice," he said slowly, "reflect upon these things. If I have failed in my duty, I have had my reward. And if you have failed in your duty, you have yours."

The Old Man turned and tramped from the room. William slumped into a chair. He stared blankly at the lead-colored walls, the high, narrow windows, the blackened winter sky that hung over the waterside like a shroud. He would have been glad if the earth had opened and swallowed up the whole roaring, flaming, living hell of the Scott Iron Works, and his father and brother with it.

Paul went down to the Bessemer to join Jim Rafferty there. He had a momentary fear that Jim would repeat his queer rudeness of yesterday. But Rafferty was one man on the job and another outside. Jim stood now as a spectator from another department, his attention fixed on the monster before him. Paul wished he could concentrate like that. He had been haunted all last night and all this morning by his disturbing experience of yesterday afternoon; by the memory of that moment with Mary which would not fade away and leave him in peace. There should be nothing so peculiar about it. He had merely gone to a certain house, talked to a man he knew well, seen a woman he knew even better—and why should this gnawing turmoil of mind be the consequence of that? He shook his head sharply and forced his attention on the converter. It was ready to blow.

And now excitement, familiar but primevally keen, swept everything else aside. The great bulbous brute towering above him began to rumble and belch. From its mouth high overhead a stream of scarlet flame threw itself at the acid winter sky. The blower gave a sign. The blow was ready, and suddenly the usual concert of barbaric noises in the shed was drowned in one fearful ear-crushing roar as the cold blast was shot into the liquid fire in the converter's belly. Element grappled with element, oxygen in a death-struggle with carbon, a battle more terrible and wonderful than man had ever made before. The flame, steady and fearfully red, began to change color, a descending scale of blinding flashes echoing from the death-and-birth agony of the elements. Inside the beast steel was being born, and from the vessel's roaring mouth the solid fire changed from red to blue, to orange, to yellow . . . the roaring subsided to echoes and heavy throbs . . . the flames faded at last to white. The ladle moved forward on the dinkey-track, paused near the converter's colossal dome. From his place fifty feet away Paul waited in suspense as tense as if he had never seen this happen before. He put on his dark goggles now, and held his breath as the enormous, egg-shaped vessel began to tilt slowly over on its axles.

This was the most unbelievable of all the fantastic sights of steel—this cascade of liquid death, beautiful with a color too vivid to believe, a salmon-red at once lovely and terrible. From it and around it streamed light and heat intense beyond endurance. As the liquid fire flowed into the enormous pot below it, a curtain of hissing sparks shot up and sprayed the scene like a gigantic devil's shower-bath. Paul and the other man and the dark shadows behind them were dwarfed by the drama that they had brought about. Paul waited until the last quivering drops plopped into the brimming twenty-five-ton ladle. The soup had the fearful fascination of Niagara for the death-leaper. A ladle of liquid steel is a lovely terror, the surface rich and undulating, creamy, seductive.

When the area nearby had cooled sufficiently, Paul followed the ladle and the crew down to the casting-shed, where a row of ingot-moulds stood ready. It was here that he and Jim had placed the special form for the sample they were drawing, and when their mould was filled they moved it away to Paul's laboratory. The cold air in the barren room struck their sweating bodies with ferocious contrast. James shuddered. It was no wonder that pneumonia was the greatest death trap of all the steel man's hazards. He told Paul that they must stop and rub down while they were waiting for their sample to cool. By now Paul could barely recall the bewildering rudeness of this same man only twenty-four hours ago. In the absorption of the work they were doing together, both forgot everything except the job in hand and the coming challenge to Paul's planning and vision, and to Jim's experience and skill.

CHAPTER X

[*1879*]

ON HER NEXT Sunday out, two weeks after Paul's first visit to the shack, Mary was amazed, while sitting alone with her father early in the evening, to have Paul appear again. He stepped inside, shaking the snow-flakes from his hat. Mary took his overcoat in silence.

"I wanted to see Jim again," Paul said rather awkwardly.

"Why, he ain't here," Mary said. "He's at his union meetin' tonight."

"Oh." Paul hesitated. He felt as if Mary must know that he knew of the union meeting as well as anyone else in the mill. But apparently she didn't. She merely looked puzzled.

"Well, I guess I'll go along then," Paul said.

Old Pat looked up.

"Sure, and I'd be glad not to see ye hurry," he said. "T'ain't often I see a visitor. Sit ye down."

Paul looked to Mary to second the invitation. She did not seem particularly cordial. But she pulled a chair out from the table and offered it to Paul. The Rafferty kitchen, like all its counterparts, was the living centre of the house, and one sat in it on straight chairs around the battered table. Paul seated himself and looked about. Supper was over and Mary had put away the dishes and food. There seemed no reason to offer him anything, though that would have tided over this unaccountably awkward moment. Mary's face seemed stern, and today she was wearing a severe dress of woollen material of an unflattering mustard-color. It was trying to her red hair. She sat down and picked up the basket of socks she had been mending. Paul hastened to make conversation.

"Where are your sisters, Mary?" he asked. "You have two, haven't you? I've never seen them."

Mary almost blurted, from some impulse that she could not understand, "I don't know a reason why ye shud have seen them." But she answered, "Me sister Kate's married and gone since last summer. She lives up the way a bit. Her husband's at Scraife's."

"She comes in to do fer me every mornin'," Patrick said. "She's a good daughter, but not like me Mary here." He spoke with pride.

"Och, Dad, ye shouldn't say that. Kate's a better girl than me."

"And you have a little sister, too, haven't you? Where's she?"

"Up at St. Veronica's in Greensburg."

"What's that, a convent?"

Mary nodded. " 'Tis. A fine place for Bridget. She's a bit wild, ye know. I used to worry about her dreadful."

"She sounds something like Constance," said Paul.

Mary laughed. Without meaning to, Paul had said the right thing.

"They're both spalpeens," Mary said. "Bridget's a year younger than Constance. I fair don't know which gives the more trouble."

"I should think you'd miss her," Paul said to Patrick. "It must be lonely for you."

"It is that. Indade, I'd fair like to have a woman around the house. 'Tis dreary the way we are, James and me. Sure, he was a fool about Annie McGlone."

Mary explained. "That was James's sweetheart. They were pledged for near five years. But James w'uldn't save money against their weddin', he wud give everythin' he earned to th' Amalgamated. So Annie got tired and married somebody else. I don't blame her," Mary said. "James'd sell his soul for Joe Bishop and all them trouble-makers." She spoke bitterly. "They're a cruel crowd, Mister Paul. They've a terrible strong idea and they think they're right."

"Maybe they are right, Mary."

Mary looked up quickly from her darning.

"If yer father doesn't think so, Mister Paul, I'd be surprised to see ye differ from him. He's a just man."

"Yes, of course he is, but Jim's union have something on their side too. Father may not take advantage of labor but most steel mills do. Father's perfectly willing to give them good wages and working conditions, he just won't have anything to do with them as a union."

"I don't blame him," Mary said. "He probably knows the way they're all possessed. They ain't reasonin' when it comes to the union."

"Neither are you when you agree with Father that it's completely bad without knowing something about it."

"Ye're talkin' pretty smart, Mister Paul," Mary said. Then she stopped suddenly and her mouth fell open. "Why," she gasped, "that was an awful fresh thing for me to say. I altogether forgot meself."

"Ye sure did," said Patrick. "Ye ought to be ashamed."

"She should not!" Paul leaned forward and rested his elbows on the table. "She ought to say whatever she thinks. She's worth listening to. Mary's got sense, Pat."

The old man looked at Paul quizzically. "I've thought that for a while meself," he said.

Mary blushed. "Go along," she said. "Don't ye think ye ought to be gettin' home, Mister Paul? I wudn't want to be hurryin' ye away, but I know James won't be home till very late. I shan't wait for him."

"Nay," said Pat. "He's always late from thim union meetin's." He reached down and began turning the wheels of his chair in the direction of the stove, where he sat huddled over his thoughts.

Paul looked for a moment at his hands clasped together on the edge of the table. He wanted to say something; Mary sensed that without taking her eyes from her work to look at his face. Neither spoke for several minutes. Then Mary, shaking the darning-egg out of a sock, said gently, "Really, I meant it, Mister Paul. 'Tis time for ye to go home. I want to get my father ready for bed now."

Paul turned his bent head toward her.

"Couldn't you walk home with me?" he asked, very quietly.

With compelling strength he looked straight into her eyes. Deep-set and sensitive, windows of truth, he knew she would have turned them away but for the power of his will. Her lips parted and she moved her right hand unconsciously, almost as if she were going to raise it and hold him off. He said in the calmest tone he could, "There's a heavy snowstorm, you know. I don't think you ought to walk up alone in it."

She meant to tell him that she had walked up and down alone for six years in all kinds of weather, often far worse than this. But his face, intent and calm, his commanding blue eyes, stopped the words before she spoke them. She knew that this suggestion of his was unsuitable and that she should tell him so. Instead she said, helplessly, "Very well, I will. Just wait till I've got me father settled in bed and then we'll go."

She put away her basket and went over to Patrick. The old man appeared to be dozing, his head fallen forward on his chest, his eyes closed, and his breathing heavy. Mary stood for a moment looking at him. Then she turned his chair around quietly and pushed it into the next room. Paul sat by the table and waited. He looked slowly about the drab little room. Not an object in it but was ugly and shabby. There was nothing to be seen except the grim accoutrements of the daily life of the poor—no ornament, no book, no picture. The only mitigation was a measly geranium which stood forlornly in a battered tin can on the window sill. Evidently Patrick was not too helpless to water it. But it was clear that the plant never felt the sun. The sight depressed Paul acutely. When Mary came back into the kitchen he looked at her fine-featured face and shining hair with newly realized amazement that this delicate human plant should have bloomed in such wretched, barren soil. He was glad when she put on her wrap and the sealskin-trimmed bonnet and tippet that became her so delightfully. He started to kneel down and help her with her overshoes, but she shook her head and refused his help, a tacit reminder that this really did seem unsuitable to her. They hardly spoke at all while they were preparing to go out. And they kept their silence halfway up the steep, slippery climb of Fulton Street, with the snow flying in their faces. Paul looked back occasionally as they mounted higher and higher away from the water-level. The Union Bridge down below them was only a dark, arched blur through the snowstorm, punctuated by dim blobs of light from its gas lamps. The snow muffled their footsteps and all other sounds about them; horses up on the avenue ahead of them could hardly be heard. Only an occasional sound of sleighbells pierced the soft wintry silence, and once there was a long, hollow hoot from a tug pushing an ore barge down the invisible river below. Mary took her first few steps with shaky uneasiness. This was, after all, not merely the unusual experience of walking home with Mister Paul; it was also the first time she had ever walked out with any man. It startled her that Paul Scott should be the first man to escort her in this way.

Paul was not content to let the silence lengthen. He was not a taciturn man and there were certain things that he wanted intensely to say. He had determined in the past minutes once for all to put himself beyond the grip of the bewilderment that had kept him in turmoil for two weeks past.

"Mary," he began. "I know you think this is rather queer, my wanting to walk home with you."

"Not queer, Mister Paul. 'Tis rather surprisin', in a way, but ye must not think I'd misunderstand ye when ye have a nice thought."

"I never would think that. You know us all so well, Mary. I don't have to tell you how we—I—all—feel about you. You're almost like—oh, you know what I mean."

Paul could have kicked himself for his clumsiness. "I just like you," he said stoutly. "I'm fond of you and somehow all this, you know, this maid business gets in the way and makes me feel queer. The point is," he said, suddenly clear in his mind, "the point is I want to be friends with you."

"Well, ye are," said Mary. "Only I wouldn't have ye get odd notions about my place in the house, and get mixed up about who belongs where. I know exactly who belongs where," she said.

"Oh, so do I," Paul said quickly. "That's not what I'm trying to talk about, Mary. I just feel that we've known each other a long time and you're so close to us and to Jim and the mill and everything we all do— well, and I want to be able to talk to you sometimes when you aren't on duty in a damn cap and apron."

"I'm not ashamed o' my cap and apron."

"No," Paul said earnestly. "Neither am I—you see what I mean. Only

I really do want to talk to you sometimes. I've got lots of things on my mind. You could be a big help to me."

"I don't quite see how."

"Well, a fellow needs somebody to talk to. Maybe that's why I try to get your brother to sit down with me sometimes and talk. You're far more sensible than he is. And—nicer too." Paul laughed a little.

"Well, I thank ye for that. I can't see the harm in talkin' things over once in a while, as ye say. It's true I'm interested in yer work, and the mill and all."

"That's just what I mean," Paul said eagerly. "And I mean about talking to you—well, I can't very well arrange a formal interview in the house with you standing at attention in a uniform."

Mary laughed. " 'Tis a funny picture."

"Well, you see. So that's what I mean—can't I see you once in a while, like this, when you're away from the house, Mary? That's all I want, just to be able to visit and talk. There's no reason why we should feel queer about it, is there?" Paul asked the question in a voice so earnest that he seemed almost to be pleading. Mary had an impulse to check him. Instead she said, softly, "No, Mister Paul. No reason at all."

They walked on in silence for a time. Then he said, "I'm glad you think that, Mary. It's just—well, when you feel the need of a friend, and the friend is right there—that's the way it is. Don't you think so too?"

"Yes, Mister Paul."

Twice he opened his mouth to ask her not to call him Mister Paul. He shrank from hearing her say it. But instinct told him to leave that point alone.

"I feel great," he said. They had reached Western Avenue now, and were close to the Scott house. "I'm so glad we had this talk. I'm glad you understand what I mean. We'll be good friends, won't we, Mary?"

He paused and looked at her closely through the darkness and the snow. The milky reflection from the snowflakes seemed to penetrate the night around them and illuminate her face framed in gleaming hair under the silvery crust of flakes on her bonnet. He looked straight into her eyes. He found in them calm and utter comprehension. They walked together slowly to the front gate, where they paused again. "Good friends," Paul repeated. "That's so, isn't it?"

"That is so," she said. "Good night." She ran up the steps ahead of him and turned off the front path to the side one, which led to the kitchen door. Paul looked after her until he heard the back door close. Then he took his latchkey from his pocket and slowly unlocked the front door.

CHAPTER XI

[*Winter 1879*]

MARY AND CONSTANCE were up in the attic making the dress that Constance was to wear to a grown-up party; her first grown-up party, really, to which she insisted on going though her mother wished she had not been invited. She had burst into bewildering maturity at the startlingly early age of sixteen. Her beauty, which had crystallized in tender curves and a dazzling pearly skin and an arrogant carriage of her flamboyant head, was matched by a terrifying defiance of all authority. Mary went to bed each night grateful that she had got through that day without losing control of Constance; she never knew when that might happen.

The dressmaking had degenerated into a quarrel. Constance stood before the pier-glass with the basted dress on, commanding Mary to cut the decolletège lower, and to dart in the sweep up from tiny waist to swelling bust in a way that made Mary blush from shame and temper.

"What's the matter with ye?" Mary cried despairingly. "Have ye no shame? Ye can't go across the river to the Duquesne Grays' Ball with the whole top o' yer body naked in the wind!"

"You nanny-goat! Why can't I? Can't you see for yourself how this dress ought to look?" Constance rattled the pattern in Mary's face. "I guess if Worth knows how to design it you needn't think you can improve on it!" Her green eyes glittered.

"There, Miss, that'll do! Maybe I'm no French dressmaker but I'll see to it ye keep a civil tongue in yer head." Mary ripped out a basting-thread with a vicious jerk. "And ye needn't try to lord it over me with yer airs and goin' about naked for the whole town to stare at. Ye're not a grown woman yet."

"For my purposes I am," said Constance with a laugh.

Mary looked at her sidelong.

"Purposes?"

"Do you think I expect to be a nice Nelly all my life? Marry a solemn old grouch like Pa and spend my life marketing and raising babies like Mama? Huh!"

Mary swallowed. There was no use answering this kind of talk; that only egged Constance on. Constance was eyeing herself in the mirror, stretching her white arms and rolling her red curls over her fingers. "I'm going to get out of this stupid place and live where it's exciting."

Mary began to laugh. "Ye had me startled for a minute. I keep forgettin' what a child ye are, with yer everlastin' play-actin' and grown-up ways. I could almost have believed ye."

"You might just as well believe me because I mean it."

Mary laid her sewing in her lap and raised her head slowly, scrutinizing Constance with a long stare.

"Ye'd better tell me exactly what ye do mean," she said coldly.

Constance came over, pushed the dress from Mary's lap, and nonchalantly sat down there herself. She twined her naked arms round Mary's neck and burrowed her face in the starched, epauletted shoulder. Mary sat stiffly. This kind of thing usually produced a bombshell.

"I'm going," Constance said in a rapt voice, "to marry a duke. Or an earl. Somebody who lives in a palace and has a hundred servants and knows all the wicked people in Europe, and keeps racehorses and—oh, everything exciting."

Mary's laughter rang out, peal after peal, until she had to gasp for breath and was wiping her eyes on the corner of her apron.

"Och, ye're a spalpeen. Dukes and racehorses."

"All right," Constance said with a strangely adult shrug. She slid off Mary's lap and began to tighten her corset-strings. "Laugh all you like, but that's what I'm going to do. You watch me."

"And how do ye propose to meet this nobleman that's to take ye out o' Pittsburgh and make a fast woman out o' ye?"

"Just leave that to me," said Constance, narrowing her green eyes. Mary stared at her. If she were to take this seriously and tell Mrs. Scott about it she would not be believed. A lot of things around here, Mary thought swiftly, were beginning to be hard to believe. Like yesterday when Mrs. Scott was so upset because Paul flatly refused to go to the Bascoms' dinner-party with Louise. He had never done such a thing in his life. Mary could not help hearing what he said to his mother. "Why?" he had repeated roughly, in a tone one could hardly recognize. "Because I'm sick of her, that's why. She's been hung around my neck ever since I can remember. I want to choose my friends for myself." Mrs. Scott had not come downstairs all afternoon. Mary was too innocent to realize what had really kept Clarissa Scott, puzzled and alarmed, brooding alone in her room.

Paul knew on what Sundays Mary was at home with her father, and on those days, as she climbed the hill in the evening, Paul appeared at her side midway up the stretch from the cinder Flat to the elevation of Chartiers Street. Usually, instead of turning right to take the direct route to the Scott house, they turned left and strolled in the opposite direction, along the crest of the ridge that paralleled the river. This way led to the mills and blast furnaces, dominated by the Scotts' Henrietta, which ranged the north bank of the Ohio just beyond its confluence with the Allegheny. They would walk slowly along Rebecca Street, pausing often to stand at a corner where they could turn and gaze down at the panorama, magnificently brutal, which both were strong enough to love. There was a point that jutted sharply just before the land swung away against the westward turn of the Ohio. A deserted house stood here, its steep front steps tottering and filthy, but pitched at just the angle that gave them, as Paul said, a box-seat view. Paul would take his big handkerchief and spread it on the top step for Mary to sit on. Sheltered by the darkness they would sit and stare at the incredible picture spread below them. They could see the whole shape of Pittsburgh, the triangle clasped in the rivers, hung with arclights, but illuminated also by the weird volcanic furnaces on the outer shores. Paul could estimate almost to the minute the progress of any blast or blow, as smoke was succeeded by flame, flame by an angry red blossoming of the darkness, the scarlet blossom by white, the white by fireworks more dazzling than the pleasaunces of Versailles. They knew of no more inspiring entertainment than this, played out for them against the great darkness in the hills around, and the spangled majesty of the sky.

They themselves were calm. This was their view of nature. If Paul's face was raptly eager before Mary climbed the bend of the street where he met her, it was peaceful when she looked at it. If her heart beat like an engine before she saw him, she seemed preternaturally quiet when she knew his eyes were on her. And when, after several weeks; after nights of lying awake; staring into the dark, of praying on the cold floor beside her bed for the strength to do what she must, she tried to tell him that this friendship must not continue, he had only the obstinate answer, "Why not?" She could not tell him. It was unthinkable, immodest and unwomanly, that she be the one to mention the fact which could only be kept at bay by elaborate silence.

"I just—well, I don't want ye to meet me any more," she said. She moved her hands with a gesture of finality. She had a way of making small movements of her head; or of raising her hands in a light, sweeping motion instead of using words. Often she broke off a sentence with a movement of head or hands that was more expressive than anything she could have said.

"Don't you like these walks? And—and—talking together?" That was unfair and he should not have asked it. She tried to look squarely at him to let him see her reproach but his face as she watched it began to grow solemn and tense. His blue eyes were wide and strained and there was no mistaking the passionate set of his lips. He stared wilfully at Mary, his eyes studying her thin face, the impalpable blonde down on her upper lip suddenly noticeable in the red glare of a blast below them.

"Don't you?" he said again, defiantly.

"I'm thinkin' about yer parents, Mister Paul. I don't like this feelin' o'—o'—" she clasped her hands nervously.

"We haven't done anything wrong," Paul said truculently.

There was a long silence. Then Mary said, "Ye know right from wrong as good as me, and ye can't fool yerself no matter how ye try."

The furnace below them belched a great scarlet jet. Paul pointed down at it and said, "Can you argue with that? Can you stop it? Why should you try to stop this?"

Mary caught her breath with a gasp. Then she said, "If that's the way ye're goin' to talk then I'll have to quit me job and get clear away from yer family and you too."

"You don't want to do that."

"O' course I don't want to do it!" she cried, suddenly exasperated. Why did he have to torment her? "But can't ye see fer yerself?" She shook her head unhappily and tried to get up from the steps; she wanted to go away. But he put his hand on her arm and drew her back on the step again. She did not want to talk about this. Couldn't he understand her struggle without talking about it? She listened to him dully while he tried to explain, insistently and too protestingly, that this was not a deception, that they were doing no wrong. His words sounded hollow. She watched him there in the spurting glare from the mills, talking in that foolish way when he knew the plain truth as well as she did.

Paul must know how she felt. In these few weeks they had learned to talk their hearts out on every subject except this. Mary loved to have Paul explain the work that was going on down in his own mill and the neighboring ones. He made it sound like a story, while they sat up there on the height and watched its living illustration unroll before them. Both had been born in the heart of this drama, and it compelled them in the grip of a fundamental need to be together. Paul, for his part, belonged to it utterly, as Mary felt she belonged to his family; that was why this wracking bewilderment gnawed at her when he persisted in the course which was the breath of life to both of them, yet which held the threat of catastrophe to everything they loved.

Mary stirred and rose slowly from the step.

"It's gettin' on for ten o'clock," she said. "Come on, Mister Paul, I must be gettin' home."

He rose and descended the steps with her. On the bottom step he turned suddenly. "Mary!" he said. "For God's sake will you stop calling me Mister Paul!" His voice was metallic.

She bent her shoulders. Her throat closed up; her voice when she spoke was strangled. Paul leaned down to hear her. Her answer was inaudible.

He could not sleep that night. He lay in bed with the gaslight turned on, smoking his pipe and trying to read engineers' specifications for the open-hearth. He could put on that act of seeming pigheaded before Mary, but away from her it was hard not to hear in retrospect her soft brogued voice: Ye know right from wrong as good as me. He did. He should know better, if standards and privileges and training meant anything. But everything else was dimmed by this new, persistent awareness of her; this fantastic sense of awakening to something that he had always known but never recognized.

Here in the house he went out of his way to avoid her. Once in a while, if he heard her voice in the pantry he restrained a quick impulse to go out there; he had a strange reluctance to see her among the other servants. He found himself listening to her brief passing greetings with an ear sharpened by surprise that this same voice could speak so hauntingly up on the height over the river. He remembered always those astonishing words she had said to him last winter in English untinged by her inborn brogue. Now she spoke as she always had. Yet if he saw her in the house, he saw not the neat maid in her aproned uniform and cap but the laughing girl in the sealskins, coming in from the cold.

She was everywhere around him. He felt her ways in the smooth, tightly-tucked linen sheets, in the fresh starched curtains at the windows; he saw her pride in his family and their home, in the shining brasses of the gaslights and doorknobs. If there was always a small pot of flowers on the marble-topped whatnot beside his morris chair in the bay window, he had not noticed it, he thought, until now. If the silver cups that he had won at Yale for rowing had ever gleamed so brilliantly before, he had been oblivious of that too. He twisted his head uneasily on his pillow, pressing his knuckles above his eyes. He had a deep desire for rest, and a premonition that his desire would not be realized.

Suddenly, as he rolled over with a groan, he had a vivid picture of her upstairs in her room; wide-awake like himself; perhaps weeping; perhaps trying to find the answer through prayer.

"My God," he muttered, reaching up to turn out the gas. "Oh, my God."

This was the day when Edgar was coming home for Christmas vacation. His arrival was anticipated with a mixture of emotions. He was in his father's bad graces because he had almost been expelled from school at Thanksgiving time. That particular crisis had been touched off by something involving a stolen bakery-cart and a nocturnal return to the Hamill House via the coal chute. But Edgar was a brilliant student. His splendid marks put him in a bargaining-position that was very awkward for anybody trying to maintain discipline.

Clarissa, who never wanted the children to be away, would ordinarily have been thrilled by the prospect of having Edgar at home for two weeks. But lately Constance had been so trying that there was no telling what she might do with Edgar there to stir her up. She had been rude and strangely excitable, breaking into fits of temper and insolently flouting Mary. Hurt feelings and tears would follow, and finally the business of Constance, wheedling and remorseful, trying to reinstate herself in favor. Clarissa was not anticipating the holidays with much pleasure this year.

She was ready to leave for the station to meet Edgar, and she went to Constance's room to call her. She had told Constance to be ready at five o'clock, but she was not there. She must be upstairs sewing with Mary. Clarissa went to the foot of the third-floor stairs and called.

"No, Ma'm, she ain't here. Not since three o'clock—she said she was goin' down to finish her—" Mary was running down the stairs. She paused in the hall, her hand on her forehead. "Begorra," she exclaimed. "She cudn't a' had no lessons to do. With school out."

"It's time to start now. I can't wait for her."

"She'll be rare disappointed. She was all excited yesterday about seein' Eddie again." Mary stuck her head into Elizabeth's room, which was empty and then went to Constance's room on an impulse and looked in the wardrobe. She came back to Mrs. Scott and said uneasily, "Her green bonnet and cloak's gone. She oughtn't to go out without tellin' me."

"She certainly should not!" Clarissa said indignantly. It was a strict rule that Constance was never to leave the house without telling her mother or Mary where she was going. For a moment Clarissa felt irritated with Mary. After all— But she forgot her annoyance as she looked into Mary's eyes, brimming with tears; she realized with a shock how thin the child had grown, and how pale. She had been noticing for a long time that Mary was looking very badly. She loved her, so much as to feel the deepest concern at the thought of her being ill or in trouble. She put out her hand and laid it on Mary's cheek.

"Don't you feel well, Mary?"

Mary's lips were trembling and Clarissa's heart ached as she saw how hard the child was trying not to break down and cry.

"I—I'm all right, Ma'm. I—it's Constance." Mary swallowed. "She oughtn't a' done that."

Clarissa started down the stairs.

"Don't worry about that, Mary. Just give her a piece of your mind when she comes in."

She got into the carriage and stared gloomily out the window as McCready started for the bridge. She had been aware for months past, much more keenly aware than she had ever admitted to herself, of a looming crisis. Why, she thought now, did one always put off coming to grips with such a thing until it was too late to act? A year ago she would have been inexpressibly shocked at the thought that Paul could be attracted by an Irish housemaid. That was the kind of thing that simply did not happen. And now here she was *worrying* about Mary instead of coldly making up her mind to send her away. Clarissa rebuked herself now for her lack of perception and realism; why had she not found another place for Mary long ago? Why, she thought, did a lady always take refuge in the belief that certain things "just could not happen"?

Nothing that Paul or Mary had ever done had led Clarissa into what she would have been ashamed to call suspicion. But she had not been able to avoid observing the two when chance brought them together in the same room. They had always been youthfully natural and unaffected. Now Clarissa pondered whether it was her imagination or a fact that Paul treated Mary with increased formality, and with a new courtesy in thanking her for small services that he had always previously, in a careless and boyish way, taken for granted. She wondered too whether she imagined that Mary was markedly distant with Paul, with a kind of reserve and deference in her manner unlike her former simplicity. No sudden or even tangible change was to be seen in either the boy or the girl. But Clarissa's instinct was too keen to escape the vibrations of a dormant, unacknowledged passion. What she could not know was its power or its scope.

Constance slipped in the side door about half an hour after her mother left the house, and tiptoed upstairs, hoping to get to her room before Mary nabbed her. She was going to be in trouble enough with her mother, without having to go through all the hoops with Mary first. She did not really care much, though. Her eyes were glittering and there were tense little dimples in the corners of her mouth. She slid into her room shutting the door noiselessly behind her, but it was no use; Mary was sitting there, her mouth hard and a merciless expression on her face. She did not say a word. Constance started to hum, hanging away her street clothes with unusual care. She began to change into her dress for dinner. It was a new dress, a stiff tan silk faille, with fine flame-colored piping. They had just finished it for the holidays.

After a while Constance stopped humming and looked curiously at Mary. If she wasn't going to start scolding, why did she sit there with that look on her face? It was too much for Constance; her love of tormenting got the better of her.

"Why don't you ask me where I've been?" she asked.

"Because yer mother will ask in good time."

"But don't you want to know?"

"Not particular."

"I'd love to tell you," Constance said jeeringly. She was playing with fire; she loved to. "I've been with my beau."

Mary sniffed. She never knew what that kind of talk meant; it could be made up out of whole cloth. Constance loved to do that.

"All right," she said flippantly. "Don't believe me. I just thought you'd be interested. Don't you want to know who it is?"

Mary frowned and still said nothing. Constance went over and took Mary's chin between her hands and turned the disapproving face up towards her. "Don't you?"

"Och, Constance, either this is a joke or it isn't. Have it over with."

"Well, I told you, I've got a beau." Constance almost waggled her slim body in triumph. "The Honourable Giles Mortimer Stephen Albert Henry Whitfield-Moulton, so there."

"And who," asked Mary, "for the love of Saint Peter is that?" Her eyes followed Constance dumbly.

"Oh, an Englishman. He's the son of Lord something-or-other. He's nice." Constance started to comb her hair, prancing a little on the way over to the bureau. "I'm going to marry him and live in London."

Mary stood up, brushing the front of her apron.

"That'll do now, ye've told enough stories fer wan day."

"This is no story. If you don't believe me now you'll just get a bigger bump later."

Mary stood by the door. She did not know what to do. She felt, suddenly, as if she wanted to hand Constance over to her mother and never be responsible for her in any way again. She felt wretched and helpless and discouraged and she wanted to get away from Constance—and from Paul too, and all the Scotts—and go away down to her father's shack and hide in a corner and cry.

"Ye'd better talk to yer mother about this, I'm not the proper wan," she said wearily. She did not really believe a word of it, but—

"Oh, no!" Constance trilled. "I woundn't tell them till it's all settled. Why—they'd spoil everything."

"Then if it ain't settled why are ye teasin' me?" Mary cried, with a catch in her voice. She felt so tormented, so bewildered and battered.

"Oh—you know, you have to tell somebody. It's so exciting."

Mary sat down suddenly on the edge of a chair. Her memory had given her a startling dig. Lately she had been so wrapped up in her own troubles that she had given only perfunctory notice to Constance.

"Was that the man," she asked slowly, "who came to the door with ye last week when I called for ye at the Morehouses' party? That light-haired chap with the—"

"Yes!" Constance nodded excitedly. "Isn't he handsome?"

"He looks," Mary said in a cold, frightened tone, "to be near forty years old. Och, Constance—"

" 'Och' your head off," Constance shrugged. "I tell you, I'm going to marry him." She twisted her head to get a view of her back in the mirror. "He doesn't know it yet, of course," she added in a worldly tone.

Mary's jaw dropped. She sat back, her hands limply cupped on her apron. A hard, calculating woman had grown already inside the exquisite body of this child. "Constance," she whispered. "Have ye any idee what ye're sayin'?"

Constance turned ond stood braced against the bureau with her hands behind her. Her voice when she spoke was curiously set and cold.

"I know exactly," she said. "I told you long ago I meant to do this. Giles is just what I want. He's old enough to be my father and I don't give a rap. I'm going to live in London where I can have some fun instead of being cooped up in this dirty old wilderness." She stared excitedly at Mary. "Some day when his brother dies he'll come into a title and then I'll be a Countess!"

Mary stood up. Her knees felt queer. She wished Mrs. Scott would come home. She felt as if she could not carry this responsibility another minute. She looked at Constance bridling with bravado, and said dully, "I'll have to tell yer mother every word ye've said. This is too much fer me." To her consternation she heard herself gulp down a sob. "I'd ought a' done better than this."

Constance stood staring, astonished at seeing Mary cry. There was a puzzled pucker between her eyebrows. Suddenly she went over and put her arm around Mary and said in a queerly mature way. "You couldn't have done anything about this. You can't change me. I know what I want, that's all. I hate flabby things and flabby people—"

"Yer father will never consent to this," Mary said, wiping her eyes.

"Do you think I expect him to?"

"But—but—nobody knows anything about this man. He might be—a—a—fortune-hunter. Anything."

"He might," Constance agreed coolly. Mary gasped again. "He might be wild, too. He might know all the wicked, fascinating people in London . . . oh, you can't stop me. So don't try. If you want to make it any easier, you might sound Mama out about it."

"Easier!" Mary cried. She flushed and clenched her fists. "Ye ought to be locked up on bread and water!"

She left the room and shut the door. Constance shrugged. "Have it your own way," she said to the door. "But I get what I want." She pranced a little. "Oh, I get what I want."

Mary dragged her feet up the stairs to her own room. Tonight she would have to go to Mrs. Scott with this whole story. As if enough other awful things weren't breaking her heart to pieces already. She meant to change to her evening uniform. But she only went over to her bed and dropped on her knees beside it and buried her face in the counterpane.

"Holy Mother," she said, sobbing. "Holy Mother o' God, what'll I do?"

CHAPTER XII

[*April 1880*]

THE NEW OPEN-HEARTH was ready for firing. More than a year had been required to complete the additions and enlargements to the mill which the new furnace involved. All this time Paul had worked night and day with the engineers, mechanics, and masons, sometimes not leaving the job for twenty-four hours at a stretch. The Old Man had backed him up without hesitation, acquiring an additional parcel of land east of the old rail mill and financing the entire construction through his own banks, without inviting Gaylord even to consult about it.

New sheds had been built to house the new furnace, the casting department, the soaking-pit, a blooming mill, and a new rolling mill which was to produce the new steel in bars and billets of special dimensions that had never been rolled before. Up to now hand-cranes worked by winch-gangs had been used in the mill for moving ladles, but in the new mill a steam-crane was installed to lift the ladle from the tapping-level of the open-hearth and carry it overhead to the ingot-platform for pouring. The open-hearth furnace was built in the partition between two parallel sheds, fired and charged from one side, tapped from the other. In the tapping-shed was a gallery, high above the ground, level with the lip of the ladle when it was raised up and swung across the shed for pouring. And across the long, dark alley, floored with tracks, there was an iron cat-walk running behind the track where the ingot-moulds stood ready. Here the ladle boss and his helper would stand with their long, clumsy tools, to open the ladle and close it and cap each ingot after it was cast. When filled, the entire train of ingots would be pulled away to the soaking-pit, which adjoined the blooming mill.

This new layout was Paul's first creative work, and he had poured himself into it with the same fanatic absorption that he would have brought to a work of art if that had been his means of expression. Not for nothing did he love the stark and terrible sights of boiling and rolling steel; they were his greatest inspiration.

The first tapping of the new furnace was to be at night. They would fire her early in the morning and let her cook all day. They could not tell exactly how long the heat would take; they would learn as they went along. Natural gas was the fuel. They fed her at intervals with scrap-iron, nickel, and chromium. They expected her to be ready sometime between dark and midnight, but they would not know the exact hour until time to start testing. All day long Paul and James, who was boss-melter, stood by their beloved furnace as if she were a wife in labor, with the Old Man hovering in the background.

The Old Man was more excited than either his son or James, but it would have been unthinkable for him to show it. He could hardly force himself to stay in his office. Every half hour he found another good reason for tramping down the long, drafty sheds and ramps to the new buildings. He would come up silently behind James and Paul, intent on watching the heat through the fire door, solemnly pull his smoked glasses from his pocket, settle them on his nose, and peer over the boys' shoulders. James stood nearest the door, bossing the gang of blackened, sweating men who strode up, one by one, to pitch in heavy shovelfuls of material. The knack of swinging correctly a heavy shovel of dolomite for making back-wall was extremely hard to master. It was not enough to pitch the load anywhere into the roaring hell, it must be placed just so, into or athwart the fire depending on the material. No old hands at Scott's knew this trick and James had had to train some of his crew from the Henrietta as well as hire new men from outside.

At the moment when the new furnace was ready for the charge of molten iron from the Henrietta, the dinkey pulling the enormous ladle came chuffing down the shed accompanied by the entire gang from the blast furnace. They marched in formation, perhaps unconsciously, but firmly in step, and ganged up around the track as the dinkey-engine stopped by the new open-hearth, where the iron would be converted to steel. The crane nosed out over their heads and loomed down to grip the knobs of the ladle, and the pot rose slowly, upward and forward, to tilt its contents into the trough. At that a roar of approval went up from Jim's old comrades. They were infected not only by the same excitement as the rest of the Scotts' workers but with fanatical devotion to Jim himself. Their tough natures and fire-tried tempers were undemonstrative usually. It was a rare occasion in a steel mill that evoked anything more eloquent than the terse profanity of daily speech. Paul had always known that Jim was a god to these men. They worshipped him because he had grown up among them and because he was their organizer, champion, and spokesman. Paul could not see Jim's reaction to the tribute. He had turned his back, lowered his head, and appeared to be more intent on the fire in the furnace than the progress of the heat required.

Late in the evening they began taking samples for tests. Jim handled the long "soup-spoon" with the same easy balance that had made him famous with the old picking-rods. He thrust the spoon squarely into the heart of the heat, drew it out, barely grimacing at the searing nearness of liquid fire, and dumped the contents into a little mould at his feet. When it had set, they turned it out in water, waited until it had solidified, and then smashed it with a sledge-hammer. This was the beginning of painful suspense for Paul, this first actual trial of the steel for which he was responsible, and on which everything, not least the financial future of the company, depended. Eagerly the two men examined the broken fragment, estimating the carbon content of the heat from the grain of the break. The steel was not yet ready but the first test augured well, and from now on they gauged the time in minutes instead of hours.

The fourth sample was perfect, and now they were ready to tap. First of all the spout must be ravelled out. Paul and his father left the fire door now, crossed over into the other shed, and climbed the cat-ladder to the long iron gallery high under the roof. They looked down on Jim and his helpers, running about in the spurting glares like gnomes in some mythical Lell. James took up the long rod and rammed it into the tap-hole of the furnace with the tough-muscled ease that it had always been the Old Man's delight to see. At the same time Paul watched the precision of Jim's feet, quick and light and skilful as those of a boxer. One instant before the spout started to belch Jim sprang aside, withdrawing his rod and his own lithe body with one motion. He disappeared underneath the gallery. Almost directly beneath the Scotts the flood of new-made liquid steel gushed into the ladle, spilling off jets of flame and showers of blinding sparks. The pitch-black cavern around them receded by contrast into one illimitable vastness, and nothing could be seen but the blazing triumph of their labor, throwing its furious glare over and around them all. The contents of the slopping ladle quivered and shone with a fierce red light. A second ladle, smaller and empty, was drawn up next to it. After the smooth, blinding stream of scarlet steel had filled the first, the blazing slag began to spill out, a hissing, shooting riot, and overflow into the second ladle.

It was not to the credit of anybody in the new sheds that not one of them had thought of young William today. Nobody had told him that the new furnace was to be fired, or what time she would be tapped. But such an event was a great day, the greatest of days, in a steel mill. And sitting at his own dinner-table that evening William had been sullen and silent with the weight of this knowledge. It was embittering and discouraging enough that his relations with his own father and with Paul were so strained. But in a way it was worse that, when his father-in-law wanted to treat William as a business equal, William did not have command of the facts to make that possible. That made him feel like a fool. In the past, Laurence Gaylord had asked him questions which he had been unable to answer. And now Gaylord would certainly question him about this new open-hearth, and about its products as well as about its financing, in a way that would make William appear an incompetent underling if he had no answers. Suppose he had to admit he had never seen the new furnace, and had not been there when it was first fired? He brooded about that all through dinner, ignoring Julia's attempts at conversation. When they left the table he was restless. Instead of settling down with his cigar and his cognac as usual, he roamed about the sitting-room and the hall and then said abruptly, "I'm going down to the mill."

"Why—*William*—" He had never done such a bizarre thing at night.

"I—I left some papers there that I want to go over." He put on his hat and topcoat and went out hurriedly. All the way down, his sensation of protest and turmoil and bitter resentment grew. He had no clear picture of what he meant to do when he got there. He only knew that he was not going to be made a fool of any longer, either by his own father or by Laurence Gaylord either.

So it was just at the moment when the second ladle drew up to the spout where the slag was gushing out that a strange figure, barely distinguishable between the total blackness of the shed and the blinding glare from the metal, appeared suddenly on the floor just under the gallery where Paul and his father were standing. In utter amazement, and in horror too, they both recognized William. He was hurrying forward towards the spout, where the slag-stream was tumbling into the second ladle. No other man was near there, and Paul's stomach lurched in a sick panic as he leaned over to shout a warning. He could not make himself heard above the roar of the slag. William would be hideously burned if he took two steps more. *Action,* Paul thought in a swift reflex, *get him quick.* Paul was on the cat-ladder and almost down to the floor, but in that split second James Rafferty had darted out almost into the stream of boiling slag, grabbed William by the collar as he would have seized a puppy, and wrenched him back into the darkness under the gallery.

Paul saw in a dazed flash the unbelievable sight of William's pale face pinched with fury, his mouth saying something outrageous and inaudible to Rafferty who stood there scowling with bewilderment. Paul saw that his brother had no idea he had escaped a fearful death and that his life had been saved by Jim. From William's contorted face it was evident only that he was furious. A common millhand, a sweating Irishman, had had the insolence to touch him and drag him away from the place where he had made up his mind to go. All in an instant he turned, swung at Rafferty and hit him. Jim's big fists came up automatically and his hard face creased in a slow, ominous grin. But Paul's reaction was quicker. He was off the ladder and landing a right on William's jaw before he himself knew he meant to do it. The squirt, his angry mind was barking, the cheap posing cowardly snob, the—

"Bring him up here," they heard in a hoarse commanding rumble overhead. They looked up dumbly. The Old Man was hanging over the railing, looking down at his two sons and James. The glare from the ladle illuminated their faces weirdly, made William's gray cheeks and bleeding jaw a ghastly sight. Paul was propping him against a stanchion. His head hung loose; he was not knocked out, but he was stupefied.

"Bring him up here," the Old Man roared again. He bulked huge in flesh and shadow, his bearded face glowing red in the light from the smoking ladle. Paul gestured to Jim and the two of them lifted William to his feet and held him until he got his balance, and helped him up the ladder to the gallery. They sat him down with his back against the railing. The Old Man gave him one brief look; awful, tragic, and contemptuous. Then he turned to look down at the floor again and said in his everyday voice, "Get on with the pouring."

The silence in the shed was punctured by hissing noises from the cooling slag. The Old Man dropped his chin on his breast as the men darted out from the darkness where they had gone, appalled by the incident.

"Jesus," said the ladle boss to his helper as they waited on the platform by the ingot moulds, "I'd hate to be in Paul's shoes. That brother of his will knife his guts."

CHAPTER XIII

[April 1880]

THEY WERE WALKING along the bluff that skirted the Ohio, more than a mile beyond the mouth of the Allegheny, where the rising slopes were still unsullied by the hulking stacks of mills. A pleasant street called Strawberry Lane ran directly inland from the river, and on a lovely April evening like this, it was a temptation to wander farther and farther along the unpaved roadway. It was barely dusk; Paul had induced Mary to leave her father's house earlier than usual. They could still see the pale new green of the slopes ahead, and the unfolding leaves of the oak and maple trees. The houses were scattered here. Some of them were simple clapboard farmhouses, still surrounded by their barns and outbuildings, which would soon be torn down to make room for brick and stone dwellings and factories. The soft spring air was deliciously moist and clear, a wonderful refreshment with the wind blowing southward, carrying the miasma of smoke from the riverside mills away from them. They strolled slowly along the quiet lane. They had not spoken for a long time but after a while Paul said, "I don't know whether the time flies or drags. Do you realize it's been more than a year—?"

Mary looked down and shook her head slowly.

"I wouldn't mind the time," Paul said, almost whispering, "if I could just see what was at the end of it."

"Haven't I tried to tell ye?" Mary murmured. A year ago she would probably have said "ain't," she thought curiously; when had she begun to speak better? She did not really know. She said, "Didn't ye promise me only a few weeks ago ye wudn't say such things any more? I thought we had it all out and ye promised."

He looked at her and suddenly put out his hand and seized one of hers. She drew her hand quietly away. He said, "I was a fool if I tried to promise something impossible."

"It was you said we was to be friends. It was all right so long as ye meant that."

There was another long silence while they wandered on. Then Paul sighed and began to tell Mary about the new open-hearth. He had not had a chance to talk to her all week. This was their first visit since the new addition to the mill had opened, and since the scene with William there. Mary listened thoughtfully, her look of delight in the success of Paul's furnace superseded by a worried, thoughtful expression when he told her about William.

"I mistrust the future," she said finally. "It looks bad, between ye."

"Oh, he can't make any trouble," Paul said carelessly.

"I wudn't be sure. Ye can't crush a man and not have yer reckoning."

Paul smiled a little. "You look so serious," he said.

She was, she realized. She wondered suddenly that he chose to spend so much time with her. He used to like gaiety and laughter and parties and pretty girls. She had nothing of the sort to offer. She had only—she swerved sharply away from such thoughts. For a long time she had been running away from them inside herself. Paul was still talking about William. "He asks for what he gets," Paul said.

"That may be," said Mary. "But yer own father and you too—ye don't help none."

"How could we? I've never picked a quarrel with Bill. But he's such a damn fool. This last thing was pure insanity, running out there into that douse of slag—" Paul paused to light his pipe. "And suppose something had happened to Jim—"

"Well, o' course," Mary said. "And ye'll be havin' trouble with him all yer days."

"Oh, shucks. We didn't come out here to discuss Bill. Mary—" He tried to take her hand again and again she drew it away, shaking her head gently.

"Ye got to think about this, Paul. Can't ye see what this is all leadin' to?"

They stopped walking. It was almost dark now and the night wind was moist, deliciously sweet in their faces. Far down in the distance the glow from night blasts began to shimmer up from the river, a strange and startling contrast to the bit of springtime immediately surrounding them. Paul stood staring at the distant light. Then his eyes turned to Mary and rested on her face. She tried to look away. Sometimes she wanted desperately to hide the look she knew he was seeking in her eyes.

"I wish you weren't always asking me to think, Mary," he said. "My God, isn't it enough to *feel?*"

"Too much!" she blurted. She wished she had not said that. She shook her head quickly as if to contradict herself. Then she said in the calmest way she could, "All I'm askin' is ye should think about William and all that the way it concerns—the—you—"

"Us?" Paul said under his breath.

"The mill! That's what I mean. Ye don't think yer father is goin' to pass on and leave the mill to Mister William to manage?"

Paul laughed.

"That's what I mean," Mary said.

"Oh."

"All I'm tryin' to say is ye know very well who'll be the head o' the mill and the family too, for that matter."

He looked down at her and smiled, a particularly tender expression in his eyes.

"And?—" he spoke teasingly.

Mary shook her head. "No, there's no use tryin' to act like ye don't know what I'm gettin' at. Paul." She paused and put her hand, in its gray cotton glove, on his sleeve. They stood for a moment, side by side. Then he turned and faced here, taking a step that brought them close together.

"Paul," she said again. Her voice was so low that he had to listen carefully. "When ye're the head o' the Scott family, this can't be goin' on, ye know."

Paul stared for a moment. Then he drew his head back almost as if in pain, and sighed, so loud and so deep that the sound was almost a groan.

"Oh, Mary," he said. "Must you bring that up again? Can't we let things alone?"

She closed her lips tightly and shook her head again.

"No," she said. "We cannot. I'm gettin' near to th' end o' my stren'th. I've got to go away, Paul, or ye've got to, or—*something!* It can't go on, I tell ye. It's not right. It's got to end."

Her voice rose unaccustomedly and her words ended in a faint wail. Paul's hands moved in a hurried gesture, grasping for hers, his eyes intently on her face. Mary backed away, putting up her hands to hold his off.

"You're right!" he said hoarsely. "It can't go on. I can't stand it either. Oh, Mary—"

She backed still further away, out of reach of his arms. "No," she said, choking. "No, that's not what I mean, Paul. We're not to meet any more, we must not meet again. Remember your duty!" she said in a sudden burst of force. "Ye must listen to me!"

She saw that he wanted not to listen. But for the first time he had reached the point of helpless silence, and she hurried to say what she had to say; what she had to say now, and quickly, before the courage to say it left her and never came back again.

"When yer father is dead," she said quickly and coldly, "and yer mother too, and yer brother William away to Boston, ye'll have the entire good name and repute of yer family in yer own two hands. What will ye do with it, Paul? Think, what will ye do?"

He shook his head behind his hands.

"What will ye give it for the future?" she asked. "Will ye give it a proper wife and children to carry on yer work and yer name? Will ye? Not if ye blacken it with gossip and strollin' of alleys in the night with a servant from yer mother's kitchen. You know and I know we've done no wrong. But we must do none. I will have no part of it. Yer father and yer mother trust me. That's the worst o' this." She choked.

"Mary—"

"No," she said, raising her hand, "I've not finished yet. I've had it in me to say this these many long months gone, and I'm goin' to say it if I never speak another word to ye me life long, so help me God. Ye've got to face this. Ye can't run from it like a coward. Ye're not a coward and ye'll not turn into one account o' me. We'll stop these walks and meetin's, Paul, and dear holy Mother—" her voice broke in a gasp but she forced herself on— " 'twill be a cruel hard road to go. But a penance fer the wrong we've done yer family, Paul. Ye've got to right that wrong. Ye always had the duty on ye, I see it as clear as day. Yer brother's acts has made me see."

Paul looked at her, emotion swept from his face by a sudden hardening, a look of defiance.

"What do you see?" he asked. His voice was cold.

"Ye've got to marry, and marry proper," Mary said. "A girl yer family can be proud of, a girl to give ye yer rightful children. Ye ought to marry Louise Kane," she said.

Paul stepped back, flushing red. "Damn it!" he cried roughly. "What do you think I am?"

Mary could no longer hold back the tears that were running down her cheeks. She made a helpless motion with her hands, shaking her head wretchedly.

"I can't help it," she sobbed. " 'Tis the God's truth I'm tellin' ye and ye know it. Ye know it, Paul," she repeated passionately. "That's why ye're takin' it this way. Oh, darlin', don't make it any harder than it is. It's so hard," she cried, turning away from him and burying her face in her shaking hands. "So cruel hard."

For a moment he stood, indecisive and stunned. He too, covered his aching eyes with his hands. He heard Mary's sobs, sharp and wrenched from the depths of bitter control. Then they stopped suddenly and another sound replaced them. He raised his head and saw her running, running swiftly like the wind, down the hill and away from him. He let her go.

Of all times, he thought angrily, for his mother to come and bother him about Constance! When he could not care what happened to any of his family. When he wished sometimes that he would never have to see them again. And his mother had had this long talk with him, and got him to find out about Whitfield-Moulton, and though Paul tried to dismiss the whole matter as too laughable to believe, the others were taking it like a melodrama. He thought that was why Constance had started all this uproar anyway, just for pure hell. Whitfield-Moulton was no adventurer, so far as anybody downtown had been able to discover. He was, as Constance had told Mary, a younger brother of a certain Viscount Tyrringdale. This connection was said to be questionable, like everything else that could be learned about the family of the Earl of Melling. Nobody seemed to know the details about "something" that concerned the head of the family and reflected on the sons. But people supposed this chap was travelling in the United States primarily for the purpose of being out of England.

Constance's first flurry over him, her mother thought, had died down after he had left town during the winter to continue his tour of America. But now, for some reason, he was back in Pittsburgh and Constance had seen him—where and how she would not say. She had been slipping out of the house, worrying Mary to distraction. Clarissa hesitated to appeal to her husband. If she did he would probably take some sweeping punitive action that would only make Constance defiant and excite her more. William detested foreigners and he thought Constance a child anyway.

Perhaps Paul could help; at least he could inquire around about the man. So his mother appealed to him.

"He seems to be harmless himself," was Paul's shrugging verdict. "But there's something fishy somewhere, and for one thing I can't see what he's doing here in Pittsburgh. He just goes around to people's houses."

"I wonder why they ask him, if these rumors are true?"

"Oh, you know. There are always people who'll run after a title. It makes me pretty sick, as a matter of fact."

"I'm awfully worried, Paul. That child—she's so *bold*. She hasn't any—" Clarissa wrung her hands. "Saying right out that she means to throw herself at his head."

"Oh, you're all making too much of this. She's probably been reading novels. Besides, she can't find many ways to see this chap. He hangs around with people older than I. Married people. They don't have kids like Constance at their houses except maybe at some big party like the one where she met him." Paul was bored with the whole thing. "Have some of her own friends around and forget about it."

But that was no solution. Then Clarissa tried reasoning with Constance and appealing to her pride and her dignity. The talk ended with a few penitent tears, and with Clarissa thinking she had finally brought the child to her senses. Two days later Mary came to Mrs. Scott right after breakfast, pale and nervous and upset as Clarissa had never seen her before.

"Please, Ma'm," she said, "I can't stand it no more. I'll have to—" She began to cry.

"Oh, Mary." Clarissa sank into a chair, her smooth brow puckering into a despairing frown. "Don't tell me she did it again."

"I tell ye, Ma'm, I can't stand the responsibility no more. She slipped out yestiddy afternoon, wearin' her best garnet broadcloth. Gone two hours, she was, while ye were at that tea-party. I was near wild. I chased her all over town, I went to the Clarks' and the McKelvies' and the Dixons'. Everywhere she's got friends. Nobody seen her."

Clarissa was beginning to look very stern; there was a set to her mouth that Mary had never seen there before. "Go on," she said.

"When she did walk in and I started to bring her to you, she managed to get me in an argiment about somethin' else and she kept me a-talkin' till you and the Master'd gone out to dinner at Mrs. Kane's. Then she went to bed airly so's she wudn't be around when ye came home. And she said she had to be at school airly this mornin' too."

Clarissa stood up with a gesture of finality.

"That settles it," she said. "I'm going to speak to her father tonight."

"I don't want the responsibility no more," Mary said again.

William Scott's first reaction when Clarissa took him to his study after dinner and told him about Constance was to dismiss the whole thing as a silly girl's prank with which women should be able to cope. When Clarissa insisted that Constance was incorrigible, her husband's brow darkened and he did the one thing that Mary, if she had dared, would have told him was fatal. He sent for Constance, took her into the the study and heavily shut the door. When she came out half an hour later, Constance's thin passionate face was scarlet, her lips were set defiantly, her eyes were hot with temper and tears which she had not and would not shed. She raced up the stairs, clutching her new long skirts in her hands, ran into her room, and slammed the door with a crash that echoed all the way down to the front hall. "Mother of God," Mary said to herself, "now he's done it for sure."

When she tried to get into Constance's room she was met by a barrage of shoes, books, brushes, and by screams of "Go away, you devil. I hate you." Mary tried to remonstrate.

"Oh, I know what kind of a friend you are," Constance screamed through the closed door. "Tattletale! Prissycat! You'll be sorry for this!" Mary heard her tramping round and round her room like an animal, throwing things and sputtering with rage. Mary knew better than anyone what the consequences of this tantrum could be. She asked Mrs. Scott, standing appalled beside her in the hall, what Mr. Scott had said.

He had pronounced, it seemed, a prison sentence on Constance. She was not to be left alone for a moment day or night, until she would give her parents her word of honor that she would never see or speak to the Englishman again. She was to sleep in the room with Elizabeth, and in the daytime Mary was not to leave her at all, unless she had been transferred to her mother's or to Elizabeth's charge. Mary listened to this in horrified silence. Finally she said, "Why, Mr. Scott might as well throw her at the man. It could amount to that, Ma'm."

Clarissa wrung her hands. "Oh, Mary, don't you think she'll get over it? This won't go on long, she never sticks more than a little while to anything."

"T'ain't the man, Ma'm," Mary said. "It's this lockin' her up. She'll do anything now to defy her father. She'd marry the—devil himself, God forgive me—"

"Oh, dear, what shall we do?" Clarissa stood looking at Mary with helpless anxiety.

"Why, only what her father said, Ma'm. You know how the master is, once he's given an order, he'll see it's carried out." Mary pushed back her front hair nervously. "I feel bad because Miss Constance has turned on me. That'll make it rare hard against the way she's always trusted me."

"Well, you'll just have to get her confidence back," Clarissa said despairingly. "You'll *have* to."

"I'll try," said Mary. "That's all I can do. But I do fear the responsibility, Ma'm. I've never had the like of it before. Whatever happens, if it's wrong it'll go against me."

"No, it won't," Clarissa said. "I'll see that it doesn't."

"Ye're very kind, Ma'm, I'm sure. Only I'll never make it right in me own mind. I'm all confused, I am, oh dear Mother and saints." Mary's brogue when she was upset came on her thick as peas porridge. "Oh, wurrah," she murmured, shaking her head like an old woman.

She went downstairs and ran into Paul in the front hall. He was just leaving for the night shift at the mill. Mary glanced at him uneasily. She had not seen him since running away down the hill last Sunday. She had nothing to say to him now, but she was so upset by Constance that she stood still, miserable and hesitating. Paul gave her a glowering look and instead of turning away she blurted, "Oh, saints, I'm so upset about Constance." She wanted to tell him her troubles. He knew it and she knew it and they stood there red-faced and flustered.

"I don't give a damn," Paul snapped, opening the front door with a vicious jerk. "Somebody might as well marry whom they want!"

Next afternoon when Clarissa rang for tea, Mary took in the tray and placed it on the low stand beside her mistress's armchair. Mrs. Scott looked up from her needlework and said uneasily, "How—what's she doing?"

"Sewin'. The—I've left the door locked." Mary blushed deeply. This seemed such an awful thing to do that a hundred commands of Mr. Scott's could not have justified it. "She's not spoke to me yet."

"She will. Don't take it too hard, Mary. After all, she's barely seventeen. Children don't stick to things."

Mary had no further reason for staying in the room and she should get back to Constance. But she had made up her mind to do a difficult, an agonizing thing today. She had been coming to the decision for a long time. She could not live another day without unburdening her soul of the terrible deceit that had been piling up on her all these months and months past. All the confessions she could ever make to Father Reilly would not free her as this act would when she had done it. She stood with her hands clasped nervously together. Clarissa, pouring a cup of tea, looked up at her and was about to give her a smile of reassurance—also of dismissal—when Mary said, "Mrs. Scott, Ma'm, wud ye think me awful fresh if I was to suggest somethin'?"

"Of course not, child."

"About—" Mary's pale cheeks began to redden but she drew a breath and made her voice as steady as she could. "About Mister Paul."

Clarissa kept her eyes on her sewing.

"He works too hard," Mary said. "He don't think about gettin' any pleasure out o' life."

Clarissa's heart began to pound under the smooth dove-gray silk of her bodice. She had known for weeks that this or something like it must come and now that it had, she thought only, "I must be wise. God help me to be wise." She tried to make her voice very easy and natural as she answered, "I've been thinking that too. He's awfully young to be so wrapped up in his work." She sighed. "He doesn't see his old friends enough."

"That's it, Ma'm. We shud have his old school crowd here oftener. The Wilkins girls with their husbands, and Joe and David Rogers. And Miss Louise."

She pronounced the last name with cold emphasis. "She ain't been here lately like she used to all the time."

Clarissa looked at Mary now. The girl had turned and was busily polishing a silver picture-frame while she talked. Clarissa knew that the picture-frames, by ancient routine, had had their regular twice-weekly cleaning only on Saturday. They all gleamed brilliantly.

"I've always been very fond of Louise Kane," Clarissa agreed.

"I always thought—perhaps I ought not to say this, Ma'm." Mary hesitated.

"Go on, Mary."

"I did think, Ma'm, that 'twas always your hope and the master's that Mister Paul and Miss Louise would marry some day."

Was it Clarissa's imagination, or did Mary's voice sound particularly precise and clear? Did the words prick at Clarissa's heart like icicles, one by one? She looked at the girl standing near her. She saw only Mary's profile, but the sensitive face was dead white, the deep-set eyes shadowed by bluish wells that were no mere reflection from the spring twilight outside the thickly curtained window. The fine features had sharpened in outline, as faces do in pain. Mary's face was frozenly calm, deathlike, in fact, but her hands still buffed busily at the picture-frame. Clarissa saw in a great opening of insight that the girl had no idea what her hands were doing.

"Oh, God," thought Clarissa in a shock of realization, "God help this poor, heartbroken child." She looked at Mary with utter tenderness. She stretched out her hand. "Come here," she said.

Mary laid down the picture-frame and walked slowly towards Clarissa. She looked at her employer unflinchingly, her eyes and mouth sternly controlled.

Clarissa searched her mind for words. Whatever she said, now, might be shattering.

"Mary," she spoke very softly. "Paul is not in love with Louise Kane. You know that, do you not?"

"I know it." Mary's tone was leaden.

"I want Paul to be happy," said Clarissa.

Mary's lips went together in a stony line. She kept her eyes on Clarissa's face, and the older woman saw that this was a gruelling effort; stern obedience of the body to unbelievable courage in the heart. Mary would not speak, Clarissa saw, until she had chosen each word that she would say, and until she knew that she could say it unfalteringly. The words finally came, tense and terrible in spite of Mary's efforts.

"Then if ye want him to be happy, make him do the right! Show him his duty to all of you. There's no happiness but that. Oh, Mrs. Scott"— Mary's hands had gone, unconsciously to her breast, clasped as they always were in prayer—"don't ye think he'd marry Louise Kane?"

Clarissa felt for a moment as if every tangible thing had vanished, as if she were alone in space with the vibrant Irish voice and the fervent gray eyes glittering with suppressed tears. Then the pounding of her heart brought her back to the familiar room. She drew herself up in her chair and looked hard at the suffering girl.

"Mary," she said, "I want to tell you something. I want you to know that I understand every unspoken word that has passed between us. I honor and respect you profoundly. Dear child, I love you too."

Those words, as they came involuntarily from her heart, sounded strange indeed as she said them to a trembling little Irish maid. Clarissa spoke them with a bitter sigh. She turned her face to the window to hide her feelings. Then she started at the sound of a strangled sob. She heard the opening of her door and the rush of Mary's quick feet down the hall towards the third floor stairs. Clarissa rose slowly, surprised to find her knees strangely weak, and followed along the hall and up the stairs to the room where Mary had run and had flung herself, sobbing, upon her bed.

Hours later, when Clarissa had seen Mary fall asleep, had covered her with an afghan, drawn the shades, and locked the door of her room so that nobody could intrude, she went and sat alone in the vine-covered summerhouse on the crest of the back lawn. Unseeing, she watched the starry darkness overtake the last streaks of sunset, the sky deepen and widen in its vast nocturnal mood, the busy mills down by the river begin their nightly drama of fire and light. She thought back over the seven crowded years since the timid and beautiful girl had first stood trembling by her chair. She thought of the growth of the strong religious nature, the steady strengthening of devotion and loyalty. She saw the drab emptiness of the girl's beginnings, and the simple eagerness with which she had filled her own cup from the fountain of abundant life among the Scotts. And she had given so much more than she had received!

Then Clarissa thought of Paul, so frankly and justly the favored of her children. There seemed something fearfully retaliative in his fate. It must be too much that he be handsome and manly, brilliant, ambitious, idealistic, already master of the destiny to which he was born. Must he pay in loneliness and sorrow for all his rich gifts? Clarissa saw now, as she had not dared to see a few months ago, and had never dreamed in all the past carefree years, that Paul would be drawn to a woman of stature and strength; that no mere gentle, adoring girl could hold him. Bitterly she regretted her blindness, her failure to foresee the inevitable and find another home for Mary before the power of her character, her personality, and her tremendous devotion had chained them all. For they were chained now; it was too late. Even if Mary tried to go, Clarissa could not allow her to. She felt responsible for the landslide that had swept down on them and the responsibility meant now, as it never had before, that she must protect Mary like a child of her own.

CHAPTER XIV

[May 1880]

THE CRISIS OVER Constance gave Mary the excuse she wanted not to leave the house. She had not been down to see her father for a month. Paul could find no opportunity to meet her, and she had told him plainly that she would never let him do so again. It was never necessary to see him in the house. She had not served in the dining-room for years, ever since Delia's departure to be married, and her own occupation with Constance.

Clarissa was haunted and tormented by Paul's drawn face and heavy eyes and his black mood expressed in monosyllables or long, glum silences. If anyone spoke to him at breakfast or dinner he answered with startling and unnatural brusqueness. His father had no patience with moods, but he had great forbearance with Paul. He believed him overtired from the long months of night work on the new furnace.

"A good summer holiday will fix all that," he told his wife, and there-after dismissed the matter. It was his way to choose the literal and con-crete of a number of alternatives. If a person's appetite was poor, it was because he was sick. If he was sick, it was because he had caught cold or eaten something indigestible. For William Scott to admit that anything so impalpable as fatigue could be legitimate cause for poor health was quite remarkable. He could see no farther than that; or he did not want to see. For years Clarissa had suspected the latter.

During the first two weeks of her imprisonment Constance had been viciously sullen and had taken a mean pleasure in making her enforced presence in the house as uncomfortable for everybody as she could. She left a mess in her wake wherever she went. Cookie crumbs, chicken bones, and fruit peels in the kitchen. Papers and torn-up letters in the parlor. Scraps of sewing materials, buttons, and trimmings in the upstairs hall. Her own room was a pigsty and she stubbornly defied Mary's directions to straighten it up. Her table manners were so atrocious that only grimmest intent could keep them that way, for actually Constance had begun long ago to develop the fastidious niceties of a fashionable woman.

Then suddenly she changed her tactics. The tantrums and scenes of fury stopped. There was no more teasing of Paul, tormenting of Elizabeth, or defiance of Mary. Even Cook revealed that Constance had stopped stealing food and coffee in the kitchen. This all appeared to Clarissa as very ominous. She roused herself violently from the welcome delusion that Constance had reformed and was about to give her parents the promise that would set her free again. There was a more plausible explanation and Clarissa sensed it reluctantly: Constance must be trying not to attract attention to herself.

On the fourth Sunday of Constance's imprisonment Clarissa called

Mary aside after midday dinner and told her she must take the rest of the day off.

"Go down and see your father, dear, or do whatever you like. I'll look after Constance."

Mary raised her blue-lidded eyes uneasily. "I don't really want to go out, Ma'm."

"You must. You'll be ill if you don't get a change. Run along." Mary's eyes filled with quick tears. Clarissa felt a sudden lump swell in her own throat.

Patrick was pathetically glad to see Mary. He fussed a little about her neglecting him so long, but he was soon pacified by the cheerful bustle she made putting the shack in order and baking scones for tea. Kate and her husband, big Dan Maginnis, a giant of a boilermaker, came in for a visit, bringing their first baby, about whom they were bursting with pride. James was not around. Old Patrick shrugged when Mary asked for him and mumbled, "Some big union shindy they got today."

Mary kept busy all afternoon and evening; that was the way to keep from thinking. She stayed at her father's much later than usual. Her mind swerved away from the reason for that, too. When she finally started up the long walk to the Scotts' her thoughts were of Dad and James; of Kate and Dan and the baby; of Bridget—Mary simply must get up to Greensburg to see her soon. For the first time in months her own kin pushed close about her to shut out all the others.

She walked slowly up the hill, deeply abstracted and conscious of a welcome vagueness, almost like fog, that had come over her tired brain and blotted out the sharp edges of her misery. Her head was bent and she looked no further than the few inches of ground ahead of her at each step. At the corner of Rebecca Street and Ridge Avenue she almost bumped into a horse that was standing by the curbstone in the dark. She looked up, startled. A livery buggy stood there.

"Get in," said Paul.

Mary's mouth opened in sharp protest. This was too cruel!

"I said get in," Paul repeated in a flat tone.

He reached down and helped her up to the seat beside him. She had not intended to get into the buggy at all. But his strange, cold tone astonished her so that she did as he ordered with a helplessness at which she herself was amazed. Paul picked up the reins and drove off at a quick trot. He did not turn the horse toward Western Avenue, but in the opposite direction. Mary said wearily, "Oh, please, Paul. Don't do that. I want to go home, truly I do."

"I can't help that. I've got to talk to you."

"But I told you I wouldn't. I—"

"Do you think your wishes are all that matter? I tell you I've got to talk to you."

Mary had never seen any indication in Paul of the hard, almost brutally curt and commanding manner that she was meeting now. He might hate her, from the cutting tone of his voice and the strained masklike lines of his face, the stony eyes, the rigid mouth, and the pallor. She bowed her head and let her hands lie limp in her lap. They rattled quickly over the cobbles and Paul turned right for the approach to the Union Bridge. Mary started.

"Paul. *Please!* Where are ye goin' this hour o' the night? I must go home."

"I'm going where I want."

He reined up at the toll house, paid his toll, and whipped the horse off again. Mary gripped the handrail of the buggy, too angry to remonstrate any more. This was so unlike him that she felt as if he were a stranger. Paul drove in silence, continuing straight across the tip of the Triangle and over onto the Point Bridge to the Southside. In all her life Mary had never been across here. It lay as remote from her concerns as a Pacific Island, yet the beckoning stretch of bridges reaching across the Allegheny and the distant Monongahela had always kept it within her sight. She could not think of a reason why Paul would do this crazy thing, so late at night, and in such a crude, wild way. She sat back. Her resentment which had been sharp as a knife a moment ago, wilted suddenly. She looked at him, stiff and determined and, she realized with a pang, just as miserable as she. They spoke no more until he had guided the horse along the precipice which skirted the southern bank of the Ohio high above the glittering water, and had turned inland to the rising ground. This district was sparsely built up and there were many trees among the scattered houses, just as there were on the Northside in the open places where Mary and Paul had had so many walks. But here the land was higher, and the view both up the river to the steel mills, and down the stretch of the Ohio, was overwhelming. As far as Mary could see, the dark intaglio of the river was emblazoned with blast furnaces and Bessemers, now beginning everywhere to dye the night sky blood-color as the heats approached midnight climaxes. There was so much to see, so infinitely more than the mere eye could absorb, that she almost forgot the calamitous circumstances that had brought her here, and for a moment was lost in wonder at the magnificent sight. Then Paul stopped the horse, jumped down, and gave her his hand to help her out.

She found herself in a small clearing, its front open to the full grandeur of the river view, its rear enclosed by a grove of trees. It was almost a calculated setting from which to see the flaming heart of Pittsburgh at the best possible vantage. Mary stood hesitating. The contact of her feet with the earth brought her back to the distressing reality of the situation, and she waited, now really Paul's prisoner, to see what he would do. He tied the horse to a sapling, brought the robe from the buggy and spread it on the ground. But he did not invite her to sit down. Instead he came over to her, in three firm, domineering steps, and took her trembling hands in his. He crushed them until she winced with pain, but she did not move, looking steadily into his eyes. Somewhere within her a prayer was going up, a prayer for help in what she knew now was to be the worst ordeal of her life.

She kept her wrists rigid, like all her bones and muscles, standing statue-stiff to warn him off. He stared at her, his eyes avid and bitterly hungry, moving from her shining hair to her delicate temples, to the clear cameo cutting of her nose and lips. He stood rigidly himself. Then his shoulders drooped in a gesture towards her and the cold bitter look went out of his face.

"I can't stand it another day, Mary." He spoke with terrible conviction. "You've got to marry me."

Now that it had come she was utterly calm, calm with the weary weakness of an old woman. Inside her she could feel the pace of her blood slacken, until it seemed to creep through her numb veins. Paul felt the cold that went into her fingers. She did not speak, because there was nothing for her to say. But with all the strength she could summon she managed to shake her head, slowly and wretchedly. He tried to rouse her. He shook her hands.

"Don't you understand, Mary? Didn't you hear? You act as if you hadn't even heard me."

"I heard ye," she said. Now she raised her head laxly and looked straight at him. "I heard ye. Oh, couldn't ye have spared me this?"

"But Mary. Please. Try to think and pay attention to me. I mean this, as I never meant anything before." He drew her forward. "Come here and let me talk to you."

He led her to the carriage robe spread on the ground and seated her on it, taking his place beside her. He never let go her hands.

"I've thought this thing through," he said. "I haven't done anything else. I haven't slept any more than you have. I've got to talk to you— dear." He looked at her bowed head and a thrust of pity for her went through him. "May I?" he whispered. "May I talk to you?"

She nodded. There was no way around this now, it was better to go straight through it.

"I know what's the matter, Mary. I'd be a fool if I didn't know why you think you can't do this. But hasn't it occurred to you that the whole world lies around us? Think." He put his right arm now about her shoulders and drew her close beside him. "Think," he said again. "I had a terrible time, oh, I can't tell you what a hell I was in, dear, every minute of the day and night. Until just yesterday. Then something happened to me, down at the mill. You see, I think the mill has been my worst difficulty anyway."

"How?"

"Oh, well, I'm getting ahead of myself. What I do know is this: we've got to marry, Mary. We were meant for each other. That's all there is to it. I've never even told you I love you, have I?"

She shook her head slowly while he pressed his cheek to her hair.

"You see, I didn't even have to do that. You didn't have to tell me. It was simply so. Like the dark and the light. The earth and the rivers. The fires down there." He spoke slowly and pointed to the flaming drama below them.

"Like all that. And you might as well try to put out a blast with Mama's watering-pot as think you can escape it."

"One can do anything," Mary said numbly.

"Not this. Oh, not this," Paul said with passion. "Only fools would throw this away. No, Mary, we will marry and go away from here."

With a cry she jerked herself away.

"Paul! Ye've gone mad! Leave Pittsburgh? Leave yer father and the mill? Why ye'd destroy the whole family!"

"What are they to me," he asked, "compared with you?"

"But I tell ye, ye're losin' yer wits. Why ye've planned yer whole life and future here. Ye've put yer heart's blood in the mill already. It belongs to you and you belong to it, and those are the things that make a man. Oh no, this talk of leavin' the mill is madness."

"It's not, Mary. You're just idealizing the damned mill. That's what I realized finally by myself. There are other mills. Hundreds of them. Why if you want to be literal about it, I could get a job in any steel plant in the world. They're scrambling for metallurgists. I could get a place as steel chemist anywhere I liked—Bethlehem, Midvale, Chicago, Birmingham, England, Germany—why I've got the whole world to choose from."

"With an Irish biddy by yer side!" she blurted.

"I can't stand that!"

They sat silent in the midst of wreckage. Paul stared at the blazing panorama ahead and Mary clutched her throbbing head in her fingers. They did not know how long the painful silence lasted. But after a time she drew herself straight and spoke quietly, in a voice so low that it was almost strangled. But she did not falter.

"Paul. Ye got no right to lose yer temper when I point out such a truth. Ye asked me to listen to you and I did, and I will. But ye must listen to me, too. I'm not refusin' to marry ye because I'd be ashamed o' meself as yer wife. I can learn. I could speak fine English and learn grand manners and—"

"Go on—"

"All right. But you don't realize what marriage is. 'Tis a fine thing to have great love in a marriage, but believe me, dear Paul, that's not what a proper marriage is founded on."

"On what, then? Money? I suppose you're refusing because you can't bring me a dowry!"

"Och, Paul, will ye be fair! 'Tis a mean way and nothing like you, when ye say these cruel things that aren't yerself. I know pain makes ye do it, but won't ye try to be reasonable at least?"

"I'm sorry. But do you think you are reasonable, Mary?"

"I'm tryin' to be. I'm bein' as honest and fair as I can think me way to be. Now listen awhile. A marriage doesn't concern just the two people who make it. It's only their little link in the chain o' the family. A family lasts hundreds of years, Paul, and a marriage only a few—in the course of time. At least one link in each generation has *got* to be sound—or the whole thing falls apart. Isn't that so?"

"I suppose."

"Well, if there was anyone else in yer family with a grain o' sense I'd not be so fixed about this. But ye're their only hope. Ye're their whole future. Think o' yer two brothers and yer two sisters and tell me honestly if any o' them will be anything but a weaklin' or a charmin' waster. So ye've got to marry the right woman to stay here by yer side in Pittsburgh where ye belong, and carry on the work yer father and grandfather passed on to ye. And that woman isn't me."

"Mary, I want to say something brutal. Do you know that the mother of one of the leaders of Pittsburgh was a cook?"

"O' course I know it. But that don't alter my feelin's a bit. Nobody in Pittsburgh is goin' to say Paul Scott's children were the sons of a chambermaid."

There was silence again.

"And that's not all," Mary continued presently. "Even if I were willin' to marry you, and even if I did agree with ye about everythin' else, there's one thing I can't overlook even if you can. That's *my* duty to yer family. You say yer life's yer own and ye'll do what ye like with it, and you don't want to be enslaved by yer family. But I am. They can't help what *you* do, Paul, ye're their flesh and blood and they've got to abide by it. But they *trust* me. Purely and of their own free will. They trust me with their name and their children and every single thing that makes them what they are. Do ye think I'd betray 'em?" She leaned towards him, frowning with intensity. "Do ye think I'd do the one thing would destroy 'em? Ye know I won't. Ye know it in yer heart." Her voice faded.

He turned to her with a sudden rough motion.

"I know this too!" he cried hoarsely. He dragged her into his arms. Whether she struggled or not, neither of them knew. His hunger was whetted to the edge of desperation. He held her high and close to his breast while he covered her face, her eyes and cheeks and ears and throat with kisses, so fierce and so violent that he felt her weaken in his arms, and he neither knew nor cared whether she were still conscious. Finally his mouth joined hers, and about them came a great quiet, a disembodiment of the world, a soaring into space that was at once silent, yet filled with a strange, pervasive thunder. Mary's lips had the passion of innocence, a passion more awesome than any he would know, and her clinging to him bound him in mortal certainty that he was the only man she could ever love. They stayed so, one thing, one feeling, until his blood hammered through his body, and still with his mouth on hers, he turned her and laid her on the rug beside him. Only then could he see her face, dim in the shadowed dark of the trees and the faint red glow thrown on the sky by the distant furnaces. Passion and peace and pain were mingled in her closed bluish eyelids, her throbbing temple pulses. His body was hard against hers, pressing with wild insistence. And then she opened her eyes.

Paul did not want to look into them. A man cannot look with ease at revelation, and Paul feared the discovery that lay waiting in the huge black pupils, the deep gray pools. He forced himself, knowing her will, to read her eyes with all their meaning. Then he turned his head, and moved.

"I can't," he sobbed. His head went down on her breast. "I can't take you now. If you had fought me, Mary . . . if you had fought . . ."

She held his head in her hands. Her lips were red as he had never seen them, her gleaming hair loose and flung about her shoulders. Never in all his life again would he see such beauty.

"I can't fight you," she whispered. "I can fight for what I believe, and I am fighting. But you, Paul—I love you."

She carried his mouth to hers. The night was ineffably delicate and sweet about them, the breath of innocence and beauty and the softness of May. But down in the riverbed was reality. Even where they lay, they heard the first penetrating rumblings and saw the spreading glare that stained the sky as a furnace went into blast. Higher, higher, straight over their heads, the crimson streamed like a battle banner. And the red light spread above them, illuminated their faces and let them see as if in brilliant sun, the features that each knew to the last shadow and hairline.

Mary's hand went up over her head, pointing to the fire in the sky.

"There," she said. "There's your answer, Paul. Ye can't escape it, my darlin'. There's the part of a man that ye've been called in the world to take. Don't fail, dear. Don't fail yerself. Or any of—them. Or me."

They embraced again, long and quietly.

"But what shall I *do?*" he groaned. "I love you. Am I to—my God, what's to become of us?"

"Paul, I don't know. I'm all bewildered, just like you. I can't think right. I've got to find a way to think, darlin', before I know."

"Not the way it's been, Mary. That's only torture."

"Only torture. Ye're entirely right. No, I'll have to go away. I couldn't be seein' ye all the time—or tryin' not to see ye, right there under the same roof."

He held her closer, and shuddered. "Don't."

"I know."

"I'll follow you to the end of the world."

"No!" she said stoutly. "That ye'll not. Yer life is here. Ye must not run away. Don't ye see, my dear darlin', there's no peace if ye run from yer own fate? Ye'd never be happy."

"Happy!"

"Look, darlin'." The red blast had soared and spread and burst into a gargantuan rocket. Showering sparks swept the heavens. "Could it be there?"

CHAPTER XV

[*May 1880—Continued*]

SHE DID NOT have to ask Paul to hurry when they started home. He knew she was exhausted, and he kept the horse at the fastest possible trot, while they sat close together, silent and doleful. Both were chilled, inwardly with the wretchedness of frustration, outwardly because the night had turned raw. The sky had begun to thicken with a damp mist. From the rivers, as they crossed each bridge, a penetrating chilly moisture rose about them, and Mary shivered under the carriage robe. She had twisted her hair into order and tied on her bonnet again, and Paul thought it was as if she had drawn down a curtain over a secret picture of unbelievable beauty that he had glimpsed once and might never see again.

They left the horse at the livery stable in the alley back of Lincoln Avenue and walked the short distance home. It was past midnight; Mary had never been out so late in her life. They walked quickly. Paul kept Mary's hand in his, tightly clasped. They did not speak.

As they turned onto Western Avenue and looked ahead towards the house, Mary started and clutched Paul's hand still tighter.

"Paul, look! Something's the matter!"

The house was lighted from top to bottom; it seemed that a light was burning in every room.

"Somebody must be ill." She started to run.

"Wait, Mary." He pulled her back and stopped. "Think. We can't come bursting in together."

"Oh."

The old sick feeling of guilt and misery swept down on her again.

"You go ahead and go in the back door as usual. I'm going to walk around the block for a while. I'll get in without attracting any attention. God knows what's going on but it must be something serious from the looks of the place. Mary." He drew her into the shadow of a big chestnut tree close to the neighbors' gateway. "Mary. Will you kiss me—good-bye?"

She took his two hands and held them tight against her breast, restraining him from putting his arms around her.

"Darlin'," she whispered. "I did—down there. Don't ask me again. I couldn't bear it, dear. 'Twould upset me somethin' dreadful."

He bent his head and carried her clasped hands to his lips and covered them with kisses. "All right," he whispered. "But try, Mary. Try to think this through and find peace for us."

She nodded, pulled her hands from his, and ran quickly up the walk and around the path to the back of the house. She let herself in and stood for a moment in the kitchen breathlessly straining to hear what might be going on. Voices floated down from the floor above her, and presently she heard William Scott's heavy bass in thunderous speech. She slipped up the back stairs and into the pantry. She had a glimpse of herself in the mirror that hung on the stair landing, where the girls were wont to straighten their caps before answering their mistress's rings. She was horribly pale, and her hair was rather disordered under the edge of her bonnet but somehow she did not care.

She opened the pantry door and stood there a moment, not knowing what to do. Whatever this emergency was, she felt she must know about it before she went up to bed. At that moment Clarissa Scott came through the door of the dining-room. Her face was red and streaked from weeping, and her handkerchief was rolled into a wet ball in her hand.

"Oh, Mary. I thought I heard you!"

"What is it, Mrs. Scott? What's happened?"

Clarissa began to cry again, and gasped, "Constance!"

Mary flung off her jacket. "What's she done? What's—?"

"Clarissa!" William Scott's voice rang through the hall. "Will you please come back here? I asked that nobody leave the room."

Clarissa turned and pulled Mary after her. "You come in too. You'd better."

They entered the long parlor. Mary gave one quick look around it and saw what had happened. The entire family were there, Elizabeth in a dressing-gown, William and Julia in street clothes, and in the middle of the room, before the fireplace, Constance and a tall blond man who stood stiffly and resentfully a little apart from her.

"And I will not be defied with impunity!" William Scott was shouting. "No, not by any child or man or woman whose life has anything to do with mine. I will not have it."

William junior, sitting in an armchair with an expression of unaccustomed sangfroid, looked up and said, "Father, we all know that, but what can you do about this? They're married now."

Mary gasped.

"Oh, Constance," she moaned, "ye didn't do it?"

Silence followed her words for a moment, caused by everyone's surprise at her presence. Then Constance lifted her head defiantly.

"Of course I did it. I said I would, didn't I?"

Whitfield-Moulton flushed. Looking at him, Mary saw that he had been putty in Constance's fingers.

"Oh my God." Mary covered her face with her hands. She could think of nothing but the past three hours. "It's my fault," she groaned. "I've failed in me duty."

"Nonsense," said Constance sharply. "You had nothing to do with it. Besides"—Mary watched her, cold and defiant, turn towards her father with one of the characteristic flings of her burnished head, "besides, you didn't seriously think you could keep me under lock and key, did you?"

At this moment the front door slammed and Paul, his hands in his pockets, appeared in the doorway. To Mary he looked self-conscious, but nobody else seemed to notice him. He stood there taking the situation in.

"So you've done it!" He said. He had used almost the same words as Mary.

Constance turned to him. Her motions were swift and pointed, and her face was coldly excited. Her eyes flashed restlessly.

"Yes," she said, "I've done it. And I wish you'd see if you can calm this tempest here."

William Scott's face reddened. And Mary felt horribly ashamed for the bewildered bridegroom, who might have been a sweetmeat that Constance had stolen, for all the volition he displayed.

"You are all here to listen to me," William Scott shouted suddenly, "and not to this girl who has disgraced us. What's done cannot be undone. But before these two leave this room certain matters are going to be thoroughly understood. It will be embarrassing for all of us. Now why," he roared at Whitfield-Moulton, "did you marry my daughter?"

The Englishman drew up his shoulders.

"I think that question insulting, sir," he said.

Mary had not expected this and she almost felt like saying "Good for you!"

"Certainly it's insulting!" retorted the Old Man. "What sort of man will run off with a seventeen-year-old child young enough to be his daughter, when he's a guest in a strange country and nobody—" here the Old Man paused and scowled and chose his words deliberately—"nobody knows anything creditable about him or his people?"

Paul took a step towards Constance's husband. The Old Man's words had been so brutally offensive that he would have stood against them in anyone's behalf. But Whitfield-Moulton only clenched his fists and looked frozen.

"If that is the way it appears to you, sir, I will not stoop to discuss it."

Julia spoke up.

"Father Scott," she said, "might it not be wise to reserve your verdict until you know more about the matter?"

Everyone turned to look at her. Clarissa's face was full of scorn.

"Considering the part you have played," William Scott answered, "you will do well to take no more action because you may be sure it will be held against you—and your husband."

"Why, what's she done?" Paul asked.

Mary held her breath.

"She was the matchmaker," Elizabeth snorted. "You don't think she'd miss a chance to get back at Father after the way you've all treated her husband, do you? Besides, she's delighted to be connected with the nobility."

"Oh for God's sake."

"That will do, Paul. No profanity, if you please."

"She hates all of us. That can't be any surprise to you," Elizabeth said. She appeared to be taking a vicious pleasure in talking, in saying things that only a crisis would give her the opportunity to say.

"She egged Constance on, not that Constance needed any urging. Julia made all the arrangements. She and William got her out of the house and went with them this evening, and lied about Constance's age so they could get the license. She—"

Mary drew in her breath with a gulp.

"So that's where ye were," she blurted, "them afternoons ye ran off—"

Constance laughed insolently.

"Ah," said Julia softly. "And where would you have had her meet her friend? *On street-corners?*"

Quiet. Quiet. Every drop of Mary's blood stood still in the terrible necessity to be quiet. Not a breath. Not a motion. Not a glance. The whole room stiffened under the pall of quiet. The clock ticked grotesquely, beat on every ear with torturing resonance. She could not look at Paul. She could not look at anyone, or up, or down; she could not close her eyes; she must not move. She must not faint, though her head began to swim.

She could not know, would never know, what that venomous question meant to each person here. Nobody dared to gasp, and nobody dared to show if he knew. "How?" thudded inside Mary's head, "how does she now? How much does she know?"

Behind the contempt in his face Paul felt sick. Clarissa's mind was in turmoil, she felt a surging, maddening impulse to rush over and cover her son and Mary with her body, like a bird or an animal, to shelter them. But Mary stood alone, apart from the group as became her situation, the target of all their intent, if not of their eyes. Elizabeth exchanged a look with William junior. Then her cold white face set, with narrowed eyes and pinched nostrils, in an expression of disgust. William Scott smashed the tension.

"Now see here!" he shouted. "I'm going to settle this." He strode over and planted himself squarely before Constance and Giles. "You've married this man, Constance, with as far as I can see, absolutely trivial and frivolous motives. You have no idea of what you've undertaken. But let me tell you," the Old Man thrust his bearded chin forward and glared savagely at his daughter, "you're married and you're going to stay married. You've done something that can't be undone. Do you understand?"

"Yes, Father."

"And as for you," turning to the shocked man before him, "you and I are going to have a clear understanding. Just what do you do for a living?"

Paul made a sound. If the situation had not been so serious, Mary would have sworn he had snickered. The question was fantastically unanswerable.

"That is hardly relevant to the circumstances," said the bridegroom.

The Old Man's eyes started from his head.

"What?" He planted his feet apart. "Now that you use the word, I'd say it's highly relevant to ask just what you've been doing around here anyway. About all I've ever heard of you," old William said, glaring, "is some connection between your not having any money and there being a lot of it in Pittsburgh."

Clarissa shuddered. She would have given her soul to have terminated this scene. But she would not have dared to interrupt. Her husband had been outraged. His loathing of idleness, of snobbery, of deception, of laziness and parasitism and sycophants; his scorn of social intrigue; his detestation of the British and his contempt for their ways combined to drive him to mad intolerance and rage. Worst of all, he was tortured by futility, there was nothing he could do; and that was the only sort of situation that could defeat him. So he had to roar and thunder, to bully and insult. And perhaps it was as well. At least this Giles would discover at the outset the nature of his fate. There would be no gradual disillusionments.

"I gather then," old William continued, "that for practical purposes you have no money. You don't do any work. Are you a remittance-man?" he asked brutally.

"How?" Whitfield-Moulton's lips were so rigid that they hardly formed the word.

"A remittance-man," repeated William. "Are you being paid a stipend to stay out of England?"

Even Elizabeth gasped and Julia clutched the arms of her chair.

"My wife and I are sailing on Wednesday in the *Britannia*," said Giles contemptuously.

"That's better news than I expected," said William. "I'm not going to support you in idleness anyway and I'd rather not do it in London than around here. Now I don't know and since it's too late to do anything about it, I don't care, what your means are, if any. I don't know what Constance told you about her expectations but you may expect the worst. I suppose you thought you were marrying a Pittsburgh millionairess. Well, you didn't. Constance will get the same allowance that she'd get if she'd married a clerk, and I wish to heaven she had. She won't starve because I'm not going to turn any daughter of mine out penniless even if she deserves it. But you won't live on it. It'll just keep Constance from being destitute, that's all."

Leaving this statement to penetrate the shocked minds of his family, William clasped his hands behind his back and turned from the culprits on the hearthrug. He began pacing heavily back and forth across the end of the room. Nobody dared to speak.

"Of course you may know some way to live without any money," he said presently to his new son-in-law. "I'm told they know how in noble circles. But we don't. We work." He paced again. Then he said, "I've got a factor in London who handles the small export business that we do. If you ever decide to work for a living, you can go and see him. He might find a clerkship for you."

Julia, Elizabeth and William junior nervously kept their eyes on the carpet. Paul stood by the windows, with his hands still rammed into his pockets, red with embarrassment. Clarissa wept quietly on the sofa. Constance stood rigid beside her husband, coldly defiant. Her green eyes were narrowed to catlike slits, and her lips were bitten blood-red. Her husband beside her belied his rather weak face and the colorless look of his hazel eyes and thin sandy hair by an erect, soldierly immobility of bearing that did him credit in an intolerable situation. Clarissa saw clearly that he was no villain but the hapless victim of a chain of wretched circumstances. He was dazzled by and infatuated by Constance. It was clear to Clarissa that it would be no easier for this harried man to return to London with an unknown American girl whom he had married as a crazy adventure than it had been for William Scott to face the situation tonight.

"None of this needed to have come about," old William went on. It was as if he had intoxicated himself with the torrent of his own words. There could not possibly be anything more to say, everyone in the room felt that, and all were in agony waiting for their dismissal. "Constance has had the standards and the training to know good behavior from bad. I think you may have had the same thing somewhere in your background. But it's too late now. You've both ruined your chances. Let Constance turn up in London an American nobody and take the consequences of her folly. She'll get them quickly enough, all alone over there."

"She is not going all alone," Clarissa said quietly. Her heart pounded suffocatingly but she had found sudden access to determination and she spoke firmly and coolly. "Mary will go with her."

"What?"

"How?"

"What do you mean?"

Exclamations and stifled sounds of surprise came from every person in the room. William Scott turned ponderously and scowled down on his wife.

"Explain yourself, Clarissa."

Mary in her corner swayed towards the wall and put her hand behind her for support. Her eyes, strained wide, were fastened on Clarissa Scott's face. Her mistress had not glanced in her direction, nor given the faintest indication what she had intended to do. But Mary knew that in five terse words Clarissa had made to her a plea of passionate eloquence. She had really said, "We are both desperate. Help me. I will help you." Neither woman dared to look at Paul standing in the far end of the room. He had turned dead white. Understanding had broken on him too with terrible clarity.

"Explain yourself, Clarissa. What is this idea?"

Clarissa sat straight on the edge of the sofa and clasped her hands in her lap. She spoke with forceful quiet.

"Constance is your daughter, whatever you have said to her tonight. And her husband is your son-in-law. I cannot ask you to provide for them financially or otherwise go against your principles. They will not be able to live according to Giles' position. But I intend that Constance shall arrive in her husband's country with her head up. She may be disgraced with you but her whole life lies ahead of her. She is not a nobody and I will not have it appear that she is."

Clarissa looked for a moment at Whitfield-Moulton who was gazing at her with the first human expression that had touched his face in the past hour. Appreciation burned in his miserable eyes. Clarissa continued.

"I do not know yet what Giles' family will think of this marriage, but I am not going to handicap Constance either by your fury or by her own youth and ignorance. Mary is our most trusted servant. She has great good sense and poise. She will go with Constance as her maid, and stand by to teach her to keep house and live up to the responsibilities that she is too young to have learned."

Old William glared in astonishment. His children looked at one another with expressions of amazement. Paul wanted only to get out; he had a fierce desire to slam out of the house and go and do the most violent things he could think of. But wisdom, cold and sickening, kept him standing in his place with the appearance of indifference. Constance heard her mother's first words with a gasp of resentment. The last thing she wanted was more of the meticulous supervision against which she had raged all her life. But in the next moment her real shrewdness brought her to her senses. The one thing that might start this off right was her arrival in England with a family servant, her personal maid. She had never known how wonderful her mother was. While Whitfield-Moulton, trembling from his awful experience, went over and took Clarissa's hand, jerking out choked words of gratitude, Constance flung aside her frozen arrogance, burst into tears, and ran across the room to Mary.

"Oh Mary, darling," she cried, throwing her arms around the shaking girl, "you'll come. You'll come with me, won't you? I'll need you so terribly."

Mary turned her head away and patted Constance's shoulder. "Sure," she whispered. She could scarcely breathe. "Sure, I'll come and help ye."

CHAPTER XVI

[Fall 1880]

GILES AND CONSTANCE were setting up their home in a tiny house of lead-colored brick squeezed between two mansions in Montagu Street, not far from Portman Square. The house belonged, with considerable complications of liens and leaseholds, to the decrepit estates of the Earl of Melling, Giles' octogenarian father. This old man had been so long a legend, and so many years had elapsed since anyone but his guardian nurse-manservant had seen him, drooling and maundering in two rooms of his shuttered country house, that nobody seriously considered him to be alive any longer. He had not died, but when he did his heir would undoubtedly finish off the ruin of the family properties which the Earl in his youth and until his collapse into incompetence, had so thoroughly undertaken. Constance quickly discovered that it was not and never had been her husband who was the blackguard of the family, but his elder brother Tyrringdale and their unbelievable father. There was one sister, the Honourable Ginevra Higgenbotham. She was the widow of a forgotten Major-General, and had lived for twenty years in India. Now, returned to London to scrimp out the rest of her life on his pension, she was the only possible thread of approach to respectable society for Giles and his bride. By dint of pointing out to the suspicious trustees that poor Giles was the only man in the family willing to present a semblance of conventional decency in his living arrangements, Ginevra managed to obtain for him the use of the little house in Montagu Street. And this was after Ginevra had succumbed to the spell of Constance on her very best behavior, and after she had observed the propriety lent the whole picture by Mary's presence and personality. If Clarissa Scott had foreseen the situation in every detail, she could not have made a wiser move.

But Ginevra still had the truth to learn about her infant sister-in-law. Constance had taken one look at the scrawny yellow widow with her crooked buck teeth and hair "the color of dusty combings—ugh"—she had shuddered to Mary—and had gritted her teeth with sudden mature cynicism. "If she's the only respectable member of this charming tribe, I'm going to be just too adorable to her. You watch me." And, with an eye fixed on the few old friends who had not made Ginevra pay the penalties of her father's and brother's sins, Constance was adorable. She listened wide-eyed and docile to Ginevra's advice about everything—furniture, house-maids, sheeting, tea, woollen underdrawers, reigning dowagers—and then went and did exactly as she pleased. She set about cataloguing everybody in London known through connection or acquaintance to Giles and his sister. She called them not only sheep and goats but finer gradations of animal characterization. But she was charming to them. And in no time at all the brown morocco book on her writing table was filled with engagements from midday to midnight.

Already it was clear that life to Constance would be a skilled game of chance for high stakes; and she regarded Giles as one of many pawns. She was nice to him those early months of her marriage. Mary remarked as much, sarcastically, one morning when she brought in Constance's tea and heard her say to Giles, who was just leaving the room, "Of course, I'll be delighted to have your Auntie Violet to dine. I'll ask her to bring Lady Brace-Freemantle too."

"Ye will!" said Mary, as the door closed. "Ain't that nice! Two old crows ye'd not 'a' looked at in Pittsburgh and here ye're givin' dinner-parties for 'em." She twitched disapprovingly at the mussed sheets on the side of the double bed that Giles had vacated. Constance yawned and stretched and flexed her pointed fingers like—Mary thought with a quick shock—an alley-cat under a hedge. The room seemed somehow indecent. Constance had no modesty now any more than she had had as a child. She included Mary in the general intimacies of her changed situation, and Giles took Mary for granted as he had always done with personal servants.

Yet he never missed an opportunity to hint, where it would do the most good, at the meaning implicit in Mary's presence. If Ginevra brought some sharp-eyed old gossip to tea, Giles found some reason for Mary to come into the room, bringing a shawl for Constance or a book for him, and he would say, remarking the notice that went to the delicate face and distinguished manner, "My wife's nurse, you know. Her mother would not let Constance leave the States without her." Mary's twenty-four years might have been the fifty that Giles implied, for the inscrutable reserve behind which she scorned the whole performance.

In a way she was sorry for Giles. He was so helplessly infatuated with Constance and she was so quickly losing the avidity for him that the novel experience of marriage had awakened. He was fascinated, almost tormented by the startling and shocking qualities of the child. He had never seen such a rocket of energy, appetites, and tempestuous charm. She ate up his days like a fever for gambling. Sometimes Mary watched Constance, shrewd and cool and clever beyond anything her age or background could explain, and once Mary said, "Do ye ever think of anythin' except what ye want?"

Constance turned around from her mirror and stared.

"Why—no. What else is there to think about?"

Mary shook her head. There was no use trying to explain. For all her stern efforts not to think about her own troubles, not to let Paul and the memory of his voice and arms and lips come stealing in to fill her sleepless nights, it sometimes seemed too much that this dazzling child should be using marriage just to satisfy her terrific greed for sensation and adventure. A body would not be human, Mary thought despairingly, if she did not fall into the temptation to make comparisons sometimes. This exile in London was a bitter makeshift. All her love for Constance and all her devotion to Mrs. Scott and all her wanting to do the right thing about Paul did not make it any easier. She missed Paul with an unrelenting, driving, penetrating hunger. Her only resort was backward into her memory. In all her interminable solitary hours, during the day when she sewed or pressed Constance's clothes, during the night when she lay rigid and sleepless, hungry and chilled, she relived the hours she and Paul had spent together. Each of these with all its distinct moments had become so precious to her that she had them tabulated in her mind, one by one, and she drew them forward to be renewed, re-recognized, and treasured like the jewels they were. Sometimes she allowed herself to recollect long conversations about his work, quiet moments on the rickety steps of the derelict house on Rebecca Street, feasting their eyes on the fiery panorama below. But the last evening held the beginnings of her great pain, and this she could not often bear to dwell upon. That hour of revelation was locked deepest in the vault of her memory. Only in the most hopeless depths of despair, when the loneliness hurt like an actual knife turning in her heart, did she resort to the memory of that night, lying in his arms in the shelter of the spring trees, knowing the meaning of desire and of her love for him.

Against those memories the adventures of Constance and Giles were desecration. Without Mrs. Scott's letters Mary sometimes felt she could not have found the strength to go on. The letters came frequently, short and full of affection and encouragement and of such news as Clarissa felt would not rouse too much homesickness. Always she closed with words of thanks for Mary's loyalty, brief words implicit with understanding and confidence. She never mentioned Paul and Mary tried hard to believe that he was resigned to her absence—perhaps even glad of it, if he was learning to do without her. She had not intended to see him alone before she left for England; for a whole day she had avoided him. But the night before she was to leave, when she went to the trunk-room in the attic for a portmanteau, he slipped in and silently took her in his arms. "Don't worry," he whispered, "I'm not going to keep you here. I won't make it hard for you. I simply had to touch you once again."

He had held her tightly in the light from the candle she had set down, looking at her face with such intensity that she knew he was engraving it on the bruised texture of his heart. She did the same. But the house about them was full of bustling people, and there was no time in which to satisfy even this minor hunger.

"I must go," she whispered. "Yer mother's waitin' for me."

"All right, darling. But we'll write—all the time, won't we?"

"Oh no!" she gasped. "No, dear. That won't help us any way at all. Ye must understand," she insisted desperately, "ye've got to understand why I'm doin' this. It isn't Constance. It's the only way to help us. We'll have to stay apart and not meet for a long, long time till we're not all weak and battered and helpless any more. That's the only way, Paul. And letters would only weaken us. Please help me, darlin'. Please, for the love of God. Please promise. Will ye, Paul? Will ye promise?"

She never received an answer. For just then they heard Clarissa at the foot of the attic stairs calling, "Mary! Did you find it?" And with one desperate touch of their lips, Mary had seized the portmanteau and the candle and run downstairs. For months she thought that she had won the promise she asked of Paul. He did not write and she tried to believe that he agreed with her.

Anyway, she said to herself, when she had dressed Constance for perhaps the fourth time in a day, and seen her sweep downstairs, glorious in her lowcut evening dress, with her hair piled in a blaze of curls and a devilish glitter in her slanting eyes, anyway this is better than not being with anybody in the family at all. Constance loved Mary and often said so. Sometimes she stalked about with a cold imperious manner and the arrogant ways of a woman of the world, but she could still plump herself into Mary's starched lap on a childish impulse and hug and kiss her. You never knew what to expect when you were alone with her. You never knew who would be the butt of her temper either. Like the day when they first moved to Montagu Street, and they were standing at the top of the garret stairs in the dark hallway under the mansard. They were peering doubtfully into the two ratholes of chambers in each of which two servants were supposed to sleep. The rooms were clammy and smelly, lighted only by slits of windows under the roof, and scarcely larger than closets. Constance recoiled and backed into the hall.

"Why Mary! These aren't rooms! They're hell-holes."

Mary was silent. Apparently she would have to live in one of these rooms, and share it with a roommate whose habits, judging by her back-stairs glimpses of British servants in these past weeks, she gagged to think about. The staff was to consist of a cook, a parlormaid, and a slavey to do scullery work, black boots and grates, and polish brasses. Presumably this latter would share Mary's room. She looked at Constance in silent consternation. But she did not protest, she did not intend to protest. She had made the decision once for all that she would endure every trial that this experience imposed; she had been sent here to perform a duty by Clarissa Scott and she would see it through if it killed her. But Constance, peering gingerly into the ill-smelling hole, was too much a Scott to let it defeat her.

"This is an outrage," she said. "If the others aren't used to anything better, let them live like animals. You're going to sleep downstairs."

"I wudn't think that wise, Miss Constance—Madam."

"You mean they'll be jealous and mean to you? Let 'em. What do you care? Would you rather be clean and comfortable and have some privacy or be popular among the bedbugs? I bet the place is crawling with them." Constance's language was not growing more refined with her emancipation.

"I'm feared those girls will take it out o' me," Mary said doubtfully.

"What do you care? I'm not scared of them, with their stuck-up snippiness. I'll show them who's boss around here. Come on, let's look downstairs."

They went down and inspected a tiny chamber back of the room which Constance intended for her own. "You'll be able to get a single bed there," Constance was pointing out, "and a wash-stand and a table and a small chest of drawers. I don't know where you'll hang your clothes, though."

"What is this?" Giles appeared in the doorway, frowning.

"We're planning Mary's room," Constance said, looking at the memorandum book in her hand.

"*Mary's* room?"

Giles' tone was sharp.

"Yes, certainly. Have you seen those filthy holes upstairs where the maids are supposed to sleep? Why, I wouldn't put a dog in one."

"They are good enough for our British servants," Giles said, implying that they were too good for an Irish-American immigrant. "And this is to be my dressing-room."

"Oh, no, it's not!" Constance's green eyes began to shine with a wicked glitter. "I told you this is Mary's room. She's used to something a whole lot better than this. So that settles it."

"That settles nothing. I will arrange this house according to my own wishes and what is suitable. The maids will sleep in their proper accommodations."

"Put your Cockneys anywhere you like," said Constance, "but Mary sleeps in this room by herself."

"I advise you not to defy me, Constance!"

"Oho. You do. Well isn't that cute of you. See here." Constance walked over and took up her stand before him with feet apart and a cold glare on her face that reminded him of her father on the horrible night of their marriage. "The sooner you learn that when I want something I get it the better it will be for you. I get what I want because I know how to get it. See? And the less you interfere the pleasanter it will be around here."

"How dare you! Before a servant."

Constance laughed. She jerked her head toward Mary with a vulgar motion that shocked Giles and Mary too. Mary was red-faced and almost in tears.

"Her? Do you expect me to play-act before Mary? You'd better get over that notion too. Nothing I did could surprise Mary, poor girl."

"Please, Miss Constance—Madam. I'd rather sleep upstairs."

"I don't care if you would." Constance now had her teeth deep in red meat and was thoroughly enjoying herself. "You could sleep in the coal-cellar for all I care. But I said this is going to be your room, and that's whose room it's going to be. And so will the rest of the house be the way I want it. Once for all," he said to Giles, twiddling her wiry white fingers, "get that through your slow old head. I've been in this country long enough to find out how you bully your wives. Well, just remember you've married an American. And you've only just begun to find out what you're in for!" she crowed, in the tone she used to browbeat Edgar.

Shame more than anything wilted him. He could not wait to get away.

He strode past her and started downstairs. But still trying to confound her with the contemplation of his rights, which as the master of the house seemed inviolable to him, he asked icily, "I suppose in making these arrangements of yours you are providing a room where I may dress?"

"Oh, I guess so," Constance answered carelessly. "If I don't you can dress in the you-know."

The furious slam of the street door echoed to her peals of laughter in the hall upstairs.

"That'll show him," she chortled, prancing up and down the hall. "That'll teach him something."

To Mary's discomfiture, it did. She was used to men like the Scotts who made all the important decisions and ran their affairs as the Old Man ran the mill. But Giles soon found that the only way to keep peace and keep Constance receptive to him was to let her have her way about what she wanted. They had almost no money, but with what little they had Constance attained a good deal of style. The money came secretly in the form of an allowance from her uncle Staunton Haynes in Baltimore, her mother's brother.

Clarissa had come to the painful conclusion that whether or not her husband was right, there was no use in shipping Constance off to England with a husband to whom an impecunious wife, no matter what his own circumstances, would be considered a disgrace and probably be treated like one. She could not extract an allowance for Constance from her own means because they were so carefully administered by her husband that no withdrawals would escape his notice. So she begged her brother to send Constance an income, however small, as a loan against her own moderate fortune during her husband's lifetime. The amount agreed upon was not large; it was only as much as Staunton Haynes could spare, and that would not suffice for Constance indefinitely. Constance's plan of action was perfectly plain to Mary. She intended to intrench herself as quickly and securely as possible with old ladies and titled dowagers whose friendship would blot out the Melling stigma. From them she meant to go on to the "wicked exciting people" over whom she had licked her chops in Pittsburgh. Dukes and racehorses, she had gloated, Mary remembered. Barely a year later that did not seem so ridiculous any more.

CHAPTER XVII

[*1881*]

ONE BITTER FEBRUARY MORNING, when she was half sick from a cold, hideously depressed by the dark dawn, and nauseated by a breakfast of scorched porridge, Mary forgot everything in the shock of the morning mail. Among other innovations which flouted Giles and her entire household, Constance had flatly refused to get up and have a proper breakfast in the dining-room as all decent wives did. She had a passion for lying in bed in the morning which she had never in her life been allowed to indulge. And now that she was her own mistress she guzzled this luxury. Of all the moments she loved best, the most delightful was when Mary came stiffly through her bedroom door, carrying the breakfast tray, her face pinched with disapproval. Constance among her pillows and eiderdown would look up and slyly jeer, "Doesn't this drive you wild, Mary? Wouldn't you just love to grab me by the ear and douse me in the water jug the way you used to?"

But there was one great advantage in Constance's plan. She had given orders that Mary was to receive the morning post from the carrier at the door, sort out her letters, and bring them upstairs on her tray. The parlor-maid had coldly pointed out that that was not the lady's maid's duty, but Constance had snapped, "That is the way I want it." And to Mary she had admitted that her real motive was suspicion of the other servants. "I bet they'd go through the letters with a fine-tooth comb," she said. "They pry into everything like vermin." Mary knew this to be the truth, so she was grateful for the chance to protect her own priva:y, though just what mail a young bride would be receiving in secrecy she had not thought to question. On this miserable morning she answered the postman's ring, shivering on the slippery doorstep, and there on the top of the pile of letters lay a thick envelope from Pittsburgh addressed to her. Mary's eyes blurred as she touched it and she was so overwhelmed with joy that she forgot all about her efforts to make Paul promise not to write.

She flew up to her room, holding the letter under her apron, and locked her door behind her. She was too happen to open the envelope right away. She stood leaning against the door holding the letter to her cheek; then she turned it over and over, examining every stroke of Paul's bold writing, even the picture of Zachary Taylor on the blue American stamp.

Finally with trembling fingers she carefully opened the letter and smoothed out the folded sheets. Her heart beat furiously as she began to read.

"Dearest Mary:

"I can't stand this nonsense any longer. If I tried to tell you how I miss you I wouldn't do anything else day and night, so I'll say that your idea of not writing was insane, and you must forget it. Either you don't know how I feel about you or you expect the impossible. I've had seven months of hell on your terms and now I'm laying down a few of my own. I'm going to write to you whenever things get so bad that I can't stand it. You might just as well know they're bad. You might as well know that my life is as empty as a blown egg and as meaningless. I'm so busy that I don't give myself two minutes at a time to think about you, and I'm so tired at night that I ought to fall asleep like a stunned pig, but I don't. I just lie there and see you and want you and hear your voice and—forgive me. I'm a selfish brute to pour all this out when you're probably having a worse time than I am, and need to be comforted instead of upset. But why, Mary? Why are we in this mess? I can't understand. You're asking something so tremendous of me, to believe in some vague ideal of yours that this is the right thing to do, and that it will all turn out for the best. How can it? This is an absolute deadlock and if you think this is the way for us to forget each other you're all wrong. There isn't any way. I didn't mean to write this kind of a letter. I didn't mean to write at all. But I can't help it. I'm doing it in spite of myself."

The first page fluttered to the floor. The pounding of her heart was almost silenced by the rush of tears she could not hold back. Mary moved blindly to the chair by the window and dropped into it and buried her face in her arms on the window sill. She could not read for a time. She could not think. She could only feel what it would be like to have Paul holding her in his arms, saying these things he had written. She could hear his voice. She cried until, suddenly, she realized there was still most of the letter to read; then she sat up and went on with it.

"I suppose you'd like to know what's really going on here in our happy home. I'm sure Mama wouldn't tell you all about it. Bill and Julia got themselves in so bad over Con that Father hasn't spoken to them since. I can't prove that Julia actually dug up this Giles but she certainly met him first and got him introduced to Connie in cold blood. She's going around over in Pittsburgh already—funny the way she knows enough not to make a fool of herself with people here in Allegheny—talking about the Earl and the Viscount as if they were her closest relations. Now that you're over there have you found out what's the skeleton in the family closet? It must be a pretty putrid one from the way people laugh at Julia.

"Mother has Louise around here all the time. I know this is what you would say is right, Mary, even though you know in your heart it isn't. I tried for a while to see it your way, honestly I did. I tried to see it from Mama's point of view. I think she misses you almost as much as I do, in a way. She's always calling the other girls Mary and stopping herself. Anyway she gets Louise over here in the afternoons and they sew together and go calling and shopping. I guess Mama is really fond of her. And she's patient with me about it. I promise you I'm not rude to Louise and I don't ignore her when she's here, but I'd like to. I never could see why I was supposed to make it up to Louise by marrying her because her father killed himself and left her penniless. I'm sure Father and Mama have paid for her education and helped her mother ever since Uncle Dick died. Isn't that enough without throwing me into the breach?

"You know the queerest thing about this experience is the way I can stand aside and look at the whole thing impersonally and *see* even when I can't *feel*. I know everybody thinks I should marry Louise, and I see why, and I'd rather be dead. Then I think, 'Well, if I won't marry her they'd probably just as soon I married some other Pittsburgh girl.' So I think about that exactly as if there were two of me, one acting and the other looking on, and no real life in either of them. I go and see other girls once in a while. I even think one of them, Virginia Neville, is very pretty and attractive and interesting, in a way. I can even see one of these shadows of myself thinking of marrying her. But actually it all has no more substance than the smoke from my pipe. Mary, darling, aren't you ever going to come to your senses? Don't you know it's you and nothing in the world but you that I love and belong to?"

Again for a while she could not read. After all this time, all these months of telling herself that Paul was growing used to doing without her, he must write the very things she had so foolishly and stupidly told herself could stop being true. He was bolder with the truth than she, he always had been; but oh, the awful, straining ache of looking it square in the face again. How could she ever have tried to hide from it? She went on with the letter; he had such a lot to tell her. Now it was about James:

"I see him all the time at the mill, but if I try to see him outside he won't have anything to do with me. I don't know whether he thinks there is any connection between me and your going away, but he certainly acts queer and suspicious unless he's actually on the job with me. And he's all wrapped up in the Amalgamated. They're gaining ground fast now in all the mills and you hear talk about their striking if they don't get their demands. Jim doesn't make any bones about the number of our men he's organized."

Mary shook her head, frowning. Other and more immediate worries had almost made her forget James and the trouble he could bring down on the Scotts once he decided to. "The fool," she muttered angrily as she read. "The wicked fool, for all that." Paul wrote, "He's so good on the job, doing wonders with the new furnace. Production is very high and we're already planning a second open-hearth. Father is delighted with the profits from the new steel; he hoards them up like an old miser against that share of Gaylord's he wants to buy back. I hope Gaylord sells out when the time comes, but something tells me he won't without a struggle. There's going to be one knockdown dragout settling-up the day Father tells off Bill and Julia. Bill knows it's coming, too. He sits around that office doing less all the time as if to remind Father he'll have to pay through the nose to get rid of him."

This was a wonderful letter. Paul was remembering to tell her every-thing she could possibly want to know. "I don't mind," she read on, "letting Father cope with Bill, but I do hate to worry him about Edgar. You know Ed better than I do, so I won't go into the grisly details. But this past Christmas vacation he came home from Princeton and proceeded to show us how a college freshman proves himself a man. It was pretty horrible and if I knew where Ed, or Constance too for that matter, got their tastes, I'd take your estimation of our proud family a little more seriously. This letter will probably make you angry but at least it's the truth. What can matter any longer between us, Mary, except the truth— about everything? I love you as I always did, which is too much to de-scribe in written words, or in any words; it will take a lifetime and all the strength I have to prove it to you, and I am determined to make you accept it.

"I feel better for having written, though I know you wished me not to. Some day you will stop denying the inevitable. You may be an angel, and superhuman in ideals and strength, but you have made an ordinary man love you with every particle of his ordinary flesh and blood. I wonder if you know yet what this means? I will not ask you to answer this letter, because I know I don't have to. I can't stand it much longer, Mary. Anything would be more endurable than this. I love you so. I love you.

"Paul."

Now Mary prayed that Constance would sleep late and give her time to get control of herself again. For never in all her life had she felt so shattered. She lay on her bed with Paul's letter crushed in her breast, her head smothered under the pillow, and wept with tremendous ripping sobs. She felt nothing except a sense of whirling; as if she were spinning inwardly in a cold black vacuum that made her very breath icy as she gasped in it. She could not even feel pain, and somewhere she had a muddled realization that she was too used to it to feel it. The sharp creases of the stiff paper scratched her breasts. Though her ears were blocked by the pillow she could hear her own horrible sobs and through them imagine Paul's voice as if he were speaking the words he had written. Time and place went out of her mind; she never knew how long she lay there.

Constance's bell rang at last. Mary hardly heard it, but in a moment it rang again, furiously. Mary jumped from the bed and glanced at herself with horror in the mirror. She slopped cold water into the basin, stripped off her uniform to the waist, and flung the icy water about her neck and breast and face, gasping from the shock. She did not know how quick she was; panic and determination made her lightning fast. As she dried her face she looked about wildly for something to hide its raw misery. She had no face powder, had never used it in her life, but she had a little sachet of orris that Clarissa had slipped into her handkerchiefs. She cut it open and flung the contents on her face and neck. Putting on her dress again, she looked at Paul's letter crumpled on the bed. Then she stuffed it inside her corset-cover and buttoned her basque tightly over it. The bib of her apron would hide it if it bulged. She made a few desperate pulls at her hair, flung on her apron and cap, and hurried in to Constance. She had not decided how she would explain if Constance remarked, as she was likely to do, about her awful appearance. But Constance remarked nothing. When Mary opened the door, Constance was leaning over the edge of her bed vomiting into the chamber-pot.

"Constance!" It took very little surprise or shock to make Mary revert to the natural address with which she had brought Constance up. "Miss" and now "Madam" were always artificial and half-ridiculous. "Constance, what's the matter?"

Constance rolled over on her back and moaned. Mary was relieved that Giles was not in the room.

"Where in hell've you been?" Constance said through chattering teeth. "I'm sick."

Mary was already fussing over her. "I see ye are. Here." She handed Constance a glass of water with mouth-wash in it. "Rinse yer mouth out. Gargle."

Constance did so, shuddering and swearing. She knew every word of profanity that Edgar had ever picked up, and was using them all with increasing abandon as she grew older. She lay back and watched Mary cleaning up. Then, carrying towels and vessels out the door Mary turned and said, "Do ye feel like having yer breakfast?"

Constance belched and shook her head. "God forbid. Mary." She sat up suddenly with a look of horror. "Mary. Do you suppose I could be having a baby?"

Mary set down her things on a stand in the hall and came slowly back into the room, closing the door. "Why, I suppose ye are. It would be natural, wouldn't it?"

"Oh my God." Constance bared her teeth and caught her knuckles in them. "How ghastly."

"Why? Ye wanted to be married, didn't ye? That's part o' bein' married, the most natural part. Why do ye act as if ye'd been doomed?"

"But I have," Constance cried. "You don't think I want a nasty squalling baby, do you? Or to be all swollen and ugly and lumbering and not be able to wear my clothes and have to stop going out just when I was getting things all fixed? Oh damn!" she screamed. "What a God damn *nuisance!*"

"Constance!" Mary walked over and seized her by the shoulder and shook her as if she had been ten years old. "Shut yer mouth. Have ye no shame, committin' sins like this and screamin' about it at the top o' yer wicked cursin' voice? Stop it! I'll not hear it!"

Constance pulled herself up to a rigid position and glared at Mary.

"Aren't you forgetting your place?"

"If I am it's because ye don't deserve any respect," said Mary shortly. "Ye're no lady and God forgive me if I wonder how yer mother ever bore ye, a wonderful woman like her."

Constance shrugged and sighed.

"Well, there's nothing like spitting it out if you feel like it," she said. "I do, so I suppose you've got a right." Sometimes she was so astoundingly honest and fair that Mary could do nothing but love her. Constance had the quality of knowing exactly whom she could bully, deceive, or patronize, and in whom she had found her match. She knew that she could neither fool nor intimidate Mary. She flounced back on her pillows and scratched her head with both hands. "Oh, what'll I do?" she muttered. "What in hell shall I do?"

"Do? Why ye'll have a baby just like all the rest o' womankind and if ye come to yer senses ye'll thank God for the privilege."

"Privilege!" Constance snarled. "Privilege! Do you realize what a privilege it is to bring a child into this family? Why they're a lot of unspeakable degenerates."

"Constance! Won't ye please stop and think what ye're saying before ye altogether lose yer immortal soul?"

"Oh, I know what I'm saying. I tell you, I could—why Mary!" She sat up and rubbed her forehead as if to bring her wits back to earth again. "Mary." Even Constance could pause abashed in the effort to find words for the thought in her mind. "Isn't there, you know . . ." she dropped her voice and narrowed her eyelids cannily. "Isn't there something I could do? Couldn't I . . . ?"

"Constance!" Mary's hands went up to her face. "I've stood everythin' on the sufferin' earth from you," Mary said in a strangled voice, "but I'll not stand this. No, so help me God, I'll not endure this."

She turned away and Constance saw that she had gone too far. She did not know where or how she had conceived this last idea, though she knew that no woman short of a prostitute could admit to knowing of such a thing. There were some limits beyond which she could not go, not if she was to keep on with her purpose of a triumphant life in London. She must never waver from her determination to keep a faultless conventional front on things.

"Oh, I'm sorry," she said grudgingly. "I suppose I didn't mean it. But it is true that nobody'd want to have this baby. I'm too young and I don't want the whole mess and nuisance and—everything."

"Ye certainly are too young," Mary said. "Ye've no idea what marriage is about. Yer husband probably would want to take a hairbrush to ye if he knew all this. After all, he has got somethin' to do with it. And in a titled family and all—why yer child might make a great difference."

"No, it wouldn't," Constance said. She spoke dully and with a strangely mature note of disillusionment. "You don't know much about this family, do you, Mary? I forget how nice you really are. You don't pry and gossip and you've got a decent mind. You ought to thank God for it."

"Why, what've they done to you?" Mary asked with sudden solicitude. It was clear to her now that Constance for all her tough exterior was a frightened and horrified child. Clear, too, that she would never admit it nor be defeated by it. "What is it, dear?"

"You know about the old man, don't you? He's insane from paresis."

She saw that Mary did not fully understand what this was. It was probably just as well.

"And Tyrringdale," she said. "Well, he's—"

"Isn't he the one ye're waitin' for the end of?" Mary asked. This was an extraordinary piece of cynicism from her. "If he doesn't ever marry won't yer husband finally get to be the Earl? And this baby would be—"

"Oh, Tyrringdale won't marry," Constance laughed nastily. "But before he dies he'll have the whole estate so ruined there'll be nothing left for Giles or any child of his to inherit. Nobody'd want to be the Earl of Melling, anyway. I've found out about that. It's nothing but an infamy."

"Well, maybe Tyrringdale will marry yet and yer husband won't ever come into the title."

Constance snorted. "He won't marry. You don't know what you're saying. I don't know which is worse—whether he lives or dies."

"What's the trouble with him?" Mary asked. "Why is he such a bogey on ye?"

"You don't know about him either, do you?" Constance spoke wearily. "He's fifty or so, I guess, and no decent person has spoken to him for twenty years."

"Why?"

"He—he likes boys."

Mary's face was a deep, burning crimson, all the way down her neck inside her collar, when Constance summoned the courage to look at her. They stared at each other for a moment of stony silence. Then Constance twisted her head wretchedly and said, "So maybe you can see why I'm not anxious to perpetuate this shining line. Oh, I admit it's mostly selfishness. I don't want any baby, even if Giles were an angel. I've been having a lot of fun and I mean to have more. Lots more. I'll not let this lick me. I'm in for it now, but just you watch me when it's over. They won't drag me down with them," Constance cried, clenching her fists. "I'm going to have a good time in my life in spite of the whole filthy pack of them!"

Mary felt tense with pity. In justice Constance's fate was probably no more than she deserved, but Mary was too fond of the child not to suffer in her behalf. She did not know a morality like the Puritanical vindictiveness of William Scott and his daughter Elizabeth. She had all the rich tenderness of her race and her faith, all of the compassion of her namesake, the understanding heart of the Mater Dolorosa. Constance, seeing the soft light in her face, burst into tears. Mary sat on the edge of the bed and took her in her arms.

"There," she crooned, "there, there. Ye're only a child yerself. I'll look after ye, dear. Mary'll take care of ye, and yer baby too. Don't cry now, dearie. Stop yer cryin'. It's bad for ye."

But Constance only sobbed harder. "I don't deserve you," she moaned. "I'm such a pig to you. Oh Mary, I'm so awful."

"Sure ye are," Mary said. "Sure, ye always were. Ye're awful. Ye're simply terrible.

But later she stood alone in her room before the mirror again, with the door locked behind her. Her hands clutched at the letter in her breast. If Paul had made her think even unconsciously of going home, if such an unlikely miracle could come to pass, she would not be able to go now anyway. She had her work cut out for her right here.

CHAPTER XVIII

[*1881*]

CONSTANCE CAME IN from an afternoon's calling a few weeks later, and met Mary in the hall, just emerging from the library with a thick book under her arm.

"Come upstairs and help me change," Constance said. "I'm pooped."

"I told ye not to go out this afternoon when ye mean to go to the Duchess o' Sutherland's dinner tonight."

Constance looked curiously at Mary's book as they climbed the stairs. "Donne's Poetical Works," she read aloud. "What on earth, Mary? Are you reading that?"

"I thought I'd look at it."

Constance stared. It was inconceivable to her that a person could want to read such a thick book by some musty old poet. Why on earth would Mary want to? Constance bent her brows quizzically and Mary began to blush.

"What put such a notion into your head?" Constance asked, as they went into her room and she began shedding her street clothes over the furniture and the floor.

Mary did not answer. She was busy hanging up Constance's lambskin pelisse in the wardrobe. Her face was hidden by the clothes. She had slipped the book into her own room. She could not possibly explain that in Paul's latest letter which was buttoned inside her dress, he had quoted, "Absence, hear my protestation," and had gone on to say:

"Read the whole poem, Mary; it will tell you everything I want you to know, but so much more beautifully than I could say it. You will find it in the works of John Donne. Some say he did not write it, but if not, a great poet did. Donne is one of my favorites."

The small library in Montagu Street was lined with books which had been sent, along with the furnishings of the house, from Melling, where they had been shrouded and unused for years. Nobody ever opened a book except Giles in occasional retreats from his convulsive existence. Constance laughed boisterously when Mary said, "Ye don't mind if I read the books, do ye?"

"Mind! Good God, is that all the deviltry you can find to get into?"

There was little enough, even heedless Constance knew, to occupy the free time of a servant in London, especially Mary, who had nothing in common with any of the others in the house. She kept to herself. Letters and books were her only recreation. Sheer loneliness, if nothing else, would have made her drop her futile idea that she and Paul should not write to each other. And from this disheartening distance she still had her own family to keep within reach. Bridget had had to leave the convent and go home to look after old Patrick; Kate could not do so any longer with her own house and baby to care for. Mary worried constantly about Bridget. She wrote to her every week, trying to remind her of the joys of a good conscience and the worthlessness of cheap pleasures, for which Kate reported Bridget had a keener taste than ever. James was a hopeless correspondent. Kate's letters after a time began to be evasive when Mary asked particularly about Bridget. She was well, she looked after Dad, she quarrelled with James. Beyond that Mary's troubled imagination had to fill the gaps.

But when she could slip away to her room and settle down with the beautiful Morocco writing-case that Constance had given her for Christmas, she could lose herself almost entirely in the joy of writing to Paul. It was fun to watch the news of ship arrivals in the *Times,* knowing there would be a letter for her when the American mails came in; it was fun to walk to the post and mail her weekly letter marked with the ship on which it was to go. That day when Constance teased her about reading books, she had a long, newly arrived letter to answer. After she had tucked Constance up for a nap she had almost two hours before time to dress her for the Duchess's dinner. Mary wrote, "I cannot send as much news as you do because so little happens here that concerns me. I hope, though, that Constance has written your mother her own news by now. She is going to have a baby, the doctor says so positively. It should be born at the end of September. Knowing Constance you cannot imagine that she is very sensible about it but I hope she will grow more so. Of course now I have no idea of coming home. Constance will need me as she never has before. She is very upset about all this and at first I thought it was pure selfishness. She has been having a gay time, going out a great deal and making many friends in London, and I thought she was only rebelling at having her pleasures interrupted. But she has told me the story of Giles's family and I must confess she has good reason for not wanting to bring any more of them into the world. It's not my place to say this but the habit of truth with you is strong on me and I don't feel able to break it. Sometimes I think it would be a mercy to go back to the old days of being near strangers, but I know I don't mean that deep in my heart.

"I could not possibly write in a letter the things Constance told me about that family. I can't think how there could be such people. And I feel very anxious not to have your father find out about them. He would tell Constance it is her just punishment for her disobedience, and that would only be a cruelty. I think she is being very brave in making the best of it."

Mary laid down her pen at that and went into the next room to look at Constance. She was sound asleep, her face buried between her milky arms on the pillows, her hair flung all about her in a burnished cloud. Her breathing was gentle and regular as a child's. She did not look old enough to be out of school, much less married, pregnant, and shrewdly following the ambitions of a woman of the world. Merely to see her as she was at this moment carried Mary back vividly to the old days at home. There was a lump in her throat when she went back to her own room. She read over again what Paul had written about Edgar; his wild habits, the secret late hours he kept with Paul's reluctant connivance, "because if I don't do that Father will find out and I want to spare Father that. Ed spends his nights over in Pittsburgh in God knows what kind of places, but you know what those houses are over on the Hill.

"Just think, Mary, if you were like any other woman I know, it would be unthinkable to tell you such a thing. And just because I do, and anything else that occurs to me too, you see?—and yet you think I could get along without you!

"Don't worry that Edgar will be expelled from Princeton. I'm so afraid the disappointment and disgrace would kill Father that I think I've really convinced Ed of this too. I've got his promise that he will study hard and not break college rules that would get him expelled, but the other side of the bargain is this promise not to tell Father what Ed does the rest of the time. It's pretty disgusting.

"I can only tell you, about Jim, that the Amalgamated has begun a stiffer membership drive than any they have put on before, and that Jim is in the thick of it, and I'm nearly desperate trying to get Father to say he will at least listen to them. Jim is far and away the best open-hearth man in the entire district and knows it, and hardly bothers to speak to any of us any more except when it's necessary. I ask once in a while about your father and he glares at me and says, 'I can take care of him all right without your interference, or anybody else's,' or words to that effect. I used to be really fond of your brother, I guess I still am, but he's changing so fast and turning so gloomy and sometimes violent in temper that it's hard to be patient with him.

"Oh, Mary, all this is a lot of empty drivel. All I really want to write is that I love you, I love you more desperately every day and if I didn't keep telling myself that some way or other I'm going to get you to come back to me I'd go stark mad. I need you so. Can't you read in these deadly letters what a hell my life is now? Please—Again, I love you. Your Paul.

"P.S. I forgot to tell you the wonder of wonders. Lizzie has a beau. Not only that, he seems to be as cold-blooded and strait-laced as she is. She met him down at the Mission House; he's from New York and spends his life on good works. And, I understand, has millions. How's that for justice?"

Mary thought for a long time and with a sigh began to write again.

"I suppose you are right about Edgar. Could you keep him out of mischief by seeing he works hard in the mill all next summer? I hope your father does not put a lot of commands on him. Ed will disobey them, just like Constance. I could seldom get at him, he's a strange lad. I should think you could do more with him than anyone just by keeping his confidence."

Mary sat idle after that. She did not really want to write about Edgar. It was time to close her letter and she always had trouble with endings. She knew what Paul would want her to write and she could never bring herself to do it. She took up her pen at last and wrote slowly,

"I am glad you are seeing Louise. It is part of what I pray for, some kind of peace for our souls. Louise will never stand in the way of that. I cannot answer the other parts of your letter. I will not tell you lies, or deny what you know to be true. But I still believe in what you call my vague ideals. They are not vague. And I am not an angel. And if you know yourself for a man, then you must realize what you are doing in this world, and why you were sent here. How can you speak as you do of us, and in the same breath point out to me your father's fury at Constance for marrying as she did? That only increases your responsibility to your family, just as your father's disappointment in William does.

"God bless you, dear. I cannot write more now. It is weak of me to do so, but I will tell you that I miss you.

"Your loving Mary."

Reading, toward which Paul in so seemingly casual a way had guided her, began to fill more and more of her time. Her education had been thorough in its way, but severely limited by the nature of the parochial school and the nuns' realistic knowledge of poor girls' requirements. Emphasis had been on religion, sewing, and useful arts, but Mary had also been trained to write a fine, precise hand and to read certain classics with appreciation. Now she realized in a few extraordinary hours that she need no longer spend her empty leisure time grinding her problems over and over in her head. She could sit on the straight-backed chair in her cramped room, with a book between her hands, and literally step off the planet of her everyday life into intoxicating space.

Donne was only a beckoning hand; she rushed forward on the course he pointed out. What she could not understand she took on faith, appreciating the majestic music it made, or she could laboriously study it word for word, with the help of lexicons and dictionaries. Poetry absorbed her for many weeks. She consumed with exquisite pleasure what she could digest of Spenser and Sidney, Marvell and Marlowe. She agonized over *Paradise Lost*, conscious for the first time in her life of the extent of her ignorance, and the bitter barrenness of her background; even the explanatory notes in the back of the edition she was reading (which had been Giles's textbook at Harrow) bewildered her.

She fell into a fit of discouragement which lasted for many days, during which she could not bear to open any book at all, because it seemed only to mock her overwhelming ignorance. Then, in fresh determination, she went to another shelf, where the books were thinner and less formidable, and took down a small book at random. This was a volume of Burns. She opened it and began to read; and presently she found herself almost singing aloud the Scottish dialect which was almost as familiar as her own inborn speech. Her own voice arrested her. Why—she thought— why—*I understand it all*. Here was wonderful poetry, full of music and beauty, which she understood. She began to turn the pages eagerly. These poems were not all in dialect. Some were in perfect and beautiful English.

Mary laid down the book and stood staring blankly out of the window at the dour gray street. A new idea was taking insistent shape in her head. It grew from something she had always known, from that deep-lying instinct which had always told her there was a finer way to speak, a better thing to make of one's life, than the crudity and ignorance into which she had been born. A poor Scottish crofter with less education even than she could point the way. She could learn to speak proper English. She would never have a better chance to learn it than here and now in London. A sense of discovery, of excitement, almost of intoxication, began to creep through her veins.

Constance noticed her efforts before long, and commented. She said sharply, one day, "You're losing your brogue, Mary. Are you trying to?"

Again, as on the day she was caught with Donne's poems, Mary blushed. She had nothing to say. But Constance gave her a shrewd look and said, "What are you up to? What's all this education you've gone in for?"

"Curiosity killed the cat," Mary retorted. "Your bath's ready."

Nothing could have induced her to answer Constance's questions. But she was startled when she thought about them later. She had never really asked them of herself. When she did, she found that Paul was in some way involved in the answers. She had never intended this to be so. Never. Was her Irish speech, she asked herself in a burst of furious frankness, the easiest to remove of all the obstacles that stood between them? If so, she had better leave it unchanged. But she went right on reading and studying and, once in a great while, listening to the most beautiful English in the world from a top-gallery seat at the Lyceum. "You cannot imagine how much pleasure this gives me," she wrote to Paul after seeing Henry Irving and Ellen Terry in *The Merchant of Venice*. She sat still for a long time and then added, her hand trembling, "I wish you might have been there with me."

[*September 1881*]

Constance lay in bed two days after the birth of her daughter.

"Tighter," she yelled, holding her breath. She lay flat on her back with her hands flung above her head. "Pull it tighter. Damn it, I could still get my whole fist inside."

The thick muslin binder already cut into her body above the waist and below the hips, until the white flesh stood out in red ridges on either side. The nurse on one side of the bed, and Mary on the other, tugged at the ends of the binder until they panted. And still Constance screamed "Tighter!"

"You'll injure yourself, Madam," said the nurse coldly. It was clear that she thought this young woman demented.

"Idiot! The only thing'll injure me is to get up and find my figure ruined. You pull this thing until I tell you it's tight enough."

"It won't pull any tighter," Mary said. "There!" She gave it one last heave and held the ends flat for the nurse to pin. Across the room the baby began suddenly to squall. Constance made a face.

"Can't you shut that brat up?" she asked the nurse irritably. "Here, give me the pins. I'll hold them for Mary."

The nurse went over to the bassinet and Constance jerked her head peevishly on the pillow. "Oh God," she groaned, "how did I ever get into this mess?"

"Didn't you promise me," Mary whispered while she pinned, "that you wouldn't talk like that with her in here? I've warned you, people like that are the worst gossips in London and there won't be a woman in the town won't know how you're acting about this baby. Will you keep still?"

Constance shut her lips and nodded. "Sorry," she whispered.

When the nurse came back Constance looked up with one of her flashes of mischief and said, "How is my dear little daughter?"

"Oh, lovely, Madam. The prettiest baby I've had in years. Shan't I bring her over now and lay her beside Mummie?"

Constance's hand conveniently covered her mouth and the sound it made.

"Well, I don't think so, Nurse Bray. Not just now. You know, I've been wondering, do I *have* to have the baby here in my room? Is it—er—customary?"

"Why yes, of course, Madam. Every mother wants her dear little baby in the room with her. Until it's big enough for its Nannie."

"How soon would you say that would be?" Constance looked so conscientious and concerned! Mary could have smacked her.

"Oh, in a month, perhaps, Madam. You'll certainly not want to be separated from the little dear before that."

Constance's expression, if the nurse had known her better, implied the contrary. But she was noncommittal for the moment. Just then Giles came in, his arms full of white chrysanthemums and lilies. He laid them on the bed as he bent over and kissed Constance with the unwontedly tender affection that he had been displaying ever since the birth of his daughter two days ago. The nurse simpered, in what she considered a suitable manner, and conspicuously left the room. Mary started to follow.

"S-s-s-s-st!" Constance called her back. "Come here."

She looked at her husband and at Mary with an expression of comical helplessness. "Look here," she half-whispered. "I don't want that puling baby here in the room with me all the time. And apparently I have to have it. It's done. What can I do?"

Giles laughed. "I'm afraid you're in for it, Connie. You'll get used to it. Women do."

"Not I. Mary, where can we put it?"

"Just where you intended to put it from the very first minute," Mary said dryly. "In with me. And you'll tell the nurse you've had terrible nightmares all your life and you're afraid you'll frighten the baby if you wake up screaming some night, or walk in your sleep. That's about what you'd thought up, isn't it?"

Constance, her eyes round with surprise, nodded slowly. She had a beautiful hothouse peach in her hands and was slowly licking the fuzz off it.

"How did you guess that?" she asked.

Mary laughed shortly. "When you have a surprise for me, Miss Con— Madam, you'd better not have seen me for a year or two beforehand. If you'll excuse me now . . ."

"No, wait a minute," Giles said. Mary paused in some astonishment. He seldom noticed her presence, much less spoke to her for any reason other than to give an order. "Do you know anything about babies, Mary?"

She looked at him with mild scorn. "Rather more than your wife does, sir, begging your pardon," she said. She was in the pleasant position of not caring, beyond the bounds of taste, what she said. She knew that Giles feared her unmercifully realistic knowledge of Constance. "I've brought up several children in my time. I don't expect to be Nannie to this one, though," she said.

"Don't you?" Constance laid down the peach and looked at Mary with alarm.

"Why no," Mary answered. "I understood you were going to engage a proper child's nurse for her and I think you should."

"But you said you'd take care of her for me," Constance reproached her, "that day last winter when I—"

"I said I'd take care of you," Mary reminded her, "and your baby too. Those were my words as I recollect them. I meant I would see that you got through this and had your baby safely in spite of all your nonsense. But I didn't mean I would turn into an infant's nurse, and I do not mean to now."

Giles looked at her with a mixture of protest and consternation. He had had no experience of anyone in a subservient—or what to him should be a servile—position who would dare to express intentions and lay down the law like this. And Constance, instead of rising up and giving Mary her orders, lay back and said meekly, "Very well. Have it your own way. But you'll have to hire a nurse for it. Don't expect me to know anything about it."

Mary laughed. "I don't," she said. She had foreseen this whole question and made up her mind about it months ago.

"Not for mine," she had said to herself. "I'll not get attached to another member of this family again, never my whole life long. And have my heart torn to pieces over it in the end."

And a day later when they decided to name the child Clarissa, Mary knew that she had been right. It was enough to have the baby this little while in her room, before its Nannie came. It lay in its basket and looked at her with its blue eyes which (she knew very well) perceived nothing, and yet which reminded her in an insistent way of everything that a child of Scott blood could mean. There was, in this extraordinary thing of waking from sleep because a baby whimpered in a cradle beside her, an awful, doomlike foreknowledge of her own destined fate.

"Dear God," she prayed into her pillow one night, "if it has to be a baby here with me, why must it be a Scott baby? Why is it not Kate's— or Bridget's?"

CHAPTER XIX

[*June 1882*]

HIS SUMMER VACATION had just begun and Edgar was in his room dressing with especial care for a night of pleasure to which he had looked forward for months past. He was to start his summer work in the mill tomorrow morning and he wanted to get out of the house now before either Paul or his father could remind him that he must get up early. He was knotting his tie at the mirror and whistling when Paul came in. "Damn," Edgar breathed to himself.

Paul strolled across the room with his hands in his pockets and stood looking over Edgar's shoulder. He watched him put the stickpin in his tie, plaster down his hair with his military brushes, and look carefully in the top bureau drawer for the handkerchief he wanted in the breast pocket of his summer suit. Finally Edgar turned around and said, "Want anything?"

"Oh—not particularly." Paul was looking at the books in Edgar's shelves. That was the baffling thing about Ed. For such a wild kid he had some surprising tastes. Books on metaphysics and philosophy; Tacitus and Plutarch and Herodotus and Homer in the original; Rabelais and Boccaccio which one would expect of him. But when did he ever take time to read? He got good marks at college but that was almost no effort for him. The rest of the time—

Paul said casually, "Be out late?"

Edgar's green eyes slid sidewise and he laughed. "Sure. Why not?"

Paul pulled out his pipe and took a long time to fill and light it. "Oh," he said. "I just—well, look here. Are we going through the same old thing every night now you're home?"

Edgar's narrow face began to set sullenly. "Didn't I get top marks in everything all year? Did I get in trouble with the Dean?"

Paul shrugged. "If you want to be literal. I don't like this business of cheating on Pa. Some day the whole show'll blow up."

Edgar was in a hurry to get away. He stared at Paul for a moment and then said sharply, "There's such a thing as being so damned good you're worse than a rip like me. What the hell do *you* do, Paul?"

Paul's heavy shoulders moved uncomfortably. He had turned away. "I didn't want to talk about myself," he said in a dull tone. "I was trying to—well, somehow this batting around doesn't make sense. You're cut out for something better."

"Don't preach," Edgar said irritably.

Paul bit his lip. "Did you think I was trying to?" he snapped suddenly. "Do you think you're the only thing on my mind?" His voice rose sharply.

Edgar turned around slowly, staring at Paul, with the corners of his mouth drawn down in a grimace of surprise.

"Say," he said drawlingly, walking across and narrowing his eyes at Paul. "What's the matter with you? Strikes me you're strung up like a cranky woman."

"Oh, forget it." Paul moved to the window and stood staring out at the freshly mowed lawn with its geometrical punctuation-marks of flowers. He felt wretched and restless; ugly of mood. For one crazy moment he thought of saying to Edgar, "I'm going over to that dive with you." He might as well. He had a lot more reason to go than Edgar. Then the thought of Mary cut across the dark turmoil in his mind like a beam of light in a dirty fog. Her last two letters lay in his breast pocket. He did not know any longer what he was waiting for, what he would do with the empty months, perhaps years, as they stretched ahead. He ran his fingers through his hair and sighed and said, "You've got some grand stuff in you, kid. I get kind of sick watching you spit all over it, that's all." He smiled awkwardly and rather apologetically. "What makes you have this one-track idea about women? That they're only—" he gestured.

Edgar shrugged. "Because that's the way they are—all the ones that don't bore you stiff. If they're worth spending an hour with, that's all they're good for."

Paul shook his head. "Do you really mean that?" he asked curiously. "Haven't you ever seen one who was—"

"Oh, there are good ones," Edgar said absently. He wished Paul would go away now and let him get out. "Like Mama. And Mary." He took a new straw hat from a box on the bed. "I guess they're about the only women I could ever look up to. What you'd call," he said with a mocking expression, "respect. But others—hell. I'm going now. I've got a beaut' waiting for me. Three shots on the lower pane, son, and expect it when you hear it."

It was a warm, starry June evening with a pleasant breeze. Edgar walked along in the height of spirits, in spite of the familiar, uneasy mixture of feelings that troubled his holidays—fear that his parents might discover the truth about his habits, and relief that he could for a while indulge them freely. He knew how to have much more fun in tough, wide-open Trenton than he could ever have in Pittsburgh, but Trenton was bounded by the single scruple in Edgar's morals. He had promised Paul that he would not incur expulsion from college, and debauchery in Trenton if discovered resulted invariably in that. So he could never really let down the bars and enjoy himself there.

He was going tonight to a certain house in the shadow of Herron Hill over in Pittsburgh, where he had already by letter ordered a fine, fancy dinner, champagne, and a companion by the name of Ruby Breen. This was the fullest measure of expensive enjoyment, and Edgar had been saving his allowance for it for nearly three months past. That was what he liked to do; then, having blown in an important sum on one magnificent night's carousal, he usually spent the rest of his holidays in more diverse and less conspicuous as well as less expensive pleasures. There was not a saloon along the dingy Bayardstown shore between Eleventh and Twenty-sixth Streets that did not know the aloof, youthful arrogance of Edgar Scott, whose imperious preference for nothing but the best old Large or Overholt rye soon became a silent understanding with the whiskered bartenders. And Edgar's preference for the kind of saloon with a ladies' entrance, and ladies who used the entrance to meet him inside, also was well understood.

He took the cut across West Park to Federal Street where he would board the horse-car that crossed the bridge to Pittsburgh. The small park seemed as delightfully inviting as everything else on this lovely evening. He walked slowly, swinging his cane and whistling quietly. Ahead of him, on the brick pathway, a girl was strolling, a slender, light-footed girl whose rhythmic step and graceful shoulders reminded him, momentarily, of some-one he knew. But he dismissed that thought, laughing; there were so many girls! He quickened his steps a little and came up beside her, eyeing her both tentatively and appraisingly. What a little beauty! She was young, her lips were an appetizing scarlet, her piquant features were lively and challenging. He saw the sidewise glance with which she made herself aware of him.

"Good evening," he said, raising his new boater with its college ribbon. "Going my way?"

"That wud depend on where ye're goin'," said the girl. Edgar was startled at her speech; Irish accents were common enough in Pittsburgh but this one stirred again the odd sense of familiarity with which he had first observed her. He looked down at her with sudden curiosity.

"What's your name?" he asked.

The girl raised her head, setting her dark curls bobbing under her flower-trimmed straw hat.

"I'd not tell ye me name," she answered, "unless I knew why ye wanted to know it. And then I'd ask ye yours."

"Oh, I was only joking," Edgar said. "I don't really know why I asked you. You reminded me of someone or other—but not anybody as pretty as you," he added.

She enjoyed the flattery, that was plain. And she was really very pretty. Edgar liked most of all the flash of her deep blue eyes. Combined with her pink-and-white coloring and smoky dark hair they made an enchanting picture in the dim light of early evening. He walked only a few steps in silence with her before she said, "Well, I'm turnin' off here. I'll say good day to ye."

"Why?" asked Edgar suddenly. He stopped walking and stood looking at her. "Wouldn't you like to come and have some fun with me?" He had been struck by a titillating idea, one with just enough promise of trouble to excite him and augur a more provocative evening than he had bargained for. Ruby Breen would be furious, and however she behaved, he had bought the right to enjoy the consequences. He would have everything he expected of Ruby and the real excitement of the night would hardly have begun.

"Where are ye goin' for the fun ye're offerin'?" the girl asked him boldly.

Edgar swallowed appreciatively. He motioned casually with his cane in the direction of Pittsburgh. "Over there," he said. "Across the river, to a, well, to a dinner-party."

"I see." She stood a minute, coolly considering the matter. Then she looked up at him with a level stare and said, "I suppose this is a very swell party? With flowers and chicken and—wine?"

"Oh, by all means," said Edgar. "Wine and bonbons and French brandy. Everything."

"Well, I'll go," she said.

Edgar's pulse was racing delightfully. The more he looked at her the more a thought, so daring that it tickled his spine like ice-cold fingers, prodded at his brain. It was a thought that he could uncover with one flip of his will if he chose—but he did not choose. And staring at the girl he saw something startlingly reflective of his own reaction in her appetizing, devilish face. He offered her his arm.

"Allow me," he said.

The horse-car rumbled up to the corner and he helped her on.

At dinner Paul felt irritable and depressed. Ben Nicholas was here from New York again, for the second time in a month. He must be getting serious about Lizzie, Paul thought, looking at the two of them sitting there. They had been telling William Scott about the new medical branch of the Presbyterian Board of Foreign Missions; Nicholas was one of the directors. He was a solemn, cold man, nearing forty, with a curious resemblance in his sallow face, bony hands, and sandy coloring to Elizabeth herself. It would only be a matter of decorous time, they all knew, before Ben would propose to Lizzie, and they would be married after another decorous interval; and that, thought Paul, is the answer to everything for them. Just as cut-and-dried as that. He gritted his teeth. Louise on his right was saying, "No, thank you, Uncle William," in her clear high voice; a voice that Paul had once described to Mary as "Curly, like her hair."

"More steak, Paul?" William Scott had the carving knife poised.

"No, thanks, Father."

Clarissa glanced at Paul's plate. He had not eaten much of his dinner. She knew he liked new peas in cream; these were delicious, the first of the season. Joel had only picked them an hour ago.

"Have another spoonful, dear."

"I couldn't, Mama."

"That's quite a big undertaking, then," William said to Nicholas. "Starting hospitals in three different provinces."

"Yes," said Lizzie with enthusiasm. Her pale face attracted all their notice by its unusual animation. "My, I'd like to go out to China."

"You would?" Nicholas turned to look at her and Clarissa saw what crossed his mind. Louise saw it, too. She stole a glance at Mrs. Scott and smiled. It would be quite exciting if Mr. Nicholas married Lizzie and took her to China on her wedding trip. Louise loved weddings and parties and the excitement that preceded them.

Clarissa sighed. She was beginning to feel uncomfortable about having Louise here so often. It was getting on Paul's nerves. For a time he had been unusually cordial to Louise, had escorted her to several dinner parties and even to the Charity Ball last winter. But recently Clarissa had seen a flicker of annoyance twitch his brows when he came home from the mill and found Louise in the summerhouse or the parlor with his mother. Louise had a way of waiting for him to speak first when she saw him. Instead of a casual "hello" or "good evening" she would look up at him expectantly, her brown eyes self-consciously warm and smiling, fixed on him until he had to give her some special greeting by name instead of including her in the general remark he would otherwise have made.

The dessert was strawberry shortcake, a particular favorite of Paul's, but he hardly touched it. He listened with artificial attention to something Louise was saying about a boating picnic to which they had been invited. Louise babbled happily about the plans but Clarissa noticed that Paul was really not taking in a thing she said. He said, "Yes," "Good," "That's nice," and pushed a strawberry around the edge of his plate and looked uncomfortably at the mantel clock across the room. Clarissa rose from the table with relief. Suddenly she wanted to help Paul, to get Louise away because his nerves were so on edge.

Paul and his father and Nicholas strolled down the garden hill. The Old Man and Paul were smoking but Benjamin Nicholas did not smoke; neither did he drink. He made such conversation as he could, but Paul saw that he was anxious for the moment when he could break away and return to Elizabeth. Paul made it easy for him. He said, "I think I'll go down to the mill now. I've got something in the lab I want to get back to."

Nicholas took the opportunity to return to the house, leaving Paul with his father.

"Where's Edgar tonight?" the Old Man asked gruffly.

Paul murmured something evasive about a young people's party. He loathed this business of covering up for Edgar but that was easier to endure than some of the other things on his mind. His father looked at him sharply. He had been worrying about Paul for a long time. He had been watching him with closer and closer attention and with growing alarm. Paul was a totally changed man. He had always had a genial and charming disposition, a certain radiance of personality at which the Old Man, though he would never have admitted it, had loved to warm himself as if in sunlight. All this was now extinguished. Paul worked harder than he ever had before, indeed with an almost fevered preoccupation which would have shown a far less observant father than William that Paul was making a superhuman effort to keep himself distracted . . . but from what? William had never once admitted to himself what this secret torment of Paul's must be. Deep, so deep that he himself could not possibly fathom it, there lay within him mute comprehension. He sensed the nature of Paul's tragedy, he knew its calendar. But he *would* not know its identity.

It had always been his way deliberately to control his mind, to put it on problems about which he could do something, and to keep himself from thinking about situations where no action could be taken. He realized now that something stronger than any such determination of his was the moving force here. He struggled with the impulse to say something reassuring to Paul; there must be some way to show this beloved son how he felt. But William Scott was without the means to exhibit compassion when he felt it. He only cleared his throat and dropped his hand on Paul's shoulder for a moment and said, "I think I'll walk down with you."

Typically, they talked about the mill and its problems all the way down. James Rafferty had been stirring up new causes of discontent among the men. "He's giving them notions about hours now," the Old Man said. "Has he said anything to you about this new holdup of theirs?"

"You mean they want an eight-hour day?"

"Did you ever hear of anything so absurd? What do they think this mill is—a day nursery?"

"The idea is spreading all around town, Father. I know Captain Jones is considering it. He told the research meeting the other night that he believed three shifts would make for much greater efficiency and production than two."

"Let him coddle his men at Edgar Thomson if he wants to. I've worked a twelve-hour shift since I was sixteen years old and I'll do it till I die. Nobody is going to dictate anything about that mill to me."

"Father," said Paul, after a silence, "have you ever really sat down and talked to Jim Rafferty?"

"What? I sit down and listen to that crackpot?"

"He's not a crackpot." Paul scowled. "I've tried for years to tell you so. I don't see—well, Father, let me say something, will you?"

"Of course."

"Well, I think you're unreasonable. You know better than anybody in town how good a furnace man Jim Rafferty is. You wouldn't let him get away from you if you had to meet somebody else's offer three times over, would you?"

"Probably not."

"And yet you call him a crackpot, just because he's got ideas about labor that make you mad. I admit he's fanatical. He's unreasonable in his way, but so are you. Couldn't you possibly see it would be good to have Jim's confidence all the way through, instead of just about his work?" Paul looked to see if he was impressing his father. "This way, if I ever try to point out to him the ways in which you do believe in him, he only snorts that you'd be a fool if you didn't, considering how much his work is worth to you."

Old William's face was inscrutable. Paul, having committed himself, pushed on. "He knows he could get a boss's job in any mill in the district. Why do you think he stays with us?"

"Since he's incapable of loyalty, I can't imagine."

"You don't understand him, you see. Naturally he'd just as soon have a bigger job with J and L or somebody else. They've all made him offers at one time or another. But he has got loyalty, Father, only of a different sort from what you approve. He's loyal to his union and it's the union that's ordered him to stay at Scott's and stay and *stay* until he's got every man in the place organized, and has signed a union contract with you."

The Old Man's face was beginning to redden.

"He'll never get it," he said through his teeth, "if it costs the last drop of my blood. And as for the union ordering him to stay with us—I'll fire him, by God!"

"No, you won't, Father," Paul said patiently. "If you did there'd be a strike."

"Strike!" Old William paused, his feet planted heavily on the slope of the steep street, and glared about him like an angry behemoth. "They'd never dare. Why, you're inventing this, Paul, you've got crazy notions from talking to that fanatic."

Paul shook his head. "I wish you were right, Father. Sometimes I think I am crazy," Paul said in an odd bitter tone, "but not," he caught himself quickly, "about this. I tell you, you simply do not realize the seriousness of this situation, and you should before it's too late."

"By sitting down and reasoning with a maniac, I suppose."

"No, Father. But if you'll let me arrange a conference between us and a delegation from the union headed by Jim Rafferty, and if you'll merely listen to what they have to say, I think a blowout could be headed off."

"But you've already told me what they'll have to say. Eight-hour day, at the same rate, meaning we increase our payroll a full third, and a union shop with all the damned collective bargaining and other infringements of my rights that go with it. Never," said the Old Man, biting off the word with a snap of his teeth. "Never."

Paul sighed. He knew inevitably what was going to happen. The only thing he could not predict was the possible length of this deadlock. It was years old already and it had begun to display the most ominous signs of acceleration to a climax. So, he thought, had the Gaylord matter also. At the last partners' meeting attended by his father, Gaylord, their attorneys, and himself, the year's accounting had been discussed with acerbity that neither of the old men troubled any more to conceal. Paul would never have questioned his father's judgment in any part of the mill management except that of labor. But Gaylord was full of questions—disagreeable, sarcastic, or protesting—about William Scott's administration and especially about his handling of the company's funds. For a business now making such strikingly good profits, it seemed very peculiar to Gaylord that it must always be necessary to plow back such a large part of the profits that the partners' percentages paid out were actually very small. William Scott's idea of a working inventory seemed to absorb a remarkably substantial amount of cash. MacTavish's books were unquestionable models of order, scrupulous accuracy, and clarity, but there was something in the Scott management that eluded the understanding of Laurence Gaylord. His idea of sound business was that its payments increase proportionately with its profits. Gaylord's greatest irritation was that William junior, who was—at least he said he was—head of the sales accounting department, appeared less able than anyone else to explain the system by which the Old Man ran the business and kept the books. Gaylord's original idea of a smart investment in a great basic industry on the threshold of a tremendous boom, with a son-in-law in close supervision of his interests there, seemed to have stumbled on grave disillusionment. It was only recently that full comprehension of all this had begun to dawn on Paul. He had been wondering just how, when he had the funds available to do so, the Old Man expected to induce Gaylord to part with his interest. Gaylord was not the man to be bought out of a profitable business if he intended to stay in it. But his father, Paul realized, was not going to be outwitted in any matter concerning the mill. There was only one quality in old William which equalled, if it did not exceed, the towering rectitude of his morals. That was his Scottish shrewdness. The Old Man, Paul told himself when the Gaylord matter began to be apparent to him, was a smart old coot.

CHAPTER XX

[March 1883]

"LIZZIE LOOKS LOVELY, doesn't she!"

Paul turned and stared at Louise. The trilling warmth of her voice made her gushing ridiculous. Lizzie did not look lovely; she was incapable of it. She and her bridegroom stood under an arch of white flowers with a wedding-bell in the centre, receiving the guests. Lizzie wore a long-sleeved, plainly cut gown of the very finest heavy white satin, with her mother's lace wedding veil draped over her drab hair. Ben stood tall and knobby in his frock coat beside her. She looked considerably older than her twenty-five years and not at all softened by the warmth of what Louise sentimentally presumed she must be feeling.

"Isn't it a lovely wedding, Paul?"

Louise did not see his jaw move, she did not know that he was gritting his teeth as he did, unconsciously, whenever she used that word. Lovely. Everything was lovely. God, he groaned silently. Louise moved away to flutter about among the crowd, and Paul turned to the table in the alcove and tossed off a cup of sweetish fruit punch that hit his stomach, on this raw March day, with a sickening thump. He looked at his mother, so gracious and dignified, her manner an effortless blending of queenliness and warmth. Sometimes he wondered what his mother really felt about her children; how much of a disappointment it was to her to have one daughter so coldly uncongenial and the other so far away. Perhaps that was why she had Louise there so much. Oh yes, Paul thought bitterly, that's why. Oh, sure. Because Louise is so gay and lovable and thoughtful. She's made herself a member of the family. That damned sweetness, he thought, for the thousandth time. If you poured vinegar over her she'd curdle like a bowl of cream. Now she was making herself charming to Ben's relatives, flitting about like a bright, curly butterfly.

Paul stood for a moment behind the plush portière that hung between the two parlors, watching the tableau. His father heavily fulfilling the functions of the host, his mother with her gracious poise, his frozen sister and her frozen bridegroom; the family friends upholstered in pounds of sturdy, rustling fabrics; the New York contingent with their veiled curiosity about the real wealth of this substantial Pittsburgh tribe; Bill and Julia present in this house for the first time since Constance's elopement, and present only to give a false picture of family solidarity; Louise with her fluttering sociability and her bright, innocent, sisterly attentions to the Scotts . . . Paul closed his eyes for a brief minute as if to wipe the whole panorama from his mind. Just then his coat-tail was jerked sharply from behind the curtain and he turned to see Edgar motioning him out to the hall. He followed, through the dining-room and pantry and down the kitchen stairs and out to the back stoop. Edgar drew a flask from his hip-pocket and unscrewed the cap.

"Here," he said. "I can't stand it another minute. Maybe you can, but you don't look it."

Paul was too apathetic to protest. He knew that Edgar had no business with a filled flask but suddenly and overwhelmingly, he did not care. He knew that they could not drink now without risking something of a scandal when they returned to the crowded, plush-insulated parlors, and he did not care about that either. He took the flask silently and swallowed down a big drink.

"Thanks, Kid," he said.

"Don't thank *me*," Edgar answered, wiping his mouth. "You look like hell, Paul. If that shindig turns your stomach the way it does mine—"

They drank again.

"It would be funny if we got drunk and went back upstairs and spoiled the party," said Edgar reflectively. "I'd love to do that."

"If it wasn't for Father and Mama, so would I," said Paul.

"Let's."

Paul shook his head. "You're right about my needing to raise hell, Ed, but I couldn't upset Mama today. Besides, oh, you know. I suppose I'm a hypocrite like all the rest of them." Seated on the top step, he put his head wearily in his hands.

"Aw, bosh. What do you mean?"

"Oh, I never get drunk and I never make a spectacle of myself so they think I'm not capable of it."

Edgar moved over closer to Paul and put his mouth close to his ear. "If you don't do something about yourself damn soon, you'll turn into a thing like—ah—our new brother-in-law."

Struck by the full weight of this idea Edgar threw back his head suddenly and roared. "Imagine!" he chortled, pummeling Paul's shoulder. "My brother! a monk. A holy man! You're on your way, son, on your way."

"Shut up!" Edgar started at the sharp despair in Paul's voice. He leaned forward and looked hard at him. "I'm sorry," he said quietly. "I—here." He handed Paul the flask again.

They sat silent for a while. Finally Edgar said, "Lord. Can you imagine Lizzie? Lizzie, the virgin bride?" He began to guffaw again. Paul wanted to rebuke him but it was not worth the trouble. Love and marriage to Edgar were all down on the same plane as his daily amusements. Love to

Paul began and ended with Mary. Half his thoughts revolved around the memory of her face and its unearthly beauty as she had lain in his arms that summer night. Her voice too—now as he sat here his memory stretched back to catch the echoes of her soft laugh, years and years ago. Edgar was still talking. He ought to shut up. Paul heard only scraps of what he was saying. He turned and looked at Edgar, his eyes stretched wide almost as if in fear. Was this kind of thing to be the end of all his dreams and longings? For the first time his own treasure of remembered passion was swept aside by a different picture. He listened to Edgar's remarks about the coming nuptial meeting of the Nicholases and suddenly his own reserve snapped like a thread. He burst into a crazy laugh and seized the flask from Edgar's pocket. Together, with their arms linked, the brothers sat and rocked wildly with laughter on the kitchen steps.

In the summer of that year William Scott had a severe attack of kidney trouble. Anyone so unaccustomed to illness would be sure to react to it badly and consider it an omen of doom. The Old Man did. He called Paul in to his study one Sunday afternoon during his convalescence, and when Paul entered the room he knew that there was something particular and portentous on his father's mind. The Old Man was sitting in his armchair in the bay window. Paul was struck with the thought that never in his life had his father ever made one of his important statements without standing on his feet, preferably in his office. But now he wore a dressing-gown and carpet slippers and sat in a cushioned chair with a tartan rug over his knees. His square beard, like his hair, had whitened, and stood out in contrast to the dark silk of his robe.

They chatted about business for a while and Paul was beginning to wonder just what was on his father's mind when Old William said abruptly, "I've decided to buy Gaylord out in November."

Paul raised his eyebrows. "What's the hurry, Father? Have you saved up all that cash already?"

"No, I haven't. I have about half of it. But I can raise the rest. The Union Trust will be glad to make me a loan. And I'm going to take one."

Paul knew that this was directly contrary to his father's idea of sound practise. So he pointed that out, and said, "Why? Can't we go along like this for a while?"

"No, Paul. I got you into this mess and I'm going to get you out before I die."

Paul stared. "But you're not going to die! You're fine. Why Doctor McClintock told Mama yesterday that your kidneys are perfectly sound, and as soon as you get your strength back you'll be better than ever."

"Just the same a man of my age cannot ignore organic breakdowns. I may live for a long time but I may not. Anyway *I* think I may die, and I'm going to leave the business without any of William's damned connections to encumber it for you."

Paul's eyes roved along the row of heavy brown books in the shelves over his father's desk. *Historical Records of Allegheny County. Early Iron*

Foundries of Western Pennsylvania. Iron and Coal Deposits of the Appalachian Range. Scott Iron Works. Scott Iron Works. Two whole shelves of bound records of the mill. One grew so used to seeing a row of books in the same place, year after year, that they lost their identity and became fixtures like the wallpaper. Strangely these records stood out now, apart from the drab brownness of the rest; year after year they stood in eloquent order, carrying Paul's thoughts back to his boyhood, his childhood, his first visit to the mill, trotting along holding his grandfather's hand. The mill was nineteen years old when I was born, Paul thought vividly; it is forty-six now. Older than I. It goes back before me, it must—and with a queer novel clarity the thought struck him dramatically as if he had never touched on it before—it must go on after me. That was what Grandfather built it for. That's what Pa's lived for. Paul stood with his hands in his pockets staring at the books. The room was warm and sunny and quiet; he heard bees buzzing in the vines outside the open bay windows. He knew that his father, silent in the chair behind him, was watching him and wondering what he was thinking. He turned around and smiled and said, "Have you sounded Gaylord out about this?"

"In a way."

"I suppose he'll hold out."

"Yes."

"You seem awfully sure you can swing it." Paul went over and dropped into a morris chair opposite his father and got out his pipe.

"I mean to swing it, that's all. I tell you I'm not only going to get rid of Gaylord but of William too." The Old Man's eyes were hard. "You won't be able to run the mill if he's there making mischief."

Paul turned his head uneasily. He said, "But after all, Father. Bill is—"

"I know. The eldest son. You don't need to point that out to me. But the mill is nothing to him so I'll see to it he's nothing to the mill." Old William shut his mouth hard as he did when he wanted a subject closed.

He poured a glass of water from the carafe beside him and drank it. Then he drew some papers from his dressing-gown pocket, closely covered with figures scribbled in pencil. "I've been making these plans for a long time, Paul," he said, "and I want you to know what I'm doing." Paul moved over and the two put their heads together and followed the point of the Old Man's pencil as it travelled down the columns. The Old Man had broken down the capital value of the business into the eventual holdings of each of his heirs. He had worked out the details minutely.

"You see," he said, "it will all be in your control. Even the partnership shares of the others. I've fixed it so there cannot be any disagreements about your policies and your management. If they don't like what you do, they can only protest by selling their share to you and getting out. But they cannot sell to anybody else whatever except by a majority vote of all the partners."

Paul said slowly, "Father, that's going to make bad feeling. You can't tell about conditions in the future. Nobody can. Sometimes I wonder—" Paul stopped speaking, uneasily.

"What do you wonder? Whether you're capable of running this business? You're better prepared than I was when it was left to me."

Paul still sat silent. But his father said presently, "Paul, are you ever going to marry?"

Paul sighed. "You ought to be concerned about that, Father. If I have no children of course the business will go out of our hands eventually. None of the others would know what to do with it."

"Exactly. That's why I asked if you ever intend to marry."

Paul groped in his mind for an answer. He wanted more than he could possibly show to take his father into his confidence, to bare his heart once for all of its intolerable burden, and at the same time to express the concern for the family and for the mill that he really felt. But, with his mouth half open, the words would not come. Old William sat with his hands clasped and his gray eyes sharply fixed on Paul. After a time, with his heart beating very hard, Paul raised his head and looked straight into his father's eyes.

"Father," he said in a quiet, desperate voice. "You know what's the trouble, don't you?"

Old William met the issue with absolute courage, though Paul knew perfectly his dread of putting anything so grave in words. He looked at his son for a long, tense time. Then he nodded his head slowly, his beard moving with it up and down on his chest.

"Yes," he said. "I know, Paul. I had hoped—well—"

"Hoped I'd get over it. Oh, Father, I've tried. I've been trying for four solid years. I've tried everything—*everything*, Father!" Paul whipped out his confession with the bitterness of despair. The Old Man did not even murmur. Paul went on talking.

"I knew how you'd all feel about it. I didn't want to disgrace you. But I'm weak compared to her. *She's* the one who's strong, Father. She refused to see me any more. She tried—oh, she talked and pleaded and even nagged—trying to make me realize. And I do realize. I always did. But what," said Paul in a strangled voice, "what shall I *do?*"

His face was gray with strain. He never took his eyes from his father. He had poured out his words breathlessly.

"Your mother knows about this, does she not?"

Paul nodded. "I suppose in a way everybody does. You remember Julia the night—that night?"

William's nostrils swelled and his mouth went down at the corners.

"That's why Mama was so magnificent. That's why she sent Mary to England. To help us, because she knew we were trying. I suppose there've been times when I'd have done anything. Times when I felt crazy because I loved her so. But she's not like—just a woman, Father. I guess I don't even have to tell you. She's got ideas that you have to be superhuman to live up to."

The Old Man's silence was heavier and more meaningful than any words. Paul sat watching him, finding in the stern, square, patriarchal face a revelation of new qualities. Old William's eyes were solemn and brave and wise. For the time being he had nothing to say. But Paul felt lax from the bursting of his pent-up sore; the bars were down and it was easier now to rush on, talking more and more. "I've gotten so desperate sometimes," he said, "that I was on the point of telling you I was quitting. The mill—and everything. And going away. But the horrible thing is," Paul sighed, his forehead creasing painfully, "if I did go, she wouldn't have me. She's said so. She said that would destroy the family and the mill and the whole thing. She said she'd rather die than have anything hurt the mill—or all of you—us—"

"James Rafferty's sister," said the Old Man bitterly.

He could not even put into words the other things about this girl that had haunted and tormented his stern, disciplined mind. Long since, he had moved past the shocking obstacle of her lowly status to the more difficult contemplation of her origin and her religion. He had been born and raised in a doctrine to which Roman Catholics were anathema and damnation. And now he said only, "James Rafferty's sister," while Paul's head went into his hands, with a groan. "There you are, you see," he said. "One awful thing on top of another. It's such a mess, Pa. Oh my God, such a hopeless mess." His shoulders moved as if they hurt him.

Old William's hands clenched tight together, one on top of the other on the plaid rug in his lap. Strangely, he looked down at these hands, gnarled and scarred and knotted from his life's work around the furnaces. He looked too with a strange soft expression at the pattern of tartan plaid that covered his knees. Clumsily he stroked the fine woollen cloth. "The clan plaid," he said, in a whisper. "My father wore it away from Scotland."

Paul raised his head and watched his father, his face filled with awe. He had never before seen his father's deepest emotions. He had known only the giant exterior of the cold, powerful man. Even as his seated position reduced the Old Man's stature, so his inner spirit expanded by contrast. His stern face was no less stern, but into it came for the first time in Paul's experience, a light of understanding and tenderness. And this, presently, was superseded by a great and singularly noble calm. His eyes rested on Paul and he spoke majestically.

"You shall marry Mary Rafferty, Paul."

Between them the quiet vibrated, and the Old Man's love was like a shining mantle, dropping down to shelter Paul. The son sat with his head bowed, tears falling on his clasped hands. Then he dropped to his knees and buried his face in the plaid on the Old Man's lap. His father's hands lay on his shoulders. Neither could speak.

Late in the day they were still sitting there, quietly feeling their way back to an everyday mood of speech and bearing. It was very difficult to talk; still more difficult for Paul to go away about any ordinary business. He thought of Mary; he thought of her so clearly, so longingly, with every memory of her sharpened now to the finest poignancy. He sensed already the multifarious problems crowding and shoving at this island of peace which for these hours, perhaps never again to be recaptured, he was sharing with his father whom he had never fully known until today. They talked a little about some of the first realities with which they must come to grips.

"It will be very hard to persuade her," Paul said. "She was always so set that anything like this would disgrace the family."

"Nothing will disgrace this family," Old William said, "so long as the members of it do their work better than anybody else, and pay their debts and keep their mouths shut. No honorable marriage with a decent hard-working woman will disgrace a family. What do you think the mothers of all these American pioneers were—duchesses? Aristocrats—like Julia?" He almost spat the name.

A feeling of excitement began to warm the pit of Paul's stomach. He saw suddenly that the Old Man loved a daring decision like this; that he was stimulated and that, once made, it started up his fighting blood.

"You let me deal with these snobs around here," William said grimly. "I'll show them who's fit to be a Scott and who isn't." His horny fist clenched on the arm of his chair.

Paul swallowed a sob. He sat watching the color rise in his father's bearded cheeks and felt himself almost a child, shaken and swept and incoherent.

"I can't believe it," he said, choking. "I just can't take it in yet. I guess I'll never dare to until I get Mary's promise."

"Well, go and do something about it!" the Old Man said, with a sudden return to his normal brusque bark.

"Oh, I will." Paul got up and began to stride excitedly around the room. "I will. But I've got to figure out how. She won't give in easily, Pa. She's sworn time and again she'd never give in at all."

The Old Man looked up at Paul as if he were about to explain the simplest procedure in a mill operation. "Go and tell your mother what I've said," he said in a patient tone, "and tell her to write Mary to come home. That's all. We'll explain the rest to her after she gets here."

CHAPTER XXI

[Fall 1883]

ONCE ON BOARD the ship Mary could think calmly for the first time in a fortnight. Mrs. Scott's astonishing letter had halted the dreary tread-mill of exile and catapulted her here to this ship as unexpectedly as she had been swept off to London over three years ago. The letter said little more than that Mary was to come home; that there was a different and a better state of things and she must trust Clarissa's judgment that there was no longer any reason for her to stay in London. Here was enclosed a draft for her travelling expenses and she should sail in the *Oceanic* on the eighteenth of October.

Mary met the surprise in a mood of surrender. It might be the greatest possible mistake to go. The thought of Paul swept everything before it, rousing doubts and fears as it went, but the chance to go was too over-whelming welcome to turn down. She felt herself riding a tidal wave of escape from homesickness and loneliness. She promised herself finally that if she did run into an impasse on reaching Pittsburgh, she would once for all leave the Scotts and find work somewhere else. Then she went and told Constance the news. Constance met it with outrage and consternation.

"What do you mean, you're going back to Pittsburgh?" she cried from her welter of lace, pillows, maribou, letters, invitations, bills, scent-bottles, and breakfast-dishes. "You must be crazy."

"No, I'm not," Mary said. There was an ecstatic gleam in her eye. "Your mother has sent for me and I'm going."

"What right has she got to send for you? She gave you to me."

"You seem to think I'm some kind of slave," Mary said. "You treat me that way often enough. But I don't belong to you or to your mother either. I work for her though, if you will stop to remember. She pays my wages and I take my orders from her."

Constance looked flabbergasted. "But what shall *I* do?" she asked.

"Do? I should think you'd get along like a breeze. Any lady's maid can keep your clothes in order and I gave up trying to make a lady of you long ago. You're too old now to bother about any more. And an English maid will probably put up with this house better than I ever could."

Constance looked rueful. "Has it really been so awful, Mary?"

"Pretty bad. I can't say I've enjoyed my stay here. You can see that for yourself. It's not been my place to open your eyes to what you didn't want to see."

Constance looked about the room as if for some desirable object with which to bribe Mary to stay.

"The baby!" she exclaimed. "You know you love the baby. You aren't going back to Pittsburgh and leave her, are you?"

"I told you when she was born," Mary said firmly, "that I was not going to get attached to that baby, and I have not. At least"—she blushed at Constance's sarcastic gesture—"not so I can't leave her. Nannie takes very good care of her and I'm nothing in her life at all. So I really am going. You'd better look for a maid right off if you want me to break her in for you."

The past ran together into one blur of confusion, now that Mary could lie in a deckchair and look back on it and—she was astounded to realize—do nothing whatever for the first time in her life. She could not remember a time when she had not been subject to the pressure of somebody's imme-diate wants and necessities. The first day out she lay for more than eight hours motionless in her chair, her eyes half closed, her mind a willing blank. When she was finally roused by the autumn darkness and the pene-trating chill of the air, she sat up slowly and looked about her as if she had been in a trance. Then she went below to her cabin, intending to wash up before dinner, and she dropped for a moment on her berth. It was four o'clock in the morning when she awoke. She undressed, too sleepy even to plait her hair or put her clothes away, crawled under the covers and went back to impenetrable slumber. She had never known of anything like this, she realized, when she did not wake until the end of the following afternoon, still feeling drugged and dazed, but hungry. She could not imagine any kind of exhaustion that would explain such an abnormal capacity for sleep.

Towards the end of the eight-day voyage she began to enjoy a wonderful sense of well-being. She had slept through a two-day spell of heavy autumn storms, and now the sun shone brilliantly all day long in a lovely burst of Indian summer. She had not felt such sunshine or seen such glorious blue skies for more than three years. In retrospect London was already synonymous with darkness—dark skies, dark buildings, the darkness of age and fog and smoke; most of all with the darkness of her spirits while she was there. She never thought of her own Pittsburgh as being equally dark, and without London's compensating atmosphere of rich ancient beauty. She was so happy to be going home that a row of blackened hot-blast domes along the Allegheny would look more beautiful to her than the most exquisite spires in Westminster.

She had felt a wrench at leaving Constance. But that, compared with the joy of going home, was a trifle. Constance was wrapped up in the dazzling details of her increasingly gay life. She had just about attained, Mary thought with alarm, the very things she had always said she wanted. The little house in Montagu Street was either crowded with some of the gayest and fastest people in London, or it was bleakly empty for days and sometimes weeks on end while Constance—at first with Giles, increasingly without him—went on visits to country houses where beauty, wit, style, and daring were the principal passes of entry.

Mary would actually miss the baby, whom they called Clarrie, far more than she would miss Constance. Clarrie was a charming child, full of smiling sweetness which had no relation to Constance's peppery temper or to the moody nervousness into which Giles had settled after the first flush of his fantastic marriage. Clarrie had her grandmother's mild blonde coloring and blue eyes (Paul's too, Mary had too often thought!) and the wide, gentle brow that was so heartrendingly familiar. Mary had always taken care of her when her Nannie was off duty. Sometimes, succumbing momentarily to all the emotions that the child's arms around her neck, or its bouncing weight on her lap could rouse, she turned away her head to battle stinging tears. A wave of deep-lying feeling would swell up and sweep over her; feeling which mingled thoughts of Paul and her own empty destiny and a strange, probing recognition of herself as a living bridge across which the generations of Paul's family might move, but through whose own fibres the pulses of creation would never quicken. At such moments she held Clarrie tight and hugged her, and sternly told herself as she must almost every day, to live for that day alone; never, never to dare the contemplation of the future. So she could not then, even in remote forbidden dreams, have perceived in Clarrie the link to the personality who would be dearest to her in an impossibly distant, unimaginable future.

Mary was almost the first passenger to debark. Carrying a small satchel and dressed charmingly in fine gray English cloth, she walked lightly down the gangway, her thoughts on quick dispatching of the customs and catching the first train to Pittsburgh.

"Mary!"

"Paul!"

She had not dreamed that he would be there. She saw him just as she stepped off the gangway and before she could fill her eyes with his face, she was in his arms. Even before the thought touched her whirling brain, she dismissed it—that he must not hold her so adoringly and kiss her so wildly before all these people, in all this confusion. He must not do so at all. She clung to him, gladly and recklessly.

"Mary! Darling, darling Mary. Let me look at you!"

"Dear. Darlin'. Oh, Paul." She tried to open her handbag for her handkerchief but he held her too tightly. The tears ran down her face and he bent over her to hide her from the crowd. Presently she stopped crying and looked up at him and he saw the shock in her gray eyes.

"Paul, you're thin!"

"You're beautiful. You're so beautiful. You're *here*."

Again his hands clung to her arms and shoulders, and hers to his.

"Let me feel you. I want to make sure you're real."

"Dear Paul. I can't believe it."

"Oh, Mary." Holding his arm about her, foolishly bumping her bag against his knees, he led her away in a helpless daze towards the pier-shed.

"Paul! To think you'd come all the way to meet me."

"I'd have gone to hell and back to meet you. I have," he added, in a sudden sharp tone.

"What do you mean?" She sensed an earthquake of news, imminent, throbbing.

"Give me time. I don't want to say or think one single thought of any kind whatsoever except how glad I am to see you. Let me enjoy it!" He dropped her bag with a thud and seized her hands again, holding them close. "Just let me enjoy it." His eyes searched her face. She knew he was looking for change in it.

"There's no change," she whispered. She did not know what words she was about to speak. "No change. I'm just the same."

Her hand went up to touch him. Her fingers ached to touch his eyes, his thick yellow hair, his warm lips. But suddenly she blushed scarlet.

"Let's—hurry. Let's get out of here," Paul said.

He stood and looked at her with worship while she finished quickly with the customs officer. She had only one small trunk. He was amazed at her speech, greatly changed and all the more startling because there was little other change in her. She was more mature, more poised, and far more at ease in a situation where she would once have been flustered or confused. But in spite of this she was still the same Mary, her clothes simple and modest but expressive of her skilful handiwork, her shining hair daintily dressed under the large hat which flattered her so much; her movements light and quick, her sensitive face radiant with inexpressible happiness. When they were in the cab, clattering down the waterfront to the ferry, he kept her hands tight in his. Ignoring the bedlam of drays, plunging horses, shouting teamsters and bellowing dockhands, he whispered again and again, "You're here. You're really here. Oh, Mary!"

"Dear Paul."

"You talk so differently!" he exclaimed. "You're not Irish any more."

She laughed. "Oh, yes I am. Nothing will ever change that, never fear."

"But how—why did you do it?"

"Oh, I—" she broke off because he was looking so deeply, so passionately into her eyes. For a moment she could not breathe. They sat tense, each searching the other's face, their eyes strained wide and the color fading from their cheeks. Paul took her in his arms then and kissed her, long and with great passion. Mary sat limply in her corner after that, her hand in his.

"You do love me," he said, almost whispering.

"I do. God help me."

He turned quickly and said, "Don't—don't say that. Not any more."

She could not speak then anyway so she sat quiet. He smiled at her. She loved the way his eyes moved deliberately, yet eagerly, as he studied every line of her face, her hair, her clothes, as if he had been starving for the sight.

"You've changed," he sighed.

Mary smiled then, a little mischievously. "Improved, you mean?"

"You couldn't be improved." That was what he said, but he meant the opposite. Her changed speech was not exactly British, nor yet American like his; it was graceful and almost musical in phrasing, keeping the undercurrent of resonance which had always rung through her light brogue; this still gave a lift and a turn to her words. But they also had a polish that had never been there before.

She would not be Mary if she were not asking all the way across on the ferry and while they were waiting for the train, about his mother and father and all the family and how they were and, above all, why: "Why, Paul, have they sent for me?"

Not until the train was clacking across the Jersey marshes, and they were settled in their places with their hats and coats stowed overhead, and Paul's eyes were drinking in the beauty of Mary's bared, shining hair, did he lean forward and in a voice dark with intensity, tell her his news.

She heard it in astounded silence. Before he stopped speaking she had drooped back against the seat, white as the lace around her neck, and numb to the ends of her fingers and toes. Her mouth opened slowly and she was, he saw, struggling to keep possession of her faculties. She looked at him weakly, almost stupidly; he realized that she was faint. He hurried to bring water, and gave it to her, sitting on the arm of her chair with his arm about her.

"Darling, I'm sorry. I didn't realize it would be such a shock. Don't cry, Mary. Dearest, please don't be upset. Here—" he laid her head against his heart, inside his coat, and held her silently while she smothered her sobs against him. "Cry if you want to, darling," he whispered. "Cry if you like. Do what you want. You're with me now. You'll never have to fight it out alone again." He was as oblivious to their surroundings as if they had been alone on a desert. He bent his head over hers and kept his left hand tight against her body, pressed to her heart.

It was several hours before they were able to talk calmly and Mary insisted on this, just as she demanded to know every happening, every idea and word and suggestion that had brought this all about. At mid-afternoon they were still at it, while Paul made real the insistence of his need for her, and Mary listened, convinced but not committed. For in spite of everything she had not yet promised to marry him.

"I feel just the way I always did," she said with a frown of concentration. "I still feel that this would not be a proper marriage for you and it would stir up a terrible tempest in Pittsburgh."

"I don't care what it stirs up."

Mary shook her head silently, several times.

"I just can't imagine it," she said helplessly. "Sitting in that house a member of the family—waiting for people to come and call—why—" she flushed with mortification.

"You won't wait, darling. Try to see this clearly. Father has made up his mind that you are the wife for me and he means us to marry soon. Do you understand why? So we shall live in the house with him and Mama, and you will be gradually introduced to all the people we know in such a way that they couldn't be rude to you, or they'd find they had to reckon with Father. And Mary, nobody in Allegheny or Pittsburgh either is going to fling down a gauntlet to Father. You realize that, don't you?"

She nodded slowly.

"He not only is reconciled to the idea, he's excited about it. Believe me, darling. I don't say he mightn't rather it had never happened at all. But the way it has happened, it gives him a chance to fight a big issue through and you know he'd rather do that than anything else in the world. He loves a fight about something he believes in, and he certainly does believe in you. I told you what he said about that—and about Julia and Giles. Look at them both—a Boston blueblood and an English nobleman and Father has kicked them both out and called them every nasty name he can think of. He'd *have* to feel the way he does about you, or he wouldn't make any sense at all."

Paul saw after that that Mary was yielding. For an hour or more she sat silent and thoughtful, her hands busy with a bit of tatting. Finally she looked up at him and asked, "Paul, who else knows about this?"

"Nobody whatever," Paul replied, "except Father and Mother. And Ed. He's home for the week-end."

He paused and then said, "Why did you ask that?"

"Oh, I don't know exactly. I suppose I feel I want to find a clean slate when I get there. No suspicions, or conflicts. And then of course, Paul—there's my family. James."

The name fell between them like a boulder.

"This is an awful situation if you look at all the sides of it," Mary said. "Can you imagine what my feelings would be—married to you, with

James threatening all that trouble on your father? Or even not married to you," she added. "It's weighed on my heart for nearly ten years."

Paul sighed. "Can't you see that's silly? After all you can't live his life and a lot of other people's too. You've got to live your own."

She looked doubtful but not resisting. "And then there's the business of James working in the mill at all," she said. "That's a queer picture—Jim a workingman in the mill and me a fine lady married to the boss. I can't think it through, Paul. I just can't."

"Well, then, don't try!" he said. "It's so damned complicated that there's nothing to do but cut a line straight through the whole tangle and make our grab for happiness. And here's Father swearing he'll make it possible. Yes, Mary?"

She looked up at him with such tenderness in her level gray eyes, and such beauty in her delicate, thin face that he could hardly breathe for watching her. "Yes, Paul," she said, and her hand went up in a kind of warning—"after I've talked to Father Reilly."

"Oh, my almighty God," he gasped, "I forgot all about that. That won't make any trouble, will it?"

She laughed, blushing furiously, and her eyes filled with tears again. "Not if—we—you—I—" she stopped.

He leaned forward and seized her hands again, and whispered, "They can be Catholics or heathens or Mohammedans, for all I care. So long as they're ours. Oh Mary, my darling."

Clarissa Scott was standing on the doorstep as they came up the walk. She took Mary in her arms and kissed her with warmth and tenderness so real that Mary clung to her and gulped and choked furiously, unable to say a word.

"Dear child," Clarissa said. "I'm so happy to have you back. Don't cry, Mary. There, now, that's better."

She raised Mary's face and wiped the tears from it with her own handkerchief. She led her into the parlor, where William Scott was standing in his characteristic position by the fireplace. He gave Mary a strong handclasp, looking hard at her with his stern gray eyes.

"Welcome home, child," he said. The occasion was so fraught with feeling that none of the four could find—or wanted to find—a word to say. Clarissa looked at Mary with obvious delight in her charming appearance, and William Scott's eyes rested on her with such grave approval that Mary's blood was warmed through and through, and presently she could smile again and say, "Oh, I'm so glad to be back!"

She looked happily about the room, noting every chair and picture and cushion and ornament with exquisite satisfaction. It seemed to her as if all the peace and safety and order in the world lay within the walls of this house, in spite of all she had suffered in it. But the suffering had been so different from the bitterness of her exile in London, and it had yielded such richness!

"You must be hungry, children," Clarissa said. "I've got some sandwiches ready for you." It was almost midnight.

She led them into the dining-room, where a cloth was laid on one end of the table, and a plate of sandwiches, some cake, glasses and a pitcher of milk were arranged.

"We're starved," Paul said. He held Mary's hand tight in his. Even before he felt its trembling, he knew how difficult she must be finding this ordeal, and how this was but an introduction to a long series of frightening adjustments. He knew it must be a fearful effort for her to enter this room for the first time from the other side of the barrier between family and servants. He held a chair for her and watched her sink into it, knowing that her knees were shaking. Clarissa knew this too, and she drew up a chair and plunged into a rush of eager questions about Constance, Clarrie, and all the details of their life. Paul ate and drank hungrily, and urged food on Mary while she talked. Presently William Scott came in, poured himself a glass of milk, and stood drinking it by the fireplace with one elbow on the mantel. He looked down at his wife and Mary and Paul with an expression of calm benevolence. Mary could not remember in many years having seen him in such a mood. This did more to reassure her about the sincerity of his decision than all the arguments that Paul had managed to bring up. By the time they had finished their supper, talking steadily about things that had happened during their long separation, Mary was almost entirely at ease, and could describe some of the episodes of life in London in a way that drew even William Scott into the general amusement. Mary did not see the occasional glances of surprise and approval that passed between him and his wife as they noticed the transformation in her speech. She could not know that this change had become reflected all through her personality, giving her poise and confidence and bringing out the instinctive refinement of her nature. Once she overcame her fright and embarrassment she revealed charm and grace that had been latent before, but that were now part of her visible quality.

"Do you mean Constance really went to Marlborough House to dine?" Clarissa repeated after her incredulously.

"Oh, yes," Mary said. "I thought she was rather like Cinderella leaving for the palace in a home-made dress—"

"If you made it I'm sure it didn't look home-made," Clarissa said, eyeing Mary's own clothes. "What was it like?"

"Pale green," Mary said. "She had me copy it from a Worth model that Lady Winchester brought over from Paris. She was beautiful in it. They said everybody in London was talking about her the next day. They said—" she stopped and bit her lip.

"What?" Paul leaned forward and put another sandwich on her plate. Mary eyed William Scott uneasily. Clarissa laughed a little nervously.

"What did they say, dear?"

"Well, you can't take those things the way they sound, you know," Mary murmured. "It was just that the—you know how he's said to—well, he admired her very much," she finished primly.

Mary could not tell them what Constance had said at three o'clock in the morning when she was undressing after that party. She had flung her arms around Mary, sleepy and bundled in a dressing-gown, and whirled her around the room (in which Giles no longer slept) and chortled, "That's it, Mary! I did it. Didn't I always say I would? My God!" she exclaimed almost in a tone of awe, "it was easy as pie."

Mary had stood and studied the gorgeous creature prancing in the gaslight, her burnished curls high on her head, her white-velvet skin daringly bared, her devilish, slanting green eyes, her slender, sensuous body, and had seen only a complication of the passionate, greedy child who had stormed half-naked around the attic in Pittsburgh.

"I can't picture it," Clarissa said. "That child."

"Bad business," Old William muttered, shaking his head.

Paul laughed. "She'll land on her feet," he said.

They heard the front door open and close and Clarissa called, "Is that you, Edgar?"

"Yes, Mama."

He came in readily, Paul was surprised to see. He was home much earlier than usual, early enough to come in like anyone else. He had done that several times lately; there had been fewer nocturnal bats. Mary jumped to her feet and ran over and threw her arms around Edgar. She wanted to cry all over again. He kissed her and asked the usual questions and tactfully avoided mention of the reason for her homecoming, since he presumed he was not supposed to know it until she told him. He dropped into a chair and took something to eat and added his questions to the barrage about Constance. He looked much older, Mary thought, and very different. But she could not put her finger on the difference. He was at once more a man, and yet there was something about him of a tentative, almost a juvenile quality; something that made him unsure of himself. Or did she only imagine that? When she gave him a typically flippant message from Constance he did not roar with laughter as he would once have done; he only smiled rather lamely and, to her surprise, looked away from Mary as if he wished she would stop talking. Could he, she thought with sudden fear, resent the thought of her marrying Paul? Was that the trouble? She would not have thought that of Edgar, as she knew she had it to expect of some of the others. She glanced at Paul to see if she could tell from his expression whether he knew what was the matter with Edgar. But he was talking to his father.

Clarissa's look at the ormolu clock warned them that it was very late. Mary began, from habit, to take the plates and glasses to the pantry, and Clarissa helped her in a matter-of-course way. But when Mary made ready to wash the dishes, Clarissa stopped her.

"Just leave them there by the sink, dear," she said. "The girls will wash them up in the morning." It was like serving notice on Mary in the kindest of ways that she must not forget the revolution in her status, and must try to act accordingly. And this was infinitely more emphasized when Clarissa took her upstairs. She had given Mary Constance's old room instead of the small one beside it. "I thought you'd be more comfortable here," she said. "There's more room to spread out." She fussed about for a moment, straightening the curtains and making sure that the bed had been made and turned down to her liking. Finally she turned to go. She put her arms around Mary and kissed her good night. Mary's eyes filled with tears again.

"No, no," said Clarissa with a smile. "It's all settled now. We all have one thing to do together. We must make one another happy. I'm happy about you and Paul." She looked into Mary's eyes. "I want you to feel sure of that."

"Oh, you're so good to me," Mary whispered. "But how—oh, Mrs. Scott, how shall I ever learn? I'm so frightened."

"Don't think about it that way, dear. Just be yourself. Be natural. If we didn't know you that way we wouldn't have—" Clarissa paused, embarrassed.

"You're so good to me," Mary repeated. She could think of nothing else.

"Well, you go to bed now and get a good sleep and tomorrow we'll talk about everything."

"Oh—tomorrow. I'd like to go down to my father's the first thing if I might."

"Of course you shall. Good night, dear."

CHAPTER XXII

[*Fall 1883*]

WHEN SHE PUSHED open the door of the shack next morning Mary had a sense of foreboding, and she saw at once the reason for her fears. The place had a close, unpleasant, ill-kept smell, and as she came in she saw two small dirty children in the middle of the kitchen floor, playing with an empty beer bottle; her father bowed and apparently asleep in his wheelchair; and Kate, enormous with child, standing over something at the stove. Kate turned as the door opened, and gaped at Mary. And Mary had to use quick presence of mind not to show how shocked she felt.

"Katie!" she went over and took her sister in her arms. "Katie, darling, how are you?"

"Ye see how I am," said Katie with a shrug. Mary had never seen her sister sullen before. She was so appalled that she turned away. She bent down and spoke to the children. "Hello, Joe. You don't know your Auntie Mary, do you?"

The child shook his head stupidly.

"And this is little Ellen." Mary picked the child up and balanced her in her arms. "My, she's a big baby, Katie."

"Too big, fer not learnin' to walk yet," said Kate. " 'Twill kill me a-liftin' o' her one o' these days, the way I am." She slammed something on the table.

Mary put the child back beside her brother and quickly took off her hat and coat. She walked over and put her arm around her sister and drew her towards the window. She was so overcome with concern for Kate that she had hardly more than glanced at her father.

"Katie," she said in a low tone. "Come on and tell me what's the trouble. It looks as if things are bad here."

Kate shut her mouth stubbornly and would not relax in the curve of Mary's arm. It was clear that she was boiling with resentment at Mary's dainty clothes, at her air of well-being, and at the changes in her which had so far delighted everyone who had observed them. But Mary refused to be put off by that. She could be stubborn too. She kept on at Kate with her questions.

"Katie, you must tell me what's the trouble. Is it Dan? Is he all right?"

Kate nodded. But at the same time she looked with fury at her own swollen body stretching the seams of a frowsy, grease-stained calico dress. Mary winced at the horrible disillusionment of that gesture; she thought for a moment of Kate's happiness at the birth of Joe.

"Ah, please, Katie, for the love of God," she insisted, "tell me why things look like this. Where is Bridget?" she asked sharply. Kate's face set heavily. "Is that why you're here?"

"Why else wud I be here?" Kate snapped. "Breakin' me back and cripplin' me legs standin' here doin' fer him"—she jerked her chin towards Patrick—"and leavin' me own house a mess half the day, with Dan on night shift and meals all the clock around and the childer underfoot—och, it's a hell it's all turned into. I wisht I was dead."

She began to cry, rubbing her eyes and blowing her nose on her dirty checked apron. Mary comforted her, but from the very hunch of Kate's shoulders, Mary was forced to realize what furious feelings were stirred up by her presence here. It was all one horrible rebuke to her for finding (even involuntarily) a way of limiting her share of her family's troubles to financial responsibility, while Kate must struggle with the wretched daily grind of cooking, picking up, and caring for Patrick in the midst of squalor. Bridget was so clearly the culprit here.

"Where did she go, Katie?" Mary pleaded. "You've got to tell me. What happened? Did she run away?"

Kate made a sound expressive of disgust. "She'd not the shame to run away," she said bitterly. "She stayed here and made dirt o' us all till the—" again she refused Patrick the courtesy of his name and thereby showed her loathing for the burden that he was—"till he threw her out. Right out in the street like the tart she is."

Mary had turned deathly pale. She stared at Kate for a moment, so incredulous that she found herself hoping that she had not understood. But she saw that no reassurance was to follow. The worst had all too clearly happened.

"You mean," she asked Kate in a stifled voice, "you mean?" She made a sign.

Kate nodded contemptuously, a single sullen jerk of her head.

"Oh, holy Mother of God." Mary covered her face and began to pray aloud. Kate stood and looked at her with stony contempt.

"Nice time ye picked to pray about her," she said. Then she lumbered across the room and back to the stove.

Mary's murmurs died away. It is all my fault, she thought. Entirely mine. I should never have gone away and left her. I would never have had to go if it had not been for Paul. If I had left the Scotts when Paul first —when Paul—when I—when— She could not really think at all. She groped her way to a chair and dropped into it and sat weeping quietly, conscious of bitter remorse and self-reproach more than of shame over Bridget.

"Oh, waur," Kate heard her moaning softly. "Oh, wurrah. Holy Mary Mother o' God. Hail Mary, Holy Mary—"

Kate turned around and said sarcastically, "So ye still talk like the rest o' us when ye ferget yer airs!"

There was a sound from the corner. Patrick had opened his eyes and was peering dazedly around the room, scratching his stubbly white head.

"Who's that ye're talkin' to, Katie?" he asked. His voice had aged to a thin, wheezy whine. His face had fallen in and was a tangle of wrinkles; apparently he had lost the last of his teeth.

Mary looked up at him, hastily drying her eyes. Her breath came in fluttering sobs as she tried to stop crying. That was the most useless thing she could do. She jumped up, shaking her red head quickly as if to clear it.

"It's me, Dad." She ran across to him and put her arms around him. "It's Mary." She knelt beside his chair and looked up at him.

"Oh. Mary, ye say." He looked at her so dully that she drew back, horrified. He seemed neither surprised by her return, nor moved by it. Mary could not tell whether his wits had dimmed during the three years of her absence, or whether he had really turned against her. She decided that the former must be true. She had always been Patrick's favorite child and he had often made a point of saying so. But even this explanation did not lessen the shock.

"Dad!" she cried insistently. "What's wrong with you? Don't you see I've come home? Aren't you glad to see me?"

He looked at her in a puzzled way.

"Where've ye been?"

"Why, you know where I've been!" She could not adjust herself quickly to this distressing situation. "I've been working in London. I just got back last night."

"London," repeated Patrick. "Ye can't be tellin' the truth. No more'n her."

Mary saw that he was coupling her with Bridget in his mind. This gave her the hint that she had better change her approach and treat him like a child. Perhaps he would become oriented when she had been there awhile. She pushed his chair to the table and Kate set a bowl of thin porridge before him.

" 'Tis all he eats now, and broth," she said wearily. "He sups it down out o' the bowl."

"Well, I'll feed it to him," Mary said. "You go along home, Kate, and try to get a little extra time to yourself today. I'll stay with Dad."

"Ye will?" asked Kate in a suspicious tone, untying her apron. "Fer how long?"

For some reason Mary turned scarlet. These few minutes in this house had thrown the previous day with all its import into such fantastic contrast that she could not think clearly at all. The idea of marrying Paul, of any life other than this, was wildly unreal. But she could not escape the full thrust of Kate's biting question.

"Well, till we find some better way of taking care of him than this,' she said. "Certainly so you won't have to work so hard, Katie."

"Nor you neither," Kate retorted. "From the look o' ye wid yer fancy airs and yer talkin' like a swell, I can't figger what ye're up to, but I can see it ain't goin' to be sloppin' around this place like me."

She bent down to pick up Ellen. Mary hurried to her, lifted the heavy baby, and put her in Kate's arms. Her first reaction to this shocking situation had been a hopeless feeling that all her plans and Paul's were only an impossible dream. But as she watched Kate shuffing off up the alley, carrying Ellen as well as her unborn burden and leading Joe by the hand, she turned back to the shanty with a sudden snapping-to of the desire for happiness that Paul had roused to such a pitch yesterday. None of this—not even Bridget—was going to defeat her. She would find Bridget and get her under control somehow. She would see James when he came home at the end of his shift today, and after giving him a good hot supper she would talk the whole thing over with him and work out some practical way of looking after him and Patrick. Sick with anxiety, but full of determination, Mary turned to feeding her father. After that she intended to clean up the shack, and then to find out what had become of Bridget.

She had no idea how to go about the search, and her first thought of cross-questioning all the neighbors on the Flat turned out to be a horrifying failure. For when she knocked next door and was answered by old Mrs. O'Brien who had been her mother's friend, she was sickened at the reception she received. Mollie O'Brien stood stony-faced on the doorsill and eyed Mary up and down.

"Well?" she asked coldly, taking in Mary's good clothes.

"I just thought—" Mary began awkwardly.

"Thought ye'd come and pay a call!" said Mollie, her tone like iron. "All dressed up in yer furrin finery."

"Why—why what's the *matter?*" Mary asked. She was flabbergasted. "I—why Mrs. O'Brien, I only wanted to say hello and ask you about—"

Coming on top of Kate's and her father's indifference to her homecoming, this treatment by an old neighbor was staggering. Mary had expected the warm Irish welcome that such a long absence would naturally call forth. Mollie O'Brien left her so nonplussed that her words trailed off to nothing and she stood dumb with embarrassment in the door-ay.

"No doubt ye're thinkin' to ask me about that sister o' yours," Mollie said flatly. "Well, I'll spare ye the pains. If ye're goin' off about yer fancy business on th' other side o' the wurrld, ye can't expect dacint folk to keep track o' yer street-walkin' kin. Yer poor Dad turned her out whin it got so every eye in the place cud see her shame. That's all I know and the less I'll have to do wid the likes o' ye the better off I'll be."

She turned into her house and slammed the door in Mary's face. For a moment Mary stood swaying on her feet, her cheeks burning, her hands clammy. Then her blurred eyes cleared, and with them her stunned mind. She clenched her fists, and clamped her teeth together. If this was the treatment she could expect from the Flat, if they were all going to identify her long absence and her good appearance with Bridget's disgraceful reputation, she would take up the challenge and turn them all down, more ruthlessly than they intended to repudiate her. She lifted her chin high, threw back her shoulders, and marched off to take the Suspension Bridge horse-car over to Pittsburgh. She was going to police headquarters to turn over the search for Bridget to the authorities.

When James came home at half-past six Mary had the shack cleaned, the stove polished, the lamp freshened, and an appetizing lamb stew simmering on the fire. Fresh soda-bread was baking in the oven, and the kettle was boiling ready for the tea. James stamped in, threw his cap on the table, and slid into his chair. Then he looked up at Mary standing by the stove.

"Hello," he said.

Mary leaned over him. "Aren't you going to kiss me, James?"

He smiled a little and kissed her on the cheek. "How are ye?"

"Fine. Just fine. Oh, there's so much to talk about, James, I don't know where to begin."

Suspicion came into his face along with surprise as he listened to her speech. "Is it a swell ye've grown?" he asked.

"Why no," Mary said insistently. She was beginning to dread hostile reactions to the changes in her. "Can't a person learn a little English if they want to?"

James shrugged.

Mary filled Patrick's bowl with broth from the stew and set a plate of food before James. She ladled some out for herself and after helping Patrick with his supper, sat down opposite James to eat her own. James bent over his food, eating so quickly and greedily that Mary saw he had not tasted anything like this for many months. He crunched the bones loudly in his teeth, sopped up the gravy with the soda-bread, and drank big, noisy gulps of scalding tea. He did not want to talk at all, Mary knew, and certainly not about any of the things that were troubling her. But she was anxious to settle as many of them as she could. Her resolution of the afternoon had crystallized into a firm decision to eliminate as quickly as possible all the hindrances of her marriage. There was no way of leading James into a conversation; one must plunge in. So Mary said, "James, I want to talk to you about Dad, here, and what to do about him, and about Bridget."

He looked up at her with a scowl. "He's done what there was to do about Bridget."

"Oh, that's outrageous. You don't honestly think he did right about her!"

"Well," James said, "ye know how I feel about them things. A woman's morals to me is just a lot o' palaver. I've got far more important things to trouble me head."

"More important?" Her brow was furrowed with incredulity. "Do you mean to tell me you've never—never gone after the *man*? Never found out who he is? Why—that would be your place, James!"

"Ah—" he brushed her away with a batting motion of his hand. "Ye're full o' notions, Mary. Ye'd not be wastin' yer time and mine on this spilled milk if ye'd a'seen what she was like. If she'd been a dacint kid at all t'wud be different. Ferget it."

"You can't throw a pregnant girl out in the street and pretend she's dead! Your own sister too." Mary's lips trembled.

"Me own sisters is no furtherance to my life," he said sarcastically. "If they were I'd be thankin' ye for a lot o' things I ain't grateful for. Now let's cut out all the jawin', Mary, I ain't in the mood."

"You're never in the mood to act human," Mary said. Then she regretted her words. She did not want to start the old bickering with James. "I just want to tell you I've had a talk with the Missing Persons officer about Bridget, and if they find her I'll try to get her in hand and see what can be done with the mess she's made of her life."

James laughed coldly. "Ye ain't seen her since she decided what to do with her life," he said. "That girl was cut out for one thing and one thing only, Mary, and ye might as well try to shove back a landslide as make her change."

Mary sighed. "Well then, the next question is Dad," she said. She looked at Patrick dozing in his chair. All the time she had been in the shack today he had hardly looked at her. She still did not know whether he was really addled with age, or determined to ignore her. "I can't find out what he thinks about anything. But he can't go on living like this and neither can you. Kate can't do all this work, James, and try to manage her own family and house too. She's in a very bad way."

He shrugged again. "O' course nobody could expect a grand lady like you to come home and look after yer Dad."

Mary jumped up irritably from her chair. "James! *Will* you be reasonable! I don't see why you've always got such a chip on your shoulder. I'm only trying to figure out some sensible way of keeping you and Dad comfortable."

"Strikes me we was always very comfortable till ye got yer notions about livin' high with the Scotts."

"Oh stop it. We're way back where we were ten years ago. I tell you I'm going to solve this without getting tangled up in your twisted ideas. Somebody has got to be found to come in here every day and do for Dad."

James looked hard at her as she dropped back into her chair. He planted his blackened hands heavily on the table. He leaned towards her.

"Mary, what are ye up to that ye weren't before?"

She colored, and swallowed hard, but she eyed him steadily and refused to be stared down.

"Nothing that I haven't got the right to!" she answered. "I'm not going to be bullied by you, either. I've got my own plans and I'm going to carry them out. They mean finding somebody to take care of Dad."

"Ah."

He slouched back and squinted at her. She did not move. But she said, "Now that I come to think of it, I've been sending enough money to Dad these three years so you could have paid some woman for a couple of hours' work a day, to come in here and keep this place clean and cook supper every night. Why didn't you think of that since Bridget—since she left—instead of making Kate nearly kill herself?"

James glowered. "I've no money to hire servants!" he growled. He put all the cruel meaning into the words that he could. Mary stiffened. She bit her lip and said, "Then there's something very queer around here. If you've been putting in the same as you used to for this house, and with me sending twenty dollars every month, you ought to have had more than enough to pay somebody. What have you done with the money? You've certainly not been buying food. That larder was bare when I came in here this morning."

"I'm no housekeeper," James muttered.

"Never mind about that," Mary insisted. "After the rent's paid on this place there ought to be more than ten dollars a week, between your wages and mine, to do for Dad. No ten dollars a week's been spent around here since I left," she exclaimed, sweeping the place with her eye. "What did you do with the money?"

She leaned forward and tried to look into James's eyes. But he kept them narrowed, squinting sullenly at the table. And his mouth was a hard, angry line. Mary stared at his gloomy face. She was baffled for a time; but presently light began to dawn on her.

"James," she breathed. "You've been giving my money to the Amalgamated."

He raised his head and glared. "Well?"

"Oh, it's a crime!" Mary cried. She sprang from her chair, and stood trembling with rage, her hands doubled into fists, her eyes burning. "It's a crime," she repeated, almost in a scream. She had never in all her life been furious like this. "How dare you steal my money, you crazy, wicked fool?"

James rose, shambling, from the table, and reached for his cap. Mary ran over and seized it from him and threw it on the floor and stamped on it. "No, you don't!" she cried. "You don't walk out of this house and get away from me."

She stood for a moment, trembling violently. Then pure fury overwhelmed her and she slapped James in the face with all her strength.

Patrick looked up, his mouth foolishly hanging open. "Wha—what—" he mumbled. Mary ignored him. Her hand stung from the blow she had struck James. And James stood there, his face dark with defiance. Presently he opened his mouth and laughed. There was no mirth in the sound, only violent mockery.

"Are ye raisin' all this hell at losin' yer dirty money, or because it's gone to fight the Scotts?" he asked.

"You—you beast! You traitor!" Mary screamed.

James shoved her aside and picked up his cap from beneath her foot. "Who's talkin' about traitors!" he said in an ugly low growl. "Traitors! When it comes to that, ye needn't look any farther than yer own rotten self. Livin' off them suckin' parasites and turnin' into one yerself. And carryin' on wid—"

"James Rafferty, shut your mouth. Shut *up*!" Mary spoke, whipped on by fury, as she had not known she could speak. She was panting, breathing through her parted lips with quick, sharp gasps.

James walked towards the door, talking to her over his shoulder as he went. On the threshold he turned and finished speaking. "I'll shut up," he assured her. "That's what I mostly do. Ye'd have been in a mess long afore this if I didn't have bigger things to think on than you and yer two-faced doin's. I'm not ashamed o' usin' yer money fer me union; no, not a bit. I'm proud o' it. I'm glad somethin' that comes from ye went to fight a just cause. Ye may be int'rested to hear we're about to ready to clinch our drive any day now. The first chance to hand I'm goin' to call a strike. I'm goin' to lick that stiffnecked old bastard and see him kneel to a closed shop in that bleedin' mill, and you're goin' to see me do it!"

"James!" Mary's voice trailed into a sob.

"Go on and cry about it!" he sneered. "That's all the good it'll do ye. As fer Dad here, I don't care what old cow ye hire to do fer him, as long as I don't have to see yer mincin' airs around here. The hell wid ye." The door crashed shut behind him.

Mary washed the dishes in furious haste. She was too violently angry to cry any more, or to give one more thought to her family and its fate. Tomorrow she would hire some woman from the Flat who would be glad of the hourly wages for looking after Patrick, and beyond that Mary intended to wash her hands of the whole horrible business and have nothing more to do with any of them, ever again. She was through with the agony of divided allegiances. Patrick's treatment, even more than James's, was the final blow. She could not get away from here fast enough, she was in a wild hurry to get back to Paul and warn him of the danger from James, and reassure herself once for all by the sight of him that she had cast her lot where it belonged.

CHAPTER XXIII

[1883—Continued]

MEMORIES CAME TROOPING in a vivid cloud as she walked quickly up the long Fulton Street hill and turned right on Western to go home. She did not feel as if she were walking alone. She felt as if a wraith, a ghost, were moving along beside her; the shadow of the timid, groping girl who had first taken this familiar walk ten years ago. Ten years?— Could it be ten?—or only yesterday, or a whole lifetime ago? Whatever it was, it teemed with scenes and talk and people, some of it to be treasured, some of it, like the awful situation down on the Flat, to be forgotten. Forgotten, she had to tell herself sternly; that is the only way. That is what I owe to Paul. The thought of him was as warm and near at this moment as he himself had been, holding her in his arms that morning and kissing her before he started with his father for the mill. That was the first time he had ever been able to do that. He had made a ceremony of it. He had called her into the back parlor before he left the house and said, "I want you to kiss me good-bye every morning when I leave the house. I want you to stand at the front door after we're married and kiss me there and stay there while I start down the street."

Her eyes filled with tears as she thought of that now. Had there ever been loneliness like that which Paul and she had endured? It was hard to conceive how there could be; theirs had had the bitter edge of hopelessness to sharpen it. And now she could not really believe it was past. She could not take in such an unbelievable miracle all at once. Especially she could not take it in when so much of life was bounded by the same familiar patterns, the very cracks of the pavements she had always trod, the crunch of the gravel as she started up the front walk and almost, from old habit, took the side path that led off to the stable and the kitchen door. There she paused, staring up at the lighted façade of the house that had been her real home, and was to be, in this incredible way, her only one for the rest of her life, hers and Paul's.

Dinner was over; she was glad of that. It would have been such an ordeal to sit down that very first evening with Paul and his parents and be served by some maid as she herself had served time out of mind in the past. Mrs. Scott had thought of all that, of course. Every servant on the place was different, Sarah and Joel and McCready pensioned, young new maids in the places of the girls Mary had known. She was so grateful to Mrs. Scott for the way she was taking her in that at moments she shook with the intensity of her feelings. She wondered how it must feel to be Mrs. Scott and have your son love a girl like herself, instead of the one you had expected and hoped for. She knew that Mrs. Scott loved her far more than she ever had Louise. But that was not the point of the thing, God knew.

She was standing there on the path thinking and in a strange way putting off the moment of going up the steps and opening the side door, which the family used as much as the front one, when the door opened, letting a flood of gaslight stream down the path, and Paul stepped out.

"Mary? Is that you, darling?"

"That's me, to be sure," she said mischievously, twisting the words with the broadest brogue she could. He laughed and took her in his arms and kissed her hungrily. "I thought you were never coming. Why wouldn't you let me come and fetch you?"

"I didn't know when I'd be ready to leave. How are you, dear?"

"Empty, without you." He smiled down at her and she put up her fingers and touched the arc of his cheekbone, just under the eye socket, where the blond hair grew downy and fine. He turned his head and caught the fingers between his lips and kissed them. With his arm around her he led her up the steps and into the house. In the hallway she drew away with a small frown; she did not want him to do anything undignified. He laughed. They went into the back parlor where Mr. and Mrs. Scott were seated on either side of the gas table lamp, he with the newspaper, she with some needlework. They inquired for Mary's family and she answered briefly that they were well. If anything could increase her determination to make the break complete, it would be the sight of this room and of the people in it, to whom anything so unholy as Bridget's sordid mess would be unspeakable degradation. She fetched her own work and they all sat together for half an hour while Mr. Scott read parts of the newspaper aloud. Business had been very bad in recent months, in some ways alarming; and Mary was reminded by that of her first day here, Black Friday ten years ago, with its tragic consequences for poor Louise.

At ten o'clock Mr. and Mrs. Scott went up to bed. Clarissa kissed Mary good night and admonished, with the smile she would have given a daughter of her own, "Don't stay up too late, dear."

When they heard the doors closing upstairs Paul got up from his chair and shut the door of the back parlor and turned out the gaslights in the wall brackets, and lowered the table lamp until it was a dim glow in its green glass shade. He went over to Mary then and picked her up and carried her across the room and sank with her into his father's big leather chair. He leaned over her face and gazed at it as if he would never see enough of it his whole life long. As she looked into his blue eyes, wide and solemn and strained, she saw them cloud over with tears. Her own eyes began to fill, and Paul put his face down with a rough motion into her breast, groaning, "Oh, God, how I've wanted you."

"I know." She whispered into the ear lying close to her lips. "I know."

"I'm not going to wait long," he said. His breath was warm in her breast. "I've waited too long already. We'll be married right away. Won't we, darling?" He raised his head and looked at her again. "Won't we?"

"Well—practically. I have some things to do. Sewing—and—"

"You can sew afterwards."

She blushed a little, laughing. "Not what I want to have ready before."

He put his face down to hers and kissed her, holding her lips long in his, holding her body up against his with steady pressure of his strong left hand. His right lay on her small breast, firm and quiet; she loved the steady deliberate motions of his hands. They never moved unnecessarily, never fumbled. There was no haste in his embrace, no clamoring urgency, but the profound passion of his love for her penetrated every vein and nerve of her body. When they drew apart she breathed, "Oh, if I could only show you how I love you."

"You will. That's why we've got to be married—now. I want you to bloom." He pushed the bright hair higher off her forehead. "In your own way. In beauty—and peace."

"You speak like a poet."

"Not I." He shook his head, smiling. "I'm just an old mill-hand. But that face"—he leaned down again and stared almost incredulously at the fine deep eyes, the awakened parted lips, the delicate cameo nostrils—"that face would make a poet of its lover."

"Oh Paul." She burst into tears. "It"—she looked about in a panicky way—"it can't be true. I'll wake up tomorrow and find it's not true. I'm afraid."

He held her close against his chest, shaking his head a little and rocking her with the motion of his shoulders. "No," he murmured, "no, darling, you'll never be afraid again. Never. Never. I'll never let you be afraid of anything . . . until the day I die. . . ."

Later he went to the pantry and fetched crackers and milk, and they ate and drank sitting close together on the sofa. Mary told Paul about James. Bridget, she had decided, was to be a closed book so far as Paul and all his people were concerned; but James—

Paul shook his head slowly. "I told Father months ago that this was brewing. He won't head it off."

"Could he, dear? What could he do?"

"I've tried for years now to get him to sit down and talk to Jim and see if they can't work out some compromise. I'm sure Jim would be satisfied if Father would only agree to recognize the Amalgamated members in the mill and to bargain with them as a union. Jim told you he means to get a closed shop, but if he only got union recognition and an open shop it would be such a victory that I'm positive he'd be satisfied. But of course Father is adamant about anything to do with the union at all."

"I think he's right," Mary said stubbornly.

"No, he's not." Paul got out his pipe, giving Mary a guilty wink, for even yet nobody was allowed to smoke except in William Scott's study. "Father is not right about this thing. And you always identify yourself with him about it instead of with Jim. Sometimes I don't understand you."

"Then you'd better begin," Mary said shortly. Paul laughed. "Don't forget nobody else knows James the way I do," she added.

"You're not even right about that, darling. I know the best of him and you apparently know the worst, and you won't make any allowances. Jim's in a queer position, Mary. It's extremely unusual for a man so expert and so indispensable to the management to be also the union organizer in a mill. I don't know why Joe Bishop picked him for the job. But probably because the men worship Jim and he is so damned intense about the union that he blotted out anyone else who might have been considered. I rely on Jim's qualities for the work he does with me. I don't see why Bishop wouldn't do the same. Jim is a very remarkable man, Mary."

"It makes me sick to hear you say it. If you could see the horrible state I found things in today, and the condition Dad is in, and poor Kate the most wretched slattern in the slums, you'd see why I'm so furious with James—when it was all unnecessary. He *stole* my money, Paul—and gave it to those crazy union brawlers."

Paul sighed. He could not very well defend Jim, for misappropriating Mary's money. It was a cruel thing to have done. But he saw why the bitter, fanatical man had done as he had. Paul saw suddenly that there was a strong resemblance between Mary's doggedness about her beliefs and her brother's about his.

"Look here, darling." He put his arm lightly about her and drew her close against him. "We've got a job to do about this and you've got to help. That is, I take it for granted you intend to help—me, I mean."

"Naturally."

"Then you and I between us must find some way of getting Father and Jim together to make a compromise settlement of this thing, or there is going to be violence around that mill and violence"—he looked down at her seriously—"could mean hell for us. Do you believe that?"

She nodded.

"And you'll do your part when I ask you to get Jim to meet Father halfway?"

"I'll be willing to try, darling, but after the way we parted this evening I can't say it looks very promising."

"You've had quarrels with Jim before. You can write off this one like all the others."

"Maybe, but James is different now. He hates the way I've changed. And I think—I know—he's suspicious about us." She looked up with a troubled frown.

"Oh, hell, everybody's been that way for years. You didn't think we'd managed to hide this, did you?"

"Paul!"

He laughed, "Darling!" He pulled her onto his lap again and crushed her against him. "What do you care anyway?" There was delicious oblivion for a while. Then she drew away and insisted on speaking, though he tried to keep her quiet with his kisses. She pushed his head back gently and said, "I've been thinking, darling. About me—living here."

"So have I. I love it."

"No, please. Be serious. I mean, until we're married. It will be terribly awkward. For everybody."

He raised his eyebrows and looked at her, rather puzzled.

"I mean," she said. She paused uncomfortably. "Well, I'll tell you. Once we are married everything that went before will be crossed out. But now, you see—"

"You're worrying about people, aren't you, Mary?"

She nodded. "That's it. When I'm here alone with your mother and father and you, we all understand and I've only to get used to my new self. But we've decided already not to tell anyone else beforehand. And meanwhile I just can't face having your mother's friends dropping in. And as for mealtimes—"

She was thinking of the traditional hospitality of the Scott table, with its constant succession of visitors.

"I haven't even seen the new help here, being away all today. But I can tell you I dread it, Paul. Really I do. Servants always know everything. You can take my word for that."

She spoke in a queer tone and he looked at her uneasily.

"Well, what do you want to do?"

"I thought if I could get a place to live all by myself until we're married," she said slowly, "then I could sleep there and eat there, you know in some nice boarding-house. And I have all my sewing to do, I must make myself some proper clothes." She smiled shyly.

He thought for a while and said, "That's not a bad idea, darling. I confess I have wondered just how we'd work all this out. Of course we're going to be married very soon; it would only be a matter of two or three months."

She nodded. "I love being with your mother, Paul, and I'd be here a good deal during the day. But I just can't face the—the—"

"I know." He put his arms around her again and pulled her head down on his shoulder. "I haven't had a chance to tell you my plan, have I, darling?"

She shook her head.

"Well." Holding her in his left arm, he lit his pipe again, crossed his knees, and leaned back in his corner of the sofa. "Ever since I finished college I've had a trip to Europe coming to me. I almost took it when you were over there, and I thought I'd go over and simply dragoon you. But I was all tangled up with the new furnaces and Edgar was raising hell, and you know. Besides you were being a stubborn little Mick and I knew I wouldn't be able to do anything with you."

She hid her face in his coat.

"You ought to be ashamed. Now listen to this. As soon as we're married we're going to sail for Europe and have that year Father promised me —all to ourselves. *To ourselves.*" He kissed her lightly.

"Do we have to go to London?" Mary made a face.

He laughed. "We'll go from here straight to Italy, and spend the spring there. Sicily. And Naples. And Rome. Oranges and palm trees and hot sunshine and we'll take a little house perched somewhere on a cliff over the water, and nobody will see us for months and months and months."

Mary's eyes were shining. She shook her head bewilderedly. "I can't believe it's me you're telling this to."

"And when we've had enough of that—"

She sat up and pulled away from him. "So you're already expecting to have enough of that!"

He laughed. "When I'm good and tired of being all alone in a honeymoon heaven with you," he said, "we'll start travelling. We'll go to Germany first."

"And see Cologne Cathedral!"

"Mary," he said, "I hate cathedrals. Get that clearly in your head. I may go to see one with you and I may act as if I like it, but for all practical purposes I am on record now as hating cathedrals. We are going to Germany to see steel mills. We will go to Essen and see Krupp's, and we will see Thyssen's, and Siemens, and all the rest of them. We will go to Austria and see the Skoda works, and when we get to France we'll go to Creusot—"

"Not to Paris?"

"I thought that would fetch you. We will not only go to Paris, but we will have a wonderful time there. If I catch you within a mile of Notre Dame I'll spank the daylights out of you. You are going to spend your time in Worth's and all those other places and when you're all dressed up you're going to make Constance look like a frump by comparison. You're going to learn to drink wine and we're going to Monte Carlo and gamble."

"Have you lost your mind, darling?"

"No, ma'm, I have not. But if you think you're going to be a little plaster saint after you marry me, you're very much mistaken."

"Don't you like me the way I am?" Mary's eyes filled with tears.

"I love you the way you are. But the way you are is just the beginning of somebody so much more wonderful—" Paul held her so that he could look into her face, and spoke with earnest intensity. "Mary, if you hadn't had all the beauty and hadn't looked the way you did, in spite of those caps and aprons you wore, I wouldn't have wanted you the way I did. The way I do. I love beauty, darling. And you're going to be the most beautiful thing God ever made by the time we get back from Europe. Your clothes are going to be marvellous and you'll look like a queen. See? And the reason you'll look like a queen is because of what will be inside the clothes."

Mary turned to him and hid her face in his shoulder again. "You frighten me so," she whispered. "I'll never be able to live up to you."

"Nonsense," he said. "You've talked this stuff to me for years about keeping up standards and all the rest of it—well, now I want you to get out in front and make a few of your own. You'll have them all at your feet if you do, darling—the whole damn town."

Something in his words made her spine begin to tingle. She sat up suddenly and looked at him with an expression of amazement. And in her gray eyes he saw the beginning of a strange new gleam—the light of ambition and of battle.

"Do you really mean that, Paul?" she asked slowly.

"Certainly I mean it. You've had the whiphand over me so long, you little bully, that I've never had a chance to know how much I meant it. I tell you, between my father and the wife I bring back after a year in Europe, you'll see that everything you ever said was a lot of poppycock."

She found a pleasant room in a house on Beech Street, only one block beyond the Scotts'. The house was the family home of a Miss Emily Mitchell, whose reduced means had led her to take paying guests. Clarissa knew her well, and went with Mary to make the arrangement. She herself had been worried, by just the questions that were haunting Mary: once Mary was no longer a maid in the Scott house there could be no possible explanation for her sudden appearance there in the status of a daughter unless the Scotts were prepared to inform their friends about her coming marriage to Paul. And everybody felt sure that this would be a mistake. When the day came Paul and Mary and Paul's parents would go to Father Reilly's study in St. Michael's parish house; the marriage would take place there, and the couple would leave at once for New York and for their year in Europe. By the time they returned, the elder Scotts would have had ample time to settle the expected furore in Pittsburgh.

William Scott too had taken a hand. For it occurred to him, as it apparently had not to anyone else, that Mary had no money except her small savings from her wages. He had a talk with her. He told her tersely that this was strictly a business matter, holding up his hand to keep her silent while she tried to protest. He was going to settle on her a small annual income for life. When she tried to thank him, though she was almost incoherent from emotion, he shook his head brusquely and waved her away.

"Every woman should have some small means of her own," he said gruffly. "Your savings are not sufficient for the purpose, that's all. As Paul's wife you will be in the same position as one of my daughters. Now say no more about it."

So Mary settled in her temporary home, surrounded by bolts of cambric and nainsook, yards of beading, insertion, and lace, rolls of tape and ribbon, and all the paraphernalia for an orgy of sewing. As she set the fine, almost invisible stitches of her new nightgowns and petticoats, and while she embroidered the dainty edges of her scalloped frills and flounces, she thought in never-lessening amazement of the unbelievable thing that had happened to her. Underclothes like this were among the luxuries that belonged to Constance; she could hardly believe that she was making them for herself. And yet, remembering Paul's words in the back parlor, she knew that he expected of her just such dainty and lovely clothing as this. Sometimes while she worked she was swept into a trembling ecstasy at the thought that she was making these things for him to see. Her hands would drop into her lap, her throat contract with the memory of his embraces and the thought of the greater, the complete ones to come. With all her modesty she had never shied away from the thought of belonging to Paul. Once she raised her head from her work and stared at herself almost with awe in the mirror across the room.

"Who—who am I?" she said aloud.

CHAPTER XXIV

[*November 1883*]

LAURENCE GAYLORD ARRIVED with profound misgivings at the semi-annual partners' meeting in November. He had regularly attended the meetings during the nine years since he had bought his interest, and he had always left them troubled and dissatisfied. William Scott had seldom consulted him about his preferences and even less often asked his advice. With his minority interest Gaylord had never been able effectively to contest any action or policy of Scott's. This meeting promised to be more trying than any previous ones. Scott had written him in advance, making the long-expected offer to buy Gaylord's share, and suggesting that they put the transaction through at the time of the semi-annual meeting. Gaylord had no intention of selling. He told William junior that. But he had made up his mind once for all to discover what lay behind that offer, and what had been shaping William Scott's policies for a long time past.

The meeting began routinely, convening as usual in the outer room of the two that comprised William Scott's offices. The inner, private office was the small, bare chamber that held only the crude, battered oak desk, the two hard chairs, and the iron safe that were the Old Man's idea of sufficient furnishings. Richard MacTavish's office connected with this one. The outer office adjoined it on the other side. In this room, also grimly barren and gloomy with its painted lead-colored walls, its bare board floor, and its narrow, smoke-dimmed windows, there was a scarred oak table, a case of wall-maps, and half a dozen plain straight-backed chairs.

Seated now around the table were William Scott at the head, with his attorney Henry Wilkins on his right; Gaylord and his lawyer from Boston; Paul as secretary of the company and general manager of the mill; and Richard MacTavish as treasurer and business manager. William junior, having no executive title, was not present. This galled him and his father-in-law and had always appeared an unnecessary piece of defiance on the Old Man's part. It irritated and outraged Gaylord as the screams of the dinkey-engine, the roar of the crusher out in the yard, and the ear-splitting clangs from the casthouse floor offended him and set his nerves on edge. Why could they not hold these meetings downtown in Pittsburgh, in an office-building or even a club? Why must they take place here in this barbaric hole, draughty and dirty and rank with coal smoke and gas fumes? William Scott had only snorted "No!" the time Gaylord had suggested meeting elsewhere.

MacTavish's clerk pushed open the door and wheeled in a creaking cart full of ledgers. Henry Wilkins rose and read off some routine questions. Then MacTavish stood up and said in his high, cracked voice, "I cairtify that these buks are in orrrder as of the close of business at the current accountin' peeriod." A few further formalities followed, and the clerk wheeled the cart back to the bookkeeper's office. Gaylord and his lawyer then asked several searching questions about the inventory and the profit percentage of the past six months, and MacTavish answered these gravely and precisely, using a great many technical figures and leaving Gaylord less enlightened, if possible, than before. But Gaylord could never put his finger on any literally contestable point in all this, and his attorney had to assure him that the Scott books were in scrupulous order as usual. The meeting ended with the formal reelection of William Scott, Paul, and MacTavish as officers. The attorneys and MacTavish withdrew. Gaylord also rose to go, but William Scott, sitting at the head of the table, looked up and detained him. "Just a moment, Mr. Gaylord," he said. "Could you not sit down again and talk over my offer to buy your share?"

Paul rose from his chair and started to leave the room. His father said, "No, Paul, I'd rather you stayed and I want William to come in here too."

Paul went for his brother and the two took places on either side of their father at the table. Gaylord had seated himself at the foot. The two older men had aged markedly in the decade of their unequal partnership. Scott had grown heavier, grayer, and much slower of body. Gaylord was thinner, so thin that his pale, slender hands had a transparent look through the fingers, and his long face, between bushy white sideburns, was a mask of skin stretched over the high forehead and the narrow, beaked nose. The two old men treated each other with grave courtesy which seemed only a curtain drawn over the reality of their mutual dislike. Gaylord's eyes went to William junior as the elder Scott son seated himself. William's expression was puzzling; there was an arrogant look in his face which mingled curiously with an expression of uneasiness and doubt. Paul's face was inscrutable. His father could see that he had resorted to deliberate impassivity, very foreign to his nature.

Scott took up the question afresh.

"I have come to believe, Mr. Gaylord, that it was a mistake in the nature of this particular business to admit an outside interest. I have tried to manage the mill in such a way as to increase the value of your investment along with mine, and the offer that I sent you represents an increase of twenty-five per cent over your original investment."

"That shows exceedingly able management, Mr. Scott," Gaylord said slowly. "I give you full credit for it. But I did not make this investment with an eye to capital increment. Income was what I had in view, as you know. That is why I have never been in full agreement with your policy of plowing profits back into inventory and allotting small—I may say, in proportion to your profits—very small annual payments to the partners."

"You have never contested my ability to run this mill at a profit, though, and that policy is the cornerstone of my way of doing things."

"It still seems to me that some upward adjustment of the payments on earnings could be made compatibly with your management policy."

"Since I cannot agree with you about that," William Scott replied, "I have taken it for granted for a long time that you are not satisfied with the status of your investment, and therefore I am offering to take it off your hands at great profit to yourself."

The two sons exchanged glances across the table.

"I have no wish to sell my share, Mr. Scott," said Gaylord flatly.

"I daresay it is not within my province to inquire into your reasons for this," Scott said, selecting his words carefully. "But in a business so closely tied to a family, it is difficult to regard matters in a purely impersonal light. I have the future of my children in mind."

"And I of mine," Gaylord answered. "My daughter Julia, as the wife of your eldest son, stands in a position where she must inherit title to my share in order to assist her husband in—er—in the event—"

"—in the event that I die and leave my holdings in equal shares to my children, which is what I would, presumably, do. In such a case your daughter's holding, combined with William's inheritance, would give him a much larger percentage of ownership than any other heir."

William junior looked up and fixed his eyes on Gaylord. "Father and Paul are determined that that shall not happen, Father Gaylord," he said.

Gaylord's face creased into a sarcastic smile. "And I," he said, "have intended for a good many years that it shall."

William Scott made one of his unexpectedly mild remarks. "You do not seriously believe, Mr. Gaylord, that William is capable of running this business if he were in control of it?"

Gaylord leaned forward slowly and pressed his fragile hands together. "How can I tell, Mr. Scott?" he asked quietly. "He has never been given a chance."

Paul's head came up with a jerk and his face took on an angry color. "Mr. Gaylord, that is an injustice. My brother has never had the slightest interest in the manufacture of steel. If he had, he would have been a vital part of this mill."

William junior opened his mouth to speak, but his father-in-law spoke sooner.

"One can hire specialists to superintend manufacture, I believe," he said. "I understand that is the policy of so astute a steel magnate as Mr. Carnegie."

William Scott stiffened and his huge frame rose halfway from his chair. His rough hand on the table closed into a knotty fist.

"Mr. Gaylord!" he exclaimed in a cold, heavy tone, "I asked you to sit down here and discuss a matter of vital importance to both of us in a reasonable manner. I consider this kind of talk unreasonable and I warn you that I will not stand for it. The name of Carnegie is anathema to me and so are all his methods!"

William junior spoke again. "You see," he said to Gaylord, "Father means to leave this business to Paul. He always meant to. Paul is his favorite."

"Paul is not my favorite except as he commands my respect!" William Scott was beginning to talk in the thunderous tone that presaged trouble. He made his obviously untrue denial with a flash of his hard eyes. "No man has any place in the steel business who cannot create steel by the sweat of his brow. That is why Paul deserves the control of this mill and that is why he is going to get it." He brought his fist down on the table and glared at the man opposite him. "That is also why I respect him!" he snapped.

There was a heavy silence. Then William junior moved from his chair with a jerk and before the others realized it, he was on his feet, leaning over the table and speaking in a sharp, tense key that rose at intervals almost to a screech.

"You see?" he cried. "That's what he respects. That's the kind of justice you can expect from him." He pointed to Paul. "Father's been taken in by that hypocrite for years."

Paul made a furious gesture but his father restrained him with a shake of his head. "Let him continue," he said. William junior took no notice.

"There's the favorite son who's cheated me out of my birthright!" he yelled, gesturing at Paul. "There's the shining angel who's going to cut me out of all my rights. The one my father respects. He hasn't the morals of a—a pimp!"

Paul's dead-white face and clenched fists were murderous, and he would have been at William's head if the Old Man's hand had not closed on his arm like a trap.

William junior waited for his words to take full effect. Then, with Gaylord asking in a horrified way, "What do you mean?" William cried, "He's been sleeping with a servant in my mother's house for years! That's the kind of man who's going to inherit the Scott Iron Works!"

"God—damn—you." Paul's words were so quiet and so deliberate that the old men's blood curdled as Paul rose slowly from his chair, staring across at William, and backing away to get clear to rush him. William junior stood grasping the edge of the table, his pale face working furiously. "With a servant!" he shouted again. "Keeping a whore right under his own mother's roof."

"Stop!" Old William's voice roared out like a thunderclap. "Speak another word and I'll knock you senseless. You may as well know right now that you've been defaming my future daughter-in-law."

Gaylord leaned forward, his face distorted with bewilderment. William junior sank suddenly into his chair with such a thud that they knew his knees had buckled under him. Paul, still standing, folded his arms and stared coldly at Gaylord. "Do you mean?" Gaylord murmured helplessly, "do you say . . . ?"

"I mean just what you think," old Scott answered, spacing his words and snapping them out like blows. "Paul is going to be married to Mary Rafferty with my full consent and approval, and my wife's."

Gaylord sank back against his chair, speechless. William junior looked stupidly at his father. Nobody spoke for many minutes.

Finally Gaylord said, "This is the most outrageous, disgusting scandal—"

William Scott shrugged. "There is nothing scandalous to me in an honorable marriage."

"Honorable!" William junior's mouth spat out the words. "Do you know what those two have been doing behind your back for years?"

"You are nobody to sit in judgment," the Old Man said, "but if it makes it any easier for you to swallow, I will tell you that Paul has never deceived me in the least degree. His feeling for Mary Rafferty is and always has been a credit to him and to her."

"A servant," Gaylord muttered, shuddering. "Oh, this is too unspeakable."

He appeared to shrink together, his head and limbs drawing in toward his body like the parts of a turtle into his shell. His expression was exactly that which would have reflected his stepping into a cesspool. His thin nose was pinched at its extremity, his nostrils flattened.

William Scott sat down again and motioned to Paul to do the same.

"That is the situation," he said presently in a changed tone. "You see exactly what my plans are and I have no wish to hide anything from you."

William junior looked at his father-in-law with a glance of despair. Gaylord sat rigid, keeping his eyes on William Scott. Presently he said, in a voice like ice, "Under these circumstances the only way I can protect my daughter is to sell you my share and take her away from you and your degenerate influence as quickly as possible."

"Julia," said the Old Man, "has hardly been under my influence."

"How much will you give me for my share?" asked Gaylord.

"Just what I said. Twenty-five per cent more than you put in. I will write you a check for the total amount of three hundred and twelve thousand five hundred dollars this minute."

Gaylord's motions were precise and slow, rather as if his hands had been benumbed and he was unable to depend on them.

"I daresay you have a bill of sale right here at hand," he said, his lips stiff.

"Certainly," said old William. "I asked you here to make this transaction, naturally I'd have the papers ready for your signature. Paul, go and call MacTavish."

They waited in bitter silence for the bookkeeper, who shuffled in behind Paul, with his hands full of papers. He laid them down before old William. The Old Man rose and carried them down to Gaylord's end of the table. MacTavish set down an inkwell and a pen at Gaylord's elbow.

Laurence Gaylord picked up the bill of sale gingerly, as if it were a putrid object, and read it through, his face frozen in lines of disgust. Without a word he took the pen and signed his name. Scott signed his. MacTavish witnessed the signatures. MacTavish handed William a check made out for the amount of the sale. William signed it, blotted it, and handed it to Gaylord who folded it after the most cursory of glances and put it in his vest pocket. He rose from his chair.

"The cancelled partnership articles will be mailed tomorrow by registered post from Boston," he said. He spoke to William Scott now in the tone that he would have used to a menial. "I am taking the night train this evening, and my daughter and her husband will go with me. You will never see either of them again, at least during my lifetime."

Young William's pale face was a painful complication of emotions, twisted, furious, and frightened. He looked at his father with baffled eyes, and at Paul with hatred. When Gaylord actually reached for his hat, and ordered William junior by a sign to prepare to accompany him, young William made one helpless, miserable gesture toward his own father. It was a gesture of appeal and of dependence, a sign even now that the filial love of his childhood had not totally disappeared. The Old Man stood, his face turned away in profile. He too was gripped by bitter emotions, and Paul knew, glancing uneasily at the tight lips in the whitening beard, that his father could not part even from a repudiated son without agony of heart. Young William's hand, stretched a few inches toward his father in an unconscious motion, revealed a world of feeling that he had never shown, and Paul knew with galling pity that his warped, misunderstood brother was now exchanging the semblance of bondage for the reality. Paul could see already the life that lay ahead of William, who would be supine under the thumb and the will of Laurence Gaylord.

Old William looked up as his eldest son came close to him. Gaylord had walked out the door, not deigning to speak another word. Young

William paused by his father, his hand still in that half-extended, half-pleading, half-unconscious gesture. His father took the hand and grasped it hard. The Old Man swallowed once or twice, and William's face reddened with the pressure of his feelings.

"Good-bye—son." Old William's lips were stiff.

"Oh, Father—"

The Old Man threw his heavy arm around William's shoulder, gave it a hard clasp, and then released it, slightly propelling William toward the door. Old William turned away and tramped to his inner office. Paul was still standing, between his brother and the door. As young William passed him, his eyes full of tears, he looked up at Paul with a sudden contorting of his face into indescribable rage and hate.

"You," William said in a strangled voice. "As for you, I'll get even with you if it takes me the rest of my life, so help me God!" He hurried through the door, leaving Paul staring after him with a fantastic, cold, hollow sensation in the pit of his stomach.

CHAPTER XXV

[November 1883]

LIKE A THUNDERBOLT the news stunned them all: James Rafferty called his long-threatened strike in the middle of that month. They had all feared it and talked about it and worried about it for so long that when Paul and his father came in late at night, gray-faced and hard-mouthed, Clarissa and Mary dropped their sewing, and gasped, "It's not true. It couldn't be true."

"It is," Paul said. His voice was bitter. The Old Man said nothing. He went at once to his study and Paul, looking after him, said, "We're going down again in a few minutes. We just came home to—"

Mary ran over to him, forgetful that they were not alone, and threw her arms around his neck.

"Please. Darling, please don't—"

Paul took her hands gently away and drew apart. "Mama," he said, "this is going to be a very nasty business. I don't know when you'll be seeing us home. But—"

Clarissa looked up, her blue eyes pained and puzzled.

"Is it"—she swallowed—"will you and Father be in any danger?"

Mary began to cry. Paul laid his hand on her arm to quiet her and said, "I don't know, Mama. I'm sure nobody would hurt either of us. But—well, we've never had a strike. I can't say what it will be like."

Old William came back into the room, buttoning his coat. Paul knew that the Old Man had taken the repeater from his desk drawer and put it in his pocket. Clarissa stood up quickly.

"I've saved your dinner for you," she said, glancing at the clock. It was after eleven. "Won't you eat something?"

"I'd rather not," William said. "I'm in a hurry to get down."

"I wish you would, Father." Paul said. And, as an afterthought, "I'm hungry myself." That was not true.

William said, "Very well, if you can feed us in ten minutes, Clarissa," and left the room with her. Mary ran into Paul's arms.

"Darling." He felt her heart pounding under his hands. "Shouldn't I run down now and talk to James? Before it's too late?"

"It is too late now, dear. Now we'll have to wait until Pa has found out what this can be like. It will be useless to try appealing to Jim until Father is willing to negotiate. We'll have to stick it out."

"Paul!" They heard Clarissa calling from the pantry. "Come and eat your supper."

"Dear God." Mary sobbed as he held her and kissed her good night. She held his face between her hands and whispered, "Don't get into any danger, darling."

He smiled and started out of the room, leading her along. "Not if— not more than I can help when I think of you." He kissed her again. "All right, coming, Mama."

Mary and Clarissa stood on the step and watched the two men out of sight. Mary burst into tears as they turned back into the house and Clarissa tried to comfort her, though she was cold with worry and apprehension herself.

"They'll be all right, Mary dear. Maybe it won't last more than a day or two."

"It's not that," Mary sobbed. "It's—James. My own brother, to do a thing like that on Mr. Scott and Paul. Oh, it's a nightmare, it is." Clarissa smiled faintly. "If it wasn't me own brother I'd not be so sick with misery."

"There, there," Clarissa signed softly. "There, there." She kept her arm around Mary and patted her cheek tenderly.

The Old Man had refused to order the carriage. Now, of all times, he would do precisely as he had always done, in the mill, and going back and forth. He did not talk to Paul. He tramped along, scowling, and Paul kept step, thinking his own tumultuous thoughts. This could have been avoided. He began reproaching himself for all the opportunities he had missed when he might have tried harder to do something. Now circumstances had played into Rafferty's hands as nobody had ever expected. The depressed business of the past few months had culminated in a violent nationwide slump, which had had immediate repercussions in Pittsburgh.

Coke ovens, blast furnaces, and rolling mills had all instantly curtailed their operations and begun laying off large numbers of men. The Old Man had ridden the fluctuating curves of business since the terrible year of 1873 without ever resorting to drastic lay-offs. Not since the lone, epochal occasion when he had banked the Henrietta after the great panic had he considered any radical curtailment of production. The ensuing decade had been one of driving expansion for the Scotts. Paul thought about it with amazement now. It had seen the installation of a Bessemer, two open-hearths, and an extensive and highly specialized rolling mill. Scott steels usually stayed in steady demand because they were all special alloy products required by tool, spring, and precision-implement manufacturers. The ordinary slumps of the business cycle did not affect them radically. But in a thorough-going depression like this, with universal reaction on all financial and industrial activity, the Scott mill could not stay on a normal basis of production. Its orders had fallen away almost to nothing.

The Old Man decided to operate some parts of the mill on a three-day-a-week basis, and to shut down the rest altogether. The Bessemer (which had been little used since the building of Paul's open-hearth department), one of the open-hearth furnaces, and half of the rolling mill were closed down. All the men normally employed in these jobs were laid off. The remaining force would operate the blast furnace, the second open-hearth, part of the blooming mill, and part of the rolling mill in the usual twelve-hour shifts; but only for three days a week.

Paul swore under his breath as he thought now of Jim's reaction to that. Rafferty had gone to the Old Man with the demand that three eight-hour shifts be substituted in the finishing departments for the usual two twelve-hour ones. He had demanded that the wage-rate be kept unchanged, and that men from the closed departments be taken on in the departments that were to keep operating. William Scott refused categorically to consider these demands. He made the refusal more infuriating by pointing out that Rafferty had no authority to make demands of him on behalf of the men, and thus the Old Man, rather than James, reopened for perhaps the hundredth time the question of union recognition for the Amalgamated members in the mill. James took up the challenge with a final ominous demand that Scott not only reconsider his refusal of the eight-hour question, but consent to recognize the Amalgamated, with James as its spokesman, as bargaining agency for all the men in the mill. Scott replied with a contemptuous refusal, and this afternoon James had called out the Amalgamated members on strike.

"Father," Paul said tentatively as they approached the mill—instead of the usual blaze of light and clangor of activity down on the waterfront, there was only cavernous dark and silence—"Father."

"Well?" The Old Man's tone was impatient.

"I know you don't want to hash this over now," Paul said, "but all the best men in the shop are out." He named some of them. "I just want to be sure you know who they are."

"I know who they are!"

"Well. I'm sorry. But the only men left are a bunch of common labor that don't know a billet from a—hell, Pa," he said angrily, "do you realize what we're up against?"

"I do." The Old Man stamped along, glaring straight ahead. "You're the general superintendent. You'll have to hire what hands you need. I'm leaving that up to you."

"That's fine," Paul said bitterly. "Scabs. A fine lot of runs I'll turn out with crews of scabs!"

The Old Man did not answer. Paul champed his pipestem and cursed.

He had set his heart on keeping the mill producing such orders as it would receive in spite of this depression. It was his particular pride that no customer of Scott's had ever been disappointed by a failure in delivery or in specifications of Scott steel. Now it looked as if he would be faced with this, which would have bad reverberations all over the country long after this strike had been settled and dismissed, if not forgotten.

For the first time since the Civil War the mill was patrolled by armed guards; but these were now private police hired by William Scott, not Pennsylvania guardsmen placed there by the Union Army. Day and night uniformed men paced up and down along the tracks beside the mill, along the river bulkhead where the ore boats tied up, through the ghostly shadows of the closed departments, back and forth over the bridge that ran from the street to the mill entrance and spanned the gulley where the tracks lay. The stacks and chimneys towered cold, dour, and lifeless. The black spaces of the rolling mill were ominous with silence more expressive than the wildest clangor of busy times. The Bessemer stood dead like an enormous blown egg. And Paul's beloved open-hearths were a pair of futile, sickened giants. One was totally dead, the other so much a problem that Paul took to never quitting the mill at all during the three days of the week when production was attempted. The scab crew in the rolling mill was just as incompetent as that on the open-hearth. No billets of precise specification could be rolled by bunglers like these. Paul had to watch every step of every rolling. Even then he could not be sure that each lot of billets would turn out fit to ship. In his heart of hearts he felt undeniable sympathy for James and the tough, devoted, marvellously skilled crews who worked with him; he could not endure the sight of the scabs who went through the motions of tending the furnace and the rolls, with results so unsatisfactory that Paul took over the foreman's functions in both departments, knowing that he could not possibly meet these responsibilities single-handed.

When the scabs came to work they were escorted down the hill to the Scott bridge by a platoon of detectives and armed guards. Bristling with rifles, clubs, and other weapons, these guards held off the infuriated pickets, strikers, and Amalgamated sympathizers who swarmed about the vicinity and kept up a continuous turmoil in the street outside the mill. There were almost as many women as men in these violent, threatening, furious crowds. Some of the women hid stones, lumps of coal, and pieces of brick in their shawls, and would stand in doorways along the steep, rutted street, flinging their missiles wildly at the scabs and guards. If any guard detached himself from the the marching platooon to chase down a person whose brickbat had hit him, he would be fallen upon by a mob of strikers, his weapons would be dragged from him, and he would be beaten to within an inch of his life. After two or three such lessons the guards had to let matters go with dodging and ducking the brickbats.

James ran the strike with cold, clear-seeing fury. The conditions under which it had finally taken place gave him and all his men the greatest possible impetus to fight. For, unlike strikes in good times, this one was taking place when most of the men would have been idle anyway, and this idleness at least might yield some permanent benefit for them all. James was everywhere that his strength, passion, and tremendous conviction were needed. He was relentlessly on the go, between conferences with Joseph Bishop and the Amalgamated officers at headquarters; turns on the picket line where his mere presence was an intoxicant to the already excited men and the crowds of sympathetic hangers-on; visits to the families of the men most affected by the situation. It was James who kept them encouraged, provided for, and above all, in the peak of fighting temper.

Mary had not dared to go near him, knowing now that her situation close to the Scotts (even though James could have no inkling of her impending marriage) would only madden him to the point of probable violence. But Paul, after three weeks of the strike, had told her that she had better prepare to get into contact with James when he told her to. He had said more ominously than ever before, "Father will have to back down from this rigid stand of his, or this thing might go on for months."

"Oh, my God. You can't mean it."

"I do. You know how I feel about the whole thing—I think Jim is more than halfway in the right. But right or wrong, this thing has got to be settled."

Mary shook her head. "It's terrible, darling. It's too horrible."

"It will be more horrible if it drags on. Not only for the strikers. The poor devils are going to have a fearful winter anyway. But if this goes on, Mary, our product will be of such rotten quality that our whole business may be undermined. You can't do our kind of work with gangs of scabs." He paced up and down, chewing the stem of his pipe. "Oh, God, how I wish I could get Father to listen to reason."

She caught Paul's hand as he paced past the chair where she was sitting, and looked up at him with strained eyes. "Darling, I'm so worried about you, I am."

"Me? Hell, I'm all right."

"You're not. You're in danger every minute."

"I'm no scab," he snorted. "My position's a little peculiar but no man who ever worked at Scott's would harm me, Mary." He spoke proudly.

Clarissa came into the room, looking tired and distraught.

"I'm so troubled about your father, Paul," she said. She sank into a chair. "He can't stand much more of this."

The Old Man was hardly ever at home, and when he was he scarcely ate or slept at all. He had had an army cot put in his office. While he was at the mill he lived on sandwiches and tea made by MacTavish. Old William stayed at the mill for three or four days and nights at a time, then came home for one night, for a bath and a change of clothes, and left for the mill again the following morning. He and Paul walked down as always, the Old Man stalking through the picket lines with his stern face immobile and his ungloved hands rammed into his ulster pockets. Paul knew that his father might easily have arranged to stay at the mill altogether, but William would never have done that. That would have seemed to him a kind of cowardice. He wanted to show himself, stubborn and adamant, defying the strikers. No possible action could be so fatal to their cause as a personal threat or an injury to William Scott. He knew that, and they knew it; he wanted to bring the fact home to them. When he tramped past them they stood along the curb, sullen and muttering, glaring at him, sometimes even shaking a fist; but nobody took a step toward him, and Paul walking by his side was torn with turbulent feelings of love for his father, futile comprehension of the strikers' rights, and despair at the growing bitterness of the deadlock.

Soon after the strike started, Clarissa was sitting alone at breakfast on a dark morning when her husband and Paul were at the mill. The front door banged open and Edgar rushed into the dining-room.

"Why, Edgar! What are you doing here, son?"

He kissed her and helped himself to a roll, cramming it into his mouth while she poured him some coffee. She rang for bacon and eggs for him.

"Came home to help," he said. "Father and Paul at the mill?"

"Yes. But why—?"

"I thought I'd better come. The papers are full of this, Mama. There's probably something I can do."

Clarissa asked him about his leaving college. He had got a leave of absence from the dean, and he intended to stay at home until the strike was over. Clarissa could not see what use he might be. But Paul was over-joyed to see him. Edgar had worked in the rolling mill all the previous summer, and Paul, tremendously relieved, put him to work there again. Edgar was not experienced enough to take the full responsibility for the finished bars and billets, but Paul could depend on him for vigilance and for protection from the bungling of the scabs whom he could never trust. Edgar worked with enormous gusto. Because of the excitement and the constant possibility of outbreaks of violence, he never left the mill at all. He worked the three-day periods when the open-hearth and the rolls were running, and the remainder of the week he prowled the dark, eerie caverns of the deserted sheds, armed with a rifle and a riot whistle. The Old Man discovered qualities in his youngest son that filled him with amazement and pride.

At the end of the second three-day run Paul announced that it was necessary to re-line the open-hearth. Nobody could be found who could be trusted to do it properly. The plant's brick-man was one of James Raf-ferty's most passionate adherents, and he had gone out taking his crew of three with him. Paul could not risk a slip in the lining job. He was finding it difficult enough to keep his furnace fired constantly at the necessary low heat level to prevent its cooling entirely between charging periods. With the other open-hearth totally out of commission, this one must be tended like a baby to forestall complete breakdown in production. Re-lining was always done in a certain amount of active fire and when Paul sent out a call for a helper who could do the job with him, nobody volunteered. He could not do it alone; two men at least had to alternate in dashes into the red-hot bottom of the furnace. Paul and the Old Man were standing by the open-hearth cudgelling their brains how to get the job done when Edgar came running down the shed from the rolling mill, yelling, "Paul! Wait a minute!"

He ran up and asked, "Why can't I do it?"

"You, Kid? Why, you've never done a brick job. This is a tough order."

"I know. What do you do?"

Paul pointed to the heap of new refractory brick lying near the furnace door.

"You have to climb inside and pry out the burned-out bricks and lay those in their places."

"Well, let's get started."

"Kid, you don't know what you're talking about. I'm not even sure I can do it right any more. I haven't taken a turn at this for years."

"It's got to be done, doesn't it?"

Paul looked at his father. The Old Man nodded heavily. "Go ahead, boys."

They went and got themselves ready. They put on shoes with wooden soles two inches thick, heavy shirts and overalls and tough hand-leathers. The Old Man stood by the furnace between the pile of bricks and the mortar-trough. A hose was attached to an overhead water-pipe and old William held the hose in his hand. Paul took the crowbar, the Old Man turned the hose on him, and Paul stepped dripping through the open fire-door of the furnace. Edgar watched him closely. Paul pitched out the smoking old brick, Edgar handed in a new one and a trowel of mortar. Paul laid the brick, and dashed out of the furnace. His clothes were smoking and gave off a horrible smell of burning cloth. His face was crimson and he was panting and choking. Edgar grabbed the crowbar, stood for a moment under the hose, and dashed in for his turn. The two fell quickly into routine, alternating in dashes into the red-hot box, leaping out again with their clothes and hair singed and smelling vilely, their hands raw from burns in spite of the clumsy protection, their eyes sore and streaming. The Old Man worked between them, hosing them before and after each dash, handing the bricks and the mortar through the door, kicking the old bricks out of the way as the boys pitched them through the opening. Edgar laid the last brick and stumbled out of the furnace. His red face was blackened with soot, his blond hair singed in patches all over his head, one eye closed and swollen from a hot cinder. There was a raw red burn, open and oozing, across the back of his right wrist. Paul was in similar condition, but not so exhausted as Edgar. He caught his brother by the arm as the boy stumbled into the stream of the hose, and held him up while the Old Man played water over him. Edgar crumpled up and they laid him on the floor.

"Pa, do you suppose he's all right?"

William put his hand on Edgar's chest and felt his heart-beats.

"He's fine." Old William's voice was tremulous.

Edgar opened his left eye in a short while and mumbled, "Jesus, that was hot!"

He was soon able to get up and he and Paul walked slowly down the shed and up the ramp to the offices. They undressed and washed. While they were sitting side by side on the Old Man's army cot, smearing carron-oil on their burns, Paul said, "I think I'll send for the carriage to take us home tonight."

"Us?" Edgar looked up from his burned knee which he was gingerly oiling. "You, if you want. I'm staying here."

"You are not. You're dead tired and Mama'll never forgive me if I don't make you go home tonight."

"You and Father go home," Edgar said. "He's more tired than we are. I'm going to sleep here."

"But Ed—"

"You don't think I'd leave the plant with none of us in it, do you? I'm not going."

And he did not. Paul asked his father to try to persuade Edgar to leave, but the Old Man shook his head. "I wouldn't interfere with him for anything on earth, Paul. This is the first real test he's ever had and it'll be the making of him." Clarissa found it hard to agree when they told her about Edgar. She looked at them reproachfully and wiped her eyes with her handkerchief.

"I think it's terrible!" she said. "You must be brutes, leaving that boy alone down there, all burned and sore. Why . . ."

"Clarissa," said old William, "it's the best thing that ever happened to him. I never expected to feel so proud of Edgar. He did a fine thing today."

When Paul told Mary about it later she looked at him with her eyes shining and said, "My, I wish I could tell James about it. He'd think it was grand. Oh, darling, I'm getting so bewildered. I keep wishing—oh—"

"What do you wish?" He was tolding her in his arms. He drew back and looked down at her. "What do you wish? That all this was over and we were married already? God knows I wish that." He gave a weary sigh.

She shook her head gently.

"What do you wish, darling?"

"Oh—oh, I don't know," she murmured. "Everything's so wild and mixed up. I just want—oh, I don't want to think any more."

"Don't," Paul whispered. "It's too late to think. I only know I need you. Oh, Mary—if this drags on—"

She raised her head and looked deep into his eyes. His fingers slipped from her shoulders and curved hungrily over her breasts, feeling them and clinging to them without fear or shame. His eyes probed hers. "Mary, if this drags on, and we can't marry when we meant to—"

She put up her hand and touched a sore red welt above his cheekbone. Her lips were parted.

"I'll have to have you," he said. "I've waited so long."

He held her tight against his hot, aching body. He pressed her shoulders back and leaned over insistently. "I can't wait much longer, Mary. Do you know it? Do you feel it?"

"I feel it," she said. "I know."

CHAPTER XXVI

[*1883—Continued*]

PAUL WAS SPENDING the night at the mill with his father. The two had made rounds at ten o'clock, tramping through the long labyrinth of pitch-dark sheds by the light of a small lantern carried by the guard walking ahead. Their boots echoed grotesquely through the hollow passages. Outside in the areaways between the sheds they would pause and look up, across the gulley, at the clusters of pickets out in the street, warming themselves by a small bonfire, and taking their turns at patrol. Paul knew that at intervals all through the night the wives of these men came stalking down the hill in pairs, carrying pails of hot coffee. The weather was bitter, the cruel piercing cold of early winter, raw with damp and the leadenness which lay on nights that followed sunless days. Bad times and strike times made horrors of Pittsburgh winter nights, when there was never a reassuring glare of light from the cold stacks, when no blowing furnace gave even the sight of warmth to flare across the bitter black sky.

Paul followed the Old Man into his private office and shut the door. A small coal-oil heater was burning here, and the stuffy hot air was almost as uncomfortable as the clammy, penetrating cold from which they had come. The Old Man sat down heavily at his desk and Paul stood, his hands behind his back, his head lowered. He was gray, fagged, and unshaven.

"Father," he said, in a grave voice, "this thing has got to stop."

Old William drew in his lips across his teeth and gave his beard a pull.

"There's no use reopening that, Paul. I will never give in to any union on the face of the earth, and certainly not to Rafferty's union."

"What do you propose to do?"

"Nothing," snapped the Old Man. He looked up defiantly.

"I'm afraid that's exactly what you will do—for longer than you think."

"What do you mean?"

"Father, won't you please believe me? I've told you day after day, the vital question for us is one thing and one thing only. Whether or not our steel is up to standard."

"Our customers know the situation now, Paul. They're all making allowances. You don't think one of them would have me give in to Rafferty, do you?"

"That's neither here nor there," Paul said desperately. "I only know that if we continue to send out stuff like this—" he dragged a pack of specification sheets from his hip pocket and flung it on his father's desk. "Read that over. I've tabulated every single run since this damned strike started. There isn't one lot, Father, not one single lot of stuff, that precisely meets specification!"

The Old Man put out his hand reluctantly and drew the pile of sheets closer. He began running his eye down the lists. Paul had checked the items in colored pencil according to their deviation from quality and standard. Ingots from the open-hearth were checked in blue, bars and billets from the rolling mill in red. There was not a column free of colored marks. William studied the lists in silence.

"Father," Paul said presently, "is that the kind of stuff you're willing to have shipped out of this mill?"

"I told you," the Old Man answered, "that our customers are all making allowances for an emergency."

"For two weeks, maybe three or even four. But damn it, Pa, if you keep this strike in a deadlock with all our men out for months, no customer in the world will make any more allowances. They'll say the hell with us and buy their steel from somebody else. Good God, we've got competitors!"

William sat like a stone image, inscrutable and cold. But Paul saw his eyes move uneasily up and down the telltale columns.

"We've got competitors,' Paul repeated. "Just because business is bad now and the orders are small, don't think we can slop along this way for long. Periods like this are used for experiment, Pa, and investigation. If Disston's decides to try out that new machine disc saw they've been talking about, do you think they'll give us future orders for carbon steel if the samples we send out now are rotten? Somebody else will get those orders."

Paul turned away and paced angrily back and forth across the end of the room.

William said, after a while, "All that may be true, Paul, but I cannot get your attitude about labor out of my head You sympathize with Rafferty, perhaps even halfway. If I give an inch now he'll take a mile."

"If you give an inch now he'll be so amazed he'll be stopped in his tracks."

The Old Man leaned back in his chair and stared at the corrugated iron ceiling.

"I don't know why I feel," he said slowly, "that the personal considerations in this are troubling you more than the business ones."

"That's unfair!" Paul exclaimed hotly. "I'm the one who's got to turn out steel in this place with a gang of thugs and muckers, and you bring up my personal feelings!"

William shook his head slowly again.

"If I did have time to consider my personal feelings," Paul said bitterly after another period of restless pacing, "I'd be kicking because I can't get married when I meant to. This kind of thing isn't—oh, hell."

He sat down heavily on the canvas cot and clutched his head between his hands. His father sat and watched him, slowly tapping his thick forefinger on the pile of papers before him. The old-fashioned clock on the wall ticked startlingly loud. The silence was ponderous. Old William said, finally, "I didn't mean to do you an injustice, Paul."

Paul raised his head. "I know you didn't, Father. But I can't help seeing all the sides of this thing Naturally I'd like to get the strike over and get the mill on a normal basis again so Mary and I can go away. But you must believe me, Father—what's really worrying me is how we'll ever get back the business we'll lose if our product goes to the devil now. And not only the business—the confidence."

William drew a very deep sigh.

"What do you suggest, actually, Paul?"

Paul knew his father too well to give any hint of the relief that welled up and broke over him like a wave. He said quietly, "There would have to be some kind of compromise with Jim Rafferty."

"What kind?"

Paul rose and went over and sat down in the straight-back chair across the desk from his father. He leaned over the desk and spoke calmly, making an effort to keep his voice from showing the intensity of his feeling.

"You'd have to sit down and think over his demands one by one. I admit that all of them together are out of the question, but singly, some of them are not so unreasonable. If you will pick any one of them and agree to accede to that one, I think Jim would give in on the others."

"What makes you think so?"

The Old Man gave Paul a searching look. Paul met it firmly.

"Mary."

Old William's eyebrows went up. After a long deliberation he said slowly, "I can't see what single demand of Rafferty's I could meet without being cornered on some of the others."

"Father," Paul said in a sudden strange burst of tense speech, "take my word for it that if you choose one point to yield on, Rafferty will call off the strike."

"I don't get your meaning fully, Paul."

They stared at each other across the desk. Paul said, finally, "Father, I'm asking you not to try to get my full meaning. All I ask is one thing. And also I ask you to trust me. Will you?"

The Old Man nodded slowly, so slowly that it hurt Paul to see the stiff old neck bend down.

At two o'clock in the morning Paul hurried up Beech Street and banged on the door of Miss Mitchell's house until the frightened lady, in her nightcap and wrapper, came down and called through the door, "Who's there?" Paul explained that he must see Miss Rafferty; a grave emergency. Miss Mitchell let him in and showed him into the parlor. In a few minutes Mary came down, holding her quilted blue wrapper tight around her, her crisp, glowing hair streaming about her shoulders. She was pale and Paul took her quickly in his arms while she asked, "What is it? Who's hurt?"

"Nobody," he said. "But the time's come, Mary. I want you to talk to Jim."

"No!" she gasped. "Do you mean it?"

He nodded, very excited. "I've got the opening wedge driven with Pa. But you must be very careful. Can you remember exactly what I'm going to tell you, darling?"

"Of course. Oh, Paul, I'm so—so—"

"Don't be too happy about it yet. It may fall through. But this is what I want you to say to Jim."

He led her over to the horsehair sofa and they sat down close together, their heads almost touching. Paul talked sharply and rapidly, in a low voice, marking off on his fingers the specific points she was to make with Jim, and watching her closely to see that she understood precisely. She listened intently, nodding slowly while he spoke. Her hair streaming about her shoulders and down over the pale blue mull of her robe was a beautiful, glowing sight in the gaslight; at any other time Paul would have been swept off his feet by the picture she made. But he did not take notice of that until she had repeated his words exactly, and he was satisfied that she was fully prepared to talk to Jim. Then he sat silent for a moment, staring at her as if the full impact of her beauty, warm and dishevelled and just risen from bed, had struck him for the first time in his life. She saw his face turn pale, his lips stiffen. Very slowly he put out his burned, stained hand and opened the small buttons of her ruffled nightgown, laying her white breasts bare. She sat rigid, her eyes wide and probing his. Suddenly he put his bristly face down hard between her breasts, gripping her light body as he had never felt it before, soft without its stays and fitted basques. "Oh, God," he groaned aloud. "Oh, God." He was dirty; he smelled of grease and smoke and sweat.

Deep and hard inside her body her blood pounded through turgid muscles and she clung to him, the whole pliant length of her body tight against his. She knew now, she had never remotely known before, the full drive of her desire for him. When he raised his head she put her hands on either side of his face and held it close to her own, staring at him, her gray eyes enormous, their pupils glittering. She spoke in a hard, strained voice, very low, sensing before she said it that she was about to cast aside the last verbal shadow between them; and that he wanted her to. "I want you, Paul." She could not believe herself capable of such boldness. But she was deeply excited, fiercely proud, because she had shown it.

He kissed her once on the mouth. "That is right," he said. "That's what it is. And soon, darling. Damned soon."

"I'll see James before light in the morning," she whispered as she let him out the door. He nodded and after she closed the door behind him she stood leaning against it, her forehead pressed against the wood, listening to his footfalls in the distance.

She did not sleep again, and at five o'clock she was on her way to the Flat. When she pushed open the door of the shack, James was already up, standing by the stove pouring watery coffee into a tin cup. Patrick was asleep in the bedroom. James looked up as she came in, jerking up his head like an angry animal.

"Wha—what the hell do ye want?"

"I want to talk to you."

"Ye've nothin' to say to me. Clear out. Back to—yer—yer—" she saw he had no words brutal enough to describe the Scotts.

"I'm going to talk to you," she said, "and I see you're in a hurry. So if you want to save time, you'll listen. You're not going to leave this house until you've heard what I came to say."

He shrugged.

Mary shut the bedroom door and from force of habit began to help James with his breakfast. But there was no porridge to cook, and nothing to eat in the house except some crusts of stale bread. She knew he had given all his food to the wives of the strikers. She poured herself a cup of the bad coffee and sat down at the table opposite him. He looked at her, at first with suspicion, and then with a strange new look of tolerance and expectancy in his dark eyes. But he said, "Ye'll have to get it said awful quick, see, I've a rare bad day ahead o' me and I'm leavin' right off."

"All right," she said. "James, will you consider a compromise settlement of the strike if William Scott meets you halfway?"

He drew down the corners of his mouth and bent his scowling eyes on her in amazement.

"And what," he asked, "is yer authority fer comin' to me with this?"

Mary swallowed and stared at him coolly. "Paul Scott."

"Ah. I thought so."

"It'll be better for us both," she said gently, "if we don't go into any details about that. But I am here because Paul told me to come, and the first part of his message is that he wants you to trust him. He thinks more of you than any man he knows, James. Do you believe that?"

The thin, bitter face opposite her twitched queerly. "I expect I do."

"Paul says he cannot run that mill without you and your men and he isn't afraid to let you know it. The trouble is the Old Man."

"Do I need ye to tell *me?*"

"Paul has got his father to consent to yield to you on some one point of the demands you're striking for. He—"

James leaped to his feet, fury in his face.

"*Wan* point!" he roared.

"Wait," Mary begged. "For the love of God, wait and let me finish, James. I've nowhere near finished."

He sat down again, doubtful and on his guard.

"If you will yield on the rest of the questions after the Old Man gives in to you on one of them, the mill can start running properly again and the business will be out of danger. The men will all get their jobs back the minute times are better."

"And a fine monkey I'd be if I let him curl me tail like that!" James snarled.

Mary leaned across the table and looked at him quietly. "James," she said. "This arrangement would only be in force for the length of the Old Man's life."

He dropped his tin cup onto the table and stared suspiciously. "What are ye gettin' at?"

Mary said, "James, who'll be the head of Scott's when the Old Man's gone?"

"What difference'll that be?"

Mary smiled. "You know just as well as I do. Paul thinks pretty nearly the same as you about every important thing to do with that mill. That is the exact truth about his offer. James, if you'll find a way to compromise about this strike with the Old Man, Paul sends you his word that you can have the rest of your demands the day he takes over the Scott Iron Works. Eight-hour day, union shop, whatever you want—so long as it's you asks it and not some outside organizer."

James sat in astounded silence.

"Well I'll be God damned," he said slowly at last.

Mary reached over and timidly put her hand on his arm.

"Will you, James? Will you?"

He looked down at her hand lying on his hairy arm; the hand white, slender, and delicately cared for, transformed from the hard red one that had helped to bring him up, washed and cooked and cleaned for him. His arm beneath her hand was scarred and sinewed, soot from a thousand firings ground into the coarse network of its skin. James looked up and his smoldering eyes met Mary's deep-set gray ones, glistening with restrained tears.

"Ye love him somethin' terrible, don't ye, Mary?"

"Terribly," she whispered.

James laid his black, horny left hand, with its broken and rutted nails and short, stiff dark hairs, over the small white one lying on his right arm. He leaned over and gave Mary a long look of deepest and most ominous intensity.

"God help ye both if ye ever let me down," he said.

Mary ran all the way to the Scott house and burst, panting, into the dining-room. Only Paul and Clarissa were there, finishing their breakfast. Paul jumped up and took her in his arms. He did not need to ask what James had said. Clarissa began to cry. "Oh, I'm so glad it's over," she said repeatedly. "I'm so glad."

"It's not over yet, Mama, but the worst is," Paul said. "Mary, did Jim say where and when?"

She shook her head. "He only said he'd be waiting at the Amalgamated office at two o'clock this afternoon for somebody to settle where to meet your father. He said to tell you he would not be willing to meet inside the mill."

Paul gulped the last of his coffee and hurried out of the room. "We can arrange all that," he said, "don't expect us home till you see us." He rushed out, banging the front door behind him. Mary and Clarissa sat on, side by side, silent while the waitress moved about removing dishes from the table. They were so carried away by their thoughts that they did not even notice the curious glances that the uniformed servant threw at Mary.

Edgar hurried back to the mill from Amalgamated headquarters where he had met Jim Rafferty. He was full of excited importance; never in his life had he been given such responsibility, and he did not know that Paul had chosen him as emissary because of his very innocence of the true nature of the agreement. He ran across the bridge and down to his father's office, while the Old Man and Paul stood at the grimy window and watched him coming.

"Jim says," he panted, "he'll come for the meeting at eleven tomorrow morning."

"Here," asked Paul, incredulously. "I thougnt—"

"Outside. Out on the bridge. He says it must be out there in full daylight, in view of anybody who wants to watch."

Paul saw in this a desire of Jim's to make as much of the settlement as public as possible, clearly in a reaction from the secrets involved. Paul himself felt the same. Every time he looked at the Old Man he had to fight down a wave of guilty uneasiness. The whole thing smacked too strongly of collusion. Yet all the past sleepless night Paul had ground the problem over and over in his mind and his conscience. He loathed deceiving his father, but always he came back to the certainty that he was right in his promises to Jim. And there was no other way to break the deadlock.

"Jim," Edgar hurried on, "says he is bringing a committee of ten men with him. All old hands—Mike Molloy and Tim Callahan and the O'Briens—men like that. He says—"

The Old Man was staring out the window, slowly shaking his head. His hands were rammed deep in his pockets and Paul knew that his hard fists were clenched. Paul's heart ached. It was agonizing to have to face this bitter humiliation to his father. The Old Man was beyond words. To have to stand there, listening to terms that Rafferty—that anybody—had laid down! Edgar in his impetuosity was rushing on with his account of the terms.

"We—you—should bring ten men of your own choice," he said. "Nobody on either side is to talk to the other, except Jim as spokesman for the Amalgamated and you, Father—"

Even Edgar paused then as he saw the dark angry color rising above his father's whitening beard. Old William locked his lips together and they heard him breathing hard and loud through his nose. Edgar looked uneasily and questioningly at Paul. All of a sudden he did not like this job any more. He wished somebody else had the duty of saying these things to his father. Paul sighed and said, "Is there anything else, Ed?"

Edgar licked his lips nervously. "One thing more. Both sides have got to agree to come without guns or weapons of any kind. Jim has to have your word for that before he'll go through with this."

Paul said, "Is he waiting down there for our answer?"

"I'm supposed to go right back and tell him what you—" Edgar turned scarlet and blurted—"what Father—says."

There was some silence, while the old wall clock ticked loud and the empty, idle yard outside the windows dramatized the hollow quiet. Paul turned to the Old Man, but did not say anything. He waited. After a time old William turned heavily from the window and growled, "You can go back to Rafferty and tell him I will meet his conditions, Edgar." Then he gathered himself together as if for a lunge at an adversary and barged out of the office, down the ramp toward the dark idle sheds. Paul stood and watched him and was neither surprised nor ashamed when he had to put up his hand and smear tears out of his eyes.

Who could know that an evil unknown tongue would wag idly, uselessly, viciously, and vanish back into the mouth of darkness? Who could find the meddler, who uncover the liar? None could; and if any had, there was to be no undoing of a dire wrong. James Rafferty himself did not know, though he believed a boy, a cinder-monkey from another mill, who rushed up to him as he was leaving Amalgamated headquarters on that dark December morning, and reported a wretched story that someone had gabbed along to him. James had not rested all night. He had sat in headquarters laying down the law to some of the union officers who were skeptical of the proposed Scott settlement. He had talked and argued until he was stiff, hoarse, exhausted, hungry, and sick from lack of sleep. Then he quit the smoky, dirty, littered offices and started out to join his men and go to the meeting with William Scott.

That was when that boy rushed up to him in the street and told him the story that was squirming from lip to lip among the millworkers in shantytown.

"I don't believe ye," James said, pushing the lad aside and walking on. James might have his own deadly quarrels with the Scotts, but he had never known the Old Man or anybody authorized by him to go back on a promised word.

The boy held on to James's sleeve, insisting. The thing was so unbelievable that James stopped in a doorway and listened against his will. He tried to tell the boy off. But the lad kept on hotly insisting. " 'Tis true," he blabbed. "Denis Naylor and them all swore them detectives wud—"

"Denis Naylor?" James scowled. That was no fool of a boy. That was an old union man from Sons of Vulcan days. "And Tom Cullen, ye say?"

The lad nodded vehemently. The look of violent bewilderment in James's dark, drawn face was followed by a sudden lowering of his heavy brows, a frozen, furious setting of his hard mouth. He turned back into headquarters, wildly pushing men out of his way, and reappeared in a moment on the steps again, his fists clenched and his eyes narrowed to inscrutable shadows. He walked quickly away through the gloomy streets.

CHAPTER XXVII

[December 1883]

PRECISELY AT ELEVEN O'CLOCK William Scott emerged from the main entrance of the mill onto the bridge. He led a group of ten men, among whom were Paul and Edgar, MacTavish, Henry Wilkins, and six of the plant guards and watchmen. Their hands were empty, and in spite of the bitter, biting cold, their jackets were unbuttoned. Nobody wore an overcoat. From the street side of the bridge a group of ten men detached themselves from the mass of shivering, solemn-faced men and women gathered on the pavement. With James a few steps in advance, they walked halfway the length of the span and stopped. James and William Scott stood perhaps fifteen feet apart, each alone, with his men grouped a dozen paces behind him.

"I am prepared," William Scott began in a firm, calm tone, "to discuss with you in the presence of these men your demands of me as owner of the Scott Iron Works."

"Let us take up the questions wan by wan," James said. "Shall I tell them off or will ye?"

"You name them," Scott said, "in order of their importance to your union."

"Furrst, we demand a closed shop in the Scott Iron Wurrks under the jurrisdiction of the Amalgamated Association of Iron, Steel, and Tin Wurrkers."

Scott's face was stony and he gave no visible reaction. "Go on."

"Second, we demand a uniforrm wage scale throughout the Scott Iron Wurrks based on the fifth district scale price fer puddlin' as agreed at the scale convention of last April."

"That scale is six dollars per ton," Scott said. "It is fifty cents higher than the present Pittsburgh scale."

"And the wage scale in the finishin' departments to be in the same proportion," Rafferty continued.

Scott turned silent again.

"Thurrd, we demand an eight-hour day fer all men employed in the finishin' departments."

"What about the furnace men?" Scott asked. There was a note of cold sarcasm in his voice.

"Boilers, heaters, melters, and puddlers to fix their own hours and those o' their helpers and 'prentices."

Scott opened his mouth to demand an explanation. But he shut it again and merely said, "Go on."

"Fourth," continued James Rafferty, "we demand the right to a joint conference at least wance a year, between the management o' the Scott Iron Wurrks and the representatives o' th' Amalgamated Association. This joint agreement meetin' shall fix wage scales and all other employment conditions fer that year."

He paused then and stared across the space at William Scott. His eyes, glaring straight at the Old Man, were laden with such explosive emotion that Paul, trying to read them, could not dare to interpret everything he thought he saw there. He could see that Jim was holding himself in the clamp of extraordinary self-control. He knew that this whole performance was, but for its hidden factors, a horrible kind of farce which he and Jim must play through, and put the Old Man through, for the sake of their mutual future. He looked at Jim in desperate suspense. Something in the expression of those narrowed, glittering dark eyes eluded him and filled him with foreboding. Paul tried hard to catch Jim's eye but the tense Irishman ignored him.

"Is that all?" Scott asked.

"Them is our basic demands."

"Then we will proceed to discuss them. First, the question of the closed shop. I will state in the briefest possible terms that I am willing under certain conditions to recognize and bargain collectively with the Amalgamated Association, as a free union in my plant. I am not willing to sign a closed shop agreement."

There. was a murmur from the cluster of men grouped behind James, which spread like a wave to the anxious, attentive crowd at the bridge-head. Both speakers ignored the sounds.

"Second, on the subject of the wage scale you demand. I will and I do pay a uniform wage scale in the Scott mill, based not on the fifth district price but on the Pittsburgh district price which is five dollars and a half a ton for puddlers, and for finishing hands in proportion."

The murmur behind James was louder now.

James said, "That wud be no increase, then, from the present wage scale."

"I pay the standard scale of the Pittsburgh district, as paid by all members of the Association of Iron Manufacturers."

Paul looked earnestly at James again. This time Paul's steady blue eyes met James's smouldering, smoky brown ones, and an almost imperceptible flash passed between them. James jerked his head in a motion toward William Scott and said, "What else?"

"On the subject of hours," old William said. "I fail to understand fully the distinction you make between the roll hands and other finishing men for whom you demand an eight-hour day, and the boilers, heaters, and puddlers who are to fix their own hours. What exactly do you mean by that?"

James stared at the Old Man for a moment, not speaking at all. He seemed about to launch into a long explanation of the question. Then he changed his tone and gave old William a shrewd look from under his lowered eyelids.

"Ye know as well as me," he said tersely, "why boilers has got to fix their own hours. Ye been about here a long time yerself."

"Of course I know!" Scott exclaimed in the full-voiced roar that was the first natural sign he had shown this morning. Paul smiled faintly. He was amused at the sudden assertion of understanding by the two deep-dyed old iron hands. "They'd never get their six heats in if they only worked eight hours. They'd never boil a ton a day."

Old William was using the vernacular of the old puddling furnaces, though practically all the pig produced now at Scott's was blast furnace iron from the Henrietta. Still, with a few variations of condition, the situation was basically the same.

"As for rollers, roughers, catchers, and helpers," the Old Man continued, "I'd need a lot more proof from your union than I've ever had that those men want an eight-hour day themselves. So long as the tonnage system is in operation, and I don't notice anybody protesting about that—your men are going to work as many hours as they need to roll the tonnage they want to get paid for."

James raised his eyebrows and behind him he heard the growls of what sounded very like approval. Old Scott had hit the eight-hour question as squarely as the skullbuster in the mill hitting a ton of slag. The eight-hour day was a burning theory in the mouths of Amalgamated officers and organizers, but the iron and steel workers really wanted none of it. They were concerned with individual pay for maximum tonnage output. It was actually technicians like Captain Bill Jones who were advocating the eight-hour day in the belief that it would increase efficiency and improve the quality of the steel.

"The present emergency," William went on, "made you open up this eight-hour question in the effort to spread the available work over as many finishing hands as possible. In normal times you know as well as I do we are all better off on the twelve-hour basis."

"Those as always has jobs may be."

"In this mill most of the hands always have jobs and you know it."

William thrust his beard belligerently at James. "Now let's get on to the next question," he said. Paul heard the Old Man's voice slacken and saw his shoulders quiver as a gust of icy wind pierced his clothing. "Your last condition is contingent on your first one. If you have a recognized union in this mill, its function would be to meet at stipulated intervals to discuss pertinent questions with the management. But this mill will remain an open shop and all joint agreements will remain cognizant of that fact. Now have you any further specific demands to lay down as points of the present discussion?"

"I have not."

"Then I make you the following offer. Taking all your demands into consideration, and dismissing the eight-hour day question as admittedly absurd, I offer you union recognition by the Scott Iron Works of the existing members of the Amalgamated Association now on the payrolls of the mill."

The reverberating murmur from the workers began to grow louder. Old William raised his voice to make himself heard above the crowd. "I will permit," he said—and the moment the word was pronounced Paul saw that it had been a bad error, for James's face contracted—"I will permit the *present* duly enrolled members of the Amalgamated employed in the Scott Iron Works to function as a union and to send their duly elected representatives from among my employees to represent them in dealings with me."

"What do ye mean by present enrolled members?" James's words were menacing.

"Just what I say. I will recognize as a union those employees now already enrolled in the Amalgamated Association. I will not countenance agitation for non-union members to enroll and I will not be restricted to union members in the hiring of men in the future."

"What's that ye say?" "The hell wid ye." "What's in that fer us?" "What'll we get out o' that?" These and many other angry protests swelled the confused roar from James's adherents.

James seemed for a moment to hesitate, bitter-faced and furious. Then he wheeled sharply to the crowd behind him and snapped, "Be still!" He turned back to face old William again. Paul saw that he was making an extraordinary effort to control his temper, and he saw too that the Old Man's tremendous, dignified impassivity was a superhuman domination of his angry feelings by his will. Paul felt the contempt that charged every word of his father's hollow proffered concession to James. He felt even more the outrage blazoned on the faces of the two impassioned groups behind James—the ominous, clamoring crowd of angry men and shawled women knotted together in the street, and the tight-lipped, bitter-tempered group of ten heavy-fisted ironworkers standing back of James. Paul looked about his father's group of which he was a part. In the swift comparison which shaped itself in his mind he turned, sickened, from the dull, brutish faces of the indifferent guards, and from the arrogance of Henry Wilkins and the pettiness of Richard MacTavish, both thinking only of the pecuniary side of the company's well-being. Edgar stood there somewhat uncomprehending, so grave were these issues which he was only now meeting face to face. Paul looked again from his father to James Rafferty. The two passionate, powerful men personified everything that made Paul's world. He loved them both, his father at this minute with desperate devotion, knowing that this experience was agony to the rigid, domineering, noble old man.

James was facing old William and was still keeping his temper, Paul saw, in the face of intolerable provocation. He said, "If there was a union like this ye describe, it wud be nothin' but a joke—a sop. How can ye have a union if ye can't stren'then it wid new members? And what good wud it be to bargain wid ye if ye say aforehand ye won't listen to no more demands?"

"Take it or leave it," said William Scott. "Partial union recognition is a lot more than none. I still have the right to do things my own way in my own mill."

"Ye ain't got the right to own men body and soul. Ye ain't got the right to tell 'em what they'll think or not think."

"I have the right to test the sincerity of your intentions. I am willing to prove the validity of mine. I cannot go a step further than my present offer. I regard it as a test of your trustworthiness."

James's control dropped from him like a curtain ripped from a window pane. Paul saw the steely muscles knot in his naked forearms and saw, with unbelieving horror, suppressed fury break like fire through the hard mask of his face.

"Trustworthiness!" James screeched, bending his legs under him like an animal preparing to spring. "Ye dirty two-timin' bastard! Ye lyin' coldblooded coward! I started out here to meet ye this day square and honest like a man I'd trust! We wasn't to bring no arms or weapons here, we wasn't." His voice was spinning from the top of his skull, a fearful and fantastic scream. He stood half crouched, crazily at bay, his mouth twisted open, his back bent, his head lowered. Paul, with his heart bucking up into his throat, his hand blanketing his mouth, moved in blind despair close to his father. The Old Man stood like a rock, brave, contemptuous, and uncomprehending.

"Pa." Paul could not get the word out.

James Rafferty still crouched, mouth open, swinging with terrible crazy rhythm from side to side.

"I have never repudiated my word in my life," said William Scott. His eyes lay fearlessly on James. "I gave my word."

"Yer word's a fraud!" screamed James. He did not change his position.

Paul tore his eyes from his father to look in desperate haste at every man in his group. All stood stunned; in each face Paul saw total perplexity. He raised his voice and shouted, "Jim! For Christ's sake, listen to me. Nobody's armed. There's no gun here." James did not hear him. Now clearly crazed from the effect of that wretched, tragic piece of gossip, he watched like a snarling animal while Scott and the men behind him stood frozen in moments that seemed to Paul each a century of horror. Then Paul lost forever the power to remember precisely what happened. The guards behind his father were stirring; this was the kind of thing they expected. They were surging forward menacingly and Paul gave a strangled cry as one of them reached automatically for the gun he would ordinarily have had on his hip.

"Stop," Paul tried to say. "Keep your hand still." But it was too late. James had seen. With an animal scream he leaped forward, and Paul's desperate effort to fling himself in front of his father came one instant after James, gibbering and squealing, had whipped a revolver from his pocket and shot straight at Scott.

Up on the hill, not many paces from the stirring, murmuring crowd at the bridgehead, Mary was hurrying down to stand where she could see the expected handshake that would mark the end of the strike and the beginning of a new world for her and Paul. She reached the vantage point as James first crouched, crazed, to the attack. Even at that distance, she knew too horribly what had happened. She could not hear a word that James was saying, but from his maniacal actions she could imagine what it was. Somebody had told him, why she was never in all her life to know, that the Scott guards were armed. Nothing—nothing else in the whole catalogue of tragedy and violence—would explain what he was doing now. She lifted up her voice, though the increasing thunder from the people below her made it a futile whimper, and screamed against the ebb of her strength, "James! Brother James! For the sacred love of Jesus and Mary —no—no—no—"

That was when she saw William Scott pitch leadenly forward, and saw the knot of men behind him rush out and fall, a mass of flailing fists and boots, on the hump in the middle of the bridge. As the pool of James's blood spread quickly, beaten and kicked out of his body, she went down like an animal on her hands and knees, and now the sound she made, so high and so wild that it rose above all the noise of terror and riot, was the fearful piercing sound of her ancestor women's keening. "Ochone. . . ." The thin, frightful wail floated high over the black morning. "Ochone. . . ."

CHAPTER XXVIII

[*December 1883–January 1884*]

ON THE FLAT all time had suspended. Mary moved through stark, stunned days and lay staring and numb through nights of black infinity. She did not know how long she had been there in her father's house; she did not remember going there; she did not remember shrieking, kicking, tearing herself from somebody who tried to lead her, and making her way to the shack where she had sunk into a dark corner, moaning and shuddering. She did not know who they were, the people who tried to break through the barricaded door, shouting to her in voices strange to her deafened ears—Kate's voice, Father Reilly's voice, Paul's voice—"Mary. Mary. Mary, Mary." She had only moaned and wailed louder to drown them out.

After a time they stopped. After a time there was silence, silence all about her, deep enough to bury the passage of days. She was alive, she was some sort of machine that saw old Patrick's clumsy movements, that knew he was there, that went in terror to the door when it realized at last that he must be fed. There on the step was a jug of milk. Blindly she took it, fed some to Patrick, retched at the thought of swallowing anything herself. One thing she wanted, she knew no other thought: to be dead.

One day she shrank from the filth of her neglected father; the next day she went automatically through the motions of making him clean. She looked at his toothless mouth wagging open, with dull surprise that it said nothing; then she remembered the collapse of the old man's senses. It seemed natural that this witless shell was all that there was for her to live with.

Mornings she found the milk on the doorstep, neither wondering nor caring who put it there. Sometimes a loaf of bread lay beside it. Sometimes she cut off a crust and sat by the table chewing it without knowing what she did. The functions of her body amazed and infuriated her. How could this thing go on defying her when she willed it so desperately to stop?

Paul was standing by his father's open hillside grave, with his knot of veiled and black-clad relatives around him, and all the occupants of the train of carriages grouped about the scene, when he raised his eyes from the coffin in its canvas hammock and looked with sudden instinct down the hill to the winding street below the cemetery. The first word of the committal was on the minister's lips.

"Wait!" said Paul. The word fell like a blow on iron.

He raised his head and sent a stony glance of command about the group. He had not looked at their faces until now. All the way from the church he had stared fiercely and blindly ahead, seeing and recognizing nothing. He saw now in a sweeping glance the veiled, bowed, black figure of his mother, supported by her eldest son and her tall, kindly brother. He saw the shapeless forms of Elizabeth and of Sophia Kane and of

Louise; and he heard Louise's maddening whimpers which would not stop. He saw his brother Edgar, ghastly pale and red-eyed but brave as William Scott's son should be brave. He felt the empty place in his own heart, the place his wife should have filled beside him here in tragedy. And then his eyes travelled back down the slope from the graveyard hill. He heard the shuffle of heavy boots as the long, long line of mourners came tramping on. He knew,—as if he had been there himself he knew that the mangled body of James Rafferty had been carried on the shoulders of these men of the Amalgamated the whole two miles to its grave. He knew the rite by which the dead man's brothers had turned the earth into that grave, passing the spade from hand to hand. He knew how his father's own men, with old Michael Molloy at their head, had turned from that graveside with their shabby, sobbing wives, and marched here to this one.

He and his stood in breathless silence while the long, motley queue wound through the gate and moved up close to the graveside. Some of the top-hatted mourners moved to make room for the grim-faced, bearded, huge-handed ironworkers, dressed in faded workshirts, dungarees, nondescript jackets and dirty caps. One by one they lifted their ragged head-coverings and crushed them in their hands. When the last of them was there, the whole crowd clustering tightly at one side of the grave, some with tears rolling unconstrained into their blackened beards, Paul made a sign to the clergyman. And when the sound broke over their bowed heads, the terrible clanking of the lowering chains following the committal words of the stern Calvinistic faith, many scarred hands went up in the sign of the cross, and rough Irish tongues murmured, "God have mercy on his soul." There was a low groan from Clarissa, a sob from Louise. Paul turned in the first spadeful of earth, then handed the spade to William. It went next to Edgar. Convention then would have had the mourners go away and leave the work for the gravediggers to finish. But Michael Molloy stepped forward and took the spade from Edgar. He turned his spadeful, handed the tool to the next ironworker in line. One by one, as they had done for Rafferty, the men who had loved old William paid him the tribute of their hands.

Riding back in the carriage Paul kept his arms folded and his jaws locked, staring at the coachman's back. If he could only keep this dumb, black insensibility, if he could only stay too stupefied to think or to feel, if he could only stop waiting for the moment which lay beyond the edge of every crucifying hour, the moment when he would see and hear and put his hands on Mary again, and begin again to remember, to think, and to feel. He wanted a silence and a solitude as absolute as that which held his father now. But on the very steps of the house as he re-entered it with his quaking mother on his arm, Henry Wilkins touched his elbow and said meaningly, "Now, Paul."

They had to gather, by a tradition like all the other horrible traditions that had been moving them about like ghostly checkers on a phantom board, in the dining-room. There in the gloomy gaslight with the dark blinds drawn to shelter the house in mourning, and the family sitting in their black clothes rigidly about the bare black oak table, Henry Wilkins stood up in his place, unfolded the thick document in its blue legal binder, cleared his throat, and began to read. Paul clenched his fists, bracing himself for the words to come. The will had been written by Wilkins, to be sure, but Paul knew as he had known every line and contour of his beloved father's head, that the Old Man had dictated this will himself, with gruff admonitions to Wilkins to keep it clear of legal terminology.

"I, William Campbell Scott of Allegheny City in the Commonwealth of Pennsylvania, being of sound mind and memory, do make, publish, and declare the following. . . ."

This, thought Paul, is Henry Wilkins' element. He likes this. His voice. His bearing. He likes it. Paul had to pull himself together to hear the words, rather than merely the pompous twanged drone of the voice as it went on reading. I must listen, Paul told himself doggedly. I must pay attention.

The others were listening closely, judging by their faces, but he doubted if his mother understood a word. She sat rigid, expressionless, both horribly harrowed and in an unbelievable way, beautiful, her stunned face presaging the look that it would wear itself in death.

Wilkins intoned the conventional provisions for payment of debts and expenses, the usual introductory passages to any will. Then the distribution of personal effects and family heirlooms, unremarkable in their equal division among the five children. A substantial bequest to Richard MacTavish. A clearing-up, Paul thought, of all the small matters that filled the periphery of any earthly life. Then Wilkins paused, cleared his throat again, sipped some water, and read portentously, "Article Five." William junior stirred and lifted his head for a narrow ominous glance at Paul. Here it comes, Paul thought. Here is the rest of my whole life, here it will be laid down for me. Wilkins's voice droned on, while Paul listened, heavier and heavier in thought and heart as the whole impact of his father's stipulations settled like the Old Man's hand itself, heavy and forceful on his shoulders. The full meaning of his father's intentions for the mill appeared to strike all the others before it penetrated clearly to Paul. Though he had known that something like this would come, he raised his head with a puzzled stare of incredulity as it became clear that he was now the arbiter not only of the mill itself but of the property of the entire family as well. As he watched the faces of his brothers and his sister, the queer veil between his comprehension and his ears lifted suddenly; his mind cleared, and with cruel vividness he had a picture of his father, stern and dour and precise, laying down these ironclad provisions to Wilkins.

In their simplest interpretation they divided the ownership of the Scott Iron Works into six equal partnership shares. Paul's share was left to him outright. Those of his mother, of William and Edgar, Elizabeth and Constance, were left them conditionally; and the conditions they must accept drew a gasp of amazement from Elizabeth, a dull snort from William. All must sign an article of agreement granting to Paul the sole and absolute control of the mill, without the necessity of consulting anybody as to procedures, finance, or policy. There were rigid restrictions on the sale of any of the partnership shares. No partner might sell his share except to Paul himself without subjecting the proposed sale to a vote of all the partners. If any partner or partners proposed to sell their share to any party other than Paul, the matter must be decided by majority vote of all the partners. Heirs signing the conditional agreement would, upon Paul's death receive outright title to their shares, or if they predeceased Paul, their shares would be divided among their issues. Clarissa's share upon her death was to be divided into five parts, each part added to the share of each of her children upon the same conditions as his original share. And finally—here everybody stirred and a wave of amazed, muffled exclamations circled the table—if any heir should refuse to sign the conditional agreement, he would during his lifetime receive his proportion of the earnings of the business, but his partnership upon his death would revert outrightly to Paul.

Wilkins himself paused at this point and looked searchingly around the table, shoving out his chin between its muttonchop whiskers and peering over his spectacles as if to make sure that each person had understood. He met a variety of reactions. Clarissa had hardly listened at all. Elizabeth, sitting beside her husband, set her lips a little more stiffly than before, and exchanged with Benjamin a look that was at once a worry and a reassurance to Paul. Clearly Elizabeth's husband had expected to become the custodian of her property. He could not conceal altogether his discomfiture that he would have nothing to do with it. But Paul was grateful that he would not have to come to grips with his dour brother-in-law. Edgar had listened dully to the reading, seemingly not much interested in its provisions; but he gathered enough of its import through the clouds of his bewilderment and misery to give Paul a look of understanding and affection. Constance's vividness was somehow emphasized by her absence. Paul thought briefly of her as he exchanged glances with Edgar. But when his eyes went, irresistibly compelled, to his elder brother, he sickened at the sight of William's pale face. Ever since William's arrival twenty-four hours ago, Paul's agony of heart and fearful preoccupation of mind had been pierced by awareness of his brother. Paul himself in those unearthly hours had scarcely grasped the fact of Mary's absence, but he remembered now the steely edge on the whisper in which William had asked where she was. Paul had not answered, and only turned on his brother a glance of horrified bewilderment. He did not know then that William had interpreted that as a statement that Paul was through with Mary because of what James had done. Paul did not know, nor did he care, that his secret was safe with William, who considered now that he and Julia were reprieved from disgrace.

There was a long, shocked silence while the family digested the hard core of the will. Then Henry Wilkins continued with the reading. The house on Western Avenue was left to Paul, with the proviso that Clarissa have a life tenure of it. The contents of the house, the furniture, the horses and carriages and all the accumulations of a substantial life, were bequeathed to Clarissa. There were bequests to the Protestant Orphan Asylum, to the Presbyterian Hospital, to the Home for the Friendless, to the

First Church of Allegheny, "in memory of my revered parents, William and Henrietta Campbell Scott."

There was finally a paragraph directing "my executors to form from the residue of my estate, comprising bonds of the United States Government, common stock of the Pennsylvania Railroad, and cash, six trust funds the income of which they shall pay out as follows:

"To Sophia Driscoll Kane, the widow of my friend, Richard Kane, the sum annually of one thousand two hundred dollars, payable quarterly for the duration of her life. If Louise Kane, the daughter of the said Sophia Driscoll Kane, survive unmarried after the decease of her mother, I direct my executors to pay to the said Louise Kane, following the decease of her mother, the sum annually of eight hundred dollars in quarterly payments, for so long as she remains unmarried.

"To the following named persons, all of whom for periods of years have served me and my family loyally and faithfully, each for the duration of his or her life the sum annually of six hundred dollars, payable quarterly:

> Peter McCready
> Joel Dunn
> Margaret Handy
> Sarah Gilligan

"To Mary Rafferty for the duration of her life the sum annually of one thousand dollars, payable quarterly."

The will concluded with the appointment of Paul, Wilkins, and another member of his firm as executors. Wilkins stopped reading, removed and folded up his spectacles, sent another inquisitional glance about the table, and slowly sat down.

There was a silence, then the rise of a continuous sibilant murmur in the room. Paul bent his throbbing head low on his chest in a peculiar motion of despair as he heard William's breath draw in in a sharp gasp, and heard the sound that escaped Elizabeth's rigid lips. Clarissa and Edgar were conspicuously silent. William asked presently in a curt tone, "When was that will dated, Mr. Wilkins?"

"On the ninth day of November, 1883."

"Ah." That was the day following old William's purchase of the Gaylord share. He had not lost a moment in making this new will, incorporating proof of every word he had said on that unforgettable day.

His heirs sat now, each painfully unwilling to reveal his true feelings. Some stared at their clasped hands, some reached for handkerchiefs. Paul's half-closed eyes were fixed on his black cravat. Old William Scott's dramatic recognition of Mary Rafferty was bitingly emphasized by her absence. Still sharper was the bitterness with which Elizabeth finally broke the silence, lifting her head to stare at Paul and say, "Of course you will disregard Father's legacy to *that man's* sister, will you not?"

Clarissa, with a moan, slid fainting from her chair. Paul jumped to her side, cushioned her fall, and holding her in his arms, started to carry her to the door. As he was leaving the room, with Edgar helping him, he spoke over his shoulder to Elizabeth.

"I will not disregard one item of Father's will or go against any wish of his."

As the door closed behind him Elizabeth turned white-faced to William.

"I never—why—this is an outrage."

William sat silent. Henry Wilkins, expressionless, cleared his throat loudly and said, "Mrs. Nicholas, I wonder if you could not be of some help to your mother?"

Elizabeth glared at him and left the room.

CHAPTER XXIX

[*February 1884*]

WHEN PAUL CAME tramping down the hill in the early mornings, his breath streaming white in the cold, the mill was a reassurance to his eyes. The pattern of straggling sheds and bulging chimneys was the only semblance of reason and order in his life. The ugly smoke-colored iron walls and the gaping, battered roofs pierced by stacks and the domes of the hot-blast stoves were concrete reassurance in a world hideous with spectres and suspense. Here in the mill Paul could touch and take refuge in the personality of his father. Once he had made the tremendous physical adjustment of sitting in his father's chair; opening, despite his confused reluctance, the drawers of the yellow oak desk, forcing himself to handle and read the papers and ledgers that had formerly been locked in his father's private safe, he was consoled by an extraordinary sensation of renewed companionship with the Old Man. There had been a deep and secret well of sentiment in William Scott which his stiff, impassive exterior had jealously concealed. Paul had only probed it on the day, agonizing now to remember, when his father had said he was to marry Mary. Paul would never forget the look in his father's face, the trembling of his gnarled fingers, as he touched the woollen plaid across his knees.

This was the worst winter in many years, paralyzing the region with hardship. For weeks there was no respite from mountainous snows, subfreezing cold, and devastating storms. Murderous, shrieking gales swooped through the suffering valleys from the frozen peaks of the mountains, and ice-jams piled crazily in the rivers, tumbling down their courses to crush everything in their way. The streams became unnavigable; ore-barges were immobile in the grinding teeth of the jams; paddleboats were powerless to push their tows against the colossal tonnage of impacted ice. Railroads too were overwhelmed. Before tracks were cleared of one snowstorm they were frozen under the piled-up violence of another. Business throughout the country had begun some weeks ago to react from the slump of the past fall but now new problems overtook the disorganized steel mills; they could not fill orders that were coming in while transportation was disrupted. Advance supplies of raw material were quickly used up. For three weeks thereafter production was at the mercy of the weather.

To Paul this situation was the climax of a nightmare. He reached a point where he could not think back to remember normal conditions in the past. His days and nights were a succession of pressing anxieties, of worried men coming to him for decisions, of endless dread of the unexpected. His single greatest difficulty was his urgent need for a man to fill Jim Rafferty's place. Someone must be found, not only to replace Jim, but to do much of Paul's former work while he applied himself to the task of learning to fill his father's shoes. Eventually Paul intended to delegate much of the mill's business management to somebody trained by Richard MacTavish for the job, so that he could turn again to the research and manufacture that were his chosen work. But meanwhile MacTavish insisted that Paul must devote himself to the office. The period of settling the Old Man's estate was no time for the new head of Scott's to be sweating over the furnaces.

Other people's troubles crowded upon him ruthlessly. Sitting in the Old Man's office was a gruelling exaction. He did not want to sit there, or anywhere, listening to MacTavish, listening to McBride, listening to the stockyard boss about burst pipes, listening to failures in coke delivery, about ore barges frozen fast upriver, about Edgar's not wanting to go back to college. Edgar wanted to stay here and help. Paul wanted him to get his degree first. That was what Paul said he wanted. What he really wanted was to know something about Mary.

The thought of her haunted, tortured, and almost crazed him. It drove him always to his feet; he was incapable of sitting unless he was figuratively chained to his father's desk. Otherwise he strode, back and forth, round and round, his hands clenched into fists or gripped behind his back. The passages of the mill echoed at unearthly hours to the tramp of his uncontrollable feet. He almost never went home. Only when the thought of his mother penetrated the wilderness in his head did he hurry up the hill to the house, look in on her where she lay in her darkened room, and rush away again, back to the mill in oblivious compulsion. Several times a day, at odd, irrational times which he himself could not foresee, he walked furiously to the Flat and paced like an animal around the locked shack through whose windows he could not even peer because Mary had covered them. After one of his furious efforts of beating and shouting at the door, he had turned crazily away to see Kate standing behind him in the alley.

"It's no use, Mr. Scott," she said in a strained voice. "She'll not open the door. Sure, we've tried every hour o' the day and night, me and Dan and Father Reilly and the neighbors. She won't pay no mind." Her voice cracked.

"Mrs. Maginnis—she may die in there."

Kate shook her head. Her body was so enormous now that her head and limbs were shrunken and distorted by comparison; she would give birth any day. She said, "She's mindin' Dad. We set a can o' milk here airly this mornin' and she tuk it in. But nobody seen her do it. She's sharp, like, the way—the way—"

Paul covered his ears. He could not listen to what this woman was hinting. No matter how Mary acted he could not believe her to be really crazed, no more than he himself, for all the horrible jungle of his thoughts.

"What shall we do?" he reached out desperately and caught Kate Maginnis by the arm. "What can we do? I want to break the door down." He eyed the flimsy unpainted panel with a look that measured the single blow with which he could have shattered it.

She gasped. "Don't do that, Mr. Scott. I beg ye not to do that. Ye don't know our—well, we're a queer folk. We do our mournin' different from what ye may understand. Ye must leave Mary alone."

Something in her brogue and her desperate will to convince him recalled grotesquely the days when Mary had talked similarly and had shown just so passionate a will.

"Oh my God," he groaned, turning away. "Oh Christ, I can't stand much more."

"If ye'll give her time," Kate pleaded. Her kind eyes were brimming with tears and she wiped them on the edge of her shawl. "Try to have patience, Mr. Scott—pray fer it if ye can. I—we'll do all we can, Dan and me. We're not leavin' her starve or freeze. Dan'll leave a scuttle o' coal on the step every day. We'll pay her mind. We—I love her too, Mr. Scott." Kate's words ended in a violent sob. Paul started and looked hard at her.

"Oh—oh—" he grabbed her rough hand suddenly. "Oh—forgive me." His voice began to tremble. "God almighty, Mrs.—Kate. Jim was your brother." He turned away and ground his fist across his forehead.

Kate moved over timidly and touched his sleeve.

"Go away, now," she said softly. "Go away home and try to rest, Mr. Scott. We'll watch over Mary. I'm prayin' fer her, we all are here."

That was why he tried to bury himself in the mill, to sit at that desk and listen to all those insistent, maddening people, while the agony boiled inside him. But in the darkest hours of the bitterest nights, he stood in the frozen ruts of the alley and stared at the covered windows and barred door of the Rafferty shack. And often he heard against the whistle of the winter wind the thin, shrill wailing of the voice within.

Edgar was going back to college that evening and he called for Paul at the mill with the buggy. Paul was going to drive him to the station. Edgar entered his brother's office with the drawn, fearsome look that crossed all the faces which had not grown used to seeing anyone else in the Old Man's hard, battered chair.

He flung himself down opposite Paul and said, "Please. For the last time will you come to your senses and let me stay here and help you?"

Paul shook his head. He was finishing the inspection of a pile of documents and he shoved them away and reached for his pipe.

"I can make out till June," he said. His voice was flat and tired; Edgar knew that he never really slept. Paul looked at the wall clock and rose and reached for his overcoat and hat from the rack.

"Time to go."

McBride, the new head heater on the open-hearths, came in. The sight of him always upset Paul. It was terrible to have to see and deal with another man in Jim Rafferty's place.

"Mr. Scott," he said, "I wun't be able to charge that run o' carbon steel in the mornin'."

"Why not?" Paul snapped, exasperated.

"The ferromanganese ain't here. We been waitin' all week."

"Damn!" Paul swung his coat on and started for the door. "Have you heard where it is?"

McBride scratched his head.

"The carload's stuck some place up by Clarion. They ain't come to since the blizzard. We ain't heard no more since then."

Paul was so irritated that his fists were working as if looking for something to smash.

"Oh, come on, Ed," he said angrily.

"Well—what'll we do?" McBride asked.

"Wait for the material," Paul said, "and use the chance to inspect your linings while you can. Good God," he said to Edgar as they walked out on the bridge, "wouldn't you think he'd figure that out for himself?"

"That's why I want to stay here," Edgar said. His voice was muffled; he found it difficult to talk out here where the memory of that fearful morning, of their father and of the utmost tragedy their minds could conceive, rushed at the brothers and overwhelmed them as they trod along the cinder-crusted boards. Paul stopped at the spot where the Old Man had fallen, and stood silent. It was bitterly cold; their fingers stiffened as they both responded to the same silent instinct, and stood there in the icy wind, lifting their hats from their heads. They felt the tears freeze in the corners of their eyes.

"Wouldn't you know," Paul murmured hoarsely. "Wouldn't you know Pa would die where you can't go in or out of the mill without crossing this spot?"

In the buggy Edgar broke a long silence by bursting out, in a low tense croak, "Paul. Say . . . it's damn near impossible to talk now. But—"

Paul, driving, and anxiously guiding the horse over the icy glare of the street, looked sidelong for a moment and felt a wrench as he saw the drawn wretchedness in Edgar's young face.

"What is it, Kid?" he asked softly.

"Nothing—not about me." Edgar's lips were blue with the cold, and pinched nervously together. "I'm just so worried about you, Paul. About —the whole thing. Where's Mary?" he asked sharply. Paul winced at the edge in his voice .

"Ed. I—for God's sake, I can't talk about it. She's—" Paul stopped and coughed and blew his nose.

"I'm sorry. I know. I was just trying to—oh, hell," Edgar blurted. "I feel so God damn awful. If there was only something I could do."

Paul stopped the horse by the station and motioned to a porter.

"It's—I can't explain much now, Kid. I'm in a terrible mess. Maybe—"

"So am—I mean—" Edgar turned away. Paul started at the hysterical note in Edgar's voice and turned to stare at him. Edgar's eyes fell and his expression changed all at once.

"I really am worried about you, Paul," he said, very controlled. "I was only trying to say—I know what it's like to be in a jam. I wish—I wish to Christ I could help."

Paul battled for a moment with the sensation that overcame him innumerable times every day; a feeling in his aching throat and eyes that he must give in to tears. But he only showed it by a tightening of his lips, a certain staring look that came into his eyes. He bent over and picked up the whip.

"So long, Kid," he said, as the horse started to move. "It's only five months till you get home for good."

Edgar smiled wanly and turned into the station. Paul drove away, rattling quickly down the cobbles of Liberty Avenue. He was so seldom, these days, in motion, so rarely outdoors except for his quick, preoccupied walks back and forth between the house and the mill, that he had an odd sensation of detachment, sitting there behind the trotting horse. The animal's breath streamed thick and white in the bitter cold. Paul's eyes rested on the plump, shiny brown flanks moving rhythmically to the pleasant clop of hoofs. There was something immensely soothing about the simple, familiar sight. Paul had often heard his mother say that she enjoyed knitting because it made her mind a restful blank. This motion of the horse apparently affected him the same way. He sat there and let his tense nerves relax. When he reached the familiar corner of Liberty Avenue and Sixth Street, Monkey (nobody knew why this horse had been given that name) started automatically to turn right for the Sixth Street Bridge. Paul let him go. Then when they reached the crossing of Penn Avenue, one block before the bridge approach, Paul reined in. Monkey paused, tossing his head in annoyed surprise. Paul sat inert, letting his tired mind edge up to the question that had woven through it for the past hour. If he drove on down Penn Avenue and took the Union Bridge, he would come out within two blocks of the Flat. He would find himself almost at Mary's doorstep. For a moment now he wanted intensely to go down there, break open that flimsy door, and tramp in to crush once and for all the whole wretched welter of his troubles. He was strong enough to pick her up like a child, wrap her in a rug, and lift her into this buggy and take her home without her being able to lift a finger to stop him. He almost twitched the left rein to turn the horse in that direction. And then the strange, cold pall of exhaustion settled once again on his brain and on his will. He sighed and picked up the whip.

"All right, Monkey, we'll go home now." His voice was leaden.

Before he reached the middle of the bridge he was relieved that he had decided as he had. He sat back in the buggy, lifting his face to the freezing currents of river wind. He felt totally a part of their bitterness. The thrusts and slashes at his ears and nose, at the tips of his fingers, benumbed in spite of his heavy woollen gloves, left him indifferent. To pain and above all to hardness, to the unequivocal cruelty of a ruthless element, he was unfeeling. Now he tried, in a passing mood of inquisitive self-torture, to summon again the excruciating sensation of his love for Mary, the yearning tension of his longing for her. And he knew, with the demoniac wind howling in his ears, that for the time, at least, he felt nothing.

Very late that night he sat alone in his father's office. The mill was almost deserted; no night runs could be scheduled with everything disrupted by the terrible weather. Paul had come down here because he could not stay away. There was nowhere else to take his tormented mind, his sore, suffering heart. He found the house unendurable. It was easier to tell himself that he had work to do down here, which, in a way, he had. The coal-oil stove was sputtering and stinking, with the flame turned high to warm the draughty room. The old clock ticked with its heavy, cracked measure. Once in a while far in the distance Paul could catch the footbeats of the night watchman as he made his rounds.

He sat at his father's desk, his head clutched in his hands, and listened to the few sterile sounds around him, and thought his horrible hopeless thoughts. He sat thus for a very long time. At last he looked up, his heavy, aching eyes examining the room. It was dark except for the single gas jet flickering over his head. The bare dirty windows on his left were a curious continuation inward of the frozen night outside, rather than a barrier against it. Paul felt himself the only living thing in a tomb of midnight silence. His eyes rested blankly on his father's safe in the corner, the private safe to which nobody else had ever had access. The combination, written in his father's hand and heavily sealed in a fibre envelope with red wax, had been turned over to Paul by Henry Wilkins.

Slowly he rose from the Old Man's chair, and slowly moved across the room, dropping on his knees before the safe. Slowly and easily, reading the combination, he opened the safe. The chunky iron door swung wide and Paul peered reluctantly inside.

He saw ledgers, private account books, his father's personal check books, stacks of papers and letters in envelopes tightly tied into packages with red cord and neatly labelled. There was a small black tin cash box in which Paul found five thousand dollars in hundred and five-hundred dollar bills. And there was another tin box, a very old handmade one, clumsily latched. Paul opened this slowly and stared at its unexpected contents. His knees began to feel numb; he rose to his feet, holding the box in his hands, and walked back to the desk and slowly sat down with it. He did not know why his hands trembled as he began with an astonishing sensation of reverence to lift the contents from the box.

He picked up a tattered stub of yellow paper, and squinted to read the notations in faded brown ink. Here was the receipt for his grandfather's packet passage to America. It was dated Glasgow, 29th August, 1821. Paul stared at it, his eyelids stinging. He turned it gently in his fingers; the paper could so easily drop apart.

He could see as if they stood before him the stern-faced young Scotsman in his bonnet and plaid, with his trembling bride, bidding farewell forever to the familiar security of the Highland village where they were born. They had landed in Boston after a terrible four-week voyage, and the young man had found work as apprentice to an iron-forger in Taunton, Massachusetts, where his only son was born in the following year. With an infant in her arms Henrietta Campbell had taken her place beside her husband in the wagon that carried them and their three small bundles of worldly goods westward across the Alleghenies. Paul had heard the story from his grandfather.

They had travelled in one of the creaking wagon-freight trains that crossed the mountains by the newly built turnpike road from Philadelphia, through Harrisburg and the wild and beautiful Juniata Valley; a trip miraculously shortened from four weeks to two by the opening of the magnificent Huntington Turnpike. Paul's grandfather had vividly remembered his early years in the wild young river town whose banks had alway throbbed to the pulses of violence. It had been only seventy short year since the British and the French had fought bloodily to possess the town, still newly wrested from the Indians. Since then the place had teemed to the drive of tremendous forces. Like its own fierce, rushing, predatory rivers which rose at intervals to reassert the violence of nature, the wills and powers of the men who dug and strove, forged and beat, fought and mastered, had colored the very earth and air with the gray and black and scarlet marks of struggle.

Life in early Pittsburgh had been ugly and violent. Paul well remembered his grandfather's description of the hideous filth and impassable mud of the downtown streets, where hogs ran wild by day and rats by night, and no child was safe; where no woman dared step from her house alone; where broad midday often found the crowded alleys, wharfs, and docksides shrouded by so black a mixture of coal-smoke and fog that robbery and murder commonly took place there. Paul had often wondered how a tow settled and dominated by stern Scottish characters like his grandfather could ever have been host to armies of thugs, gamblers, prostitutes, roving street-criminals and petty thieves, but such had been the case. The busy ironmasters had barely taken thought to provide adequate police protection. The very ugliness of the town endeared it to Paul, who saw in its steep black hillsides, sprawling dirty flats, haphazard buildings, and spidery tangle of stark iron bridges, the preoccupation with work and the indifference to æsthetics and appearances that had been the mainspring of his grandfather's life.

Paul found now in the box the original deed to the two riverside lots which had been the first William Scott's purchase with the painful savings of twelve years' toil in furnaces and forges. Here he had built, in 1837, his own forge, and here he had spent the rest of his life in earnest labor, quickly but prudently expanding with the surge of the times until his phenomenal single-handed creation of the Henrietta.

The Civil War had been the impetus for that. Paul was just old enough to remember the furious and fevered atmosphere of those days. He had been a toddler when his grandfather had overnight transformed the mill from a little puddling-shop and forge to one of the arsenals on which the

Union Army critically depended. Cannon-balls and gun-forgings had streamed out of Scott's in phenomenal quantity and speed. Paul had learned years later that shocking graft had tainted almost all transactions for equipping and supplying the Union Army. That had been interesting but impersonal, like any other lesson in history which one learned in the ordinary course of one's education. Now he looked curiously at a carefully wrapped letter, secured inside two envelopes. As a boy he had been told of such a letter, but he did not know that it really existed: a brief tribute of thanks for "loyal and tireless efforts in supplying the Army with the munitions of war." It was signed, "A. Lincoln."

Paul studied it with deep emotion. How like his unboastful grandfather to keep it hidden away instead, perhaps, of framing and displaying it as most men would have done. William Scott had scorned bribery and graft. Paul needed no proof to be sure of that. His grandfather had been fanatical about the Civil War; about the question of Emancipation; about helping escaped slaves through the Underground Railway on which Allegheny City was a principal station. Paul regretted bitterly now the combination of modesty and taciturnity which had kept his grandfather's lips sealed at a late date when almost any old man would have entertained his grandchildren with thrilling stories about escaping slaves. Paul remembered now, he had not thought of it for years, the bricked-up archway at the very back of the cellar at home, where he and Bill had loved to explore as little boys. Nobody had ever been willing to tell them what it was. Now he found proof. He had always suspected the existence of a tunnel from the river bank straight through to this cellar entrance. And here he found in primitive, half-intelligible code, a list of "goods" which his grandfather had "warehoused" in his "vault" before "transshipping" as directed to the Great Lakes.

What a grand old fighter, Paul thought tenderly. He raised his head and gazed blankly off into space. It was a fine thing, he reflected, a fine and grave responsibility to be the inheritor of such a man and of the son of such a man. I wonder, he thought solemnly, I wonder if I shall ever have to take the mill through a war. I wonder if this country will ever need our mill again the way it needed it in '61. Strangely, he heard himself say aloud, sighing, "I hope so." He sat very still and bent his head, turning gently through the other contents of the box, touching for the first time secret things that had known no other hands but his father's and his grandfather's. Through their dry rustlings they whispered to him of thoughts and loves and loyalties that could never be dead because they came alive to him at the behest of two dominant old men. A small crayon-drawing of his delicate grandmother, who had died before he was born, commemorated by so queer a memorial as the roaring brute who bore her name. A scrap of faded plain silk from some vanished bonnet. A blurred daguerreotype of his own mother as a girl, in whose features, childish though they were, Paul saw his own. A tiny lace-edged handkerchief, musty and yellowed. Had it been hers? A folded paper which almost broke in his hands, which he opened reluctantly to find a few barely-legible words signed by a woman's name he did not know. A page torn from a diary on which his father had written, "Today my dear wife gave birth safely to her third child, a healthy boy who shall be named Paul. I pray that he survives." Paul thought of the small grave near his father's new one in the family plot, where the stillborn brother who preceded him was buried. There were many more letters, a worn carnelian seal, a piece of thick paper folded about some iron filings, an envelope containing the crumbs of a sprig of heather. Paul sat at the desk late into the night, silent and pondering, knowing for the first time the deep, strange power of communion with the ineradicable dead.

CHAPTER XXX

[*February 1884*]

IT WAS KATE who broke the siege at the shack. Ten days after the beginning of Mary's imprisonment, Dan pounded on the door at four o'clock in the morning, and shouted in unmistakable panic, "Mary, come quick fer the love o' God. Katie's took."

Mary raised her tangled head from the cot and shook it dully. Something about the noise outside compelled her as none of the previous beating, pounding, shouting, and pleading had been able to do. She moved her head heavily from side to side and with great effort bent it to hear again the frantic pleas outside.

"Howly Mother and saints, I tell ye Katie's took bad. She needs ye, fer Chris' sake, will ye come?"

Mary got to her feet suddenly and with the motion her head cleared. She groped about the dark room for a candle, and went to open the door. Dan stood there panting. Mary looked at him strangely and calmly, unaware of the sight that caused his jaw suddenly to sag, his excited eyes to pop round and horrified in his face. He saw, which she did not know, a face like a death's head; a face with colorless skin stretched tight across jutting bones, vast staring eyes burned from black hollows, framed in a wild bush of torn red hair and horribly highlighted by the flickering flame of the candle. But his thoughts were on Kate.

"Come quick," he said again. "Quick."

Mary nodded, stepped back into the room, quickly put on some clothes, and started with him up the alley. Kate had been seized in the sudden hard labor of the experienced mother, and her child was born into Mary's hands a few minutes after Mary entered the house with Dan. It happened so quickly that Mary had no chance or need to adjust herself to the shock of being torn from her isolation and forced into activity. By the time she had bathed the child, tended Kate, and automatically taken up the routine of Kate's household, cooking breakfast for Dan and the two older children, cleaning, straightening up, washing, she had been lifted for good out of the iron incarceration in which her brain, her feelings, and her will had been clamped. There came a moment in the morning when she saw herself in the looking-glass. With a shudder she covered her face with her hands. Just as her only effort of energy before had gone to keeping herself barricaded, now she turned it to the grim business of getting herself in hand again.

But she could feel nothing. She could think in a certain groove related to getting things done, to taking care of people; she could clean Kate's house and her father's, cook food, feed it to people, walk back and forth between the Rafferty shack and the Maginnis one, stop at the grocery on the Flat and buy flour, tea, salt, butter, nod silently and forbiddingly to the neighbor women on their doorsteps, whose scornful glances of a few weeks ago were changed now to yearning ones of warmth and pity. But she could not, or would not, speak a word beyond the grim monosyllables of absolute necessity. She could not face a thought that threatened to lead her backward to the self, or to the world around the self, that had burst into screaming, shattered, bleeding fragments. Something as queer as the need for money drove this home to her. She bought groceries and then stood dumbly in the middle of the shop wondering why she had no money with her to pay for them. She gave a strangled groan and fled wildly back to the shack when she realized that her purse and all the money in it, and everything associated with that, were still in Miss Mitchell's boardinghouse. After that she used Dan's money. "I'll give it back to you," she told him, "when I—"

She should have known that she could not escape Paul. He had watched her minutely, fanatically; he knew what morning she had first left the shack, what time she spent with Kate. It was only a matter of hours after that before she stepped inside her father's house in the early evening and found Paul sitting at the kitchen table, his head buried in his arms. He looked up, rose, and stretched out his arms to her. Mary walked straight past them and went over and stood rigid, her back against the peeling papered wall. His face was almost as dreadful a sight as hers. Lines had dug themselves into it; it was a heavy gray color; his lips were dry and cracked.

"There is nothing to say," Mary spoke in a lifeless, muffled tone.

He kept the distance which she had so harshly indicated, but he looked at her with such eloquence in his tortured eyes that she closed her own for a moment to escape the sight.

"There is everything to say," he answered, "but I will spare you hearing it. We have nothing left but each other."

"We have nothing left at all."

"Don't say that, dear—Mary—"

"It is true. We have destroyed everything. Them—and ourselves."

"Don't say that! I can't bear it!"

"No more can I. What makes you think life is going to be bearable ever again? Do murderers know peace?"

"*Mary!*" He gripped the table, his mouth gaping.

"Live with your own soul if you can."

Paul sprang to her side and stood close to her, his fingers flexing in a wild nervous motion that reminded her astoundingly at this—of all moments—of Constance. Mary brushed her eyes with her hand. Constance! She grimaced.

"Mary, I've got to talk to you and you've got to listen."

She gave a weary, moaning sigh. Both of them were struggling with the backwash of the long labored past; the times before when they had struggled, the memories of strain and futile argument.

She looked at him and shook her head.

"I wish I had the strength to put you out of here," she sighed. She looked hopelessly at her father dozing in the corner in his chair.

Paul folded his arms and bent his eyes on her. He did not speak for a few minutes. Then he said, "The worst that I feared has happened. You've already convinced yourself that all that—that it changes everything for us."

"It has." Her voice was bitter.

"No." Paul drew close to her and let his eyes rest longingly on her tragic face. "No, that's not so. If you go on believing that, you really will bring on the total ruin of the few things that are left." He spoke sternly then, and almost coldly. "We are promised. And I am going to hold you to your word. I need you now more than ever before."

"I cannot consider that now. I have my duty to do." She stared.

"Your duty is to me."

"My duty is to God. I have the penance of my brother's crime, and the penance of our crime, to pay the rest of my life."

He looked at her with horrible, freezing bewilderment. His forehead twisted in pained lines, his eyes narrowed.

"I—can't understand," he breathed.

Mary's stony expression and rigid pose held for another moment. But with her eyes aching at the sight of his wretched, unutterably familiar, but horribly changed face, she slumped suddenly and her head fell forward on her breast. She spoke in whispers, gasping fragments of words; she put her hand up, palm outward, before her, to ward him off.

"It was wrong," she said. "The whole thing was wrong. I shouldn't ever have said I'd marry you. I shouldn't ever have let your father—God rest his dear noble soul—say we should. Anyway, it's too—late—now—" Her voice trailed away and she almost slipped forward in a faint. But she reached for a chair, held on to the back of it, with her head lowered, while Paul stood stunned before her. She raised her head with a vast effort of will and spoke again. "We sent him to his death," she whispered.

"Mary! For God's sake come to your senses. Haven't we suffered enough?"

"We deceived him," she went on, ignoring Paul. Her voice had the low throbbing ring of a voice in prayer. "We repaid his love and his belief in us—by deceiving him into the hands of his murderer."

Paul strode over and seized her by the shoulders and shook her.

"Mary!" He shouted at her. "You've lost your mind. You're crazed from all this. You're saying frightful things." He shook her again. "Do you know what you're saying?"

She nodded dully. "I do."

"Then stop it! It was a fearful enough tragedy, whatever damned meddling fool told that lie to Jim, without your losing your wits and making a melodrama out of it."

"My brother committed a crime," she said solemnly.

"And paid for it more bitterly than a man ever paid before. Now stop all this raving and come to your senses. I'm going to take you home out of here." He looked about him wildly.

"No, you're not," Mary said slowly. She stood limp in his arms. "I shall never leave this house again."

He dropped his hands with a gasp and stood staring at her. But soon he reached out again and took her in his arms.

"You can't punish me, Mary," he said. He forced her head to fall forward on his chest, and held her close to him, burying his mouth in the hair by her ear. "You can't set yourself up as God in judgment. Any wrong I've done I'm suffering for like Christ himself. I always will. But I don't have to give you up, Mary." He lifted her face and stared into it. "*He* wouldn't want that. You know he wouldn't. Father wouldn't change—now."

She only shook her dishevelled head with a hopeless motion of despair. "It's all over," she said dully. "I will not marry you."

"But you love me!" Paul's fingers dug so hard into her thin arms that she clenched her teeth with the pain. But she stood stock-still while he shouted wildly. "You love me. I love you. I love you. I love you."

The horror of the two weeks past, the grinding on his nerves, the untold hours of strain and wretchedness, backed up in one sudden flare of weakness; Le burst into sobs. "I love you."

With all her flesh, with all the terrible hoarded strength of her will, she longed to yield to him. For a moment she felt as if her very bones would liquefy and flow in a rush of love and tenderness and sympathy to melt into his. But then she pulled herself hard from his arms, leaving the tips of her fingers resting on his forearms.

"I love you, Paul. I've always loved you." She stopped speaking and her open mouth worked a little, as if straining to pour out the words she was crushing back into her throat. She swallowed and clamped her lips shut. Then she said, "I will not marry you. Not if I live alone and suffering all the rest of my life." She moved away from him and turned towards the door. Her emaciated hand pointed weakly. She did not look at him again. "Go away," she murmured, "and leave me to my penance."

Paul sat on a tufted hassock beside his mother's bed. He sat doubled over, elbows locked to knees, his head clutched in his cold hands. His mother's voice had the dull, timbreless quality of total exhaustion.

"Only time, Paul." Clarissa had wept so much that there were no tears left in her. She lay in her bed like an automaton, too utterly defeated to summon the energy to get up. She had lain like this for two weeks. Her blonde hair fell in two faded ashen braids over her shoulders. About her face it had whitened. Her eyes had dulled from their pleasant blue to a stony color reflected from enormous, strained black pupils. Her hands framed in the ruffled cuffs of her long-sleeved nightgown lay limply on the counterpane, deathly white like her face, thinned so that the blue veins stood out in age-revealing ridges on their backs.

"Only time will tell, Paul, whether she really means it. We cannot know now, son."

"I must know, Mama. I have reached the end of my endurance. I cannot live in any more suspense."

"*I* do not want to live at all, Paul."

She spoke in a chiding way, rather petulantly. He looked up at her in queer surprise. "Why, Mama." It was as if he had said, "I did not know you cared so desperately about him."

She arched her head back onto the stiff pillow.

"I hate the changes. I hate the ruin. I don't understand violence." She spoke not to him but to herself. Paul stood up suddenly and went close and looked down at her. He realized with a pang of shame that he had not really given an instant of concern to her. He had been isolated in his own agonies. He had thought she was going through something that every woman in her later days must expect and be prepared for. He had not believed that the blow of widowhood could be any such catastrophe to her as the least of his torments had been to him. He had left her to her Gethsemane because she was at the part of her life when she should expect it. And now he was trying to draw her into his.

He dropped on his knees and put his strong hands on her thin, listless, empty ones.

"Forgive me, Mama," he whispered. He held her hands closely and looked hard into the broad, wide-browed, earnest face so like his own. "I've been so crazed from everything. I can't make sense. It's such a nightmare. . . . I can't believe it and when I try to make myself, I can't see what brought it all about." He choked. "Any of it."

Clarissa drew one hand from his grasp and gently stroked the heavy blond hair from his forehead.

"You've always been so wonderful, Paul."

He shook his head. "Father made everything possible for me," he said. "That's what's killing me now. It was bad enough before—before she said those terrible things."

"She's not herself, dear. She doesn't know what she's doing now."

"Do you really think that?"

He raised his head and stared at his mother, groping for reassurance.

"As much as I can think anything," Clarissa said wearily, moving her head as if the effort pained her. "I can't give you much consolation, son. But they all tell us time heals everything. I suppose we'd better try to believe it."

They were silent for a long time. Paul knelt with his forehead pressed against the counterpane. The contact with his mother's bed, the refuge she had made for herself, was calming. A strange thought came into Paul's mind. He had been born in this very bed—conceived in it. The idea drew him into a heavy, curiously safe sense of darkness. It was as if he had found a way to go back into the security and insensibility of his mother's womb. He could not know whether she felt this. But he did not want to be torn away from her now. He stayed quiet.

CHAPTER XXXI

[*February 1884*]

THE THAW that had been dreaded for three weeks came suddenly in the first days of February, and four days and nights of torrential rain came with it. In one night the temperature rose forty degrees. Paul had been so absorbed in the mill, in the search for the men he needed, and in the pressing complications of his father's will, that he had ignored the news as it passed through town: the rivers were in alarming condition and once the big freeze broke there would be trouble. Paul should have been keen to every item of the news, for the mill, at riverfront like all others, lay exposed to the worst that could happen. But Paul had succeeded in getting several carloads of ore, coke, limestone, and other materials down the siding which he had cleared by every desperate expedient: salt, fires, gangs with pickaxes. He had an order for two carloads of rolled bars and one of pig iron; he was determined to fill it. Two full months had elapsed since the mill had produced anything in a normal manner and on regular schedule. Paul said this order must be completed and shipped without any mishap. He was in the rolling mill in late afternoon, inspecting the first lot of completed bars with Mike Hogan, the boss roller, when a boy came running down the shed, calling.

"Mr. Scott, there's a cop in your office and Mr. MacTavish says you're to come up and talk to him."

Paul swore and stalked away. He listened incredulously. The policeman had come to give him the weather bureau's warning. The Allegheny was rising so fast that by morning of the next day it would be at thirty-two feet and within a few hours thereafter would be over flood stage. This was the last official warning. The rivers had not been so high in fifty-two years, nor had there been so much ice jammed in them. The Monongahela was in worst condition still; the Youghiogheny above it had been packed tight for two weeks and had begun to move twenty-four hours ago. When this pushed past McKeesport hell would be well on its way toward town. Paul listened now with horrified attention. His own mill lay down river from the Point, square on the bank of the Ohio beyond the confluence of the rivers.

"Get the records cleared out first," he said to MacTavish. "All the stuff from your own office and here, and try to get Pa's safe out too. Never mind about the furniture, it's a lot of junk anyway."

" 'Tis no junk," MacTavish answered, "and I'll be savin' it along wi' yer Dad's papers. I'll be off to see about a dray."

Paul hurried back to the rolling mill.

"Stop the run," he ordered. "They're bringing down half a ton of grease. Start up at the blooming mill and work down this way. Soon as the parts cool, grease 'em up."

"Is it in here 'twud be comin'?" a man asked him.

"They say so. By tomorrow the whole place'll be under water. We're going to cart every movable piece we can and what stays here has got to be greased."

Michael Molloy came looking for him.

" 'Twill crack every linin' in the place, Paul," he said anxiously.

"I know it!"

Men from different sheds all through the mill had left their work if they could and come down to the rolling mill to swarm around Paul. Some of them were terror-stricken, especially older ones who remembered the great floods of twenty years ago, with their wake of death and disease, their crushing disaster. Faced with the same thing again they were stunned. Practically all of them lived on the cinder Flat or in hovel settlements equally close to the river.

"We'd better divide up," Paul said. "Some of you will have to go home to get your families moved up to the hill. I'll need about half of you here. The rest go and see about getting everybody out of the houses down there."

The men separated into gangs. Some went off to the Flat and the shantytown around the next bend of the river, and the rest stayed with Paul. For ten hours they worked furiously. There was not much movable machinery that could be carted out to an elevation high enough to escape the expected flood-level. The furnaces were in the worst danger. The Henrietta was within half an hour of a blast, and once her charge was tapped, she would have to be gutted out to get her cooled as quickly as possible. Icy water striking her while she was hot would crack her like glass. None of the old puddling furnaces was working, nor was the Bessemer, but both the open-hearths were hot, one from the heat that was now in the rolls, the other getting ready for a charge. They must be cooled. If they could escape with no damage beyond cracked linings, the mill would be lucky. Mechanical equipment might be badly damaged by water, but there was no high place to which power cranes, the dinkey-engine, the crusher, the slag-hammer, and all the ladles and moulds could be moved. All the hoisting machinery and all that in the blooming and the rolling mills could only be greased and left to fate. Paul worked with the men, crawling on his belly and lying on his back in the grease, smearing black slime into axles and between rolls. Late at night he was amazed to hear his mother's voice calling for him down at the entrance of the shed where he was working. Mac-Tavish had taken a wagonload of ledgers and papers up to the house for safekeeping and Clarissa had insisted on driving back with him to the mill, with a washbasket in the back of the wagon packed with sandwiches and swathed cans of hot coffee. Paul and his tired men crawled out from under the machinery like greasy bugs, and sat about on the frames wearily chewing their food and gulping coffee from tin mugs clutched gingerly in their slippery, coal-black hands. Clarissa moved to and fro among them, her

long widow's veil brushing the slimy corners of the machines, pouring
more coffee and urging them to eat. When she looked at Paul her pale face
broke into a wan smile.

"You look like somebody in a minstrel show," she said.

Paul helped her and MacTavish pack the things back into the wagon.
Clarissa demurred at going home, but Paul said, "Mama, there isn't a
thing you can do here, and you'll probably have people in trouble coming
to you at the house all tomorrow and the next day. You better stay there
and get ready for them."

"Everybody is ready," she said. "Mrs. Burns formed a committee yesterday when the warnings started going out. We're going to use the church
and the parish house to put the people in. We've all been allotted our
work."

"That's good. I've got to get back inside, Mama. Don't worry about
me. I'll get home when I can."

Clarissa hesitated. "I am worried about you, Paul."

"Why? I'm fine. Good night, Mama. And thanks for coming down.
The men appreciated it a lot."

By the time the rolls and machines were finished the furnaces were
cool enough to be inspected. Paul helped the gangs to scrape out the hot
cinder from the bottoms. As each job was done another pressed for attention. He could not stop when men came to ask him questions, but went on
with whatever he was doing. By four o'clock in the morning he and half a
dozen of his helpers made the last rounds, so tired they could hardly shuffle,
but satisfied that they had done everything possible to protect the mill.
From time to time somebody on watch at the river bulkhead had come
running to show the rising stage of the measure, and just as Paul turned
from the last inspection to go back to his office, the watchman came to
him again.

"Time we all started clearing out," he said, showing Paul the measure
again.

Paul went himself to look. Not two inches below the bulkhead, as he
pushed open the sliding iron door, the glittering black water slid by.
Chunks of ice and snow bobbed on its surface. Normally when one opened
this door the river lay twenty feet below. Paul's blood curdled as he gazed
at the swollen water, literally rising to eat up that last inch of space even
while he watched. He leaned far out of the doorway, holding onto the
frame with both hands, and craned his neck first down, then up the path
of the flood. Already in the distance he could see dark, bobbing, shapeless
objects, sheds or trees or something gobbled by the upper courses of the
water from the banks in the way of the flood. It was not until he could
distinguish the shape of a roof, speeding down the middle of the stream
straight toward him, that he thought—with sudden, startled, freezing
clarity—of Mary. He was too horrified to wonder why he had not thought
of her hours ago. He was exhausted. He dragged the iron door shut, turned
and ran like mad for his office.

"Everybody out," he yelled as he ran. "Clear 'em all out." He sent the
watchman to make the last inspection and make sure that nobody was left

in the mill. He seized his coat, dragging it on over his grease-stained overalls, and tore out onto the bridge. The last of the men were out there waiting for him, looking over the roofs of the sheds, appalled as the water careened down the farther side. They all turned away together and started up the steep street to the avenue on the hill. But at the corner Paul broke away from them.

"Where're ye goin'?"

"Come back here."

"Paul, ye're mad."

The men stood on the corner and yelled after him as he raced down the hill straight toward the path of the flood.

"Come back," they yelled. " 'Tis death down there. Come back."

Paul, running, shouted back over his shoulder, "Don't follow me. Go up to our house and my mother will help you look after your folks. I'll be up later."

When the neighbors began to tell Mary of the flood warnings she listened, shaking her head indifferently and saying, "Oh, I'm not frightened."

"But 'tis real bad," Mrs. Molloy insisted. "Sure, the p'lice is goin' about the whole Flat givin' warnin', and wan copper sint me here to warn ye and the three houses on each side. Ye'd better get somebody to help ye wid yer Dad afore it's too late."

She hurried away to give the rest of her warnings. Mary looked after her, quite clearly comprehending everything she had said, yet utterly, overwhelmingly indifferent. She turned into the shack and looked at Patrick, dozing as usual in his chair. Mary stood for a long time and gazed at him. It was late in the evening, a sombre winter night streaked with queer luminous color in the distant reaches of the sky, leaden and darkening overhead. She had intended to light the lamp and put on the kettle to boil for Patrick's evening tea. But now she forgot that. She stood there overcome by an enormous lassitude. She knew only that death would be the sweetest mercy of heaven. She had not expected that her prayers might be answered as realistically as this. There was no law requiring her to pull her wits together and try to save herself and her father from the flood. For all she knew, the whole catastrophe might be the deliberate intention of God to put an end to her misery. Ignoring the unlit lamp, the unfed fire, she sat down in a rickety chair by the kitchen table, took her rosary, prayed for a time, and fell into a reverie.

What hours slipped by she did not know, but a long time later she raised her head and began, in a sudden access of clear perception, to listen. Such sounds as struck her ears made oddly sharp and telling impressions. The ticking of the old wall clock, the faint susurration of her father's breathing, the muffled whisper of the dying fire in the stove, all came closely and quietly together in contrast to a different sort of sound outside. Mary listened intently now. She heard a low, throbbing roar, a noise both rhythmical and penetrating, and unlike anything she had ever heard. She had one impulse to sit on in her chair, ignore the noise, and do nothing whatever about it. But another force within her brought her to her feet and carried her over to the door. She opened it and looked out. Right and left of her the neighbors' houses stood dark and apparently deserted. The front door of one stood open; a basket of miscellaneous, untidy articles had been dropped and left on the doorstep of the other. It must be long past midnight, she knew. But this strange, empty silence was not that of ordinary night. She called loudly, "Mrs. O'Brien. Oh, Mollie O'Brien."

Nobody answered her. She called again, another name. Again silence. Then she stood, contemplating the quiet and at the same time aware of the roar, still distant, but more noticeable, more penetrating. Suddenly she knew that what she heard was the roar of the speeding river, coursing in flood somewhere just beyond the rim of the Flat which she could reach in two dozen steps if she walked straight ahead. First she felt a vast sense of triumph, a huge delight that she had stayed to meet this heaven-sent destruction and not run away to the high ground where her bodily safety would only prolong her inner suffering. Then she turned back into the house and looked at Patrick. He had raised his head and in some queer way he seemed to be listening. He could not possibly know what was happening. He had heard nothing for many months; he could not have been pretending the insensibility that had come over him. But still, he seemed to be listening now. His mouth hung open a little and one gnarled hand went behind his ear.

Mary watched him, repelled by the semblance of reason that she knew was not there. She even went over to him and said, "Dad. Do you hear anything?"

He paid no attention to her. But his attitude forced her to realize with sudden, startling rallying of her forces, that he and she were both in a danger which now loomed horrible when a moment before it had beckoned as the answer to her prayers. In one moment her nerves rebounded, from one extreme to another equally unreasoned. Instantly she was galvanized to frantic action. There was no time now to wonder which of the two impulses was the truer, whether she had really meant to sit and be drowned and let her father drown, or whether this violent will to save him and herself was and had been all along her real intention. She ran to him, noting from the tail of her eye as she did so, that the loud-ticking clock on the wall said five o'clock. She would always remember the sight and the sound of that battered clock with its cracked glass and clumsy pendulum. She seized a shawl from a bench and wrapped it round her shoulders, tucking the ends into her belt. Then she pushed her father's chair to the door and opened it.

Beneath her feet the ground had disappeared. In the few moments since she had stood and called the neighbors, something had happened. Where cindery gravel, mud, and cobbles had been visible before there was only a spreading pool of water now. Mary had intended to lower her father's chair to the ground and push it up the alley and toward the rising ground that ran into Rebecca Street. But she found now that she could not lift the wheels of the chair over the raised sill of the doorway. The front wheel stuck against it. She tried turning the chair around, and then saw that she could not push the heavy back wheels over the threshold and down the steps without losing control of the whole chair and letting it and her father tumble into the water. She turned the chair again, and, holding onto the back of it with one hand, bent down and tried desperately to edge the crooked rusty front wheel over the sill. She could not do it. The water at the bottom of the steps was spreading quickly and Mary could no longer see the ground through it. She looked at Patrick. He sat just inside the door, still cupping his ear with his hand, still with that half-crazy, half-wise expression of intent listening. And then, because the faint raw dawn light was suddenly cut off, she raised her head and looked up from the chair.

Straight before her, coming straight at her, solid as the side of a mountain, was a weaving, shimmering wall of gray. She could no longer see anything else. It blotted out the shacks across the alley; it was higher than her head. And it was moving fast. Mary stood petrified. She could not have turned and run if she had tried. Right and left, and straight before her, the towering thick gray wall rolled forward in a deafening surge.

Water, she thought, making a throaty sound of terrified disbelief. Water standing straight up in the air, higher than her head, higher than a house. . . . She closed her eyes . . . opened them. She bent again over the chair. But it was too late. The wave hit the shack with a roar like dynamite. It stunned her. Her numb fingers let go the chair, and it was swept off the steps like a crumb from a table. She was hurled back, tossed and swung about the careening cracking floor. The shack heaved and swayed on its flimsy foundation. The mountain of water wrenched it loose and swept it, on the crown of a whole streetful of debris, right off the Flat and into the course of the flood, swirling round and round. Almost unconscious, Mary clung to the kitchen dresser. As the water rushed in, she groped instinctively and half-blindly for the rickety attic stairs.

Paul was running along the high embankment above the Flat. He was bent on getting to the shack to see for himself that Mary had been removed to safety. He knew that the police warnings had covered this district, and that the shanties below must be empty by now. Yet something troubled him. His memory would not let him relax. Those last bitter words of Mary's kept ringing in his head: "I shall never leave this house again." She could not have meant them, but those were her words. He dared not disbelieve them. He must make sure. He ran down Rebecca Street, dropping steeply to the Flat, gathering speed. It was barely dawn. He could just see the outlines of the ramshackle houses below him, with water filling the alleys between. As he came to the edge of the Flat he looked upriver where the water was roaring so wild and loud. And he stopped dead in his tracks. Not half a mile away he saw that great gray wall of water, gobbling up the wreckage of everything that had lain in its way. Paul stood panting on the last slight rise of ground, measuring the advance of the water against the distance that separated him from the Rafferty shack. And as he eyed the shack through the deceiving half-light, he gulped and stood rigid with horror. For the door of the shanty was open and there was something in the doorway, which should have been empty. Something that looked like a chair, and behind the chair a bent, shadowy form moving in jerks. Paul squinted hard and looked, straining in the faint light, once more.

With one desperate glance at the advancing wave upriver, Paul plunged onto the Flat. It was a short run to the shack; he could beat the tidal wave. But he had not counted on the depth of the water that had already inundated the bottom land. The water was almost up to his knees, and it rushed past him with a strong undertow like breakers on a beach. He could scarcely make headway against it. He ran slowly and futilely, the frustrated running of a nightmare, while the roar of the tidal wave, like steady thunder, sounded closer and closer over his head. Now he was very near the house. He could clearly see in the open doorway the horrible sight of the witless old man, nodding and mouthing, with his hand cupped to his ear; and more horribly, he could see Mary struggling on the doorstep with the chair, pushing and hauling. Oh why, he thought crazily, why. . . . The water was rising fast. Now it was almost up to his chest, in a minute he would be swimming, he would have to. . . . And the thunder in his ears roared like the sea breaking to swallow him up and crush him and extinguish him . . . Mary too, he thought, gasping. Mary too. Then he was lifted off his feet. He gave one last lunge, the house was almost in his grasp. Mary could have heard him shout but for the deafening roar of the water. And his fingers missed the house. He was swung and cracked about; his eardrums rattled; the cold, thundering water closed over his head.

He could never remember afterwards what happened during his struggle with the river. He was sucked down, rolled over and over, buffeted, shot upward, sucked down again. Each time he came to the surface, with straining lungs, he took a huge breath. He was fighting for his life, and knew only that. Then, just before it was too late, he collided with an enormous timber. Breathing in rasps now, he flung his arms automatically around the wooden beam, and clung to it. The water was so cold that he felt his endurance could be only a matter of minutes more, perhaps of seconds. He did not care. He could see nothing; no Rafferty shack, no other recognizable object; only the cold black tumbling water from which he had given up hope of being rescued.

Suddenly the big timber to which he was weakly clinging struck something solid, with a shock so violent that Paul nearly lost his grip. The other end of the beam was swinging around, athwart the current. Presently it stopped, incredibly motionless, and Paul knew only that he was clutching that beam, stationary while the whole river seethed past him. He could not struggle any more. He knew dully that his arms and legs were numb, and his strength was waning. Weakly he looked around, wondering how much longer he would remain conscious. Tangled in the water around his knees he saw the beam caught in the branches of trees. Trees, he thought dully, oh yes, on an island . . . must be Brunot Island. He shook his head hard, as if to clear his wits. With one last effort he swung his trembling legs onto the upstream side of the beam, and thus was held against it and in the tree by the force of the current. He sat there, trying to rally his strength, trying to rouse his dulled mind and his will power. He opened his eyes wide to force back that dreadful dullness which kept coming over him. And then, because he thought he was addled anyway, he saw the roof of a house— in fact a whole house, submerged almost to the attic window, careening down the raging Ohio. If I could reach that house, he thought dully . . . I might. . . . But how? It was whirling down midstream, and would pass about fifty yards from his island. Suppose I tried it, he thought . . . even if I had the strength left to try. His head sagged on his chest. It was useless, he would be swept down the current much faster than the house. He looked up again. If I wait, he thought, until it passes me, and then strike out and let the current carry me down on it. . . . The house was almost abreast of him and he was fighting to keep his wits clear and work the thing out. Then his jaw dropped and he gulped in his breath. That was not just a house, some house. It was the Rafferty shack. Oh no. . . . Yes, it is, he shouted aloud, as if to rouse himself. It is. How . . . why . . . never mind that now . . . *it is*.

While he watched, gasping, he saw the shack bump something, lurch, and swirl. As it turned he saw the attic window and hanging from the window, a limp figure with red hair streaming down, almost trailing in the water. Oh God, Paul prayed through his teeth, counting the distance and the moments as the shack careened along, oh God, help me now. That's Mary. Dead or alive . . . it's Mary.

He crouched on his beam like an animal. In the few minutes since the beam had been snagged in the trees the water had risen. He could feel the treetrunks swaying in the current. He inched his way along to the edge of his precarious refuge, never taking his eyes from the shack. His fingers fumbled numbly as he wrenched off one shoe; he had lost the other without knowing it. The shack was downriver now; it seemed almost beyond his reach, but he had shrewdly let it go on ahead of him. He must let it get far enough, but not too far, or he would never have the strength to grasp it when he was swept down on it. At last, when he dared not wait any longer, he let go of the timber, drew a great breath, and struck out with the last of his strength into the terrible, murderous current.

He had judged his distance instinctively and he had judged it well. The river rolled him down on the house as he swam. Now it was only a few feet away, now his hand touched it, now the current was crushing him against the wall. He fumbled for a foothold, his eyes raised to the terrifying figure of Mary just above his head. He could almost touch her hair. His feet found the cornice of the kitchen window, and with a surge of the current he lifted himself far enough to grasp the sill of the attic window above. With a last grueling effort he drew his shoulder muscles into a strained, spastic knot, lifted himself to the sill beside Mary, and collapsed across her body as if he himself were dying.

CHAPTER XXXII

[February 1884—Continued]

PAUL CAME TO IN A few seconds, desperately aware that he must still fight. In his arms Mary was limp and icy cold. If there was any life in her, he must rouse her and fight for it; only by doing so could he also save his own. His muscles were knotted and cramped so that he could scarcely move his arms; his legs were agonizing too. When he tried to lift his head, jagged lines danced before his eyes and he almost lost his balance. Just in time he lurched the other way and fell inward, through the window, clutching Mary and dragging her in with him. The blood rushed back to his head as he fell; holding Mary in his numb arms he toppled across the sill and dropped on the slimy attic floor.

It was a short drop, for the attic was no more than an airhole under the roof. Sprawled on the floor with Mary in his arms, he looked up and saw that a nail inside the window had caught her clothes and held her; but for that she would have been swept out and drowned. Her face was lifeless but he felt her heart beating faintly. He began to try to bring her to. Her wet clothing clung to her in a sodden, ice-cold mass; he could feel the steely-cold and hard surcingle of her corsets. He ripped, pulled, and fumbled with her clothes until he could get at the stays underneath them He flung the things away. He began to chafe and massage her body and her legs and arms, at the same time forcing his own breath between her parted blue lips, and holding her close to warm her with the heat of his own body. His efforts warmed him too. His own struggle had kept his circulation going but now for the first time he felt the powerful, reassuring sensation of the second wind. He was so empty that his stomach was beginning to contract in painful cramps, yet he could not have called the emptiness hunger. He felt curiously strong and charged with super-energy that he had never before known he possessed. He opened his shirt and his undershirt and held Mary close to the warmth of his naked chest, slipping her limp, icy hands inside his damp clothing to warm them against his body And all the while he talked to her, begging, pleading, imploring her to come to. "Darling, I'm here. It's Paul. You're safe now. Mary. Darling. Open your eyes and look at me. Darling, open your eyes. . . ."

And presently she did. The blue lids rolled back and beneath them the gray eyes stared, shocked and unseeing. He shook her gently, holding her tight, and raising her head on his arm.

'Darling. Oh, Mary, I've found you."

She gazed at him dumbly for a moment; then her head fell back over his arm and she murmured, "Paul."

"Yes," he whispered. He stroked the tangled hair from her forehead and tried to shelter her from the draught with his body. "Don't slip away from me, darling." Her features looked as if they were chiselled from gray marble. He could hardly speak. His voice stuck in his throat. "Don't go."

She made a soft sound, a sigh or a groan, he could not tell, and her eyes closed again.

"Mary!" He shook her hard now and his voice roared out suddenly, startling him as much as her. She shuddered and looked at him again.

He tried to keep chafing her arms and legs while he talked; he saw now that he must keep her startled if he was to keep her conscious and get her to make any effort to stay alive.

"Darling, we're in great danger. We've got to fight. We must keep alive. Do you understand?" He spoke very loud, very distinctly.

"Ah." She made another soft sound.

"Try to understand me, darling. We'll be overcome unless we fight. We must save each other. You must try." He shook her again. "You must try. Will you, Mary? Will you try?"

She opened her eyes again. As gently as possible he dragged her to a sitting position beside him. He had barely enough strength to lift her. She collapsed in a bundle against him, and he held her, still talking and shaking her a little.

"That's better," he murmured. "You understand. Now see, I'm perfectly fine, dear, warm and not a bit chilled. I'll keep us both warm. But you must try to move, darling. Make all the effort you can."

She nodded weakly.

"Move your hands and feet as soon as you can, dear. I'll keep on rubbing them until we get them warm. The air's not very cold, darling. If we can just keep our blood going. . . ."

An hour later she was almost herself again; ghastly pale and dishevelled beyond anything he could have imagined, but able to comprehend where she was and what had happened to her. Her arms and legs were scratched and bleeding; there was a cruel, ugly bruise on her left temple; her dress hung about her in rags, the buttons and fastenings ripped off, the flounces from the skirt trailing in dirty, ragged loops. Her hair flung wildly down her back.

"How did you find me?" she asked at last.

He told her, hurrying over his own adventures to get on to hers.

"And Dad?"

He explained about the Flat.

"Ah. May God rest his poor soul." She crossed herself weakly.

Paul held her closer.

"If you had only gone up the hill when the warnings went out, darling! You knew about the flood coming, didn't you?

She nodded, her face turned away from him.

"Then why didn't you do something? Why did you stay there on the Flat after everybody else had gone?"

She did not answer at once. Finally she whispered, "I wanted to die."

He cringed; he felt a hollow opening up inside him, a bitter, empty, deadening chasm in which floated the wreckage of their lives.

"Oh don't."

"I shouldn't have said it. I'm sorry, dear. I know better now, Paul."

"Are you sure?"

She nodded again. "It isn't easy to die. We've no business tryin' to take things out o' Gods hands." She mumbled a little confusedly and slipped off at phrases into her old forgotten brogue. "If He'd meant me to die I'd be dead there in the water, long ago."

She had no remembrance of getting up to the attic of the house when the water inundated the lower floor. She did not know now why she had gone to the window; "I think," she said, "because I was sick. I think I threw up a lot of water."

"Poor darling. Poor Mary."

The day passed and it grew dark. The house was moving slowly in the flood current. Only by watching the wooded banks could Paul see that they were moving down the Ohio. Evidently this would go on all night. There was no use trying to go downstairs. The water was up to the ceiling of the lower floor, right up to the downstairs windows. The attic smelled vilely. It had never been furnished and it was now a dark, slimy, black hole. There was nothing to do, though, but sit on its rough wet planks, holding Mary in his arms and praying that she would stay alive until some kind of help came. At last he lay down on the floor and held Mary beside him. "Let's try to sleep," he whispered. "Let me try to keep you warm."

So he lay in the cold dark, holding the wraith of Mary in his arms. Only to hold her in sleep answered as much desire as he had the strength to feel. Thin and light, she lay in his arms like an autumn leaf, with the same sad promise of fluttering away. His body was numb and sore, but he prayed that there would be enough warmth in its muscle and bulk to protect them both until daylight. His bare feet were agony in the cold. Damp and penetrating draughts circled up through the floor. Piercing pains shot through the small of his back and down his legs; his arms ached leadenly but he tried not to move them. His tongue was thick and sour; a vile taste clung to his mouth; the odor of his dirty body and dirty clothes, the damp stink of the house was abominable. He slept fitfully at first, later with heavy exhaustion.

A brilliant rising sun fell on his closed eyes, and he opened them, turning his stiff neck to look at Mary curled against his breast. The sun sparkled on the wild disorder of her hair. He was aware of an agonizing cramp in his stomach. He put his hand on his belly and felt a dull surprise to find it hard and distended, blown up with gas. He had had nothing to eat for two nights and a day. Neither had she. He looked down at her. The bluish pallor of her lips, the dark purple circles around her closed eyes filled him with real terror. And here was the sun shining brilliantly, and Mary stirring and opening her eyes. She rubbed them with blank bewilderment. He saw fear coming into her face, and he spoke quickly, saying anything to comfort her.

"Look, darling! Look at the sunshine! That means the worst is over."

"What good will the sun do us?" she murmured sleepily. "We may be dead before—before—"

Just as she spoke they felt a lurch. The floor pitched downward and threw them against the wall. Mary sat up and cried, "What was that?"

Paul put his head out of the window and looked out. "I think we've stopped. I think the house is aground."

"Oh." Her eyelids fluttered wearily and she gave in to a fit of shivering.

"Don't you understand, darling? I think we're aground."

She gave a hysterical laugh. "Grand! We can go right downstairs and cook breakfast." She looked out the window at the water about two feet below it.

"Don't give up now, Mary! With this change in the weather and the house standing still, it may be very different a few hours from now."

Mary looked at his streaked face, pale under the dirt and the bristling growth of whiskers. She shook her head.

"You look awful, Paul. All in. Do you feel sick?"

He shook his head. "No. Do you?"

She pulled her rags tighter. Her teeth chattered. "Oh, no. I'm fine." As if to deny that, she closed her eyes weakly.

"Mary!" he cried, in a panic.

She opened her eyes suddenly and looked up at him. He bent down and stared hard into them. Huge, sombre pools of gray, rimmed with weary purple shadows, they met his with directness, but without candor. They were intent, but veiled. They had no answer for the silent questions in his.

"Mary—"

The blue lids came down and curtained her eyes again.

They took off most of their sodden clothes and hung them out of the attic windows to dry in the sun. Mary kept very busy about that, seeming to have found unexpected energy. Paul watched her. Several times he started to say something and checked himself, but finally he asked hoarsely, "Are you horribly hungry, Mary?"

It was a cruelty to ask that question. But he could no longer keep the thought under control; he had to prod it like an aching tooth.

"I could do with a cup of tea," she said. Her voice quavered. "There may be something I can fix downstairs when we can get to it."

The water was going down rapidly. All day they watched out of the windows as the lower part of the house began coming up into sight. By late afternoon Paul shouted, "I can see the front door. I'm going down."

He had a handful of sulphur matches in his overall pocket. Early that morning he had laid them carefully to dry on a row on the window sill in the sun, and all day Mary had watched to see that they did not blow away. Now they were dry. He struck one and by its light began groping his way down the dark, steep ladder-like stairs. Mary followed. The lower floor was still under some water. Mary gasped as the incredible mess came in sight. All the furniture was tumbled together against one wall. They both gagged at the sour, sodden smell. Paul pushed and pulled at the twisted litter of furniture until he disentangled an iron bed. The mattress on it was soaked, and gave off an unbearable odor. Paul pitched it through the window. Then he turned to Mary, to ask where she wanted him to begin cleaning up. But she paid no attention to him. She was leaning against the crumbling wall; her head was drooping: she had turned a ghastly putty-color, and her half-open eyes rolled horribly.

"Mary." He ran over and picked her up. "Darling!" She breathed faintly. She had reached the end of her endurance. He did not know how sparsely she had eaten in the shack with her father the past two weeks. Her stomach was accustomed to a minimum of food; but she was collapsing now. He laid her on the bare iron spring of the bed and looked for something to cover her. That was futile. Every thread of stuff in the house, everything he touched, was soaking wet. Finally he slipped off his filthy, foul-smelling denim shirt, folded it, and put it under her cheek so that the wire bedspring would not cut it. Then he made his way into the kitchen, stumbling over tumbled, broken furniture, clattering rusted pots and pans, sharp-cornered objects that cracked and barked his shins and bruised his bare toes. He did not dare to pause to take stock of anything. He knew now that if he did not quickly find something for them to eat they would both be overcome by starvation.

To wake to the insistent shouts of Paul's voice from the next room; to drag herself up on the bedspring to smell *smoke;* to hear the crackling of a fire; to see him coming through the door with a smile of triumph, was unbelievable. He took her in his arms and lifted her off the bed. He carried her into the kitchen and set her on a three-legged stool by the stove.

"Fire." She held out her hands, trembling; tears of weakness and relief sprang into her eyes. She looked up at Paul. "How did you do it?"

He did not answer. He was busy by the door, kneeling down with a tin dipper in his hands. He dipped river-water into the battered teakettle that he had rummaged out of the debris. He skimmed sticks, brown leaves, and bits of trash out of the water. Then he came back and put the kettle on the fire.

They hugged the stove, rubbing their hands over the heat. The sensation of warmth was overwhelming. Their faces turned from ghastly greenish-white to sudden feverish red; their eyes, which had been huge and strained, began to look normal. Once they mastered the fits of trembling that first overcame them, they groaned with the relief of the warmth.

"Oh how wonderful," Mary said. "Ah! Oh, Paul, how did you *do* it?"

"Never mind, now. The next thing is to get something inside us. Are you warm enough to come over here now and see if there's anything fit to eat?"

They sorted the soaked and jumbled contents of the cupboard. Nearly everything in it was ruined. But it had contained a set of tin canisters; one of these had held tea, another flour, another navy beans, another sugar. The sugar had melted, the flour was a cold gray paste; but the tea and the beans, though wet and swollen, were not beyond use.

"Darling!" Paul grabbed her shoulders and shook them gently. "Tea! We're not going to die! We'll be all right."

They rummaged further. In the corner, under all the debris, Paul had found a full can of kerosene. It was with that, and with some chips hacked from the attic beams upstairs, and some lumps of soft coal from the overturned scuttle, that he had got the fire going. And there too, wedged tightly under the overturned table, was a sack of potatoes. Mary's lips trembled. She looked up at Paul.

"Is it possible?" she breathed. She stared at him. ."Paul," she said. "God must want us to live."

He was standing by the stove watching the kettle come to a boil. He met her eyes, and for an instant the cataclysm that had swept over them seemed to have bound them in a new, though distant and different understanding. Paul had never felt this way before. He could say nothing.

Mary turned away to look for the teapot; then she returned to the stove. "It'll taste very queer," she said. "The canister leaked and the tea's all wet."

It did taste extremely strange. It was brackish and sour, but so welcome to their tortured stomachs that they gasped happily.

"We'll be all right now, Paul." Mary looked up at him with some of her old, calm courage. "I feel as if I could stand anything now."

He had been watching her with a queer expression, almost as if he had found a stranger standing there beside him by the stove. His eyes travelled from her torn, hanging, wild red hair, over her slender uncorseted body in its wrinkled rags, down to her bruised feet. She had lost both shoes and one stocking long ago; the other stocking was a crumpled black rag around her ankle. Looking at her, staring, Paul wondered dumbly if this could be the exquisite, delicate creature that he had loved so madly and desired so hotly time upon time in the past. He remembered moments when her slender milky neck, rising from some daintily embroidered frill, had arched back over his bent arm so that her worshipping gray eyes could look deep into his. He remembered passionate moments, like the last time he had ever been alone with her before the tragedy of his father's death; when she had been a woman both poised and voluptuous with avowed desire. There was no trace now of that lost unforgettable woman, but neither was there any loss of the quality that had always been hers—the strange sort of beauty, the luminous, unearthly inner light, which shone all the clearer through the preposterous apparition that stood beside him now. Indeed, that half-earthly, half-ghostly quality was emphasized now as it had not been for years; it was the Irish, the fantastic, the strange, the foreign; the thing that made her different, the thing that had made her haunt him in spite of all his efforts to escape.

Her eyes followed his as they moved in pity, in awe, almost in horror from her head to her feet. She looked down at her rags, and then up at him.

"It's—why, Paul—for you to see me in such a state!" She blushed slowly.

"I'd never really have known you if I hadn't." He spoke in a low, grave tone, tense and considered. "We may be here quite some time, Mary. You must understand that." He took a step toward her.

She looked about the room. There was the same subtle gesture of escape in her action that he had remarked before, the same calm evasion of something she could clearly perceive. Without a word or a gesture she held him off.

Darkness fell once again, but this time they were more comfortable.

Mary had found some candles and Paul lit one in the kitchen. Then he went up to bring down some bedding from the roof, where he had been drying it. By the flickering candlelight Mary was bending over a small rusty tin basin of warm water, doing as best she could to wash. The bodice of her ragged dress was open; she had dropped it down over her hips. She heard Paul stirring about overhead; then in the next room. And then there was entire silence.

"Mary."

He stood in the doorway, his hands hanging at his sides, his eyes fixed on her, his mouth a little open. She turned from the basin and straightened up. The look she gave him was profound. They stood and stared across the small room at each other, their eyes strained wide.

"Mary." His voice was extremely low, and in it rang the strange, penetrating resonance of a strained bass chord. She stood and stared at him; the elusiveness was gone from her face.

He walked slowly towards her, keeping his eyes on her white, tense face, on her gray eyes with their black pupils hugely distended. He came over and put his blackened, lacerated hands on her body. Beneath the ragged shift he felt her pounding heart under the jutting ribs. There was scarcely any flesh between her bones and her blue-white skin except for the small warm mounds of her breasts.

"We never knew," he said hoarsely. "We never knew anything we were talking about. We always talked too much."

She bent her head to escape his searching eyes.

"That's all over," he said, breathing hard. "There's nothing more to say. Nothing else left in the whole damned world."

He made a hoarse, heavy, anguished sound; picked her up with a quick, rough motion, and carried her into the other room.

That night; next day; another night, and another day. Only by the dark following the light, by the color of the changing sky, had they any measure of passing time. In pain and wretchedness, in cold and strain, through agony and violence, they were united at last. The poetic delicacy of their early love, the romance, the elusive ideal, were burned away in the fire of despairing passion. Life had torn from them the means to realize their love in beauty, in tenderness, in safety, in the infinite subtleties that were their natural expressions. Paul learned the power of the quality that had imprisoned him for years. He discovered now the burning, steely core of the woman whose girlhood he had shared. That girlhood had been only an exquisite veil. Behind it there was power; this tense strength pulsating in the emaciated body; this physical counterpart of the fanatical will that had tormented and challenged him for years. There was directness, clear fire, furious intensity in the passion of a woman who looked like a saint even while she lay naked in his arms between coarse gray blankets, her hair streaming about her shoulders and his.

Lying there in the early morning, with Paul's head buried in her breast, Mary stared through the gaping window at the faint rosy light in the sky; stared with her gray eyes wide and hard, fixed on space. She had managed

long since to stop thinking. Somewhere back of this whole furious immola-
tion of Nature, back of her memory, back of the confused nightmare of
death and devastation, lay buried the ordered thoughts and plans that her
life was to have been. They were buried as deeply and irrevocably as her
own brother and Paul's father. They were done. This man with whom she
was exploring—eagerly, willingly exploring—the powers of her body and
his, had the outward person of the Paul she loved. Behind that there was
mystery. Sometimes their eyes met in silent exchange of the long chain of
thoughts strung down the baffling years. Sometimes their eyes did not meet
at all. This hoarse, haggard, stubble-bearded man, with his hungry mouth,
his hard, commanding hands, his powerful masterful body was not the
yearning, sensitive Paul of the rickety old steps, the pleading, anxious
youth of the long-ago walks, the pathetic letters to London. He did not
plead that he loved her now. He did not speak in words. He spoke in a
stark and savage language. She understood it because she had the iron in
her blood, the fire in her nerves, to understand and to answer.

On that third morning, lying there awake, Mary felt as if her open eyes
were staring not at space but at a complete, supernatural panorama: the
years that lay behind her and Paul, and the years that lay ahead. She saw
it all, lying there, watching the dawn turn the window gray. She moved
carefully from Paul's arms and crept quietly out of bed. One of the shabby
gray wool blankets lay on a chair. She wrapped it around her shoulders
and walked noiselessly over to the window, to gaze out on the waste of
water which still surrounded them everywhere. The dawn was pink on the
horizon behind the stark February trees. The river was like a broad, flowing sheet of glass almost as far as she could see.

She was not alone for long. She heard Paul stirring on the bed behind
her. He was awakened and frightened by her absence; he sat up in momentary terror. Then he saw her standing at the window. He got out of
bed and crossed the room. They wrapped themselves together in the
blanket and stood looking out at the dawn.

"The water is down," Mary said. "We could wade across—I suppose—"

"Why—I guess we could," Paul said. There was dark surprise on his
face. "I'd never thought of it."

"Perhaps we didn't want to think of it," Mary said.

"That's so." Paul's arm tightened around her shoulder. They stood
silent for a long time. Then he said, "I've never been afraid of anything
before. But now, Mary—now. I'm afraid—that the water will go down."

"It will go down," she said. She was still staring out at the river.

"I don't want to go back," he said, very low.

"You—we—must. Of course." Then she turned rather abruptly and
looked up at him and said, her voice throbbing, "Paul. Have you learned
what I've learned? Here?"

He knew that he had. At moments during these weird, hourless days
he had fought against knowing. He had tried to tell himself that that was
not so. But always this strange new understanding, this acceptance of fate
—of God, Mary would put it—had come back. Always now it would block

his own passionate revolt. He looked deeply into Mary's eyes. She was waiting for him to speak. "I think I have," he whispered. "I have learned something. I don't know just what it is."

"I will tell you what it is." She drew closer to him as if she were confessing some fear herself. But her voice was firm. "This—is not the beginning of the future, Paul—"

"No—"

"It's not the beginning of the future," she said. "It is the end of the past."

CHAPTER XXXIII

[*February 1884—Continued*]

LATER THAT MORNING they were in the kitchen drinking the nauseous brew that they called tea, and preparing to eat more of the soggy, unsalted, roasted potatoes. Their supply of fuel was dwindling—Paul had torn nearly all the beams off the attic. The mildewed tea leaves in the canister were almost gone. They had triumphed for a little while over time and over thought. But as they prepared this breakfast they were deeply silent. The world was crowding in on them again.

"Hey! Hey there! Anybody in there?"

Mary started, paled, and caught at her throat. Paul raised his head, listened, and went to the window. Mary followed him, putting her hand on his arm.

"Paul—I—what is it?"

He turned, his face grave.

"Someone to rescue us."

"Oh my God." She put her face in her hands. He watched her, knowing what she felt. There was no comfort he could offer her.

"Anybody there?" The rough voice shouted outside again.

Mary went slowly into the other room. Paul put his head through the window and cried, "Here! Where are you? Here we are."

A rowboat pulled around the corner of the house. A man in it rested on his oars and looked up at Paul.

"Well fer all time! I seen yer smoke, some way upriver there."

"Where are we?" asked Paul.

"Why ye're marooned on Turtle Island. Funniest thing I ever see. Are ye all right?"

"I guess so. Can you get us out of here?"

"Sure thing. Who else ye got there?"

"My—a—a woman I saved. We were both caught in the flood."

The man pulled the boat into the mud and leaped ashore into the soggy muck. Paul went into the bedroom and spoke to Mary. She was sitting on the edge of the bed, staring at the floor; her face was expressionless. He watched her for a moment. Then he said, "We'd better go, dear."

"Yes, we'd better," she said. She looked about. The gesture was distressing and eloquent; as if to look for something that must belong to her in this room where she had known revelation. She shook her head and stood up. Paul stared at her for a moment.

"It is queer," he said. "It's damned queer to walk out of this place the way we came into it. The only place—"

"Come on," said Mary quickly. She bit her lips.

In the boat the man told them that they were twenty-one miles west of Pittsburgh. The Ohio at this point was two-thirds of a mile wide; both banks were thickly wooded. Steep cliffs dropped down to the water, and for a quarter of a mile inland, on both sides, the man said, the riverside land was uninhabited.

"Funny thing," he said, chewing tobacco and spitting into the water. "You'd think there'd been parties searchin' around here for folks like you. Guess there ain' 'nough homes right by here for nobody to bother about. This ben a bad flood."

"I don't know a thing about it," Paul said, "except this part of it I was in."

"Where d'ye come from?"

"Allegheny. What's the best way to get back?"

"Well, I'm takin' ye to my place. Got a farm downriver a piece here. Beaver's nearest town, I guess ye can get a train from there. If the tracks are down."

"Were they washed out?"

"Why, sure. Say, they's ben terr'ble goin's on. Down Wheeling way they got gov'ment rescue commissions and what all else. Most the tracks down river ben washed out. I still can't figger how come, nobody come along and found you sooner. Three days ye say ye ben there?"

"About."

"Well, well."

They watched the heavy currents as the man pulled the boat strongly against them. The river, he said, had dropped to normal level but the current was still dangerously swift.

"Wouldn't know the old stream," he said. "Most the time it's lazy's a mule. What say yer name is?"

"Scott. What's yours?"

"Mackins. Jed Mackins. Jest call me Jed." He bent to his oars again.

Mary had not said a word. She sat in the stern of the rowboat, looking behind her at the shack on the island. From this perspective it looked fantastic, stuck on a hummock of land which had caught it square beneath center. Its four corners hung at varying distances from the ground, and smoke still drifted from its chimney. She stared at the roof. Now that it was all past her, she could not believe that she had not dreamed the entire experience. She turned her head and looked at Paul. His face was solemn, and his eyes also were fixed on the house receding behind him. Mary looked at his drawn, whiskered face, and at the haphazard clothes he had put on in the house; some of James's clothes. Nobody would believe that this dirty, dishevelled, starving derelict was Paul Scott of Allegheny City; and as for her— She looked down at her scratched and stained hands, and felt of her hair which she had twisted up into a tangled ball. She took a deep breath. The fresh air, at least, was deliciously welcome; for all their efforts they had not been able to dispel the horrible dank smell in the house.

Jed Mackins pulled his boat around a bend, where the banks sloped less steeply, and rowed for about an eighth of a mile along the shore. He ran the boat aground on the edge of a small clearing. He and Paul sprang out, drew the boat up on the muddy bank, and helped Mary out. Jed tied the boat to a tree.

"My place's jest up there over that ridge," he said, pointing through the bare trees. "Jest up this slope a ways."

Mary walked gingerly, putting her feet tentatively on the ground. Paul helped her.

"It feels so queer," she said. "The ground shakes."

"You do," Paul said. "You'll only begin to find out now what this has really been like. It'll be good to get home."

She opened her mouth to say something and shut it again. They walked on slowly, Paul helping Mary, Jed leading the way. At the top of the rise he turned right and led them to a ramshackle farmhouse close to a narrow muddy road.

"Here ye be," he said. "Can't hardly see the river from here. Ye'll prob'ly be glad of that. Jennie! Oh, Jennie!"

A heavy, slatternly woman opened the door.

"Found these folks marooned in the river. They ain't had nothin' to eat 'cept sour tea 'n 'taters fer near four days. Got anything ready?"

Jennie hurried down the steps and put her arms around Mary.

"Why you poor *thing*," she cried. "You're near starved." She lifted Mary's bony, almost transparent hand. "Why you come right along in and lay down here on the kitchen lounge."

As they entered the dark kitchen the smell of stew and of boiling coffee struck their noses. Paul paled, and Mary bit her lips nervously. She dropped down on the carpet-covered sofa with a low sigh. Jennie Mackins bustled about, putting plates and spoons on the table, stirring the stew, asking endless questions full of wonder and solicitude.

"Think ye could eat now?" she asked finally.

They sat down to bowls of thick meat stew and mugs of steaming coffee. The Mackins sat with them and watched them eat, Jennie saying, "Not too fast now, ye'll get sick if you don't eat slow. Empty stummicks like that. My, my."

She cut a thick slice of bread and handed it to Mary.

"Sop that in the gravy, dearie. It'll go down easy."

"This coffee is saving my life," Paul sighed. He held out his mug to be filled again. He was amazed, now that it was all over, that his reaction was no more severe than it appeared to be. He had heard terrible tales of victims of exposure and starvation, who held up until help came, and then collapsed in hysteria, coma, or pneumonia. Neither he nor Mary appeared to be in the least danger of anything like that. They were exhausted and gray-faced and quiet, but perfectly in command of themselves. Paul saw that Mary was as grateful for this as he. Her apprehension after leaving the rowboat had been pitiful.

Jennie Mackins's curiosity was greater than her husband's. While they ate she plied them with questions, found out who they were, where they came from, how they had got caught in the flood. "My, my," she kept saying as they told their story. "My, my."

She made Mary lie down on her bed, covered her warmly, and watched her until she fell asleep. Paul asked Jed how they could get back to Pittsburgh.

"I ain't ben to Beaver sence all the trouble," Jed said, "but I heard tell yest'day they'd be gettin' through again tomorrer. A big piece was washed out here. You'd all better sleep here tonight, and I'll hitch up in the mornin' and drive you down there. You can get a train to Pittsburgh—if they is a train. I guess th' will be."

Mary slept all afternoon, while Paul wandered about with Jed.

"Good to get yer feet on dirt again, ain't it?" Jed asked. "Jeez, that must a' ben a spooky place, that house."

"Spooky! Say," said Paul, "you haven't got a razor I could borrow, have you?"

Late that night he and Mary sat alone together in the kitchen. The Mackinses had gone to bed, after many assurances from Paul that Mary and he were all right; they wanted to sit up by the fire awhile. Jennie had made a bed for Paul on the kitchen sofa, and one for Mary in the parlor. She had eyed them curiously as she bustled about. It was clear that these two were not married—they'd said they weren't; but what was there between them, anyway? Something heavy, something strong; even a total stranger, crude and heavy-handed, could sense that. She had lingered at the foot of the stairs, looking back at them as they sat by the stove.

"Sure ye're all right?" she asked. There was a curious, as well as a kindly note of solicitude in her voice. She eyed them sharply.

"Oh yes, thank you." Mary smiled at her. "You've been so good to us. Just saved our lives, you and Jed."

"Oh, that ain't nothin'. No more'n anybody'd do. Well, good-night," she said awkwardly.

They sat silent, listening to her lumbering footsteps on the stairs, and later above their heads. Finally the house grew quiet. In the distance, if they listened, they could hear Jed Mackins snore. They sat for a long time, how long they did not know. The habit of the clock had dropped completely from them. The fire made crackling noises, and they were both very still. Finally Paul raised his head.

Their eyes met. Each was surprised at the expression of the other; the calm, the weariness, the understanding. For years every glance that they had exchanged had been fraught with question, with suspense, with emotion, with longing. Now there was a strange and final quiet. They had made the journey from youth into maturity with agony and turmoil of spirit. Now for the first time they exchanged the wise, weighed glances of adults. They spoke now, to each other, and about each other, with extraordinary, objective calm. Only that morning they had lain together in the wildest ecstasy and abandon. Now these two quiet people sat and looked past those other two, and into a strange future.

"Well," Paul said, with a sigh, "I suppose we've got to decide what to do next."

Mary lay back in her chair, her hands curved in her lap. She was relaxed in every bone. "Yes," she said. And then, after a pause, "I wonder if it hasn't all been decided for us?"

"Do you believe so much in fate?" he asked.

"I believe in God," she said. "So close to us—He's been—"

"And hard," Paul said, with bitterness.

"He must know why." Mary leaned toward Paul. "It has been hard. But what is not—that is really life?"

"You're still doing penance for James," he said.

"No. Not exactly. I don't really think I have to do penance for James all the rest of my life. No priest told me that. And yet—it was a great wrong, Paul. A great sin."

"You really believe that," he said slowly.

"I do. And the one thing I always did know was that it wasn't right for you and me to marry. It wasn't fitting. It wasn't what God—life, if you want to call it that—intended. We were trying to put things together that didn't belong together, and so—something had to happen. I've always known that. Ever since—since—I knew I loved you, Paul. I've tried to explain it in all those queer ways of mine, through my feelings and my imagination and my religion—and all that. I couldn't help those ways. I suppose it's because I'm Irish. We're full of notions, they say it's in our blood. But it's always been the same to me. I've always known we could not put those things together."

Again they exchanged the deepest of glances. They looked and felt old, Mary thought. When they were healed, when their bruises and scratches were gone, when they were clean and clothed and fed and shod again, they might look no older than their actual years. But inwardly they would feel old. The texture of youth was gone from them. Violence had torn it away and burnt it up.

"That's how I can be sure I'm right," Mary said slowly. "That Irish thing, that quality you people call mystic. I'm as old now inside as I'll ever be. You see—" she leaned toward him again—"if I were young, I'd not be able to say I'd do without you. Not—now. I'd be greedy. I'd want more of you." She hesitated. "But now I'm old enough to know when I've had all I'm to get." Her voice throbbed very low. "And so are you, Paul. Aren't you?"

"Let me get it perfectly clear," he said. "You mean that you will never marry me?"

"Never," she said.

He took a deep, unsteady breath and slouched back in his chair, as if something inside him had gone flaccid. He sat there, staring at the fire.

Only a few unbelievably short weeks ago that statement would have crushed him totally. It would have been intolerable, unendurable, something flesh and blood could not bear, a decision in the shadow of which he would not have wanted to go on living. But that was not true now. He sat in the midst of desolation. But the desolation had the grandeur of true tragedy, like eternal ruins of monumental beauty, whose sadness holds a strange, pervading happiness. His was not happiness in any form that could be tasted by flesh and blood; but he sat in its presence, and it was a fragment of perfection. He was part of an ancient and incomprehensible law. It was inevitable and strange and absolutely true.

He turned his head toward her slowly. "Could you believe," he asked tensely, "that you make me feel happy?"

"Yes," she said, bending her head. "I feel happy too."

There stood complete the most momentous decision of their lives, with the making of which they had had nothing to do, in words. As Mary said, the decision had been made for them. Their part was that of recognition. To complete the recognition they had needed those three timeless days together. Without the completion of the cycle they would never have been able to see the truth. Now they could see. Now it was clear. Now they must move on, and live.

The room seemed quieter than ever. The mixture of silence and shadows, the soft noises of the fire, the loud ticking of the clock, made a luminous shell of protection around them. They had been cold and harried and tormented too long. Paul drew a deep sigh. "It's not a particularly joyful kind of happiness," he said. "But at least the battle's over. You're right about that, darling. May I call you darling? I'm used to it."

She stretched out her hand and he clasped it for a moment.

"You should break the habit," she said. Her smile was tender.

"What does it matter," he said, "what an old bachelor says to an old maid?"

Mary started. "You—you're not to be a bachelor!" she said.

"But Mary—you don't expect me to—to marry *somebody else?*"

"Of course. Of course I do. That's part of what this is all about."

"But—" he looked at her, wrinkling his forehead. "But—I can't ever love anybody else. You know that."

"I do," she said. "Nor can I. But—what has love to do with marriage —your marriage?"

Paul sat back slowly in his chair, shaking his head. But he only said, "Oh."

"Our love has had nothing to do with marriage," Mary went on. "We didn't have to marry to love each other. In fact," she stared at him, "just because we do love—we can't marry."

"You are so strange," he said.

"But it's true," she said. "You must marry, Paul. You must marry soon."

Her voice rang very low and intense. He felt again that core of steel in her. But he said, bitterly, "Who? Do you think I'll have time to go around looking the possibilities over?"

She shook her head and smiled, a strange, quiet, sorrowful smile. She knew then, perfectly certainly, that he would marry Louise Kane. He might not know it himself yet—but he would never take the time to look for anybody else.

"Would *you* marry someone else?" he asked sharply.

"Me?" she gasped. "Oh, no!"

"That's the part I couldn't bear," he said. "If you did."

"You won't have to, Paul. I shall never marry. Anyone."

They were silent while she saw him weighing this decision too. Presently she said, "You can see—that it's entirely different for each of us. I don't matter to anybody but myself. It doesn't matter whether I have children. It doesn't matter whether I carry on a family name. God knows, the name of Rafferty—" she shook her head quickly, and passed her hand across her eyes. "It doesn't matter what becomes of me in respect to any outside thing. But it does matter—it matters terribly—what becomes of you."

"So I should make a marriage of convenience," he said, tapping his pipestem on his teeth.

"You might call it that." She hesitated. "But—it's our tragedy that you couldn't fall in love with a woman who would be a suitable wife for you. I believe you, Paul. You'll never—love—her. But you could become very devoted to such a wife. And maybe that's better grounds for marriage than what we've got."

"It's so hard to take all you say and believe it, Mary."

"I know. But I'm right, and I think you know it. You'll have to do it. You'll have no choice."

Step by step she was leading him into her strange, mystical, but rigidly logical world, so logical that it was startling. He was thinking now about this marriage that she was describing as if it were to be the life of somebody else, not of Paul Scott. And after his long silence, he looked up and said, "I do mean to have children. I always did."

"Of course."

"I'm not sure I want them for myself," he said. "But I know I want them for the mill. I don't mean to die and leave that mill—" He broke off and put his face into his hands.

"There," Mary said softly. "I've always tried to say that. And you've said it better than I ever could. You *are* the mill, Paul." Her voice was very firm. "And that's why—why we've come to these decisions."

He raised his head and looked at the calm, lovely light in her face, and as he did so he felt the very last of the bitter resistance fading from his mind. She was absolutely right. If he was not the mill, he was nothing. And he could not have the mill and her for his wife too. The mill was immovable, uncompromising, fixed; it was there in Allegheny City on the bank of the Ohio and he could not marry Mary Rafferty and be that mill also. Only in another incarnation, in another place and time and world could he marry her; and then he would not have and be that mill. He sighed and let his eyes rest on her face, more spiritual and radiant than he had ever seen it before. Finally he breathed, "Lord, I'm tired. Inside. Outside. Tired all through."

Her face, he thought, watching it, came back to earth again; back to a smile for him after a visible reflection of her remote and austere and consecrated thoughts. She said, "I'm tired too. It would be nice to fall asleep now and not wake for the longest time."

They smiled slowly at each other again. Sleep meant to them now what it never had before. Even in the throes of their worst hardship, they had learned the infinite consolation of sleep profound with the weight of love. And here they were at this incredible point of renunciation, calm, reasoning, curiously poised; they could weigh and consider and speak of what they knew with ultimate quiet born of the tempests that had swept them. Paul could go still farther; his mind, so firmly trained in the ways of the tangible, the world of strong, clear realities, must move from dreams and ideals and mysteries to the actual. He asked slowly, staring at the red fire winking through the mica pane of the firebox on the stove, "What are you going to do, Mary?"

"Work," she said. "I thought I'd set up as a seamstress. I'm a good dressmaker, you know."

"Where?"

She shook her head very slowly. "Suppose we don't go into that. I don't pretend—" she swallowed— "that this will be easy."

He made a sound. "Oh, Mary. You mean—you wouldn't ever see me—at all?"

"It wouldn't be right. I mightn't—couldn't—" she broke off. He saw her tragic determination in her mouth. Somehow he recovered and took quick refuge in practicality—with which he would surround himself the rest of his days.

"Darling," he said, "you know Father left you money, don't you?"

"He said he was going to," she murmured. "I'd rather not take it."

"I want you to take it," he said. "We can't have any more crises, Mary, and heartbreaks and uproars and tragedies. I'm asking you to take it—selfishly, really. It isn't much money, after all. But if you have that income you'll never be helpless. I'm only trying to say it will save me from worrying about you. Understand?"

"I really don't want you to be in touch with me. I don't mean you to."

"Well, if you insist. I wouldn't be around in person to pay you your income, you know. The bank handles that."

"I'll need some money to start myself in dressmaking," she admitted, thinking.

"That's better. You know, I could sit here and talk like this all night. I feel so strange, Mary. If anyone had ever told me I'd sit and talk with you like this the last night before I was never to see you again, I'd say he was crazy."

"You said I was crazy once."

"Perhaps we both were."

The stove was hot and comforting between them. The clock struck one. Paul smoked in silence for a time. Mary sat quietly, her hands in her lap. A cat mewed outside. Mary got up and let it into the cellarway. When she came back to the stove Paul reached up and drew her into his arms.

"Tomorrow," he said, "it will be as you say. Tonight is still mine."

CHAPTER XXXIV

[April 1889]

MARY WALKED OUT to the entrance hall with Mrs. Dixon and stood for a moment chatting on the stoop in the sunshine. She wore a well-fitted blue challis dress and a black dressmaker's apron, with its bib stuck full of threaded needles. Around her waist there was a cotton tape with a pair of shears and a small bristling pin-cushion hanging from it. Her shining hair was twisted into a roll high on her head. Her expression just now was serious and full of concern, but her face was curiously calm and reposed. Her deep-set eyes had a quality at once luminous, yet veiled. They were wise eyes, penetrating and sentient; and they carried the power to parry inquisition. Nobody would ever read in those eyes something he was not intended to know.

Mrs. Dixon shook her head now in answer to a question, and sighed. "I'm afraid she's very ill, Miss Mary. She won't say so, of course. She insists she is only a little upset. But I don't like the look of it."

"Have you talked to Mrs. Paul? Does she know what the trouble is?"

"No, she has no idea. Mrs. Scott would not tell her, in any case. She's—— Louise is not well just now, you know."

"I didn't know."

So Louise was having her second child. Mary sighed. She was glad of that, deeply delighted for Paul. But this was such an eerie way to learn these things which mattered to her—in spite of five years' total separation from the family—more than they could matter to anyone else on earth. That was the way she had learned about Paul's marriage to Louise four years ago; even the way she had learned the minutest details of Louise's trousseau. That was how she knew when Dickie was born two and a half years ago, how she knew about the scene Louise had made about naming the child for her father, instead of for William Scott as Paul had intended. That was how she knew almost everything that concerned and happened to the Scotts—by piecing together the remarks, the news, the gossip of her customers. Mrs. Dixon was talking along now.

"Mrs. Scott," she was saying, "would never tell Louise what the doctor really says. She wouldn't want to worry any of her children—that is, if there's something seriously wrong. Or perhaps——" Mrs. Dixon paused and spoke more slowly—"perhaps she does not know herself."

"This sounds very bad to me. I wish I knew the truth. Mrs. Dixon, when you hear something more about Mrs. Scott will you be so kind as to let me know?"

"Why certainly." Her client stood for a moment smoothing her gloves and eyeing Mary under her downcast lids. She could not help speculating why, with all her intense devotion to Clarissa Scott, Mary would not be planning to go to see her immediately on hearing of her illness. But Mrs.

Dixon, like Helena Trumbull, Janet Burns, Sarah McKelvie, and all the other women who were Clarissa Scott's old friends had long ago accepted the obvious implication in Mary Rafferty's situation—that she could not bear to go on living among the Scotts after the tragedy precipitated by her brother. Nobody knew the true details of the matter.

Or perhaps the Scotts had found the idea of Mary's presence an unbearable reminder of the murder. Nobody ever said. But they all did know that Clarissa Scott had loyally befriended Mary, had urged her friends to take their dressmaking to her, and had been instrumental in helping her to establish herself in business. Yet, so far as they knew, Mary never saw the Scotts and had no contact with them. It was the natural outcome of a tragic situation. Mrs. Dixon stood on the doorstep and tried to penetrate the quiet enigma of Mary's gray eyes.

"You wouldn't go yourself to call on Mrs. Scott, Miss Mary? It might be a real comfort to her." She spoke hesitantly.

"Perhaps I might. You'll tell Horne's to send me that buckram first thing in the morning, won't you, Mrs. Dixon? I don't want to disappoint you about that taffeta dress."

"That's right. I must have it in time to take away with me on the twentieth. And the two morning-dresses, too, and the combing-jacket. Good-morning, Miss Mary. Lovely day, isn't it?"

The lady stepped into her waiting brougham and drove away. Mary stood for a moment on the step, looking up the tree-shaded stretch of Negley Avenue. It was, as people were remarking in their greetings, a lovely day, one of those rare days when the full delight of the cloudless blue sky, the gentle warmth of the spring sunshine, were unspoiled by the usual pall of gritty black smoke that hung over the city. It was all a question of wind (unless times were bad and the mills idle)—sometimes the city was in pure luck, like today.

Mary turned back into the house, walking slowly with her head bent. She was grieved to a profound degree at the news which she had just heard of Clarissa Scott; that she had been weeks in bed and seemed not to know when she would be up again. Susan Dixon happened to be the first of Clarissa's intimate friends for whom Mary had sewed since Clarissa had become so ill. Mary knew that Mrs. Scott must be dreadfully ill if she had given up any effort to be about and run her house. That was not at all like her. It would not be like her to leave things to Louise at a time like this, either; Mary had heard a good deal about that. Louise, the ladies said, took what they called "delicate health" very hard. Mary could not imagine how they were managing over at Western Avenue. She stood still, staring out the window at the budding tree outside, her mind roving through the minutest details of the Scotts' apparent situation. She sighed heavily. If Mrs. Scott was in bed with some dreadful disease she must be suffering horribly, and worrying about Louise and the little boy and— Mary put up her hand, horrified to find herself wiping tears from her eyes. This was the kind of thinking she never allowed herself. Never, she said stubbornly. Never mind whether the Scotts need me or not. I'm thinking dreams, not facts. She shook her head briskly and went back to her work.

She had succeeded beyond her expectations in making a small, separate world for herself. She had settled in two rooms in this house across the river in Pittsburgh, in the pleasant residential district between Squirrel Hill and East Liberty. She had no previous associations with this part of the city and had chosen it purposely for that reason. It was all part of the decision that she had had to make about her work and her future.

At one time she had thought of going far away from Pittsburgh altogether, to Chicago, to the West, to New York—anywhere she would be a total stranger and could try to start life over again. But she had only two ways of earning her living; if she could not be a dressmaker, she must be a servant. And she had made a final decision about that. Never again would she throw herself into the inner life of a family, never again let her heart or her mind or her will become entangled with the deep, passionate currents that shaped human beings to the intricate and agonizing patterns of the lives that she had shared. Some people, to be sure, had busy, ex‧ ternalized existences; they ran large, impersonal houses in which she might become indispensable without making any part of herself a hostage. In such a home in any large city she could undoubtedly have obtained a good position. But when she faced the question truthfully she knew that that was not what she wanted. Her need was for the simple, the warm, the familiar. Too much had been exacted of her in the packed, painful, tortuous decade since she had cast her destiny among the Scotts. She remembered now the earliest longings of her girlhood, centered about her hope of lifting herself from the miserable surroundings and companions of her birth. She had taken the only means at her disposal, and she had given, as well as received, in a sense, too much. From now on she would live her own life, alone.

Independence, she saw, could be the only key to this, and independence she would have. But to achieve this independence through plying the only trade she knew, she must get a start where somebody knew her; and that place had to be Pittsburgh. Otherwise, she could only work at sewing by hiring herself out to somebody else. And Mary was through forever, she decided, with hiring herself out.

It was not an easy thing to cut oneself off from the living human chains that had bound every day and every year of one's life. Kate was in Pittsburgh, with six children now. There was too the small old familiar world of church activities, modest good works, sociable visiting over a cup of tea. And lastly—there was Bridget to think about. Not a trace of the girl had ever been reported by the Missing Persons Bureau. Mary had steeled herself in realistic acceptance of Bridget's proclivities, and had listened impassively when detectives gave her periodic reports of the inmates of vice resorts. Mary believed firmly that some day her youngest sister would emerge from nowhere and when that happened, Mary proposed to be standing by. It was not regarded as a serious matter by the Pittsburgh police—this disappearance of a shantytown girl with a street reputation. The slums were full of that sort of thing. The police never bothered houses or their keepers or inmates too much. It was an old Pittsburgh tradition from the days of the Bayardstown Toughs and the roaring wide-open thirties and forties that business was business, and morals were morals. Pittsburgh morality was of the rigid public ·kind imposed by the stern Presbyterian citizens who kept the Sunday laws to the last blue limit, and let the ward boys and Hill girls keep the police fixed up. The mobility of the vice business was one thing that made people in it hard to find. Besides, the authorities had more than once reminded Mary, there was no reason to suppose that Bridget was in Pittsburgh at all. She might be anywhere else under the sun, or she might be dead. Still, Mary told herself that if Bridget ever did turn up, it would be in Pittsburgh, and if that happened she wanted to be there. That was unreasoning, that was instinct like the same buried knowledge that life in the same town where the Scotts lived, cut off from them as she was, was better than life somewhere else.

The one tie that she had kept unbroken was with Constance. So far away in London, so unlikely ever to come back here and stir things up— what harm if she wrote to Constance and enjoyed her erratic, spasmodic replies? Constance let the years slide carelessly by, sometimes not writing for months on end. Then suddenly she would reassert herself by some delightful Christmas surprise. Mary's two rooms were sprinkled with lovely presents from Constance, like the charming spirit-lamp teakettle and Coalport cups and saucers from which she had her tea every afternoon. There were framed pictures on the tables, mantels, and stands. Constance in this court gown, Constance in that, Clarrie in a long succession of tantalizing poses. Constance must have a good deal of money now, from her share of her father's estate, and she certainly spent it tastefully. Her letters, when she wrote them, were largely descriptions of her fittings at Worth's and Callot's in Paris; she went over twice a year for her clothes. Mary put some of the notes about the clothes to good use. She often drew from some pleased customer a "You have such lovely taste, Miss Mary; *where* did you get the idea of that bias drape?"

CHAPTER XXXV

[*1889—Continued*]

THE BREAKFAST-TABLE had a haphazard look. It was set with the same blue-willow china from which the Scotts had always eaten their breakfasts. The massive knives and forks and spoons, heavily chased and monogrammed, the thick fluted water-tumblers, the high coffee-urn, were all in their accustomed places. But the silver did not shine properly, even in the pale sunlight of this unusually clear spring morning. There was a dull film about the china and glassware, a grayish look to the linen. Things seemed not to have been placed in their old precise positions upon the table, but rather slapped down on it here and there; knife-blades were turned carelessly outward, cups set askew in their saucers. The jam-jar was sticky around its lip.

Paul put down his coffee-cup with a rattle and laid aside his *Gazette*.

"Louise," he asked in a patient tone, "is there any way of giving *you* an idea what decent coffee tastes like? If you did know, do you think you could do anything with that female ape in the kitchen?"

Louise raised her brown head and sent her husband a frightened, pleading look. "I've tried," she said weakly. Her voice was slack and thin; almost a whine. "I don't see what's the matter with this coffee, Paul."

She looked at Edgar as if to ask for support. But he was reading his mail. He kept his blond head bent over the letter in his hand. The pale tan brew stood untasted in his cup.

Louise raised her napkin to her lips.

"Oh dear," she gasped, "I'm afraid I'm going to be ill."

"Then for heaven's sake go upstairs and lie down," Paul said irritably. "I've told you not to try to come down if you feel sick."

"But Dickie—"

She looked despairingly at the chubby little boy in the high-chair beside her. His round pink face was smeared with porridge; a thick trickle of oatmeal and milk slid slowly down his chin. Louise shuddered, seized the child's bib and wiped his face. "He makes such a mess, Paul," she said.

The child gurgled happily with his mouth full. The sight and the sound curdled Louise's shaky stomach.

"If you'd only let him eat his breakfast in the nursery with Margaret," Louise wailed. "He's too little to be here, making such a mess—"

"Go upstairs and lie down, Louise." Paul rose from his place, went to the other end of the table, and sat down in the chair from which Louise had risen. "I want Dickie here at breakfast because it's the only time I ever see him."

He picked up the stubby spoon and began feeding the little boy. Louise tottered away. The waitress came in, a platter in one hand, a rack of toast in the other. Like everything else in the room, she was less than neat, less than appetizing. Her apron was spotted, one cuff was unfastened, her back hair made strings down her neck. She set the platter clumsily before Paul, and stood the toast rack nearby. He poked gloomily at the dish with the serving-spoon.

"Want some scrambled eggs, Ed?"

Edgar looked up, leaned over to examine the watery yellowish slop in the dish, and took a piece of tough, scorched toast. "No thanks, Paul."

"Wouldn't you think," Paul exclaimed, "there'd be some way of getting something decent to eat in this house? My God, it's unbearable."

He fed Dickie some more porridge.

"Well, Louise doesn't feel well," Edgar said mildly. "Don't be too hard on her, Paul—just now."

"Just now. I know. But she's got plenty of servants. She ought to be able to get proper work out of them whether she's—er—ill or not."

He stopped speaking as the waitress came in again.

"How is my mother this morning, Nettie? Have you taken up her breakfast yet?"

"Yes. She said she slept a little."

Edgar's pale lips twitched. Every time this maid opened her mouth Edgar wanted to shout at her, "Say 'Sir!'" But he restrained the impulse. He spent as little time as possible in the house; he was almost invariably out for dinner; he had little to do with anyone at home. These breakfasts were enough to drive any man away. The changes of the past five years had all but eradicated the home he had grown up in. Now his mother's illness had removed the last touch of its former warmth and order and comfort. She had lain upstairs in her bed for nearly three months. The doctor had privately given Paul and Edgar no hope for her recovery. It would be a long, wretched, pain-racked ordeal, and it might drag on for well over a year.

Clarissa lay in bed on this April morning and tried not to think about the household or what was going on in it. She had solemnly promised Doctor McClintock that she would not worry about it, or about anything. . . . She heard Paul coming up the stairs puffing and grunting. She knew he had Dickie on his shoulder. The little boy was always crying "Piggy!" and begging to clamber onto his father's back. She smiled slowly as Paul came in, and raised her thin hand in its ruffled sleeve to pat the bed beside her. Paul put Dickie there, but the lively child with his bouncing and jabbering made her uncomfortable; they rang for his nurse to take him away.

"How are you today, Mama?" Paul held her bony hand in his.

"Quite well." She spoke in a quiet, muffled voice, looking at Paul with anxiety in her faded blue eyes which she hoped she was hiding. She was playing the grim, unutterably tragic game of pretending that she did not know the truth about the fate that had overtaken her; and Paul was pretending that he did not know, and both were pretending that each had succeeded in fooling the other; a futile, terrible kind of gallantry.

"How is Louise this morning, dear?"

Paul sighed. "She feels pretty mean, Mama. I'm really awfully sorry for her. But why is she this way? Were you always fainting and crying and feeling too sick to run the house when you were having children?"

Clarissa closed her eyes with a faint shudder. The last thing one would have expected of Louise was this—that her sunny nature, the quickness of her smile, the happy lilt of her voice, would disappear under the first exactions of discomfort.

"She's so young, dear," Clarissa murmured apologetically.

"But she's not, Mama! She's twenty-eight. Why most women her age have three or four children and all the rest that goes with it. I don't understand her," Paul said. "What is there about her that makes you say she's so young? And treat her like a child?"

Clarissa thought she had better not say. She could not bring herself to face a truthful opinion of Louise in her own mind. It simply could not be true that this blitheness, sweetness, and childishness of spirit were not genuine; that they could conceal less lovable qualities; that Louise would or could knowingly use them for some purpose of her own. She must really be feeling wretched now, and not able to cope with the housekeeping.

"It's only because she's not well that things are like this, dear," Clarissa said.

"Well, I can't see how we are going to go on like this," Paul said. He looked about the room, which was the only really orderly place in the house, and which, he knew, was kept in order because Clarissa lying in bed could direct the maid as she cleaned it. The breakfast tray stood on a stand near the bed. Paul lifted the covers of the dishes and saw that his mother had hardly touched the unappetizing food.

"Look at that!" Paul exclaimed, pointing to a portion of the same watery eggs that Edgar had rejected. "Just our luck to have the cook leave after you got sick, and this woman is a fiend incarnate. I don't even blame Louise for that, I don't think anyone could cope with it. But Louise says if I fire this cook she doesn't know how to find another."

"I'll do something about it," Clarissa said soothingly. "I can keep an eye on things even from here. Bessie Cottrell is coming to see me this afternoon. I'll ask her to go to the agency and find us another cook."

Paul rose. "I've got to get to the mill, Mama." He bent over and kissed his mother gently on the forehead. "Sure you're all right? Anything I can bring you?" He lingered anxiously.

"Oh no," Clarissa said brightly. "I'm fine. Comfy as can be. I don't need a thing. Now go along, son, and don't worry about things here. I'll be up and around soon, and everything will be all straightened out."

Left alone, Clarissa closed her eyes and tried to rally her strength and her thoughts to cope with the day ahead. There was something nightmarish about the way everything had turned out, everything for herself, for Paul, everything about Louise . . . even poor Ed. What was it that kept him living here, moody and remote and lonely, instead of going on about making a life for himself? That slow, gnawing worry and concern never left her.

But now here was Louise going to pieces again. Clarissa's gentle mouth, which was beginning to grow pinched from pain, set in a straight line. Her wide, level brows shadowed her blue eyes in which memory struggled with loyalty, and judgment held the whiphand over both. If her conscience had ached bitterly about Mary Rafferty these five years past, she had tried to ignore it. She had loved Mary better than any soul except her own husband and children. She had, in spite of standards and prejudices, welcomed the thought of Mary's marrying Paul. And then violence had come, to sweep everything into cataclysm. Mary must henceforward be connected in her thinking with the crazed man who had brought disaster on them all. Clarissa would never stop loving Mary; she did not want to stop. She missed her now most painfully.

The contrast with Louise was almost unbearable. When Paul had told his mother that he was going to marry Louise she had had one dreadful moment of shock. She had always been fond of Louise. Once, long ago in a time and a way that did not matter at all, she had joined Sophia Kane in the hope that the children would marry. But when it happened, Clarissa was literally sick. She knew the reason for Paul's decision. Whatever name he gave it, propinquity was all there was to it. Denied the wife and the life he wanted, he was determined to have some kind of life, some kind of family, no matter what. And to make the least possible effort acquiring them. He had made, his mother knew, a dangerous choice, one fraught with all sorts of gloomy possibilities. Edgar understood the truth too. Perhaps that was why he so often defended Louise; he pitied her. He and his mother had had to bury their real feelings about Paul's marriage behind the convenient façade of sentiment. Mrs. Kane set the keynote for them all. This was such a suitable match, so eminently sensible a thing for dear Paul to have done; so wonderfully the realization of Richard Kane's dearest hopes. Clarissa had found it easiest to take her cue from Sophia Kane. She was glad that she had done so when, a few months after the wedding, Sophia died suddenly of acute indigestion. The thought was inescapable that Sophia had actually died of relief. She had closed her eyes murmuring, "Lord, now lettest Thou Thy servant depart in peace," as if to proclaim that she had lived only to witness the fulfillment of her lifelong hopes. Clarissa then found herself fully occupied with the burden of Louise.

The gentle, sunny, warm-natured girl threw them all into consternation by going completely to pieces, disorganized by pregnancy and seemingly shattered by her mother's death. All during that crisis she kept harking back to her father, weeping and making hysterical scenes in which his name kept recurring. Paul and Clarissa gave Louise every sort of devoted attention; they made every allowance for her. Clarissa had always intended to turn over the housekeeping to Louise, and help her with it only enough to make sure that she had her task well in hand. But that was out of the question when the poor child was so ill. Then she made a slow recovery after Dickie's birth. And then there had been one illness or upset after another, always something beyond Louise's control; and not until the incredible day when Clarissa had quietly collapsed beside her butcher's stall in the Allegheny Market, was Louise faced with any responsibility.

Paul and Edgar usually walked to the mill as old William and Paul had walked for years past, but there was no rigid rule about it now. They walked for the exercise and air if they had time, but if they were late, they drove. Today as he came out of his mother's room looking at his watch, Paul called over the banister to Nettie, listlessly dusting the hatrack in the front hall, and told her to tell Jones to hitch up. This was the third day in succession that he had had to drive; he should have left for the mill half an hour ago. He hated the daily succession of petty delays that kept him at the house too long. They were all trifles that irritated him and distracted his mind so that he reached the mill feeling snappish and nervous, approaching his day's work with tension and ill humor. He started downstairs, but paused and turned back. He felt rather remorseful about Louise. She was lying on her bed with a cold compress over her eyes. The shades were drawn.

"I'm sorry you feel so badly today," Paul said. "Is there anything I can do for you?"

Louise raised the cloth from her eyes and looked at him, blinking dazedly. "Do? Oh, no."

"Can you lie down and rest here all day?"

"Today is Margaret's day out. You know what that means." Louise's voice quavered.

Margaret was Dickie's nurse. She was the only competent and trustworthy servant in the house, a strong, stolid Scotswoman who minded her own domain and had as little as possible to do with the three slatternly women in the kitchen downstairs—the cook, the waitress Nettie, and the new chambermaid, Nora, who was the fourth in succession in the months since Clarissa had taken to her bed. Paul could never discover the reason for the transitory state of the servants. He could not understand why they were always leaving or having to be dismissed, when his mother had kept the same ones for years. Louise must be responsible for it. In his masculine way he imagined that the house should be easier to run now than years ago as he remembered it in his parents' time, with five lively children and their troops of friends, and a constant stream of company keeping domestic activity at a peak.

"Couldn't you talk to her, Paul?" Louise was asking him. "Couldn't you tell her I'm sick today and ask her to put off going out?"

"I don't see how I can, Lou," he said slowly. "I had to do that last week and the week before. Margaret is very obliging but I can't ask her to give up her free days week after week. You don't want *her* to leave, do you?"

Louise began to cry. "Oh dear," she choked, "I just don't see how I can face it. *Why* can't I let Nora take care of Dickie this afternoon, Paul? Why are you so set about that? Anybody else's chambermaid helps with children!"

"Nora is a flighty, irresponsible fool," Paul said, exasperated. "Neither she nor Nettie is trustworthy enough to mind Dickie, and until you can find a maid I can trust with him when Margaret is out, you will simply have to take care of him yourself. After all, Louise, it's only one afternoon a week. Good God, some women have half a dozen children and a whole house to mind all by themselves. And Dickie's no trouble, after all."

"Any child would be trouble if you felt the way I feel! I'm not complaining of Dickie, Paul, but only of the way I feel. It's *awful*."

It was on the tip of Paul's tongue to blurt out to Louise the whole tragic truth about his mother. So far Louise had no inkling of it. Paul and Edgar had decided that she must not know. She was too artless, too thoughtless in her quick voicing of any feeling. They felt she could not be trusted not to break down and upset Clarissa. But a few more mornings like this, Paul felt, would undo his resolve altogether. It was more than flesh and blood could bear, to go from Clarissa calmly and patiently enduring the torment of a mortal disease to Louise weeping and shuddering in her room over a collection of assorted discomforts that the doctor absently dismissed as "nerves . . . peculiar to her condition . . . some women, you know . . . may improve suddenly . . ."

Paul always turned to Edgar with relief, once they left the house behind them and got on their way to the mill. Today Edgar was waiting in the buggy, smoking a stogy. They started down Western Avenue at a quick trot. The houses set back on either side of the wide street had a fresh, swept look about them this morning. People were in the midst of spring cleaning. The lawns were the soft light green of early April, unsullied by the grime that would soon darken them. Pink and white hyacinths, yellow jonquils, and brilliant blue grape-hyacinths bloomed in stiff, neat patterns in flower-beds and borders. Ironwork gates and fences had been freshly painted black. The busy clip of hedge-shears echoed down the street. The oak and elm trees overhead were soft with pale, newly opened leaves. Edgar craned his neck up at the clean, singularly blue sky, remarking at the unusual absence of smoke.

Paul observed the familiar scene in distracted silence. He was thinking ahead to the first question of the day at the mill. Edgar read his mind and stopped admiring the weather and said, "Have you decided what to do about those Hunkies, Paul?"

"Gee. I don't know." Paul shifted the reins and leaned over to get a light for his pipe from Edgar. "I hate like the devil to take 'em in."

"Would it really make such a big difference?"

"Enormous. I showed you those payroll figures. Everybody's coming to it. You can get labor under fifteen cents an hour . . . fourteen—twelve for yard men . . . what else can I do?"

Edgar shook his head. "Some ways—" he murmured.

"I know," Paul said quickly. "I don't want to give jobs to Hunkies. And put our own fellows out. But—the difference is just too damned big."

There were many features of the big change in the labor picture that Paul did not like to think about. The single most striking development in the past three or four years had been this influx of strange, swarthy, filthy, unintelligible foreigners from wild places in Eastern Europe that nobody had ever heard of. They were pouring in by thousands, almost swamping the market at slow times, helping to turn out phenomenal quantities of steel when business swung upwards, their sweated wages undercutting the hard-fought scale of the Amalgamated and all the old-established Irish and Scotch and native men. They held no skilled jobs. The Irish had it safe there. Above the level of common labor, yard labor, and the lowest grades of helpers they kept the Hunkies out. But they quickly gave up trying to compete for the lowest jobs at the wretched wages the Hunkies were glad to take. When you needed that kind of labor now you got it not from the familiar Irish and Scotch that had sweated out the iron and steel for fifty years and more, but from teeming labor camps where contractors herded the bewildered hulks of immigrants as they arrived by the shipload. Such a labor contractor was coming to the mill this morning to see Paul. Paul shook his head slowly now, pursing his lips. He was thinking of Jim Rafferty.

"I hate to do it," he said half-aloud.

"Well—are you running the mill for profit or—"

"Oh, I know. We're not in business for our health."

Paul could not run the mill on memories of Jim. He was learning some of his father's methods, through necessity and the pressure of the times. He could not be sentimental about mill labor. He could not even keep that youthful, hopeful, impartial perspective about the question with which he used to argue with his father.

There was no Jim Rafferty now and his successors in the Amalgamated had not the same meaning to Paul. A year ago—in 1888—Paul had signed the first contract between the Scott Iron Works and the Amalgamated Association. It did not call for a closed shop, but it did recognize the Amalgamated as the bargaining agency for all union men in the Scott mill. It gave the union the other rights (with the exception of the closed shop) for which Jim Rafferty had struggled. Paul felt that he had insured peace for a long time to come. But also, curiously, the signing of the contract had once for all made in Paul's mind a final demarcation between himself as employer and his men as labor. He was as able, as eager as ever to put on overalls and hand-leathers and take a turn on a heat at the open-hearth. He retained all the physical comradeship with the men that his years of labor alongside them had developed. But with his father's responsibilities had come, perhaps, unconsciously, some of his father's ways.

CHAPTER XXXVI

[1889—Continued]

TEN DAYS AFTER Mrs. Dixon had told her of Clarissa Scott's illness Mary's doorbell jangled late one afternoon, and looking through the curtained glass panes of the front door she saw Paul Scott standing on the doorstep. She stood still, staring. Her fingers gripped the curtains and she felt the heavy pulsebeat in her throat. Her mouth felt dry. A few months ago, she would not have opened the door. But now she had no such idea. The tall man on the step was grave-faced and visibly troubled. Mary's thoughts turned to the pessimistic report of Mrs. Scott that she had heard when she delivered Mrs. Dixon's dresses. Her hand turned the doorknob even as she was thinking that she felt quite calm now at seeing Paul, but deeply anxious about his mother. Yet she was relieved to hear herself say quite naturally, "Why, Paul! Isn't this a surprise."

His heavy hand gripped hers with the firm clasp she had anticipated, and he stood holding his hat in his left hand and looking at her with a mixture of worry and tenderness in his eyes. It seemed as if a different man inhabited this powerful body. His face had grown stern and surprisingly inscrutable; his speech and movements were deliberate. He had grown a heavy blond moustache. Mary realized that he had been full of the same suspense that had set her pulse beating so hard. This coming here had not been easy for him. She waited for him to speak.

He stood holding her hand and looking at her with an expression almost of surprise and of gratitude for letting him come in. He shook his head a little and sighed, "Oh, Mary, it's good to see you."

She smiled and led the way into her parlor.

"I do want to know how your mother is, Paul." He understood that that was why she had let him in. Laying his hat on the window seat, he kept his eyes on Mary's face and said, "I can't believe it's really you. I'm so glad to see you."

She motioned him to a chair as she asked, "Is your mother really so very ill, Paul?"

"She's going to die, Mary."

"Ah. I feared that."

"Someone told you?"

"Everybody knows she's ill. No one told me what it is. I suppose I've guessed."

He nodded slowly. He could hardly believe that he was actually looking at, and talking to Mary. She looked much older, and yet in a curious way, not faded or worn. On the contrary her white skin still had its clear bloom, her strong, pale red hair still grew crisply upward from her smooth forehead, and he liked the way she had twisted it high on her head. That made her look older, more statuesque. But her figure was still slight; it always would be. It must be her expression that was so changed; it was an expression of the profoundest calm he could imagine. It was a calm like his mother's, both innate and disciplined. And, strangest of all, in these few brief minutes that he had sat here, she had communicated that calm to him, just as his mother managed to do while he was in her presence. Mary looked up and said, "Tell me, Paul. Is it cancer?"

"Yes. She's remarkable about it; you can imagine that she would be."

"Does she know?"

"Only by instinct. Doctor McClintock says he has not told her, but principally because she has not asked. She simply knows. He told Ed and me—we pretend to her we don't know anything."

"Oh, I'm so terribly, terribly sorry."

"It's very hard on us all, Mary. You see, it isn't as if there was nothing else wrong."

He spread his sinewy hands on his knees and looked down at them sharply; there was something about the gesture reminiscent of his father.

"What else is wrong, Paul?"

"Mary, I'm afraid the whole situation is a pretty bad mess. I want to talk to you about it—I've got to. But I hate to seem complaining or disloyal."

She nodded. "I understand. Don't you want to smoke?" she asked. "And I think it's teatime."

She rose, handed him matches, and moved about in the corner making ready for tea. Presently she brought the tray, with the spirit-lamp burning, and put it on a stand at her elbow. She sat down again and said, "Now tell me all about it."

Paul lit his pipe gratefully. It was in just such trifling ways that a woman's perception of comfort, and of what was conducive to it, made existence tolerable or wretched. He remarked it, telling about the hopeless disorganization at home, and of the state of things with which he could not cope any longer.

"In a way," he said, "it's outrageous for me to be here, telling you all this. I don't like to be putting the blame for my mistakes on Louise. She's not really to blame. It's just—" He was silent. Mary sat with her eyes turned away. Finally she said softly, "Paul. The only way I could help— would be for you to feel quite free—to talk to me. I"—she smiled a little— "I can stand it. And I won't misunderstand."

"You're wonderful, Mary," he said. He sat watching her make the tea. Then he spoke, thoughtfully. "This marriage," he said, "was a job I wanted to do. I wanted to do it well. Frankly, I didn't have any great hopes for it as a—a—personal relationship. You know why. But I did think I could put enough into it to compensate Louise for—for—"

"I understand."

"But I haven't succeeded. She hasn't. So it must be my fault. If it weren't for Mama I'd be doing my best to see it through—alone. I couldn't —wouldn't—have the—heart—the cruelty—to come here and dump it on you." He was speaking with great difficulty and in every line of his face, his clenched hands, Mary saw that this was an ordeal.

"It's too late to dwell on that," she said. "Now you want to make the best of it."

"That's right," he said. "That's why—I'm here." He stared hard at her. "I'm just trying to find a way to give Mama some peace—all the peace she can have, anyway."

Mary nodded slowly.

"And there isn't much I can do about the details," Paul said, "without neglecting the mill. That sounds kind of heartless, but—"

"You can't neglect the mill. That would just be adding another mistake to—to—"

"That's it. So—the point is—Louise is incapable of running that house. Maybe it's just her condition. Something about having a child makes her go all to pieces."

Mary sipped her tea, with a baffled expression. "I believe you, Paul," she said slowly, "but you'd think any woman—"

"You would think so. With plenty of help and all the money she needs. But Louise can't. I wouldn't care like this if it weren't for Mama—and Dickie."

"How is he?" Mary asked eagerly.

"That's the worst thing yet. Mary, he was almost killed last week." Paul's voice thickened.

Mary leaned forward and asked, bewildered, "How? What do you mean?"

"He was with Louise." He hurried to correct himself as he saw Mary's horrified expression. "Oh, I don't mean— But she's supposed to mind him on his nurse's day out, and now since she isn't well she says she can't do it. It hurts her back—or something. Anyway she's been trying to find a chambermaid she could trust him to when Margaret is out. Last week she had a new one. I told Louise that morning not to leave Dickie alone with the girl for more than a few minutes at a time. And instead of keeping her eye on them, she went upstairs and lay down and left them in the yard all afternoon."

Mary sat still, waiting.

"And the girl left Dickie alone in the summerhouse. He fell out."

"Oh, Paul. Not over those iron spikes!"

Paul nodded. "He climbed up on the railing and toppled over. A spike missed his eye by a hair. Ran him through the cheek. We were afraid of blood-poisoning."

Mary sat back, her mouth tightly closed. At times during this painful talk she had not had the heart to look at Paul, but now she raised her head and they exchanged one of the deep, open glances that had always carried their intimate thoughts, straight and silently, from one to the other. He sat forward, his hands clasped between his knees, and studied the carved lines of her face, her quiet, intent gray eyes. Then he said, "In a way I feel like an absolute rotter—a coward—for coming here and telling you all this. It's not fair to you—or even to poor Lou."

"I know, Paul. But you need help. You really do."

"I know it."

There was another silence. Then Mary said, looking at him, "Did your mother send you to see me, Paul?"

They exchanged another solemn look.

"Not exactly. But I can tell you she wouldn't be surprised to know I was here. It wasn't easy for her to see you go out of our lives, Mary. I see it now even more than before she got sick. Sometimes when she's in very bad pain—" he paused as he saw Mary's eyes fill. But she waited for him to finish, and he said, "At times like that, once in a great while, she mentions your name. But that's when she's in such pain that she's not thinking about—me."

Mary turned her head away. Paul coughed and began to fill his pipe again. He said, "She hasn't asked for you. Because—well, she wouldn't want to make things any harder—for me. You know her."

Mary sat silent for a long time. The dusk was deep outside now. When she looked up at Paul again he could not see her face as clearly as half an hour earlier. But her voice moved him to the core of his heart as it said, softly and slowly, "I think I'd do anything for your mother, Paul."

He moved forward, conscious of the heavy, probing ache in his heart and in his throat, as he stared at her in the fading light. She felt pain too, as she watched the sad expressions that crossed his face—surprise and yearning and sorrow and finally, relief. "You would?" he breathed. "My God. Of course you would. And—I didn't know how to find the courage to ask you."

She swallowed, and conquered the weakness that might have let her down into tears. She said, "I don't want to go back to that house. Don't make any mistake about that. I couldn't be induced to consider it—except for knowing how your mother is suffering."

Paul touched her hand for a moment. "I know," he said. "Believe me. I understand. I can't put myself under obligation to you. You know—oh, everything I can't say. I came here, frankly, to ask you to come back And now that you offer to of your own free will, I feel as if I oughtn't to let you. It wouldn't be fair. It's so damned one-sided."

"If you start digging into who owes what to whom," Mary said quickly, "you'll dig up everything that's buried and going to stay buried." She spoke with quiet emphasis. "This way—if I can make the rest of your mother's life any easier or happier, I certainly want to try. Of course the Louise part of it is beyond me. I can't imagine what would happen about that. She wouldn't want me there. You haven't mentioned it to her, have you?"

He shook his head.

"Well, I can't say I'd like to live in the house with Louise. She'd want even less to have me."

"Oh, no," Paul said. "That's not so at all. You must realize that Louise is a child."

"You can't be so blind as that. Louise is very shrewd."

"In a way. But I do know her, I know what I'm talking about. Life is a story-book to her. You grow up and marry and live happily and even if it isn't really that way, she still wants it to be. She wants everything to be nice and happy—those are her own words. She'd be glad of anything that made it that way. Then she could go on playing her story-book instead of having to cope with a sullen cook, and count the laundry and— oh, you know."

They sat and thought for a time without speaking. Presently Paul said, "If you came back to—you know, to help Mama, and keep house, and all that, it would be very different from before, Mary. You'd not be among the—the maids, the way you used to."

"I know," she said. "I wouldn't do that. I couldn't, any more. This is so sudden I haven't had a chance to think about the details, but what you need there is a housekeeper and what you're asking me to do is just that. I suppose it could be worked out—for as long—as long—" her eyes filled with tears.

"As long as Mama lives," Paul said. "After that—well—"

"There would not be any need of my staying after that," Mary said. "And I would not. I'm very content with my life as it is and I want to come back to it. I could never get over being uncomfortable about Louise, Paul. She may seem innocent and childlike to you but those people are always terribly shrewd. She couldn't possibly have been as close to your family as she always was and not have heard things—about us."

"I'll try to tell you exactly what I think she does feel, Mary," Paul said slowly. "She associates you mostly with the period when we were all youngsters together there and everything was what Louise calls 'nice and happy.' She seems to be convinced that the only reason you cut yourself off from us all was Jim and what he did. Now if she ever did think anything else—about you and me, or if she ever heard anything—you can take my word for it she's forgotten it completely. I mean she's forgotten deliberately because she wanted to forget. She's married to me. To a girl like Louise marriage is the be-all and end-all of relationships. If you're married you never think of yourself or your husband as an individual again. You're just a couple of mutual possessions."

Mary sighed. She said, "Anyway, you're trying to tell me Louise is so infantile that if I'm making the house comfortable and keeping everything 'nice and happy' she won't remember anything she may ever have heard or thought about our past?"

Paul nodded, rather uneasily.

"Well. I'd better take you at your word for a while. I'd do anything for your mother, Paul. I'm frank to tell you I've been perfectly miserable sitting here for two weeks wondering about her ever since I heard she was so ill. I'd rather be near her."

Paul looked at her gratefully. "Oh, Mary, you have such wonderful sense."

"I don't agree with you at all. I don't think it's very good sense to do this, but I love your mother and I'm grateful for a chance to do something, for her—and for you," she added softly.

Paul looked at her with tenderness, dropping the barrier of reserve that he had so carefully tried to keep between them. Mary smiled wanly, and moved her hand almost as if to warn him to remember it. She said, "There are a good many details to think about."

"Oh, fix all that any way you like. The one thing I want is for you to take that place over and run it properly. From top to bottom. You are to be the boss. Hire and fire anyone you want, market, plan the meals, see that Mama has what she needs, get people around who can do their work properly. I'm going to tell Louise that I've taken this step to relieve her of all responsibility until the baby is born, and she'll be so grateful she'll fall on your neck. You'll see. All she wants is to be pampered and not have to make any effort."

Mary sat thinking. She spoke slowly. "I wonder, Paul—this is an odd sort of position I'll be in. Neither mistress nor servant. I can't help wondering about the, you know, the living arrangements. I don't want to have my meals with you and Louise," she said hastily. She was embarrassed.

Paul stood by the mantel and stared at the floor. Presently he looked up and said, "Why don't you take Pa's old study on the first floor and use it for your sitting-room? You have to have a sort of office—you'll have all the household accounts to keep, and bills and wages to pay. You could eat there and have your friends to tea—you know, your own private sanctum. And fix it up any way you like—with your own things."

He gestured around the comfortable room, with its crisp dimity curtains, chintz and rep upholstery, embroidered cushions and tablecovers all made by Mary. He looked at the dainty English tea-things, the pictures and ornaments on the mantel, the shelves full of books.

"Bring it all with you," he said. "Do you still read a lot of poetry? Or is it novels now?" He saw several volumes of a new translation of Balzac squeezed between Whitman and *Paradise Lost*. "I wish I had time."

"I hadn't thought of giving this place up, Paul," Mary said in a low voice. "I'm not sure I want to. It's my home."

He turned from the bookcase and took her hands with one of the

THE VALLEY OF DECISION

brisk, strong motions that she knew so intimately; intimately enough to anticipate it before her hands lay in his. "Mary," he said. "Listen to me. We're never going to make things hard for each other, you and I. We understand everything, without saying a word. Don't we?"

She nodded. She had turned quite pale.

"Then come back and don't be afraid. Our house is your home. And God knows it's no home without you in it. I need you. I always needed you." He looked down at her earnestly. "I swear I won't let you be sorry."

She smiled, though he saw that she was much nearer to weeping.

"It's like a dream," she murmured.

"It is. Everything that ever happened to us. From the very first. It is like a dream, you're right. Like the kind of dream that you think about a while afterwards—and you can't tell what part of it you did dream, and what you remember from actual happening. You never know what you lived and what you dreamed. Maybe we're not supposed to know."

"I don't believe we are, Paul."

He clasped her hands very hard for a moment, then dropped them.

Outside on the doorstep they stood for a moment breathing the soft spring twilight air. It was moist and fresh and clean, but in spite of that it held a suspicion of the acrid, odorous smoke that was native to their lungs.

"I can't think now why I never left Pittsburgh a while ago," Mary said.

"I can," Paul replied. "You never meant to. Can Jones come for you tomorrow?"

"Oh, Paul. I'd be willing—but I have some work to finish. I can't just drop it."

"How soon, then?"

"This is Tuesday. Wednesday, Thursday. If I hurry I might get everything done in two days. Friday?"

"If that's the best you can do. Friday it is. Good night, Mary. I—well, I'm not going to thank you. I never could."

He hurried down the steps, sprang into his buggy, and with a quick wave, drove away.

"Friday," murmured Mary. On a Friday, sixteen years ago, she had first entered the Scott house.

CHAPTER XXXVII

[1889—Continued]

SHE THOUGHT OF THAT first Friday again as she paused with her hand on the knob of Clarissa's door. Paul stood beside her in the hall. He had come home early from the mill to be there waiting on the front steps with Louise and Dickie, when Jones stopped the carriage at the gate. It was a strange moment. Mary stepped out of the carriage and stood looking up the walk to the house, renewing her deep, dormant familiarity with every line of its severe red brick and sandstone. She walked slowly up the path, watching Paul coming toward her, leading Dickie by the hand. There was a thick bandage across the little boy's right cheek, and he looked ill. But Mary loved the way he planted his feet and marched his sturdy legs with precise energy that reminded her of his grandfather. Louise stood on the stoop and watched them. Mary leaned down and put her arms around Dickie.

"What a grand boy, Paul!" She smiled over the child's head at Louise. Louise smiled back; a flash of expression which struck Mary at that moment as meaning nothing. It lay, somehow, on the outside of Louise's pretty features; it was not insincere, yet it had no depth. Mary felt unsure of her own judgment when Louise said, taking both her hands, "Oh, I'm so glad to see you again, Mary. It's so dear of you to come and help us out."

"You're looking well."

"I'm not, though. I've been feeling awful."

"Well—we'll take good care of you."

They all spoke lamely and with peculiar tentativeness. Each knew that the others were feeling for words.

"I like you," said Dickie suddenly. "You're nice."

Paul lifted the boy to his shoulder. "She certainly is nice," he said lightly. "She's going to be nice to you, and Mama, and Granny and me."

"Not Uncle Ed?"

They all laughed. "Uncle Ed, too. She's always been nice to Uncle Ed."

"Where *is* Edgar?" Mary asked eagerly.

"Why—" Paul looked around. "That's funny. He came up from the mill with me. I thought—Hey, Ed!" he called, going up the steps.

"Coming," they heard Edgar's voice in the hall. Dickie was still staring down from Paul's shoulder at Mary.

"Who is she?" Dickie asked.

"She's Mary."

"Oh."

Entering the house with Louise, looking about in a maze of mixed feelings, Mary's mind echoed to the child's unconscious words. What a thing for him to say, she thought. How true it was. Who was she? What was this uncertainty, this sense of apprehension, this renewal of some early, urgent thought of long ago? In all the intervening years she had scarcely ever felt like this, not even at that still stranger homecoming when Paul had brought her here to be his bride. In the carriage she had driven off the memory of that. But now in the house, following Louise as she led the way, Mary felt within her own poised, slender body the thudding heart, the choking throat, of the frightened girl who had first come here to cast her lot among the Scotts. For a moment she lost the power to remember the years between.

They went into the back parlor. Edgar was standing by the mantel, waiting; it struck Mary as queer that he should have stayed in here when the others had all met her outside. She ran over and kissed him on the cheek and held him by the shoulders, laughing and saying, "Let me look at you, you spalpeen."

Edgar did not laugh so heartily as Paul. He gave Mary a hug, but when she looked eagerly at his face—it was so good to see him again!— he dropped his eyes in a strange way and turned a little aside. Mary paused, troubled and a little hurt. Was Edgar not glad to see her? She might have expected that of Louise. But her Eddie! She remembered now the queer reserve he had shown the time she came home from London, the last time she had ever really talked to him. She looked at Paul as if to ask silently what was the trouble, but there was nothing to be learned from the remote look in his face. Edgar apparently did things like this all the time now. And he looked so strange and pale and nervous. Mary turned back to the others a little sadly. Edgar was a man now, a man—goodness, she thought!—of twenty-five. You could not treat him like a boy.

The pattern of the carpet, the slanting rays of the afternoon sun in Clarissa's old bay-window garden roused the ancient memory of that first day when she had stood trembling before her new employer. Here they were in the back parlor again, she and Paul and Edgar and in some unbelievable way, Paul's wife and son. William Scott should be here, and his distant elder son; Elizabeth, cool and prim-faced; dear, tempestuous Constance. Mary stood and looked slowly about the room. In one glance she was renewing her profound intimacy with it; and also observing its state of neglect. From the smudges on the windows to the worn edges of the upholstery, the limp, sparse leaves of the dejected plants, the grimy woodwork, the filmy, unkept look of the fireplace tiles, the place was eloquent of everything that had happened to the family. Now the troubled present swept down to blot the memories from Mary's mind. She looked about and saw her work cut out.

Louise was speaking: "Mother Scott will be so glad to see you, Mary."

"I'll go right up."

Her own words echoed in Mary's mind as she ran up the stairs. She might have asked to go to Clarissa, and instead she had pronounced her intention of doing so. It was a trifle; a passing, unnoticed exchange of words, but Mary knew, approaching Clarissa's door, that it meant to her exactly what Paul had said her new situation was to mean: she was, in his words, the boss. She would not ask permissions in this house, she would make decisions. She looked at Paul as they entered his mother's room, and marvelled that Fate had twisted all their lives into this tangle. Clarissa lay in bed, her pain-racked eyes shining with happiness at sight of Mary. She stretched out her bony hand and drew Mary close for an eloquent kiss.

"Dear child," she said slowly. Mary was prepared for the shock of the changes in Clarissa, and did not show by a flick of her eye the sorrow and the pity that throbbed inside her. Clarissa was so faded; she had never been a woman of brilliant coloring or striking contours, but now her blond hair had turned colorless rather than gray, and her blue eyes had lost their hue. She had a ghostlike quality which Mary had never seen in anyone before. Clarissa Scott was a tall woman and her figure in years past had been sturdy, rather solid. Now, Mary could see, the flesh was rapidly melting away and the outline of her body beneath the bedclothes was bony rather than full and rounded as it used to be. Her voice had a hesitant, almost a strangled quality, as if she feared to start speaking lest a paroxysm of pain interrupt her and silence her. But Mary did not show a sign of perceiving all this. She drew up a hassock close to the bed and perched on it, holding Clarissa's hand and talking softly and happily.

"You're not to worry about a thing in the world, Mrs. Scott," she said. "We'll all make out beautifully here together."

"Louise," murmured Clarissa. Her heavy eyes followed Paul as he tiptoed quietly from the room, to leave his mother alone with Mary. "Can you—manage all that?"

"Of course." They looked at each other silently. Then Mary said, "Please don't worry about that, Mrs. Scott. I'm glad Paul is married to Louise. I always wanted him to marry her—long ago. Don't you remember?"

Clarissa nodded.

"I wouldn't have come back if I hadn't felt everything had turned out for the best. And I'm really happy. Truly I am."

Clarissa pressed Mary's hand. "You're a dear girl."

"I'm so awfully glad to be near you again." Mary stopped speaking as a change began to come over Clarissa's lethargic features. The bony hand in hers closed suddenly in a fierce, involuntary clutch. The dry lips set in a grim, ghastly line; the leaden eyes, sunken deep beneath their lids a moment before, opened violently and stared with horrible eloquence from the agonized face. Beads of dampness sprang out on the putty-colored forehead. Mary leaned forward, mastering her impulse to cringe at this fearful sight, and gripped Clarissa's hands hard, looking deep into her eyes. Even in the throes of mortal agony, Clarissa conveyed her relief, her gratitude at having someone by her at last before whom she need not dissemble. Mary saw all in a moment what a frightful burden of self-imposed discipline this strong woman had added to the torture that had been her fate. Mary held her breath and did not move while the paroxysm was violent. Clarissa sagged suddenly from the galvanic stiffness with which she had met the assault. Her eyes indicated a vial of medicine on the table by the bed.

"Two," she gasped, through her rigid lips.

Mary put two tablets on Clarissa's tongue and helped her swallow a little water. She sat quietly until the drug started to take effect and Clarissa's hands in hers began to grow limp. The heavy lids drooped. Mary did not know how long the seizure had lasted. She felt wraithlike, unreal; this horrible spectacle had the same effect as some other fundamental and violent devastation of Nature. Clarissa was beginning to grow drowsy, but she murmured heavily, "Thank you, dear. It won't be like this long. Later they—give—" She stopped speaking and fell into heavy sleep. Mary folded the bony hands and covered them. She reached under the blankets to feel whether Clarissa's feet were cold; slipped one pillow from beneath her head, and tucked another close to the small of her back. She opened one of the windows a little from the top, drew the dark blinds, and, carrying the hot-water bottle to be refilled, slipped from the room. On the way downstairs, her head full of plans and her heart aching for Clarissa, she put up her hand, startled to find that she had not yet taken off her hat.

There was no use, Paul told her after breakfast the next morning, in trying to be tactful with the present household staff, or in planning to make the changes gradually.

"Start in right this minute," he said, "and turn the whole place inside out. I'm not going to tell you what to do or when to do it. I'm leaving the whole thing to you." He led the way into his father's old study.

"Here are the account books and the tradesmen's books. This place has been such a mess that I can't make head or tail of the household finances but I want you to figure out a proper budget for all the running expenses and wages and I'll give it to you weekly or monthly, whichever you like. I just don't want to *worry*." Paul ran his hand nervously through his hair.

Mary stood by the desk, looking down at the pile of notebooks and the empty pigeonholes, all cleared for her use. She was about to say that she had misgivings about managing the servants. These present ones or any other Irish girls would almost certainly make spiteful difficulties about taking orders from her. And then she checked herself. Paul expected a task of her, and part of that task was to execute it without involving him in its details. He was in the front hall now, smoothing his derby with the sleeve of his topcoat and waiting for Edgar who was running downstairs to join him after his morning glimpse of his mother. Mary stood on the front steps, watching the brothers tramp off together to the mill. The moment, like almost every tick of the clock since she had returned to this house was startling and disturbing, combining the impossible and the unreal with the familiar so deeply ingrained that nothing might ever have happened to suspend it.

As she stood there the thought moved into her mind, into the forefront, the present, from which she had so sternly excluded such thoughts for so many years now. He had said, "I want you to stand at the front door . . . after . . ." and there she shut down hard on the Pandora's box of her memories . . . "and stay there . . . while I start down the street. . . ." She stood looking after him but she could not see him because of the tears that blinded her. She lifted her chin with a straining motion, as if to force down the choking lump in her throat. Then she smiled suddenly. It occurred to her now that there was no reason why she should not stand here and watch Paul and Eddie down the street every morning. That was the natural thing to do. She saw already that she was going to be having breakfast with them and Dickie. Louise had almost melted with relief at Mary's appearance with her breakfast tray this morning, and at Mary's soothing assurance that there was no reason why Louise need ever get up for breakfast while she felt like this. Mary had left her propped among the pillows, eating poached eggs on toast with her old innocent, cherubic smile. Louise would have had a turn if she could have read Mary's thoughts.

The misgivings swarmed thick as Mary descended the pantry stairs to tackle the cook. This was a tall, sour-faced, gaunt woman named Ella; a devil, as anyone could see. She was standing at the soapstone sink slamming pans and cutlery about in it.

"Now, Ella," Mary began. She hoped her voice had a suitable tone of authority. "Now, Ella. Could you come over here and go through the stores with me? I'm going up to market as soon as we have the week-end meals planned."

"I'm busy now."

"I want to do the marketing list now," Mary said. "You can finish up that cleaning after I go out."

"I'll be doin' me work when I see fit." The cook's tone was vicious and rasping. She had not turned around from the sink and looked at Mary.

"I think," said Mary, "you are making a mistake in taking this attitude, Ella. You and I had better start out by understanding each other."

"I wudn't waste me time. I'll be goin' Thursday when me week's out. Save yer breath fer givin' orders to the next wan."

Mary walked to the door, expressionless. "Very well. If that is the way you feel, go upstairs and pack your things now."

Ella whirled round. "Well!" Her wet red hands went to her hips in the classic gesture. "Quite a set o' airs ye got on ye! Firin' me, indade! I'll take me orders from the head o' this house and nobody else, see? Not from no stuck-up shanty biddy, neither!"

Mary gasped. A strange sensation, rather like a roaring noise, filled her ears. Her pulse knocked hard in her throat. Her mouth felt dry. She lifted her head high and said quietly, "Go upstairs and get your things and be down here to get your wages in an hour. If you make the slightest noise or trouble of any kind Jones will put you out forcibly." She turned toward the pantry stairs. The woman's coarse lower jaw sagged in amazement.

Mary's knees shook as she climbed the narrow, hauntingly familiar back stairs and emerged in the pantry where the slatternly Nettie was washing the breakfast dishes. From the waitress's loutish expression Mary could not tell whether or not she had overheard the episode in the kitchen but Mary presumed that she had. She stood for a moment watching the girl listlessly swish the blue-willow plates through the greasy water. Mary could see that the dishwater was too cool, that the girl was not using enough soap, that the damp, discolored dish towels flung on the rack had not been properly washed and boiled for weeks.

"You ought to rinse those plates in boiling water, Nettie," she said.

The waitress tossed her ill-combed head. There was silence for a moment. Then Mary said, "I have just dismissed Ella and told her to be out of the house in an hour. If you are not prepared to do your work properly and obey the orders I give, you can go too."

Nettie's mouth moved sibilantly.

"Well? I didn't hear what you said." Mary stood by the sink, her pale cheeks flushed and her eyes narrowed. Inwardly she was full of the most alarming starts and tremors; she hoped devoutly that she did not show it.

She had expected a certain amount of trouble, but had not realized that she would butt into it head-on the very first thing. "I think," she said coldly, "that you'd do better to go right now, Nettie. Mr. and Mrs. Scott are not at all satisfied with you, and I can't hope to teach you anything if you're going to be rude and sullen."

A plate slid from the coarse fingers and dropped on the drainboard with a crash. Mary saw that it had happened more deliberately than otherwise.

"I'll finish up these dishes after you leave," she said coldly. "Just take off your apron and go upstairs and pack your things."

She had judged that the girl would maintain her sullen silence and do as she was told. But instead she was treated to a sudden torrent of abuse.

"Who th'ell d'ye think ye are?" Nellie spat at her. "Ye're no better'n me nor Ella. Ye're only another servant like the rest! I heard her call ye a shanty biddy. Ye are. Fat chance I'd be carryin' fancy meals on trays to th' housekeeper's sittin'-room." She waggled her head and her hips in an indescribably vulgar gesture. "Miss Rafferty!" she snarled in a high, derisive voice. " 'Ye'll be takin' yer orders from Miss Rafferty in the future,' says he to me."

Mary put her hands quietly behind her and grasped the edge of the sink. She had a sudden feeling that if she did not hold onto something she would find herself laying a broomstick or dishmop about Nettie's head and face. She had a curious sensation of familiarity with this screaming, red-faced virago; her earliest years on the Flat had been spent among women who resorted to this kind of scene at the slightest provocation. And even as she stood quietly, aware of her own neat gray dress and black silk apron and shining, beautifully groomed head, Mary saw in a retrospective flash the squalid alleys and hovels from which she, no less than this riffraff, had sprung. Bridget flashed into her mind too; Bridget must be all too used to this kind of thing.

"Why are ye any better nor us?" the waitress was snarling. "I s'pose ye were born to a palace and the lap o' luxury? Fell on hard times, maybe, did ye, and had to come down to earnin' yer livin'! In a pig's snoot, ye did!"

Mary moved suddenly. In her imagination she could hear herself saying blistering things to Nettie, but she kept her face frozen and only said, "Go upstairs and pack. The same goes for you as Ella. If you make another sound I'll have Jones throw you out."

She walked quickly through the swinging door into the dining-room and hurried on into the study, closing and locking the door behind her. She sat down weakly on the edge of a chair and looked at the palms of her clammy, trembling hands. In all her doubts about this task, she had not really anticipated this core of poison, this nasty, filthy thing. It came down to one appalling point: Pittsburgh was not a metropolis, it was not so big that one could escape rigid identification with one's origin; it was a small town. Any individual who attempted to cut across the lines would be persecuted with the vigor that characterized the townspeople in all walks of life. She realized now with astounding clarity exactly what would have been her situation if she had married Paul; what infinite cruelty would have been used, even in spite of Paul's parents, to punish her.

She saw clearly that any Irish servant would feel in some degree like Ella and Nettie; and practically all the available servants in town were Irish; and whether they came from Mary's own Flat or from some similar shanty settlement, their instincts, if not the inevitable grapevine, would apprise them of Mary's situation. They would never cooperate. The perils of her anomalous position loomed like the genies of a nightmare, grimacing and threatening. She might possibly sidestep the issue by relinquishing any idea of superiority. If she were to eat her meals in the kitchen with them, do a share of the actual housework, wear an ordinary servant's uniform, give up this little sitting-room with its comforts and privileges, she might manage to get their good will.

Presently she was walking nervously, quickly and lightly, back and forth across the room. Her lips were pressed tight together and her gray eyes glittered excitedly.

"I won't do it!" she said half aloud. "I won't let them get away with it." She clenched her right hand and beat her fist softly in her left palm, striding swiftly up and down. "I'll be the mistress of this place. I'll keep the upper hand if it kills me."

There was a new and fantastic sense of excitement all through her. Scraps of Nettie's tirade echoed in her mind and at each echo Mary felt as if a stimulating drug were being pumped into the small of her back. Never in all her life could she remember a sensation like this, the sense of furiously aroused will power, the eager acceptance of challenge.

For the first time she saw just what it was that she had bought with her renunciation. She would never have Paul's name, or his property, or his body; but she would make for him the life that she had said he must lead. She would be the successor to Clarissa Scott in everything that gave the Scott house and the Scott family their meaning. Louise did not even count. Besides this enormous and challenging truth the messy jealousies and stupidities of the servants faded to mere petty problems. She stood tense, full of an intoxicating sense of freedom and purpose. Then she flung open the door and started out on her interrupted day's work in a rush of buoyant spirits. There would be plenty of pitfalls ahead; not only the servants but quite probably Louise. Mary did not overlook the likelihood of trouble from that quarter. But she was tremendously excited by the prospect of this task when she felt full of confidence in her ability to do it.

CHAPTER XXXVIII

[*1889—Continued*]

A FORTNIGHT LATER, Mary was writing out menus at her desk in the old study, now her sitting-room. The room had always been dark and unattractive, with the heavy smell of leather upholstery, massive books, and the cigars that William Scott had been wont to smoke there when Clarissa would not permit tobacco anywhere else in the house. But now Paul smoked his pipe and Edgar his stogies wherever they pleased, and the last traces of William Scott's occupancy had disappeared from the room. There was a knock on the door and Louise entered as Mary called "Come in!" Louise walked slowly and with a certain slight clumsy lack of balance which proclaimed her condition to the knowing eye even though she was still quite slender and trimly corseted. Her bosom was unusually full; it rose and fell perceptibly when she breathed. She sank into one of the armchairs, whose old brown leather upholstery was hidden now by a flowered cretonne slipcover that Mary had made. Louise leaned her curly head against the back of the chair and looked slowly about the room. It had been freshly papered with a plain, pale yellow paper, and Mary had found that her white dimity curtains from Negley Avenue fitted the two high windows very well. The heavy tomes from the bookshelves had been banished to the attic and in their places stood Mary's collection of classics and poetry and religious books and modern novels. Her tea-things, with Constance's caddy and kettle, stood on a table near the gas fireplace, and on the mantel were ranged the ornaments and pictures from Mary's former home. It was a pleasant and welcoming room though it could hardly have been plainer, and Louise's eyes roved about it appreciatively.

"You've certainly made this room attractive, Mary," she said. "You have a gift for that sort of thing, haven't you?"

Mary went on writing. "Perhaps I'm spoiled," she said. "I've got used to having my own things about me." Her pen scratched. "Shall we have a boiled tongue for Thursday dinner?"

"Why, yes, I suppose so, if everybody likes it. Why do you ask me?" There was a slight twist of emphasis on the last word.

"I just thought—after all—"

Louise's mouth opened slowly. "Oh. Am I supposed to have anything to say about it?"

"Louise! What a queer idea! Of course you are! This is your house."

Louise had a way of looking down at her breast, which was always covered with a frill of lace or embroidery of some sort. The gesture hid her brown eyes beneath the droop of her thick lashes. One could not sense what she was thinking. "It is, isn't it?" she said softly. It was as if she questioned the whole statement.

Mary looked up from her writing. "Why of course! Louise—that is—

Mrs.—Look here, I can't seem to find the right thing to call you. I'm always stumbling over it."

"Why not just Louise? You've been doing it."

"I know. But it never seems proper to me. One doesn't call one's employer by her first name."

"What about Paul?" Louise raised her head and stared hard at Mary.

"That's different. I mean, we all grew up here together and what with the twins and everything—well, we always spoke to each other that way." Mary's voice was especially quiet and casual.

"I don't remember that you did, somehow," Louise said slowly. "It all seems so long ago. You've changed a great deal, Mary."

What was she getting at? What had she come here to talk about? Mary had scarcely seen Louise to speak to in the two weeks that she had been here. Louise spent all the busy hours of the day in her room, and at other times Mary was almost always with Clarissa. She had not even had time to talk to Louise if she had wanted to. But now Louise had sought her out. Mary would gladly have avoided her, but she also felt that rather than have Louise brood and grow difficult it would be better to draw her out and put their relationship, queer as it was, on whatever basis of understanding they could effect. So she answered, in an easy, chatty way, "Yes, I have changed. That was all part of Mrs. Scott's sending me to London with Constance, you know."

"I see. That was how you dropped your Irish brogue, wasn't it?"

"In a way. I didn't exactly drop it. I just wanted to speak good English and of course I took the opportunity to learn in London. Wouldn't you?"

Louise smiled brightly. "Of course. Anybody would. You always wanted to improve yourself, didn't you, Mary?"

It could not be imagination that made Louise's voice sound devious to Mary, her tone twistingly curious, weighted with implication. It must be fact. But the more surely it was fact, the more Mary was determined not to show that she thought so. Between Paul's definition of Louise as a child, and Mary's knowledge that she was a shrewd and tense-nerved woman, there was a broad connecting measure of truth. Mary closed the menu book and turned towards Louise.

"Of course I always wanted to improve myself," she said. "I don't see how a person could be born in this country, especially in a place like Pittsburgh, and not be full of that feeling. That's what we're all brought up on. That's the great difference from England. That's what opened my eyes when I was over there. Those people never dream of rising from the class they were born in."

"You did, though."

"Certainly. That's just being an American, isn't it? We're not supposed to think of ourselves as classes."

"But we do," Louise said softly. Another twist.

"Some do," Mary agreed quickly. "But I wanted to have some education, and be independent. I wanted to go into business. That's how people get ahead."

"Is that why you came back from England?"

"Of course!" Mary clutched thankfully at the straw so innocently extended. "You see, I saved all my wages in England, and Mrs. Scott used to send me presents at holidays, so after a time I had a little money saved up and Constance didn't need me any more. Then I asked to come home."

Louise sat and twisted her fingers in the lace on her breast. The large solitaire diamond of her engagement ring sparkled between the flounces of her jabot. She seemed to be looking for something to say. Finally she looked up and said, "But this work you're doing now isn't what you really wanted, is it?"

Mary answered slowly. "No," she said, "it's not. But I love Mrs. Scott and when I saw I could do something to help her—"

A look almost of terror crossed Louise's face at Mary's mention of Clarissa's need. Louise opened her lips and Mary waited to hear what she was hesitating to say. Presently she leaned forward and whispered, rather than said, "Aren't you afraid to be in there with her?"

"Afraid! Why of course not. I don't see how you can say that."

"I meant—oh, it frightens me to see her. She's—like something—"

Mary sat very quiet, her spine stiffening unconsciously against this manifestation of hysteria. She had never before actually disliked Louise. But at this moment she was shocked and repelled by her selfish morbidity. Then she reminded herself of Louise's condition.

"She's got—a horrible disease, hasn't she, Mary?"

Mary rose with a sudden motion and flung open the window.

"She's got cancer," she said shortly. Whatever Paul had or had not told Louise up to now, Mary saw only that she must sweep the miasmic mystery from Louise's idea of this thing. "Cancer's a horrible disease," she said. "But you've got the wrong idea about it. *You* won't be affected. It's not diphtheria or typhoid fever. She's the one who's got to suffer."

Louise said, "I—I don't like to go in there, Mary. I'm afraid—for the baby."

"Well, who said you had to?"

They stared across the room at each other. Louise's anxious expression began to fade from her face; she looked at Mary attentively.

"Oh," she said.

"You didn't think Mrs. Scott wants you in there? She doesn't. I wouldn't think of going in to see her, if I were you. It would only upset both of you."

Louise seemed about to melt with relief. "She—she wouldn't think it queer if I didn't go in there any more? She wouldn't—think I didn't care —about her?"

"No," said Mary. "She's much better off without seeing people. That is"—her eyes filled suddenly with tears—"until it's time to—to send— for Constance. . . ."

"Do you know," breathed Louise, in an awed way, "when that—how long it will be?"

Mary bit her lip. If only this woman were not so devious! You could never take what she said exactly as it sounded.

"The doctor says not much above six months," she said, in the most matter-of-fact tone she could force out. "Next—in the fall, sometime—I suppose."

Louise settled back in her chair. "I'm sure it would be much better for the baby if I didn't go in there," she said. Her tone was normal again, but somehow secret. Mary's lips twitched.

"I can give Mrs. Scott all the help she needs," she said.

Louise smiled, her bright smile which for her, at least, obliterated the whole mood of the past moments.

"You're a great help to me, too," she said. "Where in the world did you find this marvellous German cook?"

"In the Allegheny Market," Mary said dryly. "Her husband used to be our poultryman—until he died. Her daughter Trude's coming tomorrow to be the waitress, too."

"Well, you certainly have made it nice here," Louise sighed.

"That's good." Mary would have shrugged if she had not checked herself. Such a gesture of indifference would be a blunder. "I don't blame you for not wanting the responsibility of the house, the way you're feeling."

"Well, I must say it makes a great difference having you here, Mary. It's much nicer for all of us." Louise sounded complacent now.

Mary thought, what is she getting at? It's as if she didn't mean a word she's saying. But she only said, "I'm glad of that. It's just because I'm used to the house. But one thing—you know, if you feel that I've taken over anything you really *like* to do—of course—"

"Oh, no." A look of panic flashed into Louise's eyes. "Gracious, no. I *hate* housekeeping. Thinking what to eat and looking to see if they've cleaned under the beds and giving talks to those nasty sulky servants. I should say not. I like it much better this way. I have a much nicer time with Paul."

Mary turned to jot down something she had forgotten.

"He used to be so *cross*," Louise said, "and now he's ever so much pleasanter. He isn't so cranky at dinner and we have lovely talks. He used to sit and complain all the time and now he never scolds me at all."

Mary kept her face expressionless. If she showed what she was thinking she would either laugh or cry outright.

"I hope Edgar is happier too," she said. "He doesn't look well. Has he been moody like this for a long time?"

Louise's brown eyes were uncomprehending. "Why—I haven't noticed especially."

Mary found herself wondering what, if anything, Louise ever did notice. She seemed to be contentedly absorbed in the remote small island of herself, wrapped in mental as well as bodily eiderdown, resistlessly sweet and impressionless as a soft pillow. And yet that was not true. Some signalling instinct, like a muffled bell tinkling in the distance, told Mary otherwise. She only said, "Edgar's fond of you, and he's such an affectionate person. I don't think he's happy."

"He's hardly ever home," Louise said uncomfortably. Nobody related to Edgar could fail to have heard something of his ways, even a woman barricaded behind smug decorum. It was the accepted thing silently to deplore Edgar and his unfortunate reputation while appearing to be completely innocent of anything he actually did.

"Poor boy!" Mary sighed. "He hasn't any life at all. Doesn't he ever see any of your friends, or bring his friends here?"

Louise colored. "Nobody knows Edgar's friends," she said stiffly.

CHAPTER XXXIX

[*Fall 1889*]

THE WHOLE TRAIN SHED was aflutter as the gorgeous lady with the little girl, the caped nurse, the black-coated maid, the Welsh terrier, the smart dust-covered luggage, the rolled steamer-rugs, the morocco jewel-case and dressing-case debarked from the Pullman Palace car, in a whirl of exclamations, excited embraces, sable-tails and ostrich-feathers. Other travellers arriving in Pittsburgh stood about by their sample-cases and gladstones gaping and staring at the beautiful woman who threw her arms first around one, then the next of the party that had come to meet her, calling them all "darling" and "dearest" in a high, crystalline, English voice.

"Eddie! Fancy *me* being glad to see you, you devil." Constance kissed him ecstatically. She reached behind her to clutch Clarrie, who stood shy and bewildered with her nurse, and dragged her towards Mary and Paul. "Here's your Uncle Paul, darling. And Uncle Ed. And Mary."

Clarrie observed them all quietly. She had huge, solemn Delft-blue eyes almost identical with Clarissa's. Mary gasped with amazement as the child turned them on her.

"Why, Constance, she's more like your mother than any of you."

"I know." Constance's face sobered quickly at the thought of her mother, but her attention jumped ahead to the next thing. "Paul, how are you? My God, you do look old and settled. How's Louise? Hasn't she had it *yet*? How do you like being married? Lester, give my brother the box-checks. Down, Taffy! Down! Oh, God, he's going to be sick again!"

They all watched, fascinated with disgust, while the terrier suffered the last of his train-sickness.

"He's been doing that all the way across," Constance sighed.

"Why did you bring him?" Edgar asked. "Travel won't broaden a dog."

"Oh, I don't know," Constance said. "Clarrie likes him. Come on, let's be going." She stalked off with Mary, leaving the others to round up the heaps of luggage, count trunks and noses, and get the expedition under way. Her green eyes were anxious and wet as she asked, "Is it true?" She pitched her voice low and bent her head close to Mary's. "Is she—"

"Yes. I wouldn't have written you so plainly if I hadn't known the end was near."

Constance's mouth turned down, trembling. "I can't believe it. I haven't the heart to face it." She bit her thin, shapely, scarlet lower lip. So shapely—so scarlet—Mary eyed it narrowly and gave Constance a shrewd look.

"No, it's *not* painted!" Constance smiled weakly. "I saw the look you gave me."

"Awfully vivid natural color," murmured Mary.

"Hot blood," said Constance.

"How's Mister Giles?"

Constance shrugged. "Do you care?"

The twins talked excitedly in the carriage while Mary and Paul sat and listened. The childhood resemblance between Edgar and Constance had only been striking when they were very animated; during their screaming quarrels or when they played rough games. Their reunion gave them this stimulus now. Their slanting, curiously-colored green eyes, their pointed chins, their white skin, were amazingly alike. But Edgar's sandy hair was no match for the riot of Constance's gleaming curls brushed to metallic brilliance under her green velvet hat trimmed with white and yellow plumes. She wore a dark green broadcloth costume, its tight basque and jewelled buttons emphasizing the tempting roundness of her breasts, and across her shoulders the sable pelisse edged with double fringes of bobbing, silky brown tails. Edgar looked at her admiringly.

"Gad, you're a gorgeous sight!" he said. "Look at her, Paul."

Paul smiled quietly and said, "I see her. She looks too full of hell for me."

"Why, Paul! I always was full of hell. Why should I be any different now?"

Edgar was fingering her beautiful furs. "If bally old Giles bought you this, I'm the Sultan of Turkey," he said.

"Personal remarks! What do you know about furs?"

"Or jewels? Or women?" Edgar narrowed his eyes and said something inaudible to Constance.

"Boor!" Constance pushed him playfully in the face with her gloved hand. "I can't believe I'm here. Mary, is Pittsburgh just as dirty as ever?"

"No worse than London," Mary said shortly. "If your ears and nose need scrubbing out I'll still take a hand to you."

Constance leaned over and kissed her with a smack.

"It's going to be fun being here!" she said. But her face went solemn. "That is—if Mama—" she looked at Paul. "Is she suffering much?" she asked. She was suddenly very serious. "Tell me all about it." She clasped her hands together.

"It's terrible, Connie."

"She has to be drugged most of the time. The pain has been the most frightful torture. You'd never know it from her. She doesn't make a sound."

"She just lies there—and when it gets so her eyes are almost popping out of her head—"

"Oh, don't." Constance covered her face and shuddered. "How long, Paul?" She spoke haltingly now, staring through the window at the muddy Allegheny beneath them; they were crossing the bridge. "Does the doctor say?"

He made a gesture. "Any time. She's never alone now. The nurse is always in her room."

"Oh." Constance thought for a moment and then said, "I'm afraid I've been frightfully inconsiderate, bringing all that caravan. I never realized, somehow . . ." She motioned over her shoulder at the hired carriage behind them. Clarrie and the retinue were following in it.

"We'll manage all right, dear. I admit I was rather appalled when you all poured off that train, but with a bit of doubling-up we can all fit in. The house is big." Mary spoke with authority. Constance stared at her curiously.

"It sounds so odd to hear you talk like that. Like Mama"—she choked —"in the old days."

"I wish your mother were well enough to see Clarrie," Mary said, shifting the conversation quickly. "It doesn't seem possible she's only seen her once."

Clarissa and Edgar had made a short trip to Europe immediately after Paul's marriage, "to give the children a chance to be alone together." That was the only time Clarissa had ever seen Constance since her marriage. Clarissa had come home figuratively holding up her hands in dismay. "Heaven only knows what she's coming to," Clarissa said. "The hours she keeps! The people she goes with! The money they spend, and the gambling, and the champagne, and her *friends!*" There was always a certain discreet evasion about casual mention of Constance's friends. Most of them had august names, but they did not behave augustly in their own circle. Edgar had been impressed and excited. He knew and matter-of-factly accepted the truths about his twin, while other people whispered, speculated, and shrugged. He had found Constance's life in London so exactly to his taste that it had been a hard wrench to turn his back on it and go home. Constance had urged him to stay. "Why not?" she said. "Why go back to that dirty old coal hole and slave your life away? You've money. Stay here and get yourself a girl. Come to Marienbad with us. Try playing at Monte. What the devil is there for you to do in Pittsburgh?"

"Paul needs me," Edgar had answered almost in spite of himself, surprised at the impulse which prompted him to speak so firmly.

"Paul? Well, good God, whose life are you living, yours or Paul's? What's the matter with you? Most of the time you only seem half alive."

Edgar had eluded her after that; there was something about him on which she could never put her finger. He seemed restless and distraught. Constance was so preoccupied with her own concerns that she gave little real thought to anyone else. Her feeling for her twin was spasmodic like all her affections, which swung between the indifference of long separation and bursts of sudden violent affection. Underneath she loved Edgar passionately. Now in the carriage she eyed him sharply as they rattled down the cobbles of Western Avenue. Edgar was pale and a strange, flat, veiled expression came over his face whenever the conversation turned and he could withdraw from it. His animation and all his teasing and taunting echoed hollowly when Constance caught this strained, mysterious expression in his green eyes. Though careless and self-centered, she was intuitive; she sensed something radically wrong about Ed. It was not in the least like him to be living like this, burying himself in the family and its everyday affairs, plodding along year after year in the mill. He ought to be off raising hell somewhere. Constance did not believe for a moment that his tastes had changed. She knew him—and herself as his twin—too well to think that.

She leaned forward as the carriage stopped. Her eyes moved quickly about the scene. She stepped out slowly and took Mary's arm going up the walk.

"It looks so strange," she murmured. "So queer and small. I can't believe I'm here."

She ignored the bustle behind her, the second carriage unloading, her brothers giving orders to Jones and the maids. Clarrie ran up and plucked at Constance's sleeve.

"Are we here, Mummie?" she asked. "Is this Granny's?"

Constance looked down at her as if she had not understood. "Granny's?" she repeated vaguely. Then she jerked her head. "My *God*, Mary! Do you realize it's been nearly ten years? It sounds so odd to call this house 'Granny's.'"

"You were a child yourself when you left." They were climbing the front steps. Constance looked about with a bewildered expression. Mary saw that she was shocked not to find her mother waiting at the door, though she knew well how impossible this must be. Constance paused on the threshold. Mary felt her hand tremble. Then she said, very low, "Mary, I can't go in. I'm afraid."

Mary put her left arm around Constance, and held Clarrie's small hot hand with her right one. "I know. You're thinking about the old days, dear. Your father and all the rest."

Constance's eyes were full of tears. "He never forgave me. I never expected to see this house again." She wiped her eyes with her tiny handkerchief. "I didn't know I cared so much."

"Your mother is waiting, dear."

They climbed the stairs slowly. At the top, Margaret, who had been waiting, come forward and took Clarrie. The little girl was so bewildered that she went along to the strange nursery without a word. Margaret made a sign to Mary over the child's head. It would be better not to suggest that she see her grandmother. Constance stood in the hall, her feet anchored to the carpet. She was milk-pale, biting her lips; her fingers twitched. She looked at Mary with terror.

Mary bent over her and spoke quietly.

"You must be brave, Constance. You must. She's been waiting for you. Hanging on."

"Is it—does she—look dreadfully?" Constance whispered.

Mary nodded solemnly.

"Yes, she does. But you must not let her know you see it. You mustn't. Nobody must." Mary spoke insistently.

Constance took off her furs and hat and dropped them with her gloves and purse on a chair in the hall. Then she turned to her mother's door. Her face was set rigidly, and Mary noticed with amazement a sudden forceful resemblance to old William Scott in the stern lines of the mouth and forehead.

Together they opened the door. The close, sickening smell enveloped them as they stepped inside the room. Mary had grown used to it, but she saw Constance's nostrils flutter, her pale face go greenish. Mary held back and watched Constance move lightly across the floor to the huge walnut bed. The figure in it was so emaciated that the outline of the body was almost flat under the counterpane; the crossed hands lying on it were like knotty gray claws; and the face of Clarissa Scott was a mask carved ready for death. The dry gray skin was tight across the jutting planes and hollows of the fine broad skull. The lips and nostrils were pinched with the look of death, but the large eyes, darkened from blue to glassy blackness, were wide open, and eloquent with expression as they saw the lovely creature approaching the bed. Mary held her breath, with her pulse knocking in her throat, as she watched Constance. Her white face broke into a rapturous smile, and in her lightest, warmest tone, her voice steady and musical, Constance said, "Mama, darling, how glad I am to see you!"

She bent over, smiling still, murmuring endearments, and kissed the ghastly face on the pillow. Tears burned in Mary's eyes; she turned away and the nurse who had been sitting by the bed, rose quietly and joined her. Constance perched on the edge of the high bed, holding her mother's hands, and listening while the stiff gray lips slowly formed words.

"Of course I brought her, darling! You can see her whenever you want to. She's been talking about her Granny all the way over. And I brought Nannie, and the dog, and all sorts of presents for everybody—we came for a real visit!" Constance never took her eyes from her mother's face, but sat smiling and softly chattering as if nothing in the world had changed since the last time she had been in this room.

"Lord bless her!" the nurse whispered to Mary. "How can she do it?"

"Don't let her stay long," Mary whispered back. "Not until—you know." Miss Calder nodded as Mary slipped outside to wait in the hall for Constance. After a time the bedroom door opened noiselessly and Constance came through it. Mary reached her just as she clutched the air with her trembling white fingers, sobbed, and keeled over in a faint. Paul was just coming upstairs. He carried his sister into Elizabeth's old room and laid her on the bed. Mary's face was streaming with tears.

Doctor McClintock came later and told them that the end was very near. Constance was calm now, extraordinarily quiet, listening closely to every word that the doctor said. She had known him all her life. Once when the doctor came out of the sickroom Constance caught his arm and gave him a dumb look of pleading.

"What is it, child?" he asked slowly.

"She can't—can't she—say—anything?"

He shook his head sadly. "Not any more."

"You mean—she'll never be able—to speak to me again?"

He put his arm around her shoulders and drew her gently towards her mother's room. "Would it help?" he asked, "just to sit in there?—for a while, for—"

"If she'd only been able to speak to me once more," Constance said numbly. She had her lace handkerchief locked in her hand. "I'd have come sooner, I'd have—"

"Con," Edgar said gently. "She only stayed alive until now so she could see you once again. Isn't that so, Doc?"

Constance drew up her slender body and squared her shoulders and again Mary saw that stern expression cross her white face, so fleetingly but startlingly like her father's.

She and Edgar went in to sit out the night by their mother's bed. Paul was there. At long intervals he looked up, his broad face haggard, so identical in bone and sculpture with the dying mask on the pillows that the sight stabbed Mary's heart. Sometimes Paul quietly left the room and went down the hall to look in on Louise. Her child was almost due, and it had been a month since she had even tried to leave her room. She had preferred not to make the effort to move her huge swollen body. Mary was glad of that; it kept her out of the way; just as she was glad of Paul's abrupt decision two days ago not to wire William and Elizabeth of the imminence of their mother's death. They might come at once and then have to stay for days or even weeks. Paul had said nobody could endure that. He would be responsible for his decision about it.

Constance and Edgar were on one side of the bed; Paul, and Mary, on her knees, on the other. It was good to be able to pray as she wanted to; it was good to pour out her heart in prayers for this beloved woman's good and peaceful death. It was a blessing to be here among those whom she loved above all others on earth. Her low voice was barely a whisper, barely a susurration as she prayed.

Her children's eyes were fixed on Clarissa Scott's awful gray face propped high on the pillows. Their hands clasped the knotty, clammy claws lying motionless on the counterpane. Clarissa's pinched mouth was slightly open, her breathing a faint, ghastly rasp, her tortured eyes hidden at last under iron-colored lids. All pretense about prolonging her life was abandoned now. Constance was able to her own amazement to listen stoically to the doctor's directions to Miss Calder—"Don't let her come out again—give it as necessary—"

"Can't you—couldn't you—?" Constance touched the doctor's arm.

"What, child?"

He looked down at the slender figure poised on the edge of the chair. The red curls were disordered, the green eyes heavy with strain and tears.

The scintillating beauty and arrogance were gone from Constance's white face and in it the old doctor saw the strong passions of temper and wilfulness disciplined to bravery. Edgar came over from the doorway, stood behind his sister, and put his hands on her shoulders. Both twins gazed intently at their dying mother. The doctor shook his head slowly. In this room, in this bed, exactly a quarter of a century ago, he had brought these children into the world for this fine and loyal and gentle woman. He thought of that painful and difficult birth, quietly borne like this dreadful death. The shocking contrast with Paul's fool of a wife struck him tellingly. He bent over Constance.

"What, child?"

"Couldn't you—make it happen—sooner? Wouldn't it be kinder?"

He nodded slowly. "It is happening now, Constance. She cannot feel any more. She doesn't know. Believe me, she will not suffer any more."

"We are feeling it now, Con." Edgar spoke quietly. The doctor watched their hands knot together, their thin faces set in identical lines. He knew the anxiety these two had caused their mother, the pitfalls into which they had flung themselves rather than take heed or accept restraint. Yet they had quality; stern nerves to meet ordeals without flinching. Doctor McClintock reflected on the mystery of twins. These two were as close as the day he had taken them from Clarissa.

Only a little while later there was a silent change; a difference in the doctor's face; a solemn remote dignity in the sad nurse's as she stepped forward and drew the high pillows from beneath Clarissa's shoulders. Edgar and Constance on one side of the bed, Paul on his, put out their hands and clasped them all together over their mother's. With their eyes fixed on the dying face Mary saw the pinched nostrils move in the faintest degree. There was no sound but the infinitesimal whisper of Mary's prayers. She saw Paul move his left arm and felt it go hard and steady around her own shoulders, his left hand doubling over her clasped ones while his right still held his mother's. Clarissa's last breath drifted quietly through her lips. Her children were silent and Mary went on praying.

CHAPTER XL

[November 1889]

DINNER WAS OVER. Elizabeth rose from her mother's old place opposite Paul and led Constance and Julia from the dining-room. Edgar went to his humidor for cigars, and Trude placed before Paul the decanters of port and brandy from the sideboard. The old days of William Scott's militant teetotalling were long forgotten, but the brothers exchanged glances of faint amusement as they gathered about the head of the table and gravely filled their glasses. Only Benjamin Nicholas stiffly refused the port. The men smoked in rather awkward silence. This whole gathering had been an ordeal difficult far beyond the strain of Clarissa Scott's death. Her brother Staunton Haynes sat here now, tall and graciously white-haired, scrutinizing his three nephews quizzically. He had hardly seen them since their childhood, when Clarissa used to bring them East for the summer, and he would visit with them briefly. Only insofar as they resembled his sister could he feel any link to them.

It struck him now that where Paul was the only one of the three who resembled his father in manner and character, he was also the only one who really looked like his mother. The other two were curiously negative. William (his Uncle Staunton had used to call him Billy) seemed unrelated to every person and every emotion in this house, while Edgar possessed an intangible quality which Haynes described to himself as *lost*. He studied Edgar behind this thin hand. His nephew was handsome, strikingly so; but in too attenuated a way. His personality had the same quality of attractiveness whose full impact was somehow weakened and dispersed at one's point of contact with it. Haynes had shrewdly noticed in his two days here how great was Paul's attachment to Edgar, almost a paternal attachment which had its dependent element too. And Edgar, while reciprocating to the utmost, while making himself indispensable to Paul, seemed nevertheless uncertain, unfulfilled; subtly unsatisfied. He was a troubled and a secretly unhappy young man. Even the consolation of reunion with Constance had not dispelled the nebulous inquietude of Edgar's spirit—a sad quality that had nothing to do with his grief for his mother. Edgar spoke to Haynes now, leaning across the corner of the table.

"You know, Uncle Staunton, I never knew until yesterday how you helped Connie after she was married. That was splendid of you!"

"Oh no, Ed. I was glad to do it for your mother. It was her money, after all. She just couldn't exactly use it as she wished while your father— while he was alive. I didn't do it for long."

"No, but it was damned fine of you just the same. Con never knew about it either. She was awfully touched yesterday when the will was read."

"Ed," said his uncle suddenly, "why don't you go home with Constance when she sails? Pay her a good long visit. It would do you good."

Edgar's face grew masked. One eager flash of his green eyes was obliterated by a pinched and resigned expression. He rolled his cigar nervously between his fingers.

"I'd like it, Uncle Staunton. Con's spoken of it already. But—I can't."

"Why not?"

"Oh, I couldn't leave Paul now. He's going to need a lot of help. He's been terribly held down with everything at home here and now that Mama's—that the suspense is over, we can throw ourselves into things at the mill. We need to, I'm afraid we've neglected a lot of possibilities. Business is booming, you know."

"Is that so?" William drawled across the table. "Is business as good as all that?"

"Tremendous," said Paul. "Blast furnace production in town has broken every previous record and in our mill I should say the sky was the limit—as far as our alloys are concerned."

The men drew their chairs closer, interested and thoroughly relieved to have the talk turn on this, their only possible interest in common, and their only conversational refuge from their sad business here.

"Are you going to increase your variety of alloys?" asked Nicholas.

"Oh, certainly. Ed, I showed you that paper of Riley's about nickel steel that he read to the British Institute? They presented it as a great departure," Paul explained, "and we've been making open-hearth nickel steel for nearly three years now."

"I wonder what effect Captain Jones's death will have on Edgar Thomson," William said slowly. He poised his cigar between his slender white fingers. William, in the few years since his removal to the bosom of Julia's family, was a changed man. Nobody knew or cared to discover what his troubles with his father-in-law must have been during the first three years of his life in Boston. But at the end of that time Laurence Gaylord had died, leaving his only child a fortune in millions. The investments were astutely divided between the most conservative possible securities, and holdings in such skyrocketing phenomena as railroads, steel, coal, and the industries related to them. It had been in the search for just such an investment that Laurence Gaylord had first hit upon the Scott Iron Works. Now William, though subject to the judgment of two cold-blooded Boston financiers as co-trustees, was one of the administrators of this fortune compared to which his own partnership in the Scott mill was negligible. William had taken on lustre in the reflection of his wife's money, and with the lustre went a kind of assurance which in a more consequential man would have meant intrinsic importance. In William it seemed mere bombast. Contact with huge and potent sums of money and intimate knowledge of the ruthless ways in which financial battles were fought had quickly hardened him and obliterated his youthful uncertainty. On the other hand, the veto of his two co-administrators hung always over any absolute decision he might wish to make.

Paul saw that Bill intended, whether cannily or not, to keep as closely informed about the mill as he could. That was the sole way in which he could demonstrate a special right to impose his judgment on his colleagues. It was also the only field in which he might ever hope to assert himself apart from them. Paul saw this while William asked unexpectedly trenchant questions about the inventories, the output, the profits, the liabilities, and the future plans of the mill. Paul answered as openly and willingly as he could, though with an uneasy sense that Bill's interest was not based on true concern for the family business. But Paul would never have challenged him with that now. Too many dogs lay sleeping and Paul was determined that they should stay asleep. He had watched narrowly when William and Julia had steepped from the carriage on arriving at the house day before yesterday. Mary had emerged from her sitting-room just as they were laying off their wraps in the hall. Her hands were full of mail and telegrams. William could not conceal his consternation at seeing her. Paul observed it plainly.

"Mary has come back to help us out, Bill," Paul had said, in the most natural tone he could muster. "She has been a godsend to Mama."

"How are you, Mister William?" Old habit stood comfortably by Mary She knew what must be transpiring in William's mind.

"Very well, thank you."

"How do you do?" said Julia stiffly.

"Very well, thank you, Mrs. William. How are the children?"

"Well, thank you."

Mary had not prolonged the encounter a moment. With a nod she had moved past the William Scotts and gone about her business. Paul had been left to face his brother's silent, startled discomfiture.

"Mary is running the house for Louise now," he said. "We've had a pretty difficult time this past year and I don't know what we'd have done without her."

"Do you mean to say she lives here again?" William had spoken in the solemn shocked whisper that seemed appropriate to all the circumstances— the house in mourning, Louise upstairs in bed, and this unbelievable reappearance of Mary Rafferty.

"Why of course."

Julia at that point had made a conspicuous move towards the back parlor, saying, "I must go and see Elizabeth. I expect she's in there."

But William had stood dumbly in the hall with Paul, looking uneasily up the stairs as if Mary's presence there was a threat to the very structure of the house.

"Why," he mumbled uncomfortably, "why, Paul. I—er—"

"Bill, I wouldn't worry about things here if I were you. We are making out very well and Louise is especially contented." Paul spoke with emphasis. He could see that William would not comprehend more than a hint of his meaning, but he could also see that the less his brother had to do with this house the more secure he would feel. Paul was reflecting on that this evening while he refilled William's glass at the table, and kept the conversation on the steel business.

In the drawing-room the three women made a strange picture. Elizabeth and Constance were so extraordinarily unlike that no eye could suspect their relationship. Both were dressed, of course, in mourning black. But Constance by her very vividness dramatized the stark lines of her dull black silk gown. Her sister could not know that Premet had only finished this simple masterpiece in time to deliver it to Constance on the ship. In spite of her strained pallor and the blue circles under her eyes, Constance was paganly beautiful. Her belted waist was small and pliant, her fiery head above her tight, high black collar a sculptured flower nodding on a dark stalk. Her glittering eyes were quiet behind her narrowed, slanting lids. She made Elizabeth feel ponderous and stupid, just because Constance sat so gracefully on a small, fat, tufted green satin chair, her elastic body seeming hardly to touch the furniture. Elizabeth was neither dull nor heavy; on the contrary, she had the same angular vigor that had carried her tireless through miles of good works all the years of her girlhood in Pittsburgh. But every line of her hard merino dress, every twist in her sandy, rather oily hair, the frank hygienic scrubbedness of her sallow skin were mute reproof to Constance. Elizabeth honestly considered her sister's whispered reputation a public scandal, and was miserably ill at ease. She could not imagine what one talked about with a woman who flouted all one's notions of decency. By Elizabeth's code Constance should be paying in bitter coin the price of her delinquencies, and instead she seemed to bask in the best of everything, coruscating and scot-free. Elizabeth was confused as much as outraged, something in her scheme of things was gravely awry. Even in her most secret thoughts she could not admit it exciting or enviable that Constance should shine so frivolously in so exalted a setting.

But Julia could. She had not forgotten her original pleasure in contriving the marriage of Constance and Giles, that pleasure compounded of snobbery and spite. Julia also enjoyed reflected celebrity. Even if the celebrity verged on notoriety it still emanated from a very impressive source. So she could sit here on the high-backed sofa, secure in her magnificence of money, flesh (she had begun to solidify markedly) and dowdy, expensive clothes, and cynically observe the reunion of her two sisters-in-law. She drew a bone of possible contention from the devious receptacle of her mind and threw it to the sisters.

"Weren't you surprised to find Mary Rafferty in the house again when you arrived?" she asked.

Elizabeth's thin mouth twitched. Constance raised her red head with her old gesture of defiance.

"Yes, indeed," said Elizabeth and "Certainly not!" snapped Constance simultaneously. Julia reacted volubly.

"I was," she said. Her eyes moved slowly from one face to the other. They held a searching question. "Wouldn't you think," she said, lowering her voice, "that Louise would have objected strongly? After all—"

"After all, what?" Constance thrust her chin forward.

"Well—" Elizabeth started to speak, thought better of it, and looked at Julia.

"Well—" Julia could not decide whether to put her insinuations into words or leave them hanging. William had never told her exactly what he knew of the matter between Paul and Mary. He would have died rather than tell. He had undergone humiliation enough at his father's and Paul's hands, and his situation with Laurence Gaylord had been difficult enough when he first went to Boston, without emphasizing the prospect of his brother's marriage to a servant. Old Gaylord would as soon have discussed the matter with his daughter as throw her into a cesspool. So she had really never been told what her father and her husband knew. All her thoughts on the subject, and they had been many and lingering, had been such as to invest it only with shameful innuendo.

"Well, I must say I would not have it in Louise's place," she said.

"Have what?" Constance managed to speak in a tone as tough as a schoolboy's.

Julia and Elizabeth exchanged a glance of exasperation.

"Really, Constance," Elizabeth looked down at her clasped hands, "you can't pretend you never noticed any, er, anything. . . ."

"I never went snooping and hinting things about people I loved, if that's what you mean," Constance said. She thought suddenly of her cigarette case upstairs, filled with tiny Turkish paper-tipped tubes. How she would love one now! She twiddled her white fingers against her skirt. She would deliciously relish shocking the eyebrows off of Lizzie, but on second thought she had no wish to outrage anybody here, for her mother's and for Mary's sake. She rose and stood with her back to the fireplace.

"I had a talk with Louise this afternoon," Julia said, ignoring Constance's retort. "I went up and sat with her while you were all down at the bank. I declare I can't understand her. She seems to *like* Mary. She lies there and lets Mary wait on her and fuss over her—it's positively unbelievable."

"Why?" asked Constance acidly. "Why is it unbelievable for Mary to devote herself to Louise and expect to bring up her children? That's what she's always done here."

"Well, of course, if you *won't* see what I mean, I can't *tell* you," Julia said. She settled her long gold watch-chain and tucked her watch deeper in her belt.

"I can see that Louise is a featherwitted ninny who's always made cow-eyes at Paul and isn't any more fit to bring up his children than a—a jackdaw. She's damned lucky to have Mary here and she knows it." Constance ignored the horrified winces that her profanity evoked. "Louise is wildly in love with Paul and—"

"Paul is *surely* just as much in love with her," Julia interpolated. Her sarcastic tone was a blend of butter and vingar.

"Like—" Constance swallowed. She started to swear again, but caught herself. "Like thin air he is."

"Ah, then, you do see what we're talking about," Julia murmured.

"Where is this getting you?" Constance asked Julia. She turned to Elizabeth. "Either of you? What possible reason can you have for trying to stir up jealousy and wretchedness around Paul? Can't you leave him alone to work out his own life? My God, it's nauseating!"

Elizabeth moved her shoulders stiffly. "I for one think it nauseating, in your words, for him to have that woman here right under the same roof with Louise and his children. It's—it's—"

"'That woman,'" snapped Constance, "is the best friend I ever had or Mama ever had, and if you'd been half the daughter to Mama that she always was—oh, you make me tired. You don't know the first thing about life. You're a walking Sunday-school lesson, complete with hypocrisy and mottoes."

Julia sniffed. "I don't see why you stand for this, Elizabeth."

"What can she do? She knows it's true. There isn't a spark of warmth or charity in her. Even poor Louise, that cushion-wit, has more human understanding than Lizzie."

Elizabeth's pale face reddened. She bit her lips and nervously clasped the arms of her chair. But she said nothing. Constance and Julia both saw that she was giving a demonstration of fortitude and self-control.

"I don't agree with you about Louise," Julia said. She kept worrying the subject like a dog a bone. "Do you mean to tell me she's never *heard* anything? Or doesn't *care*?"

"What if she has? She's married to Paul now. That's what matters to her. And she at least credits him with honorable instincts whether you do or not."

Elizabeth's mouth opened at last. "Are you a competent judge of honorable instincts?" she asked Constance, with stiff lips.

Constance laughed and shrugged.

Julia sat shaking her head. "I still can't understand it," she said.

"You wouldn't," Constance retorted.

At that point the men came in. Paul walked over to the fireplace and put his arm around Constance. "You two seem to be up to your old ways again," he said, looking from her to Elizabeth.

"Oh, we're just agreeing to disagree."

Both Benjamin Nicholas and William went to sit close to their wives, as if to protect them from dire influences. Elizabeth's flushed face was really pathetic and she gave her husband a silent look of entreaty. They had agreed not to stay in Pittsburgh any longer than necessary. The last document requiring Elizabeth's signature had been signed this evening before dinner. The Nicholases would be leaving soon now to take the night train back to New York. The William Scotts were going with them. But it was not time to leave yet. There was at least an hour more to be disposed of before they could escape upstairs and collect their belongings for the journey.

William looked curiously about the room.

"Do you realize," he said slowly, "that this is the only time we have all been together here since Constance and Giles eloped?"

Constance shrugged. "What a thing to commemorate!" she said. Edgar shook his head at her. He did not want her to show off as she loved to do for mischief's sake, and shock the family into deeper antagonism. He was very sensitive to Constance's brittle sarcasm. He hated her to display bad taste. It was too easy for her to have fun doing it.

William was still reminiscing about Constance's elopement.

"Why did you do it, anyway, Con? I never could see why, even when we went on that goose-chase that night."

"I wanted to live, Bill. Not necessarily with Giles—"

"*Constance!*" Elizabeth's face was crimson.

"Oh, that's not what I mean," Constance said carelessly. "But I'd have married anything in shoes to get away from here."

"You didn't have such a bad life," said Edgar reproachfully.

"No, I didn't. I wish—" Constance paused and turned her head away as if concealing that she was in pain. Her hand brushed her averted eyes. "I wish I'd had the sense to stay with Mama longer while I had her. That's the only thing I feel badly about." She choked.

Elizabeth moved uncomfortably. She had been desperately afraid that some time during the family gathering somebody would do just this— visibly and audibly express grief for her mother and thereby imperil the imperturbable control with which the Scotts preferred to mask their feelings. At least Elizabeth presumed that they preferred this—she did, William did; Paul could act as if he did; but those appalling twins! They were just as likely to throw emotional bomb-shells as they had been to put a litter of mice in her bed twenty years ago. Everything about this gathering made Elizabeth wretched. She mourned her mother as sincerely as any of the others, but mourning, by her ideas, should be a matter of deep inner feeling, outward solemnity and impassivity, and no manifestations of hysteria whatsoever. She had hoped to escape anything like that during her mother's funeral. Her mother's death at least had had none of the melodramatic horror of her father's. Elizabeth would never get over the awful memory of that.

And not only Constance—all the rest of them made her uncomfortable. She thought she detected a fleeting glance of satirical amusement every time her Uncle Staunton's eyes met hers. In spite of her apparent siding with Julia in the matter of Mary, it was more than Elizabeth's imagination that whenever Julia spoke of her two children she did so with a veiled but prying glance at Elizabeth's flat, angular figure. Six years of marriage, after all, and she hadn't given a *sign*. . . . Elizabeth could hear Julia voicing such speculations to any interested party. Elizabeth herself did not know why she had no children. She did not think of herself as sterile in body any more than in mind and heart; she was unaware of the truth so obvious to Constance and to Mary. They had been remarking it together in the privacy of Constance's room when Elizabeth had gone in there late last night to speak to her sister. She had not expected to find Mary there. She had not even definitely planned what she would say when she went in. But she had succumbed to a vigorous impulse of curiosity; she could only guess at the luxury with which Constance probably surrounded herself and she wanted to see it at first hand.

She found Constance sitting up in bed in a cloud of lacy baby-pillows, sipping a glass of hot milk that Mary had brought her. Her red curls tumbled brassily over the pale blue marabou bedjacket across her shoulders. Beneath it Elizabeth glimpsed a web of filmy lace and transparent silk and beneath that, the appalling, the incredible sight of Constance's pearly globular breasts. Elizabeth blushed furiously; she could see the deep pink nipples right through the lace! Constance seemed utterly unconscious. Mary, who had been (at Constance's insistence) perched on the foot of the bed, stood up and took the empty glass and bent over Constance for a moment. She pushed the brilliant hair back from Constance's forehead, and looked at her anxiously as she bent over to kiss her good night.

"Are you all right, dear? Can you sleep?"

Constance nodded, her hand in Mary's. "You're wonderful, Mary. I'd have died without you."

They kissed tenderly.

"Good night, dear. Call me if you want anything."

"Can we get Clarrie back tomorrow, do you think?" Constance looked self-conscious at admitting that she missed her child. "I'd like her with me." The children and their nurses had been sent across the street to Mrs. Burns.

Mary nodded, straightened a lampshade, and left the room. Constance looked up curiously at Elizabeth. She had not failed to notice her sister's prominent gray eyes roving about the room, taking in the gold toilet articles and the glittering row of crystal bottles on the dressing-table; the morocco jewel-box; the tooled and crested leather writing-case on the desk between the windows; the opulent pale blue satin dressing-gown and the delicate hand-made matching slippers by the armchair; the washstand covered with pots and bottles and jars of Parisian cosmetics. Elizabeth in the midst of this, thought Constance, looked like a seamy old crow. And she was only thirty-one! The sisters regarded each other in embarrassed silence. Elizabeth now had nothing to say.

There was a light tap on the door and Constance's maid came in.

"Will you need anything more tonight, Madam?"

"No, thanks, Lester. Go to bed."

"Thank you, Madam. Shan't I brush your hair first, Madam?"

Constance shook her head. "No, I haven't the patience. Go along, Lester."

"Very good, Madam." The maid went to the wardrobe, took out some clothes from what, Elizabeth could see, was an amazing array of rich fabrics and furs, and carrying them away for attention, withdrew. The silence after that was more awkward still. Elizabeth felt as if she were a spectator at a Pinero play.

"Well," she said in her flat voice, "I just came in to say good night."

Constance wished there were anything else to say. She did not want to show her indifference to Lizzie. But she would have felt more at ease with the utmost stranger.

"That was nice of you, Liz." Constance spoke gently. She was drowsy. Mary had obtained a powder from Doctor McClintock, and put it in the hot milk. "It's a pity we've only got a tragedy to bring us together again."

"It is. Tell me, Constance—did Mama know you when you got here?"

"Just for a moment. Only a moment." Constance bit her lips hard. She did not want to cry. Elizabeth did not want her to. Constance was afraid then that her sister was going to kiss her. But Elizabeth did not. She only said, "Well, I do think Paul might have let *me* know in time to get here."

"Don't be bitter about it, Liz," Constance said. "Nobody could help it—it just happened that way. I'd been a long time on my way."

Elizabeth turned to go.

"Well," she said tonelessly, "good night, Constance."

"Good night."

It was such chasms, Elizabeth sat thinking, which penetrated the whole life of her family, and kept each of her brothers, as well as Constance, apart on a little island of his own. She could not remember when these sharp divergencies of taste and personality had first impressed themselves. It seemed in retrospect that they had all had quite a normal, congenial childhood together. Now she looked at them wonderingly. William, with his lifelong aptitude for saying the wrong thing, was remarking in an artificial way, "Just think, if Paul weren't the arbiter of our financial destiny, we might never have any reason for all meeting together again."

Constance was irritated by his tactlessness. She showed it by making an ill-natured remark herself.

"I can't imagine why I'd ever come back again once I get home to London," she said. "Any of you who want to see me can come over there."

They all looked uncomfortable. Elizabeth eyed her husband, hoping that he would draw his bulky watch from his pocket, consult it, and signal her that the time had come to leave. Julia moved her plump shoulders and made a small, disapproving mouth. In William's affluent position it was hardly necessary or justifiable for him to display his resentment over Paul's authority. Edgar was sitting in the corner with his head bent and his hands rammed in his pockets; he had spoken only once since leaving the dining-room. And Uncle Staunton, who made Elizabeth almost as uncomfortable as Constance did, was stretched back in his armchair, his slender ankles crossed, his thin hand with its heavy seal ring delicately posing his cigar. He was gazing at the ceiling. Paul had drawn a sheaf of papers from his breast pocket and was looking them through, making sure that his brothers and sisters had not overlooked any detail of estate matters requiring their signatures.

"Paul." Some of them started as they heard Mary's low, lilting voice in the doorway. William and Julia and Elizabeth even winced. To them there was something inexpressibly shocking in Mary's calm, natural addressing of Paul by his Christian name. They looked at her stonily. Constance looked too, thinking as she eyed the slender, graceful, black-dressed figure and the shining hair above the cameo face, how utterly a part of the real life of this house Mary was, and how false were the natures and personalities who repudiated her.

"Paul, Louise is waiting for you to come up and say good night. She ought to go to sleep now."

Paul stood up quickly.

"I'll be down presently." He excused himself to the family and left the room with Mary. The others all sat in silence, listening to the double foot-falls, light and heavy, going up the stairs.

CHAPTER XLI

[*November 1889—Continued*]

THE CRY ECHOED sharply down the hall. Paul and Edgar and Constance were in the back parlor after dinner, Paul in his father's easy-chair with his pipe and a stack of metallurgical journals, the twins playing bezique. The Nicholases and the Williamses, as Constance called them, had been gone for several days and peace had settled over the house; but it was a tenuous peace. Paul was startled from his chair. They heard Mary's light steps running along the upstairs hall. Constance's jaw dropped and she said, "Oh, God." They heard it again, as Paul left the room; Louise's voice in a sharp wail.

"Is it like this all the time around her?" Constance asked sarcastically. She and Edgar had a certain way of speaking together, of saying things with cold humor that they would never have shown anybody else. They liked to play this humor over serious and forbidding things. Edgar shrugged. "Stick around," he said. "Anything can happen. Admission free."

Mary came running downstairs. She passed the open door. Constance yelled, "Is this it, Mary?"

"This is it." Mary was in too much of a hurry to pause long. There was a cold light in her eyes. She shut the door and left the twins staring at each other across the table. They heard her hurrying upstairs again.

Paul shot Mary a despairing glance as she entered the bedroom. He was bending over Louise with his arm around her. Sometimes when he made such a gesture Mary saw that it was a deliberate effort. Six months of living in the house with Paul and Louise had opened her eyes wide, too wide. Paul had indeed learned in the years since his marriage to obliterate every visible sign of his feeling for Mary, but in the process he had also buried many of his other demonstrative impulses. Only towards Dickie did he act like his old warm, open-hearted self. But only a man of stone would have been unmoved now by the pitiful spectacle of Louise in travail and panic.

"Is it bad, Lou?"

She nodded, her brown eyes strained more in fear than in pain.

Together Mary and Paul held her hands and tried to communicate to her strength and calmness.

"Everything will be all right," Mary said soothingly. "Wouldn't you be more comfortable to get your clothes off, and let me help you? Paul is going to send for the doctor."

"No." Louise gasped. "Paul, stay here."

"I'm not going away, Lou. I'm only running downstairs to send Jones for Mrs. Hibben and Doctor McClintock. I won't be a minute. Mary'll be right here with you."

Louise's stringy hands went to the small of her back, with a wail. "There it is!"

"I know," Mary murmured, helping her undress. "I know all about it. Now if you'll just step—that's it." She kept up a quiet flow of talk, in a soothing monotone, while she hung up Louise's clothes, braided her brown hair, and seemingly without purpose, kept her moving slowly about the room. Louise clutched at the bedpost as they walked across the floor, and whimpered, "I want to go to bed. I want Paul."

"He's coming right back, dear. Right away. I wouldn't lie down yet, you know. It's better this way. Easier. That's right—we'll get it over sooner this way."

Around and around, slowly and more slowly, she walked in step with

Louise. The pains were actually slight still, and spaced far apart but Louise was shuddering and moaning, flinging herself headlong towards panic.

"Just be calm, dear,' Mary said quietly. "Take it easy.' She stood holding Louise's hands in a rigid clasp as the trembling woman bent over, biting her lips, to meet another pain. "That's better See, it won't be so bad."

Paul came in then, and took Mary's place beside Louise.

"Jones will have Mrs. Hibben here in a few minutes," he said gently. "and Doctor McClintock is on his way."

"I don't want Mrs. Hibben," Louise wailed.

"Oh, yes, you do. You like her." He spoke as he would to Dickie.

Louise was crouching by her bed, trying to get into it. "Bed," she moaned. "I want to go to bed." She clung to Mary, clawing her arms.

Even after Mrs. Hibben, the nurse, arrived, changed into her uniform, and took Louise in hand, the frightened patient would not let Mary go. Mrs. Hibben appeared to be painfully associated in Louise's mind with the experience of Dickie's birth and she would not be left alone with her. "No," she screamed, as Mary moved towards the door. "No, no, no. Come back here. Paul, don't let her go."

Standing there, awkward and baffled, with Louise's hand in his, Paul made signs at Mary.

"She'll be right back, Lou," he said. "She'll stay with you. She's just going to see about things downstairs. She has lots to do."

Louise ignored him. "Come back," she wailed. "Mary, come back. Ouw—ouw—"

Paul glanced meaningly at the nurse, murmuring, "Can't you give her something?"

Mrs. Hibben shook her head impatiently. "Of course not. She'd be much better if everybody left her alone with me until—"

"Paul!" cried Louise. "What's she saying to you? I won't be alone. Stay here, Paul. You and Mary. I don't want that nurse. You and Mary, Paul."

He sighed desperately. If this first half hour was a sample, Louise was going to give them the worst night of their lives. Her eyes kept rolling wildly in her head, one minute turning to Paul with hysterical pleading, the next flashing panic and temper as they roved the corners of the room. "Where's Mary?" she cried. "I want Mary."

"She's coming right back, Mrs. Scott." Mrs. Hibben spoke brusquely. "I do wish you'd try to be more quiet. All this noise won't help you at all Here comes Doctor McClintock now. See if you can't be more controlled."

Paul made a welcome escape while the doctor was examining Louise. He ran downstairs to the back parlor. Constance was very pale The twins were sitting close together now, side by side on the horsehair sofa, their green eyes round with apprehension.

"Why is she screaming like that?" Constance asked, twisting her white fingers together. 'What are they doing to her? God, this is too ghastly."

"She's all right," Paul sighed. He fetched a decanter of brandy from the dining-room and poured himself a drink. Constance grabbed one too. "She just carries on like that," Paul said. "She's frightened."

"But what the hell *of?*" Constance blurted. "Any ass can have a baby. Can't you shut her up?"

Edgar gave her a reproachful look.

Constance said, after another wail from upstairs, "It's a damned outrage." She fiddled with her rings. "With children in the house. I don't fuss much about Clarrie but I don't want her to hear that."

Paul finished his drink and stood up. Constance stared at him incredulously.

"Are you going back upstairs? Back to her?"

Paul made a gesture. "You hear her."

Louise was calling and crying for Paul. They heard her door open and close, and the doctor coming downstairs. Paul found him in the front hall talking in whispers with Mary. She was saying, "Are you sure, doctor? Have you told her?"

"What?" asked Paul.

"Come in here." Doctor McClintock led them into the dining-room and closed the door. "Louise is going to have twins."

Paul sat down heavily in the nearest chair.

"How—are you sure?"

"I have suspected it for a long time. I thought it wiser not to say anything—she's too hysterical. You had better be prepared, though." Paul's face was pale and his forehead beaded. He stared.

Mary said gently, "Go on upstairs now, Paul please—" They shrank as she opened the dining-room door and Louise's shrill wails echoed down the stairs.

Paul found her tossing and heaving, flinging herself about the bed, alternately screaming and moaning. First she clung to his hands and Mrs. Hibben's, then flung them wildly aside, clawing the sheets and thrashing the air. When Mary came in presently, with her mouth set in tight lines, she too tried to quiet Louise. They all exhorted and pleaded with her.

"You must help. You must save your strength."

"Try, Mrs. Scott. Won't you please try to help us? Hold on here."

"No!" shrieked Louise. "NO, no!" Her mouth hung open; her face was streaming with tears, sweat, and saliva. "Daddy!" she screamed suddenly. "Da-a-a-ddy! Daddy Dick!"

Mary looked, startled, at Paul. "What does she mean?"

"I don't know. She did that before too. She always screams for her father if she's frightened."

"Mrs. Scott, won't you *please try*. Please be quiet." Mrs. Hibben's voice was edged.

"Please, Lou, be a good girl. It'll be so much easier," Paul leaned over her, pleading and encouraging.

She only wailed louder, thrashing from one side of the bed to the other. "No, no, no, no" — her voice rose and fell in crazy cadences. " I want Daddy. I want Paul. Paul. Daddy, pain. Pain—"

"I'm right here, Lou. Here I am."

The doctor came in and stood looking sternly at the spectacle.

"Louise," he said in a sudden, sharp tone, "you must control yourself."

Her jaw sagged lower; she fixed her rolling eyes on him; then she drew a breath and screeched louder than ever.

It was not nearly so many hours as it seemed; it was a little after two o'clock in the morning when Mary opened Louise's door after a trip down to the kitchen for boiling water, and then stood trying to rally her nerve before going into that room again. Mary's face was dead white, haggard and harrowed. Her hair was hidden under a tightly-wrapped towel. When she stepped into the room she saw to her intense relief that Louise's tossing and flailing and thrashing had stopped. Mrs. Hibben and Paul had her pinioned across hed bed, and the doctor was working over the birth which had begun. Louise's eyes, which had rolled insanely and unresponsively to all their entreaties for her help, were laxly closed; her screams had subsided to throbbing groans; and the room smelled of chloroform. Mary was surprised. She had not expected that of Doctor McClintock, who had sternly and repeatedly dismissed Paul's suggestions and Louise's shrieks for "something."

Mary looked pityingly at Paul. He was tense and gray-faced, his eyes like two stones. A heavy scowl indented his forehead. He and the doctor had removed their coats and waistcoats, their starched collars and cuffs, and had rolled up their white shirt-sleeves to their elbows. It was a weird sight. In all the crowded, tumultuous mass of her shared experience with Paul there was nothing to make this scene seem real. It could not be that she and he were struggling together to help his child into the world—his children, she thought with a start, and passed the back of her hand shakily across her eyes. Exhaustion or the creeping fumes of chloroform—she did not know—were blurring the whole fantastic sight before her. Louise's body contracted convulsively, a horrible sound parted her lips. Mary's grasp tightened on the damp shoulder beneath her fingers. The doctor straightened up, holding a greasy scarlet thing with wormlike limbs. Mrs. Hibben put her hand on Louise's sheeted belly as Doctor McClintock shook and smacked the infant. Mary and Paul looked on in horror, holding Louise between them.

There was a strange, hideous interval, with the doctor and the nurse speaking in technical monosyllables, then the whole revolting thing unbelievably happening all over again; with eight hands holding and manipulating the prostrate, unhuman, bleeding thing on the bed, and all of this fantastically unrelated to Paul. He stood there stony and shocked and clay-colored, doing what he was told. Mary did not remember afterwards the long business of helping Mrs. Hibben with the two feebly squirming infants, the horrible, exhausting cleaning up, the tottering from that awful room to Clarissa Scott's quiet empty one down the hall and sinking into the rocker by the window. The dawn was beginning to lighten the sky and far in the distance there was the red glow, too, of furnaces blowing down by the river. She sat and pressed her forehead to the cool glass of the window. Paul came in and she looked up. He walked across the floor like a jointed wooden effigy, pausing to stare dully at his mother's empty bed. His mouth moved; he said "Mama," in a tragic way. Then he walked over to Mary and dropped heavily on his knees and put his face in her lap. "Mary," he said, in a strangled croak. "Oh, Mary. I have three sons."

CHAPTER XLII

[December 1889]

CONSTANCE STAYED ON for a month. She had come from England without definite plans, never supposing that her mother's illness would terminate so suddenly. After it was over she made rather indifferent inquiries about the next sailings to England. And then, when Mary urged her not to hurry back, she concurred, really to her own surprise. The life in Pittsburgh was so profoundly different from her own tense, brilliant existence in London that once having made the adjustment it was wonderfully relaxing to let herself sink into the old ways. Now that she was participating from choice instead of necessity, it was consoling to find life the same; the calm and order of the house broken only by the shouts of Dickie and Clarrie at play; the homely routine of Mary's housekeeping, with its scrupulous supervision of dusting and cleaning and paint washing; the delicious simple meals, which Constance relished all the more in contrast to game, hothouse delicacies, rich entrées, and splendid wines. She even fell back into her childhood habit of walking to market with Mary, wandering about among the stalls of the big glass-roofed shed, feasting her eyes and her watering mouth on the tubs of fresh country butter, the crocks of soft pot-cheese, the plump chickens and waxy ducks and black-legged turkeys; the home-made sausages and scrapple and the smoke-blackened hams and bacon; the heaped baskets of eggs, the fragrant hearth-baked bread which the farm wives brought to market. It was a dream more believable, somehow, than the gilded, flunkeyed halls of palaces, realer than the card-rooms of great and famous houses. Dinner every night in the dark, oak-panelled dining-room, with her two brothers and an occasional old friend of Paul's (Louise was still recuperating in her bedroom), with the solemn, capable Trude walking sturdily around the table, was almost an adventure because of its sheer contrast with all the dinners of the past nine years, and all the people with whom she had eaten them. Paul and Edgar did not dress for dinner. Anybody who did, except for a dinner-party, would have been considered a freak in Allegheny.

After dinner Constance loved to join the boys in a glass of port, and smoke her small Turkish cigarettes while Edgar pulled at his stogy and Paul enjoyed his pipe. Paul had never seen a woman smoke before the first evening when Constance produced her jewelled cigarette-case; and if Edgar had, he was discreet enough not to remark it. Constance put her brothers completely at ease. It was clear from every word she spoke, from all her actions, her decisions, and her tastes that she was accustomed far more to the companionship of men than of women. Most masculine of all her characteristics, and most surprising in such a beautiful and feminine woman was her close-mouthed avoidance of talk about the people, especially certain exalted people, with whom she spent her time in England. She was entirely matter-of-fact about the jewels, the sables, the luxurious appurtenances and the superb Paris clothes which both her brothers knew very well were not accounted for by Giles nor even by Constance's own substantial income. She seldom mentioned Giles. If questioned about him, she shrugged. She admitted privately to Edgar that she scarcely ever saw him.

"But I have to have a name, don't I?" she said, blowing smoke through her nose. "And an address."

She also told Edgar the dreary tale of Giles's family, changed now only by the death two years before of Tyrringdale, the heir.

"So you'll be a Countess some day," Edgar said. "I hope you like it."

"Countess of Mortgages, as far as I can see," Constance said. "The title's a joke, you know. There's not only no money, there are such debts that the little remaining family property will have to be liquidated to pay them. But I don't care. I'll make out."

"I bet you will." Edgar's tone suggested that he meant more than he said. Constance stole one of her frequent questioning looks at him. He had changed so much in the past few years. He was more reserved, more mysterious than anyone she knew. And it was totally foreign to his nature to be so. She knew him, she felt, as thoroughly as she knew herself. She could feel in her own mind and emotions the identical thoughts and feelings that she read in him; all except for this new baffling curtain of mystery behind which he withdrew oftener and oftener. She spoke at great length to Mary about it. She loved to spend the late afternoon at tea in Mary's sitting-room, curled up in one of the armchairs by the gas fire while Mary sat opposite with her sewing.

One dark December day, with the blinds drawn against the impenetrable smog outside, Constance was sitting there, licking jam from the tea sandwiches off her fingertips and reaching for her cigarettes, when Mary said, "Have you spoken to Edgar again about going back with you?"

"I tried. He won't do it, Mary. He's dead set."

"It seems queerer and queerer. After all, he has no reason to act this way. Gloomy and mysterious."

"How do you know? You can't tell me he has no reason. Personally, I believe Ed's in a hellish mess of some kind and doesn't know how to get himself out. He'd tell me about it if he'd speak to anybody alive—but he won't. Something's driving him mad, Mary. He's in a shocking state."

Mary sewed quietly for a time. She was, Constance saw, thinking something over, weighing whether or not to tell Constance what was on her mind. Then she looked up and laid her work in her lap and said, "I used to wonder what he does all the time. Since he's stopped going out—running around—the way he used to—"

"He has, now you mention it," Constance said. "He's always here in the evenings. I thought it was just to be with me."

Mary shook her head. "It's a long time," she said slowly, "since Edgar has done the things he used to do."

"I'll be damned," Constance murmured, narrowing her eyes. Suddenly she sat up and asked sharply, "What does he do? When I'm not here?"

Mary hesitated. "He—" she bit off a thread. "Mostly he stays in his room. And reads, I think."

"Well, he always read a lot. That's not extraordinary. Unless—unless it's all he does. Is that what you mean?" She leaned forward and lighted another cigarette. "What does he read?"

"Philosophy," Mary said slowly.

"Oh, those old Greeks and things. He always poked about in those."

"Religious philosophy, I think," Mary said. "Certain kinds."

Constance blew smoke from her nose and asked in a shrewd way, "What are you getting at? I've a feeling you're being devious."

"No. But I—do wish I understood this thing about Edgar." Mary drew a long breath and said, as if anxious to get it off her chest, "One day quite a while ago—quite soon after I came back here—I found Eddie in this room looking through those books." She indicated a small shelf above her desk, where Constance saw a row of black leather-bound books.

Constance stared in a puzzled way. "Why—those are your prayer books," she said. "Catholic books."

"That's just it. I—oh, you know how you pass off a queer thing like that. I pretended not to notice what he was looking at, but I was awfully surprised. He made some remark and went away. But since then he's kept on doing that and lately—"

"Yes?" Constance was tense now.

"Lately he's been borrowing those books, quite frankly. Taking them to his room. And"—Mary colored unexpectedly—"asking me questions."

"Questions," Constance repeated, as if there could be no question to which Edgar would not know the answer better than Mary.

"About—certain things in our faith. He calls it," Mary said, "Catholic philosophy. The philosophy of penance." She swallowed. "It's terribly unnatural, Constance," she said in a panicky way. "Terribly. That's why —I wish you'd take him back to London and get him out of himself. He's—"

Constance was shaking her red curls slowly. "I smell," she said, "a great big rat. A monster of a rat. Look here." She leaned forward and stared compellingly into Mary's eyes. "Do you know what's the matter with him? Honest to God—do you?"

Mary did not answer. Constance insisted, "What do you think it is? What's at the bottom of all this—a woman?"

Mary looked up with an effort. "Yes," she said stiffly. Then she turned her head away.

"You think you know who?" Constance was driving at her now.

For a time Mary did not answer. Then she looked up and thought for a minute and said, "Maybe. I don't really know." She was very troubled and uncomfortable. "If I followed my suspicions I'm so afraid I'd discover something—" she choked— *"something I don't want to know."* Her voice dropped to a whisper.

"What do you mean?"

Mary whipped hard at a buttonhole. Her lips were pinched tight. "I'm not going to talk about it any more," she said.

Constance leaned back in the chair, shook her head, and stared at the ceiling. "This place seems full of things like that," she said slowly. "Edgar's a nervous wreck. And I wouldn't say Paul was exactly basking in contentment."

Mary kept her eyes lowered. She had always dreaded any mention that Constance might make of Paul. Yet if she headed her off, she might only arouse livelier speculation.

"I think Paul's happier than he's ever been," she said, making her tone as stout as she could. Constance laughed hollowly.

"Then he's been a very, very unhappy man. He never seems alive to me. Here I've been dining and talking all evening with those two chaps every day for nearly a month. And what do you think they talk about? The steel business."

"Well, my goodness, Constance, what would you expect them to talk about? What else have they got to talk about?"

"Don't ask me. I haven't seen 'em for years. But whether I know my own brothers is not so much to the point as how well I know men. And those two are not acting like men who're getting what they want out of life. They're both running away from something." Constance leaned forward and emphasized her words by a jerk of her chin. "Running to beat hell."

Mary sighed at Constance's language. "Look here," she said. She laid down her sewing and stared at Constance. "Paul married Louise for a home and children and he took plenty of time making up his mind to do it. He's got what he wanted, you must see that."

"See it? You're the home and the mother of the children, and you know it damned well." Constance watched Mary turn pale at her words and went on speaking roughly. "This place was no home when Louise was supposed to be making it one. I didn't even need to ask Ed to find that out. And for all she means to her children she might as well be a cockatoo." Constance grimaced. "The trouble with Paul is he's legally married to Louise and he's—" she paused. "Why, it's a *hell* of a mess, Mary. Did you think I didn't *know*?"

There was a dead silence. The small clock on the desk ticked grotesquely loud, though a moment before one would not have noticed it. Constance scowled, instantly regretful for the pain she saw she had caused. Mary raised her head presently. Her face was chalky, her lips gray. "Oh, Constance," she said.

Another woman might have rushed to Mary, thrown her arms about her, and through affection and sympathy reduced both of them to hysteria. Constance merely jabbed a hairpin in and out of her chignon of red curls and swore half aloud, "God, I'm sorry," she muttered. "I'm an ass. A beast. Forgive me."

"There's nothing to forgive," Mary whispered.

Then Constance sat up straight. "Yes there is," she said. "You've had the dirtiest deal of any woman on earth. Why you've been—crucified by this family, Mary. Flesh and blood can't stand what you're doing."

"I get along very well. I know what I'm doing."

"Then open your eyes a little wider and know still more. You don't think Paul is going to stand this fantastic arrangement forever, do you? My God, it's like something out of a Greek tragedy. You two are laying up dynamite for yourselves."

"Constance, you dramatize things so. You live in a world of pure excitement and you think of everybody's life in that light."

"No, I don't. You're mistaken. It's true I like excitement, I always did. I know what makes people want excitement, I know what goes on underneath, I know men, Mary—I ought to."

Mary colored, and Constance went on talking.

"I'm trying to tell you that sooner or later this unnatural situation is going to overwhelm Paul and the whole bloody thing will come down on your heads like a house of cards. Louise isn't going to simplify as time goes on, you know. She's going to get craftier and crazier every day she lives."

Mary lifted her head slowly, her mouth opening in a bewildered way.

"Crazier?" she breathed.

Constance shrugged. "Oh, I don't mean she's a raving lunatic. I'm not trying to bring *Jane Eyre* up to date. But certainly you don't think Louise is a perfectly normal woman? You're too smart to be as innocent as that. Why, if she were normal, Mary, she'd get up on her feet and throw you out."

"I—never thought of it that way."

"It's true. It's got to be true. And it's also true that Louise senses, whether she actually knows or not, exactly how Paul feels about her and about you. He'll do his duty towards her as long as he can stand it. He'll be willing to do it as long as he has you here for comfort and consolation. But if she kicked you out he'd go all to pieces—and take it out on her. She knows that. Don't fool yourself."

Mary sat quiet, biting her lower lip. At last she said, "I'm appalled. There's no use pretending every word you say isn't true. It is—horribly true. I'm so confused—oh, so tangled up." She pressed her forehead with her fingertips, shaking her head slowly. "It's not even possible to see what to do. I ought to go away, and yet—"

"If you did, you'd bring down Paul's whole life around his ears. He's walking a tightrope already. He's pouring most of his heart and soul into that mill. Let him go on doing it. Strangely enough, your being here is a kind of anæsthetic—some sort of buffer between him and Louise. But it's not going to stay that way, Mary. Life isn't like that."

"I don't know what I ought to do," Mary repeated slowly.

"I'll tell you what you ought to do." Constance leaned forward, her elbows on her knees and her face strained and serious. "This isn't easy to say, Mary. It won't be easy for you to listen to."

"Then don't say it." Mary's tone was glassy.

"All right, I won't, in so many words. You're too smart anyhow. But one of these days Paul is going to need—everything—from you—and if you're wise you'll see he gets it."

Mary shuddered. "Have you no more decency than you ever had?"

"No more prudery, is what you really mean. I'm giving you the best advice I've got, Mary, and my advice about a thing like that is worth taking. Besides, what have you got to lose? What else have you got to live for?"

"Nothing." Mary spoke reluctantly.

"Then your job is to keep Paul going. By any means the job requires. If you let him down he'll mess up his life even worse than he has already, and Louise's too, not to mention the boys. Somewhere, somehow, he's got to be free—"

"There's the mill."

"Certainly. He pours himself into that. But if you think a row of furnaces and rivers of molten steel are all the satisfaction a man needs—oh, hell, I'd better not talk any more. I'm sorry I butted in. But you know how I feel. You and Ed and Paul are the only people in the whole United States I care a damn about, and it's frightful to see you all crucifying yourselves."

Constance was cut off then by Clarrie coming in to say good night to her mother. The little girl was freshly bathed, and her blonde curls lay damp around her shoulders. She perched on Constance's lap and eyed the tea-tray solemnly.

"Would you like a cookie, darling?"

"Nannie would not like it," Clarrie said primly.

"Well, you may have half a one." Constance broke a wafer in two. "The half you eat is for me and the part you don't eat is for Nannie."

"You'll give that child a set of morals as twisted as your own," Mary said shortly.

"Rot. One thing she won't be is a hypocrite."

"When are we going home?" Clarrie asked.

"Very soon, now. Do you want to?"

Clarrie thought the matter over. "I like it here," she said, "but I think I prefer London, Mummie."

"London it is," Constance said. "I prefer it myself."

She kissed her child good night and sent her upstairs to Nannie. The two women sat on silently by the fire. Trude appeared presently at the door holding an envelope. Her face had the frightened look caused by the appearance of any telegram; but this was a *cable*. It said so on the envelope. Constance took it and ripped it open carelessly.

"Well, well," she said. She flung the paper over into Mary's lap. "So it's come."

FATHER DIED THIS AFTERNOON SOLICITORS REQUEST YOUR RE-
TURN FOR ESTATE REASONS CABLE SAILING

GILES

Constance sat still, staring at the blue gas flames.

"So now I'm the Countess of Melling," she said in a sarcastic voice, "and my lawfully wedded hindrance is a belted Earl. Without a shilling to jingle in his pocket. What a pretty picture!"

"You always said you wanted a title."

"So I did. Well, you never hear *me* grousing, do you? But I'll be sorry to leave you. And I wish I could make Ed listen to reason."

CHAPTER XLIII

[*1892*]

IN HER SITTING-ROOM next to the back parlor Mary had settled down, after Trude took away her dinner tray, to write a long letter to Constance. The house had its usual Sunday afternoon quiet. Paul was in the back parlor, taking a nap. This had been his father's habit, like so many others into which Paul had grown. Paul had the Sunday papers and his favorite pipe and the mill worksheets for the coming week, and the household account books which Mary left every Saturday night on his desk. Best of all he had his father's horsehair sofa, sagged in the middle from the Old Man's weight. Paul had never wanted it rebuilt. He liked to stretch out here and digest his dinner, smoke his pipe, read—for a while— the Sunday *Gazette,* and presently, drop into a snooze. He had a guilty sensation about that. He felt that, at barely thirty-seven, he had no right to form such a lazy old man's habit. He kept the blinds drawn and the door closed during his Sunday afternoon nap, fatuously hoping that nobody in the house knew what he was doing. He always said he was busy on the worksheets and accounts.

The twins, now two, were having their naps also, and Louise was upstairs lying down. There was not a sound to be heard except the light scratching of Mary's pen. It had been quiet in the house for so long that Mary did not consciously hear the door of the adjoining room open and shut; she only realized that it had. She did not notice when she first heard the rise and fall of Edgar's voice in conversation with Paul. It was only when she heard Edgar say, with a note of high tension, "I've got to do it, Paul. I've got to," that she laid down her pen with the sinking sensation that she was about to overhear something she was not intended to know. She rose lightly and went to the hall door, meaning to go away upstairs at once. And then she heard Paul say, "You can't mean that, Ed. You can't spring such a thing on me."

Mary's hands turned cold. She hesitated at the door. She still meant to go upstairs, to get quickly away from the chance to overhear another word. And yet she stood stockstill. This shocking moment of eavesdropping held the key to the mystery of Edgar's secret torment. Though, as she had said to Constance, she feared to know the truth, she gave in to a swift, final determination to learn it at last. She moved quietly to a chair by the wall and sat down.

"—ought to have done it long ago."

"But Ed. If I had no other right to know, I'm your brother. And your employer. I can't let you junk your whole life without even asking why."

"It's my life, isn't it?"

"Yes, but you must be—why Ed, you've got everything to live for. And look forward to. Lots of money. A fine job. Freedom." There was a bitter ring in Paul's tone. "It's all so damned unnatural," he said. "You have no burdens. No ties. My God, if I were in your place—" Mary's heart beat hard.

"If you were in my place," Edgar's voice rose almost to a screech, "you'd be wishing you were dead—like me!"

"Why, Ed." There was a thud as Mary knew that Paul had swung himself from the sofa and gone to stand close to his brother. Mary could picture Paul's arm around Edgar's shoulders, and the horrified bewilderment in Paul's grave face. She twisted her hands miserably.

The voices dropped and became an unintelligible murmur for a while. Mary rose to her feet and walked nervously and soundlessly around the carpeted room. And then she heard the question that told her the thing she had dreaded for ten years to face, the thing she could not say she knew. Paul asked, "Does Mary know?"

She opened the connecting door between the rooms and walked in on the brothers standing exactly as she had pictured them. They sprang apart. Both stood staring as Mary crossed the room and came close to them. Paul's mouth was open; he was breathing hard. He had clearly had a great shock. Edgar bit his lips. His eyes were dilated and fixed almost in horror on Mary. His forehead was damp with sweat.

"Oh," he said thickly.

"Yes," Mary said in a flat way, "I know. It *is* Bridget, isn't it, Edgar?"

Paul made a sound like a groan. Edgar only stood there, nodding dumbly.

"Did you—hear—in there?"

"Yes. But I knew anyway."

Paul said, "How?"

"How do we know all such things? How have we always known—" she looked at Paul and spoke as if Edgar were not there—"the things we know?"

Edgar opened his mouth and tried to speak. But he only made a choked sound and buried his face in his hands. Paul looked beseechingly at Mary.

"It's not a question of forgiving," she said. "If I could blame Edgar I would. I can't even be sure," she said bitterly, "that he was the man. But what I want to know is—where is Bridget? Some things nobody can stand."

Edgar groped for her hand. Paul put an arm around each of them and led them over to the sofa.

"We'd better have it all out. For God's sake, let's get to the bottom of—everything."

"Where is Bridget?" Mary repeated. "That you can tell me, Edgar."

He leaned towards her, pale and shaken. "I don't know," he said. "That's just the trouble. I've never seen her, you know—not since—since—"

"Since before—when—she—"

Edgar nodded again.

"Then what—what has happened now? What did you just tell Paul?"

"That I've got to leave here," Edgar said. "I'm leaving the mill—and all of you—all of it—everything—"

Paul looked strickenly at Mary over Edgar's head. He was trying to see what she knew that would explain this shock from Edgar.

Mary moved her hands in a strange, futile gesture. Edgar looked up presently and said, "Why don't you two start in on me? I know what you're thinking. I deserve it."

Paul said, "You do, in a way. But what's the good of that, Ed? We can't give you any hell that you haven't been through by yourself, for years."

"You're being very fair. Once there was a time when I used to defy my conscience by telling myself I was no worse than you—and Mary—" He gulped.

"You see what people really know in spite of everything." Paul looked at Mary again.

"But I was wrong," Edgar said quickly. "*I* wasn't in love." He covered his face with his hands. "I was just—you know."

"This isn't getting us anywhere," Mary said sharply. "What's done is done. But I want to know the whole story. I want to know what's become of my sister."

Paul spoke quietly. "Do you want to tell us everything you know, Ed?"

"I don't know much. That's always been the chief trouble. But I'll tell you what I can. I make no bones about it, understand. It's a rotten story."

"Do you think we've been blind all these years?"

Edgar rose from the sofa and began to walk back and forth across the room. Paul and Mary sat still; painfully still.

"I picked up a girl in West Park one evening in June in my sophomore year in college," Edgar said. "She was pretty and—say, Mary, this is going to be very hard on you."

"It always was," Mary said quietly.

"Well, I'm not trying to excuse myself, understand. I was out to raise hell and I wasn't interested in anything but the excitement. Anyway, the girl was in the same boat. I don't know, Mary, whether it was true that I was—" he stopped.

"That she was a good girl until then? That's what she told you?" Paul asked.

Edgar nodded. "But she took the whole thing in her stride. She expected it. She knew what—what she was doing."

"Of course she did," Mary said impatiently. "That's not what I'm trying to find out. What *happened?*"

"I took her," Edgar said in painful reluctance, "over to Herron Hill. I was going there anyway."

Mary pressed her lips together.

"Did you know who she was?" Paul asked.

"I can only tell you that something about her seemed familiar in a strange way but I swear to God I had no notion who she was. By that time she had got in with the—woman at the place on the Hill and she was —well, she liked it, that's all. When I did find out who she was I was scared to death and I tried every way I could think of to get her to stop. But she wouldn't. She laughed at me. I didn't want to—to have anything more to do with her after that. I was too frightened. Anyway," Edgar said, struggling with his mortification, "she told me she was through with me. She said she didn't want any college boy wasting her time."

"Ah, Holy Mother."

Edgar hurried on. He was anxious to have it all over with now.

"I never went near that place again. I never saw her again. I worked in the mill all that summer; you remember, Paul. I was in Jim's department, and I was so upset about the whole thing it used to make me sick to see him. Then I went back to college in the fall and after a while I— well, I pretty much forgot about it." Edgar paused in his pacing and rested his elbow on the mantel.

Paul and Mary had not glanced at each other. She was staring at the windows, Paul at the floor. Presently Mary said, "What about the child she had, Edgar? You know my father threw her out of the house the following winter."

Edgar sighed heavily. "I knew she had a child, of course, Mary. That was the beginning of my realizing what a terrible thing I'd done. I tell you, I didn't especially care about—about—what I did to the girl. She was," Edgar's narrow face was dead white with the strain of the relentless truth he had decided to tell, "that kind of a girl."

"I know that," Mary said. "My brother and everybody else knew it."

"It was you," Edgar said quietly. "And the thought of the child. I didn't know what you meant to me until I saw it all that way. Every time I looked at you," Edgar said, his throat closing up on the words, "I thought about what I'd done. Every time you did some tremendous unselfish thing for one of us I'd think what I'd done to that sister of yours—to you, I mean, really—and," he looked up and there was no mistaking the awful set of his face—"I've reached the end of my rope."

"But—but why go away?" Mary whispered. "Leave Paul, and the mill, and all?"

"I have to be the judge of that," Edgar said. "Every time I've looked at you all these years I've had that same unbearable thing come over me. The longer I've held it in the worse it's been. Mary," he said seizing her hand in a wild way, "you're the living personification of everything saintly and good. And I've—"

She burst into tears and buried her face in her hands. "But I'm not," she sobbed. "I'm no different—from—you—from anybody—Holy Mother, we're all alike—"

Paul nodded solemnly as Edgar watched him. "If you'd only come to us years ago, Kid," he said hoarsely. "If we'd only all—well, pooled our —our—"

"How could I?" Edgar asked desperately. "That year when Mary came home from Con's? Do you remember the state you were in that spring? How you felt about Mary? There was all that horrible thing about Father and Jim. That made it much worse. But Mary's coming home—to—" Edgar looked at them pleadingly as if to beg their forgiveness for reopening the old wounds now—"to marry you. My God," he groaned, "I almost killed myself that night she came back here."

"Poor Ed," Mary said, wiping her eyes. She stroked the thinning blond hair from his high forehead. "Poor little spalpeen." She remembered his strange cold behavior when he came in that evening and found her with his parents and Paul in the dining-room.

"It's grown worse every year," he said. "When you start to hide a thing like that the deception grows on you and grows, and the fear and the worry and the guilt—" his voice rose wildly again.

Mary and Paul sat tense and horrified.

Edgar turned and buried his head in his arms against the mantel. Mary got up and went over and put her arms around him. He clutched her shoulder with one hand. Paul sat on the couch, shaking his head. It was a horrible story; a thing that grew on one in its steady, relentless destruction of a man, and of his self-respect and his hope for a life of any kind at all. Paul waited a long time and then asked, "Have you ever tried to find out anything about the girl? Have you ever made any investigation at all?"

"Such as I could. The only thing I ever did get was proof that Bridget Rafferty did have a child in the house of a certain woman in Watt Street. She identified Bridget from a picture. The child was born in March, 1883 —well, it could have been as they claimed on Herron Hill—that's all."

"What else did you find out from the woman in Watt Street?" Mary asked. Paul knew that she would be there herself the next morning. "Did she know anything—about—them?"

"The child was a girl," Edgar said in a muffled tone, staring at the floor. "She said they stayed in the house a week. A man paid the lodging and the doctor and took Bridget and the child away in a cab. Bridget used another name and the woman didn't care who she was anyway. It was that kind of a place."

"And you have never had any proof since that she and the child are alive, or even"—Paul gasped as the thought struck him fully—"that the child was yours? Why it's incredible." Paul leaned forward, wrinkling his forehead. "It was—well, I don't mean to be cruel, but it was unnecessary, Ed. You should have told me about it."

"I should? When? When you had just married Louise? When Mama got sick? When Mary came back here to live? When Mama died? How could I, Paul? By the time you had a child of your own and Mary was here again I—I—used to—oh, it's been torment. All the time."

He dropped suddenly into a chair and passed his shaking hand across his eyes. Mary and Paul sat in helpless silence. Finally Paul said, "Would there be any use in my trying to trace that child? Would that help at all? You're willing for me to do that, aren't you?"

"I'm willing for you to do anything you can or will do, if only I never have to hear of this thing again. I've reached the end of my rope, Paul. I want to go away."

"Of course. I see now. You must go away. Take the next boat and go over and pay a long visit to Con. Stay as long as you like."

"I'm not sure that's what I want. I think I'd rather go some place absolutely quiet—and stay a long, long time."

Edgar's eyes sought Mary's in a searching look. "I'm—I've got interested in something different. I want to go away and study."

"Study what?" Paul looked from his brother to Mary with a puzzled feeling that they had some extraordinary secret understanding. "Do you know what he means, Mary?"

She could not say that she did. And yet the intensity of Edgar's tone, the meaning he had put into that long, earnest glance stirred her strangely. She sat looking at Edgar with the feeling that she really could understand by instinct what he seemed to expect her to know. Some of his questions about sin, about confession and penance and the doctrines of her religion stood out with a new and tragic meaning now. She smiled tenderly at Edgar.

"He does need a long rest, and a complete change," she said to Paul. "You want to be quite free for an indefinite time, don't you, Edgar?"

He nodded thoughtfully. "I wouldn't want to promise when I'd come back. Oh, and I don't want any money, Paul. Just take over everything I've got and settle something on—on her—them—if you ever find them. You could send me just enough to live on. Only a very little."

"But I don't understand." Paul rose and went over to Edgar and stood staring at him. "What about the mill? What do you mean—an indefinite time? No money? This is supposed to be a vacation."

Edgar did not answer. Mary put her hand on Paul's sleeve. She kept her eyes on Edgar. His pale, sad face was gray-white. His high forehead, the droop of his shoulders, were curiously eloquent.

"Don't ask him to explain any more now, Paul. You'll make it possible for him to do what he wants, won't you?"

"I couldn't stop him even if I wanted to. Of course he can go. But I need you here in the mill, Ed. Surely you realize that."

Edgar nodded gently. "I do. But don't hold me to a promise about it, Paul. First I've got to find peace." He gave Mary another meaningful look. "You've both been magnificent about this. Far, far finer and more generous and understanding than I deserve. Both of you."

Suddenly he put his face into his hands and sobbed.

CHAPTER XLIV

[*1893*]

IT WAS A BAD DAY in the mill. There had been too many such days in the past six months; too much tension, too many mistakes, too much anxiety and work for Paul. Edgar's departure had left him in critical need of a supervisor for the finishing departments. For years Paul and Edgar had divided the general superintendent's work between them. Paul had had charge of all the furnaces, in addition to the general management and his own metallurgical work in the laboratory. Edgar had been responsible for the finishing departments—the blooming and bar mills, and the hammer shop. Without him Paul was badly handicapped.

There was trouble of some kind in the blooming mill this afternoon, and on the way down there Paul was thinking of the awful confusion that followed his father's death and Jim's. This reminded him of it now. There had been a bad atmosphere in town for a long time, too. The men had been restless and sullen during the six months of the strike out at Homestead. There had been repercussions in every other shop in the district. If it had not been for his contract with the Amalgamated, Paul knew that his mill would have been struck long ago. He had been walking a tightwire of anxiety behind his apparent imperturbability. And with the men he had learned to be taciturn like his father too.

He found them starting a run. The roller boss was a hardfaced Irishman named Corbley, most of his crew men like himself whom he had recommended to Edgar. Roller, engineer, tablemen, manipulator, shearman, pit craneman, heater, and helpers, all were skilled men, sure of their jobs and solid behind Corbley. Still, something was wrong in that department. A few laborers were working around there, Hunkies loading scrap ends from the shear table onto cars and shovelling out scale from the pits under the rolls. That was hot, heavy work, sometimes dangerous. Nobody paid any attention to them. They were considered beneath it.

Paul stood watching the crew. Something had been wrong yesterday with one of the reversing gears. The millwright had just left the shop. To Paul's eye the rolls were working all right now, the great salmon-pink ingot shooting back and forth in the reversing-stands, changing shape, flattening, elongating, as the manipulator shifted it lightning-fast from one set of rolls to the next. Corbley came over and stood beside Paul. He had just given the order for a second ingot to be hoisted up from the soaking-pit to the roll-table. The first was almost ready for the shear table, where it would be cut into the blooms that went next to the bar mill for finishing. Corbley had the hard arrogance of a man in full command of his job. For the moment he had nothing routine to do; boss rollers started to work hard when there was trouble.

"Looks all right now," Paul said in the customary roar that had to carry over the crashing clatter of rolls.

"Maybe. 'Twudn't be a—" Corbley said no more. There was trouble.

Accidents happen too fast even for the most accurate eye to record. Paul could not see every detail, though he was at the roll-table in one huge stride. The gear had jammed again. There were the horrible hoarse screams, the curses, the lightning leaps here and there that repeated the nightmare of every accident. The rougher's arm had been crushed in the jammed roll as he struggled with his hook to knock the bloom over on to the next table. He was writhing on the floor, the mangled stump of the arm twitching and streaming blood, the men kneeling around him, Corbley trying to stanch the gush of blood. Somebody, Paul thought in a cruelly matter-of-fact way, while he rushed an oiler out for a doctor, somebody's bungled this shop for a long time, somebody should have—Christ!—he thought, stiffening with horror, nobody's stopped the—he looked up, across, everywhere, he felt, at once. The roll engineer—something was happening up on the pulpit too. There was no time to find out now. Roll engineers should react instantaneously, the machinery should have stopped. Instead a half-rolled bloom of red-hot steel was going wild here—Paul turned, then, stupefied with horror, to the unbelievable sight of a Hunky scrap-man standing in the manipulator's place, calmly turning and shifting the bloom and watching expertly for the second ingot to come down the table. Half the machinery was still working.

Paul felt the sweat streaming down his ribs and the insides of his thighs as he clambered onto the pulpit, seized the levers, and stopped all the rolls. The engineer lay at his feet. Not in one accident in ten thousand, shockingly common as they were, would such a thing happen again. The man had had a heart-attack. He was an old, skilled hand. Probably the shock of the ghastly thing down the line, Paul thought.

He went back to the roll-table. The doctor had arrived and, surrounded by the white-faced crew, was tying off the artery on the stump of the rougher's arm. The man was gray from loss of blood, unconscious; maybe dead already, Paul thought, retching. This business of accidents was a recurrent crucifixion. He hated it, loathed it, struggled and slaved and fought against it. He had installed every safety device known to the industry and a good many unknown, experimental ones; and still things like this could happen. He asked wretchedly about the injured man and the doctor shrugged doubtfully and Paul told him about the engineer lying up on the pulpit. Men rushed off to lift him down. Paul turned away sick and saw the Hunky still standing, stolid and watchful, his hands on the manipulating device. Paul had hardly spoken to a Hunky in all the five years since he had begun taking them into the mill. You couldn't speak to them; they spoke no English. There had to be some one man who understood enough English to interpret the few simple orders of their unskilled work to them in their own outlandish lingo. But Paul looked at this Hunky and the Hunky looked back, with glittering dark eyes.

"What's your name?" Paul asked sharply.

"Karel Hrdlička." The Hunky's voice was a throaty growl.

Oh God, Paul thought. This is going to be fine. I can't understand a damn thing he'll say, even his name. He looked around. Another Hunky, pushing a barrow of scale, was looking at them curiously. It was a sensation, a miracle, it would be all over the boardinghouses tonight. The Big Boss was talking to a Hunky.

"Boss ask name," the second Hunky said, pointing at Hrdlička. "Call him Charlie."

"Charlie?" Paul repeated slowly. "They call you Charlie around here?"

The Hunky nodded with slow gravity. "Call Charlie Liska. No say real name."

Paul stood looking at the man. He was squat, bulky, and hairy. Paul's glance moved downwards over the barrel chest, the long bristling arms, the heavy legs weighting the body low. Charlie wore stained and blackened pants, a torn black shirt, and a dirty visored cap. Small brown eyes and a tangle of hanging moustache gave him the look of a bull seal. A bitter, acrid odor of sweat and oil and metal, mingled with tobacco and garlic, hung about him. His lips under the bush of his moustache were a startling red.

Paul pointed at the cooling bloom lying on the roll-table.

"Where did you learn to do that?" he asked. He spoke as slowly and distinctly as he could. The Hunky's face was expressionless but his small brown eyes glittered. He said, "By Skoda." He pronounced it thickly: Shkoda.

"Skoda! Do you mean the Skoda works? In Austria?" Paul leaned forward, scowling with amazement.

"Yah."

"You mean," Paul said, gesturing, "you mean you are a skilled manipulator trained at Skoda?"

Charlie nodded stolidly.

"Then what in hell," Paul exploded, kicking the heap of sheared scraps the man had been collecting, "are you doing that for?"

Others were watching them now. The injured man and the dead man had been carried out. There would be no more blooms rolled today; they were going to dismantle the stands to locate the trouble. The Irish-American crew stood in a bunch across the table from Paul and the Hunky. They had ugly sets to their mouths; ominous glints in their eyes. Some of them muttered to one another through their teeth.

"Slováks no get such job," Charlie said, motioning at the machinery and the scowling crew. "Get laborer."

That was all the explanation Charlie could muster in his English. He was not capable of explaining much. He could not take the trouble to explain that he was not a Slovák at all, but a Czech. Big Boss would never have heard of a Czech. He would just about understand that the Hunkies (not Hungarians, either, and hating the ugly name which they themselves never used) were really Slováks. Boss knew well enough, though, that nobody in Pittsburgh would dream of hiring a Hunky for a skilled job. Nobody would dream a Hunky would be able to do one even if he could get it. Paul stood thinking for a minute. His arms were folded across his chest. He was staring thoughtfully at the Hunky. The crew across the table were watching him like hawks.

Paul opened his mouth slowly and rubbed his chin and pulled his moustache. Then he said, "Charlie, I'm going to put you on this job."

Charlie's face had been twisted with bewilderment and with the strain of this business of talking to the Big Boss. For a minute it did not relax. Paul thought he had not understood. There were growls and threatening sounds and curses from lip to lip among the crew over there. Paul did not care. He had weighed all that in the moment before making his unbelievable statement to the Hunky. He knew he was in for trouble, lots of it. He did not care. He was angry. Angry at the bungling somewhere that had kept this department tangled up, angry at the blind stupidity and prejudice that had wasted this superbly skilled workman on common labor. The output of a blooming mill depended on the speed and skill and judgment of the manipulator. Also on the kind of emergency behavior that this Hunky had just shown. Paul moved his chin forward and said, "Understand? See?"

Paul turned his head away then because he saw tears glittering in the corners of the Hunky's dark eyes. The man had not been able to say anything. Paul heard him gulp and clear his throat with a rasping noise and say, "Yah. Und'stand. *Rozumím.*"

"You report here tomorrow," Paul said. He looked over at Corbley with an angry, defiant glare. "To him." Paul turned away and walked quickly back to his office.

Corbley was in there alone with him in no time. He was bull-mad. The whole crew were wild, he said. There was damn near a riot going on in the blooming mill. "You can't do that to us," he shouted. "We ain't goin' to stand fer it. I'm God damned if ye'll put a Hunky in my shop." There was spittle in the corners of his mouth.

"I'll put anybody I please in your shop." Paul sat at his desk, his big hands folded, staring hard at Corbley.

"Ye can't do that. I'm doin' the hirin' and firin' in that shop and I'll have my own men there. No greasy stinkin' Hunkies neither."

"Is that the understanding you had with my brother?" Paul asked. He watched Corbley's hard face flush darkly and the eyes shift.

"I'm choosin' the crew for that shop," Corbley said doggedly.

"You mean you've been taking bribes from them to recommend them to my brother."

Corbley had nothing to say for a minute. Paul's mouth was hard with contempt. Then Corbley said, "There's no use actin' innocent in this business, Mr. Scott. You know how things is done."

"I know how they're done out at Homestead," Paul said, his voice sharpening. "If that's what you want you can clear out and work for Carnegie too. Try Braddock. They use crooked foremen there. Munhall."

He paused. Then he slammed the desk a crash with his fist and said, "This is my mill and I'm going to run it my way. It's no God damn corporation."

"Ye can have strikes here as much as Carnegie's mills, though," Corbley said, menacingly.

Paul looked up. "If that's what you're threatening over this Hunky, go ahead and strike. If you want what they got at Homestead, you'll get that. I don't run this mill like Homestead but by God I can if I have to. I can act like Henry Frick, too."

Corbley breathed loud through his nose.

"Go ahead and strike!" Paul roared, losing his temper. "If you do, that'll be the last of your damned Amalgamated around here. You'll never get another contract!"

Corbley had no answer to that. He was cursing slowly in his teeth but he said nothing to Paul. He could never get this mill out on strike now and he knew it. The Amalgamated had had a terrible defeat at Homestead. Scott held all the cards now. There were few enough mills which had contracts with the union at all. Corbley was not a very strong union man anyway. He had always played a lone and a mean game. This Hunky was an awful kick in the teeth. There was not a Hunky in a skilled job in the entire district. It was a bitter blow that the first one ever hired should be shoved down his throat, into his own shop, hired over his head. He looked at Paul with an ugly face but when he spoke he only said, rather whiningly, "That's awful tough on me, Mr. Scott."

"I can't help that," Paul said shortly. "You can take your choice. From now on I'm hiring every man in every shop in this mill. It's a small mill and I don't need your kind of—go-between stuff. You can do a job with the men I hire or," Paul said, his voice much quieter, "you can get out."

"Yer father would never have gone back on us like that," Corbley said.

"My father would never have put up with your cheap graft either." Paul took his pipe from his pocket and began to fill it. "Think it over," he said. "Tomorrow morning that Hunky—and by the way his name is Liska and you'll call him that and no dirty mouth about it—starts as manipulator. I'm going to watch you, Corbley. One try at tripping Liska and you're through. The lot of you down there."

He decided not to go home for dinner that night. He wanted to work in his laboratory. Whenever things went bad as they had today Paul's recourse was to shut himself up in his old soup-kitchen after hours and lose himself in some metallurgical problem which would blot out all the others that beset him. Jones brought him down a box of dinner, and Paul carried it out to the dirty, draughty room, with its battered zinc counters, acid baths, gas burners, blowers, scales and instruments. He sat on a high stool, eating roast beef sandwiches and studying the experimental formulæ of the new alloy he was developing. This was an extremely hard steel containing nickel and chrome, which was to be cast and sent on to a Navy arsenal for finishing into experimental armor-piercing projectiles. There had never been any such projectiles made in the United States. Only within the past two years had heavy forged armor-plate for battleships been made here. A man named Russell Davenport had produced it successfully at the Bethlehem Iron Company, and freed the Navy of the necessity of importing its heavy armor-plate from abroad. Defensive and offensive developments went together. New heavy armor-plate meant new and harder armor-piercing projectiles. This experimental order was the first work that the Scott mill had done for the Government since the close of the Civil War. Paul was tremendously stimulated by the challenge; thoughts of his grandfather often came startlingly to mind when he was alone in the gloomy quiet of the laboratory.

It was very late when he finally locked up and started to walk home. He missed Edgar in a peculiar and poignant way on these trips to and from the mill. Inside the place, all day, there were a thousand specific instances when Edgar's absence made Paul's work harder. But early in the morning and late at night, sitting thoughtfully in the buggy or striding along with the rhythm of his heels for company, Edgar's spirit, his pitiful, increasingly tormented personality, came vividly to mind, to haunt Paul and baffle him anew with the mystery of his brother. Paul's greatest difficulty was trying to accept the fact of Edgar's religious conversion. How any Scott could become a Roman Catholic was in insoluble puzzle to Paul, and a painful contradiction of his intimacy with Edgar. But how Edgar, originally the counterpart of his voluptuous, flamboyant twin, could now be seriously considering the life of a religious, was utterly confounding. In vain did Mary try to explain that such a person, having renounced his passions and appetites, was characteristically the most devoted in the religious life. Paul only shook his head and grieved.

He often remembered a letter which Constance had written Mary a few weeks after Edgar left home. Mary had read it to him, and sometimes to this day it came back entire into Paul's mind. "I have just come back from Dover," Constance had written. "I went down to the boat with Ed and in all my life I've never been through such an ordeal. He's like somebody living in another world. All the week he was here I dropped everything else and stayed with him from morning until night. He played with Clarrie, and once he evinced the very faintest interest when P. came for tea. It was the most extraordinary hour; I can't remember what we talked about, except for a while about armor-plate and the Royal Navy. After a time Ed went away upstairs and P. sat there shaking his head and saying, 'Impossible! That cannot be your brother!' I'm too heartbroken to believe it yet myself.

"Ed says he is almost positive he is right about his decision. He says he will know after these two years of study in Rome. It is too strange to hear him talk. Now that the whole thing is behind him he no longer has to pretend to be anything of his old self. He just sits, perfectly still, with his hands clasped, and listens to my chatter and smiles tolerantly as if I were his grandchild.

"I broke down when I kissed him goodbye at Dover but he made me stop crying by saying 'I'm happy. I've never been happy since we were children together at home.' And with that he went on board the boat and if you ask me, none of us will ever see him again unless we go and invade his refuge, wherever he makes it."

And then, being Constance, she had rushed on to tell Mary about her new house in Cadogan Square, "perfectly lovely, darling, just what I've always wanted. Not too large, the most delicious *pouffy* furniture, lots of space for parties. Wait until you see my bedroom! Giles actually comes here once a month and makes a very dreary appearance at dinner. After he's gone we usually have a poker-party. You'd boil over if I told you what I won from a certain party the last time. Ah well! I'll probably end in a charity lodging, the way they do in novels."

And yet, Paul thought, you were a fool if you dismissed Con for a flighty superficial scamp. In the very next breath you would run into stuff you did not often realize she had. She wrote about him, for instance, "Thank God Paul didn't have a strike. When the newspapers were full of those ghastly stories of the Homestead strike people used to look at me and remember I came from Pittsburgh and ask me the rottenest questions. I lost my temper with one man and told him before he wrote off Americans as barbarians he'd do better to look at the children in the mines here and at the working class tenements in the Midlands. I said at least Americans had the spunk to strike! That travelled where it did me no good, you may be sure!"

She had that kind of nerve, Paul chuckled; and she loved her child. For all her wildness and her dissipated life, she was a better mother than Louise. Maybe it was that hard vein of masculine realism that ran through her, which made the child a personality, rather than a possession of her emotions. "She is too enchanting," Constance had written about Clarrie. "Very tiny and dainty; her eyes are exactly like Mama's, and she speaks the most charming French. Also a little German, when she comes in to curtsey to P. Make Paul get along without you for a while soon, and come over and pay us a visit."

He sighed at the thought of trying to get along without Mary, even for the length of a trip to Europe. Sometimes it came over him like the presentiment of a nightmare, what it might be like if she were not there. Edgar's leaving had shown him what such gaps could be like. And without Mary— He had worried about it lately and even said so to her, talking in her sitting-room after dinner one evening. He had murmured about his dawning anxiety.

"You mean Louise?" Mary had asked, laying down her work.

He nodded grimly and drew a heavy sigh. "The worst of it is, I can't help seeing a good deal of her point of view. She'd like to have you gone, of course, that's no secret to you."

"Secret!"

"And I—frankly, I could not go on if you weren't here. I just want to say that. I want you to know I mean it."

Mary did not speak for a time and finally she said, "Paul, why have you brought this up? Does Louise nag about me when you're alone with her?"

"Oh no. She's too shrewd for that. She knows if she made an open issue of it she'd drive me to take a stand about you. And she knows what that stand would be. As a matter of fact, she both wants you here and doesn't want you. She knows she'd be in a mess without you."

"She is jealous of the time you spend in here talking to me."

"I've got to talk to somebody. You especially. Whom shall I talk to about the mill and the boys and everything else I'm responsible for— Louise?"

They both laughed.

"Still, you could—oh, be a little more attentive. Encourage her to entertain more. That's the only thing you have got in common, all your friends —you might get what pleasure there is out of that."

Paul turned his head quickly as he caught a catch in Mary's voice. He leaned forward and took her hand.

"You're horribly lonely, aren't you? And here I sit harping on my troubles. Lord, I'm a pig!"

Mary smiled. "Begorra," she said, "the Paddies like pigs!"

He was almost at home now, and familiar uneasy tension began to creep as usual through his veins. Homecoming every day was the same trying experience of being pushed and pulled; drawn in opposite directions; part of it welcome, part of it dreaded. He remembered a day last summer when all that had been almost unbearably vivid, dramatized as a pattern into which he knew he would be forced for years to come. It had been a murderously hot day, and he had been beset since six o'clock that blazing morning with problems precipitated by Edgar's absence. He had walked along the burning, filthy streets above the mill, his clothes plastered to his tired body, sweat streaking his dusty face. And he had rested himself by anticipating the moment of coming home. He knew he would find the house deliciously fresh and cool. The blinds would have been drawn all day. The summer matting on the floors would have the clean grassy odor he had always loved. There were cool crash slipcovers on all the furniture. There would be a big pitcher of icy lemonade on the hall table. There would be fragrant bowls of sweet-william, nasturtiums, and big garden roses in every room. The boys would have had their baths, and, clean and pink in fresh thin cotton night-drawers would be eating their bread and milk around the nursery table.

He would go up the front steps with his mind full of troubles and problems, and he would take this load, if luck was with him, to the one place where there was help. He would drop into a cushioned wicker chair in Mary's sitting-room, and drink a glass of lemonade and after a little while feel refreshed enough to talk to her about anything or everything that weighed him down. He could lie back in the wicker chair and study her thin, intent face; note the delicate lines beginning to form around her gray eyes; marvel at the perennial beauty of her hair. Sometimes he wondered when that radiant color would begin to fade. Lately he had been curiously aware of time and age. Mary, for instance, was only thirty-five. But in his mind she was infinitely older. He could scarcely remember when for him she had not personified calm, reason, order, security. He could look at her now and communicate his silent thoughts to her with a direct intimacy beyond anything they had ever known. She was the indispensable partner of his real life and his real self.

He loved her in a way universal, yet minute. He loved her for her wisdom, for her strength, for her compassion. He never asked himself whether he desired her. If he dared that, he would probe a locked vault. He knew how to keep it locked; he could not tell what tidal wave he might loose upon himself and all the complicated relationships of his life if he should ever touch the key. For seven years he had managed to be a husband to Louise. He supposed he could manage forever if he had to. He must always remember his formula; she was a dangerously shrewd child, always to be regarded and treated as one. She disliked his growing dependence on his talks with Mary. She had taken to watching for chances to spoil those. How devious she was, yet how transparent!

He had started striding up the path to the house. The burning sun had set; there was only a hot red glow in the sky which would soon be replaced by the night blasts from the mills. The hall was cool just as he had anticipated. The house smelled sweet and fresh, that welcome mixture of flowers and the delicious odor of grass matting. He had hung his hat on the rack and started toward Mary's sitting-room. Louise's feet pattered in the upper hall.

"Hello, dear!" Her high voice bubbled out as she ran down the stairs. "How nice you're home! I've got your cool bath all drawn and ready. Coming?"

He had sighed and followed Louise upstairs.

CHAPTER XLV

[*June 1895*]

THERE WAS AN early morning train from Jersey City to Pittsburgh and Paul caught it in something of a daze. He had been in New York for three days and had meant to take the sleeper home the night before. Instead, here he was. He felt very sleepy, very vague. He stretched out in his Pullman chair and smiled wryly at the thought of the champagne he had drunk. He swung his chair about toward the window, with his back to the rest of the car, drew down the shade, and went to sleep. He rested profoundly, lost in heavy daytime slumber. Once when the train stopped he awoke for a moment, dismissed the impulse to find out where he was, and fell asleep immediately again. The second time that happened he sat up and rubbed his eyes, thinking. That was it. There had been some reason why he simply had to be home by tonight; in New York it had seemed unimportant. It had nothing to do with the mill. Something else, something at home . . . that was it. Louise was planning a party. She had never taken so much interest in any festivity as this, her tenth wedding anniversary. She had been making preparations since May, though this was the twenty-first of June. She was having a dance, a real party like the one his parents had given the year Paul graduated from school. She asked if he remembered that . . . the Japanese lanterns and Mr. McGowan calling out the reel, and the lovely supper old Sarah had made?

Did he remember it! He had his own memories, etched sharper than Louise's, which twenty years had scarcely dimmed. Mary and Delia doing the Irish jig in the pantry; he could hear their squeals and giggles still. And Bill out on the porch grumbling because there was no wine in the punch. And the wonderful talk he had had with his mother that night. Paul sighed at the unequal way the burden of years was distributed. Those early, innocent days seemed like yesterday; the ten years since his marriage in 1885—good God, was it only ten years?

He was glad that he had to be in New York those days before the party. He was well out of all the mess and the endless discussions—about the menu, about wine (Paul wanted it, Louise feared to shock some of their old friends), about a hundred things over which Louise made issues and Mary quietly made order. Paul had gone to New York to see some new guns and projectiles tested at the Sandy Hook Proving Grounds. He had made the forgings for the guns; this was a new step for the mill and might lead to very important business.

He arrived early in the morning and met the Army Ordnance officers and a committee of technicians at the Waldorf for breakfast. Paul so seldom got away on trips like this that he enjoyed it almost childishly, he told himself, as the men were ordering their heavy breakfasts, which they ate slowly, with much conversation and many cups of coffee. Paul enjoyed huge dark red strawberries imbedded in crushed ice, thickly masked in powdered sugar and rich yellow cream. He had a grilled Spanish mackerel (good fresh fish was always a treat to the inlander) and a fine cigar with his last cup of coffee. Ordinarily Paul preferred his pipe, but this was that special sort of initiates' gathering that called for a good Havana cigar. The party sat long over the table. Before they left, the Avenue had filled up with the crush of the day's traffic. Hansoms and hacks and delivery wagons clopped up and down past glittering barouches and victorias with exquisite lady occupants and stiff liveried footmen on the boxes. Paul thought of his plain, faithful Jones and his two steady chestnuts when a gorgeous turnout, with coachman, footman, and tiger swept by, its sole occupant a confection of a curled and corseted lady holding a tiny lace-ruffled parasol.

What a strange life these people must lead, he thought. Here in this magnificent new hotel men and women were wandering through the lounges, and sitting until mid-morning over luxurious breakfasts, as if they had nothing more pressing to do in the world. Yet some of them, at least, were not travellers or visitors, they were New York businessmen. Paul knew a few, others were pointed out to him. When did they work? At home everybody was at work by eight o'clock. All his life Paul had breakfasted before seven and left the house at half past. He always made it a point to be in the mill before eight o'clock in the morning. Pittsburgh bankers and lawyers were at their desks before eight-thirty every day. Paul could only look with astonishment at a place where nobody seemed to have anything more pressing to do than his sister Constance must have in London.

He shook his head. This was the place where the millions garnered from Pittsburgh mills and furnaces were pyramided and manipulated to form gigantic monsters like Carnegie's steel company! Paul loathed the whole thought. Yet, as he looked about at the leisured, overfed rich men in their ample broadcloth and bejewelled cravats, he had to admit that they enjoyed life. When he walked through Peacock Alley on his way to the cab that was to take the party to the ferry he did not try to avoid the glances of two sloe-eyed, heavily perfumed women in billowing summer silks and huge flowered coal-scuttle hats. He stared at them boldly, and they stared invitingly back. One of them flicked her long darkened eyelashes. Paul turned then and began to talk to his companion. His face felt hot; could this man have marked the fleeting encounter, and could he be leering inwardly at the big awkward yokel? For that was how Paul felt. But all the way down the bay, as he stood at the rail and revelled in his rare freedom, he kept seeing the slow amused flash of those bold dark eyes.

The day at Sandy Hook was long and interesting. The men returned to town tired and hot, but pleased with the results of the testing. They would go back for another session tomorrow. This evening they met in the bar for a cocktail, dined at Delmonico's and went to Tony Pastor's for an uproarious girl show. Paul had seldom done anything like this since college, and he enjoyed himself enormously. He roared at the jokes, ogled the heavy spangle-tighted girls in the front row of the Beef Trust, and joined in the choruses of the rowdy songs, as the audience was urged to do. The illusion of a college holiday was complete when somebody slapped him on the shoulder in the lounge during the entr'acte and began joyfully pumping him by the hand.

"Well, if it isn't Paul Scott! Old Angel-Face. How are you, old-timer? Haven't seen you in a dog's age."

It was Larry Hamilton, who had stroked Paul's senior crew. Paul was delighted to see him. Larry had been famous for getting through every tight squeeze on his wits, his charm, and his money. Paul could see that he had been doing little else in the past sixteen years.

"You big ox," Larry bumbled, "why didn't you come to Fifteenth Reunion last year? Where were you?"

"I did," Paul answered. "I was there. I looked all over the place for you. They said you were too drunk."

Larry scratched his curly head. "Well, come to think of it, I guess I was. Say, how long are you in town? Want to come along tomorrow night? I'm having a party."

Paul hesitated. "I'd love to," he said. He had a sudden mental picture of Larry's party, and as he spoke, he knew that that was exactly what he wanted to do. He had not felt, nor acted, on an impulse of pure excitement in years. But he hesitated.

"The trouble is," he said, "I've got to catch the night train back to Pittsburgh. I'd have to leave in time for that."

Larry shrugged. "Well, if you have to. Meet me at Jack's at eight. Sonny Van Doren is coming, and two queens. I'll get a third for you." He rolled his eyes.

"Sounds wonderful."

"Good enough. Don't be late."

Paul was not late. But he had to hurry. He had expected to be back in town by mid-afternoon in time to do an important errand. He meant to go to Tiffany's and buy a present for Louise, something she would consider worthy of her tenth anniversary. He had decided to buy her a diamond sunburst brooch. To bring it home from New York would double her pleasure in it. And Paul knew when he forced himself to think about it, that the only happiness he had to give Louise was some material thing like this.

It turned out that he could not get away from Sandy Hook until four o'clock, and he did not reach the city until almost six. Tiffany's and all the other shops had closed. Paul swore while he packed his bag. He could get the brooch tomorrow at Grogan's; he would have to. But he had particularly wanted to give this present the extra touch of bringing it home to Louise from New York.

He finished packing just in time to meet Larry Hamilton at eight. Larry and Sonny Van Doren, who greeted Paul languidly, and three beautiful girls were seated at a small table in the lounge at Jack's drinking cocktails. The girls were indubitably, in Larry's words, queens. Paul's, with whom he was paired off by obvious prearrangement, was a tall, creamy-skinned brunette with blue-black hair built into a fantasy of puffs and curls. She had an extraordinarily beautiful figure, a slim waist burgeoning upward to high full breasts which blossomed from a deep decolletage, and curving downward to sinuously rounded hips. Her coral-pink dress, trimmed with bugles, was tightly fitted through the torso, frothing out in a mass of pink lace ruffles below the knees. She put Paul at ease immediately. He had a momentary reluctance to look into her eyes; he had a foreboding that he would find them hard and cynical and appraising.

But that was not the case at all. The four others were chattering and laughing over Manhattans, their remarks a stream of innuendo largely meaningless to Paul. The girl beside him ignored her companions. She turned towards Paul, slowly and charmingly putting out conversational feelers. Almost immediately he forgot his odd fear of meeting her eyes. They were lovely eyes, very large, liquid brown. They were soft and animated, and exquisitely placed beneath wide winged brows. She had a Southern accent with a soft slur over her n's and a slight thickening of her t's and d's. She told Paul she came from New Orleans.

"That explains a lot about you," he said. Her name was Toinette. When he asked—awkwardly, he realized—her last name, she only shrugged.

Presently they went in to dinner. Larry had ordered a Lucullan meal—lobster Newburg, squabs Eugenie, huge Long Island asparagus, an endless succession of elaborate sidedishes, a rich, heavy iced sweet, and an uninterrupted flow of champagne.

"Slightly sweet for our taste," Larry said indulgently, draining his glass, "but for the ladies—"

The ladies did justice to everything. Paul was amazed at the quantity of food and wine that disappeared inside those delicately whaleboned bodies. As the dinner progressed they all became more and more hilarious. They sat waving their champagne glasses to the music of the orchestra, humming the refrains, and drinking silent toasts to one another over the rims of their glasses. Paul became increasingly preoccupied with Toinette, or he would have been more aware of the great glittering place, the hundreds of other diners, the innumerable hurrying waiters, the clink of glassware and cutlery, the exotic mingled smells of wine and rich sauces and tobacco and perfume. The air was warm, almost steamy, but Paul liked it. There was a breathlessness, a heavy unnatural atmosphere about it all which he found intensely exciting. Paul felt Toinette's warm hand steal into his, hidden on his knee under the tablecloth. His fingers locked with hers. When he looked at her he made a self-conscious effort not to let his face reflect the tumult he was feeling. Toinette's lips were moist.

Later when they stood outside under the marquee and someone said, "Now where," Larry's girl, a blonde whom he called Cuddles, said, "Why not up to my place?"

Paul looked at his watch.

"I'm afraid—" he began.

"Oh no." Toinette put her hand on his arm and peered at the watch in his hand. "You can come up for half an hour. You'll catch your train."

Paul was about to remonstrate and make his goodbyes. But the others were paying no attention. He saw that they had no further interest in the matter, but Toinette's soft urging decided him.

"Well—just half an hour." He stepped into the hansom after her and the doorman shut the apron. Larry's carriage was ahead, with the rest of the party. Paul immediately took Toinette in his arms and kissed her. She did not hesitate or say a word. She clung to him. There was a sweet, musky fragrance in her hair and on her warm silky skin. For the past hour Paul had been imagining the taste of that skin, the ready parting of her full, moist lips. They did not speak until the cab drew up behind Larry's carriage at the door of an apartment house. Paul had not noticed where he was going. He followed the party through the lobby and into the elevator which rose slowly while they joked about the contraption and the probability of the ropes breaking and killing them all. Cuddles unlocked the door of a flat and they all followed her in.

Paul looked about with remote curiosity. His mind was on Toinette. He might have found himself in Central Park and been no more aware of where he was. The fussy, garish parlor was prepared for a party; two bottles of champagne stood cooling in restaurant buckets, and there was a covered plate of sandwiches on a bamboo table. Larry opened one bottle and began pouring the wine. There was a feeling of suspense in the room, an unnatural intensity of remarks and laughter. Paul kept his eyes on Toinette. She moved about, finding herself a cigarette, puffing her hair before the overmantel mirror. Nobody sat down. Larry paid attention only to Cuddles; Van Doren was absorbed in his girl.

Paul looked nervously at his watch. If he left right now he could just make his train. He went over to Toinette to say goodbye. She moved abstractedly towards the hall. Paul followed her.

"I must go," he said in a strained voice. "I've—I've had a wonderful time."

She stood against a painted golden-oak door, her hands clasped behind her. She leaned her head back against the panel. Paul stood staring into her eyes. Her bosom swelled inside the pink ruffles.

"Do you really mean to go?" she asked. Her husky voice dropped almost to a whisper. "That would be a pity."

They were silent for a moment. Then she put her hands with a sudden motion on either side of his face. Her dark eyes were very gentle.

"You don't have much fun, do you?" she asked slowly.

Breathing hard, Paul shook his head. His blue eyes were wide, strained and glittering. She opened the door behind her. She stood perfectly still as Paul walked past her into the room. Then she shut and locked the door.

Paul had not known what time it was when he awoke. He stirred, sat up, and for a moment felt only confusion. It was pitch dark. Before he slipped from under the covers, away from the sleeping girl, the parts of the puzzle fell into place. He groped for the window and raised the dark blind. The sky was quite light; bluish gray as he peered upward, pink in the distance beyond the housetops. He guessed it must be six o'clock. Then his watch bore in on him the full realization that he had deliberately missed his train.

He dressed quickly. He had plenty of time to make the morning train, and he would still be at home in time for the party. When he was dressed he went over to the bed and stood a moment looking down at Toinette. With her black hair loose and freed from its cage of puffs and rats, she looked far younger than he had believed her to be. She slept quietly. Her creamy breast moved rhythmically as she breathed. One hand was curved under her cheek, the other flung towards the place where Paul had lain. He stood and looked at her for many minutes. The more he gazed, the greater grew his feeling of calm and well-being. He took two large bills from his wallet, slipped them under her pillow, and tiptoed from the room.

All that came back to mind in pleasing fragments as he dozed and slept in the swaying train. In the afternoon he woke again, stretched, and looked at his watch. He raised the window-shade just as the train was pulling into the Altoona station. In a couple of hours he would be home. Suddenly he sat up. Good God! He had never wired Louise about the change in his train. He hurried out to the station, scribbled a telegram, and reached his car again just as the train began to move. Then, as he settled back in his chair, he remembered about her present.

He had never had a more appalling sense of consternation. He ran his fingers hard through his hair, as if massaging his skull could help him think what to do. There was not the slightest chance that Grogan's would still be open when he reached Pittsburgh. Even at that he would only have time to get across the river and be home in time to dress before the dinner guests arrived. He thought wildly of telegraphing Grogan's and asking them to stay open, or to deliver a selection of brooches to Mary at the house. He thought of telegraphing Mary to go and buy the brooch. Anything, any expedient at this point. But it was four o'clock already and the train was not scheduled to stop again. There was no way of getting a message to the shop before it closed.

The remainder of the trip was a nightmare. He was not in the least upset by the memory of the night, or by anything he had done. But he cursed himself for his stupid, unnecessary, damnable bungling. Why hadn't he wired Mary this morning! If he had only done that Louise's joy in her present would have obliterated any irritation or suspicion she would certainly feel about his missing the night train. Now he had thrown all the fat into the worst of fires, and he knew he would be dealing with the consequences for months to come. The clacking and swaying of the train changed from a soothing lullaby to a maddening roar of reproach and mockery. He felt like a half-baked fool of a college boy for allowing himself to be so excited by one unaccustomed party that he could be thrown completely off the track of his tightrope-balanced life. Why, why, why, he repeated to himself through grinding teeth, was I such a bloody God damn fool! He was still sitting with his head in his hands when the train pulled into Pittsburgh.

It was almost dinner-time when he reached the house and hurried upstairs. He scarcely noticed the Japanese lanterns in the yard, the white flowers, the bustle, and the rearranged furniture downstairs. Just as he had anticipated, his evening clothes were laid out in minute perfection of detail, and Louise, already dressed, was standing at her mirror with her back to him, fussing with her hair. Paul had resolved to carry the thing off with the utmost possible bravado. He breezed across the room shouting, "Hello, darling! Happy anniversary." He almost choked over the endearment. He never used such words in speaking to her ordinarily. He went over and put his arms around her, expecting her to turn and respond. Instead she stood quite rigid, and he turned her about and kissed her warmly. He saw at once that she had been crying; her eyelids were slightly swollen and she had powdered her face with fragrant orrisroot, something she did only under extreme stress of emotion.

Paul gave her a hug, ignoring her silence and her pinched trembling lips. He began hurriedly to peel off his street clothes, talking as naturally as he could.

"Too bad I missed that darn train," he said. "Gee, I felt awful about it all day long."

"You must have," Louise murmured. "I suppose that's why you didn't bother to telegraph until you reached Altoona." Paul, bending over to take off his socks, had another glimpse of her face in the mirror. She looked wretched and plain. What a hateful thing he had done to her on this of all days. There was no help for it now, though. He ignored her remark but she could not resist the urge to probe into the crack she had opened.

"At least you wouldn't have spoiled the children's picnic if you'd—remembered our existence."

"Oh, Lou." God almighty, that was worse still. He had totally forgotten the picnic, the children's share in the anniversary. This was a twist straight from the devil; he had planned the picnic himself. It was always he who thought of things to do with the boys.

"You didn't call off the picnic because I didn't get here?" In spite of himself his tone was strained.

"*I* did," Louise said caustically. "How did *I* know your plans? You couldn't expect me to go off and—and—celebrate your absence—"

"You mean the boys didn't have their picnic?" Paul asked sharply. He showed the first real concern he had manifested.

Louise tossed her head. "Oh, Mary took them!" she snapped. "You could be sure *she'd* do what—oh, I hate you!" she screamed suddenly and stamped her foot. "*Hate* you!"

Paul turned from his bureau and went over to her.

"Lou, I know just how you feel," he said quietly. "I was very busy and preoccupied and tied up with a lot of men but it was inexcusable of me to put off wiring you in time. I feel very badly about it, honestly I do.."

She dabbed at her eyes. She was making a great effort not to break down. Through the open windows they could hear footsteps on the front walk outside; the first guests must be arriving. "Please try to forgive me, Lou. I'd have cut off my hand rather than spoil your anniversary."

She looked slightly mollified. Paul noticed then that she had not put on any of her simple jewelry. He saw how keenly she was anticipating a present from him, waiting for it. He glanced wretchedly at his coat flung across a chair. If only he could go to it and take that damned diamond sunburst from his pocket and pin it on her bodice. He turned red in a sudden wave of furious mortification. Never in all his life had he felt so totally, wretchedly inadequate and ignominious. He hated her and he hated himself more. He swallowed, while she stood watching and it seemed to him, palpitating with expectation. His plea for forgiveness was a travesty without the token that would have made it real to her. He repeated something mumbling awkwardly, about how badly he felt.

Louise's face set gradually in the frozen look it would wear all evening; pain and anger and petulance masked with the sugary smile by which her friends knew her best, and for which this occasion called. She turned her hurt eyes from Paul and went over to her bureau, where with a good many conspicuous motions she took an old amethyst brooch of Clarissa's from her trinket box and pinned it in the lace on her breast. She moved toward the door.

"If you are ready," she said unsteadily, "we might as well go down. And show everybody what a happily married couple we are."

CHAPTER XLVI

[*1897*]

THE YEAR THAT Dickie was eleven and the twins seven Louise decided to try a summer on the North Shore, and at the end of June she moved with the boys to a cottage at Marblehead. One of her reasons for this choice was the proximity of William and Julia. They spent their summers there in Julia's old family home, a huge, hideous mansion of red bricks and weathered shingles imposingly situated on a bluff over the sea, surrounded by scarlet sage and blue hydrangeas. Julia was the only member of the family with whom Louise felt any kinship. Also through her there would be meetings with the best Boston people. This was a prospect so pleasurable that it overshadowed Paul's protest when the Marblehead idea was gingerly presented to him. He liked New Jersey, even if he did only get there for a week or two a year. He liked the boys to be where they could learn to swim and fish, handle a boat, and have the kind of holidays that he and his brothers and sisters had had in the old days at Ventnor, when they went East every year with Clarissa for two months. What heavenly days those were! Paul remembered vividly the cramped, noisy cottage on the strand, the hot sunny days by the blue breakers, the endless games and races on the beach, the dory over which he and Bill had come to blows, the fishing, the barnacles, the jellyfish, the smell and feel of soggy woollen bathing suits.

When Louise first mentioned Marblehead Paul reminded her of the breach between himself and his brother Bill. Why, in view of the total absence of congeniality, stir things up and deliberately pave the way for possible embarrassment? Louise brushed that aside. She had made up her mind and she always had one weapon through which to enforce her choice. She could refuse to go away at all. She had realized long since that Paul enjoyed his summer solitude, even without Mary and despite the cruel heat. She had given up nagging and teasing him to go away with her. He came for a week or two at the most; the rest of the time he never left the mill. He knew that Louise's motives were complicated and involved when she asked, as usual, how he would manage at home.

"I? Why, I'll get along fine," he said. "I'll—"

"I'll have to take most of the servants," Louise said quickly.

"Why, of course, Margaret, naturally and—"

"Mary too," Louise said. Her voice was flat and hard.

Paul's jaw twitched. He stared at her coldly. Anything he thought would touch off an explosion.

"I couldn't possibly manage those boys in a strange place without Mary," Louise said. She had an advantage and knew it. "Or run a summer house either."

It was as if she had shouted at him, "Do you think I'd go away and leave *her* in the house with you?"

"Very well," Paul said icily. "If you need Mary, take her. I want the boys to have a good holiday."

"Of course," Louise said, leaving the room, "you don't care if I have a good holiday."

Paul clenched his fists. "Did I say that?" he muttered. "Can't you be fair about things?"

"Always, if you are," Louise spoke lightly, in her brightest tone.

Paul was surprised by a cordial letter from William welcoming the family to Marblehead, assuring Paul that he and Julia would look after Louise and see that she met "our friends." He reminded Paul of the August yacht races and invited him to sail as a hand on Bill's boat. Paul showed the letter to Mary as she hurried about the house, list in hand, superintending the packing and shipping. Louise, the weather being already very hot, was lying on a wicker settee in the summerhouse, drinking iced tea, with Dickie reading aloud to her. Mary read Bill's letter and sniffed.

"He's up to something," she said.

"What? Looks to me like this is the first plain decent thing he's done in years."

"He wants something. He won't write you a letter like that—especially with Julia knowing I'm to be there, because Louise wrote her—he won't unless he's got some motive."

"Oh, hell," Paul laughed. "Let him. If I get a week's sailing out of it, it'll be such a treat for me I don't care what he's up to. But I didn't really think about Julia much or I'd have put my foot down." He looked at Mary and shook his head. "That's bad," he said. "Constance told me how she carried on about you the last time she was here."

Mary made a sound like a snort. "Do you think I can be intimidated by that?" she said. "Besides, I've got my own plans this summer."

"Your own plans? What do you mean?"

"I'm going abroad to see Constance as soon as I get Louise settled up there."

"Why, Mary." Paul's mouth hung open and he looked at her stupidly.

"Why, Paul." She laughed at his astonishment. "Why shouldn't I? I haven't said a word about it to anyone because I don't want a lot of discussion. I admit I wouldn't think of spending eight weeks in some place where Julia Scott could make my life miserable. So I decided to go this year."

"What will Louise say?" Paul asked. He still had a dumbstruck expression.

"*Louise!*" Mary laughed loudly. "You might as well ask me what President McKinley will say! He cares just about as much."

Paul reddened. He stood silently watching Mary count tea napkins into a trunk tray.

"These summers are awful," he said finally.

Mary glanced at him as she bent over the trunk.

"They're not as hard on you—as they might be," she said. "After all, you do get some—some respite." She shut her mouth firmly then.

"Louise doesn't really need you at all, does she?" he asked.

"Oh, she manages to give me the responsibility of the boys, in spite of Margaret," Mary said. "She'll be all right this year, so close to Julia's house. But you know why she really makes me go away with her," Mary said, looking straight at him.

Paul said slowly. "I don't know how—we—you—stand it. I don't know."

"It's my job," Mary said shortly. "But I'm taking a vacation this time, believe me."

"I'll miss you—frightfully, Mary."

"I'd be away anyhow. Besides, I want to go."

"Oh, I'm delighted. But it makes me think—of the time you went before." Paul's hand moved towards her in an unconscious gesture. For a moment they stood there gazing at each other, memories crowding the silence around them. Then Mary said, "Shut the book, Paul," and went off leaving him alone in the dining-room. He shook his head. He had never seen her so brusque and so independent.

William's boat, Julia IV, won the cup in the August races, and he gave a dinner to celebrate the victory. Never in their lives had he and Paul been on such a congenial footing. The week of sailing was an uninterrupted delight. William's fifty-foot sloop was easily the most beautiful boat of its kind in the club, and many summers of racing had made an expert sailor of him. He ran his boat with all the elaborate distinctions of position that permeated his Boston life. In races he carried three gentlemen and one paid hand. The gentlemen did all the severe work under the guise of pleasure, and the paid hand was occupied entirely in waiting on them and cleaning up after them.

He handled his boat masterfully, however, and Paul was ready enough to fall into place as the least important member of the crew. There was something extremely funny, after all these years, about Bill in a position of complete authority, with Paul springing to obey his orders. The other two men, friends of William's named Sturgis Greenleaf and Henry Huddleston, quite naturally treated Paul with the slight shade of condescension that seemed suitable for Scott's younger brother, and a Pittsburgh landlubber at that. Paul did not seem to them, nor feel himself, like the president of the Scott Iron Works and the sole controller of every cent of his own that William had in the world. This magnificent boat, bought with Julia's money, happily dispelled all the tiresome truths about the brothers. Between turns at the wheel and manning the sails Paul, in a cotton undershirt and dirty white duck pants, lay on his back on deck smoking his pipe and baking in the hot sun. His blond hair and full moustache bleached to straw-color, his skin burned almost mahogany; he went unshaven for forty-eight hours; he ate like a pig and slept so hard that waking up Scott became the joke of the ship. He even reached the Nirvana of literally not thinking about anything. In a week he gave not a single thought to the whole long catalogue of his troubles.

William's dinner-party was planned with as much decorum as an affair in an embassy. He took himself and all his associations very seriously. Julia, now outrightly stout and mightily armored by complacency, authority and abundant money (though still the income of her income) managed everything while William importantly presumed that he did.

The dark, ugly interior of the Gaylord summer home was a labyrinth of chopped-up rooms cluttered with whatnots and glass-paned bookcases full of first editions of Longfellow, Bryant, Whittier, Emerson, and Thoreau. Diamond-work bits of assorted stained glass appeared on unexpected windows, especially over staircases. The floors, of light-colored oak, had a perilous polish and many small, expensive Persian rugs laid in precise arrangements calculated, as Paul said the first time he slipped on one, to break your neck without further argument. The furniture was solemn and massive except for an occasional flippancy in brocade and gilt, a daring innovation of Julia's after the long mourning for both her parents had finally come to a correct end. Louise appeared to enjoy her frequent visits to the house, the long summer afternoons over elaborate teas, with many callers, on the cluttered west porch; the tennis parties when the ladies sat under striped umbrellas on the sidelines, murmuring restrained exclamations at the play. Paul said he would have suffocated if he had had to spend any time with her there.

"Thank God I was off on that boat the week I did take a vacation," he said, struggling with a stiff collar. "Who in hell," he cursed, "ever heard of dressing like this for a dinner-party in the country? Damn!"

"Paul!"

"Sorry. Thought I was still on the boat. My hands are so calloused I can't fight this." He handed her his collar button and stood patiently while she fixed it. She was bridling with pleasure at the unaccustomed small intimacy.

"There! Now we're ready. Come in!"

It was the twins coming to say good night. They bounced into the room, falling over each other in their hurry to get to Paul and be the first to leap on his back. They loved that game, or any other form of roughhouse Paul would encourage. Best of all they liked a simulated tug-of-war when each boy would grab one of Paul's hands and try to pull him off his feet in his own direction. Paul adjusted his falling with nice impartiality. Just now Louise stood fretting by the mirror, while the boys shouted and swarmed all over their father.

"Oh, Paul, make them stop. They'll ruin your clothes and you look so nice."

Paul removed a foot from his shoulder and swung Ted upside down at arm's length.

"Me too, Daddy, me too." Tommy rushed him from the other side. Paul swung him around and set him down beside Teddy.

"That'll do now. Go along to bed."

He watched the children go over and kiss their mother good night. They always treated her in a formal manner which contrasted queerly with their wild boisterousness towards Paul. Louise bent over stiffly—her corsets were tight and she did not want the boys to reach up and disarrange her hair—and gave them each a quick kiss.

"Good night. Run along quickly to Margaret."

The boys ran back to Paul and seized his hands, Teddy on the right, Tommy on the left. For some reason they always fell into those positions. Although he told them he had no time, they dragged him down the hall to the nursery with them.

"You have to put us to bed, Daddy. You got to."

Margaret smiled as the three burst through the door.

"They've missed you, Mr. Scott," she said. " 'Twas a pity ye had to go off on that boat all yer week's holiday. They'd counted so on havin' ye here."

"I know, Margaret. I was very sorry. But I don't often get a chance at sailing. Go on now, Tommy, brush your teeth and mind Margaret at once."

He was tucking Teddy into bed. But suddenly the little boy jumped up. "Why, Daddy, you forgot our prayers!"

"Oh, that was very bad of me. Come here, Tom."

Paul knelt down by the low nursery table and the boys knelt beside him, right and left as usual. All three folded their hands and said, "Now I Lay Me" and the Lord's Prayer together. Just as they finished Louise hurried in. There was a pucker between her brows. "Oh Paul, really! We'll be terribly late."

She stood and fidgeted irritably while Paul finished with the twins. They went downstairs, Louise drawing on her summer wrap, and on the porch found Dickie, flat on his stomach on the floor with his chin propped over a book.

He jumped up. Paul smiled proudly at the tall, sunburned lad. Dickie was handsome in an almost idealized masculine version of Louise's curly prettiness.

"Dad, did you remember about tomorrow?" he asked.

Paul nodded. He had promised Dickie a day's real fishing, and had hired a motorboat to take them out. Just the two of them and two boys named Waller, with whom Dick had made great friends.

"We'll leave at seven sharp in the morning. Captain Davis will have bait and everything. Will you ask Trude to put us up a lunch, Louise?"

"Well—yes, that is—" she fumed. "You might have told me sooner, Paul. How do I know whether she has anything in the house to make lunch of first thing in the morning?"

"That's all right, Mother," Dickie said eagerly, "if she hasn't, I'll run down to the store now and buy some sliced ham and things. Can I have some money, Dad?"

Paul gave him the money and they both kissed him good night. Louise began to fuss again on the short footpath walk over to Julia's.

"Really," she said, "after being away all summer and then going off on that boat the only week you have here, do you have to spend your last day off on another boat fishing with Dickie?"

Paul gave her a surprised look. "*Have to?* I want to. He's counting on it and so am I."

"Oh. I suppose it doesn't matter if I'd counted on spending one day of the summer with you."

"Why, Lou, I'll be here all evening. Good Lord, you don't want me to disappoint Dick, do you? Anyway, come along with us if you want to."

Louise shuddered. "You know it makes me sick. Ugh! Smelly, slimy old fish. And that rocking boat."

"Well, I can't sit around and rock on the porch with you, my dear. Another time figure out something you will do with Dick and me and we'll be glad to have you along. And stop fussing, please. Here comes Willy."

Willy was proceeding towards them with a slow, almost royal pace which matched his great height, his eagle nose, and his other marked resemblances to his grandfather Gaylord. He had just celebrated his twenty-first birthday after graduating from Harvard. He and his sister Angelica, who would make her debut next winter, had understandably nothing in common with Paul's small boys. But their gently patronizing attitude extended to Paul and Louise also. These plain Pittsburgh relatives were quite out of keeping with the whole studied picture of existence to which the William Scott family adhered. If, on the other hand, they had an opportunity to refer in passing to their aunt, the Countess of Melling, they availed themselves of it; even their cousin, Lady Clarissa Whitfield-Moulton, although only fourteen, was a satisfaction to contemplate and talk about.

There was a large group at dinner. William and Julia had invited a choice assortment of Boston's inner circle. Paul could not decide whether their motive had been more to flatter or to impress him and Louise. Willy and Angelica were not at the table. They went off to a young people's party after escorting their aunt and uncle up to the house. The dinner was extraordinarily good and the wines superb. Paul took it for granted that Bill did himself very handsomely, but he had not fully appreciated the Boston tradition of fine dining which was part of Julia's inherited way of life. He would have been very glad to devote himself entirely to the lobster mousse and truffle filets, but a dowager on either hand kept him all too aware of his duties. Their conversation ranged from studied comment about new books and the bird life of the vicinity to the coming winter's program of the Boston Symphony. Paul was bored. He longed to ask the Mrs. Adams on his left to tell him exactly who each of the eight men at the table was; what he did; what, if any, his business connections were. He ventured a leading question, selecting a stern-looking square-bearded man opposite him as the opening wedge. Mrs. Adams only stared.

"Why," she said vaguely, "that is Selden Middleton. I can't tell you exactly what he *does,* Mr. Scott—I believe he has an office in State Street, like everybody else."

Paul realized that Selden Middleton did just what William and the other men present did—take care of inherited money. Some of the men were lawyers; they took care of other people's inheritances as well as their own. Some were controlling stockholders or outright owners of textile mills, but Paul soon learned, after the ladies withdrew, that such men regarded the details of mill management and production as the province of hired factors and superintendents.

It was a seemingly casual reference to Andrew Carnegie that turned the spotlight of conversation on Paul. The man who mentioned Carnegie made an admiring reference to his bold vision of a vast empire of steel, and his ruthless, spectacular handling of millions in putting it together. At once Paul protested.

"I wonder if you would admire him so much if you were an independent steel manufacturer," Paul said.

"I am quite sure I would. The man is a genius, Mr. Scott, and I should think you, in your position, would be best able to appreciate that."

"I do. I concede that Andrew Carnegie is changing the whole concept of industry in this country. But I feel he is doing the gravest harm."

William spoke from his end of the table. "I think," he said, "that my brother still reflects my father's views, don't you, Paul? Our father had a violent prejudice against Carnegie."

"With good reason," Paul said shortly. "He saw Carnegie crush and swallow up two of the most brilliant men in Pittsburgh. That was the beginning. I don't believe my father"—he spoke to a man named Sedgwick who showed particular interest—"would have felt so strongly if Phipps and Carnegie hadn't *used* the iron business as they did. They used it to amass money and power for themselves. They used it to kill competition."

"They drove us out of rail-making," William explained in a rather deprecating way which indicated the paltry size of the Scott mill in his estimation.

"Did they really!"

Paul could not be sure that the man who spoke was not patronizing in his remark.

"That was a very long time ago," Paul explained. He had a sense that his mill was being faintly ridiculed by these men who admired Carnegie and his gigantic creation. "We decided in the face of that buccaneering to develop our own specialties and concentrate on them."

"My brother has done that singlehanded," William said kindly. "I showed you that list of our alloys and their uses," he reminded Selden Middleton.

"I was greatly impressed with it," Middleton said, turning to Paul. "You really have been able to develop and keep a market all your own, have you not?"

"Well—yes. Of course it's a limited market. We are dependent more on invention and technical development than on general trends. We do almost no business with railroads, for instance."

"Very interesting. In other words, you have no inclination to—to—what would you say—get into the swim of this tendency to centralize and consolidate the components of the steel industry?"

"None at all," Paul said quickly. "It can be done, of course, with tremendous efficiency and results. Henry Frick is the genius at that. But it has no bearing on my mill."

William sent an uneasy glance down towards Paul. There had been a ring of something quite like defiance in Paul's last words.

"Still," Middleton said, slowly twirling his port glass in his fingers, "these are very challenging times, Mr. Scott. It is hard to see how any man can stay out of the current as you do. Now I have never had anything to do with iron and steel manufacturing but I have been having a very active time—I may say an exciting time—with some ore interests of mine."

"I see." Paul thought immediately of the most recent crisis in the long-standing battle for control of iron ore. He found himself wondering now whether Bill had had some special motive in bringing this man here to meet him.

Middleton smiled. "Originally my holdings were in the Norrie and the

Pioneer," he said slowly. "They are small mines—of course you know how small—in comparison with the Mesaba range." He paused.

Paul leaned forward. "But there was practically a panic in those smaller mines this year," he said. "Norrie was down to $2.65 a ton last month." He bent a puzzled look on Middleton's composed face.

"Certainly. That was my point. Of course I foresaw the fate of the Norrie mine as soon as I discovered that Henry Oliver and Mr. Frick were about to make a deal with the Rockefellers. When they leased the whole Mesaba range and contracted to ship over Rockefeller facilities, the future of any competing mines ought to have been apparent to anybody."

All the men were listening intently. Paul saw that the only drama in their world was this one of battling elements, wills, and millions.

"I suppose you sold out to Oliver before he made the deal with Rockefeller," Paul said dryly.

"Precisely. I effected an exchange of stock—advantageously. Very advantageously." Middleton cleared his throat.

Paul sat back and pulled on his cigar. "I see." Selden Middleton was right now a part of the Oliver-Frick-Rockefeller ore combine which would within a few months inevitably be engulfed in the Carnegie Steel Company. Frick and Carnegie were at odds about some features of the matter, but the outcome was clearly predictable. The conversation became general, but Paul sat silent, still thinking. Presently he looked down the table at William. Now why, Paul asked himself, did this whole thing come up? Why did he have that man here tonight? And what possible concern is it of mine? Did he think it was just a natural matter of interest to me?

The men rose from their chairs and began to move towards the drawing-room. Middleton fell into step beside Paul.

"Stirring times," he said pompously. "Stirring times. We're going to see a great many more of these big consolidations, Mr. Scott. Mark my words, if we keep our eyes open we'll have plenty of opportunities for big things. Big things."

Paul stepped aside coldly and let Middleton precede him into the drawing-room.

CHAPTER XLVII

[*1897*]

MARY SAILED THE second week in July and joined Constance and Clarrie and Clarrie's Fräulein at Deauville where they were staying in a great sprawling suite of balconied rooms at the Royal Hotel. Constance was going soon to Paris for clothes, and then to Marienbad with a party of her friends. Mary suggested that Fräulein be given a holiday for three weeks to visit her family in Leipzig; Mary and Clarrie would go off alone somewhere and "really get to know each other."

"But that's not what you came for!" Constance exclaimed, while Clarrie clapped her hands and said, "Oh, Mummie, please!" "You didn't come to take care of Clarrie for three weeks while I go off razzle-dazzling. I want you to come with me."

Mary made a derisive sound. "I have a fine notion of myself taking the cure with—um. With you. This is what I want to do. I've never been on the Continent before and I'm just a rubbernecking tourist and Clarrie and I can have a lovely time gaping at things and reading Baedekers. You go off and do as I say."

"All right," Constance shrugged. "Bully me about. Have it your own way. But you're coming to Paris with me first."

Clarrie jumped up and threw her arms around Mary. "Won't we have fun?" she cried. "All by ourselves. It'll be such fun to show you things, Auntie Mary!"

At fourteen Clarrie was almost an unbelievable contrast to her mother. When Mary remembered Constance at that age, rough and wild-tempered and wilful, with her bush of blazing curls, turning the house upside down, she could scarcely bring herself to realize that this gentle, quiet pink-and-white English girl was the child of that recent tornado. Clarrie's resemblance to her grandmother Clarissa was more striking than ever. She had the same broad, serene brow, the same mild blue eyes, the same smooth blonde hair, which she wore in long braids; above all the same soft, warm, loving nature. She had not Clarissa's sturdy frame; she was slight, delicately boned, and exquisitely graceful. She had a fine mind which, under the guidance of good teachers and Constance's hardheaded naturalness, had escaped most of the hypocrisies and foibles of the time. She had always been given the freedom of her father's library. Before she was twelve she had read all the Shakespeare, Dryden, Pope, Byron, Shelley, and Keats she could hold. She read Balzac, Hugo, and Dumas voraciously in the original, and now she was absorbed in Goethe under the guidance of her Fräulein. But above all she had amazed her mother by a passion for music. Like most people Constance presumed that musical aptitude must be inherited; there was nothing on either side of Clarrie's parentage to explain it. She had discovered the piano at the age of four and thereafter spent all possible time at practising and at her music lessons. She played—"well, unbelievably, that's all," Constance said to Mary. "I mean she doesn't play or think musically like a child. Her teacher says she's a great talent."

"Your mother was very fond of music," Mary said thoughtfully.

"But that doesn't explain this kind of thing. Mama was just a parlor dabbler. Clarrie is a pianist already. I don't know what the devil to do about it."

"What is there to do—except let her go on playing?"

"Oh, of course. But suppose she expects to be a professional? Suppose she wants to appear in public—go on concert tours—all that sort of thing? My God, I can't have that!"

"Why, Constance?" Mary frowned a little. "I don't see why not."

"Maybe there's no reason. I simply feel—oh, I don't want her to be an artist. Knocking about like all those Schumanns and crazy people. She's too fine for that."

"She's too fine to do anything crazy. You wouldn't stop her, surely."

"God forbid," Constance said quickly. "She can do anything she wants. I want her to be happy. Sometimes I can't believe how much I love that child. It's not like me, you know. Remember what hell I raised about it at first?"

"Oh, that didn't mean anything. I always knew you'd feel this way about her."

"I suppose because Giles is so meaningless," Constance said slowly. "And the other thing—" she shrugged. "In other words, Clarrie's all I've got. When the rest of it goes out of my life—"

"You're level-headed," Mary said. "I suppose I always knew you had hard sense under all that gimcrackery. You realize your whole life can change in a moment, don't you?"

"It will change in a moment," Constance said. Her eyes narrowed shrewdly. "That's what I've always known, always expected." She paused. "That's why—I've lasted," she added with a laugh.

Her laugh, like her voice, was fuller and less shrill than it used to be. It was a solid laugh; there was more mirth and less nerves in it than when she was younger. She fitted the life she had made for herself as her own superb clothes fitted her. She had the best cook in London and Mary noticed instantly when she stepped from the train that her slim-lined goddess had started to fill out. There was a recently acquired lushness to Constance's hips and breasts that had never been there before. The head fitter at Worth's remarked it too when they stopped in Paris for fittings for Constance's new clothes for Marienbad. Constance revelled in the pleasure of taking Mary along.

"Just think," she kept saying, "you of all people to take to Worth's. They'll fall all over you when I tell them you made my first clothes."

"You'll tell them nothing of the sort," Mary snapped. "Do you think I want to feel like a fool?"

Constance chuckled her under the chin. "None of that, now."

It was, however, an amazing experience for Mary to see Worth's; more, to go with Constance, at whose appearance the whole staff stopped their occupations and flocked about her, bowing, chattering, hurrying here and there to bring in fittings, samples, laces, embroideries, and all sorts of oddments for her approval. She established herself in the largest and lightest of the panelled pearl-gray fitting-rooms, and stood there before the enormous triple mirror in her lace-trimmed corset-cover and drawers, smoking her Turkish cigarettes, keeping up a running fire of argument and criticism with her vendeuse and the two busy fitters, who crawled about her with their mouths full of pins. Mary sat in the corner, taking the whole scene in, noticing every detail of the exquisite dressmaking, and once, when Constance snapped her fingers furiously and called the embroiderer *une vache—une imbécile* for using the wrong kind of silk, Mary burst into peals of laughter. Everybody stopped working and stared at her.

"What is it?" Constance asked.

Mary rocked back and forth in her chair, wiping her eyes.

"Oh, Constance," she gasped, "it's just like the attic at home. You haven't changed a bit."

"Certainly not. Why should I! *Nom d'un chien, Mademoiselle, regardez ça! Vous me donnez une ligne comme la grossesse!*"

Afterwards they met Clarrie and Fräulein, who had been at the Louvre, at Rumpelmayer's for tea. Clarrie was starry-eyed from looking at the Venus de Milo; in vain, Fräulein explained, did she try to interest her in the other galleries. Every time they were in Paris they went to the Louvre and Fräulein's orderly plans for seeing the paintings were spoiled by Clarrie's going straight to the Venus and standing, staring at her, as long as she was permitted to.

"She iss so ott aboud it," Fräulein said accusingly. "She vill not haff enough of dis von statue."

"Why, darling?" Constance shook a blob of whipped cream into Clarrie's chocolate.

"I don't know, exactly, Mummie. I think it's because she's like music. I hear her."

Clarrie turned her attention to the pastries. "Oooh," she said slowly, surveying the huge trayful of glittering edible jewels. "However shall I choose? Which do you want, Auntie Mary?"

They all put their heads together and consulted seriously about the pastries. Constance chose a Napoléon, Fräulein a huge chocolate cream-puff, Clarrie an éclair, and Mary a wild-strawberry tart. It seemed, with the happy, gabbling people strolling by outside, the July sunshine filtering through the colonnades of the Rue de Rivoli, the smart turnouts spanking up and down the thoroughfare, and the four of them giggling and eating pastry around a little marble table, like a child's dream. Mary had seen so little of Constance in recent years. She had somehow not dreamed that this side of her, the same side that loved to trot along on errands with Mary at home, would grow and develop into this passionate attachment to her child and to everything that interested the child. It was almost impossible to reconcile this with the imperious, daring, notorious beauty; the dazzling woman about whom everything from scandal to envious speculation was whispered. It was unbelievable that this same Constance could burrow into this warm, silly feminine intimacy with the gusto she brought to everything else.

The three weeks' holiday with Clarrie passed like an impossibly happy dream. They took a steamer up the Rhine, they visited the Black Forest, they went to Switzerland and rode up the Alps in terrifying funiculars. They visited churches and art galleries and museums, they went to concerts and two operas. Clarrie spoke both French and German as well as English, and travelling with her was a constant amazement and delight to Mary. The child had an odd way of combining the gentle deference of a carefully-brought-up English girl with the quiet assurance of a born cosmopolitan. First she asked Mary's permission or advice about each question as it came up, then she gave directions to hotel clerks, concierges, porters, and guides with the authority born of language and experience.

Sometimes in the evening when Clarrie had gone to sleep and Mary sat alone on some hotel balcony overlooking a starlit lake, she felt appalled by the full weight of her strange life with its crushing contrasts. Here she was with Constance's daughter who at fourteen had more education, more poise, and more cultivation than Mary could ever hope, at thirty-nine, to acquire. Here she was, dressed in quiet, beautiful clothes (bought from a small Paris dressmaker at Constance's insistence), travelling about like a blood relative of Clarrie's, deferred to as the aunt, rather than the com-panion, of the titled young English lady. She could not overlook the origin of the whole relationship. Sometimes in these recent weeks her memory, jogged by some word or trivial action of Constance's, had thrown up startling reminders from the past. Perhaps it was Clarrie's compelling resemblance to Clarissa. Perhaps that reminded her, at odd moments, of the awkward gray-clad Irish child who had called this child's grandmother "Ma'm" in a brogued voice thick with shyness and fright.

But these were not the real weights in her life's burden, and Mary knew it. This was the most delightful, if unreal of interludes. The heavy, ever-present reality of Paul lay leaden on her mind, day and night, thousands of miles distant from the house, the mill, Louise, the boys. Time and again in these few summer weeks she had invited the thought of writing to him, of saying she would not come back. It could be done, she told herself; some day, it must be done. She could stay here with Constance, who would welcome her. Or she could take up her solitary life where she had left it off at Paul's plea, eight long years ago. She had never really intended the thing to drag on this way. To come for Clarissa's sake was one thing; to help Louise through the twins and the complicated readjustments was another; to stay, stay . . . for what reason? She could hear Constance's crisp, clear voice, that dark afternoon in Pittsburgh, saying awful, unacknowledgeable things . . . "you two are laying up dynamite for yourselves . . . stand this fantastic arrangement forever . . . unnatural situation will overwhelm Paul . . . craftier, crazier . . . *One of these days Paul is going to need . . .*"

Mary pressed her hot eyeballs with the tips of her fingers. Her head felt like the container of a kaleidoscope; outwardly a simple, everyday object, inside a whirl of broken thoughts and half decisions like a mess of jagged little colored fragments. What should she do? How could she go on making this vast unreality her whole life? How could she contemplate the years—how many endless, difficult, strained, frustrated years that might lie ahead? How could she go back! Sheer habit, by now, if not the unremitting discipline of half her lifetime made it more natural to renounce Paul than ever to admit she loved him. She did love him, yes, she always would. The admission, when she faced it with enormous reluctance, was like the contemplation of a colossal, burdensome treasure, incalculable in value, but an eternal worry to own and to administer. One would actually sense relief if one were robbed of it.

As for Louise—Mary gritted her teeth and shuddered. Every person affected by that pitiful, if infuriating personality was maimed by it. So much of it was not Louise's fault—it is my fault, Mary sometimes said bitterly to herself, mine and Paul's and that narrow rigid world we live in. And ignorance. And bungling. Bungling. Look at Edgar. Look at me. Look at Paul. She sighed. Louise loomed as the most formidable obstacle to going back. Louise appeared at this distance like a two-headed monster, showing one twisted face and then the other beneath her own pretty, sour-sweet smile. One side of Louise would like to kill me, Mary told herself. She is jealous enough to kill me without a regret. The other side wants me there. Wants me to do all the things I do so she can lie around and pretend to be delicate. So she won't have to come to grips with life. *So she can hang onto Paul.* I'm the only hold she has over Paul. She only keeps him by having me there.

What a fool I've been! What a fool he is! Why doesn't he *do* something, Mary asked herself futilely. Why does he settle for a mess like this? Why does he settle for peace at any price? Her mind ran on, round and round. She opened her eyes and gazed out over the lyric, peaceful beauty of Lac Leman, shimmering in the warm starlight. Its beauty had the fantasy of a scenic Easter-egg. Irrelevantly and with astounding inconsequence another view flashed through her brain—tall stacks belching fire and sparks into the black arch of a winter night.

"God help me," she said aloud. "I can't help myself."

CHAPTER XLVIII

[*1897*]

AFTER SHE WAS SETTLED at home again in the fall Mary decided to try giving more time to outside concerns than she had ever done before. She ought to get out more and see other people beside the family. Paul had often urged her to do so, but it was the sort of thing that seemed such an effort. Her sister Kate was no longer in Pittsburgh. Dan had a foreman's job in a big foundry in Johnstown and the Maginnises had moved there three years ago. That had cut her off from the last of her own family, and she had involved herself deeper than ever in the life of the Scotts. This was to stop now, she told herself. And so much chatting with Paul was going to stop too. She found ways of being busy somewhere else in the house at the times when he was apt to drop into her sitting-room.

She knew that Louise, for one, was enjoying the change. Louise had not been so gay or so good-tempered in years. She tripped about the house humming or singing in her schoolgirlish high voice, lavishing affection on Dickie and Paul, popping up to the third floor to visit Teddy and Tommy. Margaret, the old Scotswoman, had a word, unsuited to her place, to say about that. "She's no' fallen in love wi' those bairns," she muttered to Mary. "There's some whigmeleery beneath it a'."

Mary knew how simple the explanation was. Somebody—Julia, she guessed—had been giving Louise advice. It was too much to suppose that the two sisters-in-law had never touched on the question that had always titillated Julia's mean mind, while they rocked and gossipped on those summer afternoons. Mary could almost hear Julia's cool Boston voice advising Louise that her sons were her greatest advantage, and admonishing her to play those strong cards cleverly. Mary wondered indifferently whether Louise had consulted Julia about some plan for getting rid of her. If so, it would have been conceived in some way calculated not to alarm or antagonize Paul. Something to do with the boys, in other words.

Mary was writing letters in her sitting-room one dark November afternoon when Trude told her that there was a messenger from the mill at the side door. That was how Paul usually asked for his dinner to be sent down when he was going to stay at the mill and work. But this time the boy handed Mary a note which she opened curiously.

"Mary"— she read. "One of my best men is in trouble. He is Charlie Liska, the Hunky I put in the blooming mill. It seems his wife has been in labor since yesterday and is having a horrible time. Could you go down there and see if we can do anything? They speak almost no English and have no doctor—the usual slum story. Many thanks.

"P. S."

She told Jones to harness up while she went to the storeroom and packed a basket with necessities. On the way down in the carriage she wondered rather uneasily about these people; how could you help them if you couldn't talk with them? She really knew extraordinarily little about them, except that Paul had told her how he had promoted Liska and infuriated the Irish in the mill. Liska must have fought his own way since then.

When the carriage turned off at the bottom of the Allegheny Avenue hill, and Jones began guiding the horse over the patchwork cobbles that led to the old Flat, Mary sat up suddenly and caught her breath. It was incredible, impossible—she had not been down here in nearly fifteen years. It was only a twenty-minute drive from the Scott house. And for her the distance, in every sense but the physical one, was greater than that to London, to anywhere. She sat up and peered curiously through the heavy murk of smoke and dull wintry light. It could not be possible. This couldn't be the old Flat; there were just as many dreary shacks and shanties, but not the same ones. She pressed her fingertips to her eyes. This was a sensation like dreaming.

Then of course she realized why the Flat was different. The flood had levelled it. Memories came swooping down like sand pouring through a chute, a stream of bitter painful memories so sharp and swift that she could not defend any corner of her mind against them. She sat back in the carriage and bent her head and let the whole avalanche sweep over her— the flood, the unearthly experience with Paul in the shack, her last view of it perched insanely on a hummock in the middle of the river when Paul lifted her out of it into the boat. She thought of her father, of James, of Bridget—it could not be possible that such drab lives had mounted to so much drama and tragedy. Only Kate was different, Kate safe in her nice proper house in Johnstown, with her Dan and her fine family of children.

Mary looked out the carriage window again. Mrs. Molloy's house should be there, and O'Brien's beyond it, but the whole row had been replaced by a newer, though equally cramped, cluttered, ratty lot of houses. That tidal wave must have smashed the whole Flat into a pile of rubble. She marvelled now, when she had done her utmost to forget everything about it before, how their one house had been lifted clear of the whole mêlée and swept intact into the river.

Jones drove straight across the old Flat and on to a newer settlement along the bottom land which had spread with the growth of the Hunky colony. She realized now that the old Flat looked different for another reason. The signs on the meagre, dirty stores, the lettering on the saloon windows, were all in a foreign language. She could not make head or tail of them. Where were Cassidy's grocery, and McShane's saloon; what kind of names were Hlavaj and Kubovič and Baláž and Mráz? What a fool I am, she told herself. Here I've been living on the edge of this all these years, and listening to Paul talk about these new people and now when they've practically changed the face of the earth I wake up and realize it.

The situation at Liska's was much as she had expected. Charlie and his wife shared a rattletrap three-room house with another family whose three small dirty children were sitting goggle-eyed on the steps when the Scott carriage stopped there. Mrs. Liska lay on her back on a featherbed placed over a shaky iron bedstead. She was breathing in hard, quick rasps; her hair, soaked with perspiration, hung dank on either side of her face; her eyes were glassy with pain, and she was a bad, dark, purplish color. Her husband stood stonily beside her, never taking his eyes from her face, and muttering through his clenched teeth. A stout, puffing older woman waddled back and forth between the bed and a steaming kettle on the stove; the midwife who, Mary saw at a glance, was incompetent to cope with this situation and could only allow Nature to take its course. Another woman hovered in the corner. Mary touched Charlie on the elbow and said, "I'm Mr. Scott's housekeeper. Tell me, how long has she been this way?"

She was afraid from his manner that he would not answer, but when she mentioned Paul's name Charlie turned eagerly and did his best, in his bad English, to explain. All that day, since early the night before. . . . He wrung his hands.

Mary ran out to the street where she had left Jones waiting.

"Go up and get Doctor McClintock," she called to him, "quick. If he isn't home fetch him from where he is."

The trouble, as much as she could gather from Charlie's stumbling translation of the Slovak midwife's diagnosis, was that the child was turned crosswise. The mother could not give birth. From her looks, as Mary worked over her with the old woman, the child might quite possibly be dead. Mary began to feel desperate as the minutes went by and she strained her ears to hear the carriage coming back. She had never felt so helpless. She would have tried urging the midwife to do something—anything—but the woman spoke no English and would not have understood. It was probably just as well, Mary thought. She was amazed at Mrs. Liska's behavior. The young woman had been a night and a day in terrible agony, and although now almost unconscious, Charlie assured Mary, with tears in his eyes, that she had not made one sound, not a whimper, since her labor started. "And so young," he said, rubbing the tears from his eyes. "So new for eve't'ing. Oh, my Julka."

He had only brought her over from the old country last Christmas. For six years he had been waiting, living in a filthy boardinghouse with nine other men, working up from ten cents an hour, saving his wages penny by penny, until he put together enough to bring her over and marry her. This shack was only temporary, he explained in a desperate kind of embarrassment; he was supposed to get a real house for her right after the baby came. But she hadn't been very well, and the Michalčíks, with whom they shared this place, were old friends of his—Julka didn't speak English yet . . . Mary flew to the door as she heard wheels outside.

Doctor McClintock was not used to being called in emergencies at mill workers' homes. Usually they kept to their own midwives or to a rare doctor who spoke their language. Mary explained the situation as best she could while she helped him prepare Julka Liska. The doctor said he must perform an instrument delivery and he asked her to warn Charlie that it was most unlikely the child would be born alive.

"Olright," the wretched man said, twisting his blackened hands together, "anyt'ing you make it, olright, but you save my Julka. *Prosím,* you save my Julka, no?" His thick voice was a croak. He kept his eyes on his wife's ghastly face.

"I'll try," the doctor said. "I'll do my very best." He looked about, grimacing at the poor light, the cramped, cluttered room, and the lack of proper facilities. Then he shrugged, beckoned Mary with his chin, and started to work. They had to let Charlie stay there to interpret the doctor's directions to the midwife, and to hold the kerosene lamp where the doctor needed light. Mary was nervous. She was afraid Charlie would get panicky and drop the lamp.

"No, no," he said slowly, shaking his head. "Doctor need light, he get it light." He shut his mouth hard under his bushy moustache.

The child could not be saved. And by the time it was delivered the unconscious mother was in such grave condition that no one could stop to think of the mangled little body which Mary quickly hid under a sheet. Doctor McClintock worked furiously, and the old midwife who had been sullen and ugly at first, nodded and bowed and crossed herself repeatedly as the doctor brought a series of hemorrhages under control. All the time Charlie Liska stood there with his eyes riveted on his wife's face, his hand holding up the lamp steady and unfaltering. Mary stole a glance at him now and then. These Hunkies must be made of the iron in which they worked. Mary had seen plenty of things similar to this years ago among her neighbors on the Flat. But never, nowhere, had she seen such dogged, superhuman fortitude.

She told Paul all about it, and watched his face, peculiarly attentive, while she talked.

"That's it," Paul said. "That Hunky struck me that way the first time I ever took a good look at him. Those people have some kind of—I don't know. Most of 'em aren't much above animals, poor devils—but this Charlie—"

"Well, his wife is a character too. I want to keep an eye on her."

Mary began to see more and more of Julka in the next weeks, making frequent trips down to look in on her. She was a delightful young woman, a warm, calm, intelligent peasant with big, bright brown eyes and—when her strength came back—smooth apple cheeks. She was only nineteen years old. There was a solid good humor, a natural ease about her, which drew Mary as if to the warmth of a fire. Julka was quite short, stocky, and strongly built. She had worked hard all her life, and her one misfortune did not discourage her. She was entirely reasonable. She was picking up English quickly and she said to Mary, "I not vorry. I vait till Doctor say yes, I get more baby."

She showed Mary the piles of heavy round-thread linen, sheets and huge square pillowcases and tablecloths, thickly encrusted with her own embroidery, which she had brought from the old country for her marriage. She stroked them proudly.

"Is fine, fine cloth, no? Mine strýc Jaromír he gives from big land. Big place. We make ourselves, all women together." She indicated the spinning and weaving of flax. "We soak. We beat. We make for lie in sun, make lovely white."

"It must be beautiful in your country," Mary said.

Julka nodded eagerly. "Is very beautiful. So clean. So green. We love our country, love so much. But is lots trouble. We got bad people Wien come take away all men for serve in army. We got Kaiser František Procházka. Czechs not like Kaiser. Slováks not like. Czechs want free. Come America for be free."

This was pretty surprising talk, Mary thought, and Paul agreed with her. You did not think of these people as having ideas like that. You could not imagine their having had education and land and property back in the old country. Most of them, indeed, had had none. But this girl was constantly making distinctions between herself and Charlie as Czechs, and the other Hunkies who, she shrugged, were "doity Slováks." She had no intention of living like them any longer than she could help. "Come America for be free," she kept saying, and that phrase echoed in Mary's mind when she crossed the dirty ruck of the old Flat and picked her way over the stretch of mud and grit where the Liskas and the Michalčíks lived, squeezed in between other ramshackle buildings. Charlie and Julka hoped to move soon, to a small house on the hillside rising from the river bottom. There were steep, barren streets there with makeshift paving and rows of jerrybuilt mustard-yellow houses with ugly wooden stoops and open privies in the backyards. Any trees that Mary could remember on those hillsides had been cut down long ago, to enable somebody to lay out these cramped rows of hideous dwellings. The streets were dingy by day, ominous by night; they were dimly lighted by flickering gas street-lamps too far apart, and the middle houses in the rows stood in pitch dark.

Rent was the direst consideration in the lives of their tenants. For one house to be occupied by only one family was unheard of. It was usual to rent one or two of the three rooms to another family, or else to take as many bachelor boarders as could be crowded in. Entire steerage loads of strong, green young men from the Slavic Austrian provinces were still pouring into the district to fill the insatiable demands of the mills. This little patch of Allegheny was insignificant compared with the real steel boroughs where nothing existed whatsoever except through dependence on the mill. It was like that out in Braddock, Homestead, Rankin, Munhall, and the whole gloomy stretch of the Monongahela. In those places you made steel or you starved. Here in Allegheny there was a semblance at least of participation in the diverse life of a city.

Julka planned to take boarders like everybody else. Charlie protested that this would be too much work for her but she laughed at him, calling Mary, who had dropped in to see her, to witness that Doctor McClintock pronounced her strong and well now, "strong like you." She punched him playfully in his barrel chest. He blushed at her horseplay in Mary's presence. "Julinko," he whispered, "we got lady visitor. You shoon' do dat."

Mary was discouraged for them when she saw the house they rented. And they were so proud of it! Mary's interest in Julka had grown to real friendship in the space of a few weeks. And one could not be close to such a woman in such a crowded and poverty-ridden community without being caught up in the lives of all her neighbors. Mary found herself learning to pronounce strange tongue-twisting names and understand the thick, faltering English in which these clumsy shy women were beginning to speak to her. When she first began to drop in with Julka to the neighbors' crowded kitchens there had been constraint and awkwardness in every meeting. Julka was tremendously proud of her American friend, a fine-looking lady who wore a gray broadcloth dress with silk trimming, a sealskin stole, and a velvet hat with real feathers on it. But the heavy, shabby, often barefoot Slovak women with their broods of dirty children shot sullen glances at Mary's clothes and shrugged indifferent monosyllables when she tried to talk to them. Until the day when she mentioned something about her birthplace on the Flat and her memories of what it was like thirty years ago. Mrs. Michalčík turned around slowly and stared at her.

"You mean—like us?—so—you vas born?"

"But of course," Mary said. She felt a great lift inside, a sudden knowledge of how to get beneath the surface of these people, under their crudeness, their heaviness, and their enormous pathos.

"We lived right over that alley beyond the tracks there," Mary said, pointing out the window. "My brother James was the boss heater at Scott's. My Dad worked there all his life."

The three women in the room slowly laid their hands in their laps, opened their mouths, and gaped. Then, one by one, their broad, plain, shiny faces broke into slow smiles. Wonder and delight lit up their large eyes. First one, then the next, began to talk. They all crowded around Mary, babbling questions at her in their ludicrous English. They listened to her answers and nodded while she talked, wagging their heads and holding up their hands and gesturing to one another. The ice was broken. Mrs. Benko, whose husband was one of Charlie Liska's helpers, put out her hand timidly and touched the sleeve of Mary's dress. The other women took courage and began feeling the fine broadcloth, the crisp fluted silk ruffles at the neck and cuffs, the rich softness of the sealskin stole. Mrs. Michalčík even got down on her knees and minutely examined Mary's black kid shoes. They gabbed together in Slovak.

Mary looked to Julka to interpret.

"They say like fairy story," Julka explained. "Like told in old country. America for be free and rich, all say so, most time we not believe. Make happy, you first like us, now fine lady."

Hot tears sprang into Mary's eyes. She blinked rapidly.

"I'm no fine lady, Julka. I work for my living too. We all do. I've just been—lucky. It takes a little while—but you'll see—"

The women all nodded sagely. Mary's heart went out to them. She could not very well see how they could hope to improve their lives, but hope was what they wanted. Hope had brought them with their shawls and bundles and featherbeds, their songs and legends and dreams thousands of miles in hideous hardship. To the land of promise, the land of freedom and gold. And what did they find? Poverty as bitter, a lot fully as hard as anything they left behind. Dirt, sickness, cold, and meagre stringency; the horrible packing together of too many dirty, tired bodies in too few beds and rooms; the grim gray climate, the lowering pall of smoke, the damp fogs from the river; for their men the utter emptiness of the time which should be leisure, and which went only to exhausted sleep, to lounging in muddy, littered alleys, or once in an intolerable while, to getting drunk. In the old country there had been hardship, but there were green fields and trees, church and village festivals, music, good cheap beer and wine, the old ways and the old friends and the old people. Here it was too cold, too strange, too grim. Mary felt crushed by the knowledge but the women did not complain. They were strong and earthy and enormously human and sociable.

Every time she saw them Mary found herself doing some little thing for them; helping this one cut out a new calico dress, that one gather her daughter's confirmation veil; holding the baby while Mrs. Sivák sat down by the stove to peel potatoes for supper. Always before she left they shyly offered some refreshment, a cup of coffee with a piece of warm apple-cake, or a smoking hot dumpling filled with pot-cheese, or a taste of the savory thick soup simmering on the back of the stove. These women were eager and natural. Mary found they gave her something she had never known her whole life long. They and their lives and families and problems interested her intensely.

Paul said she never talked about anything else these days. She had forgotten her decision to avoid him. She was so absorbed in her new interest that she could not bother remembering why she had ever had such a notion. Paul kept track of the Liskas through her. Charlie was developing rapidly into a strong right hand, a master at his job. Paul had been praying for such a man ever since the loss of Jim Rafferty. The last place he expected to find him was in the ranks of the Hunkies whom he had so reluctantly taken into the mill. Mary scolded Paul gently for calling them Hunkies.

"Well, they come from Hungary, don't they?"

"Most of them come from Slovakia, which is a province in Hungary. A few of them are Bohemians like Charlie and Julka. They are Czechs, and very proud of it too."

"Better than the Hunkies, eh?"

"*Don't* call them Hunkies!"

"All right. Czechs."

"They aren't all Czechs."

"My God, why does it have to be so complicated? They're not Hunkies, they're not Czechs, what in blazes are they?"

"Slovaks. That's simple enough."

"All right. Mostly Slovaks. Some Czechs. Now have I got it straight?"

"Yes."

He was leaving the room. "Just the same," he said with a wink, "they're still Hunkies to me."

CHAPTER XLIX

[*1898*]

"You know," Mary said to Paul one evening, laying aside a technical journal with an article he had brought her to read, "we don't realize what an important man you are."

"Bosh," he answered. "You're used to me."

She shook her head. The article he had shown her was a report about his work in developing hard alloys for weapons and projectiles. There was even a method of hardening steel now known as the Scott Process. When a man's work was permanently labelled with his name and other mills recognized it as such, he was famous, Mary said. She smiled at Paul, standing by the mantel making faces over a new pipe. It had not been seasoned to suit him. There was a terrible February sleet storm going on outside. The wind whistled in the chimneys, and through the drawn curtains they heard needles of sleet peppering the windows. Louise had gone upstairs. She must have said something to Paul that made him feel he had to join her. He was restless and he had not sat down. Mary thought of her now and said, "Louise has no idea what a great man you are."

"Oh, Louise." He shrugged. The inference was that Louise had no idea about anything. She certainly could not grasp the outlines and necessities of his life, nor the part that she should play in them. Not long since he had told her that he had to begin seeing something of the newer people who were coming to the forefront of business and social life in town. He could not go on living in his father's generation indefinitely. Louise remonstrated. Surely Paul did not want to invite any of those men who ran the

Carnegie mills! Why, Father Scott would turn over in his grave if they set foot in his house! And Louise wouldn't know what to talk about with their wives. All the girls she had grown up with simply ignored these newly-rich women, with their huge diamonds and their dresses sent from Paris by the boxful. You couldn't tell *anything* about such people. And Louise whispered to Paul the shocking gossip that one of them—she named her—had been a *waitress* in a railway-station lunchroom!

Paul was so disgusted by her pettiness that he gave up any thought of inviting to his house certain men whom he wanted to know better. Louise would only insult their wives and make a fool of him. Paul had never been much of a clubman but now he took to driving across rather frequently to lunch at the Pittsburgh Club or the Duquesne Club, where there were always groups who were glad to have him join them. Their talk was satisfying and stimulating. Just now they were all closely absorbed in the situation between the United States and Spain. Since they all knew that Paul Scott had been supplying the Navy with armor-piercing projectiles for some years past, they had a way of deferring to his opinion about the possibilities of war with Spain. He was always mildly surprised when, after leaving his ulster and high-crowned derby at the club door, he went up the dark stairs to be welcomed with respect as well as cordiality. Some of the steel and iron men had frowned in the past on Paul's policies toward labor. They had thought him soft-headed. But the men who ran Homestead and Edgar Thomson and Duquesne and Jones and Laughlin regarded Paul Scott as a brilliant steel chemist. If you got him talking about the chemistry of alloys, you were not wasting your time.

The *Maine* was as big a surprise to Paul as to everybody else on that dark February morning when the news came. But Paul had more than furious indignation to bring to the matter. He had known for a long time that the Navy was preparing for something to touch off a war with Spain. The orders for projectiles and other armaments had been doubled months ago; now they were tripled. All through the ensuing weeks of investigation, discussion, and diplomatic wrangling, Paul ran the whole mill on twenty-four hour schedule. He was not interested in Congressional resolutions or the undertakings of the Spanish government. "Just getting set to blow the greasers off the face of the earth" was his summary of the mill's activity.

He worked every night now. If things were reasonably peaceful at home he came up for dinner and went back afterwards, but if Louise had started the day with a scene of some kind he had dinner sent down to the mill. Once he asked for a box of dinner on Jones's regular day off. Mary usually sent Flora, the upstairs maid, on errands in such cases, but on a sudden impulse she decided to take down the box herself. She had never done such a thing. Perhaps Paul would not like it. But he had been so excited lately about his huge Navy contracts, which he had won under the noses of some of the biggest mills in the country, that she could not resist the impulse to see him in the midst of all that.

It was a raw evening early in March. Mary walked quickly, swinging the box by a cord from her wrist, her hands tucked into her muff. As she drew closer to the mill she began to worry about what she was doing. No woman was ever wanted inside a mill. It was certainly bad form, and the men, by ancient tradition, thought it bad luck. Well, she wouldn't really go in, she told herself. She would just go as far as the main entrance and leave the box with the office boy the way Flora did. When she reached the crest of the hill where she had stood, that ghastly morning long ago, and seen her world shattered in one flash of catastrophe, she paused. Exactly fourteen years ago, she thought. That was something she could not believe. The fourteen years had nothing to do with it. It was lifetimes away, centuries away. This mill, in a strange sense, with Paul in it, was another world by itself too. Why—in all the years that her life had been entangled with Paul's, she had never seen him in the mill; never been inside the mill, as a matter of fact. She was dumbstruck with surprise.

The whole place was ablaze with light and fire as she approached the main entrance. The sky above her head was thick with red smoke and sparks and clouds of cinder. There was a deafening noise all about. She did not know enough to identify each barbaric voice in the concert. She did not know the clatter and crash of the rolling mill from the skull-splitting thump of the slaghammer, the penetrating roar of the crusher, the imperious shrill whistles and hisses of freight and dinkey-engines. The whole yard beneath the footbridge was a snaking tangle of freight cars and flats. A derrick was loading great clanging hunks of metal onto a flat standing by an open-ended shed. Mary approached the main entrance timidly. Now she felt like a fool for having come down here. And to her consternation she was met by an armed guard. He looked at her and waited for her to state her business. My God, she thought suddenly. Of course the mill is under guard. What a fool I was to come here! She felt as she had not felt since childhood, when she looked at the stern-faced guard and had to say, "—I've brought Mr. Scott's dinner."

It was really ludicrous. The big fellow stood there looking down on the dainty little lady in the dark gray broadcloth and sealskin furs and his hard mouth twitched. "Well," he said, "I guess you can take it in." He took a heavy steel chain of keys from his hip pocket and unlocked the iron-hinged main door.

"I—really I don't have to go in," Mary said. She was dreadfully embarrassed. "Doesn't—can't the office boy or somebody get it here?"

"He's out to supper," the guard said. "You can go in." Before she thought about it she found herself inside, and the door swung shut behind her. Now what? She stood hesitating in the corridor. If she turned left she would find herself in a furnace or something of the sort; a blast of heat snorted up the dark ramp. So she turned right and walked a short way and saw a dingy ground-glass door ahead of her with SCOTT IRON WORKS, General Offices, painted on it. Nobody appeared to be working in the row of cubbyholes she passed. They must all be out to supper. There was another door ahead of her, marked Paul Scott, Private. She knocked on it. "Come in," Paul shouted. Mary jumped. She did not know the habit of loud speech which years in a mill engendered. She opened the door and saw Paul in a dirty denim coat bent over a mass of papers, absorbed.

"Put it on the window sill," he said without looking up.

"Yes—sor." Mary could not resist that.

"What the—" he looked up and leaped from his chair. *"Mary!* What are you doing here?" He strode around the desk and seized her hands. "I'll be damned!" He was so delighted and surprised that he stood beaming from ear to ear.

"I oughtn't to have come," she said. "It was just a notion."

"Well, it was a damned fine notion," he said. "Sit down and stay while I eat my supper." His face turned serious for a moment and he said uneasily, "Anything wrong at the house?" There could hardly be any other reason for Mary's amazing appearance here.

"No," she laughed. "It just struck me I'd never seen the inside of the mill—"

"—or me in it—"

"—that's right. And with the war about to break out and all—I suppose I thought it would be exciting."

"Well, it is. Do you want to see any of the departments?"

"Oh—I ought not. I know the men hate that."

"Jim brought you up right, I see. Well—" He dragged a chair over and placed it opposite his own. "Sit down and have some supper with me." She shook her head. "I'm going home."

Paul pointed at the chair. "Sit down!" His voice was almost the same roar as his father's. Mary was feeling more and more amazed. Paul grinned at her as he went to work on a roast chicken. "Have some."

"Really I don't want it." She could not say that her heart was pounding like a child's for foolish happiness. It would have choked her to eat now.

"Look at that," Paul said with his mouth full, shoving a sheaf of papers across the desk. "Sixteen thousand of my best Pittsburgh stogies delivered since the *Maine*." He drank some coffee from a bottle and wiped his moustache with the back of his hand. "Those greasers'll wish they'd pulled somebody else's whiskers."

"I wonder if we really will declare war on them," Mary said.

"We ought not to bother. We ought to blow 'em to hell first and get around to palaver afterwards."

Mary frowned a little. "I didn't know you were so bloodthirsty, Paul."

"Me? Say, Mary, have you an idea what this mill *is?*" He shook a heavy finger at her. "One fool of a woman is enough in my life." On a sudden impulse he jumped from his chair and went over to the Old Man's private safe, standing in its corner, and opened it and lifted out the tin box and quickly but gently leafed through its contents. "There," he said quietly, lifting out the letter to his grandfather with the White House seal on the inner envelope. He handed it to Mary. She opened it, a lump forming quickly in her throat. He saw her hands trembling as she reverently held the letter, reading it with tears in her eyes. She read it several times, then folded it up carefully and handed it back.

"You see?" Paul said. He put his hand on her shoulder and his blue eyes stared deep into hers. "Anybody else might think me a sentimental fool," he said softly. "But you know me. You *really* know me. I tell you," he said, "any time this country gets in a scrap, it's my scrap and this mill's scrap. Highspeed saws and fancy springs are all right in their place—but this mill makes death for anybody that bothers the U. S. A."

"Oh, Paul, I—I love to hear you talk that way." Her eyes were wet and shining.

He smiled lamely. "I kind of—I'm afraid I got windy there," he said. "But you have to believe in something." His chin jutted out. He put away the letter in its place and slammed the safe shut and Mary rose to go. She heard doors slamming and various bustling noises out in the other offices and she knew the men were coming back from supper. Paul walked out to the gate with her. It was almost time for the night shift to go on, and the street, which had been quiet when she came down, was black with workmen carrying dinner pails. Paul guided her past the long line of them stomping over the bridge and into the mill. She looked at some of the faces curiously. It seemed another lifetime ago that she had had a brother who was one of these. It startled her that now, instead of thinking of James and the O'Briens and Cullens and old neighbors from the Flat, she found herself looking for Charlie Liska. She asked Paul how he was doing.

"Fine," Paul said, nodding at some men who stood aside to let them pass. "He's a fixture now. He's all right. How are *your* Hunkies?"

"Fine," Mary said. She smiled. They had reached the street now and she said, "After the war when you're not so busy I'm going to ask you for something for them."

It was, of all things, a house that she wanted for them. She had never asked for anything in her life, and she did not know how she would have the boldness to do it now. But Julka Liska had put the idea into her head. Mary's visits to her new friends had fallen into a certain pattern. The visits were not so casual any more. They had taken on, under Julka's persistent organizing, the nature of regular meetings. One or another of the women each time would get Mary to promise to come "next time by me." On being welcomed into that woman's house, she would find the whole group there with their sewing, their knitting, their babies, and the knotty accumulation of their problems. The kitchen table would be set with a ragtag collection of cracked cups and bent tin spoons disposed over a beautifully embroidered heavy linen cloth which was its owner's sole pride and treasure; and in the center stood a lovingly baked crumb-cake, a poppyseed strudel, or a pile of feathery jelly-doughnuts or cheese pockets. Good coffee went with these, and after Mary discovered that poverty kept the hostess from providing the cream that these women loved in it, she would slip a pint jar of cream into her marketing-bag along with spools of cotton, dress-patterns, outgrown underwear of the twins which she commandeered from Margaret, and the books which she always brought for Julka. At first she apologized for the cream, murmuring some explanation about the dairyman's leaving too much that day, but soon nothing was said about it. She knew very well that the refreshments were provided by dint of the most painful penny-scraping and scrupulous chipping-in by all the women, with much serious discussion attending the tiny weekly purchase of almonds, butter, poppyseed, raisins, or whatever such luxury was needed for the baking. The finest instincts of pride and hospitality were roused by these gatherings which had become heaven to drab and labor-ridden lives.

Most of the women were boarding-bosses like Julka and it was difficult for them to count on the undisturbed use, even for a couple of hours, of their own kitchens. The men who boarded with them worked in different shifts. Some came home at six in the morning when others were just finishing breakfast before starting to the mill. Dinner-pails had to be packed all through the day, meals kept cooking on the stove, children hushed so the night-workers could sleep in the daytime. Mary was horrified when she first realized that two men would no sooner have vacated one small, foul bed than two others, sweaty and begrimed, would fall into it. In spite of all that, most of the women made a determined, if often futile effort, to keep at least the kitchen of their house decently neat and clean.

Julka was much more of a person than any of the others. She managed her place more efficiently, she was more intelligent, more responsive, and much more ambitious than the other women. She was tremendously proud of Charlie's job. This alone would have given her distinction and made her the natural leader of the group. But she had her own ideas besides. She was avid to learn good English and under her urging Mary began giving lessons to all the women. Julka led the way in learning new habits of dress, of housekeeping and of care of children. It was she who, irritated by the intrusions of a drunken lodger who kept bursting into Mrs. Sivák's kitchen when Mary was reading *Uncle Tom's Cabin* aloud, looked up and said, "We need place for us. Own place, nobody else come. Nice place, bring children, sew, go for read books, learn eve't'ing."

Mary laid down the book and looked at Julka. The other women raised their heads and paused in their sewing.

"What a wonderful idea," Mary said slowly.

And Paul did not wait until "after the war" to find out what she wanted to ask of him. The very next evening after she had been at the mill he went looking for her when he got home late at night, and asked her what she wanted.

"A house," she said. Now that she had said it, she was amazed to see how easy it was. Paul was surprised. A smile spread across his face and he came over and sat down by the fireplace, filling his pipe.

"Sounds interesting," he said. "Tell me about it."

Two weeks later he bought a small, solidly built brick house on Nixon Street, a couple of blocks above the flat land cut up into crowded streets and alleys where the millworkers lived. It was a plain house, in a block which he and Mary remembered as much cleaner and better-kept years ago than now. They had many curious twists of reminiscence when they drove about the neighborhood looking for the place Mary wanted. Not in years, Paul kept reminding her, had they revisited the scenes of their first long walks and the treasured Sunday afternoons of long ago. Sometimes they left Jones waiting with the carriage while they went about on foot inspecting empty houses and turning up long-buried memories of their early walks and talks. Once they found themselves walking slowly up Rebecca Street towards the jutting corner on the bend of the Ohio. Paul paused and looked at an ugly new greenstone house with a mansard roof.

"Mary," he said softly. His gloved hand seized hers in the dusk. "Mary. . . . Rebecca Street. Do you remember?"

Her throat swelled suddenly; she turned her head and bit her lip hard.

"Do you?" he murmured. He pressed her hand close to his side. "The wooden steps that used to be there?"

She drew a long breath. He was waiting for her answer, standing there staring at the site of the abandoned house with the wooden steps.

"Of course I emember," she choked. "Why did you have to go and ask me?"

Just then a Bessemer across the river behind them began to blow, and presently the sky was overspread with the wide ruddy light they knew so well. They turned around and stood perfectly still in the middle of the sidewalk, hand in hand, staring at the panorama as rapt as if they had never seen it before. They did not move until the glow had faded to one blurred red ring around the mouth of the stack. It was quite dark by now. Paul shook his head with a quick motion.

"Damn it," he said in a brittle tone. "What is it about that business that gets us like this? It gives me the creeps."

"Come on," Mary said. Her voice quavered and she coughed to hide it. "Let's get on."

Julka and the rest of the club—they had decided to give the group a name some day, but so far only called it the club—were speechless with happiness and bewilderment when Mary told them that they were to have a house of their own. Some of them wiped their eyes with their petticoats, some embraced one another and Mary with noisy kisses. They crowded around Julka's kitchen table to make the suggestions and plans Mary asked them for.

They would knock out the partition between two small parlors on the first floor, and make one good-sized room in which to meet together. Upstairs they would have a sewing-room with two machines in it, a cutting-board, and all the paraphernalia for sewing and dressmaking. Mary decided to take her own equipment out of storage and give it to them. Most wonderful of all, the house contained a bathroom. There was not one of the women who had ever had running water and a toilet in her house. Some of them did not know such things existed.

Paul was almost as proud of the house as Mary. He urged her to go ahead and make any alterations, buy any equipment, that she wanted. He pored over measurements and specifications with her, insisted on buying a good gas water-heater and a new gas range, having the plumbing and the hot-air heating system completely overhauled, and even installing an icebox, which she protested they did not need. Nobody was to live at the house, she reminded him; it would only be used during the daytime when the women could get away from home for an hour or two at a time. She herself would only spend certain specified hours there because she did, after all, have her own work to do.

She did not realize how many crowded weeks had been almost completely swallowed up in her new absorption. It was less than a year, she reminded herself one evening, since she had sat on that balcony in Montreux weighing the question of not coming back to Pittsburgh at all. Why, i would have been fantastic, she saw now, not to come back. She was more deeply involved right this minute with Pittsburgh than she had been in years. This club that had sprung up around her, and these strong, colorful women with their hardships and problems were not only intensely interesting, they wove themselves back into the very texture of her own roots and background. And the most wonderful part was that it was not in the least incompatible with her job here looking after the house for Paul. She loved to get up each morning. She loved the precise fitting-together of all the details of her busy days. She liked the orderly partitions into which she divided her mind; so much time for each thing here at home, so much for each thing at the House. Nobody had thought of another name for it. Paul had asked Mary what to do when the question of title to the property came up.

"Why—I don't know," she said. "You're buying it—it's your property."

"No, I'm buying it to give to this club of yours. It really ought to be in their name, only you can't deed a piece of real estate to a dozen ignorant Hunkies. I think I'll just put the title in your name, Mary."

"Oh, no, I don't want the house."

"But somebody has to be responsible. Somebody has to pay the taxes and insurance and coal bills and all that sort of thing. If a house belongs to an organization you have to have proper officers and a treasurer to handle the funds."

They both laughed at the thought of Mrs. Baláž, for instance, acting as treasurer to the Amalgamated Mamas—Paul's name for Mary's club.

"For that matter," Paul went on, "what about funds? I'll pay the maintenance expenses, of course, but you have to have some kind of bank account. You'd better use your own until your women know enough to form a regular organization with officers and all that kind of thing. No use bewildering them now, they've got too many other things to learn. Besides—" he looked at Mary thoughtfully.

"What?"

"Well—I kind of like the idea of your having some property of your own, Mary."

"But it's *not* mine. If you take that attitude, I'll drop the whole thing."

"All right," he said quickly. "It's not yours. We'll just put it in your name for the time being."

It was amazing, with all he had to do at the mill, and the gruelling hours he put in there, that he could take the time to think about Mary's House. She had not thought how much pleasure it would be for him to go over each day's progress in the alterations with her, to look at plumbers' and painters' estimates, and decide about things like storm windows, a new backyard fence, a new cellar floor, the roof, the wallpaper, the gaslight fixtures. Neither of them had ever had such fun. And most of their sessions over bills and blueprints were enlivened with Mary's stories, told in a poor imitation of the Slovak women's broken English, of the pitifully funny things they said and did each time she saw them. Sometimes she and Paul laughed until the tears rolled down their faces.

Mary had not realized that all this would be a delightful diversion for Paul from his terrific schedule at the mill. He almost always came home for dinner now and dropped in to her sitting-room to talk about the House for a little while before going back to the mill. Then one evening in April he did not come in to speak to her. Mary was surprised. She had heard Louise go upstairs right after dinner, and a good deal later Paul had still not left for the mill. Mary sat at her desk for a long time, checking the contractor's bills for the House. Finally she put away her papers and went out to the hall to turn out the lights.

Paul was descending the stairs, slowly, with his hand opening and closing on the mahogany banister. His face was like stone. He was staring straight ahead of him.

Mary's heart lurched with sudden fear. Louise had done something. Only Louise could account for that expression. Mary went to the foot of the stairs and looked up at him.

"Why, Paul. What's the matter?"

He walked on past her into her sitting-room; she followed and closed the door.

"What is it, Paul? What's happened?"

"Louise," he said in a lifeless voice, "is pregnant."

Mary's knees began to shake and she dropped into a chair. Her mouth opened; nothing except a muffled gasp came out. She was profoundly shocked, as if something scandalous had been told her. Paul looked at her and nodded.

"Sure," he said blackly. "That's just the way I feel."

"But—Paul." Mary's composure was in hand again. She smiled. "That's all right. That's fine. You always wanted—"

He had been holding his pipe in his right hand; the stem of it cracked sharply as his fist clenched. He threw the pieces into the wastebasket.

"Listen," he said. He spoke grimly; his voice was low and hard. "I wanted children—the children I've got. They're all I've got. All I counted on—because so help me God I hate that woman with every ounce of strength in my body."

Mary burst into tears and buried her face in her hands. Paul sat staring at the gas logs. He did not appear to pay any attention to Mary. After a time he spoke again, bitterly.

"I hate myself," he said through his teeth. "I hate myself and my life and her and the whole damned rotten mess. That—that—" he looked at Mary with tragedy and brutal frankness in his eyes.

"You mean—she—" Mary stammered with embarrassment. It was not easy to take a man's attitude towards this, even stripped of prudery.

"Yes," Paul snapped. "That's what I mean."

"You didn't intend to—let her have another child."

"Intend!" Paul sprang from his chair and began to stride back and forth across the hearthrug. "Christ Almighty, intend!" He laid his arms on the mantelpiece and buried his head in them with a groan.

CHAPTER L

[1898]

WAR WAS DECLARED a few days later, on the twenty-fifth of April. Paul had hardly been at home since the awful night when Louise had told him her news. He might almost have moved bag and baggage to the mill. But with Admiral Dewey sailing from Mirs Bay against Montojo at Cavite, the war overshadowed everything else in Paul's mind. He infected the whole mill, and the boys and Mary too with his tension and his passionate concern about the performance of the Pacific Fleet. His shells were there. He knew every piece of armament on every American ship in the Pacific. He and Dick had made lists and diagrams of the fleet, pinning cut-outs labelled *Baltimore, Boston, Concord* and all the other names on a big map of the Philippines which they hung in the back hall. It was Dick more than anything else, who brought Paul home for dinner on the first of May. He was almost crazy with excitement. Dewey was sweeping the Spanish fleet from the seas. Just as Paul reached the house a telegraph boy ran up and delivered a wire. It was from a friend in the Navy Department, telling Paul of Dewey's complete victory. Paul rushed out to the yard where Louise, submerged in querulousness and nausea, was lying on her settee with Dickie reading aloud to her. Paul was waving the telegram and the evening paper and shouting.

"Come on, Dick!" he yelled. "Let's go down to the mill and give the boys the news."

Dick flung aside his book and vaulted out of the summerhouse.

"Dad!"

"Cleaned 'em out!" Paul exulted. His face was red and his hair rumpled with excitement. "Sunk the whole blooming Spanish fleet! Come *on!*" He dragged Dick along by the shoulder.

"Oh, Paul," Louise called after them, whining. "It's almost dinner time. Why don't you wait till afterwards to go down there?"

Paul was not listening. Dick was reading the newspaper over his shoulder, pounding his father on the back and giving little yips of joy.

"Our shells, Dad! We sunk 'em. Hoooooooray!"

"Come on, Dick."

They hurried away, leaving Louise, billowing in her pink muslin wrapper, behind. She leaned out of the summerhouse.

"Paul," she called fretfully. "You can't take Dickie away now. It's dinner time. Don't take him down to that dirty old mill."

By that time Dick was out in the stable helping Jones to harness up and Paul, having grabbed his hat, was hurrying out the front gate to meet them. All the way down to the mill Dick jogged up and down with excitement and Paul sat with his fists clenched, moved by a surge of intense feeling. His shells. His very own shells. No other mill in the country even made any. If only Pa could be here!

They jumped out at the mill entrance and ran across the bridge. Inside they were met by a wave of frightful heat; every furnace in the place was going full blast and out in the rolling mill the noise was ear-splitting. Dickie's face was scarlet with heat and excitement.

They hurried straight through the mill, stalking from shed to shed, spreading the news as they went. Faces broke into tough grins, big fists shot up in the air, voices bellowed in their wake. In the blooming mill Paul stopped by Charlie Liska and shouted in his ear. Charlie's fierce dark face creased into a beatific smile, and cupping his huge hands he let out a roar in Slovak that brought every Hunky in earshot on the run. From other sheds the men came hurrying; heaters and boilers and hammerers and casters running from wherever they could leave their work. They crowded around Paul, shaking his hand, slapping his shoulders, talking in a babble of English and Slovak, and finally joining together in three deafening cheers that even drowned out the racket of the rolls. Paul stood there with tears in his eyes, clutching Dickie by the hand. He did not say anything. But after the men dispersed and went back to their places he turned to Dickie and said in a thick, choked voice, "Son, I don't want you ever to forget this. Our mill is the finest thing in our lives. It's done this for our country before, and I wish your grandfather could be here tonight to know what his mill has done this time."

By late summer Paul was living on the last limit of his nerves. The protocol concluding the war was signed on the twelfth of August. For the six preceding months the mill had worked at the highest output record in its history, turning out the armor-piercing projectiles for the Navy. The award of that contract to Scott's had caused universal amazement and some bitter jealousy in the industry. How such a small mill, with limited facilities, could have had the audacity to bid for and win a contract for twenty-seven thousand precision projectiles was incomprehensible to the larger manufacturers. Still more confounding was the rigid accuracy of schedule by which the material went out. That was the triumph of Paul's management, backed up by the kind of cooperation from his men which his competitors begrudged him. He had no right to get such work out of a mill where he was actually using Hunkies alongside the Irish and Scotch and local boys. He had hardly taken on any extra labor, either. He had done the whole thing with his regular force of three hundred skilled men. He had not over-extended his facilities. He would not be faced with lay-offs when the time came to readjust his schedules to normal.

But he could not, he told himself disgustedly, manage anything else about his life so well, or even at all. Louise's behavior he found intolerable. She had refused to go away at all during the summer. Day after day from morning until night she complained, nagged, wept, snapped at the children, snapped at Mary, snapped at Paul. The boys grew troublesome and cranky, cooped up in town. Paul was furious every time he looked at them, thinking of the summer vacation they should be having. Mary took the twins to New Jersey for a couple of weeks finally, but Louise refused to let Dickie go along. Her clinging to him was intense and unhealthy; it revolted Paul and he resorted to subterfuges to get Dick out of the house and away from Louise. Her wail was that nobody but Dickie understood or loved her; nobody else ever had, except her father. One evening Paul asked Doctor McClintock why Louise kept on upchucking all through her pregnancy when normal women got over it after the early weeks. The doctor gave him a despairing look and said, "She does it on purpose. Every time she feels she's not the center of your attention."

"Almighty suffering God!" Paul exploded in Mary's sitting-room. He wrenched nervously at his moustache. "What did I *do*, Mary? What did I do to bring this down on myself?"

She turned away heartsick.

September nineteenth dawned just like any other Monday. The sun was too high and too hot for a fall day. The boys, cheated of their summer by the sea, were pale and peaked and cranky. Louise, late in her sixth month, was unbearably trying. Today was washday. Mary was halfway through fall housecleaning, the biggest upheaval of the year, and Flora was moaning in her room with cramps.

And it had been only on the Saturday before, when the mail came, that Mary realized today would be the twenty-fifth anniversary of her arrival in this house. Constance, of all people, had remembered and reminded her! On Sunday night Mary knelt by her bed in Constance's old room, surrounded by pictures and mementos of long-treasured events, memories that harked all the way back to the first journey she had taken with the family when they all went to Boston for William's wedding. Vividly Mary remembered the twins in their pork-pie hats and copper-tipped shoes. Vividly she remembered William Scott, bearded and majestic, carving the roast mutton on her first night with the family. Richard Kane's ghastly face flashed through her mind as she thought of that night; and flashing, carried a strange, sharp impression of Louise.

How could you contain the vast accumulation of these memories! Mary wondered, resting her forehead against the patchwork quilt, and quite forgetting to pray. Her fingers slipped mechanically over her rosary. The remotest chords in her mind seemed to chant *Hail Mary, Holy Mary* while all in the front of her head this mass of memories and pains and sorrows and, she thought, singularly few joys, swirled and mounted tumultuously. Paul. Paul. Paul was everywhere. Down in the shanty on the Flat; holding her in his arms under the trees the night Constance eloped; following her to the attic when she went to get out luggage to pack for London. How could she remember these moments, she asked herself, odd, single, striking things which flew at her out of the buried past, when the crowded present was heavier still with Paul's daily presence?

And James! How he would have driven himself and the men this past year when the mill was working with every expert eye in the nation focussed on it! He and Charlie Liska were two of a kind . . . but James wouldn't have liked Charlie . . . that was a strange thought. Bridget, too; would the dark abyss of the unknown yield that secret some day? Edgar; dear Edgar who had sent her the most beautiful letter, and a Missal magnificently printed and bound by the monks at Monte Cassino. Constance, above all. Next to Paul she loved Constance better than any living soul. Constance's letter, coming on the same ship as Edgar's, had gone to Mary's heart with intense poignancy. "We can't see, darling," Constance had said in closing, "why our lives take the shapes they do. I have no religion, but I do believe in something. I think it's simply you. You represent all the faith and loyalty and decency and virtue I ever knew. More than Mama, even, because Mama didn't carry the cross you bear. I know. Never forget that I know, it's the only thing I can give you."

Only Paul had not mentioned the day, and Mary dismissed any possibility that he could remember it. How could he, and why should he, with everything he had to do? She went downstairs early after telling Flora to stay in bed with a hot-water bottle. Breakfast proceeded as usual. Louise remained upstairs while Mary, in order to supervise the boys, took her place at the table. Paul finished his coffee and his *Gazette*, kissed Tommy and Teddy as Margaret took them upstairs, looked at Dick's arithmetic lesson, and left the room after Mary. He knocked on the door of her sitting-room and entered. She was just about to go down to the kitchen to make the marketing list with Anna. Paul went over and took her in his arms and kissed her gently.

"I don't know what's the phrase for the occasion," he said, "but I don't have to say it anyway, Mary." They stood for a moment, each gazing at the other's face. She had thought Paul looked just the same, ever since he had grown that impressive moustache. But he did not. Lines had dug themselves between his nose and his firm mouth; the sharp angle under his cleft chin had filled in with a little flesh; there were two heavy perpendicular grooves in his forehead. His grave eyes studied her carved features. The fine, high-bridged nose, the deepset, penetrating eyes; the beautiful white forehead with the crisp hair springing up from it—Paul put his fingers on her shining hair.

"It's fading," Mary said with a shaky laugh. "I'm forty years old. See?" She stretched her fingertips over her right cheek, turning it a little toward the light. "Wrinkles, too."

Paul swallowed. He put his hand into his pocket and brought out a purple velvet jeweler's box, with a small white envelope tied to it. He thrust it into Mary's hands and then blew his nose loudly. She opened the envelope first, very slowly. Constance's handwriting; For our Mary, on the twenty-fifth anniversary of her love, loyalty, and devotion to us. Constance, Edgar, and Paul.

Tears ran down Mary's cheeks. She stood holding the box and weeping. "Open it, Mary."

She touched the spring. The lid flew open, there was a flash of color, and her hand snapped the box shut again. She went over to her desk and sat down and put her head on her arms and sobbed. Paul went and knelt beside her. He whispered in her ear for a moment, dried her eyes with his handkerchief, and making a poor effort at recovery, said, "Come on now, Mary, let's really look at it. It's quite nice, you know."

She laughed then and opened the box once more. A watch lay on white velvet; a chatelaine watch on a bowknot pin. Three superb pear-shaped emeralds were set with their points centered to form a shamrock on the watch-case, completely surrounded by a paving of small diamonds. The pin was a twisted ribbon of emeralds and diamonds exquisitely worked together.

"It's—beautiful," Mary breathed. "It's the most beautiful thing I ever saw." She sat and stared at it. "Why, that can't be for *me!*" she said suddenly.

The door opened. Paul sprang to his feet. Louise stood in the doorway, her swollen body draped in an orchid-colored wrapper, her brown curls tousled from the pillows. Her face was puffy and grayish.

"What are you doing here?" she asked in a vicious tone.

Paul looked at her coolly.

"Today is the twenty-fifth anniversary of Mary's coming to our family," he said calmly. "I have just given Mary her present from all of us."

Louise gasped sharply. She looked from Paul to Mary with a quick snap of her head. Two expressions flashed across her face; first she started to smile, that saccharine smile of long habit; then her brown eyes narrowed and she pinched her mouth shut. Mary was still sitting quietly staring at the watch in its box. She expected to hear anything, but Louise only said, acid with sarcasm,

"Ah, an anniversary. Why didn't you tell me? We could have planned something to celebrate it."

Paul opened his mouth and started to say something. But Mary looked up quickly and said, "Oh, it's nothing to make a fuss about, Louise. I wouldn't have wanted you to bother."

Louise was moving across the room from the door. Her eyes were glued to the box on the desk.

"Let me see that," she said. Her voice sounded strangled; she had tried to make it light and casual but she was choking with rage.

Mary sat back and kept the open box between her hands. She let Louise look over her shoulder at it. Instinct told her, without her looking at Louise's twitching fingers, what would have happened if she had let her touch the box. Louise stood there, breathing loudly through her mouth. Paul watched her in a cloud of resentment and dull disgust. Louise mumbled something inarticulate, swept the desk with her sharp eyes, and snatched up the card which was lying on it.

" 'Constance, Edgar, and Paul,' " she read aloud. Then she screamed suddenly, "I don't believe a word of it. They had nothing to do with it. You gave her that piece of jewelry," she panted, walking slowly towards Paul. Her swollen breasts swung inside the loose wrapper. "Didn't you?"

Mary closed her eyes and shuddered. Paul stood staring coldly at Louise.

"I just told you," he said, "that my brother and sister and I gave Mary that watch and I will not insult Mary or them or myself by any further talk about it with you. Go upstairs and go back to bed."

Louise's hands shot above her head, fists clenched and shaking in a wild gesture.

"You're a liar!" she screamed. Paul's mouth set in a tragic downward line, too awful for mere shame. Mary sat with her head turned away, toward the wall. Paul's nostrils flared and he took a letter from his pocket, handing it to Louise with a contemptuous motion.

"There is Edgar's letter to me. You can read it and see all his directions to me about this present. Even"— Paul's voice was quavering with disgust and rage—"how I was to draw on his account and Constance's for their share of—the *bill.*" He did everything he could to put insult into his choice of words. Louise stood reading the letter, her hands shaking and her chin quavering. Her mouth hung open. She looked up dully and said, "Sometimes I'd like to kill you."

Paul stood perfectly still. "I wish to God you would. Since I can't hope for such a happy release, will you please go upstairs and let me get myself in hand before I go to the mill."

He opened the door and pointed. Louise hesitated, her glance darting from Paul to Mary and back. She moistened her lips. Then she appeared to realize suddenly what a dreadful spectacle she had made of herself; she drew herself up clumsily and said, leaving the room, "I will be waiting for you when you come home this evening. I want to talk to you then."

Mary sat wretchedly at her desk. Paul walked the hearthrug. Mary said finally, "You aren't going to let her put on another scene like that tonight? Don't subject yourself to it, Paul. I'm leaving."

He did not really take that in. If he had thought she meant it he would have gone to pieces himself. He was hideously shaken. He only said, "Oh —well. Yes. For the time being."

Mary knew better than to argue about that now. She was leaving. It was entirely unthinkable to do anything else. But she would try to do it without too drastic punishment of Paul. She at least would be as undramatic as it was humanly possible to be.

Paul stopped pacing. He said, "Once for all this thing is going to be thrashed out. Sick or well, pregnant or not, she's going to get what she's asking for. I'm going to the mill now"—he looked hastily at his watch— "I'm late for an appointment. But I'm coming back here tonight and tell Louise precisely what her orders are from now on. I've had enough."

"But, Paul." Perhaps she should try to explain.

"Yes?" Even to Mary his tone was sharp and severe.

"I don't think I can stay here under these circumstances. It's always been—difficult. I think I can't cope with it any longer."

"The circumstances will be different," Paul said firmly, "and you will stay. Unless you'll go away with me, Mary?"

"Holy Mother of God!" She covered her face with her hands.

."I admit it would be impossible now on account of the boys. So—"

There was no use trying to argue or explain anything to him now. She had never seen him in this mood of didactic command. Her own mind was made up, her own will just as stubborn as his, but this was no time to set the issue. She merely said, "I'll be away—later—Paul—"

He nodded silently, turned, and left the room.

CHAPTER LI

[*1898—Continued*]

THE DAY PASSED curiously fast. Down at the mill Paul drove himself at double speed, avoiding even a possible five minutes in which to think. He saw as many people, listened to as much talk as he could. He drove over to the club for lunch and thoroughly enjoyed the comments of the men who were still talking impressively about Scott's remarkable feat with the Navy projectiles. Promptly at six o'clock he closed and locked his office, put on his hat, and walked briskly home. He had a romp with the twins in the yard, helped Dick to do his homework, and ate dinner alone with him in the cool, dark dining-room. They talked about open-hearth alloy processes the whole time. Paul had a strange sense of detachment from some major segment of his own mind. Louise was upstairs in her room, perhaps a pulp of hysterics. He had not thought and would not think of her until it suited him to do so.

After Dick went upstairs to bed Paul sat and smoked his pipe for a while in the back parlor. Once he opened the door into Mary's sitting-room. He lit the gas there and walked slowly around the room, reading the titles of the books in the shelves, idly picking up and setting down a tea-cup, staring at her silver-backed blotter with its traces of her fine, pointed handwriting. He did not believe for a moment that she had left here for good. He was actually too stunned for such a thought to penetrate his head. It was only natural for her to go away now. She must be down at the House, he thought. That was where she would go. Thank God he had bought the House. Thank God for anything that might give her a fragment of peace and respite. He knocked out his pipe, turned out the gas, and went upstairs.

Louise was sitting up in bed knitting a pink baby-jacket. Her hair was brushed and tied round with a ribbon and her face, puffy and unhealthy though it was, freshened and powdered with orris-root. She lifted her face as if expecting Paul to kiss her. He ignored the motion and went and sat down by the hearth. Neither of them spoke for some time. Then Louise said, "I'm sorry about this morning, Paul. I didn't mean what I said."

Paul said, "Those are not things you can say and take back afterwards, Louise."

She sniffed. "Well, I'm apologizing anyway."

"I accept your apology for myself if it's any comfort to you," he said, "but I cannot forgive your insulting Mary."

Louise laid down her knitting. It was irregular and full of lumps and holes. Even a man could see that.

"Always full of concern for Mary, aren't you?" she whined.

Paul ignored that.

"Aren't you?" Louise repeated sharply.

He looked up and stared at her.

"The time has come," he said, "for you to pull yourself together. I've tried my level best for thirteen years to—"

"Oh," she said. "So you even know how long we've been married? Since you forgot our tenth anniversary and remembered this thing of hers today I'd have thought you wouldn't notice—"

"Louise!" Paul had never spoken to her in such a thunderous tone. She looked at him, startled, and began to cry.

"Well, it's true," she wailed. "How do you think I felt seeing those emeralds? Emeralds—for a *servant*—after the way you treated me?"

"The watch was not my idea. It was Constance's."

"Oh." Louise drew herself together in bed like a cat about to spring. "I suppose your whole behavior toward Mary was Constance's idea. I guess the way you've been in love with her all your life was Constance's idea. I—"

Paul braced himself. "Something's got to be done to straighten you out," he said. "You lie up here brooding and inventing things and feeding yourself on them until you're poisoned through and through and incapable of a decent thought."

"Oh, I do? Maybe I like to lie here alone and brood. Try it sometime. Try it, instead of sitting down there in that nasty room talking secrets with her. Try remembering I'm your wife and see how that feels!"

"As if I could forget it!"

"There. You see?" Louise heaved her heavy misshapen body from her bed and lunged across the floor. She stood swaying in front of Paul. Her toes curled down on the carpet.

"I told you I was going to talk to you and now I'm doing it. Now you'll sit there and listen to me." She licked her lips. "I'm going to throw her out. I've stood it long enough. She's got to go."

"She has gone." Paul ignored Louise's gasp. "But she'll be back," he said. "I mean her to come back."

"You would have the indecency to say that. Why, you're admitting right now what she means to you. And I won't have it!" Louise's voice slid upward to a shriek. "I won't have it. Flesh and blood can't stand it. That—that—" she gargled thickly. "Under the same roof with your own sons. I was crazy ever to let you bring her here."

Paul looked at his wife with loathing. "It was because you are crazy that I had to bring her here."

"Wha—" she drowned her own words in a drawn-out scream. She dropped on her knees and began beating her clenched fists on the floor. Her tangled hair fell over her eyes. She began to sob and gulp in long, shuddering breaths. Paul rose, grasped her by the shoulders, and propelled her back to bed. She kicked and struggled, but let him seat her on the side of the bed, swing her swollen legs into it, and draw the covers over her. She flung herself on her side and sobbed into the pillows. Paul stood and watched her for a time. Then he sat down on the edge of the bed and put his hand on her shoulder.

"Lou," he said quietly. "I don't claim to be all in the right and you all in the wrong. We've got to work something out. Something at least that will keep things together on account of the boys. But one thing you must get through your head. You have never acted like a grown-up woman about your house and your children and your responsibilities. That was why I had to bring Mary here when Mama was dying. Somebody had to—"

"*My* house? *My* children?" she cried, gasping. "I never had a chance to call them my own. You took them away from me and gave them to her!"

Paul sighed. "That's not true. You had your chance. I let you go on by yourself for five years, remember that—before I had to step in and do something. Even then you didn't protest her coming here. You liked it. It left you free to—"

"To have more children for you. To be sick and miserable twenty-four hours a day. Too bad you can't have a baby and see how I feel now. *You* ought to know what it's like."

She clutched her breast with her veined, edemic hands. Her brown eyes had no trace of their softness or brightness; they were hot, clouded, and red-rimmed. She was, Paul thought, the most awful sight he had ever laid eyes on. He pressed his hands to his throbbing head. Nothing, he knew perfectly well, could come of this scene. All his firm talk of the morning was meaningless. He knew desperately that he was trapped. For the first time he realized that Mary would have to go. To give in to this mass of shuddering, noisy flesh on the bed would mark the last milestone of his undoing. But he would have to do it. After this Mary could not, even if she would, be subjected any longer to life in the house with Louise. Then he thought of the boys. How could he, how could any rational person, leave three—no, four—children in the house with this slobbering hysteric? He could get another housekeeper, he would have to; but who on earth, without Mary's compelling motive, would stay in such a place? He shook his head wretchedly and sank into a chair, clutching his skull between his hands. Louise sat and eyed him through twitching, narrowed lids. He looked up presently and said in a dead voice, "The awful thing is, I've tried so hard."

She gave a shrill cackle. "Tried? Yes, you've tried. Tried to fool me all these years while you carried on with a servant right under my roof." Her jaw wagged. "Liar."

Paul clenched his fists and rammed his gritted teeth against them. Louise sat hunched and tense in the middle of the bed, her mouth open and moving. He looked at her and said hoarsely, "I'm damned sorry that isn't true."

She caught her breath with a sharp noise. "So you admit it!" she screamed. "You admit you're in love with her. You always have been.

Everybody knows it. Everybody in your family, everybody in town. It's been a scandal for twenty years."

"Then why in the name of Almighty God did you marry me?" Paul's voice was leaden.

"I don't know," she wailed. "I suppose because I've always loved you. Daddy always wanted me to. I always did what Daddy said. I thought your—your affair—was all over. Mama told me all young men did things like that. And then you brought her—her"—she ground her teeth—"right into the house where you could—"

"Shut up!" Paul sprang from his chair and roared.

"I won't. It's true. It's all true. You've done—those things with her—"

"*You* didn't keep me from her," Paul said slowly through his teeth, spacing his words. "Not you. My boys did. I tried to make a home for them. I had only her to help me—"

"Help?" Louise screamed. "That's why you bought her that house in Nixon Street—so she could help you there. Go on and keep your dirty biddy of a mistress, go on, go on—"

"All right!" Paul strode to the door. "So help me God, I will!"

The house shook as the street door slammed with a shattering crash.

He strode bareheaded down the hill to the mill district, his feet moving in great pounding stamps, his coat flying open as he walked. He was not thinking. He did not know what was driving him, what might be the end of the seething fury in his body and his head. He wanted only motion. No thoughts. When he did look up and focus his eyes away from the toes of his boots, he found himself staring at the dark front of the house in Nixon Street. He stood there. He thought he meant to walk up the front steps and put his big thumb on the doorbell and hold it there until she came and opened the door. He meant his hands and feet to do those things. But nothing happened. He stood in the street and stared at the plain dark green door with the polished brass handle, at the neat, drawn window shades. He knew she was in there. He did not think she had gone anywhere else. He belonged in there too. He belonged wherever she was. Why did his numb hand not raise itself and ring the doorbell?

He turned slowly away, his head bent, his heavy shoulders sagging. He could not do it. If he had done it he would have asked one thing more of her when she had already turned the whole stream of her life into a tortuous false channel which he had dug. He had left its true course dry and barren. The one he had shaped was painful, too deep, too jagged. He could not ask anything more. He never knew that he had stood two hours in that street.

He moved on down the hill now, still blind to his whereabouts, still going by instinct, making his way through the maze of alleys that converged on the street leading to the mill. A raw wind ruffled his bare head and swept through his light suit. He stalked along looking neither right nor left, sensible only of a desire to hold his mind closed—closed, he told himself over and over, against the merest possibility of a thought. He would not think. Sooner or later he would have to do the hardest, longest, most painful thinking of his entire life. He could not face that yet. It took all the strength he had to keep from thinking or feeling anything now.

His laboratory, off at the end of the casting-shed, had a door of its own opening out on the yard. Paul took his keys from his pocket, unlocked this iron door, and stepped inside. Part of the mill was still running on night shift, but not this part. From the farthest end of the buildings he could hear the clatter of the rolling mill. He lit the gaslights, hung his coat on a hook, put on an acid-proof apron, and immediately plunged into a formula on which he had been working for some time past. It was complicated and absorbing; but from time to time the furiously suppressed volcano in his brain stirred and rumbled and threatened to erupt. Each time Paul cursed and rammed it back. He had been there several hours, bent scowling over his burners and retorts, when he heard running footsteps outside in the cindery yard, then pounding on the laboratory door. Paul looked up, twitching with anger.

"Who's there?"

"It's me, sir—Jones."

"What do you want?"

"Open the door. Please, Mr. Scott, please—"

Paul opened it. Jones was panting, terror in his face. He stumbled over the threshold.

"What's the matter, Jones?"

"Please, sir—I—they sent me—" his Adam's apple bobbed inside the collar of his nightshirt, over which he had dragged on his trousers and broadcloth coat.

"Jones, tell me at once what's happened."

The man began to blubber. "Mrs. Scott, sir. Jesus—it's Mrs. Scott."

CHAPTER LII

[*December 1900*]

WILLIAM SCOTT had not been inside the mill for seventeen years. This December afternoon, gray and gloomy and thick with the acrid fumes of soft coal, reminded him startlingly of the day he had last walked from this place. Nothing might have changed, he thought, driving in a livery hack from the Pennsylvania Station across the Manchester Bridge to the mill. He sat silent, quite ignoring his companion who leaned forward from time to time to look up and down the stretch of the many-bridged river and exclaim at the blazing furnaces which trimmed it like devil's jewels. Nothing seemed to have changed here, William thought. But this was the first year of a new century, and the age had shaken itself and come to birth a full-grown giant. This hill-jagged region of belching stacks, bare stripped coal lands, mile upon mile of sprawling, wildly illuminated sheds from which endless trainloads of rails and girders and bridge spans and pigs and sheets and bars and billets and ingots streamed out across the country—this region too had come of age. It was visibly scarred and torn, aged and blackened. Its riches of money and power, vast beyond any kingdom's, were not to be seen among the stacks and cinders and flatcars and fires. They lay in a different world of banks and offices, where William felt at ease. For years he had watched in wondering admiration while wealth joined with wealth, force with force, to weld and compress these galvanic forces into ruthless bludgeons of financial power.

He looked curiously at the Scott mill as the horse clopped along the cobbled approach to the entrance. It did not seem possible that this tangle of dirty sheds and blackened stacks and the bulky monstrosity of the old Henrietta could comprise anything anybody could want. He had loathed it with every nerve and fibre the first half of his life. But he saw it in a different light today.

He was fifty now, and he looked all of that descending stiffly from the cramped hack and escorting his companion over the bridge to the main entrance. William had not seen this bridge since before the tragedy of his father's death here. He looked curiously at the oft-renewed coal-black planks as if they could hold some trace of the Old Man's presence.

Paul met them at the door of the outer office.

"You remember Selden Middleton, Paul."

They all shook hands gravely and took places around a fumed oak table which replaced the older one of William's bitter memories.

"Well," said Paul tentatively, "this is quite a surprise."

William cleared his throat.

"It's very natural to see you here at the old stand, Paul. How are things?"

"Pretty good. I can't complain." Paul was handing cigars round and filling his pipe. "We've had a busy year. I suppose you know I sent samples of our new rapid-cutting tool steel to the Paris Exhibition last summer, Bill. It seemed to make quite an impression."

"I know about it," Middleton said with a smile. "I was there. It made more than an impression, it was a sensation. Of course," he said gruffly, "I don't understand much about the technicalities of these things, Mr. Scott, but this mill of yours has attracted remarkable attention the past two or three years. Remarkable."

"Well," Paul said, "we work hard."

There was an awkward silence. Then William said, "Paul, I suppose we might as well come to the point. Middleton came out here with me because he has something he wants to talk over with you. It concerns all of us in the family and I—well, I'm deeply interested."

Selden Middleton looked from one of the Scotts to the other, shooting his heavy-browed eyes from William's faded, narrow face to Paul's broad, serious, kindly one. William Scott's high forehead was accentuated by sparse gray hair. Paul's head had a look of abundance and solidity; his blond hair and full moustache were as thick as ever, though faded in color. He bent his head and stared back at Middleton from lowered eyelids.

"Why don't you start right in and talk?" he asked.

Middleton examined his cigar.

"I suppose you know," he began slowly, "that all these big consolidations in the steel industry in recent years have been moving toward a climax lately."

Paul nodded, quite expressionless. William watched him closely, turning sidewise in his chair to avoid facing his brother directly. Middleton spoke very slowly, choosing his words and keeping his eyes on Paul. He had a feeling already that nothing he was about to say would come as a surprise to this man, or would elicit any spontaneous reaction. He had come prepared to play his cards very close to his chest; he was a bit nonplussed to find that Paul Scott already gave indications of doing the same thing. Somehow he had sized him up differently at their one meeting in William Scott's house. Perhaps it was the surroundings, grim and noisy, with a freight engine hissing outside the dirty windows, that set him unaccustomedly ill at ease.

"Now you may remember," Middleton continued, "that when we met a few years ago I mentioned to you my interest in the Oliver Iron Mining Company. That was the beginning of a series of moves by which I acquired holdings in the H. C. Frick Coke Company."

He paused. Paul still listened attentively and inscrutably.

"You will forgive my going back into certain personal details," Middleton said with a deprecating gesture, "but I want to give you the background of this whole picture."

"By all means," Paul said.

"Good. Of course you followed the negotiations last winter when the Frick Company was merged with the Carnegie Steel Company. That resulted in the arrangement by which we—I mean the Frick stockholders, who supported Mr. Frick during Carnegie's attempt to oust him—have now acquired stock and bonds of the Carnegie Steel Company in exchange for our previous holdings."

He paused to relight his cigar.

"I have some four hundred and fifty shares of stock in the Carnegie Company," Middleton said slowly, "and approximately an equal holding in bonds."

He stopped speaking as if to allow Paul to calculate the value of these holdings, which Paul promptly did. The Carnegie stock had been issued at par value of a thousand dollars a share; Middleton's interest therefore was about a million altogether. Paul's eyebrows moved slightly. He smiled a little and said, "And the next step is this billion-dollar consolidation they are putting together in New York and calling the United States Steel Corporation."

Now Middleton smiled.

"Correct," he said.

"We watch these things out here," Paul said, "in a kind of a way. That was quite a junket those bankers made to visit Henry Frick here."

"There have been quite a few meetings in New York also," Middleton said.

"Oh yes. Bill here thinks I hate Carnegie so much I don't even notice his existence, but I hear about it when he gives those little dinners for J. P. Morgan and Charlie Schwab. Well, Mr. Middleton, what next?"

Middleton felt more on the defensive than ever. But, imperturbable in his bearded dignity, he took an alligator-skin letter-case from his breast pocket, extracted a memorandum from it, and held it in his hand.

"The plans," he said, "for the prospective steel corporation include some dozen or so companies and mills. Let's just run over them—it would be informative, I think."

He cleared his throat and read from the memo in his hand.

"First, the Carnegie Company. One hundred and sixty million each of capital stock and of bonds."

William swallowed and turned toward Paul.

"Think of it!" he exclaimed. "Think of the size of it!"

"I am thinking," Paul said shortly. "Go on, Mr. Middleton."

"Then comes the Federal Steel Company, with forty-six million in common stock, fifty-three million preferred. These are round figures, of course. Then the National Tube Company, about forty million each of common and preferred. National Steel Company, around thirty million of common and of preferred. American Bridge Company, thirty million of each. American Steel and Wire Company, forty-nine million common, thirty-nine preferred."

William was leaning forward, fascinated by the recital of astronomical figures. Paul sat back, smoking his pipe.

"Next the American Tin Plate Company, with thirty million common and eighteen preferred. American Steel Hoop Company, nineteen million common, fourteen million preferred. American Sheet Steel Company, twenty-four and twenty-four. The Lake Superior Iron Mines, twenty-nine and a half million common." He paused. Then he said, "As you of course see from this list, Mr. Scott, the basic idea is to put together a corporation which will contain at least one of every kind of major steel producing unit. We have covered the field thoroughly. Ore, coal, coke, transportation both land and water, blast furnaces, plants devoted to Bessemer and open-hearth steels; crucible steels; rail, bridge, sheet, plate, tube, and wire mills—well, I need not bore you with details about which you are infinitely better informed than I. The point is, finally—" he hesitated.

"That you want an alloy and specialty-steel mill," Paul said dryly.

"Precisely." Middleton sat back and smiled. William heaved a sigh as if of relief. He was unexpectedly grateful to Paul for coming out with the thing himself.

Paul champed his pipe-stem reflectively.

"Well, now, Mr. Middleton," he said, "don't you think my—our—mill is a bit smallish in that kind of company?" He pointed to the memo. "We're just a little family concern. This isn't our kind of speed."

William broke in.

"It isn't the size of the mill they care about, Paul, it's the quality. They haven't got a unit where anybody does research like yours."

Paul's lips twitched. He had not looked for anything so obvious from Bill who was, after all, pretty smooth after his years in Boston.

"Well, I'm not going to waste your time," he said to Middleton. "The idea looks ridiculous to me, but what's your offer? I gather you are representing the crowd in New York. Or did Bill think this up?" He smiled at his brother.

"Why—" William had no answer ready.

"Oh—it was—just one of those things," Middleton said, waving his hand. "Your brother and I have had a good many dealings in recent years, what with Laurence Gaylord's estate and one thing or another. I've been interested, naturally, in your mill here. It's quite unique, after all. Those Navy projectiles you made, and that stuff I saw last summer. Quite unique."

"Well, are you making an offer now?" Paul asked.

"Oh, certainly. Now I understand that this is a partnership business. You—ah—have no stock, that is, you are unincorporated?"

"I know Bill has told you all the details," Paul said easily. "You don't have to feel your way, Mr. Middleton. We are a partnership business owned entirely by my brothers and sisters and myself. So any offer would be on the basis of a straight sale, not an exchange of stock or anything of that sort. Bill has also doubtless told you what he thinks the company is worth, and he's probably right about that. What figure did he give you?" Paul asked suddenly, in a sharp changed tone. He leaned forward.

Middleton looked at William, who looked uneasily at Paul.

"Why," William said, looking uncomfortable, "I think I said about two and a half million, didn't I, Selden?"

"Three would be more exact," Paul said, "but it doesn't matter when you're dealing with stuff like that." He pointed again at Middleton's memorandum.

"In that case," said Middleton, visibly making a mental revision of something he had decided before, "I would be instructed to offer you two and a half million in seven per cent cumulative preferred stock of the projected corporation, and a million and a half more in United States Steel common."

He sat back and looked at the ceiling. William looked at Paul.

Paul gave no indication of surprise or any other marked reaction, but he did turn his head and stare for a minute at William.

I bet he's palpitating with eagerness, Paul said to himself.

The silence lasted quite a long time. Then Middleton coughed and said, "Of course this is just a talking proposition so far, Mr. Scott."

"Of course," agreed Paul. He was thinking of his father. If the Old Man were here now the glass would be rattling in the windowpanes and these two chaps would be scurrying around looking for their hats and overcoats. Paul almost laughed at the picture. He was also quite startled to find how calmly he really took this; it must be because he had always expected something of the kind and he had learned long ago not to rush out and meet issues headlong. They caught up with you soon enough.

"I don't want to commit myself too far at this preliminary stage of the matter," Middleton was saying. "but in general you could expect to realize the total book value of your company in preferred stock, and we would about match that in common. In other words—"

"Not quite double our holdings," Paul said.

"Approximately. Of course it would depend on the condition of your property—" Middleton raised his eyes and looked doubtfully around the bare, ugly, dun-colored room as if it had anything to do with the mill's capacity to make steel.

"Of course," Paul said again.

Both men waited for him to say something more. William leaned forward and clasped his thin, perfectly groomed hands on the table before him. He wanted very much to get a real reaction from Paul. He wanted desperately for Middleton to pull this thing off successfully. He wanted beyond endurance the three quarters of a million or more in United States Steel stock that he would get out of this, and he could not conceive that Paul and all the others would not be just as eager to have like amounts themselves. Whether the mill lost its identity and Paul his life work had really never crossed William's mind. He said finally, to break the silence, "How do you feel about it, Paul?"

Paul put his pipe carefully down, balancing it on the edge of the table. For one fleeting instant he looked at William with the full impact of scorn that this whole thing roused in him. Then he resumed his calm good nature and said, "Of course I couldn't possibly give an answer now. For one thing, Mr. Middleton, since Bill told you so much else about the company, did he explain the stipulations of my father's will in respect to partnerships?"

"More or less."

"Then you understand that this sale could only be consummated through a two-thirds or majority vote of the five partners?"

"Yes. I understand that."

"And it would take a certain amount of time to call a meeting and poll the partners about this."

"Naturally." William said that, with a look of satisfaction. He was relieved at Paul's calm reaction to this offer. He had feared that Paul might make a quick refusal and force him into taking legal action to bring the question to a vote. He murmured something about his gratification that Paul was being so open-minded about it.

"Oh, you can't dismiss an offer to double your property," Paul said. He said it so consideredly that for a minute William felt as if there must be some barb in the remark and he was not quick enough to perceive it.

"So we will consider it very carefully," Paul said, rising from his chair, "and that will take some time. We have a brother and sister in Europe. That takes time. And finally, there is the voting."

William and Selden Middleton exchanged a heavy look.

Paul took out his watch.

"It's nearly seven," he said. "We will just get home in time for dinner." He took Middleton's fur-collared overcoat from the rack and held it for him.

"Why—er—" William said uncomfortably.

Paul turned to him with surprise.

"You aren't staying somewhere else, surely? I took it for granted you'd stay with me. I can put you both up."

"That's very kind of you," Middleton said quickly. "As a matter of fact I am taking the night train to New York. I must be in Boston to-morrow."

"I have to take that train myself," William said, a little too quickly. "I told Julia—"

"Well, you have plenty of time for dinner," Paul said casually. "The train doesn't leave till nearly midnight. Jones must be waiting up at the gate. Come on."

William had hoped somehow to avoid this. He did not want in the very least to go to the house for dinner, or at all. He was afraid Paul might have Mary at the table. He really knew very little about the status of things in Paul's house, and he wanted to keep his distance. He did not want to be reminded of Louise's ghastly suicide, which had taken place when he was abroad with Julia. He had been spared the funeral and any first-hand contact with that hideous thing: poor Louise with her unborn child lying with her head against the gaslogs in her bedroom—Mama's bedroom. William had scowled and held Julia off when she tried to tell him what details she had learned. Terribly strange details—Louise had been found holding a picture of her father in one hand and an awful, incoherent letter to him in the other. "To her *father*," Julia had said, pursing her mouth and shaking her head. "That man we met at your house—that very first time —dear, dear, isn't it too *dreadful*, William?" It was. William really suffered agonies in the carriage, driving up the hill. But he could not possibly have refused Paul's hospitality without offending him, and this was no time to offend Paul.

CHAPTER LIII

[1900-1901]

WILLIAM'S FEARS WERE unfounded. He had to admit before dinner was over that not since his childhood had he known such calm, such warm, orderly comfort, and such a deeply contented atmosphere in his old home. Cheerful bright light gleamed from the front windows through red-ribboned Christmas wreaths as they walked up the front path. The Christmas tree still stood in the corner of the back parlor where the boys had found it loaded with presents the week before. Dick was waiting for his father at the front door and shook hands cordially with his uncle. He was tall for his age, and very handsome, with Louise's warm coloring and curly brown hair. Only the four of them were at the table together; when Bill inquired for the twins Paul said they would come in after dinner to say good night.

William examined the dining-room with interest. Certain pleasant changes had been made. The flickering, hissing gas-jets had been replaced by the new Welsbach mantels. There was a large Persian rug on the floor instead of the flamboyant Turkey carpet William remembered. The scratchy, slippery horsehair seats of the high-backed oak chairs were gone, and the chairs upholstered in corded red velvet. They ate with the old, massive chased family silver, but in addition to the ice water in the old Waterford goblets they drank an excellent Deidesheimer from thin, pale green Rhine wine glasses. The dinner was unexpectedly good too. William had to concede that the light, creamy cauliflower soup, the roast venison— "Joe Rogers shot it up at Ligonier, you remember him, don't you, Bill?"— the delicate potato dumplings, the rum soufflé could not have been bettered in his own house. He looked at Paul with a new and almost a respectful sort of interest.

"I say, you have a first-class cook," Selden Middleton said when Paul carved a second helping of venison for him.

"I didn't know there were such cooks in Pittsburgh," Bill said.

"Oh, we get along," Paul remarked with a laugh. "Trude, open another bottle of wine, please."

William gazed about the room.

"You've kept the house up well, Paul," he said. "I had an impression the Northside was going down."

"I'm afraid that's true," Paul said. "It was dark when we came home so you couldn't see much. The neighborhood is running down, no question about it. Too many boardinghouses and things. But I like it. I wouldn't think of moving."

"I should think you'd be interested in Sewickley," Bill said. "On account of the boys. There's a very good school there, isn't there?"

"Yes," Paul said, "but Allegheny was all right for us and it'll have to do for them too. Won't it, Dick?"

"Good enough for me," Dick said. "They've got what I want at Prep."

"What is that?" asked Middleton politely.

"Math and football, sir."

"That's all he's interested in," Paul explained with pride. "He's going to Sheff, of course."

"Are you not going away to school before you go to Yale?" asked Middleton. Paul saw that any boy of Dick's age who did not go to Groton or Middlesex was incomprehensible to him.

"I was planning to go to Andover," Dick said. He colored slightly. "But since—I mean—now—I think I'd rather stay home with Dad."

"Dick spends every Saturday morning with me at the mill," Paul said. "He knows his way around very well."

"I'm going to work there next summer if Dad will let me," Dick said eagerly.

"How old are you now?" William asked. "Fifteen?"

"Nearly. I will be next month."

"Well, he's too young, Paul. He can't work in the mill yet, can he?"

"Maybe another year," Paul said. "We weren't more than sixteen when Pa took us on, were we? Lord, how you used to hate it!"

William laughed rather shamefacedly. "I'm afraid I did. I fear I was not cut out for an ironmaster."

"Dad was," said Dick. It was a tactless remark, but made with such stout pride that they all smiled.

They had coffee and brandy in the back parlor. Tommy and Teddy came in when they left the dining-room. William exclaimed with surprise when they appeared. "My word, Paul," he said, "what are you raising, a houseful of giants?"

The twins were embarrassed. They were just as tall for their eleven years as Dick was for his age. But they had no other resemblance to one another at all. Tommy had a bush of straight, unruly hair, reddish enough in color to suggest a fleeting resemblance to Constance's, but much darker. His face was thin, tightly put together, with ears lying close to his skull, very white skin heavily peppered with freckles, and restless green eyes. Teddy looked enough like Paul to be his miniature. Here were the broad brow and clear blue eyes and thick blond hair which Clarissa had given to Paul and to her granddaughter Clarrie; the same dreamy expression and gentle—too gentle, for a boy—disposition. When they walked into the room together even a stranger like Middleton could see that Tommy made the decisions for both. Tommy took the lead, ordered Teddy about, imposed his will on his brother. They were a striking sight, in spite of the lumpy clothes, the ugly black stockings, the clumsy shoes, and the chapped stained hands of small boyhood.

Paul made the sort of conversation with them that fathers make when children come in to speak to company. He was not sorry when the mantel clock struck nine and Mary appeared in the doorway.

"Come, boys," she said. "Bed."

William looked up, rising involuntarily to his feet because Middleton was doing so. Mary wore a gleaming, rustling dress of dark brown silk with a high collar edged with malines ruching. Her hair, twisted up in its severe high chignon, shone brilliantly in the white light from the Welsbach mantels. The emerald watch was pinned on her left shoulder. She smiled at William and came across the room holding out her hand. She was slenderer than ever, very light and quick as she moved.

"Hello," she said cordially, "how are you?" William noticed that she avoided speaking his name.

"Splendid, thank you."

Paul was introducing her to Middleton. She paused for a moment, chatting with William about Willy, whose engagement had just been announced; she hoped he was happy? And Angelica? No, William laughed, she was quite fancy-free. Mary turned to the twins.

"It's past bedtime, boys," she said.

Her voice was low and full of authority. The boys said their good nights and went away. Mary followed them presently and Dick went to his room to finish his homework.

"Fine chaps you've got there," Middleton said, helping himself to brandy. William looked conspicuously at his watch. "Now about the matter we were discussing this afternoon, Mr. Scott—do you think you can give me some idea of the time element?"

"Well—" Paul pursed his lips. "Frankly, I don't think I can commit myself on that just yet. But I won't make any unnecessary delays. I'll keep in touch with you right along."

Middleton nodded. William said, "That's good. Well, Selden—" He looked at his watch again.

Making small talk, they moved to the hall to get their coats. Paul saw them out to the carriage. Neither man spoke until they were in the middle of the Sixth Street Bridge. Then Middleton turned suddenly to William and said, "Who is that striking woman in your brother's house?"

William jumped.

"Oh," he said. "Her name is Mary Rafferty. She's my brother's housekeeper." And then, to his own amazement, and quite involuntarily with pride in his voice, he said, "She's been in our family nearly thirty years."

Paul went back to the parlor and put another log of wood on the fire. This open fireplace was an innovation precipitated by the tragedy of Louise. Paul had always taken the gas fireplaces for granted. They were commonplace fixtures, familiar all his life. But after Louise's death he was unable to look at gas logs or gas fireplace heaters without sickening. He went through the house with a contractor and removed them from every room. He wanted open fireplaces, but could not have many without ripping the place to pieces to rebuild all the chimneys. So he compromised with bricking up most of the hearths and facing them with decorated tiles which were much in style. But in the back parlor, because it was in an ell at the rear of the house, he was able to build a real fireplace. It gave him great pleasure, and around it Mary refurnished the room. Paul still clung to his father's old sofa, but now the room contained two brown leather morris chairs, a large, practical desk, a new dark green carpet, a pleasant neutral wallpaper, and curtains of heavy English crewel linen. Paul dropped into a morris chair by the fire and lay back with his pipe.

Presently Mary came in with her sewing and sat down opposite him. She chose a straight chair with low arms; it was comfortable for sewing and it stood beside a table in good light. She poked in a small tin box for shirt-buttons, threaded her needle and set to work on the twins' clothes. She knew that presently Paul would begin to talk and tell her what had brought William and the Boston financier to Pittsburgh.

Before he was halfway through his story Mary forgot all about the mending and sat stiffly on the edge of her chair, with her eyes fixed on his face. Most of the time she had an expression of incredulous protest. When he finally paused, having brought her completely up to the moment, she threw her head in the air and sniffed.

"That's the most preposterous poppycock I ever heard of," she said.

Paul burst out laughing. "Poppycock! A billion dollars' worth! The biggest financial brains in the country put together the biggest corporation in the world and you call it poppycock!"

"Well, that's what it is to us. You surely don't take this offer seriously?"

"Hold on, now. I don't say I'm going to snap it up, but I just tried to explain what this means in money. It's a lot of money, Mary."

"Yes," she said acidly. "A lot of money. What will you do with three quarters of a million dollars? Go and sun yourself on the Riviera? What are the boys supposed to do? Grow up and ask Mr. Carnegie for jobs?"

Paul's lips twitched. "Why not? Somebody might even give me a job."

"*Paul!*" Mary sprang up and stamped her foot. "Are you out of your mind? What's William said to you, the blatherskite!"

Paul stretched his arms over his head and chuckled.

"I never knew you were such a mark," he said. "Go on and give me some more hell."

She blushed suddenly. With a sheepish expression, she sat down. Paul laughed. Then he said, "No, the question simply is how to go about this with the least amount of uproar. You know there'll be a showdown."

"I don't see why. William and Elizabeth vote for the sale and you and Constance and Edgar vote against it. Where's the uproar in that?"

"What makes you so positive Ed and Con will both vote with me?"

"Why—they—because— Why Paul, they're with us—that's all. They *belong* to us."

"Three quarters of a million in cash or the equivalent can have a very surprising influence on people. I don't really think Ed would vote for this sale, but"—Paul spoke more slowly and sucked hard on his pipe—"I'm not so sure about Con."

"I'm amazed at you. Constance has no use for William. Or leave him out of it and think of her going in on anything with Lizzie. It's preposterous."

"Maybe so," Paul said. "But I have a strange feeling about this, Mary. If anything about Con would be preposterous it would be her turning down a chance to realize so much money. She wouldn't want to hurt me, I don't say that, but money—well, you know how she burns it up."

Mary still looked incredulous.

"What's more," Paul went on, "you must think of Con's connections in London. That set she runs around with. Some of those fellows are the biggest money-brains in Europe. She'll ask their advice about this, beyond any doubt, and what do you think they'll tell her? Why, I myself would tell her to jump at this offer if I were in their place and didn't have any personal bias about the thing."

Mary shook her head. "I still think you're underestimating her loyalty."

"My dear girl, loyalty has a saturation-point like everything else. This won't be put to Con in the light of her loyalty to me or of my differences with Bill. It's a business proposition and business"—Paul got up to stir the fire—"is business."

The five partners were informed of the offer simultaneously in a formal notification. All the notices went out so that they should be received on the same day. Edgar's and Constance's were dispatched on the fifteenth of

January. Elizabeth's and William's were mailed on the twenty-first. All were asked either to come to Pittsburgh to cast their votes at a meeting at the mill on Friday, February the fifteenth, or to send their votes by mail or cable on or before that date, if they should be unable to come in person.

Now, thought William up in Boston, there was nothing to do but sit back and wait. He was sure of Lizzie. Certainly Constance with all her luxurious proclivities could not resist this offer. And even Paul, William had reason to believe, was so impressed with the chance almost to double his fortunate that he would find it irresistible. And if Paul wanted to go on making steel, the Scott mill or any other unit of the new corporation would offer him far more salary that he had ever paid himself. He must be seeing this as a magnificent opportunity. As for Edgar—he simply did not count in William's calculations. Poor Edgar was an embarrassing encumbrance whose vote in this matter could not make any difference, and whose existence in a Benedictine monastery was elaborately overlooked by the Episcopalian William Scotts and the Presbyterian Benjamin Nicholases.

Mary doggedly refused to consider the possibility that Constance and Edgar would not automatically vote against the sale. But the more she encouraged herself in that attitude the more she remembered Paul's doubts. At first she told herself that it was merely typical of his judicious mind to see all sides of the question. Then she began to defend her own blind faith in her twins against Paul's realistic analysis. Finally she decided to write to Constance. She knew that Paul would be angry if he found out that she had. If William were to find it out there might be an all-round explosion.

She mailed her letter on the next ship after the one that had carried the notification to Constance. It was a brief letter, in which Mary took the bull by the horns and acknowledged the undeniable financial attractiveness of the offer. But then she went on to point out what an irreparable catastrophe such a sale would be to Paul. She appealed to Constance in brief, sharp words which must impress themselves on her mind and her intense loyalties. Then, praying that her action would never be found out, she too sat back confidently to wait.

She could not foresee what would be the circumstances of the dark twenty-fourth of January when the carrier handed her letter to the footman at Cadogan Square. To be sure, Mary and Paul the previous morning had sat shaking their heads at the breakfast table over the black-headlined news of Queen Victoria's death. It had been expected; it touched them only through the cosmic sense of the passing era; it dramatized the year-old new century in a way that no other event conceivably could. This towering symbol of majesty and permanence and power had dominated their concept of the foreign world ever since they were born. But only now, in a sudden, incisively shocking way, did Mary sit up and realize that this had something to do with Constance, something Mary would not mention or speculate about or discuss even with Paul. She sat silent, breaking a piece of toast to bits and mechanically watching to see that Tommy did not sugar his porridge too thickly, while Paul read the historic news aloud.

She received Constance's cable next day.

HAVE THOUGHT DESPERATELY STOP TERRIBLY AFRAID I SHALL HAVE TO VOTE FOR SALE AS I WILL NEED ALL POSSIBLE MONEY STOP TRY TO FORGIVE UNDERSTAND AND RECONCILE PAUL ALL LOVE CONSTANCE

Mary stood in the front hall, reading the message over and over. At first she could not believe it; she frowned and pored over it as if it were in a strange language. This *could* not be from Constance—Mary thought wildly for a moment that it was some kind of a hoax. Then she remembered Paul's earnest warnings. She had simply not dreamed they could be true. She had thought to dispel any possibility of their being true by writing that letter to Constance. Perhaps that had been a mistake. She saw now that it could be a worse mistake to tell Paul about this, or to try to "reconcile" him.

The loud striking of the grandfather clock made her realize that she must have stood here in the hall more than half an hour. She began to think quickly and furiously. She hurried to her desk, consulted the calendar, and counted off the days until the fifteenth of February. Twenty-one days. That should be plenty of time. Mary put on her hat and coat and hurried out. She took the trolley-car over to Pittsburgh and spent the next two hours downtown.

She did not dare weigh very carefully what she had decided to do. She had never deceived Paul in her life and if she thought too hard about that aspect of this matter she might not have the courage to go through with it now. But she felt determined, pushed on by desperation. Paul was not going to lose that mill. His very quietness, his stern reasonableness about all this, showed deeper feeling than all the protest and talk in the world. If he were to have an inkling of Mary's intentions he would forbid them categorically.

That evening Mary told Paul that her sister Kate had had a bad fall and broken her leg. Kate's eldest daughter, Ellen, was about to have her first child, and the two youngest of Kate's own children were in bed with measles. (God forgive me, Mary prayed wildly as she talked. Some of this was true and some was not, she had jumbled it all up together.)

"So I'll have to go up to Johnstown tomorrow and stay until they're all through this safely," Mary said. She forced herself to look matter-of-factly at Paul. She hoped desperately that she was getting away with this. She must be, because Paul only looked concerned and said, "That's too bad. If they need you I guess you'll have to go."

"Oh, they need me badly."

"Well—how long do you think you'll be?"

Mary gestured. "Why—a broken leg. You know—I suppose three weeks or a month at least. Before she can get about."

"I hope the boys will be all right," Paul said doubtfully. Margaret had been dispensed with nearly two years ago. The twins were too old for a nurse.

"They'll be all right," Mary said reassuringly. "Trude can manage them. They're at school most of the day anyway."

"Well," Paul said slowly, "Dick and I'll keep an eye on 'em as much as we can. But you'll hurry back, Mary?"

"Why, of course," she said. "Just as soon as I can." Oh dear, she thought, I do hate telling lies. I'm no good at it at all, at all.

CHAPTER LIV

[*1901*]

CONSTANCE MET HER at Waterloo. She was dressed entirely in dull black and looked subdued and pale almost to the point, had that been possible, of plainness. The streets as they drove through them were draped in black; shopfronts and gateways were shrouded, and window-blinds uniformly closed. It was a depressing sight.

"How long does this keep up?" Mary asked curiously. "I never saw such a thing."

"Six weeks," Constance said. "That's the official period of court mourning."

They spoke with unusual constraint. Mary had not been able to evoke one natural exclamation or a spontaneous laugh from Constance. Surely she could not be feeling any bereavement for the old Queen. Mary decided that Constance was really sick with guilty remorse for the stand she had taken or was about to take. She was relieved when they pulled up at Cadogan Square and entered the house. Inside, behind the drawn curtains, it was warm and cheerful with bright fires on the hearths, masses of roses and carnations everywhere, and a delicious tea waiting on the low table by the fire in Constance's boudoir. Constance ripped off her black clothes and flung them to her maid.

"Phew!" she exclaimed, stretching herself. She wore her usual exquisite hand-made lingerie rich with real lace, from which her pearly breasts and white shoulders rose like parts of a lush flower. She slid into the blue velvet teagown her maid was holding.

"Where is Clarrie?" Mary asked eagerly.

"Out," said Constance. There was a strange note in her voice. "Out at a music lesson. You may go, Hargrove." She flung herself down on the chaise longue and began to cry. "Oh Mary, she's in love."

"*What?*" Mary's face puckered with amazement. "Why, that's too ridiculous."

Constance shook her head. "No, it's not. She's eighteen, that seems a child to you and me, but she's deadly in earnest."

"You mean she wants to get married?"

"She *is* going to be married."

Mary leaned back and opened her mouth stupidly.

"Why—I—why—"

"I know," said Constance wretchedly. "That's the way I felt. But I can't oppose her. I can't make her unhappy. I want her life to be as lovely as she is."

"Who is he?"

"A boy named Evan Gregory. He's only twenty. He's the youngest child of a big, poor, ancient Welsh family. He hasn't a sou. He'd be a singer if it weren't for all the rot about gentlemen not doing things. He has the most beautiful voice you ever heard. She met him at the Royal College and I wish to God I'd never let her go there."

"But, Constance." Mary stirred her tea. "I just don't understand. It's so sudden. You never wrote me about it."

"It only happened a month or so ago. I tell you, I was never so flabbergasted in my life. She came in one afternoon and sat down here and just said, 'Mummie, I've fallen in love.' And the worst of it is I knew damn well she meant it." Constance blew a thin trail of smoke.

"You know him—of course—"

"Of course. He's here all the time. I'm not going to break that child's heart."

"You were only seventeen when you were married," Mary said slowly. "By the way, what does Giles say about it?"

"How in hell should I know?" Constance shrugged. "He lives in the country. Rents a cottage from the millionaire the creditors sold Melling to. What has he to do with this?"

Mary gestured. "Nothing. Only—"

"Only I'm Clarrie's father as well as mother. Here she is about to marry a charming pauper and what do you suppose they'll live on? Me."

Mary raised her eyebrows. "So that's why you need more money."

"That—and the other thing. I've not really thought for years where anything came from. I've always had what I wanted and done as I pleased and now—well, it can't be the same. You see that. Oh God, Mary, let's not talk about it now." Constance ruffled her hair nervously. She stared at Mary and her green eyes lighted on the emerald watch. "Come over here and show it to me," she said. "I've never seen it."

She unpinned the watch from Mary's dress and examined it with the concentration of a jewel expert. "Paul has taste," she said finally. "I'm not sure I'd have thought it of him. Oh, here comes Clarrie. Let her tell you about Evan herself."

But Clarrie, as she hurried in, pink-cheeked from the cold air, with her blonde hair curling delicately under her black hat, flung her arms about Mary ecstatically and dropped to her knees beside the chair. She looked quickly at her mother and then back at Mary.

"Mummie's told you!" she exclaimed. "Oh, Auntie Mary, isn't it too wonderful? And isn't she the most perfect, understanding, darling mother in the world?"

Mary smiled at her. It was impossible to grasp all at once the change in Clarrie. Hair up, yes, and long skirts; a tiny, trim, curving figure in place of the up-and-down young girl; physically one would expect such changes. But there was a far profounder difference in Clarrie. It was all intangible, all in the expression of her blue eyes, in the warm maturity of her voice; even her hands, clasped on Mary's knee, small and square and blunt-fingered in queer contrast to her delicate wrists, bespoke intensity and purpose.

Mary tried for two days to pin Constance down for a talk about the mill. In childhood Constance had been diabolically clever about evading issues which she dreaded to face. Mary saw she had not lost that talent. She gave unnecessary attention to trivial and passing things, but if she sensed that Mary was making or grasping an opportunity for a serious talk she flitted off, actually or mentally, about some concern of her own. She was hugely demonstrative, more than ever before. She expressed minute concern for Mary's comfort, critically inspected her room, sent up fresh flowers and bowls of fruit every day, and showered Mary with hugs and kisses at every encounter. They could not go out to the theatre or make any kind of public appearance because of the court mourning. The weather was too vile even to permit a daily walk or drive, and so they stayed almost imprisoned in the house.

It was now the fifth of February and if Constance's answer were to go by mail it must be sent on the ship sailing tomorrow—only twenty-four hours off. At that, it could only be delivered in Pittsburgh the night of the fourteenth or the morning of the fifteenth. While dressing for dinner Mary pondered what to do. She must have it out with Constance tonight. At home it had seemed as if there were plenty of time to bring Constance round; here it looked too late already.

Evan Gregory came to dinner and the four of them sat in state in the candlelight, with the butler and the footman circling the table serving one of the superb dinners that were almost as much a part of the Constance legend as her wicked speech or her red hair. For Mary, and for Clarrie who was too meltingly in love to eat a mouthful, and for Evan who had to tear his gaze from Clarrie to notice anybody or anything, the whole gastronomic ritual was a ridiculous ordeal. Constance, in a black velvet dinner gown and great pearls, sat at the head of the table critically attentive and judicious as perfect soles followed perfect turtle soup, a garnished filet of buttery red beef followed the soles, artichokes from the South of France followed that, a huge *pâté en croute* appeared with the salad, and a frozen bombe masked in golden spun sugar brought—Mary hoped—the formidable meal to a close. But no, there was the savory to cope with, peppery devilled mushrooms on thrones of toast. There was sherry with the soup, Meursault with the fish, Richebourg with the beef, and Mary actually shuddered when Constance, helping herself to the sweet, said "Champagne, Radford. The Cordon Rouge."

So she had not ordered that beforehand. Mary realized now that all this profusion of luxurious food and wine, these great decorated platters which—but for Constance herself—went back to the kitchen barely touched, this incredibly wasteful display was, although quite the usual procedure in this house, intentionally mounted tonight for Constance's purposes. It was a way of saying, "You see? I told you I had to have enormous amounts of money. I must have it. Look around and see why I must." Whether there might be any alternative would never have crossed Constance's mind. Not so long as she wished to live like this. She watched closely while the butler filled the champagne glasses and when Mary raised a finger to refuse, Constance shook her head.

"No," she said, "you must. I insist. I want to drink a toast."

She raised her glass and looked from Evan on her right to Clarrie at the other end of the table.

"To you both," she said. "You darlings. I want you to be happy."

Mary had to join in that, with all her heart.

"Coffee in the music room," said Constance, rising.

"Very good, m'Lady."

"So the children can play for us," Constance said, slipping her arm through Mary's. That sounded insincere in a way, but it was not. She was really eager for Evan and Clarrie to play, Mary knew; she also saw it was the best way to put off conversation. To hear Constance mention "the children" in that tone almost made Mary laugh out loud. It was half-act, half-genuine; and it was certainly no wool over Mary's eyes.

She kept marvelling at the change in Clarrie. Only three and a half years ago she had been all child—serious and poised and sensible, but artless enough to grow wide-eyed over the treats she was allowed. Mary had never been able clearly to follow Constance's reasoning, if any, in her plans for Clarrie. She was being prepared for such a debut as any Earl's daughter should make, yet she was allowed to bury herself as deeply as she wished in the music which was the greatest possible contrast to all that. This should have been the year of her debut and her presentation, but now there would be no Courts because of mourning. And Clarrie, turning with utter relief to ever more serious study, had fallen maturely—of that Mary was sure—in love. Her expression when she looked at Evan Gregory was that of a wise and intensely absorbed woman. There was nothing childish about it.

She seated herself at the piano and looked up at Evan, standing beside her, with silent inquiry. He smiled. Mary watched the two of them with the sudden pressing realization that she wanted to cry. This boy was as beautiful in his way as Clarrie—tall and firmly built, dark of hair, with warmly colored skin and deep gray eyes. Like Clarrie he was quiet, confidently relaxed in manner, yet fundamentally intense.

His voice was all Constance had said. It was a full, ringing baritone with a luminous poetic color which shone through every phrase of the songs he chose—English songs with words by Ben Jonson and Shelley and Shakespeare, which Mary could enjoy utterly. She had supposed he would sing in German or Italian, and after a time he did sing some songs from the *Winterreise.* Clarrie played magnificently. She was a polished artist, and Mary, knowing nothing of music, was conscious principally of a profound sense of confidence in Clarrie as she played. There was an authority in the very set of her shoulders, bent slightly forward over the keyboard.

After about an hour Mary began to look uneasily at Constance. It was quite late. Evan and Clarrie must be tired of singing and playing. Constance had been urging them on, begging Evan for this or that until it was all too clear that she had some ulterior motive in stringing the evening out. Mary knew that the young people were wishing desperately to be left alone. She saw that Evan would only be able to bring the concert to a close by making his goodnights. Constance would then take both Clarrie and Mary upstairs and contrive to keep them together with her, to forestall being left alone with Mary. Mary chose the end of the next song to rise from her chair and stare meaningly at Constance. She said, "Why don't we go upstairs now; I have some things I brought from home to show you."

Constance stared back, stubborn, yet embarrassed. She was about to sidestep the suggestion, but Evan was too quick. He had moved courteously from the piano as soon as Mary rose, and was waiting to open the door for her and Constance. There was nothing to do but leave the room. Constance paused to kiss Clarrie and shake a playful warning finger at Evan.

"Don't stay down here too late," she said. She swept from the room, her black velvet train swishing behind her. Mary followed. She felt exactly as if this were twenty years ago; as if Constance, banished from the parlor for some typical misdemeanor, had been set upstairs in her custody. Constance swished into her boudoir and Mary followed and closed the door. Constance flung herself peevishly into a chair and said, "Well! I do think you're turning highhanded. What is this, anyway?"

Mary stood on the hearthrug.

"This is," she said coldly, "the reason I came over here to see you. I've been here forty-eight precious hours waiting for a chance to talk to you and you've been playing cat-and-mouse with me every minute. You know as well as I do you must mail your ballot tomorrow and I want to know what it is going to say."

Constance sighed. "Didn't I wire you? Haven't I explained? Can't you see the situation? Must we stage a drama about it?"

"Apparently," said Mary, "we'll have to. I'd prefer to talk it out quietly but if you're going to take this attitude then I suppose we'll fight it out. First of all, I can't believe you'd do anything so contrary to your own nature, Constance. You've always been greedy, but not to the point of harming anybody else."

"Why does this have to be a damned moral issue? Why am I my brother's keeper? You're such a sentimentalist, Mary, and so full of these holy ideals about loyalty and duty and all that—you can't understand business is business."

"I understand a good deal more about business than you with your spoiled extravagance! Have you any idea how much good money was wasted on that disgusting dinner tonight?"

"Well, I'll be damned." Constance glared up at Mary.

"I'm not impressed by the famous, dazzling Lady Melling, if that's what you mean."

Constance's nostrils swelled. For a moment she looked furiously at Mary; then with one of her sudden unpredictable flashes she burst out laughing.

"Oh, the hell with it," she said. "We're doing our best to work up to a second-act curtain and it's perfectly absurd."

"Certainly it's absurd. This is a dreadfully serious thing, and I'm frank to tell you I'm nearly desperate. *I want to save the mill for Paul.*" She leaned forward and fixed her tear-filled eyes on Constance. "Can't you realize what this means—don't you *know?*" Her voice broke.

Constance sat pulling a rose to bits. Her scarlet lips were tightly pursed. She did not answer at once. Finally she said, "I see your side of it, you know that perfectly well. My God, you know that's what's been driving me crazy. You don't think I *like* being in this position?"

"Then what—why—"

"Look." Constance sat up and reached for a memo pad and pencil. "Just come and sit down here and let me show you. My share in the mill is now worth I understand about four hundred thousand dollars." She began jotting down figures.

"And that's a good substantial increase since your father died," Mary said. "Your income has increased steadily the past five years or so, hasn't it?"

"Yes. It averages perhaps eighteen thousand dollars a year now. Sometimes more, sometimes less. That's one thing about this that bothers me. Not having a fixed dividend rate. Paul just pays us out our share of the net profits at whatever rate he thinks best. So we can't tell from one year to the next what the income will be."

"But the amount is always large enough so you oughtn't to be bothered about the difference over and above the minimum you know you'll get."

"That's what you think. But you don't realize how much money I need. Why Mary, you don't think I could live on eighteen thousand dollars a year—a bit over *three thousand pounds?* Don't be a child."

"You could if you wanted to."

"But I don't want to!" Constance flared. "I'm damned if I will. Why should I?"

Mary bit her lip. She had a scorching answer ready but thought better of it. She only said mildly, "Lots of people do."

Constance shrugged. "Oh, if you're going to talk rot there's no use discussing the thing with you. I am not 'lots of people' and I've no intention of being. If you'll get that through your head once for all I'll go on explaining my side of this to you."

"Go on."

"I've always had lots of money over and above what Paul sent from the mill. You understand that."

"I wish I didn't," Mary said acidly.

"Well, the point is, I've had it. And it—ah, I—I shan't have it any more. In fact it will be quite out of the question. The Queen's death and—oh, the devil. I'm not going into the details with you. I never have. They're none of your damn business." Constance was charming about that, not insolent. She picked up her pencil again and went back to her figures.

"You see," she said, "all in all I've had about as much again as Paul sent me. Between six and seven thousand pounds a year altogether."

"From which you did not buy jewels, furs, wines and sundries."

"From which I most certainly did not. But I've spent every cent I did get and it will cost me as much to live in the future as it has in the past. Particularly with Clarrie and Evan to support."

There was a long silence. At last Mary said, "Did it ever occur to you that you might change your style of living? You could live a great deal more simply and still roll in luxury."

"Of course it occurred to me," Constance answered, "and if I recollect correctly, we talked about that the last time you were here. Mary, you don't really think I'm a heedless, improvident fool, do you? You know me better than that. Some day I'll get bored to death with all this and then I'll do something else. In fact some day I'll probably find it smarter to leave London. Any day, perhaps."

"But you would still want piles of money badly enough to get it by breaking Paul's heart?"

Constance flushed. "Isn't that a bit thick? After all, Paul would get as much money out of this as the rest of us."

"Paul doesn't want money," Mary said bitterly. "Paul only wants his mill. For you and those two coldblooded brutes to take it away from him—"

"But, Mary, if Paul is the greatest metallurgist in the world, as you say, why should he waste his talents in a silly little backwater like our mill? Why, this new Steel Corporation would snap him up—make him the head of all their invention or whatever you call it—they'd pay him hundreds of thousands of dollars instead of the fool pittance he pays himself."

"And take all the meaning out of life for him."

Constance's finger moved slowly forward and tilted Mary's chin.

"Why is that all the meaning life has for him?" she asked in a low voice. "You know the answer to that."

Mary turned a deep scarlet.

"You just said something was none of my damn business," she said. "I'll return the compliment."

"*Touché.*" It was Constance's turn to blush now. She picked up the memo pad and made more figures on it. "Now look here," she said. "I need at the very least six thousand pounds a year. It's out of the question that I can get it from my share in our mill. I've talked this all over with Ernie Cassel, who's the smartest man I know. He advised me to vote for this sale. He's been watching those fellows put this corporation together and he says I'd be an ass not to get in on it now. If I do, I shall have stock worth nearly three quarters of a million dollars. I'd have perhaps thirty to thirty-five thousand dollars a year in dividends—in other words, about the same as I've had up to now. Now I ask you, Mary, how can I refuse?"

Mary sat silent, shaking her head. Constance tapped her gold pencil on the memo pad. A lump of coal broke in the grate with a sputtering noise. Presently Mary looked up and said, "Is there nothing in the world that would move you? Can't you *feel*, Constance?—can't you?"

"Of course I feel!" Constance's voice was sharp with strain. "You put me in a frightful position. If this meant Paul would be ruined, or anything like that, naturally I wouldn't vote for it. But he'll be so much better off—once he gets over—the—"

"The heartbreak," Mary said cruelly. "You haven't got the courage to admit it."

Constance began to cry. "Oh, you're devilling me so," she sobbed. "Why does this have to be all tangled up with the people I love? Why can't it just be business? It's only dollars and cents, after all."

"Only dollars and cents," Mary repeated angrily. "I'd like your father to hear you say that. I wish he could see what you're trying to do to the mill—and the family—"

"Oh *Jesus!*" Constance cried sharply. She was seldom as profane as that. "There you go: off on your horse again. The family! That God damn family. Hasn't it messed up your life and Paul's life enough—without using it as a club over me?"

"I'm disgusted with you," Mary said coldly. "You're no better than William and Lizzie. You make a mockery out of all the things your mother and father brought you up to be. You don't understand the mill any better than William. You don't see that the mill and the family are all the same. Ruin one and you ruin the other. *You'd* just as soon." Constance kept on snuffling and mopping her eyes like a child. "I thought you were one of us," Mary said bitterly. "Paul and Edgar. And me."

"I am," Constance sobbed into her handkerchief. "You know I am."

"But you love your fleshpots better than you love us."

"Oh, you're beastly to me! How can you say such a thing?"

"Because I'm afraid it's true," Mary said wretchedly. "I thought I'd be able to move you. I thought—you'd—" now Mary broke down in tears.

"Don't," Constance clutched her arm. "I don't want you to take on this way. Please—"

"How can I help it? The only thing I've ever asked of you. The only time I've ever—admitted—what—Paul—" Again she choked her words off. Then she drew a long breath and asked, "Do you remember the letter you wrote me three years ago? On the anniversary?"

Constance nodded sadly.

"Then where *are* you?" Mary asked piteously. "What's happened to you?"

Constance was silent.

"I don't know what to do," Mary breathed at last. "I just can't let you do this. If only I knew what to *do*."

"This is a hell of a situation," Constance groaned. "To sit here holding the balance and be torn in little pieces. If only somebody else would vote for the damn thing then I wouldn't feel guilty of everything you accuse me of."

"That's so preposterous," Mary said impatiently. "Who else but William and Lizzie would vote for it? Certainly not Paul. Or Edgar. He's probably sent his vote by mail long ago."

"Poor Eddie," said Constance. "He's so simple and ineffectual."

Before the words were out of Constance's mouth Mary's spine stiffened.

Something pricked at her mind, some idea, vague, distant, formless—but an idea. A feeling that Edgar might be the last resort which could miraculously influence Constance. He might appeal to some streak in her, something buried as deep as his own mysticism had been buried in the years before misery brought it to the surface. Mary leaned forward and looked into Constance's eyes. They met hers without flinching. They stared honest and clear and frank—but stubborn.

"Will you do one thing for me?" Mary asked in a low voice. "Promise me one thing?"

"What?"

"Don't mail the ballot tomorrow. Plan to send your vote by cable in time for the fifteenth."

"Why?"

"I can't exactly explain," Mary said, "but I've got to talk this over with Edgar. I don't know myself exactly what I'm getting at. But I just know I must talk to him before you vote."

"Well—" Constance shrugged. "I'm not going to change my mind, Mary. I've explained the basis of my decision—it's flat cash—and you've explained everything you can. Nothing Ed can say will influence me either. I've gone through hell coming to this decision and now my mind's made up."

"But you will wait and cable your vote?" Mary begged.

Constance shrugged again. "Very well, if it's any comfort to you."

CHAPTER LV

[1901—Continued]

EDGAR SAT QUIETLY with his hands clasped before him on the oak table in the stone reception hall. The dark, vaulted chamber was cold with a deadly, penetrating chill. Though the winter sun shone feebly outside, no warmth could penetrate these massive walls. A small charcoal brazier burned in the corner.

Mary had finally overcome her emotion at seeing him again. She had been full of hesitancy and uncertainty during the painful moments of waiting for Edgar to join her here after she was admitted to Monte Cassino. She had trembled all over when the low door in the wall opened and he entered the hall and strode over, holding out his hands in the warmest, most natural kind of greeting. He was dressed in a long hooded habit of coarse black cloth belted with a heavy leather girdle. A crucifix hung from it. His feet were bare, shod in crude leather sandals, and his hands were brown, hard, and stained and scarred from heavy work. He had seen Mary's eyes go to his head and he smiled slowly.

"No," he had said. "I am not tonsured yet." He was still a lay brother, but he was about to become a canonical novice. Mary was amazed at his eyes. They had grown deep, warm, and profound in expression. The strained, haunted look, the tendency to stare anxiously, had completely disappeared. His face was as thin as ever, but neither drawn nor pale. They had sat down here and Edgar had told her something of his life, of his extreme contentment with it, of the early rising, the long, regular hours of prayer, the reading and meditation, the ample, peaceful sleep, the hard, satisfying work. He was in the forge where all metals used in the community were worked and repaired. The time of Mary's visit was limited and she had had to begin then to tell him why she had come. She talked while he listened attentively. "And," she finished, "that's where it stands now."

Edgar raised his head and looked at her. During the first part of her story he had listened with his brow puckered as if the effort to throw his mind back into the mundane world of money and its struggles was painful. Mary saw that he never thought in English any more. He pondered each point that she made and sometimes asked to have it repeated. When she finally finished, he sat quiet, staring at her.

"I feel very sad about Con," he said slowly.

"I feel so sad," Mary said, "that I've come to ask you to do something. Anything, Edgar—I have absolute faith there is something you can do."

He thought for a time.

"Of course," he said quietly, "Paul must not lose the mill."

They looked deep into each other's eyes.

"I feel that way too," Mary said. "I ask you not to let him lose it."

"You know of course what I can do," he said. "Even if you had not thought it out, you had an instinct about it. I shall have to do it, if there is no other way to influence Con."

"You mean you'd—" Mary hesitated.

"This is rather serious for me too," Edgar said. "It is not strictly honorable. It may be"—he bowed his head and crossed himself slowly—"a sin."

Mary caught her breath.

"Oh, why?" she whispered.

"It is against the terms of Father's will for any one of us to bring pressure on any of the others to decide his vote in the event of a proposed sale. If I induce Constance to vote with Paul, that will be the first dishonest thing I do. There will be more, too—alas."

"But we are only trying to do what is right," Mary pleaded. "It is right to keep the mill for Paul. It is right not to let mere greed for money take it away from him."

"Who are you to decide what is right?" Edgar asked slowly. "Is that not blasphemy?"

"I will pray," Mary said earnestly. "I will pray and do penance all the rest of my life if this is sinful now. You too, you will pray. You are a holy man now, Edgar. I cannot feel you would do what is really wrong." She paused. "And there's no time to lose," she said in a panicky way. "Today is the seventh of February. The votes must be in Pittsburgh one week from today."

"Mine should be there already," Edgar said. "I wrote the day I received the notice. There was not even a question of choice."

"Thank God."

"There is one reason aside from the great question of dishonesty, why this is hard for me," Edgar said slowly. Mary waited for him to explain. He thought for a time, and continued.

"I had always intended when I was received into the Order to arrange with Paul to buy my share in the mill. Under the terms of Father's will, you remember, any of us is permitted to sell our share to Paul if we wish. I wanted to take that money and give it to the Order."

Mary nodded slowly. "I am not surprised at that. It is a magnificent thing to do for the Church."

"Nothing compared with what the Church gives to me," Edgar said simply. "But I also thought of it as the proper way to terminate my worldly existence, I wanted very much to do that, Mary."

"And now?"

"Now, of course, I shall have to give half my share to Constance," Edgar said. He spoke quite matter-of-factly, as if he had thought this out long ago. Actually it could only have occurred to him in the few moments since Mary had told him about Constance. He had thought at first, like Mary, that Constance would automatically vote against the sale.

Mary drew in her breath with a sharp gasp. This was what she had felt, the elusive thought which would not take shape for her. She began to cry.

"Oh, Edgar," she said, holding her handkerchief to her face, "You are too good, too wonderful."

He shook his head slowly.

"On the contrary, I fear I am doing something very wrong. It is a dreadful thing, a shocking, wicked thing to take money one had meant to give to God and turn it over to Mammon—which is certainly Constance's use for money. I should not make it possible for her to be more worldly and ‍spoiled than she is already."

‍She wants some of the money for Clarrie," Mary said weakly.

"She and Clarrie could live good honorable lives with much less than they have now," Edgar said sternly. "No, frankly I am not thinking of Constance. I am thinking of Paul—and you. I did you a very great wrong through your sister. I have never had a chance to expiate that to you. This is my chance. You want Paul to keep the mill. He shall keep it."

Mary cried quietly.

"Besides," Edgar said, "I have tried Paul sorely, and made his work harder for him by leaving him to run the mill alone when he needed me. And also—" he paused, feeling for words. Mary realized again that he was thinking in Italian, perhaps in Latin, certainly not in English.

"I feel," Edgar said slowly, "that this is the only thing I can do to—to help insure the continuity of the family." He chose his words thoughtfully. "My being here out of the world—I know that has distressed Paul. But I see clearly from here, Mary."

He leaned forward and smiled gravely. "I see," he said, "what is valuable in our family and what is not. What has given it identity and character, what helps it to keep those things." He reflected. "The mill does that," he said. Then there was a long pause. "And so do you."

The tears rose quickly to Mary's eyes and spilled over on her pale cheeks.

"I don't deserve that," she said softly.

"But it is true. You have held us to the best in ourselves—where we have been able to rise so high. I think in a way that is true of the mill too. I should not like to contemplate a future for Paul and his sons—without our mill."

"Then you cannot have any doubts about your method of saving it for them!"

"There is no time to ponder that now," Edgar said. "I shall go into retreat as soon as you leave, and talk about it with my confessor. Now we must act. If you would not mind waiting here, Mary, while I go and get permission to go to Rome—"

"What are we going to do?" Mary asked.

"We are going to the American consul, to get his help in drawing up a deed of gift. Father's will," Edgar said slowly, with a look in his eye which reminded Mary dimly of his mischievous ways of long ago, "Father's will said nothing about any heir's *giving* his share or any part thereof away. The restrictions were all about selling the shares."

"You are wonderful," Mary said again.

"You will take this deed, dated some time after February fifteenth, back to London, and tell Constance I offer her the gift of half my share if she will vote against the sale. This will give her a total holding about equal in value to the amount of steel stock she would receive if the sale were made. If she accepts my offer, see that she cables her vote at once. If she refuses it destroy the deed, or return it to me."

"God bless you, Edgar," Mary said, wiping her eyes.

"I shall pray most earnestly for Him to do so," Edgar said, "and Our Blessed Lady also. I fear I am committing several grave sins."

"You are saving—the dearest thing—in the—world—" Mary sat down by the table and buried her head in her arms as Edgar went away and closed the small door in the wall.

The meeting was scheduled for three o'clock on the afternoon of February fifteenth. William was to arrive in Pittsburgh at noon and Paul sent Jones to meet him at the station and take him to the Duquesne Club for lunch. Paul joined him there. Elizabeth had been supposed to come with Bill, but she had wired the previous evening that she was not well, and that William was bringing her vote with him.

"What's the matter with her?" Paul asked over the pepperpot soup. He was not so much concerned as making family conversation.

Bill looked uncomfortable.

"Why—ah—to tell you the truth, Paul," he blurted, "I don't quite know how to put it."

Paul laid down his spoon.

"What's the matter? Is she seriously ill?" He thought quickly of his mother.

"No." William coughed behind his napkin. "To be frank, Paul, she's ah—er—really you can't imagine it," he said.

"What *is* it?"

"She's"—Bill turned a dull red—"going to have a child."

Paul's mouth dropped open. "Go on. You're kidding."

Now that it was out, Bill laughed. "No I'm not. Ben told me about it yesterday. It's no mistake."

"Well I'll be damned. How old is Lizzie, anyway?—why Lord, she's forty-two years old!"

"I know. It's almost unbelievable. Like Sarah in the Bible."

"Why, it'll kill her," Paul said.

"I understand it is rather—dangerous for a woman her age. Who never had any children."

Paul sat shaking his head and buttering a roll.

"Bible is right," he said. "The barren fig tree or something. It gives me the creeps."

"Are all the votes in?" Bill asked, changing the subject abruptly.

"I guess so. Harry's put a letter from Monte Cassino in the safe at the mill, and a cable which I suppose is from Con. You've got Lizzie's vote with you—and here we are."

"Here we are," agreed Bill. "Who else will be at the meeting?"

"Just Harry Wilkins,"—this was Paul's lawyer, old Henry Wilkins' son. "And one of his clerks. And two men from the bank. Just as well Middleton decided not to come—there was no real reason."

"I suppose not," William said. He seemed about to say something else, then to think better of it. Paul was signing the check.

"Well, if you're ready, Bill—"

They chatted desultorily in the carriage driving over to the mill. William still seemed to have something to say which he was holding back. Probably making plans for transferring the assets of the company, Paul thought to himself.

The other men were already seated around the conference table in the outer office when the brothers arrived. They all rose and there was general handshaking. Nobody had ever seen William Scott in such an affable, confident mood in these surroundings. Paul motioned Bill and the bankers to chairs and walked over to the safe with Harry Wilkins. They opened it and took out a heavy manila envelope with thick wax seals.

For the record, Wilkins read aloud a copy of the offer from the projected United States Steel Corporation, as transmitted to the five partners of the Scott Iron Works. He then read the portion of old William Scott's will covering the questions of any sale of the Scott Iron Works or any partnership thereof. Paul gazed out of the window during the reading, his eyes resting on the bridge stretching from the street to the front entrance of the mill. Even today the strong will of his father, expressed in these hard legal words, had the power to hold his closest attention. There was something so immediate about the Old Man in these words; Paul felt as if he were here in the room. Burning with scorn, too.

"Now," said Harry Wilkins, "we are ready to open the votes. Is there any preference as to the order in which we read them?"

Paul listened in complete detachment. He could not feel as if the mill were at stake, though it was still perfectly possible that five minutes from now he might find the whole thing gone, finished, done. He tried to believe that, but he knew perfectly well he was fooling himself. He had had his bad and hopeless moments, but they were over now. He felt completely calm.

Bill was leaning back in his chair with a comfortable smile.

"Why not open them in the order they arrived?" he suggested.

Everybody nodded.

Wilkins picked up the letter with the Italian stamp. "This came first, didn't it, Paul?"

He slit open the envelope and extracted one thin sheet written in Edgar's hand, and the enclosure, the ballot that had been sent to Edgar to mark.

"Edgar Scott, lay brother of the Order of Saint Benedict, Monte Cassino, Province of Lazio, Rome, Italy, votes against sale of the Scott Iron Works to the projected United States Steel Corporation," Wilkins read. Everybody took that for granted. Wilkins laid down the ballot in the center of the table. "Signature of Edgar Scott duly attested," he said.

Next he picked up the cable, Constance's cable, they all knew. William still sat smiling a little and quite expansive. He knew what this would say. Paul smoked his pipe, perfectly impassive. Wilkins opened the cable.

"I cast my vote," he read aloud, "against sale of Scott Iron Works to projected United States Steel Corporation. Stop. Ballot duly signed witnessed posted London February eleventh nineteen one. Signed Constance, Countess of Melling. born Constance Scott."

William leaned forward, frowning. "What?" he asked, as if he had not heard correctly. Paul's eyebrows twitched. Nobody else spoke. Wilkins handed Constance's cable to William, who read it, his pale gray eyes moving slowly along the lines. He moistened his lips and laughed a little.

"Rather a surprise, isn't it, Paul?" he asked in an artificially easy tone.

"Very much so," said Paul. "What's the next ballot, Elizabeth's?"

Wilkins picked up the sealed envelope addressed in Elizabeth's handwriting.

"Elizabeth Scott Nicholas of Thirty-six East Thirty-seventh Street, City and County of New York, State of New York, votes to sell the Scott Iron Works to the projected United States Steel Corporation on the terms stated in the notification of January fifteenth. Signature of Elizabeth Scott Nicholas duly attested."

William looked relieved. It made a difference in the atmosphere for the positive votes to appear now. He was really glad that the twins' ballots were opened and finished with; from now on it would be straight sailing. His own ballot lay next on the pile, Paul's on the bottom. William was so sure of Paul that he had urged Selden Middleton to feel out the men who were putting the Corporation together, concerning a highly-paid executive post in one of the Pittsburgh mills for Paul.

"William Campbell Scott of 147 Beacon Street, City and County of Boston, Commonwealth of Massachusetts, votes to sell the Scott Iron Works to the projected United States Steel Corporation on the terms stated in the notification of January fifteenth. Signature of William Campbell Scott duly attested."

There was no comment. Paul's ballot lay alone on the table in its sealed envelope. William was smiling outrightly now; palpably congratulating himself and Paul. The envelope crackled as Wilkins slit it open. He read aloud in his sharp Pittsburgh voice.

"Paul Scott of 1203 Western Avenue, City and County of Allegheny, Commonwealth of Pennsylvania, votes against sale of Scott Iron Works to the projected—"

The rest of his words were drowned in the long, hoarse gasp that came from William. All the men turned their heads and looked curiously at him. Paul was still perfectly expressionless. William recovered his poise and leaned forward, clutching the table with his long, veined hands.

"There must be some mistake," he said.

Nobody answered.

"Some mistake," he repeated. "Is there not, Paul?"

Wilkins said, "I had better read the last ballot aloud again." He did so.

William was half out of his chair as Harry Wilkins laid down the paper; he leaned over the table towards Paul, with his pale face working. For one awful moment Paul remembered the last such meeting in this room, the meeting where the Old Man had bought out Gaylord and broken with Bill. Paul was afraid there would be an outburst from William now. But his brother was too old for that; too mortified in the presence of these witnesses. He was, however, inarticulate with outrage. He stared at Paul, while Wilkins and his clerk and the men from the bank self-consciously shuffled papers, lit cigars, blew their noses, and tried to look the other way. William's hands trembled on the edge of the table.

"You've tricked me," he said at last, half aloud. "I might have known you'd do such a thing."

Paul shook his head gravely.

"I beg your pardon, Bill, I have not tricked you in the least."

"You let me think you'd vote for this sale! What is that if not deceit?"

"I did not let you think so. I never said one word," Paul replied.

"But—but—why did you let me take it for granted you'd sell? You did do that!" His voice was thick with anger.

"I can't help it if that's the way you interpreted my attitude. I was trying to be fair and impartial in respect to everybody else, but if you seriously thought I'd vote to sell this mill you are unrealistic, that's all. You ought to have known me better."

"I know you," William said bitterly. "I know you well enough to think there's something rotten about this."

He reached out and seized the pile of ballots with Constance's cable among them. He ruffled through them, his narrow gray eyes flicking across each one as if he expected to find something he had not known before. He took the cable and slapped it down on the table in front of Paul.

"How about that?" he asked furiously. "There's something queer there if I know you and that—that—" he paused, seeking an epithet for Constance. Paul had to restrain a smile. When Bill approved of Constance he was only too pleased to be the brother of a Countess. "Why did she cable?" William snapped. "What's she been up to? If she'd voted honestly she'd have mailed her ballot in proper time the way Edgar did. At least he's honest, if he is a poor deluded fool."

"You know Constance as well as I do," Paul said coldly. "You see more of her than I do; I've never even been in London." As he spoke, he saw in a sudden shocking flash who had been in London and what had happened there. He felt shaken and weak. Now his composure was entirely artificial and his voice harsh as he turned to Wilkins and asked, "Would you say Lady Melling attended to her correspondence and business regularly, Harry? Or promptly? Have you ever had a signed receipt or other document from her on time?"

"Never," said Wilkins.

There was a long silence. The men around the table stirred uncomfortably; the meeting should be dismissed; there could be nothing more to discuss. But just as Paul was about to rise and break up the gathering William said, "You'll regret this to your dying day. This Corporation will get something in place of your piddling mill and crush you out of existence."

"I'll be expecting that," Paul said.

"Well, you needn't have dragged the rest of us down with you!"

"I hope I won't. So far we've made out, I think. Incidentally, Bill—"

The men all looked up expectantly. They sensed what Paul was about to say. William sat glaring at the table.

"—any time you are dissatisfied with my management," Paul continued, "I'll be glad to buy you out."

"I'm sure you'd be," William answered with hate. "I've no intention of selling—to you."

Paul exchanged a glance with Harry Wilkins, who stood up with palpable relief. "This concludes the business before the meeting, I believe," he said.

Paul stood at the head of the table while the men gathered their hats and overcoats and filed out. William was in a hurry to get away. He had quickly accepted Wilkins' invitation to drive him to the station.

"You won't come up for dinner, Bill?" Paul asked. He had been undecided whether this was wise or foolhardy. After all, Bill might come. But his brother only replied curtly, "No, thank you. I hardly think we'd have anything—congenial to talk about." He said good-bye abruptly and followed Harry Wilkins out. When the last of the men had gone Paul went into his private office and shut the door. He sank slowly into his swivel chair, and putting his hand to his forehead, was surprised to find it damp.

"Whew!" he said slowly. "Oh—Mary. Oh, my God." He leaned his elbows on the desk and dropped his head on them. "Oh, Mary," he said again. He knew now that he had, in a way, known where she was going and what she meant to do from the very minute she had told him her queer-sounding story about her sister. "You little devil," he said, with a choke in his throat. "If I'd known what she was up to," he said to himself, "I'd never have let her do it."

He raised his head and stared hard at the big framed picture of the Old Man which years ago he had hung on the wall between the windows. The bearded face, the strange, hard, slightly slanting eyes, so dramatized in Constance's wilful face, seemed almost ready to come to life and speak to him. Paul stared for a long time. Then he swallowed and found himself wishing the Old Man could know what Mary had done. Suddenly he jumped to his feet, ripped off his coat, and ploughed into his dungarees which he kept hanging on a hook. He hurried out of his office, ran down the ramp to the open-hearth shed, and went to Number One Furnace where Jim Rafferty used to work. The boss, in purple goggles, was squinting through the fire-door. The gang were waiting near him with their shovels. The boss opened the door and yelled "Shoot!" The crew swung past the open inferno, slinging in their loads of ferro-manganese. Paul grabbed the shovel from the last man, his heart pounding with wild happiness.

"Let me take a turn," he said. "I need a workout."

The Hunky heater protested. "No good, no uset', bad for you."

But Paul swung the shovel anyway. He could have burst for happiness. Down by the yard the big ladle loomed in the entrance, brimful of blazing red soup from the Henrietta. Paul leaned on his shovel and looked at it and thought of the Old Man.

CHAPTER LVI

[*Summer 1901*]

THE DAY BEFORE Mary was to leave for Cape May with the twins Paul took Dick to Charlie Liska to begin his first summer's work in the mill. Paul had finally yielded to Dick's pleading to start work this summer, a whole year younger than Paul himself and his brothers had been when they began. Dick was to have four weeks' taste of it, and then he and his father were going to Cape May for the whole month of August. Paul had never taken such a long vacation. He had chartered a sloop, and Dick was planning to have friends to visit, and they were all looking forward to a wonderful summer.

Charlie was expecting them. He was an old hand in the blooming mill now. Once in a while some kind of nastiness among the men still flared up, but Charlie's work was so expert and his output so high that his record spoke for itself. Corbley had long since dropped out of the picture; a quiet man named Smith was the roller-boss and Charlie second in command. He had to be better than any other hand in the shop in order to keep the men working peacefully with him; and he was better. Paul had decided to put Dick in Charlie's crew for a starter.

"Here he is, Charlie," the boss said.

Charlie looked the tall boy up and down, measuring his strength and weight with his eye.

"Looks like fine boy you got, boss."

"We'll see what kind of a worker he is."

Dick shifted his feet.

"Not lots fun, vork by mill hot summer. Sveat plenty, plenty tired."

"I guess I can stand it," Dick said. He was uncomfortable. He wanted to be given something to do. He did not realize there was very little he could do at his age. Years ago when the puddling furnaces were working there was a cinder-monkey on each of them, a boy who ran up and down the line wheeling a barrow full of cinder which was shovelled into the molten iron just before time to ravel off. Paul had done a turn at this, and most of the older men had started in by doing it. But puddled pig-iron had not been made at Scott's in years, and cinder was hauled to the blast furnace by the dinkey-engine.

"Couldn't I work in the open-hearth department, Dad?"

Charlie Liska spread his hands protestingly. *"Vaht?"*

Dick bit his lip. He was irritated by this hulking Hunky who seemed to have the right to decide where he should work, and to whom his father appeared to defer quite willingly. Dick looked pleadingly at Paul. He wanted his father to understand how he felt. Paul smiled at him and said, "You don't mind if I take Charlie's advice about this, son? He's closer to the shop work than I am now, and I don't think you realize how heavy most of this stuff is. All we want is to work you in gradually."

Charlie nodded, beaming. Dick felt better, and smiled and said, "Sure, Dad, I understand. You and Mr. Liska fix it up."

"Nah!" Charlie protested, reddening with pleasure, "no Mr. Liska. Charlie, *prosím*, like Papa say. You call me Charlie, hanh?"

"Sure," said Dick shyly, "Charlie."

"Olright. Vy you don't stay here my shop, learn for oil, learn for check rolls with Štefan? No?"

Dick nodded.

"Kubovič!" Charlie turned and bellowed.

A grease-stained face with a broad grin emerged from behind some machinery. Charlie volleyed a mouthful of Slovak.

"You go with Štefan," Charlie explained to Dick, "take oilcan, do like him. Learn for grease gears."

Paul and Charlie stood and watched Dick, in his brand-new blue dungarees, swarm up the cat-ladder after Štefan Kubovič. There was a lump in Paul's throat, but he could not help laughing along with Charlie.

That afternoon Mary went down to the House to say good-bye to her Mamas before she left town for the summer. She was dog-tired. Packing for the summer exodus was always exhausting, but at their present age the twins were fiendishly inventive of ways to complicate everything. Nothing ever happened without an explosion, an uproar, or a fight of some kind. They were always in trouble. Tommy had all the ideas and the explosive energy to put things into action, but Teddy had the prosaic persistence to carry them out. Ever since Dick had acquired the dignity of a promised job in the mill this year, he had scorned any contact with the twins. This morning at seven-thirty he had proudly left home with Paul, ignoring the excited shouts of the twins as they stood on the steps with Mary and watched their father and brother start down the front walk.

"Don't get burnt!" Tommy yelled after Dick. "Don't fall in the soup." "Don't get run over!" Teddy echoed.

"Aw, shut up!" Dick had called back. He had not been able to suppress that. He had not meant to notice those brats at all. Paul's lips twitched. He turned around once and waved at Mary.

Julka was waiting for her at the House. Half a dozen women were there, some sewing, some drying their hair in the back yard. Four tots were playing in the sandbox under the plane tree. The shades were drawn in all the rooms and the House was quiet and fairly cool. It was heaven by contrast to the dirty, crowded hovels the women had escaped to come up here today. They were all glad to see Mary. She could not spend as much time with them nowadays as she used to. They understood that she had to spend more time at home with the motherless Scott children whom she was bringing up. When she did come down, there was rejoicing, and much sage shaking of heads over eleven-year-old boys.

"Davils," pronounced Mrs. Baláž. "All davils. All same, rich and poor."

Julka was having her third baby. Her eldest, a boy now nearly three, was outside in the sandbox, and her fifteen-month-old girl was upstairs asleep in a crib. Julka was at the desk in the club room writing a letter. She beamed at Mary.

"I write to my Uncle Jaromír and Aunt Ludmila," she said. Her English had improved markedly. She now spoke much better than Charlie, in spite of his longer time in America. Her accent was still pronounced, but she had worked hard over her grammar and she made fewer mistakes year by year. She read so many English classics that her speech was a little stilted; sometimes it had a quaint and charming quality. She was always trying to get the other women more interested in learning English. Most of them would not or could not make the effort; many of them could not read or write at all.

"What else to expect?" Julka often remarked with a shrug. "Ignorant Slováks."

"Why are you always running them down like that, Julka?"

"I will tell you. They are Slavs like us, but their country is wild and poor. They don't read and study like us. Most don't go to school. Czechs are better," Julka said firmly.

Mary reproved her gently for that. Their poverty was not the Slovaks' fault. It was wrong of Julka to be so arrogant. Was it not?

"Maybe," Julka shrugged. "I'll try different."

Mary had asked Julka long ago to tell her something about her own background and Charlie's. They were, obviously, cleverer and more intelligent than their neighbors and the masses of illiterate Hunkies who lived so miserably in the courts and slums of the steel towns. "Well," Julka had said, "that's a long story."

And it was several years, really, before Mary pieced all the facts together. Julka had told them in many leisurely talks over sewing and coffee-drinking after her English lessons. Mary always marvelled that these strange foreign tales studded with tongue-twisting names of men and women and places should stay so clearly in her mind, and impress her so strongly. Perhaps it was because Julka used them as she did; they meant so much to her, not only in the light of the past, but in terms of the future she dreamed about.

"Karel's papa," Julka had said long ago, when her English was still sketchy, "vas Czech. A real Czech, from Brno. He went up in the Tatras, that's in Slovakia, see—vaht you say, Hungary—to vork by the wood business. He married the mama there. Yah, *she* vas Slovák." Julka made a face, sticking out her lower lip. "She vas the only Slovák we got. Everybody else—real Czech." Mary had laughed. She still could not understand why Julka made this distinction with such vigorous prejudice.

"They vas poor," Julka went on. She clucked her tongue and wagged her head a little, trying to describe to Mary, who knew plenty about poverty, the incredible hardship of life for these Slovak peasants. Julka described the Tatra mountains, a wild and primitive region owned entirely by great Hungarian landowners in whose service the peasants were little better than serfs. Most of this mountain territory was given over to vast hunting-preserves for the nobles; the peasants scraped a wretched living from woodcutting and sheepherding. They were intense, race-proud, poetic people who considered their Hungarian overlords robbers and persecutors, and who brought up their children generation after generation in the religion of independence for their country and revolt from Hungarian enslavement.

Their lives followed the ancient, stringent pattern, uninterrupted century after century except by incessantly recurrent wars. It was only during the past twenty-five years that the rising ferment of industrial revolution had reached out and touched them. It had stretched all the way from America in the persons of labor contractors who appeared in the isolated villages, as in all the provinces of the Empire, west, south, and north of here, with stories of abundant, well-paid work, quick riches, and independence in the mines and mills of Pennsylvania. By hundreds of thousands, Slovaks and Ruthenians and Croatians and Slovenes and Serbs and Poles flocked to the seaports, to fearful steerage voyages, to the pitiful bewilderments of the new world, to the hardest, most dangerous, worst-paid jobs, to the squalid mining-patches and company towns of western Pennsylvania.

"You seen them," Julka said, shaking her head. "Animals. Like regular animals, so, they live. But the Czechs," Julka said, lifting her head proudly. "*To je* difference!"

The Czechs, Bohemians and Moravians had been emigrating from their lands for over a hundred years past, to escape the same intolerable serfdom at the hands of Austrian landlords which the Slovaks suffered from the Hungarians. Czechs, Julka said "always got to learn. Always they want better. They want free, too, like I always say. They work good, they try right away get land where they go. At home, in our country, my people don't get land, all belongs these damn Austrians." She had begun to spice her English with a few common words. "Fürstenbergs and Esterházys and Kinskys and Schwarzenbergs and you know—all that." She made a disgusted mouth. "Once a while, some Czech get lee'l piece land. Maybe some gift, maybe he buys. So mine strýček Jaromír got land, old Fürst Schwarzenberg gave him piece after Königgrätz."

Mary had not fully understood why, and Julka explained that her uncle as a young man had been a servant of Prince Schwarzenberg's and had saved his life at the battle of Königgrätz. The farm that Julka grew up on was his reward, along with the stewardship of one of the neighboring Schwarzenberg estates.

"So beautiful!" Julka said of the farm. *"Krásný!* Down in valley, where the river flows. That is *Vltava,* our own river. Near Hluboká, nice lee'l town." She tried to describe the country, magnificent and fertile, where the principal crop was hops for the great breweries of Plzeň and of České Budějovice nearby. She laughed and licked her lips when she spoke of the beer they made there. "Such beer!" She sighed. "Here by America they try copy, they say Pilsener and Budweiser—" she shrugged. "I wish you taste our beer once," she said. "I hope I taste *ještě jednou!"* She rolled her eyes fervently.

"Well," she said on another occasion, "there I grew up." Her brown eyes filled with tears and she wiped them away. "So happy, we vas. Not like poor doity Slováks starving in hills. I was, vaht you say, *sirotek,* orphan. My mama and papa die when I vas baby. So my teta Ludmila takes me. She vas my mama's sister. And so I vas like her own. Nine, we vas—eight from teta Ludmila and strýček Jaromír—and me. Their name is Dvořák," Julka said proudly. That was a fine, ancient Czech name. The composer Antonín was a distant family connection. "Where you find a Slovák with such a musician in the family?" Julka remarked.

Mary asked her when and how she met Charlie.

"In Plzeň," Julka said, "I vas only lee'l girl. Only thirteen. Vas vonderful day! We have big *svátek,* vaht you say—holiday—every year for time when hops ready. Lots people, all families together, big parade in streets. Come from every place. They make music, they dance, they sing. Streets all full with flags, flowers, green leaves—oh, is vonderful. Beautiful. And every body wears *Český kroj.* Own costume, you know. We always make ourselves, so much vork, so much embroider!" She wagged her head. "Only for festival days. National days. So there vas great feast after parade, hams—" she sucked in her cheeks hungrily. "Big. Pink. Sweet. Oh, is nowhere ham like mine strýček makes! From own pigs. And goose. And *kachna,* vaht you say, duck. All kinds *zelenina.* All kind *pečivo*—those things you like, vaht we make—all baked things. Is vonderful. And beer!" She rolled her eyes once more. "In barrels big like a house. You could walk around inside!"

"So we vas all there together in beer garden," she said. "Strýček and tetička and all cousins, ten Dvořáks, and *mnoho* friends, lots relatives. Even babička, my grandma, she's dead now. She vas maybe ninety. And babies. Everybody. *Každý*. And Karel comes along."

"But what was Charlie doing in Plzeň?" Mary could not pronounce the name of the town properly at all.

"Ach, he vouldn't stay and starve up in the Tatra all his life," Julka explained. "He left there already five or six years before. He vas smart, he liked machinery. He wanted to vork in factory. He went to Plzeň because we got factories there—like here." Julka pointed out the window. "The Skoda works are there. Big machine shops, and foundries and rolling mills. They make all guns for army. Big guns." She gestured. "Charlie vorked by Skoda then. He saw me in beer garden. I vas so funny!" She blushed and wagged her hands deprecatingly. "So fat and dumb. Long braids and *eleven* petticoats!"

"But Skoda not much difference from here," Julka went on, shaking her head. "Karel not get on quick enough. He learn rolling-machine but good jobs only for Austrians. Germans. *Fuj.* They tell him, *hloupý Slovák.* Dumb Slovák. He only stay long enough save money for America. And before he go, he ask me promise I wait for him, come America marry him when he sends money. So I promise. I wait. I was only lee'l girl. I wait six whole years. I vork by fields, vork by geese, make linen like I show you. Strýček gives me linen for my *věno*." Mary gathered she must mean her dowry.

"And so I come," Julka finished, "and next thing I make friend like you. I am lucky, no?"

It was interesting and touching, Mary thought this hot summer afternoon, to look back over the changes in Julka. Now she spoke more correctly. Many of the funny and clumsy turns of her speech were gone. In a way she had had more distinction before. Now when she talked to Mary she was very apt to branch out into passionate enthusiasm about the national revival that was going on in the old country. Though she was glad to be in America and vociferously proud of Charlie's job at Scott's, she dreamed always of her own country. She loved to talk about it, to tell of the struggle for freedom that was going on there. "In our schools," she said. "Our universities. You know, Mary—you know about our university at Praha? The oldest one, I guess, on the Continent. Such fine teachers we have there, such scholars!" There was something touching about her pride in that, considering that she herself had only a primary school education. But that, she told Mary, with more of her strange, fierce pride, was Czech. "Every Czech feels like that. And our young people—now they learn in our own language. Read Hus and Havlíček and Komenský and Palacký. Learn how to make the revolution."

Mary was surprised the first time Julka came out with that word.

"Really?" she said. "You mean they will break away from Austria—the way we did from England?"

Julka nodded emphatically. "You wait," she said. "Maybe it takes years, maybe a hundred years. But we will. That's why we study now.

Everybody must study," she said, in her almost fanatical way. "To be ready when our country is ours again. So we can make a fine life there, fine and free for everybody, even the dumb Slováks."

She admitted that was the reason why she took so much interest in the Slovak women here. Even out here in Pennsylvania, in Ohio, in the West, in Chicago, in every place where Czechs and Slovaks lived they must work and struggle to emancipate themselves. So said the hardworking young boarding-boss, strong and calm and confident, big with child, her large hands and sturdy forearms muscled with work.

"Even here in America?" Mary asked wonderingly. "Even over here, when you've moved away from the old country? Does it matter here?"

"But sure!" Julka said earnestly. "Here especially. Wait and see. America is the place to learn these things. America will help us when the time comes. Some day," she said, her big brown eyes bright with tears, "some day my country will be free!"

That seemed fantastically unreal to Mary, almost as remote and incomprehensible to her as—she thought once—Edgar's religious vocation was to his brothers and sisters. And just as little related to the everyday world. It was a fine dream to have, without doubt; everybody was better for some such inspiration in his life. She liked to hear Julka talk about it. But it had no reality. It could not have, in a world so grandly and ponderously established as the Europe she had glimpsed. It was really ridiculous if you thought of it in the light of Constance's London with its counterparts of wealth and power and royal privilege in the imperial capitals of the Continent. These funny little ants of people taking their dreams so seriously!

When she left that afternoon Julka stood on the steps with her and held her hand tightly while saying good-bye.

"You come back first September, sure?"

"Sure." Mary smiled.

"We don't see you enough any more," Julka said in a troubled way. "Not like it used to be. This last couple years, you don't spend so much time here like before. We miss you."

"I have my boys to look after now," Mary said rather lamely.

She had never been able to explain to Julka that the House in some strange way had troubled her a little ever since the horrible night of Louise's suicide. Mary never went into the House now without remembering that one night that she had spent there; the reason for her being there; and the awful dark dawn when she had been brought the ghastly news from home. She had gone back to Paul's house that morning, because he needed her then as never before. Not a word had ever been said about her absence.

"In the fall," Julka was saying, "your boys go to school all day. Then you come oftener, like old times, no?"

Mary squeezed Julka's hand and promised. Walking home she busied herself with last-minute mental lists of things she must do before leaving tomorrow. She avoided the thought of why it troubled her sometimes to be at the House now. She wanted to keep on going there, she wanted to keep up the work she had begun. She would not desert Julka or her Mamas.

CHAPTER LVII

[*1901–1902*]

WHAT A STRANGE YEAR that was, Mary used to think much later. Looking back on it she always felt baffled in the effort to understand the workings of fate. For one thing, Elizabeth Nicholas had a son at the beginning of September. That, at her age, and after her eighteen years of barren marriage, was a sensation throughout the family. Constance wrote about it in remarks that were only less derisive than they were ribald. Paul had of course told Mary of Elizabeth's miraculous expectations back in the winter when William had told him. After the voting-down of the Steel Corporation offer Paul took it for granted that he and his would never hear again from William's branch or from the Nicholases either. William would be too bitter to bother about amenities any more. He never had indulged in them except for ulterior reasons.

So Mary was astonished when she received a letter from Elizabeth early in the summer. It was so shy a letter, so stiff and awkward and revealing in what it did not say that Mary's heart was touched. Elizabeth, she gathered, was scared to death.

"I am sure," Elizabeth had written, "it will surprise you very much to hear from me. I feel diffident about writing, since I never have kept in touch with you. I have always been frank as you know, and this is no time to be otherwise. I find myself in a situation where I must ask some help. I am asking it of you.

"There is nobody else I can ask. I do not mind the discomfort of an ordinary illness or operation, but there is so much about all this that I do not know. If I had had children when I was first married, or if I had been with sisters or friends who were having them, I would not feel so worried and so anxious now. I do not like strangers. I have two good nurses already engaged, but I feel the need of someone who is at least connected, since I have nobody who is related.

"I would not blame you if you refused to come, Mary. I admit I have never given you the slightest reason to feel kindly towards me. But I am quite frankly throwing myself on the devotion you have shown to the rest of my family. When I was younger I did not understand the nature of that devotion and what I misunderstood I resented. I want to apologize now, in the light of my great necessity. I never dreamed a day would come when I, like the rest of my family, would admit I felt dependent on you.

"If you could plan to come here about the middle of August and stay about a month, I would be so grateful. I have no right to ask it, but I am putting such considerations aside."

"Of course I can't refuse to go," Mary said to Paul. "She's terrified."

"Poor old Lizzie."

"It's no joke for a woman her age, let me tell you."

"She must be a sight," Paul said cruelly. "Old as Jehovah."

"She's exactly my age," Mary retorted. "Two months younger."

Paul's jaw dropped. "Go on! Why you're—just the way you always were."

"Forty-four next January."

"Well, you dye that hair then, and strop your tongue every morning before breakfast." He squeezed her shoulder as he walked past her down the porch steps. He was going fishing with the boys.

"Don't bring home any catfish," Mary called after them.

And so, on account of Elizabeth, of all people in the world, she had to miss Clarrie's wedding on the first of September. Constance was furious. Instead of condoling with Mary for her bad luck in having made that promise to Elizabeth, she sent a stream of protesting cables and letters. Clarrie wrote and pleaded, there was even a note from Evan, but Mary would not change her mind.

"Couldn't somebody else take over Lizzie?" Paul asked, when he saw how badly Mary felt. "Or couldn't those kids wait and be married a few weeks later?"

"Certainly not! They've waited all this time already, just because Clarrie promised her mother she'd not get married before her twentieth birthday."

"That's typical of Constance," Paul said. "She runs off herself when she's barely seventeen and then quibbles about Clarrie being a few months older more or less." He frowned. "And Lizzie has to spoil our summer too —after I'd counted on the whole month of August. Damn my sisters."

"Now, Paul—"

"Well, why do they suddenly crop up and yell for you? They keep quiet enough when they don't need anything."

The months she spent in Elizabeth's house was one of the strangest experiences she ever had. The Nicholases lived in a gloomy brownstone front on Murray Hill. The house had high steps and a basement areaway and tall, narrow windows shrouded in layers of Nottingham lace, velour, and opaque shades. There were folding shutters, too, which collapsed into casings in the deep window recesses. The front hall was narrow and dungeonlike, like everything else in the house. Mary had never had such an impression of narrowness—in everything from Benjamin Nicholas's long, hollow-cheeked face to the very rooms themselves—all long and dark, cluttered with heavy black walnut furniture and much dark green and dark red plush upholstery. Elizabeth, when Mary arrived, had taken already to the seclusion of her bedroom, but was not staying in bed. She was sitting in an armchair by the high front window, reading a book. She rose slowly and with difficulty, very self-conscious and embarrassed. She held out her hand, thin and heavily veined and lined, and said, "It was good of you to come, Mary."

"I was glad to. How are you feeling, Elizabeth?"

She hardly needed to ask; she could see that Elizabeth was really ill and desperately uncomfortable. She had taken on no weight except for the sudden sharp bulge of the child she was carrying. Her shoulders and limbs and neck and face were thinner than ever. Mary had not seen her in eleven years. Her sandy hair was streaked with gray and her skin looked like whitish leather. She was utterly pitiful, Mary thought.

They got along well enough. Elizabeth had lost all her sharpness in the anxieties of the moment, and was pathetically grateful to Mary for whatever she did for her. Actually there was very little to do while they waited. Elizabeth had had the layette made by a seamstress and the nurses had installed everything necessary for the birth of the child. It was just the lack of feminine affection at such a time that had driven her to drop her prejudices and her pride and turn to Mary. Her husband was inarticulate both by nature and from an overwhelming sense of embarrassment at the intrusion of such a thing into his life at this late and incomprehensible date. He and Mary ate their meals in the cavernous basement dining-room, served by a hardfaced fiftyish Irish waitress. She shot rude inquisitive glances at Mary as if she knew her whole story, and sometimes set a plate before her with a silent jerk which as much as implied that she would have liked to slap it down. It was so many years since Mary had thought in these terms that she was amused rather than affronted.

She would have liked a chance to see a little of New York, to go to some theatres, to sightsee, and do some shopping. But that was almost out of the question. Nobody begrudged her an afternoon walk, but most of the shops were down below Twenty-third Street, and she had no time to wander about and do as she liked. Elizabeth lived in hourly terror that her labor would begin, and in her awkward way she clung to Mary and showed her relief when she returned to the house.

The boy was born in the evening on September third, after an awful twenty hours' struggle. Mary was amazed at how well Elizabeth behaved. Mary knew that there was no time when a woman more totally revealed the stuff of which she was made. Elizabeth acted like Clarissa's daughter, which was the best tribute Mary could pay her. She said so several times during the course of the ordeal and was rewarded by the dumb gratitude in Elizabeth's agonized eyes. There was one point when Elizabeth's pulse grew so faint that the doctor began exchanging significant looks with the senior nurse, and thinking of Benjamin Nicholas silently twisting his bony hands in the next room, Mary's heart sank. But Elizabeth pulled through and the dreadfully homely, wizened, undersized infant was named Benjamin junior.

Mary was inexpressibly glad to go home. She stayed until Elizabeth felt strong enough to manage without her, and until she could assure the bewilderedly belated mother that the nurse was doing just what she should in caring for the baby. For all her good works and her activities at hospitals and missions, Elizabeth had scarcely ever touched a baby, and was thoroughly afraid to now. But she quickly developed huge pride in the miraculous achievement of her unexpected son. Mary had never looked for anything to humanize her so much. Mary was still reflecting on the wondrous ways of maternity after her return to Pittsburgh when Elizabeth continued to write her friendly letters and give her minute reports of Benjie's progress.

At home Mary found a packing-case just arrived from London, full of pictures of Clarrie in her wedding-dress. There were beautiful cabinet photos framed in silver and morocco, and a miniature on ivory, as delicately perfect as Clarrie herself, in a jewelled onyx locket. It was like Constance to send them this way, as elaborately and expensively as possible. Clarrie looked to Mary the most beautiful bride in the whole world. Next to the miniature the loveliest picture was the big one of Clarrie and Evan standing together before a bower of flowers in the Cadogan Square drawing-room. Evan was turned toward his bride, who barely reached his shoulder. She was looking not at the camera, but up at her husband with a smile of heavenly beauty and radiance. Mary studied every detail of the lovely face so startlingly reflective of Clarissa Scott. She pored over the marvellous wedding gown which Constance had described in her letters down to the last medallion of Point de Bruxelles. Clarrie was wearing a string of pearls whose extraordinary beauty was plain even in a photograph. Mary knew who had sent her those. But dress and jewels and flowers were obscured by the rarer beauty of Clarrie's inspired face.

"It could hardly have been quieter," Constance wrote. "With Clarrie's not wanting any fuss, I was cheated out of all the folderol I'd have splashed about if I'd had my way. The Bishop married them at St. George's Hanover Square and here we had only about a hundred people afterwards; just champagne and little bouchées, Clarrie would not even have a proper breakfast. She has some quaint notion that being in love with Evan is supposed to shut the world out rather than invite it in. His family all came up from Wales; really they are darlings. So many of them, all with great solemn gray eyes and the most beautiful speaking voices. They looked like figures out of an old print. His mother wore a Paisley shawl that was worth three hundred pounds if I know anything, but they are so poor Evan said it was a puzzle for them to eke out money enough for the journey. Something or other happened about twenty years ago and they got done out of most of their land—full of coal, of course, on which some bounder has grown rich. Thank God I've plenty for Evan and Clarrie both. They can go on making music and living in their clouds and though I know you think I've gone batty, I love it.

"I wish you could have seen Giles walking up the aisle with Clarrie on his arm. He looked so presentable I thought I'd dreamed it. I suppose I've been a rotter to him. Oh well. Poor thing, he's quite frail and so damned decent."

There were only two or three letters after that, telling about "Mr. Evan and Lady Clarissa Gregory, did you ever heard of anything so absurd?—" travelling in Germany and Austria and making Constance meet them there and dragging her to the opera—"my God, I was bored!"—before the startling, somehow incredible news that Clarrie was pregnant.

Constance did not take kindly to that aspect of Clarrie's romance at all. It was like her never to have thought of it. Clarrie was too young, Clarrie was too lovely and exquisite just alone with Evan. Constance had wanted the two of them to have an idyll of perfection, wrapped round with love and music and beauty. And now this had happened! Besides, she wrote, "who the devil wants to be a grandmother at my age? Thirty-seven

—no, thirty-eight when the thing is born? Did you ever hear of anything so disgusting and preposterous?"

Mary wrote back instantly.

"Please remember," she wrote, "how you carried on before Clarrie was born—and after—and what a fool you made of yourself and how wrong you later admitted you were. All your love for Clarrie does not mean a thing if you aren't going to love her baby and her having a baby as you love her. I want you to promise me you'll control your tongue, Constance. You don't mean any of these outrageous things you say. Clarrie worships you and so does Evan, and it would be unspeakable to shock them with your talk.

"Nobody but me is to make one stitch of that baby's clothes. I can't help it if people send Clarrie presents for it, but you are not to order one thing made by anybody else. I know just what it will need and just what kind of thing you'll want it to have, and between the two extremes I'm using my judgment. Send me some fine real Val insertion and edging, very narrow; and a bolt of the finest cambric you can get in Paris. Also some very thin pure wool English flannel. I can't get anything like that here.

"Take care of Clarrie and do behave yourself, dear; you worry me dreadfully."

Mary never had a busier winter. The house seemed to be bursting with small boys. Tommy and Teddy usually appeared home from school at three o'clock at the head of a swarm of yelling dervishes who swept through the place like a herd of buffalo, gobbling the cookies and milk, or sandwiches and cocoa that Mary had set out in the pantry, then debouching on the yard for baseball, cops and robbers, touch football, snowfights, or whatever else the season and their whims suggested. Dick, who was very grown up, and taking extra work in physics and mathematics, often roared at them to douse their noise so he could study, but Mary let them alone until the time she called them in to wash up for dinner. This year, now that they were twelve, they had dinner every night with Paul and Dick, and Mary sat at the foot of the table serving the vegetables and keeping a stern eye on the twins' table manners. When Paul had guests to dinner the twins and Mary had their supper an hour earlier at the gateleg table in the dining-room window.

She was planning to sail early in May. Constance and Clarrie were both eagerly counting on her being there when the baby was born, and Mary often thought that of all the children she had ever waited for, this one of Clarrie's had taken the strongest hold on her imagination. Sometimes she wondered why. Perhaps it was because Constance would never look or feel or behave like a grandmother. Mary would be doing that for Clarrie's child instead.

She sewed more and more furiously through the spring, and by the end of April she had four boxes packed ready to take with her, filled with the most beautiful baby-clothes that she—she admitted quite shamelessly—or anyone else had ever seen. Often during the winter when she had carried her work down to the House for the afternoon, the Mamas had crowded about her, gingerly picking up the exquisite wisps of lace and beading and gossamer cambric and minute hemstitching and exclaiming over them with awe.

"Look a' dat," Mrs. Baláž or Mrs. Michalčík would marvel, wagging their heads from side to side. Their coarse, work-scarred fingers would touch the lovely things timidly. "Not for real baby!" Mrs. Sivák said once protestingly. "Baby womit, spoil ev't'ing!"

And then, two days before she was to leave for New York to board her ship, Teddy sat at the dinner-table eating nothing and scowling when he was reproved for it. That happened twice. The third time, when Paul said sharply, "Ted, sit up straight and eat your dinner!" Mary eyed the boy with a sudden uneasy suspicion. His face was flushed, his eyes were heavy. He was sick. She took him upstairs and took his temperature and looked at his throat. Putting him to bed, she kept telling herself, "He's all right. He'll be all right in the morning. He's just got an upset."

Oh, yes, her better sense jibed at her, just an upset. With those spots on his throat. . . . She tried not to think too hard about it. Doctor McClintock looked doubtful when he examined Ted; shook his head when he sent for Tommy and took his temperature too, and said, "I'll be back about eleven tonight on my way home."

"What do you think it is, Doctor?"

The old doctor smiled at her encouragingly. He knew all about her plans, he had been following the news of Clarrie almost as eagerly as Mary herself. "Don't cross any bridges," he murmured evasively. But when he did come back later, after Tommy had been vomiting for half an hour and both boys' temperatures were a hundred and three, the doctor could not put off the truth any longer.

"Scarlet fever," he said reluctantly to Mary and Paul. "I'm so sorry, Mary. Dreadfully sorry."

"Oh for God's sake!" Paul exclaimed. "Isn't that the damnedest luck! I could smack those kids."

Mary swallowed hard to force down the tears of disappointment. What a blow! She only realized now how eagerly she had been counting on this trip to Constance's. She closed her lips tight and blinked a bit to keep the tears out of her eyes and said, "It doesn't matter. They don't really need me in London anyway."

"Sure it matters!" Paul said. "Of course it matters. Say, Doc—can't she go anyhow? We can get a raft of nurses in here, the kids will be all right."

The doctor shook his head sadly. "I know that, Paul. I wouldn't keep her here on account of them. But she can't go near Clarrie now—after exposure to scarlet fever."

"I wouldn't go anyway," Mary said quickly. "I wouldn't think of leaving the boys."

So she had to wait, day by day, for news from Constance, while the boys writhed through bad cases of scarlet fever and the house was full of nurses and antiseptic sheets and the smell of carbolic acid. Mary left the boys sleeping in their darkened room one brilliant, sunny June afternoon— it was the fourth of June, she would never forget the date. She went out to the yard to get some fresh air after the horrid antiseptic smell of the house. She was out there cutting roses from the red ramblers on the summer-house. She had a sunbonnet on; the sun was blinding. Trude came hurrying down the garden walk.

"Miss Mary!" she called. "Miss Mary, cable!"

Mary dropped her shears and ran to meet Trude. The sun was so hot. It made the letter jiggle as she unfolded the paper.

CLARRIE DIED THIS MORNING GIVING BIRTH TO DAUGHTER
CONSTANCE

CHAPTER LVIII

[1907–08]

CLAIRE HAD A very early memory of a hot sunny garden high on a cliff over the blue sea. It was a big garden, with many paths that had small shiny white pebbles and tiny seashells sprinkled on them like the coarse sugar on the flat cookies she liked. There were fat round bushes along the paths with shiny, dark green, pointed leaves, and bright little oranges that she could hide inside her hand. They had thick, starry white blossoms too, which smelled delicious. Claire was always thrusting her nose into the blossoms.

Everything grew in the garden. Everything smelled spicy and sweet in the clear hot sunshine. Claire trotted about all day long after Jeannot in his blue blouse and flapping sandals. Sometimes he brought out his wheelbarrow and then Claire screamed with joy, because he always gave her a ride. Best of all she liked to play in the shade of the thick currant hedge which stood between Jeannot's garden and the other place where artichokes and cabbages and beans and lettuce grew in rows. There were red currants and white ones, huge plump clusters of clear veined fruit, hot from the sun, which Claire loved to suck slowly, letting the sour juice run down her throat while she held the seeds captive in her small teeth. She was not supposed to eat the currants. If Nannie caught her she was punished. But Jeannot let her eat them. And Jeannot taught her to lift the round tan snails from the stalks of the currant bushes and stand still and hold one in her hand and sing to it

> *Escargot, bigorneau,*
> *Montrez-moi tes cornes!*

And sure enough in a little while the pointed head and soft, squishy horns would come peeping out of the shell! Claire would jump up and down and shout and her brown curls would jump up and down too. She was a fat little girl and in spite of all Nannie's efforts to keep bonnets on her head, she always managed to get the bonnet off as soon as she started to play. So she was sunburned; her short nose and her round arms and legs and her pudgy little hands were cocoa-brown. She tried to make her kitten wear her bonnet. Sometimes she dressed him up in dolls' clothes and wheeled him around the garden in dolly's pram. Or else she sat under a bush with kitty in her arms and hugged the breath out of him and rocked him back and forth and sang to him.

"She'll kill that poor cat," she once heard Daddy say, up on the terrace where he was sitting.

"Nonsense," Mère Constance told him, "the cat loves it. Don't fuss so, Evan."

There were always many people on that terrace with the red paving and the blue umbrellas and the big straw chairs. Mère Constance always sat in a special chair, with a high back like a pretty fan, and Claire could hear her laughing voice in every corner of the garden. Usually her voice was quite loud, but sometimes Mère Constance said something Claire could barely hear, and then there would be shrieks of laughter and remarks in English and French and German and Italian from all the ladies and gentlemen. Henri the fat butler and Luigi his helper, dressed in monkey jackets and striped waistcoats were always stepping about, handing wide stemmed glasses on silver trays. Mère Constance sometimes gave Claire a taste of the fizzy yellow drink in the glasses. It was quite nice; not so sour and tangy as the juice from the currants, but it prickled nicely going down. Claire liked it mostly because Nannie was so cross with Mère Constance if she found out.

The nicest person in the wrold was Daddy, who didn't make so much noise as Mère Constance's friends. He sometimes sat for a very long time not saying anything, staring at the red flowers on the white plaster wall and the brilliant blue water beyond. Sometimes he would get up and put his hands in the pockets of his jacket and walk slowly away down the garden towards a grove of big trees with silvery gray leaves. He would walk in between the trees and sometimes he disappeared from sight. One day Claire followed him. He did not hear her pattering along behind. He wandered about for a while and then he sat down under one of the trees and leaned back against it and closed his eyes. He was very quiet. Claire stood and watched him for a long time. Then she went over softly and leaned close to him and said, "Daddy, are you tired?"

He opened his eyes and looked at Claire and his eyes were wet.

"Oh!" she said. Her own eyes opened very wide. "Why, Daddy, you're crying. Are you hurt?"

He smiled and took Claire in his arms and settled back against the tree trunk holding her tight.

"No," he said, making a funny noise in his throat. "Not a bit. I was just dreaming about something."

"What, Daddy?"

"About Mummie."

Claire clapped her hands. "Oh, that's your nicest dream. Tell me all over again."

She had heard the same dream lots of times before. But she loved him to repeat it; the more familiar a story the better she enjoyed it. Before he reached the end she was reciting the nicest part with him: "And she had long golden hair and beautiful blue eyes and pink cheeks and a lovely voice and now she's an angel."

Claire loved Daddy best of all, and Mère Constance next. She knew she was supposed to love Nannie next after that, but didn't. She often thought about who came next. Kitty, she usually decided.

"And next?" Mère Constance sometimes played this game with her.

Claire would think for a little while and then say "Mary."

"But you can scarcely remember Mary, darling." She had only been to visit them twice since Claire was born. Claire was five years old now.

"Yes, I do," Claire would say, nodding her head so hard that the brown curls bobbed up and down her shoulders. "I want her to come back now, too."

"I wish she would."

"Well, make her. Make her come here. So she can play in the currants with me."

Mary had only been to London to visit them. And Claire did not like it much there. It was dark and cold and she was always stuffed into so many clothes before Nannie took her to the Park. She always carried something to play with, a diavolo or a hoop and stick; but after a little while she grew tired of toys and wanted to go home. The only thing she liked in London was the nursery fire. She liked to lie on her stomach on a rug by the grate and color pictures with crayons in a big book. There were words under each picture and Claire could read them all now.

The London house was full of people too. There were maids in rustling aprons and funny caps like fluted custard-cups, and Radford and Simons and Monsieur Gonneau in his tall white cap whom Claire was sometimes taken down to see as a great treat. Claire liked that better than going to the drawing-room at tea-time, dressed in embroidered white batiste over a pink slip with a wide pink sash and pink bows in her hair. She hated those clothes. She was to curtsey, Nannie taught her, to each person, and stand quietly by Mère Constance while she ate one small cake, and then go about and curtsey all over again, and go back to the nursery.

When Claire was five Mary came to London again. It was springtime and Claire noticed that this was the part of the year when there was most bustle and fuss about the house. There were more people coming and going, more glittering carriages with shiny horses and tall footmen, more noisy parties downstairs when Claire lying in bed could hear loud talking and laughter through the hours until she fell asleep. But this year she hadn't noticed any beautiful new gowns, gleaming with trimming, on Mère Constance when she went down to say good night. Mère Constance seemed to wear only black, and though she was as gay and funny as ever when she talked to people, sometimes she stopped short and seemed to remember something and bit her lip.

She took Claire along when she went to the railway station to meet Mary. Claire was very excited. Stations were perfectly familiar to her with their high glass roofs and dingy iron railings and the puffing, hissing engines of which she wasn't afraid a bit. She loved engines and trains and all the places you went on them. She stood by a gate clutching Mère Constance's hand and jumping up and down with impatience as they watched the faces streaming by. They did not have to wait long. There she was— walking quickly up the long platform with her full skirt swishing behind her. She was looking for them just the way they were watching for her. She gave her ticket to the guard and hurried through the gate to meet them.

Claire flung herself into Mary's arms and was swung up off the ground as lightly as if Mary had been Daddy, instead of a thin little lady. Mary kissed Mère Constance and Claire kissed Mary and all three of them squeezed into the brougham laughing and talking at once. But Mère Constance shook her head a little at Claire. That meant she was to be quiet now and let the grown-ups do all the talking. She sat clinging to Mary's hand while they talked about her the way all grown-ups do.

"How she's grown, Constance!"

"She's certainly not going to be a Dresden doll like Clarrie."

"She looks like Evan. How is he, dear?"

"Just the same. Quiet and sweet. He's in Vienna now, has been most of the winter."

"Daddy sends me a present every week," Claire told Mary proudly. "Last time it was a whole Noah's Ark made of chocolate. Two of every kind of animal. I've eaten one bear and two giraffes and a duck."

"It was too bad to eat up both giraffes at once," Mary said.

"Yes, but their necks are such fun to suck."

After Claire's bath that evening Mary came up to the nursery and Claire sat in her lap and read Little Black Sambo, which Mary said she did very well. Claire knew it by heart but it was nice to act reading anyway. And she loved to sit in Mary's lap. Mary wasn't fat and soft like Mère Constance; she was quite flat and bony. But when you cuddled up under her high collar her cheek was soft and smooth and smelled a little bit sweet like candy. Mère Constance came up while they were sitting there and stood and looked at them.

"My God," she said with a laugh, "I can almost remember myself in her place."

"You might also remember your language," Mary said. Claire was a little puzzled by that.

After Claire was tucked into bed Mary went downstairs to Constance.

"Well, tell me all the news," Constance said, stretching out on her couch and lighting a cigarette. "How's Paul?"

"Fine. I was worried about him last fall. That panic came so suddenly and a lot of people were caught."

"He must have been to some extent. I had to take an awful cut."

"You should be thankful you got anything. That was just Paul's good management. He might have been caught with carloads of rolled steel he couldn't dispose of. Or bank loans he couldn't meet."

"I hope to God everything's all right now."

"For Paul's sake, no doubt," said Mary.

"Oh, go on. Sarcastic as ever, aren't you? *Is* business all right or must I plan to go into genteel poverty?"

"Of course it's all right! You idiot! Dick's working full time now, and Paul is so proud he simply struts. It reminds me of the year he went to work with your father."

"Is Dick any fun, Mary, or is he a prig?"

"Where did you get such a notion? Just because he works hard and graduates with honors he doesn't have to be a prig. He's a grand boy. He has loads of young people up in the evenings, and we have open house every Sunday night now. I never know how many there'll be or who's coming. They all invite their friends—the twins too. They went to their first dance this Christmas vacation."

"Sounds nice," Constance said, "if you're cut out for it. My God, I'm bored this year. Did you ever know such a time for poor old Giles to kick off—just at the opening of the Season?"

"And you wear mourning. Hypocrite."

"What do you want me to do? Dash about in a red hat and be a scandal?"

Mary burst out laughing. "Be a scandal!" she repeated. "What else have you been for twenty-five years? You're beginning to show it, too, my love."

Constance bounced irritably on the couch. "Why the hell I ever ask you over here," she growled.

"Why I ever come is more like it," Mary retorted. They smiled at each other. Constance ran her fingers through her hair. She glanced across to the high mirror screen which reflected the whole room—herself, spreading and billowing on the tufted satin couch, the clutter of flowers and perfume bottles and bric-a-brac; Mary slender and immaculate in a *café-au-lait* moiré dress.

"I am getting fat as a pig," Constance said ruefully. She looked down the length of her own body. "But what the hell. How do you keep your figure—and your hair?"

"I was about to remark about yours. You're dyeing it."

"I suppose," replied Constance, "it would be chic to let it turn spotted like a hyena? That's what it started to do."

"Not before you helped it along someway or other."

"Yours is hardly changed at all. Just turning a little sandy."

"You are forty-four years old," Mary said, "and I am fifty. I don't expect to fool Nature, and you'd do better if you didn't try."

"Fifty," Constance murmured. Then she sat up and reached for another cigarette. "Mary, why have you never married Paul?" she asked suddenly.

Mary started. She turned a pained red and for a moment her eyes flashed angrily. Then she sat back in her chair and sighed.

"Must we go into that?" she asked. "It ought to be pretty self-evident."

"It's been self-evident to me ever since Louise died that the natural thing for you and Paul was to marry."

"We don't happen to see it that way."

"But *why not?*"

"I suppose," Mary said slowly, "if I tried to explain something to you on the grounds of thinking of someone else before oneself, you'd have trouble understanding, wouldn't you?"

"Probably."

"Then there's hardly any use my trying to explain."

Constance was looking solemn. Her green eyes lay heavily on Mary.

"I think I really do understand," she said softly.

"Thank God, then. I shan't have to rake up a lot of painful memories and go into everything with a microscope."

Constance lay back and squinted at the ceiling. The line of her chin was blurred; she was filling out rapidly there, and Mary remembered vividly the swanlike beauty of her throat when they first came to London. And even until quite recently. Constance was talking slowly.

"You think I'm a selfish, gross, spoiled, lazy old—" she swallowed the word she was about to use. "And I daresay that's right. But even wicked old bags like me can feel, Mary. I just keep my feelings locked up in compartments to suit myself. Other people stir them all up together."

It was extremely unlike her to talk about herself. Mary listened quietly.

"For me," Constance went on, "love has nothing to do with marriage and marriage has nothing to do with a man I'd want and children have nothing to do with either. And the people you love you love for themselves and not because they come in a package tied round with the strings of your feelings for somebody else."

"Few people would understand that."

"I know. But that's the way I am and that's the way I feel about you. You are in one of those compartments. Clarrie was in one and Claire can't ever take her place. Maybe she'll make one of her own. I love Evan. And Ed. And Paul. I loved Mama. That's all," said Constance.

"And you've had more friends and more attention that any woman alive."

Constance shrugged. "Probably because I didn't give a damn. They like being kicked about."

"You're *brutal*."

"I suppose that's why I wish you'd marry Paul and make the rest of his life happy? Because I'm brutal?"

"Paul is happy," Mary said. "So am I. I told you once years ago you live in a perpetual melodrama and other people aren't like that. We live and poke along and worry about the boys' reports and whether to install electricity and a new water-heater. We talk about boats and fishing and the mill and baseball when the boys are around, and about business and family matters when they're not."

"Marriage," said Constance bitterly, "in all but name and bed. What in hell kind of life is that for Paul?"

Mary ignored the remark, but Constance refused to be parried.

"Do you mean to tell me Paul has nothing to do with women? That he lives like Ed?"

"I did not say that." Mary's lips were stiff.

"Well then, don't be so prudish about the thing."

"You could hardly call me that."

"Then why the devil don't you marry? It would be honest, anyway."

Mary sprang from her chair. "Constance," she gasped, turning pale, "you didn't think—I—we—"

"What else should I think? That's what I mean. If you live with him—"

"But I don't! That's the whole point."

"Oh." Constance sat back limply and looked at Mary with her mouth open.

"How did we ever get onto this subject anyway?" Mary cried. "You've pried and prodded till everything's strewn all over the place and now nobody makes any sense." Her eyes filled with tears.

"Oh, Jesus, I'm sorry." Constance spoke jerkily. "I didn't mean that. I wouldn't have started all this for mischief's sake. It wasn't just gossip. I *care*, Mary. You know damn well I do. I love both of you and I don't want you to waste any more of your lives."

"They're not wasted. We know what's best for us, we found out years ago. What's best for the boys. You told me just now what you think about love and marriage—do you think nobody else has anything figured out?"

"Why—"

"We have, you see. We've always had other people to think about and now we're used to it that way. The boys and everybody—"

"But the boys would love you to marry Paul."

"I'm the judge of that."

"And poor old Paul gets the short end of the stick. What the hell does he *do*—he's not senile yet, for God's sake!"

Mary bit her lips. They were almost white.

"I don't pry into Paul's concerns the way you're trying to," she said stiffly.

"You're a smart card," said Constance.

CHAPTER LIX

[*1912*]

GOING ABOUT THE HOUSE on a July morning in 1912 Mary was stirred by a deep sense of change. Most changes happened so gradually, or she had expected them for so long, that she did not precisely remark them when they came. But today for some reason everything impressed her sharply. Everything from the telephone and the electric lights, which had been in the house for years now, to the way she missed Anna in the kitchen. The old German cook, Mary's right hand and loyal friend, had died after sixteen years of devoted service. Trude was taking her place; not so good a cook as her mother, but better than anyone Mary could have found now. There was a new chambermaid, third-generation Irish to whom the old jealousies and gossip could have no meaning; and a waitress named Stella. It seemed like a large staff just for Paul and Dick, with the twins away almost all the time. But cleaning was more work than ever in Pittsburgh. Mary did not imagine more dirt than ever before; there was more dirt. There were more mills and bigger mills, up and down both sides of the rivers.

Once young people started to grow up, Mary thought, they went about it in a bewildering hurry. The twins were twenty-two this year. It seemed only yesterday that they were gangling hulks with tousled heads and stained corduroys and a troop of obstreperous cronies at their heels. Now they were men like Paul himself; like Dick, who was coming home from his honeymoon today!

The twins had not been at home together for almost seven years, and that gave Mary a turn when she counted back through those years now. She remembered a winter evening soon after their fifteenth birthday when Ted was lying quietly on the parlor floor reading *War and Peace,* and Paul was working on an article for the *Metallurgical Review,* and she was sewing, as usual, Tom was not there, he had gone out right after dinner. It must have been about ten o'clock when they heard a commotion on the front steps and Paul had stood up at the furious ringing of the doorbell, and gone to let in two policemen and several angry neighbors of his, all holding Tom by the elbows. Mary could feel still the wave of horror that had shaken her.

Paul had stood pale with rage and glaring at Tom, waiting to be told what this meant, while Mary and Ted hovered anxiously in the doorway of the back parlor.

"This boy of yours," Paul's old friend and neighbor George Cottrell said, red in the face, "has gone far enough. I called the police, Paul, and I'm going to prefer charges against Tom."

"What for?"

"Vandalism, wilful destruction, disturbing the peace."

The two policemen stood bulky and impassive, Tom defiant and sullen between them.

"Tom," Paul asked in a voice none of them had ever heard before, "what is the meaning of this? What have you done?"

Tom shot a contemptuous glance at Mr. Cottrell, as if to brand him a bum sport, and said, "Oh, we were just razzing around. Just the gang."

"What did you *do?*"

"Broke windows."

"Whose windows?"

"His." Tom jerked his head rudely at Cottrell. "Burns's. McKelvies'. Roberts'. Thur—" Paul interrupted him. "Do you mean to say," he roared, "every house in this block?"

"About."

Mary and Ted exchanged a look. Ted was if possible more shocked than Mary. He and Tom had not spent their free time together for some years. Ted was oftener in the house reading than playing out in the yard.

Paul turned to George Cottrell. "I'm sorry about this," he said. "I'm going to let you go ahead and handle this whatever way you intended. Do anything you want about Tom."

"Oh, I—" Cottrell was embarrassed now.

Paul shook his head. "I'm washing my hands of the whole thing. Do whatever you'd do if you didn't know Tom or me either."

The thing ended next day in Paul's paying a heavy fine for Tom's misdemeanor, and the cost of replacing all the broken windows in the neighbors' houses. Paul was deeply upset. The whole business was more than a prank, there was a wild, alarming character to it. For a couple of years Tom had been the ringleader of a gang of boys, all well-bred schoolmates of his, who were getting a bad name all over the Northside.

Paul turned as usual to Mary for advice and they quickly made the obvious decision that Tom must go away to school. Tom's trouble was really sheer animal energy, a furious, tumultuous force whose outlet was violence when it could not be violent activity. He was almost incapable of staying indoors. No ordinary house and yard could hold him. He had extraordinary athletic skill of every kind and unless he was absorbed in using it, he stormed about the place with his restless green eyes looking for trouble. He never went through a door; he crashed through it. He never walked or ran up and down stairs; he catapulted. His voice was a sharp-pitched bark, as if every word he had to say was part of the quarterback's signals in a football game.

Paul sent Tom to Exeter, where he promptly made the football, baseball, indoor track and hockey teams. He excelled particularly at hockey, which he played with diabolical fury and daring. But he was in constant trouble with his teachers. He flunked his courses over and over again. Only the incentive of playing college football and hockey drove him through the entrance examinations and by the narrowest possible margin into Yale. He went to Sheff because his father and Dick had done so, but he scarcely made a gesture of studying.

Meanwhile Ted stayed at home and graduated from Allegheny Preparatory with top honors and passed his college entrance examinations brilliantly. Only in Edgar as a student could Paul and Mary remember any precedent in the family for a boy like Ted. He had a real love for books, and especially for classics. He skipped the inevitable Rover Boys and Frank Merriwell which his schoolmates read, and devoured Hugo, Balzac, Tolstoy, and Dostoievsky. He did his school work easily, though he disliked science and mathematics, an incomprehensible thing to Paul. He did not want to go to Sheff and for a time he was anxious not to go to Yale at all. He thought Harvard promised a more scholarly atmosphere and at one time begged to go there. But Paul seemed very disappointed, and Ted was finally shouted down by Dick and Tom. They roared at him that it was bad enough to have a grind in the family; if they had to have a Harvard one they would be massacred every time they stuck their noses inside their club. So Ted gave in and settled for the Academic department at Yale.

Paul often felt grateful that his eldest son, at least, was no mystery to him. The twins were each baffling in his own way, but Dick was everything

Paul understood and had confidence in. Dick had majored in electrical engineering at Sheff, and after graduating he went almost at once into the mill, where his mechanical talent and modern technical training were a godsend to Paul.

Mary had really not felt so full of excited anticipation in years as she did this morning. Not only was Dick bringing Ruth home from their honeymoon, but Ted was coming home for good too. Mary had written and asked him particularly to come that day because it would please his father so much. Ted had graduated from Yale a month ago and had been up in Canada at a fishing-camp with some of his friends. He was to start work in the mill the first of August. Mary often suspected that this prospect was a grim one for him. If the circumstances had been different she would have urged Paul to let Ted go on and take a Master's degree in English at Harvard, which he really wanted to do. Ted could not ask Paul for this now, and Mary could not encourage him to; Paul had had enough disappointment in Tom. Mary had a pang whenever she thought about it.

Tom flunked out of Yale in the middle of his junior year. He could perfectly well have done enough work to get by, but he would not do it. He literally lived for football and hockey and was deaf to all efforts to interest him in anything else. He was willing enough to work in the mill for a month during summer vacations as Paul expected him to do, but he acted like a caged animal dying of confinement. After putting in the month, he would make a bee line for the wildest, roughest place he could find, and stay there until the day he had to be back at college.

When he flunked out Paul had a wretched time. He had not realized how much his heart was set on each of his boys graduating from Yale, starting in at the bottom at the mill, and working under his guidance to the permanent berth he was best suited for. Long ago Paul had it all planned out. He used to talk to Mary about it by the hour, sitting with his pipe by the fire and dreaming out loud.

"Dick will be president and general manager," he would say. "Tom will be production superintendent. We'll work the hell out of him, he'll be responsible for so many different things he'll never have a chance to get restless. And Ted"—that was obvious. Quiet, brainy Ted would be the head of the business department. A good intellect, Paul believed, could be just as valuable in business as in postgraduate study and in newspaper work, which Ted had said once he would love to do. He really wanted to write, he confessed to Mary, but "how can I say that to Dad? You know how he'd feel about it."

He would feel very bad, they both knew. It was not as if he had had to swallow only his disappointment about Tom's flunking out. Far worse, and far more serious, was the sequel. Tom did not want to work in the mill at all. That was a stunning blow to Paul. He had never remotely conceived that Tom, with all his energy and his craving for action, would not find just the outlet he needed in the surging vitality of the mill. But Tom had said, "Dad, if you shut me up in that place I'll—well, some day I'll jump into a furnace if I stay long enough to go that crazy."

Paul shuddered; this was a bad thing for a son of Louise's to say.

"What *do* you want to do, Tom?" Paul's voice was lifeless and his face tragic.

Tom stalked the floor, running his hard brown fingers through his coppery hair. He had the slanting green eyes which reminded Mary so intensely of Constance, and all the ungovernable instincts that went with them.

"I don't know," Tom said roughly. "I don't know. I've got to be away —somewhere where it's wild and nobody gives a damn what I do. Somewhere *big*." He made a sweeping gesture with his right arm.

"But that's not work," Paul said slowly. "That's not a life for a man. You're talking like a kid."

Tom had been so intent on his own desire that he did not even try to understand his father. He only said, "I don't want anything else, Dad, money or a job or anything. You can cut me off without a nickel if you want to. Then I'll bum my way where I want to go. But I'm going."

There was no stopping him and it was not Paul's nature to be punitive —especially about a thing so vital as this. He could only hope that Tom would work it all out of his system and come to his senses and come home. That was what Mary felt sure he would do. So Paul gave him a moderate allowance and let him go. It was now a year and a half since they had seen him. He was punching cattle on a ranch in Texas—the biggest ranch in the world, some Westerner told Paul—and no dude business about it. Tom never wrote a letter; the most that ever came was a rare postcard to Paul with a few scrawled words ending in "Love, Tom." Mary could not find the courage to look at Paul's eyes on a day when she put one of these cards by his plate at breakfast.

The bride and groom had been gone for three months, on a wonderful honeymoon from which Ruth had sent Mary and Paul a constant stream of letters and postcards. They had travelled all over Europe, from the English lakes to the Austrian Alps, and had visited Rome and Venice and Paris and Dresden and Brussels—a real Grand Tour. The climax was their visit to Dick's Aunt Constance who gave Ruth a pair of diamond earrings and a Persian lamb coat and took them gambling at Monte Carlo. Ruth had never seen anybody like this, or anybody who brought up a child the way Aunt Constance was rearing Claire. She let her drink wine and stay up late at night listening to her father sing, and some of the things Aunt Constance said with the child right there taking it all in! Ruth had written Mary all about it. Mary smiled when she pictured gentle, pretty little Ruth Chilton from Montclair, shocked and dazzled by Constance and her cheerful madhouse.

Paul had a surprise for Dick and Ruth and Ted. When the train pulled in and the bride and groom, with Ted behind them, walked through the track gate, Paul and Mary were standing there beaming. It was very hot. Paul wore a thin tan summer suit and a wide-brimmed Panama. Mary had on a thin muslin in a fine black-and-white stripe, trimmed with white silk braid. She embraced and kissed Ruth and admired her Paris clothes.

"I see Constance's hand in that," she exclaimed, admiring the full-skirted suit of blue silk poplin.

"You certainly do," Ruth replied, "can you imagine me having the nerve to go into Paquin's alone?"

The three men, arm in arm, were walking ahead of them. Paul at fifty-six had lost his elastic step of years ago, and walked with a firm, sedate tread that reminded Mary a little of his father. He had not the imperious, inflexible quality, either in mind or body, of the Old Man, but he was—as Tom had said once after a clash with him—no lightweight. Paul's blond hair and moustache had faded gradually to a sandy gray, and his strapping figure had thickened through the middle. Mary liked all that; it added importance to Paul's appearance. But in recent years he had taken to stooping a little, and his broad shoulders were growing round. He no longer stood his full six feet one, and Dick topped him by an inch while Ted was taller still. But Paul between his sons was a heartwarming picture.

Mary could see that Ruth was thinking the same thing. Her quiet eyes rested adoringly on the back of Dick's handsome brown head, and on his great shoulders perfectly set off by a London suit. Ted walked close to Paul, bending his head to hear what his father was saying. There was something almost protective in his attitude, and this was not the first time Mary had noticed it. It had been developing during the past year or so. Every time Mary thought about it she also thought of Tom, and her face grew stern.

They walked through the main waiting-room and came out at the station entrance where Jones should be waiting with the big carriage. But he was not there. Dick stood and craned his neck while Ted hurried from the driveway to the street to see if he was out there. Paul called him back. He took Dick and Ted each by an elbow and led them to a scarlet touring-car which was parked in the driveway. A young chauffeur stood cap in hand beside it. The boys, and Ruth walking along with Mary, paused and stared at Paul.

"Get in," he said.

Ted's mouth was open.

"Whose is it?" he asked, just as Dick said the same thing.

"Ours."

"No."

"Go on."

"Why *Dad!*" Ruth threw her arms around his neck. "It's the most beautiful thing I ever saw."

Ted was walking slowly around the car, examining it inch by inch. He came back to the others and whistled.

"She's a beauty."

"It's a Lozier," Dick explained to Ruth.

"Gee, I can't believe it."

"Dick, this is Stanley," Paul said, indicating the chauffeur. "My son, Mr. Dick, Stanley. Mrs. Dick. Mr. Ted." Stanley touched his cap.

"But where's Jones?" Ruth asked. It was like her to think of that.

Mary laughed. "Jones is relegated to the garden," she said. "Your father offered to have him taught to drive this thing but he turned up his nose and said he'd rather starve. So he putters, and drives me to market, and one thing or another. He's too old to work hard anyway."

They were all seated by now, Mary and Ruth in the back seat, Paul and Dick on two folding seats which Stanley proudly demonstrated, and Ted in front. Stanley set knobs and levers on the steering-gear and dashboard and hurried round in front to crank. He had to make four tries before she caught. Then there was a roar, a magnificent spurt of noise and blue smoke, and Stanley sprang into place and let the car into gear. They all sat forward, breathless with excitement, while he steered the snorting machine around the drive and out into Liberty Avenue. Passersby paused and gaped at them on the majestic progress down the Avenue and across the Sixth Street Bridge. Automobiles were no longer a rarity by any means, but one like this would be a sensation anywhere. The boys had been begging Paul for years to buy a car, and Dick had even talked of getting a Ford runabout of his own, but this exceeded any notions of a car that they had had. It was like Paul to put them off all this time while everybody they knew grew used to automobiles, and finally to buy this huge, beautiful red thing with the glittering brass lamps and trimming, the folding top with its straps and buckles, the huge brass horn with the black rubber squeeze-ball. Stanley squeezed it now to warn a delivery-wagon out of the way and they all roared with laughter at the driver's panic. He leaned forward clinging to the reins while the frightened horse plunged and skittered and the driver shook his fist and swore at the Scotts.

"This is going to be fun," Ted said, turning around. "Can Dick and I drive it, Dad?"

"Why not? Stanley'll teach you. We'll go on trips in it and all take turns driving."

Paul had another disappointment of a sort when he found that Dick and Ruth did not intend to live at home with him. He had taken it for granted that they would. He and Mary were both very fond of Ruth. She had paid many long visits to them since Dick's junior year in college, when they first met, and she had won their hearts completely by her warmth and the way she slipped into the family circle. Above all, Mary saw with satisfaction, Ruth encouraged the intense bond between Dick and his father. She might have tried to draw Dick away and monopolize him herself. But Dick had had the sense to choose the right wife, Paul often said happily to Mary. They liked everything about the marriage, and Ruth's people, quiet and moderately fixed, who lived in a yellow clapboard tree-shaded house on a pleasant suburban street.

So Paul was really shocked when Mary—put up to it by Dick—told him that the children would not live with him. Dick had said quite frankly, "Mary, if you think it would hurt Dad really badly I guess we could settle down with him but—"

"You want your own home," Mary said. "Ruth wouldn't be natural if she didn't."

"But I don't want to disappoint Dad," Dick said. "If he really has set his heart on this."

"You leave your Dad to me. If he's set his heart he'll have to unset it. You and Ruth will be here a lot and you'll be at the mill all the time— Ruth's got to have elbow room to make her own friends and her own home."

Paul took it reasonably when Mary pointed out the fallacy of his thinking they could all live together. She convinced him quickly that no two women could both run a house and said, "Of course if you're absolutely sure you want Dick and Ruth, I'd rather go to Cannes and live with Constance."

Constance had given up her London house in 1910 and moved permanently to Cannes. Mary went over almost every year now to visit her and Claire.

"When you move to Cannes it'll be time for me to quit work and go along," Paul said. "You're absolutely right about Dick; I was a selfish old fool."

It was no accident, Mary knew, that they had built this solid, strongly-knit family, she and Paul. Sometimes she contrasted life as it was now with the days when Louise was alive. What a commentary on that twisted, bitter soul; even her children had shed their tenuous feeling for her as they had outgrown their clothes. With Paul to absorb their filial love and Mary to keep their home a bastion around them they would have been a world sufficient to themselves except for Tom. And even there Paul had been wise enough never to close a door behind him. Even in his worst disappointment Paul had been generous and patient. If Tom ever did decide to come home and settle down there would be no breaches to heal.

Mary was struck by that when William Scott died a few weeks after Tom left college and went west. It was quite shocking that the news of his brother's death did not grieve Paul; he certainly could not be hypocritical about that with Mary. He went to Boston to the funeral, taking Dick with him and meeting Ted who went up from New Haven.

William's share in the mill was divided, by the terms of old William Scott's will, between Willy and Angelica. They were at that time aged thirty-four and thirty-one respectively. Willy had been married for nine years to an eminently suitable wife born Georgina Hall of the best Beacon Hill blood. They were so thoroughly absorbed in Julia's world that their Pittsburgh relatives never impinged on their existences at all.

Angelica had not married and it was clear that she never would. Paul called her the triumph of militant virginity. She and her mother lived precisely as the Gaylords had for sedate generations past, giving the approved allotments of attention to good works, society, and to intellectual pursuits which in Angelica's case took the form of an interest in genealogy.

But if William Scott's rôle had been to disperse one branch of the family, a startlingly different thing had happened in the case of Edgar. This was the more surprising, Paul and Mary saw, because of the irrevocable finality with which Edgar had withdrawn from the world. They had grown used to thinking of him in retrospect. Only Mary had a common bond with him in the present; only she could understand to this day why he had taken the step he had. Only she had ever seen him in the years of his exile. Even if he had asked Paul to visit him, Mary knew that Paul had a curious dread of ever having to see Edgar as he must be now, largely a stranger. Paul preferred to remember him as he had been. It shocked Paul if Mary spoke of Fra Anselmo, which had been Edgar's name since his profession into the Benedictine Order. But one remarkable action of Edgar's had gone a long way toward reassuring Paul about the wisdom of his brother's judgment. This was a letter that Mary had received out of the blue, one fall day seven years ago. She read:

"MY DEAR MARY,

"I know you will join with me in prayers of humble thanks and joyful gratitude to Our Lord, to our Holy Mother, and to all the blessed Saints who have interceded for me and brought about the inestimably precious blessing I am about to receive. I am to be received into our Holy Order of Saint Benedict within the month, and in contemplation of this step, for which I have worked and prayed so long, I am arranging my remaining personal affairs in accordance with the Rule of the Order.

"As I explained to you at the time when I saw fit to deed half of my inherited property to Constance, it had been my hope at one time to convert my share in our mill into funds which I could give to the Order. At that time, however, when you made clear to me that it lay within my power to help my brother Paul, I chose to do that as a compensation for depriving him of my help in his work, on which he had hoped to depend.

"Since that time I have devoted earnest and prayerful thought to the question of the disposition of the remaining half of my share in the mill. Though it would give me profound satisfaction to cede this property or its financial equivalent to our Order at this time, I have come to the conclusion that I have certain other responsibilities which must be discharged if I am to continue the effort to expiate the sins I committed and the consequent anxiety I laid upon my beloved brother and upon you.

"I bear deeply in mind and upon my soul the consciousness of the debt owed to you by every member of my family. I know that no material recognition can be considered recompense for the gift of your life to them. I know the Christian loyalty, self-sacrifice, and self-denial which have armed and guided you in your long years of devotion first to my mother and now to my brother and his children.

"It is in awareness of these facts that I now, upon renouncing the last of my worldly property, choose to leave it in your hands, secure in the confidence that you will use it wisely. I leave to your sole judgment the ultimate disposition of this property according to events or necessities as they may arise. I leave with you the discharge of any responsibility I may have incurred. I leave with you the knowledge of my absolute devotion to Holy Church and to this Order into which I am about to be received.

"I send you my blessing and my devoted gratitude for the faith and understanding through which you have supported me these long years past.

"Lovingly yours in Christ,

"EDGAR SCOTT, hereafter ANSELM, O.S.B."

The letter was folded around a document which Mary opened with shaking hands. It was a deed of gift for the second half of Edgar's share in the mill. She showed the letter and the deed to Paul. He and she were both too moved to say a word.

CHAPTER LX

[*1914*]

EVAN AND PAUL were playing chess at one end of the terrace. Claire was cutting out paper dolls at the other, sitting cross-legged on the tiles at Mary's feet. Constance and three friends were playing auction bridge under the blue awning, their usual chatter stilled by their concentration on the cards. They spoke only when bidding, or when some exclamation was called forth by the play.

Mary had some sewing in her hands, but she was not working. From behind her glasses (she had taken to gold-rimmed spectacles for reading and sewing) she was quietly scrutinizing Constance. She sent piercing glances at the other bridge-players too. They were smart and sleek and superbly confident of themselves. None of them looked as if anything could ever disturb the beautifully complicated texture of his life. This was not really the season for Cannes, of course; this late, intensely hot July. But the "regulars," the smallest, richest, most amusing clique often kept their houses open the year round.

Paul and Mary had arrived here ten days ago, on the second real vacation Paul had ever consented to take. Business was not too good at home, but Dick was equal to most decisions that might come up, and he could always keep in touch with Paul by cable. Since reaching Cannes Mary had heard a good many rumors of trouble in Austria as the result of the shooting of Franz Josef's heir in Servia last month. Evan talked about it; it was the kind of thing Julka Liska would be all excited about; but nobody else seemed to worry, and it certainly did not impress itself on Mary. She was far more interested in the people around her, particularly in the never-palling pastime of watching Constance. That was equivalent to an evening in the theatre.

The Countess was fat, there was no question about it. She filled out the chair she sat in, her corseted curves squeezed cozily between the arms. Her hair was by now a cheerful brightly dyed henna red, marvellously waved and dressed in a coiffure which took one hour of her maid's time whenever it was concocted. During this operation Constance sat stark naked, her white body billowing over the cushioned chair, with a mirror in one hand and a cigarette in the other, directing, criticizing, and commenting in a stream of mingled English and French heavily spiked with profanity. Any female in the house was at liberty to visit her room during the hairdressing, and that seemed to be the time when Constance most enjoyed chatting with Mary. Claire was almost always there, sitting happily in a corner trying on her grandmother's jewels or draping the cats in ruffles and gilets of priceless laces. Sometimes Mary held her breath when Constance came out with a hair-raising expletive or a scandalous reference to somebody's latest affair. Mary would look nervously at Claire, hoping she had neither heard nor understood, and Constance would sit grinning in the mirror at Mary, shrugging her thickening shoulders and winking her wicked green eyes.

But Mary found Claire strangely untouched by her grandmother's bawdy talk. It was amazing, Mary said to Constance, simply amazing, that the child was as innocent and natural as she was.

"It's not so amazing," Constance said. "She's intelligent and she has taste and imagination and plenty of good stuff to occupy her. Why should she ape me?"

"Most children would."

"Oh. Most children. Strikes me I told you bloody years ago I was not 'most people' and I'll thank you to remember that my offspring aren't either."

Mary sighed. "I wonder if anything will ever take you down a peg?"

"I daresay. Someday I'll come a classic cropper."

"Oh no, Mère Constance!" Claire exclaimed, craning her neck to get the effect of a ruby earring on her childish brown ear. "You'd never be so commonplace."

Mary found it just as baffling to consider the difference between Claire and Clarrie. Claire's mother had always been the model of a sheltered young English girl, for all her talent and her intellectual emancipation. This child Claire had been turned loose mentally and socially into the rough-and-tumble of Constance's life as early as she had been left physically free to roam the big garden. She had no playmates of her own age and never showed the slightest desire for any. She was perfectly happy with Mère Constance; with Daddy who was often, though not always there; with her books and her cats and her paper dolls and her secret cave down under the cliff by the water, where she spent a great deal of her time.

She was not a pretty child, nor superficially a winning one, but she was fascinating to Mary. She did not resemble anyone in the family. She had curly brown hair with a deep chestnut cast, and flecked hazel eyes and brown skin even when she was not sunburned. Her face was broad and firm, with square planes and high cheekbones and a broad jaw; there was a trace of Evan there. She spoke English and French and Italian equally well. Nobody had taught her the latter, she had picked it up from the servants and under-gardeners who were mostly Italian by birth or propinquity. Last year Evan had taken her on a holiday to his beloved Vienna, where he really lived as much as he could be said to have a home anywhere. In six weeks she absorbed enough Wiener-Deutsch to throw Constance and her friends into convulsions when, on her arrival home, she gave imitations of low comedy from the Josefstadt.

"*Habi 'ne Schwesterrrrrl,*" she would sing in a throaty leer, and when Mary, hearing it for the first time, gasped, "Evan, you didn't take her to a cheap music-hall!" he only smiled and answered, "My dear, her home rather resembles one. I'm not afraid of her learning anything her grandmother hasn't taught her."

Constance looked up from the game she was playing and blew him a kiss.

"There's my boy."

Mary feared that Claire would be a horrid child, over-wise, oversmart, precocious and sophisticated. But she was not. Like her mother she read anything she wanted, and was always asking her grandmother to buy her books, since the big villa at Cannes would have contained few but for her. She had a passion for Greek and Roman mythology which, combined with a fantastic imagination, resulted in extraordinary games that she played all by herself. It was nothing out of the way to come upon Claire down behind the olive grove, standing on a stump wrapped in a white tablecloth, with a shiny pudding-mould on her head, a light oar in one hand and the cover of the copper washboiler in the other. She would be declaiming a long stream of half-intelligible words and phrases, in a jumble of several languages, accompanied by grandiosely dramatic gestures. Once Mary made the mistake of asking who she was.

"I am Athena!" Claire replied in a dark tone, "and you, common mortal, dare not approach me without prostrating yourself."

She was really much like Constance, but she had a tougher, more serious mind. She was peculiarly fearless. At a time when children were shepherded into the water to paddle and breast-stroke on water-wings and safety-belts, Claire would dive off the yacht-float on the end of Constance's pier and strike out into the harbor like a boy. The first time she did that for bravado, expecting to give her father, who was sunning himself on the rocks, a dreadful (and pleasantly exciting) fright. But he only looked up and called, "If you'll just hump back here, Baby, and let me show you how to do that properly you won't look such a fool."

He always called her Baby and no name could have been more ridiculously inappropriate.

All pretense at a nursery existence for Claire had been dropped long ago. She did not keep nursery hours; she would not eat nursery food. She never drank milk. If—especially before they moved away from London— she were served milk puddings and messes considered suitable for children, she would not touch them. She vomited promptly if confronted by soft-cooked eggs.

"What *does* she eat, m'Lady?" the last governess had asked icily. (No governess stayed more than a few months with Claire, and the final one departed when the child was ten.)

"*Petite Marmite*," said Constance, blowing smoke at the governess. "*Sole Colbert. Poulet en Daube. Filet de bœuf sanglant. Tripes à la mode de Caen. Pont L'Evêque. Camembert Pontet-Canet. Clos Vougeot.* Green almonds. Green figs. Green peaches. Green anything. Leave her alone, you ramrod."

There was the problem of Claire's education. Evan had presumed that the governesses were necessary for that; Constance soon found them unendurable. There was one period when Claire had no lessons at all, when she read Bulfinch and Shakespeare and Dumas and Lane's Arabian Nights and nobody bothered about grammar or spelling or arithmetic. Evan gave her a piano lesson every day. She was not nearly as talented musically as her mother had been but she had a workmanlike approach to the drudgery of scales and Czerny's exercises. When Evan was away travelling or in Vienna, Claire's music continued with an old German named Professor Blasius. He was tall and stooped, with a long pointed white beard and a kaiserlich moustache. He was a martinet, but Claire would accept that from a man while she had long since learned to flout any kind of female teacher. Professor gave her a Chopin Étude once and when he asked for it at the next lesson Claire said, "I haven't learned it."

"*Wie?*" The professor taught in German.

"*Ich mag's nicht,*" she said sullenly.

"So," roared the teacher. "You don't like Chopin. So!" He thrust his stern face at her and sneered, "Pray, who are you?"

Presently Evan protested that she must get on with her education. Constance was indifferent. She was tired of struggling with governesses and she could not conceive of sending Claire to school. So Evan found a tutor, a young Cambridge man who was living on the Riviera for his health. He was poor and he lived *en pension* in the family of the local haberdasher. Every morning he arrived at the Villa Bellevue with a green flannel bag of books. He and Claire set up school in the garden pavilion. She would not sit there without her cats. She had two now; a big orange-colored tom named Zeus and a tortoiseshell kitten named Jupiter. Somebody who lacked imagination pointed out to Claire that these were two different names for the same person. She withered the visitor by asking if he could call off the double names of the entire hierarchy of Greek and Roman gods and goddesses. Claire could.

At intervals Evan asked Mr. Cranwell, the tutor, for a report of Claire's progress. He could not have got much satisfaction from the answers.

"She learns exactly what she wants to learn," Cranwell said. "She speaks faultless French but won't study any grammar. She can recite whole acts of *Macbeth* and *Henry VIII* and *Julius Cæsar* but she says *Midsummer Night's Dream* is tommyrot. She does multiplication like lightning because she's memorized all the tables but she can't solve the simplest problem in percentage or fractions. When I tell her to do something she doesn't like she sits there hugging and kissing Zeus and Jupiter and talking to them in some fantastic lingo of her own—Jove, I never heard such gibberish!"

"I know," Evan said. "She sings to 'em in it too."

Lessons stopped at midsummer when Mr. Cranwell went home to England for six weeks. Claire loved that part of the year best of all. Mary almost always came for a visit, and this was the second time Uncle Paul had come. She had never known anybody like Uncle Paul; so big and solid and quiet, sitting there smoking his pipe and looking at Mère Constance as if she were a gnat and he a big dog who could swallow her at a snap. Claire was puzzled by her uncles anyway. She asked Mary to tell her about them. When they still lived in London, she said, a tall, stern-faced man with a fat wife and a thin, ugly daughter had come to call. Claire could remember Mère Constance saying, "Come here, Claire. This is your Uncle William. And Aunt Julia. And your Cousin Angelica."

They shook hands stiffly and Aunt Julia offered her cheek to be kissed. She was fat, but not fat like Mère Constance, with her curls and laces and jolly laughter and the nice way she smelled. Aunt Julia was hard all over, like a balloon tightly inflated. Her gray hair was skinned up into a hard round pompadour with another hard round thing on top of that. Her bust was a hard, shiny shelf, and her upper arms were thick and hard inside her shiny sleeves. She wore an ugly cameo breastpin and a plain thick gold wedding ring on her hard fat hand. Claire could not understand why Mère Constance rolled her eyes when speaking of Aunt Julia and said, "With all those millions! Can you bear it?" If people had millions, Claire presumed, they would have beautiful jewels and furs like Mère Constance, and their daughter, instead of looking like Cousin Angelica, would be curly and pretty and gay and have lots of beaux.

Nobody bothered to tell Claire when Uncle William died. It happened just at the time when Mère Constance decided to give up Cadogan Square and go live at the Villa Bellevue all year round. Claire was so excited by the wonderful news and the bustle of packing and the house full of men taking everything to pieces that she never knew the reason for the move. She did not realize that another death had preceded Uncle William's. She knew only that Mère Constance had cried several times a few weeks before. Mère Constance so seldom cried that Claire could only stare curiously and watch her and finally ask, "Why are you crying, Mère Constance?"

"I have lost a very old friend," Mère Constance replied.

"Who was it?"

"Just a very old friend," Mère Constance had repeated. "Go away and play, darling."

It was not until much later, after they were settled at Cannes, that Claire thought one day about the massive bearded man with the German accent whom she had once—no, twice—found at tea with Mère Constance when she came in from the Park. That was long ago. Mère Constance had whispered to her to make a very deep curtsey. And the old man with the big stomach had rumbled that this little one did not resemble her poor mama. Claire had gone up to the nursery after that. She never thought particularly about the old man—there was always someone at tea with Mère Constance. But now that she did try to remember, he certainly did look like the photographs with black borders in the illustrated magazines. But he had no crown and no ermine robes, so he couldn't have been a King. But—she thought—he must have been. . . .

"Grand slam!" said Lady Tattersfield. "Such fun!" She leaned across the table, her ornaments and jewels jangling on their chains. "How much do we win, Michel?"

The young Frenchman appeared to be politely unconcerned in the score.

Charles Harriott was adding. "Thirty-two, thirty-three—" he looked up at Constance. "We owe sixteen hundred fifty apiece, m'dear." Constance shrugged. She looked about for Henri or Luigi; she wanted some champagne and she wanted Clémentine with her purse. No servants were in sight.

"Hen-reeeee!" she called. "Claire, darling, run and ring the bell. What those lazy louts do all day—"

Paul stared at Evan. "Sixteen hundred and fifty what?" he asked in a tone of awe. "Dollars? Pounds?"

Evan laughed. "No, francs, but they wouldn't care."

The sun was very hot out over the water, although it was late afternoon. The brilliant vista was blinding if one looked straight at it. Electric-blue sea, dazzling white buildings, emerald lawn, riots of scarlet and yellow and salmon and purple in the garden. The shade of the dark blue awning was grateful.

"Can you drop us, Charles?" asked Lady Tattersfield. She looked at Michel de Rochambeau with possessive adoration. She was old enough to be his mother. "We promised to run by and see Sylvia."

"Is she still putting up a front?" Constance asked. "I can't think how she does it."

"Oh, I don't know," Sir Charles drawled. He stroked his white moustache. "Others have survived *flagrante delectu.*"

Mary looked nervously at Claire.

Sir Charles laid down a pile of gold pieces and pretty franc notes.

"There you are, Sybil. Ill-gotten too, by God."

"Where's that damn Henri?" Constance fumed. "Did you ring, Claire?"

Henri appeared from the dining-room. He ran stiffly down the long terrace and stopped beside Constance. He had no tray with him, no champagne, no purse. He was holding a piece of paper and it was rattling in his hands.

"*Regardez, Milady. C'est arrivé!*"

Constance stared vaguely and took the printed paper with the crossed French flags on it. But Michel de Rochambeau was on his feet.

"*Mobilization générale!*"

Evan seized the paper from Constance and read it together with Michel. Henri was palpitating at Constance's elbow.

"I must go at once, *Milady,*" he said in French, very fast. "I regret. Adieu. Adieu." He bowed in several directions and started away.

"Come back!" Constance shouted at him. "You can't walk out like this. We're sixteen for dinner tonight."

"*Mais, Milady.* You do not understand. I am called to my regiment."

Constance gaped. Paul and all the others were on their feet. Mary for some reason put her arm around Claire and held her tight. She held her breath. Constance said, "What does this mean, Michel?"

The Frenchman exchanged a glance with Evan.

"It means war, Countess."

There was excitement and confusion all that night and all the next morning. The household fell apart. Constance's great chef, Gonneau, was cook to the officers' mess of a reserve regiment. He and Constance both wept when he said good-bye, standing over her chair in his high white hat and snowy neckcloth. He and Henri and Raoul the chauffeur and Claire's beloved Jeannot, the head gardener, all left together.

In the uproar over the tearful departure of the servants Mary noticed that Evan and Paul had both disappeared, that Claire sat on a hassock dumbly hugging Jupiter with a stricken look on her face, that Constance was too flabbergasted even to swear. Evan came back on his bicycle at lunchtime and said Paul would not return from town for hours. He was down there in a madhouse at the bank trying to arrange passage home and get money on his letter of credit.

Lunch was a pickup affair on the terrace. Mary watched Claire with a sick and heavy heart. The child did not eat a mouthful. She cut up her chicken into bits and slipped the pieces to the cats under the table. Her eyes opened wide every time she looked at Evan and when he caught her staring, he smiled at her so tenderly that all the tragic fear went out of her face and she smiled back for a moment. After a time he pushed back his chair and held out his hand to her.

"Let's walk down to the olive trees, Baby."

Mary and Constance sat and watched them go. Claire's thick brown curls bobbed up and down her shoulders. Mary sat turned a little away from Constance and kept her head bent over some tatting she had taken from her bag. She never sat with empty hands. Constance was perfectly quiet until she suddenly burst into tears and said, "Oh, Jesus, go ahead and cry, Mary."

"I can't believe it," Mary said wretchedly. "Not—not—*England too!* Not Evan!"

"Why in hell he has to go and throw himself away," Constance stormed. "He won't be any use in this mess. He's an artist. Why should he go and kill Germans? Dammit—he loves 'em."

Mary was surprised at her own voice when she heard it say solemnly, "His country is at war. Or will be."

"But he can think, for God's sake. How can he do this—*and think?*"

"How can there be war at all?"

"Oh, don't be a damn fool. Questions like that. Evan's thirty-four years old and not very robust and he turns pale if somebody shoots a rabbit. I ask you."

"I'm worried about Claire."

"Did you think I was exactly happy about her? Suppose he does get killed—he will, you know. They'd have had such a life together, those two—knocking about and listening to music—"

"That's the way you talked about Evan and Clarrie."

"Oh, don't." Constance gasped and covered her face.

Evan did not say much after they sat down with their backs to the big olive tree. Claire held his hand tight in hers and waited for him to speak, but he only said, "Baby, there's not much to say about this. I can't fool you."

"No, Daddy."

"You're twelve years old, Baby," he said, "and I never have to explain anything to you. Must I?"

Claire stared at him.

"No, Daddy." She gulped. "Not now, anyway."

But almost at once she forgot that and said, "You couldn't explain why this had to happen, could you?"

He shook his head. "Men have been trying to find that out since the beginning of time. I can't explain, darling. I can't even say we're all good and the others are all bad."

"That's what I meant," Claire said slowly. "Why should Josef be killed now? Or Herr Winkler?" Those were friends in Vienna.

Evan sighed.

"They're probably asking themselves the same thing about us. It's no good to think about that."

There was a long silence while she held his hand tight in her two and tried not to believe what she knew to be happening. Finally she looked up at him and said, "Daddy. If England comes in—will you—would you—"

He nodded slowly, his strong wide mouth tightly closed.

"How—" Claire asked a little wildly, trying not to cry—"how do you go away to fight? What do you do?"

"Uncle Hugh," Evan said briefly. "My eldest brother, the one who lives in Cardiff. He's getting me a commission in his regiment."

"What's a commission, Daddy?"

"It means that I shall be—an officer—after I've had the training. Don't think about those details, Baby. Just—"

Claire sat frowning a little. Presently she said, "Somehow I still can't understand why. When it's so—when you might—" she choked.

Evan spoke very slowly, thinking hard over each word. "Baby," he said. He put his hands on her upper arms and gently turned her towards him until she was facing him, staring into his eyes in her strange solemn way. "There are certain things a man—every man—has to be willing to die for." He paused. "Sometimes a man lives his whole life through without coming up to face them. Sometimes— There. That's the straightest answer I can give you."

Claire sat quiet for some time. Then she looked up and asked slowly, "Why do people die for their country, Daddy?"

Evan shook his head sadly. "There's no sense in a man's dying for his country," he said. "Any more than there was sense in your mother's dying for you. But it had to be. Men and women have to be willing to do it. They have to expect to do it."

Claire's eyes opened very wide. "Why—I see."

He stood up then and swung Claire from the ground and put his arms around her. "We shan't drag it out," he said. "Will you be brave, Baby?"

She nodded, keeping her eyes on his face. He hesitated a moment, and then he said, "Whatever happens, don't be bitter about it. You're too smart. You're awfully smart, you know."

"I think you had better kiss me good-bye now, Daddy."

He kissed her, and she clung to him with her arms around his neck. Then she drew away and stood and looked at him with her queer flecked eyes and the wise, unchildlike expression he loved.

After he left she went down to the currant bushes, walking slowly with Jupe on her shoulder. Zeus stalked along behind, his tail a perpendicular red candle. Jupe purred, very loud and fast as young cats do, rubbing his moist gray nose in Claire's ear. Claire stared straight ahead at the thick green hedge; the currants were all gone now. She sat down slowly in the grass. Zeus dispatched a butterfly. Jupe spread-eagled himself on Claire's chest, his front claws hooked carefully to her shoulders. He purred louder than ever. Claire sat perfectly still with her brown hands on Jupe's rumbling flanks. Presently she rolled over on her side and buried her face in Jupe's stomach and sobbed bitterly.

CHAPTER LXI

[September 1915]

THIRTEEN MONTHS LATER Mary stood in the crowd on the end of a steamy New York pier-shed, waiting for Claire's ship to dock. It was a small French ship out of Marseille and had come across in convoy, tripling the length of the normal voyage. Mary had had so much trouble obtaining a pier permit that she was almost sick from fatigue and the horrible unseasonable heat. Her face was flushed, her clothes felt glued to her body, her stomach heaved at every blast of hot stale air from the pier, and at the puffs of bad cigar smoke that a sweating man blew in her direction as they stood in the jostling crowd watching the dirty little camouflaged vessel being warped in.

Though she was eager for the sight of the child, Mary knew that her first glimpse of Claire would be heartrending. Constance's letters had been telling her to expect that. Evan had fallen heroically at Ypres last April, in his first engagement after going to the front. Constance's cynical expostulations about the war stopped with tragic abruptness after that. Overnight she turned serious and bitter. She turned the Villa Bellevue into a convalescent home for wounded British officers, and for a time had let Claire help her there. Mary had worried dreadfully; that was no place for a heartbroken child. Constance soon agreed with her. She had written, "She never speaks of Evan, but I know she broods over him frightfully. And I couldn't keep her from seeing the *blessés* here even if I wanted to. Every room in the house except hers and mine and the servants' is full of cases. I let her read to them at first to take her mind off her own tragedy. But sometimes now when she's reading to a blind one I see her look up at him when she pauses and I see her thinking, 'Why are you alive and my Daddy dead? Why couldn't he only have been blinded or maimed—he'd have come back to me and I could have taken care of him the rest of his life.' I *know* she thinks that.

"I've been feeling her out—I'd rather die than let her think I want to send her away. First I thought I might induce her to go to Evan's people in Wales for a visit—which we'd manage to stretch out till the war was over—but she went to pieces at the merest hint of that and clung to me and almost broke my heart with her sobs. She's only seen Mrs. Gregory once in her life and detested her. That was my fault for being such a freak and making any normal grandmother a frozen old crone by comparison. Well—you've got the point by now, dear. I want you to write to Claire and invite her to come over and visit you—all as if I knew nothing about it. Don't mention any special length of time—just say 'a visit.' Say you need her or something like that so she won't think she's being taken away from here. She's full of this passion for helping just as we all are. At first I thought this might be just the thing for her here but she's too young. At night sometimes I stand in the bathroom and listen at her bedroom door and I hear her sobbing her heart out. If I open the door she stuffs the pillow in her mouth and pretends to be asleep.

"Don't offer to come over and get her. That would make her feel she's being treated like a child, and she'd refuse to go. She feels very grown up —I must say her tragedy is enough to kill the childhood in anybody. I'm quite willing to let her go over alone—it will be a new experience and take her mind off everything here, and she has got sense, you know, lots of it. Perhaps you could induce her to go to school at home, that would be a novelty for her and you could always be telling her how you brought me up—oh, I don't have to suggest anything. She loves you and that's all that matters now."

The ship was in now, and Mary stood watching the passengers, a harried-looking lot, coming down the gangplank. Mary's heart thumped as she watched for Claire. She came in sight quite soon—taller than Mary expected, very pale, with weary-looking eyes, her bushy brown curls tied at her neck with a black ribbon. She wore an unbecoming brown dress with a loose cape and a brown leghorn mushroom-shaped hat. She carried a pocketbook in one hand and in the other—Mary might have known!—a covered wicker basket from which indignant miaows rent the steamy air. When she saw Mary she started to smile with what proved, in a moment, to be a pitifully gallant effort; for when she stepped off the gangway into Mary's arms she burst into tears and clung to her.

Mary swallowed hard and tried not to cry herself. She kept Claire's arm in hers and made as much talk as she could.

"Did you see any submarines?"

Claire shook her head. "But I wouldn't have noticed if we had. I was too sick."

"What a shame. What did you do about Jupe?"

They were standing under G at the customs inspection now and Claire had taken Jupe from the basket to quiet him.

"He was sicker than I. I had to clean up after him all the time."

"Oh, Claire."

Jupe was glaring balefully at the porter bearing down on them with the handtruck full of Claire's luggage. He was sweating profusely.

"Sure is heavy," he said, dumping the truck.

"It's all books," Claire said indifferently.

"How's Mère Constance, dear?"

"Fine. She's so busy with her *blessés* I hardly see her to talk to. She sent you her love."

It was awkward, trying to talk about nothing. And it was sickeningly hot. Even Claire, used to the blazing sun of the Côte d'Azure, stood pale and breathless, her upper lip beaded with damp. She shoved her thick curls from her neck.

"Is it far where we go from here?" she asked.

"Overnight," Mary said. "We have a drawing-room on the train and we'll be quite comfortable, I hope." She looked at Jupe, still clinging to Claire's shoulder, with his ears laid flat. She opened her mouth to say something about putting him in the baggage-car, but thought better of it.

Jupe, it turned out, slept in the upper berth with Claire. Mary offered to give them the lower, but Claire wanted to climb up the ladder and sleep on the shelf; she had never seen such a queer train. Mary was touched by the pathetic blending of wondering child and grief-stricken woman in everything Claire said and did. One minute, with her cat and her marvelling at all the strange sights, she was the little girl she had always been; and the next minute, when she lost interest in everything about her and sat remotely silent during dinner, she was the living tragedy of war stabbing Mary's heart through and through. She was ready enough to tell Mary about Mère Constance who, Claire said, "would like to wipe every German off the face of the earth. So would I," she added.

"I can't exactly picture her as a Florence Nightingale," Mary said.

"Oh, she doesn't do any of that. She has a lot of good nurses to take care of her *blessés*. She just—you know. Keeps their spirits up." Mary could indeed imagine Constance as Claire described her then—barging about in a starched white uniform and a long veiled coif, chortling, telling tall ones, lighting her cigarettes from her boys', downing drink for drink with them, and playing any games, at any stakes, according to the guests' means and preferences. The Villa Bellevue had become the most coveted spot of all the Riviera refuges where shattered men were sent to lie in the sun and regain, if they could, their health and spirits.

Paul had told Mary that Constance had never spent so much money in all her extravagant career. She was keeping up and adding to everything on the place that could please her boys—the gardens, the boat, the stable, the cellar, which she let them enjoy unstintingly. But for once, Paul said, it did not matter how enormous her drafts had to be. Never in the history of the mill had business been like this. They were working twenty-four hours seven days a week, and still could not keep up with the orders that were swamping them. He was coming to the reluctant decision that he would soon have to enlarge the mill.

He met Mary and Claire at the station in the morning. Mary was reassured by the way Claire clung to his arm and kept looking up at him as if he personified the only masculine security in the world now. He gave Mary a look of secret consternation when he caught sight—and sound—of Jupe's basket, but he concealed his feeling from Claire. He even asked her why she hadn't brought Zeus too.

"He was too old," Claire said primly. "Too set in his ways. He wouldn't have been a success in a strange place."

"How do you know Jupe will be?"

Claire turned a stare on her uncle. "You understand *your* children, don't you, Uncle Paul?"

In the car Claire sat up straight and looked out curiously as they approached the Sixth Street Bridge. They crawled across the noisy labyrinth of Duquesne Way, with coal trucks, drays, trolley cars, and a huge brewery wagon massing confusion around them. When Stanley finally guided the Lozier onto the bridge, Claire turned around on the seat and knelt like a small child, looking backwards at the waterfront behind her. Factory chimneys and packing-houses and the Pennsylvania freight yards and blocks of warehouses crowded the banks strung with the tentacles of iron bridges. Black barren cliffs rose inconsequently from tangles of buildings, spotted with ramshackle houses and denuded of all surface save cinder and soot and rock. Claire craned her neck to look up the Allegheny, and suddenly she clapped her hands and cried, "Oh look, a *Drahtseilbahn!* Mary you didn't tell me this was like Switzerland!"

"Switzerland!" Paul said. "That's the Penn Incline."

She was watching the little car crawl up the side of the cliff.

"But nobody told me there were things like that in Pittsburgh. I thought it was all steel mills and coal mines."

"It is. Would you like to see our mill, Claire?"

She turned around and plunked back on the seat.

"Oh, yes."

"Well, just look down there."

He pointed to the left, down towards the Ohio. The view was almost completely shrouded in a pall of thick black smoke. From the centre of the bridge it was difficult to distinguish anything on either bank of the river. But following Paul's finger Claire looked down at the heaviest blanket of swirling black. In the midst of it she could distinguish the outlines of roofs and chimneys and some strange-looking dome-shaped things and one especially thick stack which, just as she looked, belched a jet of red smoke.

"Oooooh," she said. "What's that?"

"That's the Henrietta, our blast furnace. Your great-great-grandfather built her in 1861."

"He did! What was his name?"

"William Scott."

"Why did you call that thing 'her'?"

"All blast furnaces are called 'her.' "

"Why?"

"I don't know. They're always given women's names. Ours is named for your great-great-grandmother Henrietta. There's a Lucy furnace in Pittsburgh, and a Carrie and an Isabella—lots of them."

Claire was peering up and down the river.

"It's so smoky you can't really see anything, Uncle Paul. Why is that?"

"The mills are all working at capacity. It's the war, you see."

"You're helping us in the war, aren't you?"

"Of course. We're making steel for guns and shells—all kinds of things. I'm going to show you the mill if you'd like to see it—How about it?"

"Why—I think I should like it." She sniffed. "It smells exciting here."

"Wait till you take your bath," Mary said dryly. "And wash your ears and nose."

They were driving up Western Avenue now, almost home. It was really a pleasant, sunny day. Once they climbed away from the river level it was possible to see what things looked like. Mary found herself gazing at the familiar street with different eyes—Claire's eyes. Nothing could contrast so utterly with every vista the child had ever seen before. Now that she thought of it, Mary realized that the wide, handsome street had changed startlingly in the past couple of years. It was the war, she supposed. Too many of the fine old houses had erupted into the ragtag disorder of boardinghouses. She had not realized how many families on their block had recently moved or drifted away. The Georges and the McKelvies to Sewickley; the Burnses and the Dixons and the Cottrells to Squirrel Hill. That was only five, but it meant five big places slipping into shabbiness. Working people—the Irish, one said contemptuously, to Mary's shame—were being pushed up here by the swarming Hunkies who crowded the river banks and bottoms. Out in boroughs like Braddock and Rankin there was hardly an "American" family left. They had all fled to the East End and Shadyside and Squirrel Hill.

Claire stood on the front steps and looked up at the severe brick façade of the house. The windows glittered in the dusty fall sunshine. Uncle Paul was unlocking the door with his latchkey on the end of a heavy gold watch chain. Mary rang the doorbell too; as the big door swung open a neat maid came hurrying through the hall. She smiled at Claire.

"Welcome, Miss Claire," she said. "I hope you had a good trip."

"This is Stella," said Mary, "and this is Jessie"—as the chambermaid, in her morning blue-and-white stripes came running downstairs to help with Claire's luggage. Claire stood in the middle of the hall and looked slowly and thoroughly about her. She had never seen a house anything like this. She had never seen a vestibule with this sort of patterned tiled floor, or a wide centre hallway with walnut panelling, or massive intricately carved mahogany stairs like this, or such fancy electric chandeliers. It was no bigger than any house she was used to, nor any handsomer; but it was totally different. She stood still, a solemn island of strangeness, while people moved about taking luggage upstairs, speaking in accents that fell oddly on her polyglot ears. Presently she looked at Mary and sniffed again.

"It smells good here," she said.

It did. It had the indefinable smell of a perfectly-kept, well-loved American home; the smell found nowhere else on earth. A smell of cleanliness and polish and Ivory soap and potted plants and baking bread—the sweet, warm smell of simplicity and abundance. "You must be hungry," Mary said, "and Jupe too. Why don't you just run up and have a lick and a promise before breakfast? Then we'll spend the day getting unpacked and settled."

She put her arm around Claire and walked upstairs with her to her room. She had decided on Elizabeth's old room for Claire because it had a cozy deep bay window with a cushioned seat and, as it was over the back parlor, a real fireplace. Mary had had the walls papered with pale blue paper with bunches of field flowers on it. The woodwork was painted white, and the furniture too. Instead of the old brass bed there was a new white one with canework in the headboard and footboard. Mary had made the dimity curtains (two sets, of course) and the ruffled bedspread over a pink sateen underspread. She had thought of every detail that Claire would like: a desk with lots of pigeonholes, a row of tiny china cats on the mantel, a roomy bookcase, a grown-up dressing table. She had even found, for the chair-cushions and the upholstered window-seat, a cretonne with currants on it—bunches of red and white currants on a pale gray ground. Claire would love that. And beside the bed there was a snow-white sheepskin rug with wool long enough for her bare feet to sink in to the ankles. Tom had sent that, with a note to Mary: I wish we could really do something to comfort the kid. I'm not going to wait much longer to get back at those damned Huns.

While she washed her hands, Claire looked wonderingly at the plumbing. It was all new; Paul had had it done over a year ago, and two extra bathrooms put in, and an automatic water-heater. Claire stared at the dirty suds in the basin.

"I *can't* be that dirty," she said.

Mary laughed. "You'll get used to it."

Ted had already left for the mill; Paul would have been there by now but for Claire's arrival. He had breakfast with her and Mary. Claire had said she was not hungry but she found herself eating a big meal. It was strange and oddly delicious. She had never tasted waffles before, or these fat, crisp brown sausages, or the maple syrup that Uncle Paul poured in a thick golden pool over his buttered waffles. Claire tasted it gingerly.

"It's good by itself," she said, frowning a little, "but why do you eat it on meat?"

"You don't. You pour it on the waffles and it runs over on the meat."

Claire shook her head; that was an American taste she would never acquire.

Dick and Ruth came to dinner that night. Ruth was expecting her second child; she already had one little girl two years old, whom they called Ruthie. Now she and Dick had set their hearts on a boy. They wanted to name him Paul, which they knew would please Dad more than anything in the world. Ruth sat on Paul's left, opposite Claire, and Dick and Ted faced each other on either side of Mary at the foot of the table. Claire had never seen a gathering like this. Only once, on her visit to her relatives in Wales, had she ever seen so many people all related to one another. She was amazed at what good friends they all seemed to be. They had so much to talk about, and they argued with so much vigor and so little temper.

Her two tall cousins made a fuss over her, and she knew she had a particular standing in their eyes because her Daddy had been killed in the war. She liked Dick much better than Ted. He was gayer and handsomer and he laughed more. He seemed awfully in love with Ruth. Claire liked to watch him when he looked at Ruth. His eyes were so warm and full of expression. It would be wonderful, she thought, to have a man look at her that way some day. She wondered how Ruth felt, how it must feel to be having a baby. Ruth was so quiet, with her ash-blonde hair piled in a Psyche knot, and her cornflower blue silk dress with the ruffly front which, Claire knew, was supposed to hide her figure. It didn't; Claire saw that Ruth's stomach bulged like a balloon. Her face was pretty but nothing like the faces Claire understood best—witty, sharp-lined, delicately painted faces like those of Mère Constance's friends. When Ruth and Dick were visiting at the Villa Bellevue on their honeymoon Claire had overheard Mère Constance saying something about them to her friend Sybil Tattersfield.

"They're *good*," Mère Constance had said. "So damned good it cloys like caramel custard."

Now that she was here among them Claire saw what Mère Constance had meant. They were good, yes; everybody and everything in the room felt kind and gentle and safe. But Claire felt strange among them. For a little while it was novel to watch them and listen to them and compare them with the people she was used to. Yet the sight of any man only reminded her with a cruel stab of Daddy. He seemed so terribly far away from here. At home at the Villa Bellevue there were people who had known him, people who had shared the little daily experiences with him that kept him vivid in Claire's mind. Here everybody had his own concerns to think about. At home everything revolved around the war and around the men who were fighting and dying in the war. Uncle Paul's mill was helping them, to be sure. But it was an awfully far cry from that tangle of ugly black sheds spewing smoke and fire on this hard American air to the tortured fields of Flanders, or to the hot white rocks, the cool secret shade of the olive grove, the deep shadows of the currant hedge which had been her refuge. When she lay in the strange white bed that night, after Mary tucked her in and kissed her, Claire cried as even Mère Contsance had never found her crying up to now. If it weren't for you, she told Jupe in French, with her wet face buried in his fur, I couldn't stand it at all.

CHAPTER LXII

[*1915*]

CLAIRE HAD MISSED the first three weeks of school by the time she made up her mind to go there. She had never been to school in her life and had never, but for the occasional artificial gesture of an afternoon, had the companionship of anyone her own age. She had not wanted to go to school. Uncle Paul told her she ought to go, but he hoped she would decide to of her own free will. "Why should I go?" she asked him finally. It seemed such a queer question to him that he hardly knew how to answer right off.

"Why—you don't want to be a freak, do you, Claire?" He looked at her quizzically. "We want you to have a happy time with us here but you can't if you're going to be different from everybody else."

She sighed.

"Just remember," he said, "boys and girls dislike what they don't understand. They'll—"

"*Boys?*" Claire breathed, horrified.

He nodded. "If you go to Allegheny Prep where the boys went, there's both boys and girls there."

"Oh, Uncle Paul, I shouldn't like that."

This was a poser. He had taken it for granted that if Claire was to be a member of the family she would do as they all had done.

"Your cousins went there," he said.

"I see." He could not tell whether she was troubled or just sulky. Her face was clouded.

"Why don't you try it, anyway? If you don't like it—" he shrugged. He realized that the child was, after all, only visiting. If she really hated living here she could write Constance that she wanted to go home. And Constance would let her. But he did not want the thing to end that way. He wanted a chance for this kid with her queer jumble of strong feelings and strange moods to become something better than the frivolous sophisticate that she must be if she were given nothing else now. Besides, he loved her and Mary loved her.

"You try it," he said again. "If you find you hate it, tell me and we'll try something else. But all you have to do is stand up to 'em. Do you think you can?"

Claire was so fond of Uncle Paul, with his kind, broad, quiet face and his gray handlebar moustache and his watch chain with the gold seals (her great-grandfather's, he told her) which he let her have for Jupe to play with, that she looked at him for a while and said, "All right, Uncle Paul. I'll try it."

He patted her shoulder.

"But I can't promise I'll like it," she warned him quickly.

She hated it. She hated the big, barren, begrimed brick building with the echoing floors and the stuffy classrooms that smelled of dust and chalk and gas and people. She hated the ugly varnished desk fastened to the floor, with the uncomfortable seat attached to it, into which you slid. She hated the dirt. Pittsburgh dirt, like that on your face when you came in from the yard, was funny and you were almost proud of it. But this school dirt was repulsive. It clung to the crannies of the hideous furniture and stained under your fingernails and smudged the pages of your copybooks. Claire was extremely neat about her work and took almost too much pride in the perfect appearance of her themes and written lessons. She was annoyed by mess and dirt and ugliness and there was little else in school. Even her desk which, if it were to be hers she wanted really for her own, was scratched and scarred and cut with the markings of all its previous occupants. Silly girls who had scratched boys' initials and hearts with arrows through them. And some boy who had whittled a deep hole surrounded by smaller holes, for some mysterious purpose, which now made only a catching-place for dirt.

But she had worse troubles than that. From the very first the teachers made it hard for her. She was put in a French class which was reading *Le Médecin Malgré Lui.* It was senior French; there was no sense holding her back with the class her own age. These boys and girls were all three years older than Claire at least. The teacher was a stout woman with oily brown hair and a flat-footed stance by the blackboard. Her very rear elevation put Claire's teeth on edge. Her name was Miss Walker. Her French was the appallingly ground-out, malpronounced product of the American school and college. Claire knew that she had never really spoken it in her life, and that it had no meaning to her as a language. Her method of teaching was insufferable. Two or three sentences or a paragraph would be read by a student—a victim, Claire said to herself—standing at his place; then he would translate the butchered words into dreadful, plodding, infantile English; then another victim would have to stand up and take the tortured French apart and analyze it grammatically, naming every mood and tense and structure. On the second day of this Claire was called upon to recite. She stood up and read off a page. The boys and girls in the class gave each other meaning looks. This was a freak, this was somebody to be put through the torture of punishment for being different.

Miss Walker sucked her lips as Claire came to the end of the page. "Translate, please."

Claire did so, reshaping Molière's phrases in her polished British English—Daddy's English—which had made her the victim of stares and snickers and nudges the first day of school. As she paused, one boy cleared his throat loudly and whispered to his seat-mate. The second boy tittered. Claire flushed and stood stiffly, staring at the blackboard.

"Walter!" said Miss Walker. But there was no conviction in her tone.

Other boys shuffled their feet and several girls opened up on Claire with cold, challenging stares. The whole room was becoming infected. The teacher had no wish to control the thing. She felt with these barbarians, Claire saw that. But she went on with a semblance of routine.

Instead, however, of asking the next victim to analyze the grammar of the page Claire had read, she told Claire to do it.

Twenty pairs of eyes moved from the teacher's pasty, malicious face to Claire standing rigidly beside her desk. Her cheeks were pale and the thick bush of her hair framed them startlingly. These unspeakable creatures were waiting for her to do something to put herself in the wrong. Her hands began to perspire and she flexed her strong brown fingers along the sides of her skirt. There was a bad feeling in her stomach. But she began to speak rapidly and colloquially, in French. Everyone else had done this grammatical butchery in English. But Claire gave a quick, contemptuous summary of the stupid grammar in French. She knew it accurately, more because of her unconscious absorption of Mr. Cranwell's lessons than because she had ever willingly learned it.

She came to the end of the grammatical summary and paused for a moment, watching the gaping faces of the class and a queer flush rising over the heavy features of the teacher. It struck her that she was certainly in wrong. Well, she thought, I'll give them their money's worth. Without changing her tone of voice, hardly with a pause, so that most of them were not aware of a difference in what she was saying, she continued to talk, rapidly and in a studied monotone. But she had switched to the tough coastal argot that Jeannot had spoken with his fellow servants and which he and his wife Lizette, a Marseille fishwife's daughter, had long ago taught Claire.

"For pigs like you," she said, "it wasn't worth while my bothering to remember all that ordure that any educated person knows without grovelling in it. You make me sick. You make me spit. You make me vomit. I spit on the lot of you." Certain phrases of Luigi's and the other Italian servants shot through her mind. Bastard Italian was dirtier than anything else she knew. She stood there, respectful and expressionless, like any reciting student. "You are a pack of animals," she said. *"Un amasso di stupidi animali.* But that's too good for you. *Voi siete 'merda'.* You," she said at the teacher, though she did not look at her, "are an ignorant female dog. A despoiler of poetry, a stink in the nose of gentility. Your school," she said, raising her eyes with a blank stare, "is a *porcheria. Fogna immonda di esseri viventi."* She laid down the book, flashed one glance at the bewildered faces in the room, and walked out.

She had done something dreadful. She did not care. Her hands were clammy and shaking, her knees wobbly, as she went to her own classroom, collected her books and notebooks, took her hat and coat from the rack, and started home. She had not been out alone yet in Pittsburgh; this was only her second day at school and Uncle Paul had had Stanley take her and call for her. She was to walk back and forth alone just as soon as she was sure of the way. Everybody did. She would meet her friends on the way to school, Uncle Paul said, and they would all walk together. Friends, she thought scornfully. Oh yes.

She followed her nose going home, but paid no attention to her whereabouts. She never expected to go back to that unspeakable place again.

Uncle Paul would be angry when he heard about this, but Claire did not care about that either. The worst that could happen would be his sending her back to Mère Constance, and now that she began to think about it, that was what she wanted to do. She thought more and more. She decided she loathed this whole dirty, noisy, ugly, barbaric place; these stupid people with their twangy voices and their ground-out R's; the irritating decency of Uncle Paul's house, with its precise hours and incessant cleaning and Mary and that saccharine Ruth sitting sewing baby-clothes in the back parlor. She loathed the busy, earnest maids and that beast of a German Trude—all Germans were the same bloody Huns who had killed Daddy. She wanted to hear a good resounding mouthful of sarcastic profanity from Mère Constance. She wanted to lie on the rocks by the salt water and bury her hot face in the strong, cool brine. She wanted a *langouste* and a salad high with garlic and a glass of iced champagne and a hell's brew of bitterly black Italian coffee. She wanted Daddy. She wanted to be with him under the olive trees, talking long and intimately and slowly. She wanted to hear him sing *Wir Wandelten*. She wanted it desperately. She heard in the sore bruised core of her heart his deep, beautiful, shimmering voice, singing their song.

Wir wandelten, wir zwei zusammen.

But it was the Germans who had killed Daddy. The Huns. Claire stopped for a moment on the dusty street, looked about as if all the horror on earth were crashing down on her, and broke into a run. She ran all the way to the house, through the side door and up the stairs to her room. She flung herself, dirty and crumpled, on the ruffled white bed and sobbed. Her sobs were wrenching gasps that began in her stomach and tore through her whole body. They made a frightening and heart-sickening noise and that was what Mary heard, coming up the stairs.

When Paul came home for dinner Mary told him that Claire was in trouble, and she said, "It's mostly homesickness, but she's done something she says is dreadful. She says I'd be too shocked if she told me what it is."

Paul went upstairs where Claire was lying in bed with Jupe crouched possessively on her chest. He laid his ears flat when Paul came over and stood by the bed. "Don't you want to get up and come down for dinner, Claire?" Paul asked.

She shook her head. "I want to go home," she said.

"Mary asked Trude to make potato pancakes for you." That should tempt her; she loved those. But she only shook her head and said, "I'm not hungry."

Paul sat down slowly on the edge of the bed, proffering his watch chain with the gold seals to Jupe. Claire watched Jupe batting the bright things and springing after them.

"I can't go to school any more, Uncle Paul," she said. "I've probably been kicked out by now anyway."

He waited for her to tell him why, and presently she did. She told him what she had done. "If she hadn't been such a—a *greasy* thing," Claire said about the teacher, "I might have stood her not knowing any French. But they were all so—so—mean—"

"Well, what did they do when you said all that?" Uncle Paul asked. Claire had told him exactly what she had said. He listened open-mouthed. The kid had certainly got herself into a peck of trouble, if he knew Joe Holloway. Holloway was the principal of the school. Paul had known him all his life. Together they had steered the three Scott boys through school, and Paul would have thought there could not be any such problems that they had not run up against already. But this was a poser. Mary appeared in the doorway and said, "Mr. Holloway is calling you on the telephone, Paul."

Holloway apparently did not know all that Paul had just heard and was calling to ask why Claire had walked out of school as she had. Paul asked him to come over and have dinner with him. He found the schoolmaster strangely at sea about the thing. So, over a cocktail, Paul told him what the child, by her own account, had said. Then he stopped suddenly and asked, "But—Joe. Why should I be telling you this? Why didn't the teacher tell you?"

Holloway looked embarrassed for a moment and then burst into a laugh. "She—you won't believe me, Paul. She didn't understand the child."

"Didn't understand? Go on! What is this, anyway? I thought she was the French teacher."

"What this thing really is," Holloway said, "is a very sad commentary on our educational system. Our teaching of foreign languages is a travesty. We take these teachers because they can double in some other department, or for an equally poor reason. Real fluency or cultivation in the language simply isn't part of the picture. It's a dreary mechanical grind that's utterly useless if the kids ever do want to use the language. Your niece," he said slowly, shaking his head, "was quite right. Insolent and insubordinate. But right."

Paul was bewildered by Holloway's attitude. He had expected to be asked to take Claire out of school at once.

"Right?" he asked. "When she tells me she called the teacher a pig, a dog, a butcher, a despoiler of French poetry, the leader of a pack of hyenas? And a lot more, in French and Italian, that I can't remember? That's pretty strong stuff, Joe. I think you're awfully casual about it."

Holloway began to laugh again while Paul was talking. He laughed until he had to dry his eyes. He rolled about in his chair. "Oh," he gasped. "Oh, Paul, if you could see Miss Walker! And I can't help admiring spunk like Claire's. Lord, she's exactly like your sister Constance!"

"All right, but what are we going to do about her?" Paul asked.

Holloway rubbed his chin.

"If anybody really understood what she said," he said, "we'd have to take some severe disciplinary action. Probably put her out. But since they didn't know, that's our fault, not hers. She can't be in a French class, that's self-evident. What she needs is a little real toughening-up in other things. She's spoiled, of course, and conceited. If you want that taken out of her I'll try."

"She probably won't cooperate," Paul said doubtfully. "She says tonight she wants to go home."

"Let her decide. Her education so far has been a fantastic hodgepodge. It hasn't fitted her for any kind of a life in this country but maybe you don't care."

Paul was looking very thoughtful.

"Some day," he said slowly, "she'll inherit the single biggest share in our mill."

"Then for heaven's sake don't let her become a parasite and an international waster living off American dividends. Look at Europe. Is that what you want to subsidize with earnings from your mill?"

It was queer, Paul thought, as he stood on the steps saying good-bye to Holloway after dinner, that it had taken somebody else to suggest the way to show the real Pittsburgh and its real place in her life to Claire. The kid loved drama and she was all wrapped up in the war. Well, he thought, he would give her a taste of that which she would never forget. The mill was heading into production pressure so terrific that there could be no solution except a major enlargement, which Paul had always dreaded to undertake at times of emergency. You were only bargaining for future trouble when you did that. Paul knew too vividly the inevitable deflations that always followed periods of frenzied expansion. But he did not know what else to do now. Sometimes when he ran his eye down the weekly production sheets he felt like a Frankenstein. Twice before, indeed, the mill had become an arsenal, but always as part of its own nation's fate in a war. Now it seemed at times simply a monster grinding out trainloads of slaughter for unknown, unimaginable, disturbingly anonymous humans somewhere on the other side of the earth. One called them Boches and Huns. If one were as violent a man as Tom, one swore and promised oneself a chance to get a crack at them. To Paul the whole rocketing increase of output seemed fantastic even though he himself had decreed it. He could stand in the office with Ted and look at these figures and pass his hand across his eyes and still have trouble believing it all.

He went back to Claire's room. She was still lying there, pale and self-consciously dramatic.

"I've got to go down to the mill tonight," he said in a matter-of-fact tone. "I thought you might like to go with me."

"*Me?*"

"Sure. I've been meaning to take you down and this is a good chance. Come on, get up and put on your clothes."

Claire hesitated. She had reached the point where she meant to write to Mère Constance tonight and say she was coming home. She was tired anyway, and very low, and quite weak (she was hungry) and there seemed no point in this idea. But Mary came in just then with a small tray. There was a plate on it with chicken sandwiches and a glass of claret. Mary had hesitated over the wine. She always did, with Claire. She always winced a little when Claire expected to share Paul's occasional bottle of wine at dinner. It seemed so unnatural somehow; so absurd. But Claire never touched milk or any drink suitable for a child and Mary was not prepared to undo her upbringing.

She set down the tray on the bedside table. Jupe immediately got up, voiced a mild "Prrrraow" and delicately licked at a sandwich. Claire pushed him away and took it herself.

Paul started downstairs again. "You be ready in fifteen minutes," he said.

CHAPTER LXIII

[*1915—Continued*]

GOING DOWN IN THE CAR he told her how steel was made. He began at the very beginning, with the melting of iron as it had been done in the old days when her great-great-grandfather had started his forge in 1837.

"Seventy-eight years ago," Claire said, counting.

"And I remember the first time I was taken to the mill," Uncle Paul said, "just the way I'm taking you. Only I was much younger. Grandfather took me down one day when they were making cannon-balls for the Union Army in the Civil War."

Claire's eyes began to shine. History was her passion. She had only a hazy notion of the American Civil War but that was the kind of defect in her education that Joe Holloway had told Paul he would remedy. And Claire's idea of the American Revolution, derived from Stephen Cranwell, was ludicrous. Paul realized suddenly that a whole world of excitement and fascination and discovery lay ahead of the kid right here in Pittsburgh. Fort Duquesne. Fort Pitt. Fort Stanwix. The French. The Indians. General Braddock. George Washington. McIntosh and Button Gwinnett. The opening of the West. The story of the rivers. The wagon trains of the Huntington Turnpike.

For a child who loved stories this place was a treasure-house. Right at home in the attic were William Scott's old books, the earliest records of the Monongahela country, the Indian Wars, the settlement of Allegheny County, the beginnings of mining and manufacture and river commerce and trade. Claire listened enthralled while Uncle Paul told her about these books, and the things she ought to know to understand why this black, jagged, sprawling town at the confluence of three rivers had become the living heart of modern industrial America. By now Stanley had stopped the car at the mill gate and opened the door for them to step out.

Uncle Paul led Claire across the bridge, stopping in the middle. "Here," he said, in a low voice, "is the spot where my father died."

Claire caught her breath, staring at Uncle Paul with huge round eyes. "Why, Uncle Paul," she breathed, "was *your* father killed too?"

"Yes," he said. "He died fighting, like your Daddy, Claire."

"In a war?"

"Not what you mean by a war. But a cruel, terrible struggle between men. My father may not have been entirely in the right. But he was a fearless man."

"Why did they kill him?"

"It was a horrible mistake. A misunderstanding. But he died for what he believed in, Claire. So did your Dad."

"You have to be willing to," Claire whispered. Uncle Paul bent down to hear her.

"Your Dad said that to you, didn't he?"

Claire nodded slowly, feeling for her handkerchief. Uncle Paul patted her shoulder and led the way into the mill.

While they were in the car Claire had been sitting on the edge of her seat, as Stanley drove through the dark streets and along the crest of the hill overhanging the riverside. Paul, watching her, remembered the sights of the old days, when blast furnace gas instead of being recovered and used, had been allowed to blow off in the spectacular explosions that dyed the night skies red. Bessemers too had added to the dramatic picture. Now it was different. He had discarded his only Bessemer years before, and his mill had no such sights to display as the blasts and blows of twenty years ago. But it was still a heart-stopping thrill to come down the hill in the dark and see the mill, a tangle of slanting roofs and stacks, illuminated by a dozen different kinds of fire. There were moments when the blackness of the night would be rent by lurid flashes of red or orange or angry white, as a heat was poured, a crucible tapped off, or a forty-ton ladle of molten blast furnace iron chugged across the yard behind the dinky-engine on its way to the mixer. Most spectacular of all were the dump-cars of blazing slag, standing in the yard to burn off before being routed away to the cement plant which bought the slag from Scott's.

Down at the finishing departments where some of the old corrugated sheds had been replaced by modern structural iron with glass-paned roofs, wonderful colors dyed the sky above the incredible clamor of the rolling mill. Claire had looked down that way, while standing on the bridge.

"Do they always work all night, Uncle Paul?"

"In times like these. Now you wait here just a minute while I speak to Ted."

Claire stood in the middle of the outer office and looked about wonderingly. She had never seen a place like this, so crude, so grim, so ugly. Dun-colored walls and shapeless yellow furniture and a big, forbidding safe in the corner with Scott Iron Works painted on it in faded gilt lettering full of curlicues. The floor was dirty and littered with cigar butts and bits of torn paper. Claire did not know that a conference in here had broken up only just before Uncle Paul went home to dinner; a meeting of Allied purchasing agents and Paul and Dick and the department heads. It was the outcome of this very day's conference that was to settle Paul's reluctant decision to enlarge the mill.

Claire tiptoed over and looked into the room where Uncle Paul had gone. He was bending over Ted who sat at a big desk piled high with papers and huge gray-bound books and sheafs of thin typewritten papers bound in light-blue folders. Ted was scratching his head with both hands.

"How in hell can we do it, Dad?" he was asking.

"I don't know," Paul said. He was wrenching his moustache in the way he did when he was bothered. Every week the rate of output kept on rising. Last week they had shipped a new total in thousands of chrome-nickel gun-forgings, projectiles for howitzer and trench-mortar shells and armor-piercing naval projectiles not very different in specification from the famous ones they had made in '97 and '98. They had shipped extra carloads of alloy steel ingots, billets, and bars to machine tool and specialty plants and carloads to ordnance works for machine-guns and rifles; also hundreds of tons of silicomanganese and tungsten-valve steels for motors. And as soon as they had the new furnace capacity to turn it out in quantity, they would start shipping a new lightweight steel just developed by Paul, a steel of beautiful texture, impervious to rust and stain, which would go into the engines of the airplanes that crazy gallant boys were to fly above the Western Front. Liberty motors, they were called in the plants where they were being developed; and they could not have been built without the steel over which Paul had spent weeks of consecutive nights in his laboratory.

He straightened up from Ted's desk and began to take off his coat. Claire saw him changing to another coat, a queer stiff dark-blue one with bulging patch pockets. He started to join her and then turned back to Ted. He leaned over and whispered. Ted nodded and got up and went out. Paul had told him to go to the foremen in certain departments and explain that the boss would be around soon with his grand-niece. There was an ancient, rigid superstition among iron and steel men that it meant bad luck for a woman or girl to set foot in a mill. Paul was hoping to jolly them out of that for the time being before he got there with Claire.

First he took her to the Henrietta. If she had been a boy he would have taken her right down into the stockyard and shown her the raw materials, the ore, coke, and limestone, being shovelled into the skips which the hoist carried up to dump into the furnace. He took her into the casthouse where the keeper and the crew watched and tended the heat and prepared it for the blast and the pouring. Claire was too excited and bewildered to understand more than the bare outlines of what Uncle Paul explained; besides it was very near time for tapping and Uncle Paul promised she should see that. She did, from a safe distance, her hand clutching Uncle Paul's spasmodically while, through the purple goggles he had put on her, she stood and saw the terrifying sight of a flood of molten iron stream with a deafening roar and a blinding curtain of sparks into the huge ladle on the buggy.

When it was over and Claire was panting with the heat and the excitement Uncle Paul said, "Now we'll go and see what they do with that iron."

He showed her the mixer invented by his old friend Captain Bill Jones, and explained its purpose. Then they walked a long way, on a gritty crunching black floor which Claire thought was just plain earth with cinders ground into it. Railroad tracks ran up and down the length of the place. Claire asked about them. Did the railroad run right in here?

"Yes," Uncle Paul said with a smile. How else could you move forty-ton ladles and carloads of ferro-manganese, one of the heaviest minerals in the world?

The open-hearth shed was a different place, Paul thought with a start, from the scene of that first heat of his—let's see—twenty—thirty—no *thirty-five years ago.* "My God," he exclaimed aloud "My God, I'm an old man." But Claire did not hear that. She was staring at a man who was perched up on the back of a queer-looking sort of car which shoved other, smaller cars full of material straight into an open hole full of fire. The man was pushing and pulling levers. She pulled Uncle Paul's arm "What's that? What's he doing?"

"That's a charging-machine. That man is the operator. He's loading limestone into that furnace."

"Furnace?"

Paul followed her gaze at the hot, dark, blackened brick wall with its symmetrical rows of iron doors. Eight of them, four on each side, he thought, shaking his head. The two at the end were brand new. They were electric furnaces which were Dick's special pride, his first big job. Dick was working now on a pair of crucible furnaces for the production of specially hardened chrome steel. Was there to be no end to this expansion? In a sense it frightened Paul rather than pleased him. He was going to have to pay an exorbitant price for additional land beyond the north end of the mill. And God knew what kind of money for the labor and material to build the new sheds.

"Those don't look like furnaces, Uncle Paul," Claire was saying.

"They are, though." He nodded at a young man who was running down the shed with a coil of heavy wire over his arm.

"Who's that?"

Paul smiled at Claire. She was not missing a chance to ask a question. "An electrician's apprentice. His father is the roller-boss in the blooming mill. We have men here whose grandfathers worked for my grandfather."

One of the open-hearths was ready for its charge of blast furnace iron from the mixer and Claire, staring through the purple goggles, watched breathless while the big ladle slid down an overhead track, stopped at the door, and on the melter's signal, swung slowly on its axles to pour its beautiful liquid death into the trough against the open door. Paul was standing a good fifty feet away, holding Claire's hand in his, and he had to restrain her as she tried to move forward to see into the furnace door.

"It's just like soup! Like one of Gonneau's big pots of soup," she cried.

"That's what we call it. Soup."

When he took her up on the gallery in the next shed to watch a furnace tapped and the ingots poured she was so excited that he had to hold her by the shoulder for fear she would topple over the rail. She screamed with excitement when the setter opened the stopper and the scarlet liquid shot into the mould, roaring and throwing up a rocket of sparks. "It's beautiful!" she cried, jumping up and down. "It's wonderful! Oh, look, Uncle Paul, what's that man doing down there?" She pointed at a man on the pouring platform looking through a bulky thing he held up to his face.

"Taking the temperature of the steel."

"What?"

"That's an optical pyrometer he's looking through. They can tell the exact degree of that soup just by the way it looks."

Claire's mouth hung open with amazement. In the burning heat of the shed, and her excitement, her brown face had turned scarlet and her upper lip was beaded. She stood gaping as the dinkey chuffed up and busily pulled away the train of ingots.

"Now what?" she sighed, as the crew dispersed to wait for the next pouring.

"Now I think you'd better go home," Uncle Paul said, taking out his watch. "Stanley is waiting outside for you."

"But is that all there is to see?" she asked anxiously. "What happens to those—that soup they poured into the long pots?"

He laughed. "That's a long business, Claire. They take those ingots out there"—he pointed toward the cooling shed—"and strip the moulds off them and dump them into a big hot pit."

"Why?"

"To keep them the right temperature until they are ready to roll them."

"Where do they do that?"

"In the blooming mill."

"Why?"

"Well, you can't do anything with a big chunk of cast metal, you know. It isn't any use until you roll it. That's what shapes it and makes it hard and gets it in form so they can go ahead and make things out of it."

"I want to see them do that."

They were walking down past the soaking pit now.

"It's after ten, Claire. Mary will be very cross if I keep you out any later."

"I'll attend to Mary. I don't want to go home now."

All right, he thought. I didn't realize this would turn out so well. He smiled at Claire and said, "But you'll have to pacify Mary."

Charlie Liska grinned delightedly when they appeared in the entrance to the blooming mill. He had been watching for them. He came down the shed holding out his thick blackened hand. He appeared, Paul thought, to have an old-worldly kind of punctilio about this first visit of the Boss's young niece.

He had been roller-boss for four years now. And he knew all about Claire, and about her father being killed in the war. Mary had told Julka, and Julka was all wrapped up in the war. Claire shook hands with the fierce-looking man while she tried to get used to the terrific noise in this place. Paul shouted, "Jerry like his job?" and Charlie shouted back, "Sure. Fine. I hope he learns good."

"That was the boy we saw back there," Uncle Paul explained to Claire. She saw that Uncle Paul seemed to notice these people particularly. She wondered why, trotting to keep up with Uncle Paul on the way to the casting department. She had asked particularly to see something made that was really going to be sent to France, something you could recognize for the actual weapon it was, which would actually kill Germans. She licked her lips when she said that. Paul wondered whether it was the heat or real bloodthirstiness that made her do it. So he took her to the shed here they were casting trench-mortar projectiles. Claire stood and watched with a grim set to her mouth. Sure enough, that long row of cigar-shaped moulds into which a small ladle was shooting liquid steel, was perfectly easy to recognize. Anybody could imagine those things landing in the German trenches, blowing them and their beastly occupants to shreds of mud and blood.

"That's grand," she said. "What happens to those now?"

"They have to be machined," Uncle Paul explained, "to make them smooth and polished and accurate to a thousandth of an inch. Then we ship them away. To be capped onto shells filled with explosives and finished."

Claire sighed. "That's grand," she said again. "Are you making *lots* of them, Uncle Paul? Lots?"

He laughed rather bitterly. What a world this was, he thought suddenly, when a thirteen-year-old girl was urging him to make more and more of these barbarously deadly things, when he was being driven to expand against his judgment and all the wisdom of his experience. If he could have found a way to adjust war production to his existing facilities he would have done it gladly even at the sacrifice of enormous profits.

He walked Claire out to the car, telling her to keep her coat tightly buttoned and the laprobe pulled high around her on the drive home. She was bubbling with excitement and enthusiasm. "I had no idea what it was like," she said, as she stepped into the car. "It's really wonderful. Oh, Uncle Paul!" she called, as Stanley started the car, "I think I'm going to like it here!" He smiled at her and watched her, craning her neck for a last glimpse of the mill as the car climbed the steep hill.

Paul went back to his office and tackled the big problem of the expansion that he could no longer avoid. He was going to have a tremendous job on his hands. He had never dreamed a day would come when more than a thousand men would work at Scott's in each twenty-four hours. The question of hours had always been knotty and insoluble. But Paul's labor policy, involving an open shop and as wide Amalgamated membership as the men wanted, created a situation where most departments worked twelve-hour shifts with the gruelling long turn of twenty-four hours at the seventh day, and a few finishing departments worked eight-hour shifts of three turns. Paul thought the twelve-hour day brutal. He had hoped all his life to see it universally abolished. But as he had said to Mary long ago, you saw these things differently when you ran a mill. So long as competitive prices were based on the twelve-hour day he could not increase labor by a third even if the wage-rates were proportionally reduced. Most of the men would not have that in any case. Of the devil's choice they preferred the longer day and the higher wage. But wages were mounting steadily anyway. Scott's was now paying a basic rate of $2.40 a day to common labor, and steeply sliding scales upward to the $12.00 and more earned by rollers and department foremen.

The Pittsburgh banks were amply willing to finance the expansion. In the next weeks Paul left the technical supervision of the mill to Dick and the department heads while he spent day after day in town working over the details of the huge loan he was negotiating. It would be a loan large enough to swing the new land and buildings and machines, the increase in payroll and operation expenses, and the vastly increased contracts for ore, manganese, tungsten, nickel, chrome, coke, and other raw materials. And on the urging of the banks and of government and foreign purchasing agents, he consented finally to open a business office in the Triangle as a convenience and time-saver for everybody concerned. He took an unpretentious suite of three rooms in the Oliver Building and put Ted in charge there as well as in the accounting and sales department at the mill.

Sometimes during this frenziedly busy period, when Paul lay exhausted and too keyed up to sleep at night, he thought of the Old Man and tried to imagine what he would do and say and think if he were here now. Sometimes Paul felt as he knew his father must have felt at critical times when his own sons were young. Ted, for instance, was no such worry as young William had been, but his heart was not in the mill and Paul knew it. One could not complain, though, of a boy as decent and generous and self-sacrificing as Ted. Not a word had ever been said about it, but Paul knew that Ted was trying to make it up to him for the bitter disappointment of Tom. If it had not been for his brother's selfishness Ted would have felt free to ask Paul to let him go and devote his life to the intellectual pursuits he craved.

"I have a lot to be thankful for," Paul told himself, lying in the dark in his vast walnut bed. This was his father's and his mother's bed; here he had been conceived and born and here, he told himself nowadays, he would surely die. He was sixty years old. He had used his years hard. He had his beloved Dick, on whom he leaned with profound confidence. He had a grandchild and would have more. He had his twins who would, somehow or other, come through all right. He had Mary. He had always had her. Now, in the calm of long years gone, he could lie alone in the dark and see how the parts of his strange life pattern had fallen into place.

> *There is an evening twilight of the heart*
> *When its wild passion-waves are lulled to rest.*

She had read that aloud to him one evening as they sat by the fire not long ago. Her voice was beautiful when she read poetry; she chanted a little, and through her words there rang the faintest echo of a brogue.

CHAPTER LXIV

[*1915*]

ONE MORNING the week before Christmas Paul and Mary and Ted and Claire were at breakfast when there was a commotion in the front hall. The door slammed, a sharp voice greeted Stella boisterously, and Paul, throwing down his paper, rose in his place. Tom strode into the dining-room barking "Hiya, Dad!" Everybody stopped eating and crowded around him. Paul wrung his hand, running his eyes over Tom's thin weatherbeaten face. Mary flung her arms around his neck and kissed him. Ted pounded him on the shoulders. Claire sat with her mouth open and stared. Tom smiled down at her.

"Hello, Claire," he said, "here's the prodigal sheep." He bent over and kissed her. She had never seen such a tornado of a man. He took her for granted as if he had always known her. Mary was bustling about laying another place at the table while Tom roared at Stella, "Rustle me up a big one, gal, I'm empty."

"What do you want for breakfast, Tom?"

"Steak. Potatoes. Lotta coffee."

Mary looked doubtful. "I don't think we have a steak in the house."

"Steak?" murmured Claire. "For breakfast?"

"Sure, why not? Well, got any ham?"

"Yes indeed. We had one baked Tuesday."

"Fry 'em up."

Mary went down to the kitchen. She thought she had better slice the ham herself. Trude would make it too dainty.

Tom dropped into a chair between Paul and Ted and sprawled under and above the table.

"Gee, it's good to see you, Dad."

Paul was so moved with surprise and pleasure that he had nothing to say. He patted Tom's hard forearm; the muscles through the cloth of his coat were like steel straps.

Ted bombarded his twin with questions. Tom answered some briefly and passed over others. He kept staring at Claire with his glittering green eyes. She stared back. Presently she said, "Your eyes are like Mère Constance's."

"That's right, I guess they are. I guess I can cuss as good as Aunt Constance too, from what I hear."

He sniffed impatiently as Mary came back from the kitchen.

"Like it here, Claire?"

"I do now."

"Pretty tough at first, anh? Y'oughta see where I live. That's real America."

Stella came in with a big blue willow platter and a bread tray covered with a napkin. She set them down in front of Tom. On the platter were four thick slices of crisp fried ham, four cheerful fried eggs, and a steaming mound of crusty German-fried potatoes. Tom helped himself to half the platterful, broke open a hot roll, and sighed happily.

"Gee, this is wonderful." He began to eat ravenously.

"You can have some hot cakes afterwards," Mary said dryly, "if you can hold them."

"Can I!"

Paul was still silent. Mary knew that he had one question, and only one, to ask of Tom. He was afraid to ask it. He wanted to ask whether

Tom had come home for good. Ted was full of suspense too. He began holding back on his questions. Tom asked for Dick and Ruth and Ruthie and all the news of the mill, and when Paul reluctantly looked at his watch Tom said, "Aw, call up and tell 'em you're taking the day off."

"I don't see how I can, son. The pressure's fearful now."

"Why don't you come down with us?" Ted said. "You wouldn't know the place."

Tom shrugged. "I'd a lot rather chin with you and Dad here. I've only got today."

"What?" Mary said. Paul turned pale.

"Gotta shove on tonight. New York."

"But Tom," Mary cried, "didn't you come home for *Christmas?*"

Tom pursed his lips, shoved his hands in his pockets, tipped back on the rear legs of his chair, and shook his head.

"Sorry. I'm sailing the day after tomorrow."

Paul started from his chair. "Tom!"

Claire gasped. "You mean—France?"

"Yep." Tom took a packet of cigarette papers and a bag of Bull Durham from his pocket and began to roll a cigarette.

Paul sat back in his chair and drew a long, broken sigh. Mary's eyes met his. He looked stricken; he looked weak and wretched and old; weak because he could do nothing. His mouth twitched and trembled a little at the corners.

Ted was leaning over Tom.

"What's up? What've you done?"

"Joined the Lafayette Flying Corps."

Paul moved his head as if his neck hurt. "Have you been flying out in Texas, Tom?"

"Sure. We got a crate on the ranch. Couple of us been flying it since last summer. Say," he said suddenly, turning to Paul, "you didn't think I'd sit around and read about this show in the papers, did you?"

"I suppose not." Paul made a gallant effort. "Tell me your plans, Tom."

"Well, I don't know much. We train at some place called Le Buc and if we're any good they use us, that's all."

"The French Army?"

"Um."

Claire's eyes were shining.

"Oh, Cousin Tom, you're wonderful."

"Shucks. I want to get in the scrap."

But Paul knew that there was more to Tom's decision than the driving restlessness and appetite for adventure that made it seem obvious. Mary knew too. Though Tom had hardly ever been articulate about anything, he was the one of all the boys who had had a violent personal reaction to the war. He hated bullies and anybody who picked one someone weaker than himself. He had fought his way through school licking boys like that. In his brief and sparse scrawls to his father and Mary he had been savage about the Germans ever since the invasion of Belgium.

Ted sat pale and thoughtful, listening to Tom. His head rested on his hand, and in spite of all his bulk and his resemblance to Paul, there was something infinitely pathetic about him. Mary knew what he was feeling. He was indeed, as he appeared, worried at the awful danger into which Tom had chosen to go. He loved his brother dearly, so dearly that he had given up his life to leaving Tom free. But Mary knew too the deep, secret well of bitterness on which Ted's soul must feed. Why, he would think when he was alone with his thoughts, should Tom always elect the course of glory and excitement, heroics, startling dramatization of himself? Why did people like that always get away with it while somebody like Ted obscurely footed the bill?

Paul went to telephone Dick, who must be at the mill by now. He told him to take over for the morning; Paul wanted to spend as much time as he could with Tom. He gave Ted the afternoon off. The twins could have that time alone. And in the evening Dick and Ruth would come for dinner.

It was the last time Paul was ever to sit down with all his sons together, but he did not know it then.

Mary realized with a shock that Claire had never seen a real Christmas. Nothing could be more unlikely than an old-fashioned Christmas in Constance's rakish menage. Sometimes when Claire came in contact for the first time with some simple, unaffected tradition of the family, Mary watched with trepidation to see what her reaction would be. Once or twice it had been derision, which Claire quickly checked. Mary was annoyed, but not at Claire who could not help it. Nobody but Constance would turn out a thirteen-year-old girl who had so many attributes of a woman of the world. These, in her child's body, against the intense emotions of her mourning and her homesickness and her love for her cat, were pathetic and ridiculous. But there was a sweep to Claire, a gusto for everything real and imaginative and new, which Mary hoped would blow out the hyperculti-vated tendrils of exotic tastes and ideas which clung like plant parasites to the sound stuff she really was.

Mary's way with Claire was always to go about things matter-of-factly. Claire belonged to the family and the house and the mill and everything all Scotts belonged to; explanations and introductions were therefore superfluous. Claire liked that. It gave her a sense of discovery, and at the same time of being firmly held by the same big roots that had built the mill and built this house and bought its heavy, substantial furnishings and dictated all the inflexible funny traditions like roast beef on Sunday and lamb stew on Monday, window-washing and clean curtains on Wednesday, that huge daily seven o'clock breakfast for everybody, Uncle Paul's Sunday afternoon nap and Mary's Saturday morning trip to market, on which Claire loved to go along.

Jones had finally retired a year ago and died within three months; with him went the last of the horses. After that Stanley inherited the duty of driving Mary and of following her about between the stalls of the Allegheny Market on West Diamond Street, carrying a big basket in which he collected her packages. Mary told Claire how Mère Constance had loved to go along in this very way when she was a girl, and how she would stand on the corner of Diamond Square staring at the cast-iron oxen's heads on the corners of the market building, calling them Eeenie, Meenie, Minie, and Moe. There were so many different places to go, Claire kept saying. Why couldn't you buy both butter and cottage cheese at the same stall? Because Uncle Paul insisted Mrs. Heisinger's cottage cheese was better than anybody else's, but Mrs. Slingerland's butter was exactly what he liked—salted just enough, and moulded in a round print with a sheaf of wheat on it, which he liked to see on the table in the pedestalled butter-dish with the glass cover. One fat toothless old woman sold flowers in a corner of the market—winter primroses in round bunches and dried straw-flowers and coxcombs and stiff bright red carnations. Now for Christmas she was selling holly wreaths with bunches of bright red berries. Mary had ordered hers several weeks ago, and Stanley collected them in four big piles from behind the stall. There were armfuls of green spruce boughs for decorating the house, and a thick piece of mistletoe.

When they reached home that noon after selecting a twenty-five-pound turkey and all the things that went with it, there was a Christmas tree propped out on the side porch, waiting for Stanley to attach the stand and bring it into the house. He set it up in the back parlor. Mary had spread a sheet on the floor underneath it. The tree just grazed the fourteen-foot ceiling, and its branches spread out so far that they took up a whole end of the room. Mary told Claire how in the old days when the house was full of children only those older than sixteen had been allowed to help trim the tree on Christmas Eve; everybody else was sent to bed early. Now it was no use sending Claire to bed because—she and Mary laughed together —she would not go. So after dinner on Christmas Eve Ted and Stanley brought down four big cartons from the attic, full of Christmas-tree trim-mings, and Claire fetched the new things she and Mary had bought. Every year a few new ornaments were added to replace those that had been broken. There were new candles for the shiny tin holders that clamped to the boughs of the tree. Fifty of them. They were always lighted with wax tapers fastened to the end of the old extension pole that had been used to light the gas chandeliers years ago. Mary remembered it from her very first day in the house.

"How long ago was that, Mary?"

Claire was with her in the pantry helping to take down the big turkey platter from the top shelf where it was kept in a bag between state occa-sions. Claire was sitting on top of the step-ladder, looking down at Mary who was counting tumblers and goblets at the glass closet.

"Let me see." Mary calculated. "Forty-two years ago last September."

"Ah-h-h-h—" there was a long incredulous gasp from Claire. "Why—that's not possible." She frowned. "How old are you, anyway?"

"Fifty-seven, dear."

Claire rested her chin in her hands and looked down at Mary.

"I can't imagine spending my whole life in one house," she said slowly.

Mary laughed. "Never fear, you won't. Now hand me down that plat-ter, Claire. Be careful, it's very heavy. Slide it forward over the edge of the shelf." They held their breaths during the operation. "That's right."

Claire stayed thoughtful all that afternoon. Mary saw that she was following some new train of thought which must be pushing through her mind loading up questions all the way. Several times she started to ask Mary something and then changed her mind.

She helped Mary put Christmas decorations on the dinner-table after Stella had finished setting it. There was so much holly and tinsel and red ribbon and red candles and fancy candies that Claire became quite intoxicated. She tried to tie a red bow around Jupe's neck. He had been sitting in the window sill watching the proceedings. He was not supposed to be in the dining-room for fear he might get caught in the swinging door. That had happened once years ago to a kitten of Clarissa's. Jupe objected violently to being decorated, and bolted away upstairs. Claire turned thoughtful in her unpredictable way and looked at Mary and said, "Is it true you were a maid when you first came here?"

Mary set down the epergne on the sideboard and looked over her shoulder at Claire.

"Certainly. There's no secret about that."

"Then why," asked Claire in a low voice, "are you like Uncle Paul's wife now?"

Mary sighed. "That's a long story, dear. Some day when you're older I'll tell you all about it."

She thought Claire would be satisfied. But after a moment Claire said, "Who was Uncle Paul's wife? What became of her?"

"She was your Aunt Louise," Mary said shortly. "She died a long time ago and I brought up the boys. The way I did your grandmother."

Of all times for the child to start asking questions like this! But just then they heard the car at the door and Claire jumped up and ran out to meet Uncle Paul and Ted. Mary heard her excitedly telling them about the day she had spent getting ready for Christmas. Then Dick and Ruth arrived, and Mary had last-minute things to see to, and the next thing she knew they were all sitting around the decorated table with Paul saying grace and the oyster stew steaming in the tureen in front of her.

When Claire awoke at six the next morning, she saw one of her long black lisle stockings tied to the foot of her white bed. Though it was still pitch dark outside she saw that the stocking was bulging. She switched on the light. Jupe uncurled from his place by her shoulder where he always slept and looked about, very indignant at the disturbance. There had been no nonsensical talk about Santa Claus last night, but nobody had mentioned the magic of finding a filled stocking on Christmas morning. Claire was almost happy enough to believe in Santa Claus anyway.

The stocking held a wonderful collection of things. There were lovely things, silly things, pretty things, things to eat. There was a big red papier-mâché Santa Claus sticking out of the top. There was a set of real tortoise-shell barettes; there was a lovely little manicure set; there was a topaz ring in a box marked with the name of a jeweller in Cannes—so that was why she hadn't received a package from Mère Constance, Mary had hidden it; there were long thin boxes of delicious caramels and chocolate cherries from Reymer's; there were china cats and funny puzzles and a joke book; there was a catnip mouse for Jupe; and in the very toe of the stocking a ten-dollar gold piece. She knew Uncle Paul had put that there. She weighed it in her hand. She polished it on the blanket. Money was nothing in particular itself, she had always had what she wanted by asking Mère Constance. But this was such a nice piece of money, and the American eagle was more imposing than the profiles of Napoleon and Queen Victoria and King Edward on French and English money. Sitting there with the gold piece in her hand and Jupe purring ecstatically while he pounced the catnip mouse all over the bed, Claire thought suddenly and vividly of Daddy. He would have loved this kind of a Christmas. They should have had them while he was alive. Tears sprang to her eyes as they so often did; things were always coming up that she wanted him to share.

After breakfast—Dick and Ruth had come over in time, of course—they all trooped into the back parlor where, with the curtains still drawn, Stanley had lighted all the candles on the tree. It shimmered and winked at them, all standing silently admiring it as if this had not happened every year of their lives. Only little Ruthie squealed with excitement, sitting on Dick's shoulder. Stanley and Trude and the maids stood at one side, smiling and pleased with themselves. Uncle Paul had one arm around Claire's shoulder and the other around Ruth's. After they had all admired the tree in silence they broke into the annual chorus of remarks—"Prettiest tree we ever had"—"Oh, there's the angel we couldn't find last year"—"I told you we needed more tinsel rope, Dick"—"I always like the blue things best"——

Then they turned on the lights and Uncle Paul told Claire to distribute the presents. She had never seen so many packages in her life. They were heaped round the base of the tree, and strewn over the sofa and chairs, boxes of every imaginable size and shape done up in colored and fancy papers with red and silver and green and holly-flowered ribbons. They were all jumbled up together so that Claire had to read off the name on each package and take it to the person it was meant for; this took more than half an hour. Nobody was allowed to start opening until all the presents were given out. Each servant had a huge armful, five or six packages and one very small, heavy one which Claire knew contained a gold piece. When they had received them all they went around to each member of the family and shook hands and wished him a Merry Christmas. Then they went away downstairs and everybody settled down to opening presents.

"Oh, Dad, you darling!" Ruth was ecstatic over a jewelled wrist watch. "Just what I wanted."

"Oh, *thank* you."

"Gee, this is wonderful."

"You shouldn't have done that, Ted!"

"How did you know I wanted one?"

Thank you. Thank you. Thank you. Claire had never seen people make such a fuss over one another. Ruthie sat on the floor in a pile of toys, screaming with delight and flopping from one thing to the next, hugging a teddy bear to her breast. Uncle Paul and the boys were surrounded with piles of socks and handkerchiefs and neckties and cigars and pipes and tobacco and books and slippers and cuff-links and bottles. Claire looked at one curiously. It said Old Overholt, Bottled in Bond, and Uncle Paul told her it was forty years old and a Mr. Mellon had sent him a case of it.

Claire's own presents were breathtaking. She had never received such a quantity of gifts in her life. Of course Mère Constance and Daddy had always given her lovely Christmas and birthday presents, and Mary had always sent them, but never in her wildest dreams had she imagined anything like this. There were nineteen presents not counting her stocking! There was a whole set of Mark Twain and another of somebody called Frank Stockton. There was a caseful of exquisite lingerie from Mère Constance's woman in Paris. There was a beautiful brown leather purse from Ted, a camera from Dick and Ruth, an ivory and silver desk set from Mary, and she couldn't even keep track of the smaller things. Jupe had the best time of anybody. He went from box to box, leaping in, burrowing under the papers, staying awhile and moving on to another box whenever somebody opened one.

Then it was time for church, and although Claire had been allowed these past three months to do as she pleased about attending church, Uncle Paul made it plain that he expected her to join the family today. Mary had been to five o'clock Mass at her church and would go again early in the evening. Now she wanted to stay at home to supervise the cleaning up of the parlor and the setting of the table for Christmas dinner. Stanley had the car especially well polished—it was a new car, a dark green closed Pierce-Arrow in place of the red Lozier touring-car. He had hung a small holly wreath inside the back window.

Claire liked it in church because there was such a crowd and everybody seemed so glad to be there. She had always thought of churches as dark, mysterious, mildew-smelling caverns where you followed a French or Italian or German guide through echoing stone passages, to be shown awesome sights of architecture and stained glass, and sometimes gruesome things as well, like the preserved cadavers wearing robes and jewels in the crypts of cathedrals in Italy. Once after seeing the one in the Milan cathedral, on a trip with Daddy, she had tugged at his coat as they climbed upstairs. The great madonna window faced them, and Claire pointed to it and said, "Daddy, is that that gentleman's wife and child?"

You would not think of things like that in the First Church of Allegheny. Here the interior was bare and austere, but the sun shone brightly through the high windows, there was lots of light, there were cheerful Christmas decorations, and a big choir of men and women in caps and gowns. Everybody sang with them. Claire sang as loud as she could. "Hark the Herald Angels Sing," she chanted, in her childish soprano, while Uncle Paul, sharing his hymnbook with her, sang in his rumbling bass and people in the neighboring pews smiled at them. Claire loved this. She even enjoyed the sermon because it gave her plenty of time to look around and study all the people. Most of them, Uncle Paul had told her, he had known all his life. They were not very smart-looking, and it was fun to imagine what they would talk about with Mère Constance if she should suddenly appear among them. They would not have anything in common, but a lot of them must have gone to school with her. Claire looked at a stout, severe-faced woman in a black silk dress and an elaborate hat, who had been staring at her. She was surrounded by a huge family. That woman must be about Mère Constance's age, and she certainly knew her. Was it Pittsburgh that made her look like such a ramrod, or would she have been that way anywhere?

Claire's eye caught a carved oak tablet fastened to the wall. She read: In Loving Memory of William Scott, Who Departed This Life on the Fifth Day of November, 1866, and of his Wife, Henrietta Campbell Scott.

Claire touched Uncle Paul's hand, and pointed to the tablet. Great-great-grandfather? He nodded, and pointed to a corresponding tablet on the other side of the church. Claire squinted and read: Erected in Loving Memory of William Campbell Scott and Clarissa Haynes Scott by Their Children, December 25, 1890.

At Christmas dinner only Mary knew what Paul was thinking as he rose in his place to carve the colossal turkey which made its entrance in a chorus of admiring gasps and exclamations. He glanced around the table, counting noses and filling his eyes with the good sight of his family gathered about him. The habit of missing Tom had worn thin long ago, but when Paul looked at Ted, Mary felt the ache in his heart. He was thinking of Tom on the high seas on his way to war.

•

CHAPTER LXV

[*February 1917*]

CLAIRE WAS WRITING one of her long letters to Mère Constance. She wanted to get it off this afternoon and she was hurrying, because later she and Mary were going down to the Liskas' for supper. Claire enjoyed doing that almost more than anything else in this queer new life she was leading. A year ago she would not have believed she would ever find so much to interest her and keep her busy in Pittsburgh, which she had expected to find a dull, dreary hole. Now she had spent her second Christmas here and was just beginning her fourth term at school. She had passed her midyear examinations with high marks, all except Algebra, which she had flunked, and she had all that to tell Mère Constance. Then there was Ted. Ted was engaged. That was exciting.

"She's that girl I told you about before," Claire wrote, "the tall one named Lauchlan McIntyre. Did you ever hear such an odd name for a girl? It's really her middle name, her first one's Margaret. American girls seem to think that very smart. It does suit her. She's almost as tall as Ted. She has dark, flat hair that looks as if it were blowing away from her temples, and dark eyes, and her face has that set look about it like Tom's —as if she were walking into a high wind. She's very good at games, tennis and golf and all that sort of thing, and spends most of her time on a horse. She's supposed to be very tosh here, her family have pots of money and live out in Sewickley in the most hideous pile of masonry I ever saw. We drove out there in state two Sundays ago for dinner, Uncle Paul and Ted and I. Mary didn't go. Uncle Paul was in a bad humor. He hates to be away from home for Sunday dinner and I know he was upset about Mary. I couldn't tell whether she hadn't been invited, or whether she wouldn't go if she had been."

Claire had not known that Uncle Paul could swear almost as well as Mère Constance, until that day when she had overheard him say to Mary, "I'll be damned if I'll go out there without you."

Mary had murmured something and Claire had caught the word "family" and Uncle Paul had almost roared, "*I'm* not marrying into that bunch of snobs. If Ted's going to, I'll keep my distance a hell of a lot further than they." But he had gone anyway, and if Mary had been there in person she could not have pictured his cold aloofness more clearly than Claire described it later. Mary's lips had twitched and Claire saw an amused, faraway look in her gray eyes. Claire had asked what Mary was thinking and Mary had said, "Nothing. I was just remembering Uncle Paul's father at your Uncle Bill's wedding in Boston."

"Anyway," Claire wrote, "I can see why Uncle Paul doesn't seem delighted about Ted and Lauchlan. Ted is simply moony about her, he just sits and gawps 'at her and she is very brisk and bossy and decides everything. Just the opposite of Ruth—in fact you never saw a funnier contrast. Lauchlan looks at Ruth as if she were a funny little caterpillar. Mr. McIntyre is building a house on part of his place for Lauchlan and Ted, and she has it all planned that Ted will commute to town every day. Uncle Paul was very patient and tried to explain why he'd prefer that Ted live nearer the mill at least until the war is over, because there's such masses of work and Ted has to be near both the mill and the downtown office. But Lauchlan just laughed and said, 'Oh, Mr. Scott, I *couldn't* live in town,' and that was the end of it. I heard Uncle Paul tell Mary yesterday that Ted would have to get up at five o'clock every day after he was married and Mary sniffed and said, 'You'd better go and hire a sales manager or you'll be up every day at four o'clock yourself.'

"I just can't imagine Ted married to Lauchlan and coming here all the time the way Dick and Ruth do. Lauchlan would be bored to tears. I daresay Mary will be quite content if she never comes. Lauchlan's mother told me I must come out and stay with them and meet some of the young people—as if I'd been living in an old ladies' home here. I know she meant to be polite but there was something about the way she spoke that made me furious."

Mary came in just then with some clean laundry and laid it on Claire's bed. She winked as she did so. Claire had had to learn to take care of her own clothes, put away her laundry, hang up her dresses, keep her bureau drawers neat. Mary had said so. Claire was sometimes surprised to find herself doing as Mary said about things like that. At home she would have flung a bedroom slipper at anybody who suggested such a thing.

"Give my love to Mère Constance," Mary said. Claire nodded and bent over her desk again. She really loved this funny-looking desk with the slanting top which let down to form the writing table, and the pigeonholes, some open, some with doors, where she kept her treasures. Jupe leaped into her lap and settled down and she hurried to finish her letter.

"I have enough friends right here, though the girls are rather bores. Once in a while I still have some trouble."

She laid down her pen then and sat deliberating whether to tell Mère Constance about the latest trouble she had had. She thought she'd let it go. It seemed rather silly now, but it certainly hadn't at the time. She and two of her classmates were walking home from school when they passed a knot of boys on the corner of Ridge Avenue and Irwin Avenue. They were public-school boys and the girls ignored them; but just as they passed, they were horrified to see Claire stop and say, "Hello, Anton," to a short boy in funny-looking clothes. "Hello," the boy answered, and Claire had said, "I've got some more stamps from France for you, I'll bring them the next time we come to your house." "Thanks," the boy had said, and then he and Claire had waved their hands casually and each turned back to his friends. But the girls with Claire had thrown their heads in the air and sniffed.

"Well!" Betty Jarvis had said. "I call that the limit!"

"So do I!" Dorothy Denny had said indignantly.

They both threw scornful sidelong glances at Claire. She returned them.

"Wait till I tell my mother *that!*" Betty Jarvis said.

"What?" Claire asked. The girls missed the sarcasm in her voice.

"A Hunky! You ought to know better than that, Claire," Dorothy Denny said. "Why, nobody ever speaks to a Hunky. Nobody knows any."

"Well, *I* know a lot." Claire's mouth snapped shut on that.

"I'd be ashamed to admit it, if I were you," Betty said. "Everybody knows you're a freak—but you needn't be seen talking to Hunkies when you're going some place with *me!*"

"Me either."

Claire stopped walking and the two girls, instead of going on and leaving her, stopped too. They thought they had her cowed. Instead she laughed roughly and said, "The Hunkies are about the only people I've seen in Pittsburgh who aren't a lot of dried-up prunes. I'd far rather be friends with them than with snobs and bores like you." She had turned on her heel then, and strolled around the corner, leaving the two girls gaping after her.

Their mothers had spoken to Uncle Paul about her and Uncle Paul had apparently done some apologizing for Claire. It seemed to her that everybody had made a lot more of the matter than it was worth. So she would not bother to tell Mère Constance about it. Instead she wrote, "In the afternoon, we usually do something outdoors, at which I'm wretched, like skating on Lake Elizabeth or coasting down our back hill here, and then we go to Kennedy's Drug Store on the corner of Irwin and Western and have sodas. Can you imagine me sitting on a stool in a drugstore lapping up chocolate ice cream and the goo they pile on it? Goo is an American word, by the way.

"I've funked dancing school. I loathed it so much that Uncle Paul finally had to tell Mrs. Robinson I wasn't coming any more.

"Yes, Aunt Lizzie and Benjie did come for Christmas. The boys snorted a bit about it before they got here, but Mary scolded them and said they should be ashamed. Uncle Paul said he'd never forgive himself if he didn't invite his sister home for Christmas the first year she was a widow.

"They are rather terrible, darling. *How* can that old sourpuss (another American word I learned in school!) be your sister? She looks old enough to be your mother, and then that spindly little boy who looks like her grandson! I don't like Benjie. Everybody supposes we should be great friends because we're almost the same age. I will admit he's bright. He can do Algebra like a flash and showed me two or three short-cuts which he said should make it easier for me at school. I haven't noticed much difference. I still flunk it.

"Aunt Lizzie looked at me as if I were a walking case of measles that Benjie might catch. She kept asking Mary if I was really allowed to drink wine and coffee or whether I was just wilful like you. Somebody told me she's very rich and does a lot of good with her money—she certainly doesn't have any fun out of it. Or Benjie either as far as I can see. We had one fight. About the war. He says it's none of America's business and he doesn't care which side wins."

Mary put her head inside the door and said, "It's almost time to go dear."

Claire nodded and said, "I'll be ready in a shake," and scribbled very fast.

"Ruth finally decided to name the baby Pauline. She was so upset about its being another girl she's taken all year making up her mind about its name. Dick kept telling her it was silly to name her Pauline because some day they'd have a boy they'd want to name Paul and whoever heard of a brother and a sister named Paul and Pauline? But Ruth did it anyway.

"Uncle Paul says to tell you to write him *everything* about Tom, no matter how busy you are. How grand for him to have that leave with you! I got so homesick thinking about it I almost packed up and sailed. Mary says she's sure it's her prayers and Fra Anselmo's that have kept Tom safe. You should see Uncle Paul combing the newspaper for news of the Escadrille. He's stopped worrying so much about Tom getting killed and now he gets just as excited about the fights as if he were in them himself. He's terribly keen on the war, says we (America) must come in soon to help us (Allies) and he rages about the U-boat sinkings and sometimes swears so I could think it was you.

"Darling, I think I'll come home this summer. Do you mind? I'll stay and finish the school year, but then I want to leave. Mary and Uncle Paul are wonderful to me, and I've loved it here in many ways, but I've had enough for this time. If it weren't that I keep telling myself why we never see the sky or the sunshine I'd be frightfully low. It is gloomy, you know, and the dirt is horrid. But when I think it all comes from making guns and shells and steel to kill Boches, I feel better.

"Jupe sends his love. He wants to come home too, he misses his catnip bed and his eschalots. And I miss you. I feel as if I'd been on my best behaviour for a long time and now I want to come home and let down. I haven't really been very good, lots of times I've been horrid. Especially about Benjie. But you'd have been worse.

"Je t'embrasse, je t'aime, je te baise mille fois.

"Claire."

The Liskas lived in a cramped, grimy, two-story brick house in a row on Liverpool Street, just up the hill from the mill. There was a kitchen and a front room on the ground floor and three bedrooms on the second floor—one for Julka and Charlie, one for the boys, and one for the girls. Claire had never seen people living so close to poverty, and she could not realize that, as steel-workers' lives went, the Liskas were extraordinarily prosperous and fortunate. Having a whole house to one family was a rare privilege. Having a job like Charlie's, a key job which would not fold up under one in slow times unless the entire mill shut down, was the height of security. Charlie was almost a legend in the Slavic community. To most Slavs he was the personification of the dream they had all cherished in the beginning and which some, in spite of hardship and the cruel ganged-up prejudice of the Irish-Americans, had kept alive. His work was respected; he was in Paul Scott's confidence; above all he was one of the exceedingly rare examples throughout the entire Pittsburgh district of a Slav in a skilled job where native-born Americans, as well as immigrant Hunkies, worked under his orders. He had been more than twenty-five years in the Scott mill, and by sheer seniority had reached a place where everybody accepted him.

Now, at fifty-two, he sat at the head of the crowded round table in the kitchen, with Julka opposite him, and Mary and Claire and his children grouped around the sides. Jerry was the eldest, nineteen now, whom Claire had first seen at work in the mill. Next came his sister Míla, then Anton, then little Jenny. Their names were really Jaromír, Ludmila, Antonín and Libuše.

They had all been born right here in Pittsburgh and they all spoke ordinary everyday English, as well as the Czech that their mother insisted be spoken in their home. And Claire liked them because in spite of the tremendous gulf between them and everybody else she knew, they made her feel more at home than any of Uncle Paul's friends or even her own cousins. They were all wrapped up in Europe and the war, and the children drank beer and coffee like civilized people, and Jerry, who was a lot younger than Ted Scott, seemed to Claire to have more sense and be more independent than Ted. Naturally Claire could not perceive the corresponding contrast between herself and Míla, the eldest Liska girl, which brought amused smiles to the faces of Mary and Julka. It was seventeen-year-old

Míla nowadays who ran the house, washed the clothes, cleaned, marketed, and cooked under her mother's supervision; for Julka had been too busy with her political work for two years past to do much housekeeping. Míla was serving the supper now, making quick trips from the stove to the table. She did not sit down until everybody was served.

For a time nobody talked much. Claire ate her soup slowly, watching the Liskas from under her downcast eyelids. Charlie and Jerry never talked when they first sat down to eat. That was the way they showed their fatigue after their day in the mill. They bent over their steaming plates of noodle soup, resting on their elbows and carrying their spoons to their mouths with heavy hands black in spite of careful scrubbing. Charlie's graying head and Jerry's smooth brown one rose from the open collars of their clean blue shirts like two well-shaped rocks. Claire saw the tender look in Julka's brown eyes when she looked at them. Julka's glance moved to her younger son. He was fifteen.

"How was your lesson today, Anton?" she asked.

This was the boy to whom Claire had spoken on Irwin Avenue, incurring the scorn of her friends. He was different from the rest of his family, blond and short, and rather delicate-looking. He liked books and he collected stamps, so Claire saved the envelopes of all her letters from Europe for him. He looked up at his mother with brown eyes like hers, and said, "It was good, Mama. Professor Wollner said I should go ahead to the Allegro."

"You learned first movement *good?*" Charlie asked, wiping his full moustache with the back of his hand. He wagged a heavy forefinger at Anton. "No go ahead till last thing perfect—*výborně*——"

They were speaking English in deference to Mary and Claire. But Claire always listened eagerly for the words in Czech that dropped into the talk. Her ear, accustomed to a mêlée of languages, welcomed anything beside the flat sharp-R'd twang of English that she heard all the time now. And this language was so utterly strange, so bewilderingly unrelated to any of the others she knew. She was a born linguist, not yet fully aware of her own remarkable talent, which was closely related to the musical gifts of both of her parents. It seemed incomprehensible to her that anybody confronted with a strange language would not automatically try to find his way about in it.

"*Ano, tatínku,*" Anton said respectfully.

"He's working on the Beethoven Concerto," Julka explained. "Why don't you play us the first movement after supper, Anton?"

"If you want," he said shyly. "Only—without accompaniment? Without Professor?"

The Liskas even had a piano, a shrill, tinny, second-hand upright in the crowded front room. Julka had stubbornly hoarded coins for years before she had saved enough to buy it.

"Maybe I could accompany," Claire said.

"You?" Jerry looked at her and laughed, she thought, a little derisively. She flushed and started to say something withering in retort, but thought better of it and only said, "Why not?"

Jerry shrugged, conscious that his mother was scowling at him. For some reason it had seemed unlikely to him that this niece of the Boss's, whose coming here with Mary Rafferty made him vaguely uncomfortable, should be able to sit down and play the piano part of the Beethoven Concerto. They saw that he thought she was just showing off. Her face was still pink with mortification and anger, and Mary was watching her rather anxiously; in any other such circumstance Claire's tongue would have shot sparks by now. But Míla got up then to bring the rest of the supper and everybody's attention went to that. She brought a big, deep, covered pot from the stove, and placed it before Charlie. Julka said, "Are you too tired to dish, Papa?"

Charlie raised his head and smiled, wiping his moustache again.

"No, no, not for company. Is honor."

Míla took the cover off the pot and a mouthwatering pungent steam filled the room.

"Oooh! Pork and sauerkraut"—Claire looked at the dish—"and *houskové knedlíky!*"

"She remembered it," Julka said to Míla. "I told you she would."

"How come you learn Czech words so easy?" Jerry asked. His manner was different now. Apparently he felt sorry for embarrassing her. "It's a tough lingo."

"Oh, I don't know. Through the skin, I guess. Go on and talk Czech, all of you, I want to listen."

"Not polite," Charlie said firmly. He spooned up helpings of rich boiled pork, sauerkraut creamy with grated potato and spiced with caraway seeds, and slices of big, feathery dumplings. "Rude for talk Czech when Miss Mary don't understand."

"I don't mind," Mary said quickly. "I like to hear it."

They all laughed self-consciously. Julka was slicing the black bread, holding the loaf against her chest. "You can be sure we don't say anything about you," she said to Mary. "Except nice."

They ate hungrily. Claire had a second helping when Charlie asked her. There were two quart pails of beer on the table; Jenny had gone to the corner for them just before dinner. Everybody had a glass except Mary, who did not like beer.

"Mama," Jerry said, pushing his empty plate away, "did you find out if it's true about the brigade in Russia?"

Everybody looked at Julka, with a kind of deference quite unrelated to their old-worldly respect for her as their mother. Mary herself sometimes felt a little in awe of this side of Julka; this busy, public, authoritative side. For three years she had been running a veritable hotbed of sedition against the Austro-Hungarian side in the war. She had taught Míla to take her place at home so that she could travel and keep in touch with the rising Czech and Slovak separatist groups that were working all over the United States. Charlie was earning the highest wages of his lifetime—$14.50 a day—and even Jerry as electrician's helper on the new open-hearths was bringing in $4.00 a day. So there was money enough for Julka to go to New York, to Bridgeport, to Detroit, Chicago, Cleveland—wherever awakening and organizing groups were holding revolutionary congresses and meetings. She was much in demand as a speaker at these congresses, and as Mary had always observed, her organizing talents were boundless.

Julka was no longer pretty and apple-cheeked, but she was a striking woman, big of frame, with broad, high, prominent cheekbones and the shiny unwrinkled skin of a peasant. Her hair was sprinkled with gray and combed back into a plain knot. Her large brown eyes were deep with wisdom and warmth. Her hands were dry and heavy and thickened with work, but when you talked to her you did not think of her as a steelworker's oman and drudge.

She nodded at Jerry's question and reached over to the dresser for a pile of papers.

"There's no doubt about it any more," she said. "Last night I got the latest report." She ran her eye down a list of figures. "About fifty thousand of them. And Professor Masaryk is on his way from Paris to help them."

"Who do you mean, Mrs. Liska?" Claire laid down her fork and bent toward Julka.

"Our troops. They have been deserting across the lines to Russia for six months now. In battle they simply surrender and walk over, then they fight on the other side."

"But can they shape up a separate unit?" Jerry asked. "Those Russkis are punks, it won't do us much good to fight with them."

"They're not punks!" Claire interrupted sharply. Every head turned and every pair of eyes stared at her in surprise. Again that sardonic look came into Jerry's face and this time he shrugged and said, "Oh, no? What do you know about it?"

Julka put up her hand. Maybe the child was butting in and showing off, but she could not tolerate Jerry's taunting her. To her surprise Claire, instead of reacting with temper, said, "Is it their fault if that horrible government of their sends them into battle without arms or ammunition or—or anything—to be slaughtered like cattle?"

Charlie laid down his knife and fork, and Anton and Jenny stared at Claire with wide, round eyes. Charlie leaned forward and said slowly, "Jaromír, young lady say right. She say trut'." Jerry shrugged again and Julka said, "Our men are not trying to stay with the Russkis anyway. They want to fight in the West. That's why Professor Masaryk is going to Russia now, to tell them what to do next."

"I wish he come here," Charlie said. "Could show dumb Slováks what for do too."

"Papa, don't call them names," Julka said impatiently.

Mary smiled faintly. She could remember vividly how she used to reproach Julka fifteen years ago for talking that way about the Slovaks herself. Nowadays Mary was always answering Claire's questions about those times, and about the beginnings of the House, which was now The Slovak Women's Friendly Society of Pittsburgh, organized and chartered, with a membership of two hundred, and all sorts of projects and activities that had outgrown Mary's personal touch. And Julka had learned her early lesson well. A Czech in a Slovak community, she used the circumstance as a lever to work for joint Czech and Slovak action in sabotaging the Austrian fronts of the war, and laying the groundwork for an independent republic.

"Mrs. Liska," Claire said, "I don't understand about these different organizations you have. Why can't there just be one big group all working together?"

Jerry cackled. "You don't know what you'd be bargaining for," he said. "They wouldn't have any fun if they all curled up together. They gotta scrap and call each other names. They're built like that."

Julka shrugged and nodded. "It's too bad too," she said. "But you can't change human nature all at once. Don't we have enough trouble, without we should invite the League to join the Alliance?"

She meant, Claire knew, the Slovak League, to which all the Pittsburgh Hunkies belonged, and the Czech National Alliance, whose headquarters were in Chicago, to which Julka belonged. She was doing her best, she said, to get the two groups to pull together and lay aside their age-old jealousies and their jockeying for priority. Professor Masaryk and his committees in Paris and London, and the underground workers in the old country at home desperately needed the help of both organizations and the money they were always raising at these meetings in America. Julka was in touch with the Masaryk committees all the time. If anybody knew exactly what was going on, she did.

She was stacking the empty plates before her now, saying, "All right, Míla darling." Míla took the pile away. Everybody sat back looking full and contented. Míla had the secret pleased look of a cook who is about to spring a sensationally welcome surprise. She reached down a set of small, pretty plates from a high shelf and dusted the top one with her apron. These were company plates; Mary had given them to Julka one Christmas shortly after they moved into this house.

Míla put the plates on the table and then produced a huge pan which she had been hiding in the back kitchen. They all sat up, appetite renewed, and grinned delightedly. Míla was pouring the coffee into mugs at the stove.

"Jeez!" said Jerry. "I bet you can't say what those are in Czech, Miss Gregory."

"I asked you all to call me Claire," she said, "and those are *tvarohové taštičky*, so there!" She bit into one of the tender, fragrant cheese pockets and sighed blissfully.

Jerry grinned at her now. "I guess you win," he said, with his mouth full. And, to the others, "She's smart."

They sat for a long time around the table, talking about the war which was the thing nearest their hearts. Mary admitted that Paul was getting pretty rabid about it. "He says the purchasing commissions tell him they can't hold out through the spring if the sinkings keep up at the present rate," she said. "Of course I will say I don't altogether trust the British—they'd claim anything to get us in the war."

"Well, why not?" asked Jerry hotly. "Do you blame 'em?"

The younger children still listened in silence.

Mary bit her lip.

"You don't really feel Irish, do you, darling?" Claire looked at her shrewdly. "That's what's the matter with you."

Mary looked embarrassed. "I'm American," she said. "Above all. I just can't help wondering what there'd be in this for us."

"You shoon' talk like dat," Charlie said slowly. Mary was an old friend; he felt quite free to reprove her even though his attitude toward her was respectful. "We got very great cause here, all good people together. We win war, we get nation, all Slavs get nation, no more empire, no more oppress', no more Habsburgs and Hohenzollerns. President Wilson, listen to him. He got right idea."

"I suppose so," Mary said slowly. She sighed. "But war never really settles anything."

"It vill this time. Jeez, I can't wait to get over there," Jerry said. He made a fist on the table.

Mary turned and looked at Julka. Whatever she had expected to see in that broad, earnest face, she was surprised to find calm pride in it now. She would have thought a mother would shrink to hear her son say such a thing. But Julka only smiled remotely at Jerry, and Mary knew that she had no greater hope for her son than the chance to join his people's fight for liberty.

Then Julka turned to Anton and said, "Go and get your fiddle, Anton. Claire, can you really play for him?"

"I can try," Claire said. "I don't read very well at sight but—"

"Fine," Charlie said gravely, rising from the table. "*To bude hezké.*"

CHAPTER LXVI

[*1917*]

WHEN THE DECLARATION of war came on the sixth of April, it was as great a shock as if it had not been long expected. Even to Paul, who had been intellectually and emotionally convinced for over a year past that the United States must enter the war, the sight of the afternoon papers with their fatal headlines was paralyzing. Younger men were wildly exhilarated and a few were truculently opposed, but Paul was made very sober by the real meaning of the awful step. He was inhumanly pressed at the mill at that time. Ted's wedding had taken place the previous Saturday, an enormous, ostentatious, crowded, noisy function. The ceremony, embellished by two bishops and sixteen bridesmaids and ushers, had taken place in St. Stephen's Church in Sewickley, and the reception at the McIntyres' had been for Paul an unmitigated ordeal. The big house was filled with hundreds of dressed-up people milling about drinking champagne and exclaiming about Lauchlan's beauty in her wedding dress and the magnificent display of presents on the second floor. There was a marquee built over a dance floor in the garden with an orchestra from New York playing from afternoon until the early hours of the next morning, long after Ted and Lauchlan had left for White Sulphur Springs in the Buick roadster that Paul gave them for a wedding present.

Lauchlan had wanted to go to Honolulu and Ted had acted as if he really thought that quite possible until Paul had had a serious talk with him. It had hurt Paul to have to speak to Ted like this. Ever since Ted's engagement to Lauchlan, Paul had hoped that the natural excitement and distraction of the thing would wear off in due course and Ted resume his reasonable and reliable way of going about his work. But that, Paul saw finally, was not going to happen unless he took some step about it. Even though Lauchlan had grown up in the midst of traditionally hardworking Pittsburgh men—she came of a fine old settler family—she seemed to assume that there was something different ahead for Ted. Paul finally had it out with him.

"This is a decision you've got to make, son," he had said. "If you want to cut down your working hours and be at your wife's disposal for long vacations and evenings and week-ends—well—" he shrugged.

The inference was clear: Ted could not do that and stay at the mill.

"The point is," Paul went on, "I have to know where I stand. Either I can rely on you to take the sales department and the books off my mind or I can't. I have to rely on somebody—*twenty-four hours a day.*"

"You can rely on me, Dad." Ted's voice was low and he looked shamefaced.

"Mind—I'm not forcing you, Ted. This is an extreme emergency and you know conditions will only be like this during the war."

"I know."

"Your work is almost entirely confidential and I can't go out and hire a bookkeeper or sales manager to take it over—now."

Ted nodded.

"I'll make it up to you, Ted. When the emergency is over I promise you can have a long vacation, go any place you like and stay as long as you want to. Do you think you can satisfy Lauchlan with that?"

"Sure."

"Well, then, don't take more than two weeks for your honeymoon, and don't go so far I can't reach you by telephone in case of emergency."

There was a silence. Ted knew perfectly well what Paul meant by "emergency."

"Do you think we'll be in it soon, Dad?"

Paul nodded slowly. But it was still a shock when a boy rushed in with the papers that Friday afternoon.

The American colossus roused itself slowly and blunderingly. For a good many months things went on in Pittsburgh much as they had before. Industrial activity intensified and speeded up almost to the breaking point, and many young unmarried men went into the service. Dick's and Ted's friends found themselves with commissions and orders to report at officers' training camps. A certain number of the younger men in the mill went off, but since they were workers in the most essential war industry, and since their wages were at all-time highs, there was not much incentive to quit work and join the army now. But Jerry Liska came to Paul on Monday morning following the declaration of war.

"I'm joining up, Mr. Scott," he said.

Paul liked the boy immensely. He was the best kind of tough-fibred young mechanic.

"I'm sorry, Jerry. You're doing a fine job here," he said.

"I hope I can come back to it. But I gotta go now."

"I know. You people feel this is your fight." Paul had heard Claire's accounts of her visits to the Liskas'.

"We sure do." Jerry moved to his feet. This was awkward for him.

"Well, good-bye, Boss," he said. He thrust out his hand.

Paul shook it hard. "Good-bye, Jerry. Good luck." Paul hesitated. "Just a minute." He was thinking of Julka's work, about which Mary and Claire had been telling him for months past. He knew that she might find herself pinched without Jerry's earnings. Paul said, "I want to ask you something. I'd like you to take this to your mother and tell her it's my contribution to her work and please not to mention it any further. Okay?" He was writing a check on his personal account; he signed and blotted it quickly and folded it before handing it to Jerry.

"Okay." Jerry's face was red and he blinked his eyes.

He left the office and shut the door. Then it opened again and he stuck his head inside.

"Anybody tells me you're a bastard like those Company managers, I'll murder 'em," he said.

Paul laughed. But he wondered queerly whether the men ever did say things like that about him among themselves.

Late one night almost at Christmas time Dick and Ruth were in bed talking. Ruth's blonde hair was plaited in two fat braids tied with blue ribbon, ending in bunches of curls. There were matching baby-ribbons in the insertion in her cambric nightgown. Her smooth white arms and round breasts swelled softly from ruffled sleeves and square neckline. She was propped against the pillows, knitting. All the girls knitted in every possible moment of their waking hours; Ruth regularly finished a sock a day. She usually spent the evenings over at Dad's with Mary, now that Dick and Dad always went back to the mill after dinner. Dick drove home late with Dad and picked Ruth up, and Stanley brought them over to their house on Cedar Avenue. Dick would fall into bed exhausted. Sometimes he had blueprints and specifications sheets and technical drawings to study, and then he would sit up with a glass of milk trying to keep awake for another half hour. He had just laid a sheaf of papers on the floor and turned on his side, flinging one arm across Ruth.

"Put out the light, honey, we've got to get to sleep."

"Just let me finish this needle."

"How's Ruthie's throat?"

"Much better. They were so disappointed not to say good night to you."

"I know. I told Ted I'd see a fellow for him at six."

"So he could catch his train to Sewickley," Ruth said.

"Oh, what the hell."

Ruth finished her needle, slipped out of bed to open the windows, put out the lights, and came back and lay down. Dick curved his long length around her short, plump body and relaxed with a low growl. They always slept that way. He closed his eyes now but he was too tense to sleep. Ruth could feel that. She said after a while, "I wish you could sleep, Dickie."

"Got so much on my mind."

She hesitated. "Is it—anything more than usual?"

"Oh, I guess not."

"Why do you do any of Ted's work when you have too much of your own?"

"I don't really do anything for Ted. He's okay, dear. After all—he's got a right to want to get home for dinner. They're still star-gazing. And they didn't get a real honeymoon."

"They've got everything else under the sun."

"Aw, I wouldn't be jealous of Lauchlan, honey."

"I'm not. I just don't like her."

Dick laughed. Ruth thought she had better maunder on a little longer. Dick would relax sooner.

"Why do you suppose she fell for Ted? You'd think she'd want some millionaire with a string of polo ponies."

"My little candy angel, your brother-in-law Ted is a very beautiful young man. Lauchlan has fallen for his godlike body and he has as good a chance to wind up with a string of polo ponies as anybody else in these woods. Lauchlan will always be able to buy them for him anyway."

"He probably wouldn't want them. In fact I don't know why he fell for her. Bossy old snob."

"That one is easy. Hadn't it ever occurred to you she's very much like Tom?"

"Tom's no snob."

"I don't mean that. He's hard and energetic and decisive and Ted's been used to that since before he was born. He feels lost without his dynamo. Lauchlan has his mind made up for him before he knows it. So he never has to decide anything." Dick sighed. "Gee, what a break."

Ruth pulled up on her elbow and looked at Dick in the dark.

"What do you mean by that, darling?"

"Nothing."

There was a very long silence. Ruth was almost asleep. Dick breathed regularly. Ruth's mind wandered in the last scattered fog of thought. Red Cross day tomorrow . . . Pauline's white shoes for Christmas . . . write to Mother . . . a fresh shaving-stick for Dick . . . must remember to telephone . . .

Dick rolled over suddenly and groaned. Ruth jumped.

"Darling, I thought you were asleep."

He buried his head on her neck and said through his teeth. "I don't know what the hell to do."

Ruth felt cold and shaky inside. She had thought for a long time that Dick was looking more tired and anxious than the heaviest strain at the mill could explain. Now she knew she had been right. But she did not know what to say. Strange and awful fears flashed through her mind, things that happened to people's marriages. Maybe Dick didn't love her any more. Maybe——

She put her arms around him. "Please tell me. I have to know."

She felt his muscles tighten, heard his teeth click. He had a way of shutting his mouth hard when he was tense. Then he said, "I want to go to France."

"Dick!" Ruth did not know that a thin, desperate wail would rise from her throat. She gasped with shame when it did. She ought not to have done that. But nonetheless she burst into tears. Dick held her tight.

"I was afraid you'd take it that way."

"What else should I do?" she sobbed.

"I'm sorry. You asked me to tell you."

"I meant that. I'm sorry I was such a coward."

"Ruth, don't you think you could understand?"

"It's pretty hard. Between Dad and the mill and us there's no reason in the world why you should go."

"Except that I want to. And I'll always feel yellow if I don't."

"But you're needed here. We can't get along without you." Her voice quavered.

"Ruth." Dick sat up straight and lit a cigarette in the dark. "How many English girls would talk like that?"

"They're different."

"That's a bum thing to say. You're not really like that."

"But why *do* you want to go? Just to get killed—for the excitement of it?"

Dick got out of bed and began to pace the floor.

"I'm pretty sick about this," he said. "I should have thought you'd understand." His voice was cold.

"Why should I understand? Why should I get up and cheer because you want to rush off to the war and leave me with two babies? And Dad with the whole mill? He can't get along without you, even if I could."

"Yes he can. Dad's got more guts than you have."

"How *can* you say such a thing!"

"Maybe I'm wrong. I hope so."

"But what would he do? Literally?"

"I can get him a better general superintendent than I am. Gray Simcox. That fellow with the lame foot the year before me in college. He's chief engineer at Lackawanna. He could do my job and a lot more."

"Dad wouldn't think so. He depends on you like his own eyes."

"Something tells me Dad would make this easier for me than you do."

"It's not fair!" Ruth said passionately. "Married men don't have to fight. There are plenty of others to do it. You don't see Ted rushing off to France, do you?"

"That's quibbling. I'm not Ted. I'm not making up his mind . . ."

"And it would kill Dad. You know he's aged ten years since Tom went over." Ruth shivered and added, "Please shut the windows."

Dick shut them and went on pacing. His striped pajama jacket flapped.

"I don't think it's fair to hold Dad over me," he said. "Or you either, since there's plenty of money for you and the girls. If you were going to be destitute without me—"

"So it *is* just adventure you're after," Ruth wailed. "Dad can support us while you—"

Dick strode over to the bed and clamped his heavy hand on her shoulder.

"Look here," he said. "I told you I was having an awful struggle with my conscience. I know all the arguments against this better than you do. You're not even trying to see the other side."

"What is there to see?"

"Are you blind?" Dick shouted. "Can't you read the papers? Or don't you give a damn? The whole U. S. Army's in a hell of a mess and you ask me what there is to see. They aren't getting brains out of the draft, Ruth. They're swamped with confusion. There's a desperate need for technicians and engineers. Here it is Christmas and they want to get going in the spring—hell, we've been in the war nearly eight months and they're still falling over their own feet. Brest is a three-ring madhouse over there. I'm the kind of a guy they need and I don't do a thing in the mill Gray couldn't do and besides if you don't understand what makes a man want to—oh, God, I'm not going to give an oration about my country, right or wrong."

Ruth was crying quietly, humped in the middle of the bed. She stretched out her hand when Dick paused and said, "Come here."

He went over and sat down beside her.

"I'm sorry," she said. Her face was muffled in the pillows. "I do understand."

Dick put his face down and pressed his cheek to hers. She gave a loud sob and said, "I'm—I'm proud of you."

All the breath went out of him and he sagged down beside her with his arms around her. At last he said, "I knew you had the stuff, darling."

Ruth tried to stop crying.

"You'll help me see it through, won't you?" Dick whispered. Ruth nodded. "Help Mary look after Dad?"

She nodded hard.

Dick kissed her desperately. "You're wonderful."

"No I'm not," she gulped. "I'm a coward."

"You never were. You're wonderful," he said again. "Ruth, I love you so much."

"I love you, Dick. All my life."

"Darling."

CHAPTER LXVII

[*February 1918*]

PAUL WAS TIRED. In all his life he had never felt like this. He had always had health and energy enough to meet every demand of the mill, even at the most crucial times. Like the Old Man, he had never thought of sparing himself. When the mill needed him he was there, whether at ordinary hours of the day or through long stretches of the night.

Every other fundamental of his life had somewhere, at some time, been shaken; his tie with the mill never. He loved the place now with intensity born of the knowledge that he must carry on alone in heart and see the mill through its greatest effort without Dick. Nobody could take Dick's place. If Paul allowed himself to question the rightness of Dick's decision he would open the doors to weakness. He would waver in the throes of indecision, of regret, of a will threatened by encroaching age, even of a lack of simple patriotism. Paul decided from the moment of Dick's departure to discipline himself against any such yielding to weakness. At sixty-two self-discipline should be second nature. But it was also a cruel burden to a tired, driven man; to a desperately anxious father. Tom was safe and unhurt still. Mary tried to strengthen Paul in the faith that her prayers would protect Dick also.

It was strange to be alone in the house, just Mary and Paul.

"After all these years," he said to her as they sat by the fire drinking their coffee one February night. He would be going back to the mill in half an hour. Lately he had been taking increasingly large amounts of strong coffee. Mary was worried. She was troubled about the deepening lines of fatigue and anxiety in his face. She was more troubled because she sometimes saw his hand tremble, and by the quick way he hid this if he caught her eyes on him. He had grown very gray in this past year; the last of the sandy color had faded from his hair and his moustache, and they were almost white. But his blue eyes were as clear as ever and right now they were studying Mary with an expression almost of surprise, as if he had really not had time to look at her for months past. That was almost literally true.

He saw in her face the quality of resolution which must carry him through this awful period of strain. She was looking much older. The soft brilliance of her pale red hair had dimmed to straw-color. Paul realized that her hair was just as faded as his own, but strangely, it had not faded to gray. Its light, halo-like tint gave her a startlingly spiritual expression. She had no deep lines in her face like his own, no furrows worn by stress. It was in Mary's eyes that he could read the whole long story of their lives. Deep under the fine white brow her gray eyes looked out, level and wise and brave and patient. They had always been penetrating; they were, if you feared them, mercilessly probing now. They could be cold and indignant too, sometimes cynical, sometimes scornful. They were dark with tenderness when they rested on Paul.

He lay back in his leather chair and looked at her, thoroughly and slowly. She saw what was in his mind. She took off her glasses, put down her knitting, and let her thin body sink against the straight chair-back. She was still very erect, carrying her small head at an imperious angle above her high collar. Her skin was white, her forehead and cheeks threaded with very fine wrinkles. Her hands were old; quick and busier than ever, they showed in strong ridges and sharp, small bones and blue veins the ageing that her face resisted.

"All these years," Paul repeated. "Do you realize it is exactly thirty-four years since you refused to marry me?"

"I do."

"And you have been a wife—to me—"

"For longer than that."

"For ever, I think."

Sometimes when he looked at Mary, Paul's mind stumbled backwards to an effort to remember Louise. That twisted and pitiable soul had never held him in more than a moment of reality. It was all dark, all distant; the unbelievable fact that he had married her, that he had slept upstairs in his parents' bed with her, and fathered his boys through the protesting mechanism of her body. That was what it had been, he told himself once; a mechanism. No breath of the imaginative, the spiritual, the beautiful, the maternal. Mary had given all of that, all of it that he and his boys and their home had ever had. Her thin ascetic body with its secret core of disciplined passion had been diminished in the consuming strength of her spirit. He looked at her wonderingly, grateful for a moment in which to think.

"It would sound very strange if I asked you to marry me now, wouldn't it?"

Mary shook her head slowly.

"No."

"Would you?"

"No."

"I thought not." He sighed. "The boys are all gone now."

"Dear Paul. I see what you're thinking. But we can go on to the end in the peaceful way we know. Any change would not be peace. Somebody would—" she stopped.

"You're thinking of Lauchlan, aren't you?"

She shrugged and smiled.

"Isn't it good," she said slowly, "to come to the time when we never need to explain anything?"

"I thought we'd always been there."

She nodded slowly. Paul looked up at the mantel clock and lifted himself from his chair.

"Must you really go down tonight, Paul? You look so dreadfully tired."

He stooped over her chair and kissed her lingeringly.

"Ted is helping a lot more since Dick's gone. I think he really feels this intensely."

Mary rose and walked out to the hall with Paul.

"Ted isn't—hasn't—" she paused in her question.

Putting on his wool muffler and heavy overcoat, Paul shook his head.

"He won't go," Paul said. "If the circumstances were different he might want to, but he knows it's out of the question. If Lauchlan can make him happy we oughtn't to judge her too hard. In some ways," Paul said suddenly, "Ted's situation isn't so very different from ours."

Mary handed him his wool-lined gloves.

"I've got to confess I haven't always been sure you realized that," she said. "Ted's given up his own choice for Tom at every turn I can remember."

"For Dick too now," Paul sighed. "But—well, he isn't Dick, that's all."

"Try not to stay too late, Paul."

"I've got a lot of new troubles. There are so many men sick with this damned flu."

"You'll be careful—" she put her hand on his arm. He smiled.

"Good night, Mary dear. I wish you wouldn't wait up."

"Well, I will, and I'll bring you your hot milk in bed."

"With a big slug of Overholt," Paul said, opening the door.

Mary went back to the parlor and sat down again by the fire. She picked up her knitting. Her small veined hands went swiftly and noiselessly to work, while the quiet remoteness of her face reflected its complete unconcern with mundane things. It would be impossible for anyone who knew her to think of her without some sort of work in her hands. Yet they were never obtrusive. They went along in their busy detached way while her attention stayed entirely with people when they were about, with her thoughts when she was alone. She was thinking of Paul now. Not for a long time had she let her thoughts roam so far back into the poignantly remembered past. What would she have done, she thought now, without the wonderful resource all her life long of people to love? First Clarissa Scott. Paul supremely and unwaveringly. Constance—there was always a tender expression of amusement in her face when she thought of Constance, but beyond that, there had been nobody in all her world so completely commanding of devotion. And now Claire. No child in all the family, not even one of Paul's boys, had made such a place in Mary's heart. She hoped she would always see a lot of Claire, but she sighed as she foresaw the improbability of that. The girl would be swept into a glittering, high-keyed life after the war, you could expect nothing else. It had been in a way an extraordinary experience to have her here in this quiet house, tied to the staid, solid traditions of the family. She had adapted herself surprisingly well, Mary thought, remembering the first few weeks of Claire's rebellious presence here.

Mary missed her dreadfully. It had been one of the hardest wrenches of her life to say goodbye to her on that day in New York last June. She had begged her to stay longer, until the war was over and there would be nothing horrible to which to go home. But Claire was firm. "I love you better than anyone in the world next to Mère Constance," she said, "but I do love her most of all, and I want to go home."

When Mary thought about it, she supposed it was really better for

Constance. No matter how cheerful and trifling her letters, running a convalescent hospital was a tragic undertaking. A few months of it, perhaps, could be taken in any woman's stride, but here she was stretching into her third year. Mary had read lately between the lines of Constance's letters that her nerves were wearing thin. She had once suggested that Constance come over and visit them and take Claire home if she wanted to, but Constance had only said, "I'll stick this to the end."

So it should be a real lift to her to have Claire at home again, full of new experiences and full of the terrific exhilaration of American excitement about entering the war: above all, inspired by Pittsburgh's contribution to the struggle. On her last night with them, Claire had asked Uncle Paul to let her go down to the mill with him.

"I want to see them at work once more," she said. "I want to remember every single thing you're doing, so I can tell Mère Constance's *blessés* about it and make them feel you're winning the war right here."

She had stood and watched the fiery drama of shell-castings being poured. She could have stayed there on the gallery for hours, her square brown hands gripping the railing, her eyes hidden behind purple goggles. She had grown much taller in the past year, and had lengthened out, losing her childlike squatness. Paul often thought that she was going to be a marvellous-looking woman. Her bones were good, square, and firmly put together. Her face was arresting with heavy brows and strong planes and a firm, large mouth. Her eyes were shrewd and alert. Her expression, her whole physiognomy, were both sensual and intelligent.

She had the nature of a salamander with her passion for watching fire and the miracles it made. She liked to be as close to the processes as she was allowed, to stand sweating in the glare of a hot job, licking her lips with the same avidity that she brought to a plate of boiling soup. She jumped at any chance to go down to the mill, although Paul very seldom allowed it, because the men really hated to have a female inside the shops. In her whole twenty-one months in Pittsburgh Claire only visited the mill four times. But she made the most of those visits. And she listened carefully at the dinner-table when Uncle Paul and Dick talked about their work. She liked the terminology of steel even when she could not understand the technicality.

Her reaction was always excited and intense. One thing she loved was riding down with Paul in the car when he went back to the mill at night. She hung on the spectacle of Pittsburgh's mills ablaze in the dark. She often teased Stanley to drive her up high on the bluffs over the river where she would get out of the car and sit on some grimy rock with her chin cupped in her hands, staring at the unforgettable picture with her lips moving in some whispered reaction audible only to herself. The vicinity abounded in vantage points where one could see the whole panorama spreading in perspective: the gloomy Monongahela with the thickest smoke, the blackest jungle of mills and furnaces, the wildest flares of fire, twisting to meet the duller Allegheny and join it down by the bend of the Ohio where the Scott mill clung to the northward curve, pouring its columns of dyed smoke into the black arches of the sky. Claire often thought, and sometimes said to Mary if she had come along, as she occasionally did, "I suppose the Front looks like that. I can picture men lying out there in the filth, watching sights like that, trying to kill one another, waiting to die—"

It was very strange to have her gone. When they saw her again she would be grown up.

Mary looked up at the clock and was startled to see that Paul had been gone almost three hours already. He should be coming home soon. She had not moved from her chair by the fire. It was cold in the other rooms of the house, it had to be. Everybody had to save coal for the sake of the war, even in a coal-producing region. That seemed ridiculous in a way, here where every hill for twenty miles around was disfigured with a rattletrap coal-tipple, where the level ground was bare and blackened from ruthless, wasteful stripping. The whole district was solidly underlaid with coal. Like Wales, Mary thought, with a curious flash of reminiscence, where Claire's father's people lived still, had always lived. There, she said aloud, there I am thinking about Claire again.

She went upstairs to put a hot-water bottle in Paul's bed, so that it would be warm and restful in spite of the chilly room. She would not go down to the kitchen to heat his bedtime glass of milk until she heard the car turning in at the driveway. She went back to the parlor to wait. One reason, she had been thinking, why she missed Claire so much and why she had so much loved having her here was Claire's enthusiastic sharing of Mary's own personal interest, the only part of her life that was separate from the family. That was the Mamas, of course; their bustling activities down at the House; and, above all, the Liskas. It was natural for a European child—and Claire was that, in spite of her Scott ancestry—to fit in with foreigners and their ways. But Claire had certainly never known any people like the Liskas in Europe. Or had she? Mary did not realize that some instinct in Claire had always drawn her, curious or sympathetic, toward peasants and working people when she had the chance to talk to them. That was where she had learned much of the tough talk she knew. That was where she had got her taste for coarse thick soup and black bread and garlic, which Constance's Gonneau had certainly never served up. Claire had eaten more snacks in Jeannot's kitchen than anybody suspected.

And so she felt at home with the Liskas. They had none of the austerity that marked Uncle Paul's friends. And beside all that the child had this real passion for history, she had always had it, and had always had the dramatic tendency to personify it in her games and in the people she knew. So when she saw Julka Liska actually working to make history, to help create a new state, patterned on the American democracy which Claire had only understood since going to school in Pittsburgh, it fired her imagination. She had gone away making Mary promise to write her all the news about the Liskas, and all about Julka's progress with her work. There had been plenty to write, too. There would be more. Julka kept telling Mary so, and Mary dutifully wrote it all to Claire.

It was very late now, long past midnight, and Mary was beginning to worry about Paul. He really should not stay down at the mill so late. He should not get so tired. This was such wretched, dangerous weather, and the hazards of pneumonia in the mill were never so grave as now. The influenza epidemic on top of it all, too—Mary began to wish desperately that he would come home. She was beginning to grow apprehensive, all the pleasant reminiscences of the evening were being driven out of her mind, when she heard the car in the side driveway at last, and she jumped up, quick and lightfooted as ever, to meet Paul.

CHAPTER LXVIII

[*September 1918*]

IT WAS A mid-September evening, foully hot, the cruel early fall heat which finds one's endurance almost exhausted. Mary was down in the kitchen at half-past ten, chipping ice to make a cool bedtime drink for Paul. The front doorbell rang. Mary laid down the icepick and went upstairs automatically, wondering why anybody should be dropping in so late. It was not some friend of Paul's at the door, or Ted and Lauchlan, though Ted had a latchkey and would not have rung anyway. It was a telegraph boy. Mary thought nothing particular about that as she signed for the telegram with her initials beneath Paul's name. Then as she carried the telegram to the back parlor a thought slashed at her mind. She stopped and stood still in the hall. This could not be—stop that, she told herself sternly. This must be about business. There was nothing special about a telegram. This wasn't twenty years ago. Yet she stood hesitating in the hall, reluctant to take in the telegram and rouse Paul. He was resting now, and he had been so tired this evening when he came home.

He had come up the walk so slowly that her heart ached as she stood in the doorway watching him. She had taken his Panama and hung it up, saying, "Your bath is ready, Paul." She always had a cool bath drawn, with a big handful of seasalt dissolved in it. He would lie there for fifteen or twenty minutes, then slowly dress in a soft shirt, a clean linen suit, and white shoes, and come downstairs for dinner.

They had eaten dinner slowly and almost without speaking. It was good not to have to speak. Paul liked to look up and see Mary sitting there in her crisp sheer voile dress, the personification of calm and peace and quiet. This evening he had been too tired to talk at all. After dinner he went slowly into the back parlor and sat down by the open window with the evening paper. He read every word of the war news, noting the terrible fighting at St. Mihiel, following the correspondent's account minutely on the big map tacked to the wall. The Americans were in real action now —God knew it had taken them long enough to get there. And the Germans were falling back. There was no longer any doubt that when the Americans went into the big push the Germans could not stand against them. How long would this have to go on? How long would it take? Could it be done? Would the end ever be in sight?

Paul looked at the clock from habit when he finished the paper. Ordinarily he would be back at the mill by now. But ever since the dead heat of summer Mary had prevailed on him not to go to the mill at night any more. He knew that he was too utterly tired to drive himself to night work unless there should be some extreme emergency. Gray Simcox had proved quite capable of handling the decisions that came up. And Paul was always there at eight in the morning to check on them. He dropped the newspaper beside him on the floor and drifted into a heavy doze.

Mary stood in the parlor doorway watching him. She decided not to wake him now. She would leave the envelope on the table at his elbow and he would find it when she woke him up for his drink. But he opened his eyes as she stood beside him. He saw the yellow envelope in her hand and asked in a sleepy voice, "What is it?"

"Oh, just a telegram." That was good; casual.

His tired blue eyes opened very wide for an instant; she saw his fingers go round the arm of the chair. His lips drew in against his teeth. Then he looked straight at Mary with despair in his face and said, "Open it."

"It's for you, Paul."

"I said open it."

He sat looking up at her, rigid, terrible, questioning; leaning on her as literally as if his legs had given out and he was clinging to her thin shoulders for support. Mary slid her forefinger under the flap and kept her eyes lowered as she took out and unfolded the sheet of yellow paper.

She did not know that one could lose all sense of feeling, of contact with the floor, with one's clothes, with the horrible thing in one's hand, and still stand there, dead white, motionless, tearless, speechless. Paul's chin began to tremble as he watched her. She heard him say in a ghost's voice, "Which? Which is it? *Tom?*" He said Tom because he knew she had to tell him worse.

"It's Dick, Paul."

Ted came at midnight. Paul was still sitting rigidly in his chair, staring at nothing, his hands cupped emptily upward on his knees in an unnatural way. Mary met Ted in the hall. She had not dared to cry. Her eyes were strained and dim behind her glasses. She was a ghastly color and her skin was damp with sweat. Ted went with her into her old sitting-room and insisted on seeing the telegram with his own eyes before going in to Paul. He stood in the middle of the room clutching the paper and squinting at it as if it were written in a strange language.

DEEPLY REGRET TO INFORM YOU THAT CAPTAIN RICHARD KANE SCOTT COMPANY F 15TH ENGINEERS IS OFFICIALLY REPORTED AS KILLED IN ACTION SEPTEMBER 13TH. WILL REPORT FIRST INFORMATION RECEIVED.
                    WALTER S. JOHNSON, ADJUTANT GENERAL

"Christ. Jesus Christ." Ted swallowed and choked and said it again. "Christ." Then he looked at Mary and said, "This will kill Dad."

"Holy Mother!" Mary wiped her lips with a quaking hand. "Don't say that."

Ted stood, still looking at the telegram and shaking his head. Suddenly he made a noise and turned away. Mary went over to him.

"Ted." She touched his hand. "For God's sake hold onto yourself now. Try to help me with Dad. And Ruth."

"Oh, the poor kid."

"She hated his going so."

"I'm glad she's still away," Ted said dully. "She'd make it even worse for Dad." Ruth and the children had been away all summer with her mother in New Jersey.

"God have mercy on us all."

There was a sound from the next room. Ted stiffened his heavy shoulders and went in to Paul. Mary followed slowly, groping her way. She could not see the familiar strip of summer matting along which her feet were dragging. Ted was kneeling by Paul's chair with his arms around his father and the two were weeping the terrible silent tears of men.

Paul lay upstairs in his bed for two days and two nights without saying a word. Sometimes when Mary went in—she allowed nobody else but Ted into the room—she had a swift and cruel recollection of Clarissa Scott dying in this bed. Paul's face on the pillows, silent and staring, was enough like his mother's to turn Mary's blood chilly when she opened the door. Paul was stonily aware of her presence. He looked at her with bitter revelation. He ate nothing, but when she brought a cup of broth or tea and fed it to him by spoonfuls he took it without a word, staring at her as if her face was the last reality he ever expected to see.

Ted had moved to the house to stay for a while. Lauchlan came in with him the day after the telegram came, and was so gentle and understanding that Mary found her lovable for the first time. Lauchlan said, "I'm not going to stay here with Ted, Mary. I think it will help Dad more to have him here alone." She wiped her eyes. "More like—when the boys were all at home."

"You're a dear, Lauchlan."

"No."

Mary looked up quickly as she heard the frightened tremor in the girl's voice. "What is it, dear?"

Lauchlan burst into tears. She covered her face with her narrow brown jewelled hands, and mumbled behind them. "I'm a pig. I feel as if I'd stolen something."

"Why, Lauchlan!"

"Yes, I do." Her clipped voice came in gulps behind her hands. "Here I am with Ted safe, and everything in the world, and poor Ruth—and Dad—"

"They couldn't have stopped Dick, dear."

"But he ought to have known Dad needed him—and loved him best."

"I wouldn't say—"

"Oh yes. Dad did love Dick best. He was Dad's whole world."

"See how he clings to Ted now."

Lauchlan reached for her handkerchief. "Of course. Naturally. Tom may get killed too. Ted's all—Dad's got—" she sobbed violently.

Mary put her arm around her.

"Tom will get home safely. I know he will. He's got a charmed life."

"But he's not Dick!" Lauchlan said. Mary knew how many times Paul must have said that to himself. "I feel so awful about Ruth. She's so soft—"

It was almost as if Lauchlan had declared herself tough and better able to stand such a blow than Ruth. "You've talked to her?" Lauchlan asked.

"To her mother. Ruth was too crushed."

"Who told her?" Lauchlan seemed to want to dig into this, into every cruel detail. As if it were some kind of penance for her own fortunate lot.

"They wired her too. It was arranged there'd be simultaneous notices if—it—"

Lauchlan looked up, her sleek face ravaged and streaked with tears. "Is there anything we can do for her, Mary?"

Mary shook her head slowly, "Ruth is in Gethsemane," she said slowly, crossing herself. "The loneliest place in the world, where nobody can help her but God."

She had never dreamed of being able to say such a thing to Lauchlan.

On the third morning Paul rose at his usual early hour, dressed, and appeared at seven at breakfast. Mary would have protested his making the effort if she had not been warned by a look of stern resolution in his face. He refused anything except two cups of strong coffee and a piece of toast. He did not look at the folded newspaper by his plate. He had not looked at a newspaper since that night. But the news was already known all over town. The worst part of Paul's ordeal lay ahead of him. To face the mill, and all the men—Mary would have cut off an arm to spare him that. She thought of Charlie Liska, who had loved Dick, who must still live in momentary anxiety for Jerry. She thought of all the good, hard, kindly men who were feeling Paul's bereavement and the mill's irreparable loss, and the painful futility of conveying what they felt.

Paul rose in his place and looked at Ted. Ted said, "Dad—must you?"

"I'm not going to the mill," Paul said in a toneless way.

Mary looked up quickly. This was the most alarming thing Paul could have said. She half rose from her chair.

"Not today," Paul explained. He saw what Mary and Ted had thought. "I'm going to town to see John Purcell." Purcell was Paul's lawyer, the present senior partner of the old Wilkins firm.

Ted and Mary exchanged glances. Paul must be thinking about his will. But he dropped a thunderbolt. He stood in the dining-room doorway and said, "I'm going to incorporate the mill."

"Paul!"

"Dad—what?"

He might as well have said he was going to dynamite the mill.

"The mill is a business. From now on it will be run like one. By business men. By hired men." He spoke with bitterness. Mary stared at his tragic face. There was a sudden groan from Ted, the clatter of a cup, and he burst into sobbing, the most horrible sound a man can make. He buried his blond head in his arms on the table.

"Oh, Christ," he groaned, "why couldn't I have died instead of Dick!"

Paul strode across the room and put his hands on Ted's shoulders. He lifted him from his chair and looked him deep in the eyes.

"Forgive me, son," he said thickly.

Ted shook his head.

"Don't."

"I am ashamed," Paul said, clutching Ted's shoulders. "You are the finest, most loyal son a man could have."

"But not Dick," Ted ground out through his teeth. "Not Dick, or you —or grandfather—"

Mary sat and wept silently.

"Don't say that, son. I have been blind and selfish about you. I have let you give years of your life to the mill already. I know why you did it. You are not going to give up anything more for me—or your brother—"

"But I want to work in the mill, Dad."

"Then you shall. But it will be voluntary. You will not be shackled to it. I am going to turn the mill into a possession—" Paul said sternly— "instead of a possessor."

Mary shook her head. He might as well have said he was committing suicide. Until his last breath he would be possessed by the mill. It would live in and with him, its fire and metal his flesh and blood. He had fertilized it with his labor and his love; he had created for it a son to carry on its life. For him that life had died with Dick.

"The mill will work for you—" Paul said brokenly. "Not you for it."

Ted clenched his fists. Paul did something very strange. He drew Ted's head down between his hands and gently kissed his forehead.

CHAPTER LXIX

[*October 1918*]

IT WAS SO shockingly simple to make the change. There stood the mill, its stacks and domes and chimneys smoking, its rolls crashing and clattering. There it stood, pulsating, clamoring, belching thick purposeful smoke into its hard native air, spewing out implements of death to strike back at the murderers of its son. But one day it was the Scott Iron Works, the dirty-faced, tumultuous, sprawling, live creation of two William Scotts and a Paul and a Richard; and the next day it was the Scott Steel Company, Limited, a Pennsylvania Corporation.

Paul insisted on changing the name.

"No," he said, when his lawyers and Ted and Joe Rogers (who was on the first board of directors, along with seven other old business associates) protested. "No, that's the way I want it. Scott Iron Works meant something that doesn't exist any more. We don't make iron anyhow, to speak of. We make steel and that's what this corporation is going to be called."

It was a closed corporation, of course. Paul had quickly obtained consent to his plan from all the partnership shareholders. Some were profoundly glad to have old William Scott's mortmain lifted. Others— Constance and Mary—were willing to consent to anything Paul proposed. He had no idea of floating the stock for public sale. He had simply been able to decide on no better future for the mill than this, now that it would have to be run, as he had said, by hired men.

Only Paul and Ted and officers of the banks with whom the big loan had been placed three years ago were really aware of the present value of the business. Everybody in Pittsburgh thought of it as a little business, a little family concern which, indeed, it was. But to the family it looked astonishing to see in documents that the book value of the corporation was to be placed at $15,000,000.

"Most people wouldn't realize we were worth that," Ted said.

They were sitting in Paul's office, the Old Man's office, with the Old Man's picture eyeing them vividly from high up on the wall. Paul's glance kept straying to it now. He had a lot to say to Ted, and much of it was the same sort of thing that his father had said to him, that summer afternoon so unbelievably long ago. Ted leaned on the desk watching his father, watching the soft but inscrutable look that came into his eyes, the vacant expression on his face, as memory roused the echo of the Old Man's gruff, cold voice. It had been husky then, and hushed. "You shall marry Mary Rafferty, Paul." Ted saw his father's lips tighten under the full white moustache, and the heavy ironmaster's hand close slowly in a fist on the scarred desk. Outside a locomotive whistle screamed and a shadow fell across the barren room. A big swash of smoke rolled against the windows. Paul moved his head and sighed, "What did you say, Ted?"

"I said people probably didn't realize we were worth that much." Ted pointed to the papers lying on the desk under Paul's hand.

"We are—under present circumstances," Paul answered. "But after the war—" he sighed heavily. "I've made the best provision I could."

He had arranged to issue the corporate stock in the form of twelve million dollars' worth of common at par of $100 a share. This was to be divided among the partners in amounts equal to their former holdings. One hundred and twenty thousand shares of common stock were issued. Paul himself, with his twenty per cent share in the business, received twenty-four thousand shares of common stock. Willy and Angelica, of whom nobody but the bookkeeper had thought in the years since their father's death, received twelve thousand shares each. Elizabeth, like Paul, got twenty-four thousand shares; Mary, with her ten per cent interest from

Edgar, twelve thousand shares; and Constance the largest block of thirty-six thousand shares.

Paul shook his head as he sat studying the figures with Ted.

"There are a lot of things I don't like about this picture," he said sadly. "Look at this, for instance." He pointed to the margin of the ledger sheet where he had scribbled some notes. Ted saw his father's forefinger tremble as he poised it.

Paul had made a little diagram—a bracket around his twenty-four thousand shares, divided four ways.

"This is the final irony," he said wearily. "You and Tom—my own sons—will have the smallest common holdings of anybody." He drew his hands across his forehead. "Thank God Pa never saw ahead to that."

Ted raised his eyebrows. This was not a very pleasant situation any way you looked at it. Paul's shares must be divided among Ted himself and Tom and Ruth of course. But why should there be a fourth block, obviously intended for Mary? Hadn't she more than enough already with half of Edgar Scott's original share? Ted looked uneasily at his father. Paul stared back. In his tired blue eyes there was a stubborn and almost a stupid look wilfully set there. Paul knew exactly what Ted was thinking. Very seldom in his life except in the early stages of his courtship had Ted run head-on into the strange question of Mary's place in his father's life and in the family. She had been closer to the twins since the moment of their birth than their own mother at any time in their lives. It was unnatural to question her right to a widow's share in Paul's property—for that was plainly the way Paul was thinking of her. But Ted was questioning now. Paul saw it clearly. He went on speaking in a low tone.

"I see what you're thinking, son," he said. "In a way I don't blame you. But I have my reasons for what I am doing." He filled his pipe and lit it carefully. "I have my reasons."

Ted opened his mouth to speak. Then he thought better of it and his jaws closed slowly. After all, there were some things you could not say even to your own father. You could not reproach him for his feeling about the woman who—Paul was speaking still.

"You would probably rather," he said, "that I had married Mary long ago. It would make it all much clearer and easier to understand—maybe—less embarrassing."

Ted made a protesting gesture. Now that Dad was talking about this he wished the subject had never come up. But Paul had something definite to say.

"You see," he said, staring through the grimy window, "you see, in a way Mary means even more to me than if she were my wife." Ted looked puzzled, but he waited for Paul to explain. Paul leaned across the desk and asked, "Have you ever heard any gossip about us, Ted, or were you—too close to—us?"

"Well." Ted began drawing circles with a compass he picked up from the pen-tray. "That's—kind of a tough one, Dad."

Paul nodded slowly. "Yes, I realize now I ought to have talked to you boys frankly about this years ago. Mary was so much part of my life that I didn't want to raise any feeling of her being an outsider by talking to you kids as if she could be one—or ever had been.'

Ted laid down the compass and lit a cigarette and leaned back in his chair, suddenly relieved and at ease.

"You were always in love with her, weren't you, Dad?"

"Always. From the time I first laid eyes on her, I suppose. I didn't realize it for some years. By that time—"

"You were just a kid ' Ted said softly.

"That's right. She was the loveliest thing a man ever saw," Paul said dreamily. "She just—well. she glowed, she was so shining and– well, i. I said pure I'd sound like a fool. But that's the way she was She looked like Saint Barbara in the San Sisto Madonna. And yet—"

Ted had been looking quizzical. Paul nodded at him and smiled

"She was no saint, of course," Paul said quietly 'She was just a little Irish girl from shantytown. But she had her own ideas They were big, hard, serious ideas. God knows where she got them but she had them. The main one was about this family."

"She's always had that."

"Yes, and long before you were born. She was absolutely hellbent that nothing should ever happen to reflect on this family.' Paul spoke very slowly. and paused. Ted listened. Then Paul said, "Now—after all this time—I think I see what she really did with those ideas."

He looked out the window again. Ted sensed that in those tragic silent days and nights while Paul had lain like a stone in his room, he must have thought and weighed and pondered this whole question. with its tentacle; involving so many lives, and he must have seen clearly what he had bee : too near and too active to see before. He must have come at last to the sombre high plateau from which a man looks back. perspective complete, upon all his life.

"There was a time," Paul said slowly, "when I would have left the mill—except for her. She made me stay. She," he said, "has made me do— more, I think, than I ever knew I could. She's held her ground against the most inhuman obstacles, fiendish obstacles. She's been—as they say themselves, the Irish—possessed."

"Isn't that queer," Ted murmured. "A little Irish maid."

"That's just it,' Paul said. "I think a lot of her notion came from the poverty of her own background. When she came into our house it looked to her like all the security and established position in the world. So she began making us in her own mind the kind of family we seemed to her. She's a very creative person, Ted. She's always making something." Paul thought for a moment and returned to the family. "I honestly do not believe," he said slowly, "that we were such a family as she said. I only think she decided we were. We were just plain Americans. We had no particular sense of dynasty, but she did. That's why she wouldn't marry me—basically. There were more immediate reasons—tragic ones."

Ted looked up curiously. "Like—"

"Oh, some day I'll tell you the whole long story if you want me to," Paul said. "Fate kept stepping in and putting in reasons why Mary would say we couldn't marry. Anyway—the point is this. Out of all the turmoil and disappointment of nearly fifty years one thing is perfectly clear to me. Mary *is* the family she insisted we all were."

Ted's face began to express his comprehension of this strange idea. Paul went on. "We have dwindled and scattered and turned into ghosts like Uncle Ed or scarecrows like Willy and Angelica or bums like your aunt Constance—"

"Dad!"

"Oh, we all love her," Paul smiled. "That has nothing to do with it. But she is a bum so far as that idea of Mary's is concerned. And right here in our home—"

Ted sighed. "I see. Dick was the only one who had the stuff."

"No," Paul said quickly. "Don't say that. Dick happened to be the one who was suited for the mill. You've got qualities and character, Ted, the things some of them didn't have when they should. Tom hasn't, in spite of the way I love him. He's nervous and unreliable. He's out, so far as all this is concerned. And you—" Paul looked deeply into Ted's eyes. "Well, it's simply this. If you had the bent for the mill that Dick had, I wouldn't give this another thought. You haven't got it though, and there's no use tying you up with a lot of responsibility when you might want to be free of it any time. How do we know?"

"I guess we don't."

"I only know that I've fought against something all my life, and I'm not going to see the same thing happen to you. In your case it would be the mill. In mine it was—I've told you."

There was a long pause. Then Ted said, "I don't quite see the practical application of all this." He pointed to the ledger sheets on the desk. "And what's the connection with what you said—that Mary means more to you than if she were your wife?"

"Just that she stands for all the ideas and all the standards that none of us have had the luck or the stuff to live up to. It's a queer notion, Ted, but you'll have to believe me. Only Mary and the mill have the qualities she stubbornly believes we have—as a family. And she has pumped those qualities into us. She has always fought to protect the family and keep it the thing she believed or wanted it to be. She will do the same for the mill as long as she lives—and that's why I want her to have some of my stock. Now do you understand?"

Ted nodded slowly, his eyes on his father's face.

"The common stock," Paul said, "has voting powers. I can't predict the future but if it's anything like the past, times will come when there will be disputes about the mill. There may even be a time when each stockholder's vote is a matter of life or death to the mill. I am frankly trying to put what voting power I can in Mary's hands. The value of the stock has nothing to do with it. Don't worry about money, Ted; you'll be all right."

"Lauchlan's—" Ted spoke reluctantly.

"I don't mean that," Paul said quickly. "You'll have money from me —and preferred stock, of course."

"I see."

"There is to be an issue of three million dollars in six per cent cumulative preferred callable at one hundred and five. This is about equal to the amount of the bank loans now."

"I see."

"I'm buying as much of it as I can. Joe Rogers and Walter Whitley and John Purcell," Paul said, checking off the names on his fingers, "and three of the men at the Union Trust are all taking some. I think it will all be held among the directors. Anyway, I will leave mine to you and Tom, and financially that will be far better for you than any other arrangement. Only of course the preferred has no vote."

Ted sighed.

"I feel like an awful slouch, Dad."

"You shouldn't. Now one thing—I am very anxious to get the preferred paid off as soon as possible. If we keep on making money at this rate it shouldn't be hard to call it in at the rate of about two hundred thousand a year. We can spare that out of the net under all normal conditions. And that will mean you'll have some choice about your own future. If you find after I'm gone—"

Ted sighed.

"I'm only being honest with both of us, son. If you find after I'm gone that you're more attached to the business than you expected to be—if you really get to love it from your desk as my Pa and Dick and I did from the floor—then you can take the money from your preferred stock as it's bought in and stir around and pick up some more common. There will be places to get it."

"Tom?"

"Probably. Willy and Angelica. Maybe your aunts. Maybe any of them. You might like doing that. At least it would be *you* going out and building up your hold on the mill—not the mill with a death grip on you. And on the other hand you might want to quit altogether. Go away somewhere and do—what you used to think you wanted."

"I'm afraid it's too late for that."

"It's my fault if it is. And Tom's. That's what I'm trying to tell you— I'm trying to leave things so as to square myself if I can and still insure that the mill will be run—well, like our mill."

CHAPTER LXX

[*1918*]

PAUL WAS LISTLESS and chilled now. It seemed impossible to Mary that he would voluntarily stay away from the mill, but he began to do that as soon as the articles of incorporation were ratified. He was the chairman of the new board of directors and president of the company, which he ran as he always had. He began to parcel out his former work among those to whom he saw the responsibilities would soon fall in any case. He made Gray Simcox general superintendent. And he had a curious way of keeping his interviews with Simcox as brief and pointed as possible. It was clear that it hurt him unbearably to deal with an outsider filling Dick's place. Simcox was unquestionably capable. Production by now was at the absolute extreme of pressure, and Paul had learned through his bitter days of mourning that this output could continue in his absence. So he simply let it run on on momentum, under Simcox's supervision.

"What hurts most of all," he said sadly to Mary, "is that there won't be any more creative work done in the mill—like we used to do."

"Oh no." She hastened to reassure him. "You mustn't say that. The mill will always be ahead in new inventions."

He shook his head.

"It won't be the same. Dick's machines and processes and my formulas were all developed through—well, through love. That sounds like a crazy thing to say about a steel mill, the toughest kind of shop there is. But it's true. I'd never have had some of my best ideas if I'd been working for somebody else."

"Simcox will have the ideas because of competition if nothing else. He can't let other mills get ahead of ours, can he?"

"I suppose not." Paul sighed. "Oh, I'm so tired, Mary. So horribly tired."

She was always trying to give him a lift, a gentle one that would exact no undue effort or attention from him. In one way it was good for them to be alone in the big, quiet house, served by the deft and devoted Stella and fed the simple, nourishing dishes through which Mary and Trude plotted to get strength into Paul whether he had appetite or not.

He leaned on her with pathetic dependence. And all her tender smiles, her gentle encouragement, were a cruel effort for her. Her task was made excruciatingly hard by a tragic secret that she had to keep from Paul. At all costs, it must be kept from him. She would have taken that responsibility even if she had not been ordered to. Late in October she had received a letter from Constance—thank God, she said to herself, it had chanced not to come at breakfast time with Paul sitting there waiting for her to read snatches aloud as she usually did. Mary was alone in her sitting-room when she opened the censored envelope and unfolded the sheets to read in Constance's sprawling hand: "Tom is here. He is hurt and doesn't want his father to know about it. I can't tell you how bad it is, partly because we aren't sure ourselves, and partly because Tom is determined Paul shall not find out about him. He heard about Dick very soon after it happened. He was frightfully broken up, and right afterwards he had a cable from Ted telling him how heartbroken Paul is and how he's giving up and how he's changed. This business about the mill is apparently very hard on the twins. Poor lads, they can't help it if they aren't like Paul and Father. But now that Dick's gone they are desperate because they're themselves.

"Anyway you can see what the shock did to Tom—he's always been reckless but after Dick's death he went—so his sergeant told me, who brought him here—completely insane with wanting to kill Germans. The fighting has been hell's shambles around the Meuse and in the Argonne, and Tom's squadron is right in the thick of it. They're up in dogfights all day and every night. Tom has apparently shot down more Boche planes in the past fortnight than in the whole year previous. He has become a legend on the whole front.

"It seems he went to his command and had his papers changed after Dick's death and put me down as next of kin—because he didn't want Paul to be notified if he got his. Then he went off and simply loosed a personal suicide offensive on the Boche air force. He took on a whole covey of them singlehanded and shot down all but the last, a week ago; and that one got away leaving Tom's plane flaming. He crashed behind our lines. God only knows why he wasn't killed outright. He was badly burned about the head and he has a spine injury which may or may not have consequences—we can't tell yet. He never lost consciousness and when they picked him up he insisted on being sent here. Billings (the sergeant) says they thought Tom was raving with pain and fever when he screamed to be taken to Cannes, but he made such a frightful scene that they had to give in and put him on a train with Billings and send him. He threatened to kill anybody who tried to drug him so he wouldn't know where he was. He was determined not to get into some hospital where they'd send out reports about him which would reach Paul. He's utterly obsessed with this idea about Paul. I think it may be a mistake, but this is not my responsibility. I'm easing my conscience by telling you because none of us can see what may happen and I do feel somebody at home has got to know the truth about Tom.

"Claire is grand. She's quite grown up. I wish I'd had her sense at sixteen. She's wonderful with Tom. He can't see, you know, his head is covered with bandages, and Claire always knows what to say and do with him. Think of that poor boy—that steamboiler of energy—lying there burning himself up inside.

"So now you know. For God's sake take care of Paul, not that I have to tell you to. How are you, darling? You never mention yourself. This is a wretched letter but I can't put on an act with you. Claire sends her love. I'm so afraid she's going to go soft over some chap here, she's changed a lot and is so striking. Don't think my *blessés* don't notice it too."

There was little else. The whole letter was fraught with the same fear that haunted Mary steadily now, the chill knowledge that Paul, in heart and mind, and in his big tired body, had given up. Tom's instinct was right. If Paul were to know the truth now his heart would literally break. Mary took the letter to her desk and locked it up, her hands going through the commonplace motions while her brain went round and round over this new reef in the widening whirlpool: Tom was hurt, Tom was burned. *Could he be blind?* Constance must know the truth, she had a fine medical staff at the Villa. She must be trying to break the news gradually. Oh, Holy Mother of God, Mary said half aloud, why is this happening to

Paul? Why must he die feeling his life undone? What was all our sacrifice for—if the sons and the mill—the whole long forty years of Paul's lifework—are to be nothing? This, she told herself sternly, could not be true. The mill was there, Ted was there, Tom was alive and out of the way of further danger—she must not dramatize the tragedy of Dick any further. She must keep a grip on things for Paul's sake. She must be cheerful and matter-of-fact and brisk. It was about as easy to put up such a front as to look like a sixteen-year-old girl again.

Now that he spent all his evenings at home with Mary, Paul liked to have Charlie Liska come up once in a while after work. There was nobody else at the mill whom Paul wanted to see. Gray Simcox was only an agonizing reminder of Dick's death, but Charlie was the tie to the old days. Charlie's view of the mill was what Paul wanted to hear. Sometimes they talked shop and sometimes they just visited. Charlie was none too young or energetic himself any more. His lifetime of exacting work in the fearful noise and heat of the rolling-mills had left him stooped and grizzled, lined, weary in his heavy body and in all his ways. Even his voice was lower and slower. His accent was as strong as twenty years ago. But what he said was worth hearing. He never spoke until he had weighed and well considered his thoughts, and then, sitting with Paul over a pipe and a tall glass of beer, he gave forth peasant wisdom inborn and broadened by a hard-lived life. His handlebar moustache and thick shock of hair were iron gray, and his brown skin set them off strikingly. He had clever eyes, narrow and sharpened by years of precision judgment.

Sometimes Julka came up with him, if she could take the time from her incessant meetings. Once Mary thought in a startled way how very strange it was that now, in the evening of their lives, with all the crowded course of time behind them, she and Paul should sit visiting with these two old friends who were the very substance of everything they had shared in the beginning. She could almost relive the emotions roused by Paul's visits to the shack when she went there to see her father on her Sundays off. Good Lord, she had not thought of her father in years. Not of the crippled old man who had once boiled iron at Scott's, only of a disembodied soul whom she duly remembered in her prayers.

And James! It was uncanny to think of him now, lowering and ugly of temper, burning with a passion of belief no less intense than Julka Liska's for her ideal. Mary could not think of James without opening the floodgate of the whole terrible stream of memory which long habit had enabled her to bypass. If she had not learned control from her strange life, control of her mind, of her will, of her body, her heart, and her memory, she had learned nothing.

Mary looked up from her sewing to see Julka smiling at her with peculiar, grave tenderness. Julka's eyes had gone from Paul, down at the other end of the room, deep in reflective talk with Charlie, to Mary in her high-backed chair by the reading lamp. Mary's gray eyes and Julka's brown ones met in one of those exchanges of profound honesty which are rare revelations even between the most intimate friends. Slow tears crept into Mary's eyes. Julka nodded, a heavy, earthly motion of deep simplicity. Julka knew. Mary saw at this moment that Julka knew her whole story, hers and Paul's. She had known it for years. Certainly she had never questioned anybody. She knew because her humanity and her tenderness and her warmth would tell her. Mary smiled tremulously. Her own eyes moved to Paul, and Julka saw the pain in them as they studied his sad, tired face, intent on Charlie's talk, but veiled by grief. The Liskas were reluctant to talk about Jerry. So far he had come through unscathed and as Charlie said to his wife, "It makes for shame we talk about him to boss. Why we have all luck, all t'ings come our way now, and he dying for sorrow. *Ach!*"

This was early in the first week in November, this quiet evening when the Liskas were sitting with Paul and Mary. Julka radiated a deep and wonderful pride. Only a few days ago the Czechoslovak Republic had been formally proclaimed and recognized, and Thomas Masaryk elected its first president by the National Council. He was in Washington still, working with President Wilson, but Julka told them he would be leaving for Europe soon. The Germans had been suffering terrible reverses on the Western Front. The Eastern and Balkan points of resistance had collapsed completely. It did not seem possible that the war could drag on through another winter. Yet one never knew. One thing was certain; the Habsburg Empire was destroyed.

There had been a time when Paul had not seen so clearly the connection between Julka's fanatical work and the lives of his sons in France. But in recent months all that had become very plain indeed. Ever since last spring Paul had followed the rising fortunes of the Czechs and Slovaks as eagerly as Mary. There was no story of the war that for sheer daring and courage exceeded the exploits of the Czech Legions on the Eastern Front. Julka had told them all about it. It was wonderful to hear the story in her own words. After the collapse of Russia, and the German invasion of the Ukraine, the Czechs fought every mile of their way eastward to Siberia. Isolated and desperate for supplies, they had not only fought the Germans but somehow managed to maintain themselves as an army in the midst of the bloodiest terror of the Bolshevist Revolution. What they wanted was to get to France and join their Allies; what that meant was the incredible Anabasis of the armed march around the world.

"So they just keep on going," Julka said with one of her characteristic shrugs. "Every place they go, they fight first, then go on. Trotsky orders them stopped and disarmed when they reach the Trans-Siberian Railroad, so there they fight the Russians too. Before they can advance on a section of the railroad they have to fight and capture it first. Then they go on until somebody stops them and they get out and fight for the next piece. That's the way they are going all the way around the world. Heroes!"

"Do you suppose you have any relatives in the Legion?" Paul asked her.

"Sure! I got to have. Where else would my cousins and nephews be? Lots probably killed already, but we've got plenty of men in our family. Uncle Jaromír had six sons, my mamma and Aunt Ludmila had brothers and sisters with sons."

The climax had come last May, when Professor Masaryk landed in Vancouver. He had crossed Siberia with the Legions, to come to America to get the new state proclaimed and its constitution ratified. Julka had been almost beside herself. But in all her excitement she had never dreamed that her name would be known to Thomas Masaryk as one of the earliest and hardest workers from the Pittsburgh district. He had asked her to stand by as a member of his personal committee during the Convention in Pittsburgh which was to draft the pact guaranteeing equal rights to Czechs and Slovaks in the new republic. Paul had shaken his head incredulously when Mary told him all this.

"I just can't take it in," he said, "Old Charlie's wife. Do you remember how I used to make fun of your Amalgamated Mamas, Mary?"

"I know. I told you then Julka was something remarkable. But I admit I couldn't believe all this would ever come true. I thought she was just dreaming."

Paul urged Mary to go to the first big meeting of the Convention at which Masaryk presided and Julka was one of the committee. He was deeply impressed at last, and he wanted Mary to tell him all about it. There was something fantastic in the idea that all this was happening right here in Pittsburgh where the very word Hunky had always been synonymous with ignorance, poverty, and misery. So Mary went to the meeting with Charlie and his children and told Paul about it afterwards. She had not been able to understand a word except a few short formalities in English. "But you didn't need to understand the language to know what Professor Masaryk was saying," she said. "You never saw such a man, Paul. He looks as wise and gentle and quiet as—well, a priest. You can't believe he's led the fight he has. And the people simply went crazy over him."

She related how the hall was so crowded that they were sitting two on a seat in places. "And the way they sang!" she said, with her eyes shining. "Really, when you see them that way, homely and poor, with that awful language and the hard work they all do—"

"The thing that gets me is the way they pattern all this on the American Revolution," Paul said.

"And they're copying whole blocks of our Constitution. The Bill of Rights—almost word for word."

"I'd never have thought it," Paul said. "Not in a thousand years."

"I just wish you could have seen Julka on that platform. I thought Charlie would burst with pride."

Now, on this late fall evening, Julka had been telling them about the new constitution which would go into effect the day the war was over. Paul sighed and said thoughtfully, "If only they make a wise peace! This new state of yours can be a Utopia, Julka, and so can the other new countries you've been talking about. But they can go awfully wrong, too."

"They will be the new world, you will see," Julka said.

"If the economic basis of Europe is sound. Politically your Habsburg Empire is—was—a monstrosity, but with a sensible federal government of all its different parts it could be a miniature United States."

"We don't want that," Julka said sharply. "We Czechs want our own nation."

"Of course you do. But if you have to put up tariff barriers around your country, and multiply that by all the different nations you say will come out of this war—how can you reconstruct trade in Europe?"

"We will have all the industries from the Empire," Julka said inconsequently.

"That may be fine for you, but where will it leave Austria? A pauper. Mind you, *I* don't care if Austria is wiped off the face of the earth and Germany more so. I'd like"—Paul's face flushed—"I'd like to murder twenty Germans for every life they've taken the past four years—"

"Me too," Charlie said. "Murder too good for the damn *barbars*."

"—but that wouldn't solve anything really," Paul said. "I can't go along with the President on some of his ideas, but I guess his zeal to spread democracy is the only hope for the world."

"We will show them all what democracy can do," Julka said. "You see what it will be like."

"Are you still planning to go over?" Mary asked her.

"The minute the war is over. I'm going to take Anton and leave him there to study with Kubelík and—"

"Yah!" Charlie interrupted, nodding and beaming fiercely. "Anton will be Czech fiddler! Real Czech artist, you'll see."

"And I want," Julka said, "I got to see our President begin the new government. My whole life I worked for this. Remember what I told you, Mary?"

Mary would never forget now. Some day, the eager young immigrant had said, some day my country will be free! And Mary had thought her dreaming.

"Your country better be a model for all the others over there," Paul said. "Or the world won't be safe for democracy."

"It will be," Julka said passionately. "It's got to be. Such a war couldn't be for nothing, Mr. Scott. We make a better world or we are all—"

"—or Dick and all the others will have died in vain." Paul's voice trembled and he put his face in his hands. Charlie signalled Julka with his eyebrow that it was time to leave.

A few days later Paul caught a cold. For the first time in a year he had had the urge to spend an evening in his laboratory as he used to do. There was a problem in an electric furnace where a certain cobalt alloy was not turning out to specification. Simcox brought it to Paul's attention, and Paul said he would do some work on it that night. Mary begged him not to go down after dinner when he said he was going, but he only smiled at her and put her off. She watched him step slowly into the car, with Stanley tucking the laprobe over his knees. That was no way to be going down to the soup-kitchen.

It was good, he said to himself, to see the mill at night again. He realized with quite a shock that it was the best part of six weeks since he had been down at night. Every department was going full blast, and on his way to the laboratory it made Paul feel warm to see the hearty smiles and waves with which the men welcomed him back. He stopped for nearly an hour at the electric open-hearth that was turning out the defective steel. In his concentration and the sudden burst of activity he got into a sweat. When the sampling started he worked right with the furnace boss, and after a time had three different samples ready to go to the laboratory. Paul followed them there and immediately set to work.

He found the defect in the steel and spent the next three hours revising the formula, testing, and making notes. Satisfied at last that he would be able to give Simcox a perfect formula tomorrow, he put away his measures and instruments and started to go home. He felt a little queer, rather throaty and very tired. He must be catching a cold, he thought indifferently. His glass of hot milk and whiskey would fix him up at bedtime. He stopped in his private office for a moment to file his revised formula in his safe, which was a habit of years' standing. The whole reputation and business of Scott steels depended on these metallurgical formulas of Paul's. He stooped by the safe and his eye fell upon the old tin box, the queer old handmade box which held his grandfather's, his father's, and his own most secret mementos. On a sudden inexplicable impulse, Paul pulled it out and carried it home with him.

Next morning he woke with a high temperature. Within twenty-four hours he lay in a soaring fever, his breathing a ghastly, barking rasp, his eyes glazed, his big hands clutching and clenching the bedcovers. Mary did not need the doctors to tell her how very serious his pneumonia was. Now, as at other times in her life, she whipped her will power to a thin, hard blade of decision. She would be calm, she would be brave, she would face the inevitable with all the combined strength of her disciplined character and her absolute religious faith. If he must die, she prayed in the age-old words, let him have a good death, a peaceful and a Christian one. She cabled Fra Anselmo and invoked his prayers. She cabled Tom and Constance and Claire. Ted moved back to the house as he had in September. There were three nurses by day and by night, and the ablest doctors in the city. The house, she realized ironically, had not been so full of people and activity—though this was a ghastly, muffled, whispered activity—in years. She was on her feet all day except for the hours she spent sitting in a chair by Paul's bedside, with her eyes riveted on his face. At night she sometimes let one of the nurses induce her to go to bed, but after sleeping less than an hour she would be up again, bathed and dressed, sitting at attention in Paul's dressing-room, waiting—waiting. He did not know anyone. His fever rose to a point at which it seemed he must burn to death from within. Still the nurses worked, still there were the jackets and poultices, the medicines, the oxygen. And all the time Mary knew silently, tearlessly, mortally that he was about to die.

She could sit rigidly beside him, gazing at his distorted, burning, stubbled face, his dry lips and gaunt square chin and cheek bones which now horribly resembled his mother's on this very bed, and she could think with a certain fantastic application of reason in a pattern underlying this tumult of grief and pain. When Ted tiptoed in and stood for a while at the bedside his swollen eyes would go from his father to Mary and he would marvel at what he saw: the thin, colorless face with its cameo lips closed as if upon all the secrets of the human heart which, indeed, they were; the burning gray eyes levelled steadily at the dying man; the bony hands clasped tight over a small rosary. He wondered what she was thinking. He wondered what she would do. He wonderel what it must feel to be a woman of whom a man said that she was more than wife. He saw in her eyes that his father had made her understand that that was so.

There were several days of this. Paul's condition grew worse. No hope was held by any doctor. There was no chance, they told Mary frankly, for they saw she had to know, of one of the crises which broke certain types of this disease.

Then there was an afternoon—Ted was down at the mill on imperative business—when the quiet street outside burst into a pandemonium of unearthly noise. Whistles blew by the thousands in all the teeming mills along the rivers. Tugs and barges loosed their steam whistles. Men and women and children poured into the streets shouting and shrieking and waving flags and snatching newspapers from vendors and from one another. Somebody went out desperately from the house where Paul lay dying to the bedlam in the street and came back and told Mary—who barely grasped its meaning, standing in the hall outside Paul's door—the news.

The door opened then and a nurse touched Mary's arm. She stepped quickly into the room. Paul's eyes were open and wild. He was struggling in bed. Mary hurried over and put her arms around him. She felt his body burning with fever as she clasped it. A most dreadful, ominous odor wrung her throat and nostrils.

His lips were moving. His eyes rolled wildly. "Noise," he gargled. He made strangled sounds.

Mary put her lips to his forehead and tried to hold him quiet.

"Ah, darling," she murmured, "macushla, it's all right, dear. The war is over."

He made another convulsive motion. She could have sworn his eyes knew her.

"Yes," he gasped. "The war is over." He was dead in her arms.

CHAPTER LXXI

[The Twenties]

"WHY," people sometimes asked Mary Rafferty, "do you go on living all alone in that museum of a house?"

She never answered that question, never gave a reason. She would smile quietly, or raise her bony shoulders in a delicate shrug. When she was seventy years old, she still carried her white head erect, at a certain proud angle that belied the quiet unobtrusiveness of her clothes. It was difficult for any person to read her eyes. Set exceedingly deep, they had been sunken by age still farther beneath the fine carved projection of her forehead; and her spectacles increased their inscrutability. She knew this; she used it. She could read the tawdry affairs of the world as it was now, the public world of crazed finance and vicious lawbreaking and cynical corruption, the private world of nasty talk and thought and action in which most people revolved. But they could not tell what she knew or what she thought, unless she wished them to.

The old Scott house was indeed a preposterous place for a solitary aged woman, a shuttered pile with one high room closed against the next. But it was not empty to her. The small modern flat that Ted occasionally urged her to consider would have been desolate by comparison. The old house was, in fact, the only thing in this grotesque world that did not seem desolate to Mary. Here she had a striking vantage-point from which to observe the futile and sometimes ugly convolutions of the lives that touched hers. Here, perhaps because of her solitude in this enormous place, people were drawn to pause in their bat-witted rushing-about and look in on her. Ted did that, coming from the downtown office at the end of a day, perhaps once, perhaps twice in a month. His children spent one afternoon a week with Mary, which, she often thought, was not enough to be an antidote to the influence of their mother and the atmosphere of their home. Mary had long since made a quiet arrangement with Lauchlan that on the nurse's day off the chauffeur should bring Paul and Peggy in to spend the day with her. If they forgot to be condescending toward what she had to offer, and succumbed to the natural fascination of the old carriage house and the coasting hill and the attic full of inexhaustible treasures, which were such a contrast to the sleek stables, kennels, and playhouse of their home, they had a good time. But when their mother's custom-built motor car appeared, to take them home, they bade Mary a languid good-bye and stepped, like two infant caricatures of Lauchlan and her friends, into the tonneau, to wait for the man to spread the broadcloth robe over their smart bare knees.

Of all the thoughts that colored her days, the one that struck Mary oftenest was what Paul would think of the world as it was now. What would he think of the mill, to which he had said good-bye at the apex of its fight, the ultimate, furious fighting pace spurred by the death of Dick? What would he say if he were to know the present-day uses of his stainless steels; the plated skyscraper towers, the two-hundred-and-fifty-dollar sets of matched golf clubs, the tricked-out automobiles—one for every garage and often two or three—for which, along with refrigerators and console radios and new chromium plumbing, the people were careening in a hoopla of spiralling debt? What would he think of the stock market, into whose seething pot of 'prosperity' there had been three different proposals to toss the stock of the mill, all turned down by Mary and those she had been able to influence with her reminders and warnings? If the mill had not been coining money anyway, like every other American business, it might have been harder for some of the family to resist the dazzling offers of the slick promoters. It was, however, natural for people like conservative Eliz-

abeth and stuffy Willy and Angelica, and tragic, shattered Tom out in
Texas, and pathetic Ruth living obscurely in Montclair, and mild, easygoing Ted, to fall in with Mary's insistence that the mill stay as it had
always been, entirely the property of the family. As for Constance . . .
Ah, Mary would think, smiling wryly and shaking her head. Ah, Constance!
So long as she had all the money she wanted to burn she did not care
about the status of the stock. Instinctively she would always do what Mary
asked; for Mary had never, in all the unbelievable fifty-five years, asked
her for anything except the preservation of the mill.

It was when Mary observed and considered the lives of the children—
as she called all the present generation of the family—that the real futility of the World War was most oppressive. For what, she said to herself,
watching the dizzy extravagances of Constance and Claire, or the terrific
drinking, the cold excitement-eating of Lauchlan's set, in which Ted was
little more than a property; for what had Claire's father and Dick Scott
and Paul himself laid down their lives? Was this the world they had died
to preserve? The world, in America, of gangsters and bootleggers and
drunken young people, coupling—you could not read their books without
encountering their own words for this in cold print—in dark automobiles
at country clubs? Or driving these automobiles at seventy miles an hour
to screaming death and headlines? Was Europe now—the Europe where
Constance and Claire gambled and frittered their lives away, the Europe
of perverts and esoteric vices and painted men and trousered women and
utter political decadence—was that, too, the world for which eight and a
half million men had died? Mary did not know. It was a strange thing
that now, when all her time was her own, when at last she could read as
much as she wanted, she could find little written in the present that did
not appall, revolt, sicken, or mock her.

Certain ideas and identities stood out from the soiled confusion and
held the suggestion, if not the assurance of decency. Her old friend Julka,
for instance, who lived now in Czechoslovakia as she had always said she
would some day, and who wrote regularly to Mary, had escaped this foul-
ness that seemed to pervade the world. That country and its people really
appeared to be what its idol, Woodrow Wilson, had hoped so tragically
and frustratedly, that the whole new world should be. But that was no
mitigation of the decay that appeared to pervade the rest of exhausted
Europe; or of the cold cynicism which made decent Americans exultantly
brag of shady stock deals and feats of petty lawbreaking.

Mary had made a last trip to Cannes to see Constance in 1925; and
what she had observed there had brought her back soul-sick to the empty
old house. They appeared to have a wonderful time at the Villa Bellevue—
Constance, corpulent and jolly, dripping with jewels and terrible language;
Claire with a one-year botch of a meaningless marriage chopped off behind
her; a stream of brilliant, gabbling, reckless people following on one
another's heels through the salons and grottos and gardens into which
Constance latterly had been pouring a fresh stream of crazy cash. Mary,
had sat with her tatting or her knitting, her eyes unreadable behind those

gold-rimmed spectacles, and had known how 'quaint' and 'extraord'n'ry' and *'originale'* and *'fabelhaft'* chattering men and women had found her, as they played out their emptiness against the extravaganza of Louis Quinze and Louis Seize chairs and tables and cabinets and commodes and *poudreuses* and great upholstered beds in which celebrated sins had been —and still were being—committed.

And for all of that, Mary could receive such a letter from Constance as had come lately, now in the last spiral of this dreadful decade. A letter in which Constance wrote: "Darling, do you remember years ago before I bought this place you asked me, 'I suppose you know all this can end in a day?'—and I said, 'I know it will.' That was London. Well, that was a lovely life, a serene and dignified thing, for all my dreadful reputation: this is a cheap sideshow compared with it. Yet what else should I do? Sometimes it comes creeping over me in the night when I can't sleep that this can't be all there is in life—for Claire, anyway. I'll die full of my fat and my fun and my wickedness—what about her? She does all the things I do, Mary, but she doesn't mean them. The trouble is I don't know what she does mean. Sometimes she gets up about three in the afternoon, after having stayed up until daylight playing with some fool over at Monte— and she wanders about for a bit, with a stare in those lion-eyes of hers, and then she says, 'Darling, I think I'll blow for a while.' So she spends half an hour kissing her cats goodbye, and gives me a hug and gets into her car and 'blows.' She may be gone a week, or a dozen weeks. That's the way she leaves when she goes to see you."

Mary sighed. She herself never knew exactly what brought Claire drifting in to Pittsburgh when Mary did not know on which side of the Atlantic she was. Four times she had done that in the past seven years. She had never stayed long; she seemed to have no interest in seeing anybody but Mary, and anything she could see of the mill by plaguing Ted to have her admitted there. She often disappeared into the attic where she would sit for hours on end, forgetting time and place and food and drink, poring over the books that were stored up there: William Scott's books, the bound records of the mill, Paul's technical books, the old early nineteenth-century histories of Western Pennsylvania. She would lavish affection and companionship on Mary for a week or two or three, and then one morning she would be off again, saying she was going to Palm Beach to drop in on somebody whose name Mary knew to be dubiously notable; and the next thing Mary would hear of her would be that she was back in Cannes. Or Julka, in a letter, might write that Claire had startlingly appeared in Prague or down in the old homestead in the country to visit her. Constance sometimes mentioned that, too. "She's restless, Mary," Constance wrote. "She's after something, but to save myself from damnation I couldn't say what. She wanders off to outlandish primitive holes in countries whose names I don't know how to spell, and pokes about in smelly places and comes back all abstracted and dishevelled and goes up to Paris and buys out Vionnet's and Chanel's and comes back here and throws a holy terror of a party that lasts for twenty-four hours. But don't ask me the answer.

I haven't got it. I haven't got anything except a bad name and a sense of humour and a lot of love for her and for you. The hell with the rest of it."

And yet, Mary thought, people could ask her why she went on living all alone in that museum, that other-world of a shuttered house!

CHAPTER LXXII

[January 1933]

EVERY WINDOW facing on the Wilhelmstrasse was wide open and packed with people, though it was a freezing night. In the Presse-Abteilung of the Foreign Office the correspondents were congregated in cliques, the Americans in one window, the British in another, the French and Swiss and other Continentals in knots of their own. Some sat on the sills with their legs dangling outside, while the rest pressed close behind them and peered out over their shoulders. They were directly opposite the window where the old field marshal stood, looking like a granite effigy (some said he had a high stool behind him) reviewing the ragtag parade which had been streaming by for three hours. Down in the Chancellery, half a block away, a comic-strip figure in a brown shirt stood in the balcony window with its arm raised and held its pose as if frozen there. Each platoon of marchers with torches and banners turned heads right when it passed the balcony and greeted Hitler with a roar and a straight-arm salute.

Claire squirmed on the window sill. She had had a half-hour turn of sitting there and was cramped and stiff with the cold. She told somebody else to take her place and clambered back into the room.

Jack Thomas gave her a drink from a bottle of Asbacher Uralt which stood on a table. She was shivering.

"I've caught my death, I know," she said.

"It's nowhere near over."

"Can't we leave now? I think I will anyway." She pulled her beaver coat tighter.

"Better not. I've sent two cables since it began but they say there's no sign of an end. The damn thing may go on all night. There are hundreds of thousands still down at the Sportplatz waiting to fall in."

Claire frowned. "What do you make of it all, Jack?"

"Ask me a year from now."

His tone was sober. It was like trying to discuss the early symptoms of a disease when somebody you knew was already dying of it. He never made snap judgments. He was one of the ablest newspaper correspondents in Central Europe, writing for a Chicago daily and a large syndicate affiliated with it. He was stationed in Vienna, but yesterday he had flown up to Berlin to meet Claire who had just driven in from Bremen.

She had been in America for several months. There had been a special stockholders' meeting in Pittsburgh at which her presence had been required. She had not seen Mary for over a year. There was something of a crisis about money—the mill had not paid a dividend since the last quarter of 1930. Her old car was so far gone that she had had to get another and bring it back with her. She was planning to drive the new one to Vienna, with Jack for company, and to spend a couple of weeks there, and then to go down to Italy and so make her way by casual stages to Cannes. She was in no hurry to get there. Without Mère Constance the place was ghostly, especially now that Claire lacked the income to keep it up. The house was closed and she had let the servants go. Only old Jeannot and his wife Lizette stayed there as caretakers. Claire camped in it when she was there.

It did not seem possible that this was the fourth year since Mère Constance had died. Claire missed her intensely still, but sometimes when irritating decisions attendant on the new poverty pressed for attention Claire thought how relieved Mère Constance must be to have escaped the whole mess. She had lived that burlesque decade after the war, rolling in money, glorying in the reputation which brought the whole celebrated world and its wife and its mistress and its lover to the Villa Bellevue. She built a dramatic grotto of a swimming-pool as a piece of redundant extravagance right beside the blue sea where they had always been content to swim before. There, enthroned in a priceless inlaid camphorwood chair, the gift of a departing Maharajah, Constance sat out the last years of her life under a striped silk awning, engulfed in sweet-smelling white flesh. She had cut her hair short during the war and she dyed it increasingly startling shades of red, so that at the last her shrewd old green eyes twinkled from under a frizzled bush of vermilion curls.

She was one of the real legends of Europe. Everybody knew her story, a story once so discreetly whispered, and finally talked forth in a triumphant crescendo of recognition. If you knew Lady Melling and had the magic entrée to her house, you could breathe the last authentic perfume of the Edwardian age. If you were somebody who could walk across the emerald lawn to the canopied throne, to be greeted by a chortle of "Darling! I'm so bloody glad to see you! Where in hell's acre have you been?" you were part of a world of fantasy, which you cherished the more, knowing it must vanish on some approaching gust. And one hot, exotic day late in the summmer of 1929, after a luncheon for twenty-odd, with carved ice swans full of caviar and magnums of Cordon Rouge 1911, Lady Melling looked up from her cards at the table beside the pool, and called to Claire who lay half naked in the burning sun nearby and said, "I think I'm going to faint, Baby." And in the instant that Claire leaped to her chair Constance was dead, her painted mouth open and her fat white hands with the vermilion nails shedding a slam hand of hearts on the grass at her feet. She died marvellously, her friends said; exactly as she should have died; and even in her stunned grief Claire knew that that was true.

Less than three months later the whole sideshow was over for everybody who had been riding the wild crest of the boom. Claire's inheritance, Mère Constance's property intact, consisted of the Villa Bellevue with its furnishings, Constance's jewels, a few thousand pounds in Consols and cash, and her thirty-six thousand shares of stock in the Scott Steel Company. When

Constance died this block was worth many millions. When Claire got it after the estate was settled, its value was under a million and the depression had brought production in the mill almost to a standstill. Dividends were suspended soon thereafter. Claire was the largest stockholder, with thirty per cent of the stock, and Ted asked her to come to Pittsburgh and vote in person on questions dictated by the crisis. She was glad to go. She fell into the way of going as often as she had a reason. She loved to be with Mary, to lose herself in strange, quiet days in the big empty house.

A paralysis had come over everything that Claire had always known and accepted as integral in life. Her own house in Cannes, Uncle Paul's in Pittsburgh, the mill which had no wonderful sights to show her now, nothing but cold black stacks and dead chimneys and echoing empty caverns—everywhere she went it was the same. Shivering beggars selling apples on the streets of Pittsburgh and New York were the same breed as the shivering beggars on the cathedral steps of Vienna and Berlin and Paris. It seemed not to matter much where one was. Claire was both apathetic and restless. If she was in Europe, trailing about from one familiar place to another, she wanted to be in the United States. When she went back to Pittsburgh and spent a few weeks in the queer miniscule world where Mary lived, she wanted to get out and go back to the lax disorderliness of the Continent. She had just enough money to move about if the mill suspended dividends indefinitely. But when she did move she wondered why.

She had drifted into a group whom she found more congenial than anyone in Mère Constance's orbit. These newspaper people were good company. In Vienna she had met some of them a couple of years before and in their easygoing way they had included her in their comings and goings, their gatherings in bars and cafés, where, after filing their dispatches, they congregated to talk and smoke and drink and speculate about the weird things working up to the surface of sickly Europe. Jack Thomas had made rather an impression on her. She liked him. Perhaps she more than liked him. She seldom thought very clearly about the thing. But it was good to have the kind of friend whom she could wire: "Meet me Berlin thirtieth drive new car Vienna." No particular reason for such a trip; one had to do something, be somewhere; she was glad of company.

But when they met at the Bristol that afternoon the news was on the street: Hindenburg had made Adolf Hitler Chancellor. It was unbelievable, in some ways it was ridiculous, but it was a story which made Thomas glad of the chance that had brought him to the spot. Instead of the evening they had planned, the superb dinner at Horcher's, the round of dives afterwards, they joined the stunned crowd of Jack's colleagues at the press meeting in the Foreign Office to which they had all been requested to come. Claire had no business there, and no credentials. She used her Pennsylvania driver's license, waving it at the guards who were too busy to read it, and would not have understood it if they had. Never in all his fifteen years at this game, Jack said, had he seen anything so ominous as this development in Berlin today. There was something about the temper of the crowds that made your blood run cold.

They went to the window once more and craned their necks over the people's heads. Already they must have seen a quarter of a million of those brown-shirted hoodlums with their torches and banners, their intermittent *"Heils!"* and their dreary repetitions of the ugly Horst Wessel song. Claire felt sick. She knew that she was catching cold, but that could not account for the leaden feeling in the pit of her stomach. She looked down at the packed crowds along the street. As far as she could see they lined this side of the Wilhelmstrasse, standing on one another's feet, waving their small swastika flags. A few hours ago this symbol had been illegal. Now it sprouted from every hand and every window. The whole population must have had them hidden away waiting for this night. They were dreadful people, Claire said to herself, looking down at the jam of men and women and children. They were fat and lethargic and ugly, the housewives worst of all, with their red shiny faces and greasy blonde hair and the rapt way they looked at the monkey on the balcony while they chanted that horrible song. Where were all the real Germans, Claire found herself wondering. Why were the streets crammed with these cattle when Berlin was full of real people? Where were they tonight?

It was past one o'clock and she told Jack Thomas she was going to leave. He said he might as well go with her. A good many of the newspaper people had left already. Those who still stayed were held by curiosity about the endurance of the two men across the street. The old one had not moved a muscle and the younger one still stood holding up his arm in that idiotic salute. Claire had had enough. She wanted desperately to get away.

They made their way by inches through the mob. Jack kept Claire in front of him and forced an opening between packed people shuffling their feet in the bitter cold. They squirmed around the corner at last and into Unter den Linden. It was a vast relief to get into the Adlon bar. Friends made room for them at a table and Claire ordered a double hot toddy. Everybody was in the bar. All the American correspondents had filed their stories—including the first official one from the new government handed them early in the evening by Frick—and were ready to spend the rest of the night in talk. The room was thick with smoke and heat and excitement, with the swirling babble of talk, with hurrying waiters taking their orders in clipped Prussian syllables.

"Nochmal!"
"Vier Helle!"
" 'Stimmt!"
"Jawohl!"

It was all perfectly familiar, all part of a scene they had lived time and time again, but Claire felt lost. There was a terrible sense of threat through all this. The busy bartenders and the scurrying waiters were no longer the same hardworking, efficient Germans she had seen in this place for years past. Their faces looked different. Their cropped heads, which were as much a part of this scene as the steins and glasses on the tables, lost their amusing familiarity and stirred in her mind an impression she had not recalled for years: the memory of the cartoons she used to see in the British and American illustrated papers years ago during the war. Germans were not harmless or amusing or *gemütlich* then. They were beasts and Boches and Huns. They were the barbarians who had killed her father and her cousin Dick and broken Uncle Paul's heart and sent Tom Scott home a blinded, crippled wreck, to fume out his life on the porch of a ranch house in Texas. Why, that was only fifteen years ago, and what kind of drug had the world taken that it could have forgotten so much in so little time? What was this feeling now, Claire thought, if not the coming-to after a drugged and futile oblivion?

She was profoundly glad to get out of Germany. The weather was abominable, Continental winter at its worst, with lowering black skies and the penetrating wet cold that made each day an ordeal. She had caught a bad cold, and she had spent two days in bed at the Bristol while Jack Thomas rushed about covering the news story whose magnitude they could as yet only sense. One thing they saw already: the membership of the Nazi party was tremendous, its penetration among the people infinitely deeper than many observers had thought. There were still some who tended to shrug this off, but not the wise ones. There were some who had never believed the plainly stated tenets of the leader. They said that theoretical anti-Semitism had always been a Germanic philosophy and presumably would continue to be. When a *New York Times* man predicted the imminence of pogroms and violence before this new government had been in power a month, the crowd at the Adlon bar laughed at him.

There was something horrible in the air, though, and for all her attachment to the German world, for she had spent much time here in recent years, Claire could not wait to get out of the country. They started early on the morning of February second, and drove down through Leipzig and Dresden over nerve-racking icy roads, through villages plastered with swastika flags and banners, through endless groups and knots and crowds of people standing on street corners reading handbills, while bullies in brown shirts with arm bands and knee boots swaggered about giving orders and *heiling* one another with the straight-arm salute. They stopped to buy cigarettes at a village outside Dresden and Claire read incredulously a lithographed strip pasted across the shop window: *Hier grüsst man nur mit Heil Hitler!* The storekeeper did so to them as they left. Claire's mouth opened automatically and she snapped over her shoulder, *"Guten Tag!"*

When they went back to the car a crowd had collected around it. That was nothing unusual. Claire always had a good American car and it always drew the same audience in any village in Europe: the gaping urchins, the giggling, pointing girls, the half-dozen sidewalk loungers who argued about it knowingly, handling the doors and radiator cap and hubs and the steering wheel if they dared, sometimes even boldly opening the bonnet and touching the motor. This was going on now. Claire was used to it but this time she was annoyed. She asked the people curtly to get away from the car, and slid into her seat behind the wheel, slamming the door hard. She pulled away from the curb with a roar.

"I'd go easy on that," Jack said after a moment.

"What do you mean?"

"Did you see the faces on some of those men?"

"Ugly customers, you mean? I shouldn't think so, Jack. They're harmless."

"They used to be."

"You don't think so any more? You're all stirred up about this thing."

"It's a revolution, Claire. It's in the air. You can feel it, or smell it if you want to put it that way. I've seen it before. Russia. Italy. Lots of places."

"Surely that can't have anything to do with my car."

"Maybe not. But I'm damn glad I'm here instead of you tooling around alone in the middle of this. If I were you I'd keep my brave new Cadillac out of this country from now on."

"You really think so?"

"I tell you, it's a revolution. Unless I haven't learned a thing in fifteen years. I give it about a month before the violence starts."

She looked at him sidewise.

"What kind of violence? What will they do?

Jack did not answer immediately. After a time he said, "Hitler has written a book called *Mein Kampf*. It is compulsory reading for every member of the Nazi party and it ought to be for everybody in this neck of the woods. It is a plan for world revolution and domination by these ruffians. You read it when you get to Vienna. Then sit back and wait to see if I'm talking through my hat."

"God!" Claire breathed.

"And countries with revolutionary mobs in them are no place for lone rich women with expensive American cars."

"I'm not rich," Claire said with a rueful laugh.

"Not by your own decadent standards, my poor little newly poor. But you are the kind of party that makes mobs see red."

"All right, Jack."

They talked very little while Claire drove the rest of the way to the frontier. By mid-afternoon the winter dusk was closing in, and in the higher turns of the Erzgebirge she had to drive very slowly, hugging the insides of the hairpin turns and keeping the car in second all the time. Jack offered to drive but Claire shook her head. She liked this kind of driving, anything that was a challenge to her concentration and her skill. They pulled up at the frontier, where the red and white painted barrier closed the road. The *Zollamt* was a small, scrupulously neat little house with the seal of the German Republic on a plaque over the door. But a large swastika flag had already been raised on the roof flagpole. Beside the customs officer at the counter inside were two storm troopers who eyed the travellers curiously and insolently. While Claire and Jack were showing their passports and the automobile papers one of the storm troopers lumbered outside and inspected the car.

Jack picked up Claire's American passport which lay on the counter.

"It seems queer for you to have one of these," he said. "Nobody ever thinks of you as an American."

Claire laughed. "I got that much out of marriage, anyway." She held out her cold hands to the potbellied stove, rubbing them together. One of

Constance's diamonds sparkled in a heavy ring on her left little finger. Claire had interesting hands, and she was rather vain about them. They were square and strongly muscled, with straight, sturdy fingers and soft brown skin. She wore her nails short and kept them beautifully manicured and finished with dark red lacquer.

The Czech custom house was not so clean or orderly as the German one, but Claire gave a growl of relief when they pulled up at the door. Inside the air was close and steamy and the place could have stood an airing, but the customs officer smiled when Claire greeted him in his own language, and invited them to sit down. Jack looked at her curiously when she chatted with the two Czechs at the counter. The passports were stamped and the car cleared quickly. There was a small sort of inn at the back of the customs shed, a single room with a stove and a couple of rude tables where some workmen were sitting over drnks.

"Let's have a cup of coffee in there," Claire said. "I'm cold."

The place smelled of soft coal and coffee and sweaty bodies in winter clothes. But Claire seemed to like it. "It's not that I like the smell," she said, "I like the frankness of it. It's just what it is, that's all."

A stout woman in a lot of woollen petticoats brought two mugs of coffee and two glasses of slivovitz. Claire threw her coat over the wooden chair-back and lifted the mug of coffee between her hands. She drank it in big greedy gulps.

"How can you drink the stuff scalding like that?"

"I like it. I always like things boiling hot."

The slivovitz began to warm them and Claire rolled hers on her tongue. It was a crude distillation and stung her mouth but its warmth spread comfortably through her veins. Jack lit a cigarette and rested his elbows on the table. He had an interesting face, Claire thought. It was narrow and nervous, with sharp blue eyes and a bush of sandy curls. His ears were small and pointed and carved close to his skull. In a certain way he reminded her of Tom Scott, perhaps only because of the quickness and sharpness of his voice and manner. Sometimes Claire thought he was in love with her and at other times—strangely enough, the times when he approached eloquence in talking about her—she felt sure that he was not. She was always aware of her own lack of desire for him. He simply did not appeal to her as a lover, though she could wish intensely that he did. She liked him. He was good, tough, stimulating, interesting company. He had an agreeable gregarious quality which Claire lacked and which enabled her to enjoy his friends without having to make much effort herself. But if he wanted to make love to her she had to refuse in spite of herself and so far he had been willing to let the thing rest on her terms. But Claire did not believe he would leave it at that indefinitely. She dreaded the next step.

He was staring at her now. She was damned good to stare at, as he had put it not long ago. She was so well put together. Her coloring was well blended; the dark chestnut of her curly cropped hair, the soft tan of her skin, the dark lipstick she used on her wide mouth. Her hazel eyes were level and clear. Sometimes one could read them like print, and at other times they appeared to glaze and turn into flat tawny stones, expressionless and inscrutable as the eyes of a lion. There was much in her manner that reminded him of a big cat anyway; the quick shifts from gentle, lazy, sybaritic warmth of mood to unaccountable coldness and a sudden withdrawal into aloofness. When she was like that it was no more use to try to get at her than to hold an unwilling cat on your knees trying to make it relax and purr.

She was looking contented and reflective now. She understood some Czech and was listening to the conversation around her. Jack said suddenly, still thinking of her American passport, "Who in hell *are* you anyway, Claire? Who was Wood? How long were you married to him? Why do you talk American with an English accent, live on the Continent, call Pittsburgh home, and speak six languages?"

She set down her glass and laughed.

"You make me out to be an international mystery, don't you? I wish to God it was true. There wasn't even anything nice and tragic about my marriage. It was just a youthful little mess so I called it off."

"Who was he?"

"Well, his name, if you care, was Joshua Wood. He was a young Greek god from Harvard with the most beautiful body and the most empty head. He was a Lieutenant in the American Army and he was wounded and somehow or other got sent to my grandmother's place which she ran as a convalescent home for British officers. I don't really know how Josh got there, no other American did except my cousin Tom. I was sixteen when I first saw him and if you know what a *Backfisch* can do to her wits over a beautiful dumb blond giant, you know the whole story."

"You didn't marry him at that time?"

"Oh, Lord, no. He got well and went home to the States and used to write me nice college boy letters in a round fat hand, and I used to take them down in the garden with my cats and lie in the grass and dream over them—oh, Jack, you can't be serious! You can't want me to tell you all that rot!"

"I do," he said. He was leaning over the table listening to every word. "Maybe I'll find out what makes you the way you are."

"Frigid," she said derisively.

"The hell you are."

"Anyway, like the prince in the story book, he actually came back to Cannes three years later after he took his degree—for God knows what—at Harvard, and believe it or not he married the childhood sweetheart. We had a magnificent wedding with all the proper tommyrot and then"—she shuddered—"we went to Boston to live. Boston—*me*—in Boston. In Brookline. Meeting the five-eighteen every night. Having his old clubmates to Sunday supper. Making gin in the bathtub. Having Sunday lunch with his family on Louisburg Square. Oh my God, Jack," she blurted, motioning for another slivovitz, "it was bleeding. Positively, utterly bleeding. I stood it for nearly a year and then went home to Grandma. That's all."

"Didn't you—love him?"

"No," she said, with a snort. "Love! At twenty. How in hell should I know what love was at that age? Or learn it from an all-American half-back? Don't be ridiculous."

"You poor kid."

"Well," she said with a sigh, "as you say, I did get an American pass-port out of it. And at least learn what not to bungle into again."

"I'm surprised you didn't have a kid," Jack said slowly. "Most girls would in a set-up like that."

Claire shrugged. "God was on my side for once. Or Mère Constance, if you want to know the truth. My grandmother."

"She must have been a wonder."

"She was. She was utterly incomparable. When I started to marry Josh she shrugged her fat shoulders and said, 'You'll be back in a year, darling, and I do hope you're quick about it and get all this rot out of your system, but if you bring a brat with you I'll drown it, so help me God.' So she jolly well saw to it there wouldn't be any brat, bless her."

Jack sighed. Claire turned her head and looked at him quickly and said, "I believe you're shocked."

He smiled. "Maybe I am—in a way. But not the way you mean. That seems to me like an awful raw deal for a woman like you. Do you mean to say you've been knocking around ever since without—well, just on the loose?"

"I don't notice you rushing home every night to a vine-covered cottage and a wife and kiddies."

"Hell, that's different. This kind of life's my business."

"Maybe it's mine."

"No, that's phony. If you really did any work I wouldn't talk like this. You could, you know. You could write anything you damn pleased if you'd take a grip on yourself and do it."

"I suppose I could," Claire spoke thoughtfully.

"Then why don't you? You're restless and bored—I'm not any surer than you are that a man's the answer. But I'd bet my last shirt a job would be."

"I've had too much money," Claire said sadly. "It's been too easy to be a bum."

"Well, you're honest anyhow," Jack said quickly. "That's why I like you. You're a big woman—got a big mind and a big point of view and I'd guess—" He paused and bit his lip.

"I know."

"Well then if you can't fill all that up with a man, for God's sake fill it with something. You're too good to be rattling around empty."

Claire's eyes were unusually soft and she stared at him.

"You're a grand friend, Jack."

"No I'm not. I'd like to be a—a grand—something to you if you'd have me. Claire—" He reached over and covered her hand with his.

She smiled gently.

"I wish I could be in love with you, Jack."

He took out two cigarettes and lit them and gave one to her. "Can I have a little more time to work on you?"

She laughed and reached behind her for her coat. "If you want to waste your own."

"I'll worry about mine," he said, "and I wish you'd get a little more sense about yours. How old are you—thirty?"

"You just looked at my passport."

"Well. Don't fritter away any more years. Live 'em."

"Yes, doctor."

They went outside to the car. It was pitch dark now, not a star in the sky, and bitterly cold. They stood and looked about them for a moment. Like all frontiers this spot was desolate and bleak and forebodingly lonely.

"Where do we go from here?" Jack asked cheerfully.

"Prague. It's only about a hundred and twenty kilometers. And we'll go to the Piskáč and have dinner—" Claire sucked in her cheeks with a gluttonous noise. "Mushroom soup and roast goose and *knedlíky* and—"

"Have a heart. I'll die of hunger before we get there."

"You'll die of overeating after we've been there."

CHAPTER LXXIII

[*1933—Continued*]

IT WAS A LONG STORY that Jack Thomas drew from Claire on the drive to Prague, the long and fascinating story of the Scott mill, and of her American relatives. He had asked her to start back at the beginning, and she had done just that, even going back to the first William Scott, her great-great-grandfather, who had supplied the Union Army in the Civil War and sped escaping slaves through his cellar station of the Underground Railway. It was a fantastic span from that world and that time to the awful, troubled present. And Claire had dwelt on the past war as she had seen it from two strikingly contrasted points—Pittsburgh and the grim determination of Uncle Paul, and France under the impact of devastation and excitement and suffering. And now, she had just said, would Jack please tell her the use of any of it? The whole world was paralyzed, nobody had the things we had been told we were fighting for, men were taking refuge in blind barbarism or in refusing to see what lay before their noses. "They won't believe it in America," she was saying. "Millions of men idle and their families starving and everybody supposes it'll snap back to normal any day now."

"This is just the beginning, for the U. S." Jack said. "They're getting the backwash from here. Believe me, I know. I've been in this mess here since 1920 and what we saw yesterday in Berlin is just the eggs beginning to hatch."

"If you could see them!" Claire's mind was still running on the crisis in Pittsburgh. "Men who've worked all their lives and their fathers before them, in steel mills—highly skilled men—dumped out by the thousands without a bloody cent in their pants."

"Something will be done after the new administration goes in in March," Jack said. "What will Roosevelt's New Deal be, if not that?"

"Oh, sure. They'll have to have government relief of some kind. They found that out in England long ago."

"You can't put American labor on the dole."

"You can't put it on its tail on the curbstone either. It gives me this hellish feeling on account of our mill. I ought to be able to do something, Jack."

"You!" He could not help laughing a little.

"Don't make fun of me. God knows the stock's not worth a thing right now. If I did get any dividends I wouldn't have the gall to keep them. But there are none, so that's that. We're losing money at some appalling rate, I never know anything about figures, but I know that after they pay the operating expenses and taxes they're in the hole already."

"What is your mill actually producing now?"

"Oh—a few specialties like steels for tools and machine parts and certain things for aircraft and automobile factories—but not enough to keep anybody really working. They average about eighteen per cent of capacity. Think of that—and when I was there during the war they ran the whole place at a hundred per cent on twenty-four hour schedule!"

"Oh, in the war. What the hell."

"Yes," Claire repeated gloomily, "what the hell. Look how they fixed the world for us. As a matter of fact this country is about the only place that's better off for the war having been." She waved at the dark landscape through the window.

"I'm so sick of Vienna," Jack said after a pause. "I've been there five years and it's been like watching an old, decrepit friend die by inches. The place makes no sense whatever. A capital without a country. That was a fine way to fix things, your friend Mr. Wilson and his buddies."

"Wilson didn't mean it to turn out like this. That was Clemenceau. And Henry Cabot Lodge."

"Whoever it was, they gummed up the world something fierce."

They drove on in silence and after a time the lights of Prague began to flicker up, tiny points down in the distant valley. Claire exclaimed with pleasure.

"What makes you like this country so much?" Jack asked curiously. "Far as I'm concerned it's something only a mother could love. God-awful language and those stubborn, dour people."

"You just don't understand them," Claire said. "They're remarkable people. They haven't much finesse, it's true, but did you ever know any of them well?"

"No, and do you?"

"I'll take you to see a friend of mine tomorrow," Claire promised.

The friend was Julka Liska, of course. She was known correctly in Czechoslovakia as Julka Hrdličková, though her American friends could never have learned to say all that. She had been widowed nine years before, just when she had induced Charlie to fulfill her lifetime dream of taking their savings, enough to enable them to live carefully the rest of their lives, and go to Prague or to Suchomel, her birthplace, the village on the Vltava, and settle there. She had been back once, on her long-anticipated trip in 1920, and she had seen the new government established and had left Anton in Prague to study with Kubelík at the Conservatory. Then she returned to Charlie in Pittsburgh, but he saw and Mary Rafferty saw that Julka's heart had stayed behind in her own country. So it was a foregone conclusion after Charlie's death that Julka would go back to Czechoslovakia. Her children were all grown and independent. Jerry was boss electrician in the open-hearth department at the mill. He was married and had three children. Míla was married and living in Cleveland. Jenny was a nurse at the Magee Hospital in Pittsburgh.

When they reached Prague, Claire telephoned Anton to ask where his mother was. Down in the country, he said, with the Dvořák relatives and she had left word that Claire should come right down there. He knew that Claire had just been in America and he asked after Jerry and the girls. Claire asked him to come out and have a drink, but he had friends at his house and could not leave. So Claire and Jack had a glorious late dinner of goose and dumplings washed down by *Plzeňské pivo* which, she said, was the correct name of the exquisite Pilsener beer that Jack was enjoying so hugely. He put down his fourth empty pint flute and sighed and ruefully patted his stomach.

"Jeez," he said. "That beer is too good to be true."

"You've drunk it before."

"Sure. Lots of times. But you forget how marvellous it is." He grinned. "Or maybe you flavor it up for me."

"I want a slivovitz with my coffee."

"I don't. I want another beer."

"You'll burst. I see suds coming out of your ears already."

Jack asked her about these Czech friends of hers on the way down to Suchomel next morning. "Who was the man you talked to on the phone?" he asked.

"That was Anton Hrdlička, the son of the woman we're going to see. He's the first violinist of the orchestra in Prague. He wanted to be a virtuoso—" Claire shrugged. "You know how that is."

"Was he born in Pittsburgh?"

"Oh, yes. I don't know him as well as I know his mother. I used to see them all there when we were kids. His brother works in the mill."

"That must be kind of tough," Jack said, musing. "To want to be a big shot like Kreisler or Heifetz and end up playing in an orchestra."

"That's just life," Claire said. "A chap turns out to be a good violinist, not a great one. What should he do—" She was keeping her eyes carefully on the slippery macadam road. "It's a shame we're here in winter," she said. "This countryside is a paradise in summer."

"Why does your friend Julka live down here?" Jack asked.

"She doesn't—always. She's in the government, in the Land Reform

Administration. Some of the time she lives in Prague with her son and the rest of the time down here where they all came from. She's full of hell, you know, always up to something. She'll go out in the fields if she feels like it and take a hand with the poppy-sowing or the hop-harvest. But she's really a district administrator for the Land Office."

Jack knew that that was the agency through which, after the over-throw of the Empire, the peasants had acquired and paid for land formerly owned by the great Austrian landlord nobles. The land had been expro-priated by the new Czech government and reissued to peasant farmers in limited parcels calculated to prevent the accumulation of land by absentee or other non-working owners.

"And Julka's good at that," Claire explained. "She knows all the people down there and she just uses common sense when they get into disputes about property—instead of tying them all up in red tape."

Jack looked out at the dreary winter landscape. He was perfectly familiar with it. Time and again as he had crossed and recrossed Europe on assignments he had seen these rolling valleys dotted with red-roofed villages, each with its onion-spired church. The fields spread out, brown and stubbled now, as far as the eye could reach, carefully measured into strips worked this way and that. The sky was gray and the air clammy. It was about as unattractive a prospect as you could find. Jack thought long-ingly of Sicily or the Dalmatian coast, which would be bursting into warm bloom now. He wondered why on earth he should be doing this with a week's stolen time, when he could have flown down to some sunny, relaxing place where he could have lain on a beach and got a tan and rid himself of the nagging vestiges of a cold. He always had this dragging cold during the deadly Central European winter. No wonder Vienna was full of nose and throat specialists. He looked up gloomily at the leaden sky.·

"It's going to snow," he said resentfully.

"I'm sorry," Claire smiled at him. "I·didn't plan it that way."

He shook his head, muttering something about a Godforsaken wilder-ness. At that point Claire turned the car off at a crossroad and began negotiating a narrow mud road, frozen and rutted and coated thinly with ice.

"For God's sake, Claire, why didn't you tell me we were going to ex-plore Tibet?"

"You should be glad this isn't March," Claire retorted, "you'd be help-ing me jack up the car in the mud. And running around looking for a team to haul us out."

"Jesus! And you like it here."

The wheel slithered between her hands as she let the car ride in the deep ruts. Jack clutched the doorframe and swore.

"Never mind," she said. "It's not far."

He saw a village around the next bend, huddled on both sides of the road, with the inevitable church lifting its spire from among the low roofs. This church had a needle spire instead of the commoner bulbous one. It had been built, Claire said, by the Schwarzenberg family who had orig-inally owned the village.

She drove slowly down the single village street. The houses on either side seemed almost lifeless. They were all two-storied, built of light gray plaster with tightly shut double-casement windows and ridged tile roofs. An occasional face peered curiously out at the big mud-spattered car advancing down the street. Each house had a center front door and to one side another door, high and wide as a gate, tightly closed. These were the courtyard doors which always stood open in summer, to let the busy farm traffic in and out. Now the village was hibernating; even the ubiquitous geese were not in sight. They were all packed away in the closed courtyards.

There was a large house, set a little apart from the close-shouldered neighboring ones, toward the end of the street. It too appeared tightly closed. But Claire stopped the car outside the door and jumped out. Before she could knock the door flew open and Julka hurried out, crying *"Nazdar!"* She wrapped Claire in a delighted embrace. They held each other tight and kissed one cheek, then the other, exclaiming and beaming. Julka let go of Claire presently and shook hands with Jack, whom she had never seen. She had not seen Claire for over two years. These visits had always been sparse and spasmodic.

"Come right in," she said, "you must be frozen."

Jack was surprised to hear her speak English. She called inside the house in Czech and a boy of about fourteen came out, shook hands shyly with Claire, and began to help unload the bags from the car.

"My nephew Jan," Julka said. More people appeared from the house; a stout smiling woman who greeted Claire in Czech, followed by several boys and girls who clustered about the car, wide-eyed and silent. Then a tall, grave, bearded man appeared and ceremoniously bowed them inside the door. That was František Dvořák, Julka's cousin and foster brother. He was about sixty, Jack judged; a remarkable-looking man who felt about for words in which to speak to his male guest (he spoke no English) and finally decided on German which, he explained, he used only when there was no other choice.

They all moved in to the large central room of the house. It was low-ceilinged and rather dark, with an enormous blue tile stove in the corner. An old woman sat in an armchair beside it with a knitted blanket over her knees. She was brown and shrivelled like a mummy. She paid no attention to the bustle in the room.

"František's wife's mother," Claire explained to Jack. "She's nearly a hundred."

Julka and Anička Dvořáková, František's wife, directed the young boys as they carried the luggage up the dark staircase. The girls—there seemed to be four or five of them and Jack was bewildered by new faces which kept appearing from other rooms—were taking coats and wraps, laying the center table with a richly embroidered cloth, and setting out cups and dishes. František stood by the stove talking to Claire. His face was very serious. Although they were speaking Czech Jack knew that Dvořák was asking Claire about the ominous happenings in Germany.

Jack stood a little apart by himself, taking the scene in. He watched Julka Liska curiously. What a grand-looking woman she was, he thought.

Her strong plain face was alert and beaming with happiness at seeing Claire. Her body was erect and vigorous. She had iron-gray hair parted in the center and knotted at her neck. She wore a dark cloth dress and an embroidered apron thickly gathered on a wide waistband. She looked so utterly a part of this house that Jack had difficulty picturing her in an American mill town, running political meetings in dingy Slovak meeting halls, sitting in on the councils of state which had created this country. But she did speak English, Pittsburgh English at that, tinged with characteristic words and phrases.

Presently they all gathered round the table for afternoon coffee. Jack could not hope to disentangle the relationships of the eleven people who, not counting the old grandmother, comprised the members of the Dvořák family present. This house, Julka explained, was really a sort of homestead. They were gathered in one half of it, occupied by František and his family and his widowed sister and her children. In the other half lived one of his brothers with his family and dependents; and in other houses in this village and elsewhere in the valley were half a hundred connections and relations stemming from Jaromír and Ludmila Dvořák and their brothers and sisters and children. Jack remarked almost at once on the absence of young men, as he looked about the table at the women, the girls, and the boys.

"They are never here in winter," Julka said, pouring delicious coffee into a cup for Claire and adding hot milk and whipped cream. "František has four big sons. Two are married and two in Praha at the University."

"One is studying to be an engineer," Julka said, "that's Otakar. And Tomáš is in his last year of agricultural science. They come home for the plowing in the spring, of course. Their courses are arranged for that."

"Nearly all the Czech families do that," Claire explained. "Everybody goes to the University, whether they are farmers or live in towns."

"I am going too, next year," a slight, very pretty girl said shyly in English. She looked about seventeen.

"She is going to study medicine," Julka said.

"You didn't do your preparatory work here in the village, did you?" Jack asked.

"Oh, no. I go to the gymnasium in České Budějovice. It is only twelve kilometers. I go every morning with the bus."

Jack raised his eyebrows. So far every young person he had heard about in this family was either in High School or the University or had already graduated. He had expected this to be a backwater where people could hardly read or write. Claire laughed at him. Julka laughed too. She passed a big plate loaded with coffee cake and poppyseed cake and said, "Here, eat something old-fashioned and you won't have such a foolish expression on your face."

Jack was still talking to the girl who was going to be a doctor. "Where did you learn to speak such good English? In school too?"

"Teta Julka," said Dora, "she's teaching us."

Claire said, "Can't you ever stop improving people, Julka? Why don't you let somebody be a bum once in a while? You taught me Czech, then you teach your nieces English, what will you do when there's nobody left to improve?"

"There will never be such a time," Julka said. "And there's room for plenty of improvement in your Czech too." She winked. "Tell me all about Mary and everybody at home. I want to hear all the news."

When she was in Pittsburgh she had called the old country home; now that she was here, she called Pittsburgh home. "I'm worried about Jerry," she said.

Claire bit her lip. She did not know how to tell Julka how frightful conditions were in America. Up to last month Jerry had not lost his job. That was because a skeleton staff of electricians and mechanics had to be kept on for maintenance whether the mill was shut down or not. But Claire knew that his wages had been cut, and that he was only working part time. There had been a wage slash straight through the mill from Gray Simcox down to the yard labor. She knew that Jerry was very hard hit by this. She did not usually see him when she was in Pittsburgh except for an arriving and a parting visit to bring and take messages for his mother. Somehow in Pittsburgh, without Julka there, it was awkward to intrude on Jerry in his house. He had his own life, his wife and children and friends, and they were solidly established on the other side of the proverbial tracks from the Scott family. It was artificial to seek him out. Something about the thing made Claire feel uncomfortable, perhaps because his wife Bella seemed to resent her appearance and think her patronizing. Mary Rafferty and Julka were the only people Claire knew who had ever bridged the gap between mill owners and mill labor and moved successfully between the two. Otherwise that was an unnatural thing to try to do. Claire was forced to admit it. She would have liked to feel free to make her friends as and where her instincts guided her.

Julka had once tried to explain to her why that could not be. The barrier lay not only in tradition and prejudice and the rigid natures of most of the Scotts, but in the stories of Constance's dazzling, extravagant life with all the overtones of gossip that had seeped down even to the men in the mill. They felt, if they thought about it at all, that the Countess of Melling ate and drank and wore the sweat of their bodies when she blew through the money that came out of the mill. You could hardly expect them, Julka reminded Claire, to feel at ease with anybody who tried to step from her world into theirs.

"But I'm not like Mère Constance," Claire had said in a troubled way.

"You can't expect them to appreciate that. They don't know anything about you except you're a Scott and her granddaughter. It wouldn't matter which Scott you were, though. They'd feel the same. People shouldn't cross the tracks."

"And I'd like so much to know some of them," Claire said.

"You got to think straight about a thing like that," Julka said. "Suppose I only see you driving around in a big Cadillac in a fur coat, and somebody tells me you live in a palace on the Riviera and your grandmother is a Countess—what do I think? Do I think you mean it when you want to be friends with me? No, I think you're looking for something new to amuse you "

"Amusement," said Claire bitterly. "Listen, Julka, I'm so damned fed up with amusement and amusing people and—" she shuddered.

Julka nodded wisely "And every place you go it's the same faces and the same talk and the same old amusement, no?"

Claire nodded and said, 'It's a habit, a nasty old habit you want to break and even if you're making headway nobody wants you to succeed. They come at you and shove the damn drug down your throat 'Darling,'" she mimicked suddenly in a high brittle voice like those of the international set, " 'wheah've you been? Not in that dihty, vile Pittsburgh! Fahncy!' Oh, the hell with them!'' she said savagely.

Julka had studied Claire's sombre face with her strong wise eyes— eyes that held much the same wisdom as Mary's, but were earthier and more worldly.

"You're lonely, aren't you?" she asked "Lost. You can't find yourself, no?"

Claire sighed heavily and nodded her head.

Nobody appeared to understand as well as Julka what it was that Claire was groping for. Mary ought to understand, but her mind was bounded by her own small world. She was always overjoyed when Claire came back to Pittsburgh, and always newly disappointed when Claire went away again. She could not understand why it was that Europe, which was in Claire's blood, could neither satisfy her and give her secure anchorage, nor relinquish her and free her of its tastes and habits.

But it was quite clear that Claire's extraordinary childhood had had a great deal to do with the way she was today. So had her experience of the war and so had the fact, more clearly perceived by Julka than anybody, that Claire had a tremendous capacity for reality which nothing in her life with Constance had ever satisfied. It was enough to hear Claire talk about the mill as she had first known it; to see her come into a place like this homestead of the Dvořáks with its plain, honest sights and sounds and odors; to see her apply herself to a steaming plate of boiled beef with horseradish. She was fundamentally a direct human being with intense natural instincts. But they lay beneath a façade of intricate complication.

Claire was happy right now, with the family tomcat purring in her lap and the Dvořáks talking good sense around her. František was still gravely weighing the meaning of the Nazi victory in Germany.

"Don't you think you tend to overstress all that?" Jack Thomas asked in his fluent, flat, badly pronounced German. "What concern have they with you?"

František stroked his beard. "I do not trust them," he said soberly. "I explained to you about the three million right here." He waved his left hand at the west window, toward the foothills which rose a few miles away to the Sudeten mountains. "We did not want them in the first place, did we, Julka?"

She shook her head. "Professor Masaryk warned about them right in the beginning," she said. "He always said they would make trouble."

"So we keep a strong army," František went on. "Every Czech is a soldier. We have forts over there in the mountains and now I believe we will have to build stronger ones. That costs much money, wastes much good manpower. We could do better in a civilized world than use up our substance on fortifications to keep out barbarians."

"I still think you exaggerate the danger from a mere political party in Germany," Jack said. "Why, in Vienna they've tried to make some converts among the young hoodlums and nobody takes them seriously. They laugh them off."

"Ach, *Vídeň*," said Dvořák with a shrug. "What can you expect? Lightweights. *Nemám pravdu, Julko?*"

"Hanh?" She started. She had lost track of the talk. She had been sitting there quietly eyeing Claire and Jack Thomas and weighing the conclusion in her mind and, from her thoughtful expression, finding it wanting.

CHAPTER LXXIV

[October 1934]

MARY STOOD on the doorstep looking up and down the street. Claire should be arriving any time now. She had telephoned from Greensburg saying that she would be in well before dinner. She had not been back from Europe in almost two years. Her letters were frequent, but the stretches between her visits were lonely. Lately Mary had been wondering what became of the time as the years fled by. It was certainly true that as you grew old your years seemed shorter and shorter. And it was true too that no matter what your resolutions not to yield to the ways of old age, you did live largely in the past. Mary sometimes scolded herself for that. And, living all alone, there were times when she felt as if she had developed a second personality, an interrogator who sometimes jogged her will or her memory or, she was ashamed to realize, her tongue. Once in a while she found herself speaking aloud, as if another person were with her.

She stared now at the familiar street with suddenly conscious eyes. It was so much a part of her that she took no more ordinary notice of it than of her hands and feet. But she thought at this moment how it was going to look to Claire. Awful, Mary said, shaking her head; simply awful. She realized that the street had about completed the descent into outright shabbiness. She kept her own place trim and clipped, but not planted and formally landscaped as it had been years ago. For one thing the coal dust and gas in the air kept any flowering plant from blooming. But she had a man by the hour to keep the grass and the hedges in order. Out in the street, though, she saw sadly that when a tree died nobody was doing anything about replacing it; most of the friendly oaks and elms had disappeared.

Of course nothing could look well on a day like this, a dour autumn day with the surviving trees bare, and a clammy chill in the air. Mary made allowance for that. What really startled her was the number of families that had died out or moved away since she had been living here alone. They were all gone, the Georges and Cottrells and McKelvies and Browns and Dixons, all gone and mostly dead. And all their houses had slipped into dereliction. Not one had been disposed of to anyone you could call a desirable neighbor. The Cottrells' was a boardinghouse; the McKelvie mansion had been cut up into a ragtag two-family arrangement, its spacious yard cluttered with bent tricycles, rusty hoops, broken toys and—horror of horrors—clotheslines flapping their ugly secrets for the world to see. What had become of the drying-yard? It must have been gone for years, Mary saw now with a start. But that had never really impressed her until now.

As if in shocked defiance the Scott house with its blinded front windows, and two other fine old places in which their owners still lived, were kept in the most exemplary condition. Their bricks were pointed, their roofs repaired, their ironwork gates and fences carefully painted every spring. Mary went on doing this as a ritual no more to be abandoned than her regular visits to Uniondale Cemetery, where the Scott plot was kept and tended under her direction, an island of green peace and beauty. She often went there just to rest beside the low railing and reflect and remember and pray. She told herself recently, with incredulous amazement, that it was sixty-one years since she had first entered this house and the life of this family. And even now there was something unbelievable about the fate which had brought her from that beginning to this ending. Ted understood and appreciated her feeling about the house and cemetery, but Mary had come to the worried conclusion that he was beginning to be restive about the cost of keeping up the house. He had made a trip all the way over from town not long ago to ask her if she could do anything to hold down the annual maintenance bills. Mary knew that he was pressed for cash. Without any dividends he must be embarrassed in many ways when he ruled out any reliance on Lauchlan's money. There was Tom, for one thing. If his expenses rose above the rigid minimum which could be negotiated on his small means other than his mill stock, Ted would have to make up the difference. He at least had a salary.

Mary herself was pinched. She had for years allotted a large share of her income to a dozen or more good works and private benefactions which had come to depend on her. Now at a time like this, when people needed help more than ever before, she could not cut them off in order to keep funds for herself.

So she did without this and did without that and found how exceedingly easy it was for a solitary person to economize on every sort of living expense. She drifted from running the house with well-trained maids who had too little to do, to one strong woman whose principal work was cleaning; there was no end to that in Pittsburgh. One after another, Mary had closed the large front rooms downstairs and most of the bedrooms upstairs. She had her meals on a tray in the back parlor, where she lived almost entirely. It had always been Paul's favorite room; it was still full of his personality. She dusted and tidied it herself, and aired the other big, dark, shrouded rooms at regular intervals, and all these duties and details served to fill up her days.

She heard the throb of a motor down the street, and turned happily to watch as a big car rolled up and Claire turned it into the driveway and stopped at the side door. Claire got out with the stiff motions that come from long sitting behind the wheel, and threw her arms around Mary with a cry of "Darling!" Mary felt like an ivory figurine to Claire; so light and tiny, the bones so fragile and sharp, the flesh so impalpable.

"You're too thin," Claire said anxiously. "What's the matter?"

"Nothing, dear. Leave the things right in the car. I told George to come back at six o'clock to carry it all upstairs for us. I knew you'd be here by then."

"I can't leave this till six o'clock," Claire said, reaching back into the car. She pulled out with a covered basket in her hands.

Mary smiled. "Another one?"

"This one's for you. Something very special."

Claire carried the basket into the back parlor and opened the lid. A very mussed and draggled red Persian cat leaped out and scooted belly-low behind the sofa, a flash of long fur and angry topaz eyes. Claire crawled under the couch on her stomach and retrieved the cat and sat on the floor smoothing and stroking him and talking to him in her lingo. He dug his claws into her shoulders and looked around him with his ears flat. Mary watched noncommittally. She was used to this scene, with innumerable variations.

"This one's for you," Claire repeated, kissing the cat's snub salmon-colored nose and crooning to him. "He's really the cat of all cats, Mary. Wait till you get acquainted with him."

Mary sighed and smiled wryly. She did not want a cat and Claire ought to know it.

"Never mind," Claire said. "I know I'm the little boy who gave his father the electric train for Christmas. But wait till you really know this cat."

"What's his name?"

"Oriflamme. That's his real moniker, I call him Flam for short."

"Claire," said Mary accusingly, "did you bring that animal all the way from Europe?"

"All the way," Claire said cheerfully. "I know I promised you I wouldn't do that any more but I went to the cat show in Paris the week before I sailed. I was all out of sorts and—oh, low in my mind, I don't know. I didn't really look at anything, I was just wandering around and down by the door just before I left something caught my skirt and made me stop. Here was this cat—deliberately reached out of the cage and grabbed me. Well, Mary—you wouldn't just laugh that off and go on! If you could have seen that face turned up at you—I couldn't have left him there. I was elected."

"So you brought him to me," said Mary dryly.

"You have to have a cat," Claire said decisively. "He's really a joint cat. But he's going to stay here and attend to you when I'm away."

"He'll never look at me when you're around."

Claire laughed. "If you care enough to be jealous you're overboard already." She jumped up and dumped Flam in Mary's lap. Mary scratched his rump gingerly and he began to wash his frill and heavy front paws, working hard.

"Why do they do that, wash their vests if you scratch the ends of their spines?"

"You ask him when you're alone with him."

Mary had been worrying about Claire for a long time. On the face of it there seemed slight reason to be anxious about a young woman who had, in the most banal phrase, everything. Claire scoffed affectionately when Mary showed her uneasiness.

"I used to think," Claire said, "that you were a wise old party who never fussed or got shocked by anything. I thought Mère Constance had you all nicely educated and now I'll have to start from scratch all over again."

"Impudent."

"I'm right, though. You fume because you can't put me in a nice neat box with HUSBAND AND CHILDREN on the label and know I'll be there the next time you go to the shelf for it."

"But don't you *want* a husband—a home, Claire?" Mary's old face was wistful and puzzled.

"Well, yes, if this were fairyland. But if you weren't crazy in love with a man you wouldn't want him in your hair, would you, darling?" She put her fingers under Mary's chin. "Would you?"

"No."

"There you are. Your own life has been queer enough, God knows, yet you want to straighten mine all out nice and proper when I don't need it."

Mary's life was still queer, now that she was seventy-six years old, a frail framework of small, erect bones and fine white wrinkled skin and a cloud of soft white hair. She seemed in most ways to exist completely out of the present-day world, but that was not true. When she wanted to participate in something, that matter felt the firm impact of her will. There was no place where her presence was more emphatic than at the annual October stockholders' meetings at the mill. She had never missed a meeting since Paul's death and would not miss one until her own. Claire, as the largest stockholder, had the most reason of anyone for attending, but she did not always do so. This year she would be here; two years ago she had been; and as long as business was in this critical condition most of the stockholders, anxious and apprehensive, would pay very close attention to the mill. But Mary had been surprised in the past few years by the sudden interest that Ben Nicholas, Elizabeth's son, had been showing in the mill. She was quite curious about him. It seemed strange to her and to Claire when they talked about it that this rich, preoccupied young man who was known as a stock manipulator of genius should suddenly begin taking the time to come to Pittsburgh for the annual meetings of such a small company.

Elizabeth Nicholas died in 1927, leaving Ben the sole heir to his father's fortune, in which she had had a life interest. She also left him her twenty-four thousand shares of Scott stock. He was five years out of Harvard at the time. His first step was to buy a seat on the Stock Exchange (he had been a customers' man in a large firm for some time) and his second was immediately to increase his patrimony by some quarter of a million dollars in one brilliant turn. He had an instinct for money which was the despair of his acquaintances even at a time when everybody was making tremendous profits. He was enormously shrewd, with cold precision of judgment inherited from his father, and an unimpressive exterior—Elizabeth's legacy —which belied his wealth and his business daring. He looked, as Claire said to Mary, like a Y.M.C.A. worker in the war. That was only Claire's opinion. There were women who found Ben's imperturbable blond personality very attractive. The most phenomenal thing he ever did, which left his cousins gaping with incredulous envy, was to sell out every stock he held, with the sole exception of his Scott stock, in the late summer of 1929. When the crash came Ben was sitting coolly upon millions of cash, with which he soon thereafter began going short of the tobogganing market. By early 1930 he had amassed millions more.

To Ted Scott, in the anxiety that overwhelmed all Pittsburgh, Ben's performance was disconcerting in the extreme. It was only because the mill's stock was unlisted and entirely family owned that Ben had not sold his block of that too. As a matter of fact, though Ben had not said so to Ted, his Scott stock in comparison with his major holdings in motors, utilities, and industrials, was so small that he had really almost ignored it. It was not until the stock market had about finished its wild spiral downward that Ben showed any interest in the mill at all. Then, finding himself with masses of idle cash and very little other holdings to absorb his passion for manipulation, he showed up at the stockholders' meeting in 1930 instead of sending his signed proxy as he had done before. That was the meeting at which dividend payments were indefinitely suspended, and they had not been resumed since.

Mary did not mind doing without income from the mill when conditions dictated it, but she worried about other matters there. She had grown into the habit of talking these things over with Claire, partly because she wanted Claire to understand clearly what Paul's intentions about the mill had been during his lifetime and what they would be if he were here now. There had always been a problem about the choice of officers since Paul's death. Claire had often remarked how unfit Ted was to succeed his father as chairman of the board of directors and president of Scott's. Ted had not been experienced enough when Paul died to step into his shoes. The directors had appointed John Purcell as chairman, and it had become a matter of custom automatically to reappoint him every year. In the same way they named Gray Simcox president of the company. That function was so interwoven with the general superintendent's that it was best to keep both in one man's hands. Ted was not jealous of Simcox. Ted did not have the deep-rooted proprietary love for the mill which would have made him feel that way. He was absorbed chiefly in Lauchlan. She was an intensely demanding woman, requiring the utmost in attention, in time, and in love. Ted poured his whole body and soul into the effort.

And he needed money for Tom. So they had all been feeling more or less anxious the last time Claire had been here for a meeting. That was the time Claire had asked Mary how she would manage, and Mary had countered by asking Claire the same thing, and Claire had shrugged and said, "I have a few bits and pieces from Mère Constance. I don't want anything but a car and some place to leave my cats when I'm travelling, and a pittance for Jeannot. Hell, I can always sell a bond or a diamond if I get in a jam. Don't worry about me."

Mary looked shocked.

"I know that sounds reckless," Claire said, "but what's the difference?"

That was one of the times when Mary had begun to fret about Claire's vagabond life. "It isn't right," she insisted, shaking her white head. "It isn't natural."

Claire came as near exasperation as she could with Mary, whom she adored.

"What do you want me to do?" she cried irritably. "Marry some pompous ass or another sap like Josh just to get a label pinned on me? Or some old lecher in Europe? Or a kept boy?"

So this year it was not easy to dismiss Claire's latest cat with a laugh. Of course Mary subscribed to the fiction that Flam was a present for her. But the moment she saw him she knew that Claire must have been restless and unhappy and emptily disappointed about something. It was in that mood that Claire always turned to the surest consolation she knew: her cats. Mary often deplored this seeming waste of a rich emotional nature. Having poured her own life into the deep stream of a beloved family she could not understand the skeptical instinct to hold oneself aloof. Once when Mary ventured to say something of that sort Claire said sharply, "I wish you'd leave all that alone. I haven't found people the darlings that you have." And later she murmured, "I know where I stand with my cats all the time." It hurt to hear her say such things.

Mary suspected that Claire's friendship with Jack Thomas—if that was what it was—had gone awry. She had never seen Thomas, and Claire had been uncommunicative about him. But Julka had written Mary about his trip with Claire and their visit to her. Julka hinted hopefully that 'something' might come of this—"something" to the two devoted older women meaning whatever would make Claire happy and get her settled. Marriage, preferably.

But Claire had told Mary abruptly that that was all over. And then, rather surprisingly, she talked about it a little.

"It just wasn't anything," she said. Her voice was dull and discouraged. "Jack is a nice guy. Awfully bright and a good newspaper man. Interested in the things I am. We ought to be a good team, as a matter of fact."

"I take it he is—was—in love with you."

"Oh yes." Claire was doing her nails. She always did them herself, an odd commentary on her years of care at the hands of Constance's skilled maids. She pushed carefully at a cuticle now. "I was probably in the wrong.

I don't know what I expect, Mary, but I can tell you it will have to tear the heart out of me every time I think of a man, or he'll make me sick."

Mary's face was thoughtful. "So that's what it was."

Claire shrugged. "Just as simple as that. We had a lot of fun knocking about together and he really had me quite enthusiastic about the idea of trying to write. In fact I wrote a few human interest articles about Prague and the Czechs, and Jack got his syndicate to buy them. Of course the more he did for me the more of a cheat I felt for leaving him on the short end of the deal."

Mary made no comment.

"He was damned patient, when you think what people are really like. He didn't press me. He was just always there—hopeful. You know. If I'd said I'd marry him hands down he'd have jumped at it. Of course I wasn't going to do that," Claire said with a sour laugh. "Will you tell me," she burst out suddenly, "how the whole so-called genteel world has kept itself going on this nauseating mockery of 'innocent' marriage? How does a woman dare marry if she doesn't even know whether a man suits her sexually?"

"I suppose I ought to be shocked," Mary sighed.

"You? You're an adult woman. Like Julka. And Mère Constance. She tried to show me the ropes, God knows."

"She wasn't choosing her men for their sex appeal," Mary said.

"Why, Mary! You little old cynic, you."

"She seemed to manage very well without making that the prime consideration."

"Oh, everything was different then. Most women didn't want it and the others didn't know they did want it, and when somebody like Mère Constance came along she was clever enough not to get her signals switched. Anyway"—Claire returned abruptly to the subject of Jack Thomas—"he was so damned nice and companionable I thought perhaps he'd turn out all right. So I said we'd try it—and—ugh." She shuddered and reached for a cigarette. Mary sat sewing, without saying anything. Presently Claire said, "It was a mess, that's all. It's pretty damned humiliating to have to let a man know he makes you sick. Especially when you like him and it's a swell idea every place but in bed."

Mary was still silent. There was nothing to say. It seemed a bitter disposition of fate that Claire must fritter away the richest years of her life on experiences like this. Either her standards were impossibly exacting or there must really be some deficiency in her nature. It was not for lack of charm, God knew, or attractiveness, or opportunity that things turned out this way for Claire. Mary looked up finally and said, "Couldn't you have—well—grown to be in love with him? That's what really happens in most cases, after all."

Claire shook her head. "I tell you I tried. I hung on and put on an act and was pretty good at it if I do say so. That was a mistake too. Because I let him feel happy and settled and he was beginning to ask when we'd get married and make plans about where we are going to live—and then I had to tell him. Oh, hell," she said, "let's have a drink."

"You have one."

"I'll make you some tea."

They sat by the fire in Claire's room with the tray between them.

"Look," Claire said, "here we are two old maids drinking tea by the fire with our cat between us on the rug and I ask you—I *ask* you!"

CHAPTER LXXV

[1934—Continued]

THAT SAME EVENING Ben Nicholas was having dinner and spending the night down at Sewickley with Ted and Lauchlan. He accepted their invitation quickly. It was like him to be thorough about everything he did, and to participate in things entirely or not at all. From no interest whatever in his Pittsburgh relatives and in the Scott company, he swung to the opposite extreme of wanting to learn as much about them as he could. Anyone knowing him well would know that he must have some cogent motive for this.

Lauchlan was a superb hostess. She had been born in a tradition of constant, lavish hospitality, in this very house with its innumerable sprawling rooms opening one on the next. When Ted and Ben arrived from town it was late afternoon. The weather was raw and wet, the trees bare and dripping, the lawns littered with sodden brown leaves. But inside there were crackling log fires in every room, masses of cut flowers and blooming plants from the greenhouse, and the luxurious invitation of large, soft couches and armchairs upholstered in leather and English chintzes. Three beautiful springer spaniels lay sleeping by the fire in the largest room.

Lauchlan was finishing up a bridge game with three smart, sleek matrons like herself. They all wore English tweeds and sweaters and smoked incessantly and played excellent bridge, which Ben observed as he stood looking over Lauchlan's shoulder at the final hand, with which she won the rubber. She only glanced up when the two men came in, tipped her head for a sidewise kiss from Ted, and shook hands with Ben over her right shoulder.

The silver teatray was waiting on a lace-covered table by the fire and near it a tray of drinks.

"Help yourselves," Lauchlan said, "I'll be with you in a minute."

Ben poured himself a cup of tea and Ted took a whiskey and soda. They stood by the mantel admiring the dogs while the women finished their game. Lauchlan won forty dollars, for which Mary Prince scribbled a check, saying, "It'll probably bounce, Lauchlan, I've been broke for weeks."

Introductions were made and everybody shook hands. Ben was struck by the peculiar inflections of speech which he had noticed before and which he heard again now as the women chatted over their drinks. Pittsburghers had an odd way of accenting a question: "Are you going in *town* tomorrow?" they said, stressing the penultimate word and letting their voices fade out on the final one. They all did it; the taxi driver at the Penn Station had done it this morning, and now these girls, all products of smart Eastern schools, did the same thing. It had a singsong quality which Ben thought rather Germanic. He knew a man from Lancaster, Pennsylvania, who spoke that way and who was Pennsylvania Dutch. These Pittsburghers were almost all of Scottish extraction, and they all had a Western edge on their speech which mingled oddly with this cadenced mannerism of interrogation.

The girls—they were all married women in their thirties, but girls by definition nonetheless—went home presently, two of them telling Ben they'd see him later at dinner. Lauchlan showed him upstairs to his room. She preceded him up the wide, shallow oak stairway, giving him an interesting view of her slim hips and long, fine legs and trim ankles. Her back was flat and her shanks long and graceful; she was a pleasure to look at from any angle. Ted, Ben observed, seldom took his eyes off her when they were in the room together.

Ben followed Lauchlan down a wide, thickly carpeted centre hall furnished with massive old mahogany, and into a very large, inviting room with another cheerful fire burning, and everything he could possibly want ready at hand. His bags had already been unpacked. Lauchlan told him to ring twice for anything he wanted, and gave a quick, practised glance at night-table, desk, and bureau. She went over to the dressing-table, picked up Ben's comb which had been laid out there, and casually ran it through her sleek dark hair, looking at him in the mirror as she did so. He was startled. She should be gone from the room now in the ordinary course of the moment; it was queer for her to be here still. But she was perfectly unconscious and at ease.

She paused at the door, standing in profile so that Ben was struck by the same impression she so often made—a tall, taut creature heading into a high wind. She seemed always to be on the verge of some action; not a mere gesture to absorb nervous energy, but some planned, integrated motion with a purpose. She smiled and said, "Dinner at eight, but come down about a quarter of for a cocktail, will you?" and shut the door behind her with a thud. Ben stood staring at the polished mahogany door for a minute as if she had left a reflection in it. She was as decisive and sharply etched as a pattern in deeply cut glass. A very hard and wilful and spoiled woman, said Ben to himself, removing his coat, with the power to command whatever she wanted. She wanted a lot, he reflected, though she could not have many material demands unfilled.

This place was certainly the setting for her, one of the very first big places built in Sewickley. She had always had a passionate attachment to it, which pleased her father so much that he willed the house to her, thereby for a time alienating her brother who had expected it by rights. But that had soon worn off. Ted had brought Ben up to date on all this, while driving down from town. Between them Lauchlan and her brother had inherited money enough from their father's holdings in oil, aluminum, coke, and banks so that it mattered very little who got the old house and who built a new one. Lauchlan's mother had moved after Mr. McIntyre's death to the small house he had originally built for Lauchlan when she and Ted were married. There was a kind of dynastic procedure about all this, like the retiring of a widowed noblewoman to a dower house, which seemed oddly out of place in an American city. Ted would have thought it more suitable for Lauchlan to postpone moving into the big house until her mother voluntarily relinquished it or lived out a life tenure in it by Lauchlan's invitation. But Lauchlan had nipped that idea with eight crisp words: "The house is mine, I want it now."

Ben sat on her right at dinner and on his other side was a very pretty woman, the wife of the president of a big refractories company. There were a dozen others at the table, the men all cut from the same decisive pattern. They were hardworking officers of industrial corporations and banks, with well-dressed wives who had known one another all their lives and whose conversation largely excluded anyone who was not, either by birth or long acceptance, one of them. Everybody was cordial to Ben, because they all felt well oriented with him. He was Ted's cousin, and the story of his phenomenal performance in the crash had preceded him here, well dramatized by Lauchlan, who made no secret of her envy. From her restless dark eyes she gave Ben frequent looks freighted with admiration and a certain challenging curiosity which he found exciting. She looked at him as if he must have some special or peculiar power of mind or will or—he came to the conclusion with some surprise—body, which she might find it interesting to explore. From his unimpressive exterior nobody would have suspected his thoughts. He appeared the most retiring and conventional of guests. But even while he was listening to the small talk of blonde Mrs. Stevenson on his right, he was concluding that he had never known a woman to flash so bold and quick a hand so soon as Lauchlan.

He looked down the table at Ted, and then back to her. A very odd business, Ben said to himself, lighting a cigarette for Lauchlan. Ted was desperately in love with her and hopelessly dependent on her. They must have been married fourteen—no, fifteen—years; Ben remembered his mother writing him at school about their wedding just before the war. And Ted sat there hanging on her words, spoken in a hard, drawling, fashionable-school voice, and clinging to her with his eyes as if she were a devastating novelty. There was something almost beseeching in Ted's expression when he looked at his wife. It made Ben uncomfortable. He had a sensation that he was looking through a keyhole at something nobody ought to see. And then when he turned his attention to the other people at the table he realized that whatever it was he knew the others, who had known Lauchlan all her life, knew also. Only Ted had no idea.

The talk was all along one line—the crash and its consequences. It seemed not to matter where they started, they soon got back to the same track. Everybody was either broke or related to someone who had gone broke, or about to wake up and find himself broke. The women were all bewilderedly resentful at the necessity to retrench after having vied with one another in the greatest spending debauch of all time; and the men were soberly shaken by the frightful state of business and industry.

Yet it all sounded empty and twaddling with two menservants and two parlormaids in the room, with excellent champagne, with everybody talking about Rolling Rock, which they assured Ben was the newest, finest, most luxurious, most perfectly appointed hunt club in the country, and didn't he want to come out for the week-end with them, they'd be delighted to arrange it? You went only by invitation, as a guest of the Mellons; and it was exactly like staying in a country house, only no other house was in the class with this. When you left you got one quiet bill for everything, which disposed of the bothersome question of obligation and all that sort of thing. And nobody was there except people you knew and wanted to see—personal friends of the Mellons, really, which was so much better than all the rigmarole of a regular club with the questions of admissions. And of dues, somebody remarked.

Ted, who said very little while everybody else talked, was uncomfortable. He was in no way responsible for Lauchlan's money or for her expenditures. He was used to living as she decreed and since she had not proposed to economize he presumed her fortune had weathered the crash better than those of his redundant dinner guests. He did not take seriously anyway this chatter about going bankrupt, but he was deeply disturbed because it revealed such a shocking abyss of insecurity beneath the smooth luxury of life as they all lived it. The state of mind of these people set him thinking. These men were all high-salaried officers of great companies which had continued to pay their salaries, with a cut here and there, long after hundreds of thousands of laboring men had been dumped out to beg, sell apples, or starve.

For a long time Ted had felt nightmarish about this. After all, the Scott mill had been no more immune to the universal paralysis than any other. It had been running on skeleton staffs at an absolute minimum of production. When Ted went there from the downtown office he had to drive through the river-level streets where the men lived, and where he had to see them, clustered in silent groups on the squalid street corners, bitter, derelict, and desperate. The same thing had been going on, terrifyingly multiplied, in the black company towns and back streets and courts and tenements of Homestead, Braddock, Munhall, the coal towns; upriver, downriver; in fact in every industrial district in the United States. But right here they had as thorough a cross-section of the catastrophe as there was to be seen. The only way you could live at all, Ted had been telling himself for a long time, was to shut your mind utterly to the human aspect of the thing, and concentrate on trying to get what business you could. But there was no streak of Bourbon or Habsburg mentality in Ted. A dozen and more years in Lauchlan's orbit had not altered the fact that he was a Scott. In the fourth generation of a living, self-regenerating thing like that mill, you could not, even if you wanted, shrug off its troubles and enjoy your filet mignons and champagne while men you had known all your life, and their wives and pallid children, grew grayer and thinner and steadily more desperate on hopelessness and idleness and charity soup.

A fortnight later, Ted dropped in at the old house one evening, clearly with something on his mind. Mary and Claire had finished their dinner which they ate on a small table by the fire in the back parlor. Claire had never had occasion to cook, and had never really learned to do it, but she had a natural gift for it. When they were alone like this she loved to fuss in the kitchen. Mrs. Tschuda, who came to clean every day, was supposed to stay and cook dinner in the evening if anybody was at the house with Mary, but Claire often sent her home and cooked dinner herself. She had made a *poulet en casserole* with vegetables, artfully seasoned to tempt Mary's frail appetite, and a *zabaione* for dessert—another light and nourishing delicacy which she insisted Mary eat.

Afterwards they were sitting by the fire, Claire with a thermos pot of Italian coffee and plenty of cigarettes, when Ted appeared. He took a cup of coffee and lighted a cigar. They chatted about things for a while. Mary often looked at Ted searchingly as if to find beneath his marked physical resemblance to Paul some traits of character to bear out the striking surface similarity. There were few. Ted was good; loyal and kindly and completely reliable—and, on the other hand, soft. Mary knew that any major decision was torture for him. He had always been that way. From her earliest memories of the twins, it had been Tommy in the lead, Teddy in the rear. Even now Tom could write to Ted (he dictated everything except his faltering signature) expressing a decision or a wish without regard to its feasibility, and Ted would fall in with it at once. He did this not so much from the wish that Tom should have whatever he wanted as from liking to carry out a flat decision made by somebody he loved. Long ago Dick had shrewdly divined to Ruth that the basis of Lauchlan's hold over Ted was her similarity in temperament and will to Tom.

So it was startling when Ted, looking so like his father there in the old brown leather armchair, said, "Mary, how would you feel about selling this house?"

Claire gasped, but Mary, who was just as shocked, only looked up from her sewing and said mildly, "Why, have you had an offer?"

Ted did not answer immediately. He said finally, "There seems to be a real-estate syndicate interested in the property. Of course it has no residential value any more and—" he paused awkwardly.

"They would tear it down, I suppose."

"I suppose."

Claire moved abruptly in her chair.

"Doesn't Uncle Paul's will say Mary is to have life tenure here?"

"Of course—unless she voluntarily recommends to Tom and me that we sell it. If we do she gets twenty per cent of the proceeds."

"I wouldn't care about that, Ted."

"I know you wouldn't. You'd have it, though—in times like these you oughtn't to overlook such matters."

"My wants are simple. If I didn't live here I'd only want a room or two somewhere—"

"You'd live with me!" Claire exclaimed quickly. "Room or two my eye!"

Mary smiled. "I'm too old to transplant, dear. I really wouldn't fit in Europe." She was silent.

Ted looked uncomfortable. Both Mary and Claire saw that he was broaching this question as the emissary for somebody else. Tom, most probably, and others whom it still remained to reveal. Ted might worry about the cost of keeping up the house and paying the taxes, but he himself would never have instigated something so radical as a plan to sell it. Mary looked at him hard for a moment and said, "My feeling is chiefly a matter of wanting to know all about it. I tell you frankly, Ted, the way I feel about the place I'd only be willing to sell it if I knew exactly what was to become of it. I wouldn't think of letting it turn into a disgrace and heartache like the Cottrells' or the Dixons' or any of the old places." Her voice trembled a little. "I'd rather—well . . ."

"Oh, no," Ted said quickly. "No—I didn't mean anything like that."

Claire eyed him sharply. She saw that he was avoiding a good deal of plain fact about this proposition. She even suspected that he did not know the whole story himself. In any case he was uncomfortable about it.

"Then why don't you tell me exactly who this real-estate syndicate is and what they would do with the place if they bought it? Put up stores? Apartments? What?"

"Well—" Ted spoke tentatively. "To tell you the truth I don't precisely know. I—"

"Do you know anybody in this syndicate? Who made you the offer?"

"Oh—a fellow who came into the office and seemed to know a lot about the Northside. You know, he was just sort of feeling us out on the idea."

Mary studied Ted's broad face. He was forty-four years old, she realized suddenly. It seemed a ridiculous idea. He did not have the personality or the qualities of mind or will or character that a Scott man should have at such an age. Mary thought of Paul at that time of life—just at the turn of the century, after he had put the mill through the historical feat of arming the Navy for the Spanish War, just before he had—with her help, he would remind her if he were here—defeated William's effort to sell out to the Steel Corporation. She shook her head at her thoughts and Ted leaned forward and said, "Does that mean you wouldn't consider it, Mary?"

"Goodness no!" She smiled. "I was shaking my head about something altogether different. Old people do queer things, you know."

Claire made a noise which could have been interpreted as an observation that queerness was not confined to old people. She reached down and lifted Flam into her lap and made her remarks into his whiskers.

Ted was getting ready to leave.

"There's no hurry about this, Mary," he said easily. "Think it over and—"

"Have you written to ask Tom what he thinks?"

Ted hesitated. "Well—yes."

"I mean," Mary said, "have you and Tom agreed that you both really want to sell the house to get rid of the expenses?"

"More or less."

"Because if that's true and you honestly can't afford to keep it up without cramping yourselves I don't want to stand in your way."

"It's not as bad as that—yet."

"I won't stand in your way unreasonably, Ted. I just feel—"

"I understand."

"Well, you tell me whatever you can find out about the people behind this and then we'll talk it all over."

Ted kissed them both good night and got into his Packard coupé at the side door. He drove this car himself; Lauchlan always had the limousine. Mary and Claire stood watching him drive away. Then as she shut and locked the door, Claire said, "Mary, why do I smell a rat in this?"

"Do you?" Mary asked innocently.

"And so do you," Claire replied.

Actually it had not originally occurred to Ted to sell the house. The idea had evolved from a talk he had had with Ben Nicholas a week ago. There was no question that Ted was feeling badly pinched for money in every quarter which had no relation to Lauchlan. Tom's expenses in Texas were never negligible and at times they became quite heavy. He lived in a cottage he had built on a tract of the ranch where he had worked before the war. He was a hopeless and difficult invalid. The spine injury which Constance had never truthfully described until after Paul's death had left Tom with one side paralyzed. The head burns had almost entirely destroyed his sight. He required constant attendance, but could not endure to be made aware of his helplessness. Consequently his existence was a complicated routine of keeping him cared for without the obvious presence of nurses, companions, or anybody paid to be near him. As the years went by Tom became so nervously unbalanced on this question of his care that Ted, keeping the closest, most devoted watch over him in spite of the great distance, was put to all sorts of elaborate and expensive subterfuges to find people who were acceptable to Tom. Tom never knew anything about his property or his finances. Ted took entire charge of that. Up until the panic of 1929 there had been ample money for Tom from his own property, but thereafter the income had declined steadily, while Tom's expenses increased. Ted had resorted during the past two years to making up Tom's deficits from his own pocket. With considerable surprise Ted had realized not long ago that this could not continue indefinitely. If he could not hope soon for some restoration of income he would have to make some curtailment of outgo.

He had been rather diffident when he decided to talk to Ben Nicholas about his dilemma, but he had such awestruck regard for Ben's financial wizardry that it seemed the best advice to seek. Ben listened carefully and looked very thoroughly at the books and accounts in Ted's office. Then he pointed out as the first thing to be eliminated, the obvious wastefulness of maintaining the Western Avenue house for a solitary old woman.

"That's preposterous," he had said tersely. "You should sell the place quickly, for whatever it will bring. Especially if it's true that the neighborhood is going down so fast."

Ted pointed out the personal and sentimental considerations involved. He had an uncomfortable feeling of guilt, almost as if his father were sitting across the desk silently rebuking him. But Ben had waved that aside. You could not allow sentiment to interfere with your business judgment. Houses were houses and money was money; as soon as you thought of them in terms of their hold over your emotions you were licked.

Ben had not penetrated far into the history and finances of the Scott family, linked at every turn to the fortunes of the mill itself, before he became keenly interested. His interest was all objective and very inviting as a field for the exercise of new ideas and modern financial techniques. The mill had not had the benefit of anything like that for a great many years. In a way it had never had it. Ben found himself agreeably excited and challenged by the realization that he already had one foot rightfully established in this field. The other itched to follow. Already his mind was beginning to stir over the provocative notion that it might not be necessary for this mill to accede supinely to the present benumbed state of American business. Maybe there was business—somewhere. Maybe the mill could produce on some basis other than the old one, which held it at the mercy of the main business cycle. Ben was already very thoughtful about all this when he advised Ted to dispose of the old house.

Characteristically, Ted listened to Ben and said he would think it over and then did nothing particular about it. And characteristically Ben, who had only been in Pittsburgh half a dozen times in his life, immediately set about the business of spading up a buyer for the house. He always went about such things quietly. And particularly in a case like this, where the commodity in question was specialized, something nobody would want except for highly individual and private reasons. Nobody in the open real-estate market would want that queer old place on the Northside enough to pay real money for it.

CHAPTER LXXVI

[*1934*]

A COUPLE OF WEEKS passed without their hearing anything more from Ted about the offer for the house. Claire knew that Mary was in a state of constant inward suspense, and that she avoided discussing the question because it hurt her even to think about it. It seemed too much to hope that the whole thing had fallen through. Claire did hope, but in her own mind she knew better. Mary was spending a good deal of time at her desk .over her accounts. She was clearly trying to find new ways to economize and cut corners in the upkeep of the house. She might even be trying to assure Ted that she would carry the expenses all by herself. That would be impossible with business in its present condition.

Claire said one morning that she was going over to the Cadillac place to leave her car. It needed a lot of work done on it. Mary looked up from her desk and asked, "Why don't you let Jerry Liska fix your car for you?"

"Jerry? How come?"

"Well, he's a wonderful mechanic. He can do anything with an engine. And he's terribly hard up. He only has three or four days' work a week at the mill and I don't know how they live on that. With three children and all the debts they've piled up these last years."

Claire opened her eyes wide. She said slowly. "Do you mean Jerry and Bella and those kids live on—what—eighteen or twenty dollars a week?"

"Plus any work he can get by the day," Mary said sadly. "He'd rather starve than go on relief."

"*Relief*! Jerry Liska on relief! It makes me boil!" Claire cried. "I could blow the whole goddam system to hell if that's what it's doing to people like Jerry."

"Oh, now, don't go talking like a parlor socialist. You don't mean it. But it would be good to give this work to Jerry."

They sent word to him and he came around that evening. Claire had not seen him for over two years. He was looking much older: very gaunt and dark with a stern, bitter look on his thin face. His black hair was sprinkled at the temples with gray. That startled Claire. She calculated quickly that Jerry was only a couple of years older than she. And he looked over forty. He entered the house awkwardly at the side door. There had always been constraint in Jerry's contacts with the Scott house. In the old days when Claire used to go down with Mary to eat supper at Julka's Jerry had been cheerful and sure of himself and, though always of a serious turn of mind, full of the same warmth that ran through all the Liskas. There was none of that in sight now. He stood uncomfortably, holding his cap. Claire took it and hung it on the hatrack and walked him into the back parlor. He smiled wanly at Mary. His clothes were a sight.

The natural instinct was to ask Jerry how things were, how Bella and the children were, what was new. But they knew the answers to those questions without asking for them. Things were terrible with Jerry. It hung about him like a veil. Claire had deliberately neglected to clear away the remains of supper from the fireside table. She looked at it now, pretending to fuss about it, and poured herself another cup of coffee. She poured one at the same time for Jerry, which she filled up with cream and three lumps of sugar, and handed it to him without comment while she talked about his mother. Without seeming to be doing so she and Mary got two pieces of apple pie and three cups of coffee into Jerry. Then Claire asked him to help her carry the dishes out to the pantry. He was much more at ease now and sat by the fire for a while, smoking cigarettes from the leather box by his chair.

Gradually they began to recapture the easy congeniality of the old days. Jerry was deep in relief at the momentary respite from his troubles. The warmth and quiet and simple comfort of this old room loomed tremendous in Claire's mind as she contrasted it with the probable condition of Jerry's home now. And there was so much to talk about. Jerry was interested in his mother's work. From that they got onto conditions elsewhere in Europe. The Nazi party was in brutal control now in Germany. The Jewish persecutions were fiendish, as Claire's friend had said they would be. She had seen this herself.

"It's completely unbelievable," she said. "It gives you the blue creeps."

"Plenty here gives me the same thing," Jerry said. "I will say it's different now. At least the government knows there's been a hell of a mess. Before, we were all supposed to ignore it."

"This head in the sand business," Claire said. "It's the same everywhere."

Jerry stood up.

"We'd better get to your car," he said. "That's what I came for."

They went out to the old stable, now the garage, and Claire switched on the lights. She began telling Jerry some of the things wrong with the car. Then she said, "There's no use talking, you can see it all for yourself, driving it. Wait till I get a coat."

She ran in and put on a fur coat and the small hat which matched it while Jerry backed the car out and brought it to the side door. Claire got in beside him and said, "You really ought to give it a workout. If you take it up some stiff hill you'll see what's the matter. That gas in Europe is full of garbage and it ruins the carburetor."

"I guess Aliquippa Street's the stiffest hill there is," Jerry said, "but it's over across the river."

"What's the difference?"

Crossing the bridge Claire remarked about the depressing sight of the waterfronts at times like this. An occasional mill had a furnace in blow, some specialty furnace which could not be allowed to go dead, but largely the banks of the river looked, she said, "Like the Styx. It's so awful. Do you remember how it's supposed to look, Jerry?"

He laughed bitterly. "Remember! Do I remember what it's like to have the rent paid up and the kids full of milk and oranges?"

"Aren't things any better?"

"Well," he said, "I guess they will be. Only not before we've raised an awful lotta hell."

"You mean labor? Strikes?"

"Sure. We're gonna get organized this time. And stay organized."

"Don't you belong to the Amalgamated in the mill, Jerry?"

He made a rasping noise with his tongue. "Phooey," he said. "I said a real union, not a doddering old bunch of—say, they never had a real union, Claire. If you're interested you ought to learn something while you're around here."

"I am," she said. "It seems incredible—that the Amalgamated never could organize the steel industry."

"Aw, you've heard all that stuff about Mary's brother. That's the dark ages. Nobody ever had a real union in steel. And the men are nearly as much to blame as the companies. The Amalgamated's just a joke. They used to buy 'em off with fat jobs in politics. Gee," he said, doubling his hard fists, "I wish I'd been around in 1919."

"Can you picture Ted Scott around our mill in that strike?"

"He wasn't," Jerry said succinctly. "He was in Indo-China on his belated honeymoon with that slab-shanked houri of his. Ted Scott in a strike?—don't make me laugh."

They put their attention on the car as Jerry started up the steep incline of Aliquippa Street. The motor knocked hard and they sat forward, listening to it, as they wound their way up, past the University buildings and on to the crest of the hill. At the very top there was an embankment close to which Jerry stopped the car, with its nose facing forward toward the view. A street lamp shone into the car from overhead. It was a cloudy, sullen November night, and except for the lights in the buildings below, and the tall, dark tower of the laughable skyscraper University below them, they missed much of the panorama that this magnificent vantage point should reveal.

"This goddam depression," Claire mourned, in a voice like a pettish child. "This place ought to be blazing like a thousand little hells. That's the way I like to see it."

"You—disappointed in the view!" Jerry muttered.

Claire turned to him quickly. "I—I'm sorry," she breathed. "That must have sounded—lousy to you. With all your—your—"

"Aw, forget it. I'm touchy. You get awful raw after a turn like we've had."

"How is Bella, Jerry?"

"Ah, it's a hell of a thing. You can't ask a girl to take four years of tough times and not go sour sometimes. We were doing okay there when we got married and for a stretch afterwards. I don't ever expect to be in the money—but a feller counts on having a house and things—you know."

"I know."

"We haven't had enough money to feed all five of us all at once since 1930," he said. "I don't care for myself. Bella'd be okay too if it wasn't for the kids. She used to work in Kaufmann's. She'd rather have a job than anything. But that's out on account of the kids. She couldn't find one anyway now, probably. So she gets it on the chin."

Claire studied his dark, frowning face. He was staring out through the windshield. He had deepset, strong brown eyes, direct eyes trained to examine and weigh and judge without dissembling anything. He was used to machines. Claire said softly, "You're awfully fair about her, Jerry. I guess the truth is—she's pretty mean-tempered with you, isn't she?"

He nodded stiffly, still staring through the windshield.

"But I don't blame her," he said stubbornly. "Poor kid. She can't help crabbing me—when she hasn't had a new dress or a pair of shoes or a night out since—"

Claire felt now as if they were children again, talking around the Liskas' supper table. She felt close to Jerry. Her love for his mother came over her in a wave. He was like Julka, he had the same deep wells of tenacity and fortitude, the same earthbound quality which had always drawn her toward these people. They were like good black bread, like the bread she used to steal as a little girl from the servants' table because she preferred it to the delicate white rolls served Mère Constance. Jerry was breathing loudly through his nose. Claire knew he had said more than he meant to say. She had glimpsed his sore heart.

She put her hand on his arm. The cloth of his coat felt thin and shoddy and full of grit. Under it she could feel the hard hairy flesh tight against the strong bone. He turned his head slowly and looked at her. His eyes were dark slits staring into hers. Her pupils were dilated, the hazel irises sickles of light. Her lips parted. Jerry's jaw rippled as his teeth locked. Claire sat in suspense, holding the moment open between them, knowing as he knew what must come. His face was gray in the cold arclight. He was putting up a struggle inside. He opened his mouth slowly and started to shake his head, but Claire said, "Kiss me, Jerry."

"I—don't want to. I mean—if I do—"

"I know."

He laid his hands on her shoulders. She stared at him. It seemed like a very long time that they waited, sitting there waiting almost as if for a signal to strike. Claire felt the moments coursing through the arteries in her wrists, the heavy numbness of her fingers as she touched him. She bent her head slowly back against the cushion.

"I want you to kiss me. I want you."

His hands slid down the shoulders and front of her fur coat and roughly shoved it open. His arms around her were hard. His mouth driving down on hers was hard; his strong teeth, his lips, his tongue. There was a hard smell about him. There with her ears ringing, with the cold core inside her belly bursting into sparks, with the sound of her own gasping breaths filling her ears, she could notice the hard smell: not dirt, not sweat. Her spine arched beneath his hands; her arms were numb around him.

"Where can we go?" he said hoarsely into her mouth. "Where can we go?"

Claire crossed her room in the dark, dropping her clothes about her, and flung herself naked on her bed, burying her face in the warm musky bundle of Flam curled against the pillows. She was heavy, saturated, drenched with the torrents of satisfied passion. Lying there, with Flam's sensuous rumbling against her throat, she flexed her strong fingers slowly, as if to keep in them the tactile ecstasy roused and re-roused these past climactic hours. She sighed aloud, slowly and long. It was as if a great light had been kindled inside her, she whispered to herself. She could feel it now in every cavity in her body. She could feel its warmth in the outermost surface of her skin. It was too miraculous to believe yet. Believing was thinking, and she was not yet ready to think. She did not want to;

she wanted only to feel. In all her life she had never known such magnificent exaltation of body.

"Jerry Liska," her lips murmured against the back of her tingling hand. "To go through all those years of hell and find the answer here—" She rolled over on her back and stared at the window. The pale late winter dawn was beginning to streak the sky. It crept up past a cluster of lifeless stacks in the distance. "Jerry," she sighed half aloud. "Jerry." She was heavily drowsy but reluctant to fall asleep and miss the reminiscent swellings and surges of ecstasy which swept her. "Jerry." She flung one hand across her eyes as if to hold in the memory of his thin dark face burning with amazed and voracious discovery.

Mary was out when she came downstairs late in the morning. Mrs Tschuda was cleaning the kitchen and had left a tray with a thermos pot of coffee in the back parlor. Claire drank her coffee standing up. She could not sit down. Her feet felt elastic, her legs taut and springy. She was full of energetic purpose and vibrating with excitement. Plan after plan had swept through her mind while she bathed and dressed; one had this advantage, another that. She had not made up her mind. But she would when she talked to Jerry.

"Tell Miss Rafferty I'll be back this afternoon," she called down the pantry stairs to Mrs. Tschuda, and ran up to her room to put on her street clothes.

The sun was bright when she stepped out the door. She lifted her head and sniffed the air hungrily. No rich coal dust, no prosperous-looking banks of smoke, but the cool sunshine was welcome nontheless. She started briskly down the walk. The car was not in the old stable. Jerry had it. She felt a hot surge of reminiscent excitement at the thought. He had it in an empty detached garage which belonged to one of the mill foremen who had long since lost his car through unpaid installments. The man had a work bench and tools and Jerry had arranged to use the place as a shop while he worked on Claire's car. That was where they had driven last night. Claire's face turned scarlet at the crude thought. A garage, a derelict garage. Jerry was there now. He was not due at the mill again until the day after tomorrow.

She thought furiously as she walked toward Ridge Avenue. She could pick up a taxi near the Bridge. There was so much to think about that she had to hold her whirling mind in check. The one thing she was sure of was that they must have some place of their own . . . some place to go. She was going to find such a place today. She was so full of excited plans that, in spite of her impatience, the taxi drew up at the garage door in the alley before she expected it to. She paid the driver in a daze, leaving half a dollar in change with him, and was astonished to find that her feet, so quick and restless all morning, lagged involuntarily as she crossed the pavement. She could hear him working inside. The sliding galvanized door was a few inches open. Claire caught her breath as she put her gloved hand on it and started to open it further; wide enough to see him; wide enough to go inside to him.

"Jerry." Her voice stuck queerly in her throat.

He was under the car, lying on his back with his head out of sight, his overalled legs sprawled toward her.

He grunted something unintelligible. Claire felt suddenly embarrassed. One moment she wanted to fling herself down on the greasy concrete beside him, crawl under there and find his face and quickly, quickly rekindle the blaze dormant in his thin lips. The next moment, standing awkwardly beside the empty car with the man hammering at something underneath, she almost shrank at the thought of what she had done. But the first impulse overrode the second. She crouched down beside him and peered under the car.

"Hello—darling." She spoke in a loud whisper.

" 'Lo, Claire." He went on hammering. She squatted there so long that her bent legs began to tremble and ache. He seemed in no hurry to come out. Finally she said, "Will you be long under there?"

"Quite a while."

"Well." She rose took off her gloves, and lit a cigarette. "I—well, I'll be glad to see you when you come out." There was a catch in her voice. He heard it and drowned it out—inadvertently, she wondered?—with a round of curses at a stubborn bolt.

There was silence, punctuated only by Jerry's poundings and curses. Claire could count her own thudding pulse. She smoked nervously, staring at Jerry's feet in their cracked workshoes, twisting this way and that as he balanced himself now on his shoulders, now on his hipbones. At last he wriggled out, shoving the big oil pan ahead of him. His hands were dripping thick black oil. There were smudges of it on his face. His head was covered by a greasy mechanic's cap. Claire caught her breath at the sight. Could this be? Could this have happened? But his eyes meeting hers answered her bewildered questions. It was so. The merest flash from those narrow dark eyes kindled her blood and set her nerves tingling. She ached to touch him. Her fingers stretched toward him. He did not or would not notice. He walked over to the bench under the caged droplight, and immediately became absorbed in looking for a special wrench. Claire felt idiotic standing there staring at him. Wasn't he going to say anything? Wasn't he going to look at her—grin—say something?

"Jerry—"

"What?"

"I—I—haven't you anything—to say?"

He looked up then and his eyes were hard. "What's there to say?"

Her brows puckered. She did not think she had heard right. "Why—" She swallowed. This was horrible. This was unbelievable. This was not what this morning was supposed to yield up. He was putting her in a sickening position. He stood there, still staring, rather truculent; impatient to be let alone with his work. Claire sat down suddenly on the running board and fumbled for her handkerchief.

"Oh, Jerry."

There was a loud bang as she realized he had flung the wrench on the workbench. She looked up and saw him standing near her, legs apart, hands hanging at his sides. He was scowling and making no attempt to mitigate the shock she now saw he was deliberately giving her.

"Look," he said. "Let's get this straight, Claire. I—well, I want you to get it straight. We wanted it and we had it and that's that, see?"

She felt her breath going out of her in a wheeze. Her chin was shaking and she knew she would crumple up and make a fool of herself unless she was very careful now. She said dully, "I see."

He was looking rather unnerved himself. He tried to soften the blow by talking a little, clumsily.

"We've got to get it straight," he repeated. "One thing about you. You don't kid yourself. You didn't kid yourself about last night. You got what you wanted. You've got to take what goes with it." He licked his lips.

"I thought—" she began weakly.

"No you didn't," he snapped. "You didn't think I was going to start something with you. Maybe I'd like to—but I'm not going to."

"I—I—nobody would know."

"My God," he exploded, "that's not the idea. *I'd* know. You'd know. That's enough for me. I'm not cut out for that. Maybe you are where you come from, all those rich bums sleeping around, but I'm not going to. It don't add up. I'm not kidding myself about last night. I wanted it. I knew I had no business with you but—"

"*Why* didn't you have any business with me?" Claire cried. "I started it. I was honest enough for that. I wanted you. I still do—" she looked at him desperately. "Terribly. I want you with every nerve in my body. I'm not ashamed to say it."

"You oughta be," he mumbled. He looked nervously at the work-bench and then at her again. "It's out, see. Once for all. I don't want to be tough but I'll have to be if you push me. Look, Claire. Life is a hell of a pain in the neck already and this kinda thing will only make it worse. You've got your own world, I've got mine. Mine stinks, but—"

"What do you think mine does?" she cried harshly.

"Well, maybe it stinks too. But it's where you belong and you've got to stay there. Anyway you can't come over into mine. You stay out." He shut his hard mouth.

She began to cry. She did not want to. She fought it. She did not want him to think she would descend to that. But she cried brokenly and said, "Can't you try to understand? Can't you see what's the trouble? All these years groping, feeling my way, all alone in the mess. I don't *like* that, can't you understand? Did you think I wanted—just—a—a—"

"A piece of tail?" he supplied brutally. She shuddered. Then she stopped crying and drew herself up and said, "If I can't find a way to really live, among real people, I'm going to kill myself. I can't stand this any longer. Why does everybody else find a way to be alive?"

He stood there and shook his head and looked at her with awkward compassion.

"Jesus, I'm sorry," he said softly. He leaned over her. "But this wouldn't be the answer, can't you see that? You might be awful crazy about

me and me about you, but you can't change what we are. It would be
phony as hell, Claire. We'd go on for a while having a lot of excitement
but pretty soon I'd start eating myself about Bella and the kids and you'd
start wondering how in Christ you ever got mixed up with a millhand—
aw, you can see for yourself, you're no dope."

She sighed brokenly and did not speak.

"Can't you, Claire? Can't you see?"

"I suppose so." He had to lean over to hear her. But she jumped up
suddenly and began to beat her hands together.

"But what about me?" she cried wildly. "What's supposed to become
of me? You've got Bella, even with all the worry. Everybody has somebody—only what's to become of *me?* I can't bear it," she moaned, twisting
her body as if in pain. "I can't bear it. I wouldn't mind if I was in Bella's
place," she cried. "I'd rather be broke and dirty and hungry and sick and
all she is and worse—if it was only real—*real*—" She paused and gasped
to bring her breathing under control. "Do you know what I'm talking
about?"

"I know."

"So what do I do? I tell you I want you. I want the way I feel about
you." She put her hands on her body, one on her breast and the other
on her belly. "I want to feel like this," she said thickly. "I've never felt
it before. I need it. Oh God, how I need it."

"Somebody—" he began lamely.

"Stop!" she cried. "Don't say it. 'Somebody will come along.' I know,
I've heard it all my life. Nobody will. Nobody will ever come now—after
I've found out what it's like to be real. Oh Jerry—" she put out her hand
toward him. He seemed not to see it. He was staring over her head at the
scarred wall, his dark eyes brooding.

"You just see something in me on account of you're all upset," he said
slowly. "I'm just a slob. Can't even—"

"No," Claire said in a low tone. "It's not that. It's got something to
do with the way I feel about your mother. Because she's real. She's been
real all her life. The only kind of person that's got a right to live. You're
her kind. I want to be, Jerry." She looked up pleadingly. "I want to be
that kind too."

She began to weep again, wearily. He made a gesture toward her with
his blackened hand and said lamely, "You're real, Claire. My God—you
are."

"Only if I get help. You could make me real. This way I'm a ghost—
outside in the nowhere—looking in—" she sobbed bitterly. He still stood
dumbly, staring at her with pity and a kind of fear.

"I wish I knew," she said after a long time, "what to do. I can't think
of a goddam thing in the world to do except kill myself."

"If you do that," Jerry said in a queer flat way, "you *will* be a punk."

"And this way I suppose I'm a going concern!" Her voice rose hys-
terically. "What about this?" She struck her breast with her clenched fists.
"What am I going to do about this? Empty, I tell you. Empty. It hurts—"

He reached down and pulled her roughly from the running board and held her hard against him, dirty and greasy as he was. He pushed her hair from her forehead and stared at her for a minute.

"For Christ's sake," he said softly, "be yourself. You're big enough to take this."

"This?" she whispered.

"I can't talk any more. I don't want to say good-bye. Give my love to Mama when you see her. Your car—"

"Don't."

"I've got to. I'll bring your car around and leave it day after tomorrow. Give my love to Mama," he said again, dropping his hands and turning away. Claire stood staring at him.

"If you got to talk to somebody, talk to Mama," he said, going toward the door. "She'll understand."

"But—she can't do anything," Claire whispered with stiff lips.

"Go and see her soon anyway." She heard the flimsy door rasp behind him and his quick steps beating down the street.

CHAPTER LXXVII

[*1934—Continued*]

IT WAS DUSK when she dragged her feet slowly up the walk. She opened the side door and moved quietly inside. She did not want to be confronted by Mary. She heard voices in the back parlor. That was good; some friend must be there having a cup of tea. She could get to her room unnoticed. She was so tired that the backs of her legs pained and throbbed as she put one foot slowly before the other climbing the stairs, pulling herself up by the banister.

She had been walking all day. She had no idea where. She had a jumbled memory now of the big, noisy Point Bridge with traffic roaring and crashing around her. Already she saw that a melodramatic instinct had taken her there on foot, where some truck might run her down. Or maybe—no, she had not intended to jump off. She was too good a swimmer to have any such fool idea as that.

She knew very well that she would never do anything of that kind. Either she didn't have the guts, she told herself, or she was too literal-minded. She was not having a broken heart now, either. That was one thing she had admitted, tramping hours later up the ugly miles of Bigelow Boulevard, with the traffic roaring past her and the magnificent expanses of jagged hillside hidden behind billboards braying about Teaberry Gum, Iron City Beer, Rieck's Ice Cream. No, she did not have a broken heart. She was quite straight about that. You had to be in love to have your heart broken. She wanted to be in love. She could have been wildly in love with Jerry. But he had smacked her down. Right now she could see that he was being the tough, decent, brutally honest man she wanted by acting that way. I could settle for that, she had been telling herself wretchedly all day, if it hadn't been so wonderful. Once for all she had found the man who could—she remembered saying the words to Mary—tear the heart out of her. And now what? *What?* she had been groaning to herself all day long. She was so exhausted that she flopped across her bed throbbing with weariness but still it travelled round and round inside her head. That damned eternal *what?*

Her head kept on buzzing but presently she heard Mary calling her from the foot of the stairs. She dragged herself off the bed and went out and leaned over the banister.

"Will you come down here a moment, Claire? There's someone I—"

Claire nodded dully, hesitated about going back to her room to try to make herself presentable, and decided against it. She knew she looked like the wrath of God. It would take too long to do anything about it. She was too tired. She went slowly downstairs. Mary was standing at the foot of the stairs waiting for her. She looked up, her eyes sharp behind her spectacles, and said in a muffled voice, "There's a—a person here in the parlor. I think—I'd rather you knew about this."

"What, Mary?" Claire whispered because Mary had.

"It's—" Mary's pale lips trembled a little—"about the house."

Claire turned suddenly attentive. "What's up? Have the boys—?"

Mary shook her head. "No. This is the man who—whom—well, I'd rather he told you himself." She led the way into the back parlor. A man sat on a straight chair by the fireplace, stiffly, with his hands planted on his knees and a curious inquiring expression on his face. He looked very ordinary, like a salesman or a gas-meter reader, Claire thought. He was middle-aged and commonplace. He got to his feet as the two women entered the room. His movements were awkward and self-conscious.

"This is my—niece—Mrs. Wood," Mary said in a small dry voice. "Mr. Hinchman."

"How do," said Mr. Hinchman. Claire stared. He did not look like anybody with whom one would exchange amenities. She felt this, not from snobbish motives, but from the completely mechanical impression of the man's personality. He was the sort of man, one felt, who knew nobody except as a client or a customer. Mary answered the silent question in Claire's face by saying quietly, "Mr. Hinchman is the party who made the offer for the house."

"I see," Claire said, lighting a cigarette. She motioned Mr. Hinchman permission to do the same if he chose. He did. Claire sat down slowly on the edge of one of the leather armchairs and Mary took her usual chair by the fireside table.

"Mr. Hinchman wanted—was interested—in the house for his business," Mary said in the same small dry voice. It was not like her so pointedly to color her meaning by inflections. She was conveying a great many questions to Claire, the answers to which lay in Mr. Hinchman. So Claire asked matter-of-factly, "What is your business, Mr. Hinchman? What had you planned to do with the house?"

She looked at Mary as she asked that and was surprised to see a wave of troubled color rise up the delicate wrinkled throat and suffuse the pale old face. She could not see Mary's eyes; the light was shining into her spectacle lenses. Mr. Hinchman cleared his throat and said, "Well . . ." He looked uneasily at Mary. "Miss Rafferty here seems to know all about it." He blew his nose. "I sure would like to know how you found out," he said suddenly, turning to Mary.

Claire looked at her too. Mary's lips were pinched and her face reflected a combination of disdain and disgust. Also there was an imperious set to her small head. The white hair made a soft cloud around her forehead.

"What did you find out, Mary?" Claire asked softly.

"I'd rather Mr. Hinchman told you."

He shrugged. These were two of the strangest women he had ever encountered. The old one ought to be doddering, from her frail looks, and instead of that, the only time he had ever clapped eyes on her was yesterday when she had appeared in his office on Diamond Street and calmly informed him what she had already discovered about his business and his plans for the house if he bought it. In his dingy one-room office with "C. T. Hinchman, Realtor" painted on the door, she had looked like an apparition. He had gaped at her and listened while she, rather than he, did the small amount of talking that was done. She had said she wished he would come to the house next day and explain the matter to her niece.

"Well, why?" Mr. Hinchman had asked. He had no wish to go to the house. If these people wouldn't sell, they wouldn't sell. Somebody else would.

"I think she should know all about this," Mary had said. "She is one of the owners of the house," she had lied calmly. She wanted to put all the details of the matter directly in Claire's hands. She wanted Claire to know how she might expect things to be done in the future—perhaps after Mary was no longer there.

"Well," Mr. Hinchman said now, sitting with his two baffling interrogators in the back parlor, "Miss Rafferty mightn't want me to explain all the details. My business is kind of peculiar, see. I buy quite a few houses in the towns where I operate."

"Oh," Claire said. She narrowed her eyes. "A chain, is that it?"

"Yeah." He lit another cigarette. "Detroit. St. Louis. Cleveland. I kinda thought I'd open a branch in Pittsburgh. This is a pretty good town for the business," he said reflectively.

Claire looked at Mary and almost shrank from the cold, contemptuous comprehension in her face.

"You mean—" Claire said.

Hinchman moved heavily. He said, "We might's well get it over with." Obviously he resented the position in which he found himself, but the old lady had actually shamed him into coming here and going through with this. "You got to understand a little about the business in Pittsburgh," he said, in a queerly apologetic way. "Every town is different. Some places you pay protection regular, some you rent, some you buy. Here you move."

Claire was staring, utterly fascinated. "What do you mean, move?" she asked softly.

"Well, they leave you alone in one address for a certain len'th of time —of course you're paying 'em while you're there—and then some women's club or election time or sometimes just a scared ward boss stirs up the cops—and then you move. Just to another house, it ain't so bad," he said casually. "So I thought I'd kinda combine stones or birds or whatever you kill twice. If I bought up some properties I'd use 'em for the business till I got tipped off and then I'd move to another one and rent the empty place to some store or outfit on the level. On a short lease, see. Then later I'd use it for the business again."

"Mary," Claire said faintly, appalled almost to incoherence. "Mary, they wanted this for a whorehouse."

"*I* don't need to have it explained." The old voice was edged and reedy.

Claire turned to Hinchman with a puzzled scowl. "How did you happen to choose this particular house?" she asked slowly. "It seems very—"

"Well," he said again. He seemed incapable of beginning a sentence without that fencerail to lean upon. "Well, I'd been looking things over here on the Northside. It's kinda right for the business, see. I operate quiet, you keep it dark who really owns the stuff. So I was real surprised when this Mr. Nicholas comes to me a while back and wants to know would I be in'erested in this here house."

Claire gave Mary a long, naked, horrified look. "The bastard," Claire said quietly. Hinchman jumped. "Jeez," he said. "I didn't expect to hear that here."

Claire turned red and bit her lip. Hinchman looked at Mary and said, "I wasn't too hot about coming here and spilling all this," he said. He spoke in almost an accusing way, as if to inform Mary that he had kept his end of an embarrassing compact and now expected her to keep hers— though surely she had made no such assurance. He said again, "I sure would like to know how you found out about all this. I thought I always kept way out of sight."

"You do," Mary said. She was anxious to get rid of him now. "You'll never find yourself in any trouble on account of me, Mr. Hinchman. So far as I am concerned this is a closed book."

He got to his feet, unsatisfied, but blocked in the effort to discover anything more. The sooner this was all signed off the better.

"Don't you worry any more about your house, lady," he said. His clumsy attempt at kindness was almost pathetic. "Honest, I don't want this perticler house. There's lotsa others, see."

"I see," Mary said, letting him out the front door. "Thank you very much for coming, Mr. Hinchman. It was a great help to me."

"Don't mention it," he said. He put on his derby hat, moving down the steps, and gave them an embarrassed nod and went away. Mary shut the door and turned to see Claire, dishevelled and distracted-looking, standing beside her in the hall. There was a shrewd gleam in Claire's eye, and tucks in the corners of her mouth. She put her arm around Mary and led her back to the parlor, saying, "Come clean, darling. How did you really spade all this up?"

Mary smoothed back her hair and sat down primly, folding her hands.

"I've known some queer people in my time," she said vaguely. "Once there was a woman over in Watt Street—" She paused and said sharply, "Never mind about the past, Claire. I just wanted you to know what to look for in the future."

[*February 1935*]

Ben Nicholas's secretary restrained an impulse to raise his eyebrows when he saw the Mrs. Gregory Wood who had telephoned and made the appointment to see Mr. Nicholas that afternoon. The secretary was a pallid young man with thin hair and a foxlike expression. He was discreet and impassive. But it had quite surprised him to hear a woman's voice, polished and authoritative and perfectly confident that Mr. Nicholas would speak to her and see her. Apparently she did not know that Mr. Nicholas spoke to very few people unless he sent for them.

Mrs. Wood was a stunner, the young man said to himself, as he ushered her into the private office. She was dressed in the kind of unrelieved mat black which everybody knew came from Paris. She had a pair of silver foxes slung across her arm and huge single pearls in her ears. Either women bought those pearls in the ten cent store, or they were real, the secretary reflected; and these were real. He could tell that by the way this woman walked, by the angle of her head and chin, and by the way it seemed not to occur to her that there was any particular privilege about getting in to see Ben Nicholas.

Ben rose from his desk and said, "This is quite a surprise, Claire."

"Yes. Isn't it?"

She dropped into the chair he held for her and crossed her shapely legs in their clocked French stockings. Noiselessly and regretfully the secretary closed the door. Mr. Nicholas had never had an office visitor like this. Not until he was back at his desk did the young man realize with sudden disillusionment that this was his employer's cousin.

"Have you been in town long?" Ben asked. He did not like such an obvious way of sparring for time but it might make an opening a little awkward for Claire. Ben knew perfectly well why she had come to see him.

She lit a cigarette and blew smoke from her nostrils, saying, "I'm sailing tomorrow on the *Normandie*. Before I go I want to get it straight about Mary and the Pittsburgh house."

"Why, so far as I know there's nothing to see me about. Don't Ted and Tom own the house?"

"Certainly. And I came to tell you I'll thank you not to sell it for them —to a badhouse syndicate or anybody else."

"Why Claire." Ben looked out the window at the distant skyline. "Isn't that—ah—"

"Rather. I think it was the dirtiest lowdown trick I ever heard of."

Ben assumed a mild sneer. "Don't you think you're going somewhat beyond your own business butting into this?" he asked. "I wasn't aware you had an interest in the house."

"I haven't," Claire said "But I have got an interest in Mary She wants to stay there and I'm going to see she does."

"A very fine and empty sentiment," Ben said quietly, "since Ted doesn't intend to pay the taxes any longer If he and Tom want to sell the house they'll sell it."

"Not unless Mary consents."

"I'm afraid Mary's consent or refusal wouldn't amount to anything in a tax sale procedure."

Claire narrowed her eyes and looked at Ben scornfully. She had disliked him ever since the first time she saw him that Christmas years ago when his mother brought him to Uncle Paul's. He looks, she said to herself, as if he had salt water in his veins instead of blood. So cold and cut and dried and irritatingly smooth and—handsome, in spite of it all, in a strange way.

"You realize of course," he was saying, "that I haven't the slightest interest in the house one way or the other. I have no time, I assure you, to bother with a Victorian relic in a rundown neighborhood in Pittsburgh." He laughed coldly at the thought. "I—Ted merely asked my advice about it."

"So you gave him a hell of a piece of advice. I say, Ben—the place is just as much of a white elephant as Ted says. Nobody needs it. But Mary's going to spend the rest of her days in peace there."

"What about the taxes? And other expenses?"

"I'm paying them now."

Ben shrugged, but raised his eyebrows and looked curiously at Claire. "Have you money to throw away while—ah—business is in its present state? I envy you."

She hated the sarcasm in his tone. But she only said, "I'll worry about that." She picked up her purse and made gestures preliminary to leaving. But Ben found himself impelled by curiosity. Without really intending to he said, "I think you're being very rash, if you don't mind my saying so. Unless of course your income—" he suggested vaguely.

"Oh, no. I'm not getting dividends from the mill any more than the rest of you."

"That's what I thought. I understood the bulk of Aunt Constance's estate was her stock in the mill."

"It was. I have a few bits and pieces besides," Claire said calmly. "And a job."

"Well." Ben put the tips of his fingers together and looked at her with renewed surprise. "Is that so. Isn't that new?"

"Brand new."

Claire herself was still astonished at the fact that only twenty-four hours ago when she arrived in New York on her aimless way back to Europe, a casual meeting with the head of Jack Thomas's syndicate had resulted in her being hired to work full time as a roving correspondent in Europe. She had never realized that the few special articles which Jack had sold for her were very well written. She had tossed them off scarcely noticing what she was paid for them. But they were concise and clear and peculiarly colorful. They had the unusual quality of seeming to have been translated from the language of the place of their origin into vigorous newspaper English. That was because of Claire's ability as a linguist and her complete fluency in six languages. It had never occurred to her that this could be a very valuable asset if she chose to sell it.

She had listened almost in bewilderment yesterday as the syndicate editor, Mark Monroe, discussed his increasing problems in Central Europe where the machinations of the Nazi party could be traced to the root of much that was happening behind the scenes. He needed very badly somebody who could get about and into things cleverly, somebody who had wide contacts and unlimited entree and a Continental background and many languages. It had been almost uncanny, she thought afterwards, as they sat there in the dimly lit cocktail bar talking about all this with no reference whatever to her, until Monroe put down his glass with a clink and leaned over and said, "Why don't you have a crack at it?" Before she could really grasp the idea he was describing her first assignments and putting forward her sailing five days and telling her she would start at fifty a week, but needn't stay at that if she proved to be worth more.

Not until she was out on the street, lightheadedly walking back to the St. Regis, did she feel the full intoxication of what had happened to her. All the past weeks, ever since that harrowing twenty-four hours haunted by Jerry, she had been going about in a stunned and wretched frame of mind. Her own misery had been intensified by the threat that hung over Mary. In the end Claire had pleaded with Mary to go back with her to Europe and let the boys dispose legitimately of the house and write the past all off, once and forever.

Mary had only smiled and shaken her head. "The house does not really cost so much," she said. "I can squeeze things a little further and simply ignore it when repairs need to be made."

The taxs were only a few hundred dollars a year, after all; that was one reason for being glad that the city had grown so fast in other directions. Claire had not seen very clearly how to carry out her intention, but she said, "From here out I'm paying the taxes. You tell the boys to go to hell. We'll manage it some way."

"How, dear? You have none too much cash yourself."

"Never mind. Leave that to me."

It might mean borrowing money or selling something, but she was not going to discuss the details with Mary. When business improved and the mill started paying dividends again there would be no problem anyway. And it put her mind at rest to have Mary's promise not to allow Ted to pay any more maintenance for the house. If his best judgment had been to let Ben Nicholas proceed as he had, Mary was better off without anything from Ted.

But it had never occurred to Claire what it would actually feel like to earn her living—or even a small part of it. The money she was to receive was negligible as money; compared with her normal income it was a pittance. She had often spent many times that sum in a day on whims and foolishness. But walking up Fifth Avenue in the sharp blue winter dusk, with her hands in her coat pockets and the tap of her heels setting an agreeable rhythm, she discovered a feeling of excitement and pride and eagerness such as she had never known before. Her heart was still sore and heavy from the mortifying experience with Jerry. She could not say she had forgotten it, or would. But two hours ago she would not have believed anything could happen to give her a complete new view of everything.

In spite of her excitement she was a little frightened about the job. Maybe she would be a failure at it. Maybe they would change their minds after they received a few of her pieces. Maybe she could not write at all. It might only have been Jack Thomas's urging and editing that made the articles saleable. And how on earth could she crash into government bureaux and political-party headquarters and the homes and private offices of powers behind the European scene, and get—much less write—the stories that Mark Monroe wanted? He had told her not to think about that. She should put her eye on the ball and keep it there, he said.

"But one thing, Mrs. Wood, you'll have to do. Get rid of that swank car you travel around in. You want to be obscure in this job if you can. Look tacky once in a while. Leave your jewels here in the bank. Get yourself a ratty old Ford—or better still, get a cheesy foreign car when you get over there."

Claire agreed and her Cadillac, so beautiful and in such marvellous condition after Jerry's overhauling, went to dead storage the next morning. She could at least use it when she came home—no, back—no—she found herself stumbling over the thought. Where was her home, anyway? Certainly not the great closed palace in Cannes, yet her cats were there. Not Pittsburgh, though in Mary she had the strongest of ties—she closed her mind sternly at the thought of Jerry. Well, for once there was going to be a good reason why no particular place was her home. She had to control the thrill of pride in her voice when she said, so casually, to Ben Nicholas that she had a job. She had risen and was about to say goodbye when he cleared his throat and said, "Claire, do you pay much attention to the business? The mill?"

She dropped back onto the arm of the chair she had been sitting in and said, "Why, I don't know. What made you ask?"

He shrugged. "Nothing particular. You are the largest stockholder of course—I should think you'd be interested."

"I am," she said. "But what can I do about it if the world is paralyzed? I'd love it if the mill could keep going at a decent rate, but I don't see what we can do about it. If there were anything, Gray Simcox would be on to it."

Ben pursed his lips. "Well, I don't know," he said slowly.

"I don't follow you. Gray does a good job."

"Oh, very. But he's a technical man, after all. He doesn't concern himself much with the business end. That's supposed to be Ted's lookout."

Claire took out a new cigarette and lit it slowly. It occurred to her for the first time to what extent any business concern of Ted's might be a matter for Ben's influence. Judging by the thing about the house—she left Ben looking at her in silence for a while and then said sharply, "Just what are you getting at?"

"Nothing. Only I can't help thinking about this, you know. Here we have this mill capable of making certain specialties for which there is always a market somewhere in the world and—"

"You don't think Ted does very much about it."

"No, I don't."

"I suppose you have an idea—"

Ben got up and stood behind his desk chair, half turned away from Claire and looking out the window. "You know," he said slowly, "I bet I could sell as much lightweight alloy steel as that mill could produce."

"To whom? Aircraft factories?"

"That depends where you mean. I understand the American aviation industry is taking all the lightweight alloys it can use."

"And that's not much. Not enough to get us above forty per cent capacity."

He turned and looked at Claire. "You know more about this than I thought you did, somehow."

She shrugged. "You pointed out yourself why I ought to. Naturally if you're not getting any income you make some effort to find out why."

"I'm trying to tell you I could fix that. There are buyers who'd grab our steel if they had the chance."

Claire stared at him for a moment and then said, "Well, what are we waiting for?"

Ben glanced down at her sidewise. He paused as if weighing his words very carefully and said, rather uneasily, "There are complications. Matters of world exchange. Difficulties in trade arrangements. A lot of excitable fools in this country who can't see—"

Claire's wide mouth set in a scornful line and her hazel eyes began to turn stony and inscrutable in their leonine way.

"If people didn't have prejudices against trading with Germany," she said in a flat undertone. "The German boycott is beginning to be an obstruction to profitable trade, isn't it?"

"It's a lot of sentimental tripe," he said angrily. "These snivelling refugees coming over here stirring up the Jews—by God, I wish we had some way of cleaning house of 'em right here. Hitler has the right idea."

If Claire let her feelings get the upper hand now she would start a quarrel, with far-reaching and probably disastrous results. Only the slow dilation of her nostrils showed her disgust and anger as she said quietly, "You ought to see some of his work at first hand."

"I'd like to! I bet it's wonderful. I'm thinking of running over and seeing how they do it. Unemployment nearly eliminated—damned Bolshevik labor unions smashed—by God, that's what we ought to do with that bunch of thugs in Pittsburgh. John L. Lewis and that henchman of his—what's his name. Murray. Starting a Steel Workers' Organizing Committee! Why, they're nothing but a bunch of Reds. We ought to clean 'em out! Shoot the ringleaders and smack the rest back where they belong."

Claire closed her eyes as the vision of Jerry's face twisted with murderous fury swept across her mind. He ought to hear this. She intended to write him every word of it. Ben was still talking, almost orating, walking up and down the office with his hands in his pockets. Claire held herself rigid and contemptuously silent. Ben evidently thought she was enthralled.

"And instead of behaving like red-blooded Americans and being tough with these dirty Jews and Reds, what do we do? Listen to 'em! Coddle 'em. What's our board of directors doing? Has anybody in that mill taken a he-man stand about this? Ted listens to Simcox and that old dodo Purcell—"

"—and you," Claire murmured.

"Not about this. Why, the next thing you know those soft-soap fools will be wanting to sign a contract with these racketeers."

"You seem to forget Ted isn't the president of the company," Claire said mildly. "He has no authority to sign labor contracts. I wouldn't worry about it if I were you."

Ben stopped pacing and shot a sharp glance at her.

"It seems to me," he repeated slowly, "you know more about this business than you let on. So far I'd like to ask just who is going to decide the company's policies about these things? This labor racketeering—and whether or not we do some real business."

"I'm really very stupid about all that, Ben. I supposed the board of directors more or less decided things like that through the president they appoint."

"Then they ought to appoint a different one from Gray Simcox. We'll never get out of this standstill until we have an aggressive realist in there. Simcox is all right as a technician—but how can you expect tough two-fisted action from a—a—cripple?"

"I think Gray Simcox does a very fine job," Claire said. She spoke with disdain.

"Well I don't! It makes me boil to see that fine little property going to hell for want of some brains and management. This isn't the good old days. That mill needs a housecleaning the way—the whole country does! We'll never get on our feet until we throw that gang of radicals and Jews and crackpots out of Washington. Same thing with the mill. If Simcox and this board of directors is holding us up let's kick 'em out. We're the stockholders. We've got the say in the end."

"So we have."

"Let's get going then. Let's get together and tell 'em what we want. If they don't like it—"

Claire rose abruptly. She knew that if she stayed another five minutes there would be an explosion. Her one fatal misstep now would be to let Ben know the absoluteness of the opposition between them. Pursued to its utmost extreme this could turn into a struggle for control of the company. Well, she did hold the largest block of stock. The rest of the stockholders would have to be watched and steered at every turn. Ben Nicholas would take the most watching of all. Suddenly she was very glad that Mary had refused so adamantly to leave Pittsburgh.

CHAPTER LXXVIII

[*November 1936*]

THE ONLY TROUBLE with Claire's work, Mary often thought regretfully, was that it kept her from coming back to Pittsburgh as she used to come. It was getting on toward the end of the second year since Claire had last been here. And she had not taken a week's vacation since beginning her job. She was totally absorbed in it, more even than the gripping drama of the news she dealt with might explain. Mary thought that the restlessness, the boredom, the emptiness which had tortured Claire were of the past now. Perhaps it was possible, after all, for her to find all the intensity of life she craved in this job she was doing. Nobody else had written articles of this kind from Europe. Her dispatches appeared regularly in the Pittsburgh *Press,* among many other American papers, and to this day Mary had not overcome her recurrent amazement at the sight of that line under the heading: by Claire Gregory.

Today Mary had a letter from Claire, and since this was a particularly horrid winter morning, almost black with smog, Mary lingered over her breakfast by the fire in the back parlor, thoughtfully reading and then rereading the letter. Claire had written from Vienna. That was interesting; she was out of Germany, then, after almost a year there.

"I've got a case of mental indigestion," she had written. "I'm never really convinced that my pieces are any good and every time a cable comes from New York I expect to find I've been fired. It still seems queer they were willing to trust their reputation to a beginner like me. I love it but I'm still terrified of the responsibility. I've lost four kilos—thank God my shape will benefit anyway.

"Those months in Germany were the most disturbing experience I've ever had. Compared with what I remember during the war this thing that's happening to the German people is infinitely more horrible. I'd rather have Tom's fate for a son or brother of mine than see him turn into one of these bestial fanatics. I used to think Nazis were just the poor wretched scum of the people driven to their belief in Hitler by desperation. The original ones were, of course. But now the thing has infected the whole nation, from the top crust down. I'm haunted by the frightful things they're doing to their own minds and brains and souls—let alone what they do to the Jews and intellectuals. Germans can't all be primitive beasts intoxicated by violence and brutality—or can they? I don't know. I do know that what I wrote about their secretly building an army is true—hideously true.

"You have no idea how hard it was to do that series. Going about interviewing women in their homes and getting into village schools and Hitler Jugend meetings and folksing up with the Deutscher Mädel—Monroe kept wiring the pieces were swell and I can't believe yet that the Nazi government was so stupid they couldn't see between the lines. They actually believed I was writing a marvellous piece of propaganda for them! All about how German women and children have been booted back into the middle ages!

"I left last Friday, with groans of relief. It's wonderful to get where you don't have to be afraid to breathe. When I really wanted to talk to one of my old friends in Germany we'd go into the bathroom and turn on all the water taps and keep flushing the toilet and sit on the edge of the bathtub and whisper. Suspected people's houses are wired for dicta-phones and all the servants are spies. Most of my old buddies are still here and we waste as much time in the Café Louvre as we ever did. Jack is in Russia. They sent him back to head the Moscow office. I'm glad of it. I miss him in a way—we used to have a lot of fun here together—but I'm glad he's gone.

"I suppose if you ask me questions you want them answered. You wanted to know if I am happy. Well—yes and no. I'm lonely. Most of the time work keeps me from thinking about it. I shudder to think what a state I'd be in by now if it weren't for my job. I love my friends here—they're grand people. Brainy and gay and tough and compassionate. I think news-paper people are magnificent, the American ones anyway. And so superbly generous you can't believe it until you've seen them work together. All that amounts to a lot. But I must be getting old, Mary, or I'd never bend enough to admit I want something more. You used to try to make me confess it. You win. But where does that leave the score?"

Now there, Mary thought, laying down the letter and absently stroking Flam who lay asleep in her lap. There, she's come right out with it for the first time. I did think this job was all she could possibly want. But now that she seems to have mastered it—Mary leaned back in her chair and gazed at the fire. She had tried hard enough to tell Claire that life could not possibly be empty if you gave yourself fully to it. She thought of Paul; she was always thinking of Paul. Any outsider might have thought that Mary had been cheated of the full measure of experience. But Mary knew better. And she must still wonder and speculate uneasily about what was to become of Claire. She was not so very happy after all, then, when she could write, "Oh, Mary, I'm horribly low about the world. When I was in Salzburg in August I met some of my English relatives. I'd almost for-gotten I had any—David and Gillian Gregory, these were, my Uncle Hugh's children. They were always running over to Munich and coming back with rapt accounts of how marvellous it all is—the Party and the Brown House and how much the Führer is doing for Germany . . . they went to Berch-tesgaden and spent the whole day parked on the side of the road waiting for him to pass. It makes me sick to the bottom of my soul. This thing will creep and crawl and infect the whole world unless somebody wakes up and begins to do something about it. And they did nothing—nothing—last March when this beast, this maniac, sent armed troops into the Rhine-land. I've never stopped thinking about it since. France, our France, did absolutely nothing. Daddy should know that, and all the others like him and Dick.

"Oh, hell, write me about something different to take my mind off this.

Tell me about Jerry and how his S.W.O.C. is doing. I suppose there was a time when I would have been as much of a bloody jackass as Ben about all that. But believe me, my eyes would have been opened by Germany if I had been stone blind before. Just to see what's happened to German labor and their families is enough for me. The frightening thing is how many people in the U. S. are just like Ben. What's the difference what they're called—Fascists—Nazis—if it hadn't been for them the riffraff wouldn't have been financed and organized in Germany.

"And be sure you keep tabs on B. N., and write me all you learn. If it hadn't been for your tour-de-force about Monsieur Hinchman I'd never have known what a high-class detective you are, you little wretch. If my hunch means anything Ben will begin sniffing about looking for loose crumbs of stock one of these days. Keep me posted. I'm off for Praha to see Julka next week, taking a few days off at last. I really am fed up. I've got to get some respite or I'll start Heiling myself in the mirror. I wish you could be there with us!"

Putting the letter away Mary enjoyed the thought of Claire's reunion with Julka. That should give her a real lift. She really had been working much too hard and keeping at it too steadily if she had not even taken a trip to see Julka in all this time. After all, that was no great distance from where she was. And distance was nothing to Claire . . . My goodness, Mary thought, looking at the clock, I've been dreaming and dawdling here half the morning. And Peggy coming from Sewickley for lunch.

Lauchlan seldom appeared at the old house, but that afternoon it was she who called for Peggy instead of the chauffeur. She was driving herself, and to Mary's surprise Ben Nicholas was sitting beside her when the glittering new convertible coupé drew up at the side door. These visits of Ben's to Ted's house had been growing more frequent lately. Perhaps they seemed perfectly natural to Ted, Mary thought; perhaps he and Ben were really congenial. But she found that hard to believe. Ted had just enough of his father's simplicity and warmth and Ben had just enough of his mother's cool impassivity so that Mary could not believe they had any more in common that Paul and Elizabeth themselves had had. She stood watching the two inside the car as they switched on the interior light and Lauchlan bent her head, apparently rummaging for her purse. When she looked up Mary saw her dark eyes meet Ben's cold gray ones in a peculiar, consciously lengthened look. There was a strange expression of cynical satisfaction in both their faces; Lauchlan's with that sharp-cut swift look in profile, Ben's veiled as always by a cleverness that would never imaginably leave him off his guard. Mary as she watched them felt the two interlocking parts of an idea come together almost as if with a click of precision in her mind. There was no suspicion about this, only certainty; and her old face set in a mask of inscrutability, while contempt and scorn, and pity for Ted mingled and moved just beneath.

She opened the side door as Lauchlan stepped from the car and said, making an effort not to let her tone betray her, "Good evening, Lauchlan. How do you do, Ben? Isn't it a mean night?"

They chatted in the hall while Peggy was upstairs putting on her hat and coat. Mary offered them a cocktail—if Lauchlan wanted to go out to the pantry and make it herself—but they refused and thanked her and presently Peggy came downstairs and thanked Mary for taking her to the movies, which she had done after lunch, and then they all went out to the steps and Mary stood watching the three of them get into the car. Peggy was beaming with pleasure. "Oh, you've brought the new Packard!" she cried. "Isn't it a peach, Cousin Ben?" It was, Mary thought, shaking her head. And only a little while ago Ted had been ready to sell this house because he was so hard up. Now—but Lauchlan had bought herself this car, Mary realized, turning back into the house after waving them good-bye. It did not matter to Lauchlan whether there was a depression or a boom. She had money enough for whatever she wanted.

It was a good thing for Mary's peace of mind that she had not seen and heard more of the actions and the conversation between Lauchlan and Ben that afternoon. Her indignation for Ted's sake might have paled in comparison if she had merely had a glimpse of the memo that Ben had taken from his wallet at one point, and gone over with Lauchlan. In general Mary suspected that Ben was keeping tabs in just such detail upon the owners and directors of the mill. She knew that it was her task to discover exactly what he was doing and planning to do, and to report all that to Claire. Even if Claire had had nothing to do with it, if Claire did not exist at all, Mary would feel the same necessity to protect the mill from Ben's undertakings. The real obligation was to Paul. That was always clearest of anything in her mind.

Ben had made a little diagram showing all the owners of the Scott stock and the number of their shares. He did not explain his idea in detail to Lauchlan, but he did make it clear that he knew ways to make enormous new business for the mill if he could get a majority of the directors to agree with him. Now they probably would not. Business, surprisingly, had rebounded sky-high since the low levels of the recent depression. Orders had begun the early part of this year to pour into the mill. They came from all over the country; immediate demands for special steels and alloys, steels for airplane engines and bodies and parts, steels for machine tools, chrome and nickel alloys for every kind of industry.

"So I don't have to shove this through as fast now as I'd first thought," Ben said to Lauchlan. "This" was his plan for controlling the board of directors. At present there was not enough dissatisfaction with the mill's business, there was too much optimistic relief over the recovery, artificial though it was, to furnish the impetus that Ben would require to put his plan into effect. "But it'll work along," he said confidently. "It'll take quite a while to set things up around that fool of a woman . . ."

"You mean Claire?" Lauchlan had drawled. She knew enough about the ownership of the mill to know that Claire held the most stock.

Ben nodded. "She's a sentimental crackpot," he said. "About the mill and about Ted's father and the old woman and—in fact—everything that's going on in the world. Do you ever read that tripe she writes from Europe?"

"I?" Lauchlan gave him one of her looks, and a sly, intimate laugh.

"I've got more important things to do." She laid her long brown hand on his thigh, and moved her fingers slowly.

"Well—" There was no point in talking about Claire to Lauchlan. Ben was much too shrewd not to be able to evaluate Claire and Lauchlan both for precisely what they were. But he was going to have trouble with Claire some day, and he was going to use Lauchlan. That was the difference. Claire's reaction to his feelers, the time she came to his office, had not promised much. And now that she was over there, writing what she did about Germany—Ben was going to have to do this job cleverly, he told himself. But then he always did everything cleverly. At the time he talked to Claire he had already been approached by a commercial agent of the German government, whose precise information about the Scott mill, its products, facilities, and ownership, had struck Ben with reluctant admiration. These Nazis were thorough and smart, whatever else they were. The man had a perfectly clear offer to make to Scott's if the proper avenue could be opened up. He had even been smart enough to know whom not to approach about it. So these chaps must have dug up the details not only of the mill ownership, but of the characters of the owners. Ben said to himself as he so often had occasion to, that you had to hand it to them.

Ben had been explaining to Lauchlan that a housecleaning of the board of directors and the company's officers could only be pushed through by vote of the stockholders. Now the directors were in a mood to make the most of the business recovery while it lasted, and the chairman, John Purcell, was still doing things according to the basic financial plan laid down by Paul Scott at the time of the incorporation eighteen years ago. There still remained six hundred thousand dollars' worth of the preferred stock to retire in accordance with Paul's plan, but for the past six years this had been impossible. The preferred dividends had been passed too. And now these had accumulated as a prior obligation before any common dividend could be paid at all. That was another thorn in Ben's flesh and another quarrel he intended to open up with the directors.

So, on his little pocket memo, he had classified all the stockholders under the three headings of Yes, No, and Possible, according to his estimation of their positions when he brought all this to a head. That was what he was showing Lauchlan.

"These are the 'yes' items, you see," he said. Here were listed his own twenty per cent of the common stock; then Willy's and Angelica's ten per cent each.

"Imagine a man of sixty who's always been called 'Willy'!" Lauchlan exclaimed. "I've never seen him, not that I care."

"I haven't seen him since Uncle Bill's funeral. I was just a kid, I wouldn't know him now. He lives in Pasadena."

"I saw Angelica once," Lauchlan said with a snort. "In Boston. My Gahd. But you're sure they'd go along with you?"

"Yes. So far they're the only ones I could say that of. The next batch, each with five per cent, are what I call 'possible.' "

"Meaning—?"

"Either that I could get them to vote my way, what with one thing or another, or else sell their stock to me. Anyhow, there's room for a little action."

"And *they* would be," Lauchlan said with sarcastic impressiveness, "my wonderful he-man of a husband, my wounded hero of a brother-in-law, and my pathetic churchmouse of a sister-in-law. Right?"

"Right."

"Then what's all the shooting for? You can practically do as you like right now."

"Oh, no." Ben laughed and shook his head. "You've overlooked a mere matter of forty-five per cent, my dear."

"Claire—"

"—with thirty per cent," Ben said, "and what burns me up, that scheming old servant that everybody treats like a priceless antique. Fifteen per cent!" he growled. "Blackmail, that's all it was—the stock your father-in-law left her. And as for Mama's brother Edgar—why if that weakling hadn't fallen for her crooked Catholic plotting . . . well, there you have it. I intend to get control of more than half those votes sometime during the next year. Just as simple as that. And then," he said, "you can have the fun of watching some real footwork and brainwork around that miniature of a so-called steel mill."

"I suppose you'd always know where to sell steel even when nobody else did," Lauchlan said. She wanted to flatter Ben but she was not very interested in any of this. She was in a hurry to get him to their destination and she pressed her foot harder on the gas.

"I'd know," Ben said with a short, sharp laugh. He knew exactly where to sell lightweight aviation steel to buyers who would take all they could get and were prepared to pay anything for it. Their motives and reasons, the plan behind their buying, did not concern him in the least.

CHAPTER LXXIX

[November 1936]

CLAIRE SNIFFED HAPPILY as the car rounded the turn of the hill and she could look down and see the sharp spires of Prague piercing the gray haze which seemed always to hang over the city. The air had the most pungent, unforgettable odor. And how different, Claire thought, from the smoky smell of Pittsburgh. She put the rabbity little car in second gear and steered it noisily down the grade. It's a strange thing, she reflected, that I have this queer love for two of the smokiest, grayest cities in the world. London is gray and smoky and smelly too. But it leaves me cold.

She drove as slowly as she could because she wanted to fill her eyes with the ancient, beautiful vista—the broad winding Vltava spanned by lacy bridges and crowned by the jewel of the Karlův Most.

Beyond, the Hradčany brooded on its bluffs, the stern pile of centuries where the wise old coachman's son had lived and guided the nation he had led to freedom. Claire smiled tenderly as she though of Julka, received and honored in that castle; another peasant whose hands and body and eyes had known the hardest, ugliest things in life, but whose heart brimmed with the passionate ideal that had restored this land to its people. She drove down the wide Vyšehrad, crossed the Palacký Bridge and turned left on the Smíchov Embankment. The river flowed along, steel-colored and heavy in the dank November air. Tugboats and steamers puffed about their business. Handsome buildings and monuments lined the banks, punctuated by the noble Gothic towers of the bridges. Claire looked back over her shoulder at the imposing pile of the Národní Divadlo; the national opera house, the quintessence of nineteenth-century pomposity, and wondered for the thousandth time why European city-builders had the vision to line their rivers with architectual magnificence while in America—she grimaced at the thought of Pittsburgh. All its riverbanks were a shambles of ugliness; stacks and sheds and chimneys and railroad tracks and miles of dingy warehouses to obliterate the beauty God had put there. Yet she loved it. She would feel this same inward happiness, this eagerness to throw her arms around a beloved friend, if she were reaching Mary in Pittsburgh instead of Julka in Prague.

Yet as she stopped the car outside the neat gray façade of Anton's apartment house, she had a twinge of retrospective pain; of doubt, too; and was this fear that she was feeling? This queer fluttering in her throat, this tension in her wrists. This was what had kept her away from here for almost two years. This was why Julka's letters to her in Berlin, in Nuremberg, in Vienna, in Warsaw, in Salzburg, had been so troubled and so puzzled. Why didn't she come oftener, Julka would write. Why hadn't she come since her last trip to Pittsburgh? Yes, it was fine that she had a job and was so wrapped up in it, but did that mean she had forgotten her old friends entirely? Or had she lost interest in them? That wasn't like her. When was she coming?

Claire had not only not taken Jerry's parting advice to talk to his mother, she had sternly repressed the impulse to think back to him or to anybody connected with him. Sometimes the urge to open up the hurt, like the temptation to lift a half-healed scab, had been almost more than she could resist. But she was sure she had mastered it now. The humiliation had never hurt so much as the empty ache of knowing fulfillment only to have it immediately snatched away. The right and wrong of the matter had never haunted Claire. She had not lived in a world that judged these things that way. Perhaps she ought to have done so. Perhaps that was why now, when she really had outlived the impact of the blow, she should be standing on this doorstep quivering a little inside, hesitating before her gloved finger pushed the bell marked "Hrdlička." The name had always been crowded with meaning for her. Now it had the power to hurt her too.

Julka gave her the delighted warm embraces she had been hungry for, beaming and exclaiming how thin she was, and studying Claire with her keen brown eyes as if to learn all there was to know about the long interval since she had seen her last. And this time Julka was not asking the questions about Jerry and the girls; it was so long since Claire had been in Pittsburgh that Julka had the most recent news.

"Bella's got another baby," she told Claire, along with the latest about Jenny's promotion to night supervisor at the hospital, and Míla's husband's going into business for himself in Cleveland. "Another boy," she said.

"Wouldn't you like to see him?" Claire asked, giving Julka's heavy shoulder a squeeze. "What kind of a grandmother are you, anyway—running a government office way over here instead of clucking to your grandchildren?"

"Let their mamas cluck," Julka said, grinning. "I done my share of that already. When they're big enough they should come see me here and I'll do them some real good. Clucking!"

Claire took the news of Jerry's new baby without a flicker. It was so plain what had happened, so clear that Jerry had turned to his wife in a desperate snatch at reassurance, at rehabilitating himself in his own eyes after the madness of his abandonment. That was fine, Claire thought, just as it should be. How fantastic that there is no originality in this pattern, she thought swiftly, none whatever, whether it repeats itself in a palace or a hovel, in the great world or the small. She drew a deep breath. She felt now for the first time as if a door were slammed, locked, and sealed on the entire thing. The fluttering and the tension were gone. She and Julka were laughing and gabbling together when they heard a latchkey in the door and Anton came in from his rehearsal at the Filharmonie. Claire had not seen him in years. They shook hands and Anton asked about her job and how long since she had been in Pittsburgh, and they made the inevitable discovery that both had been in Salzburg last summer without ever meeting there . . . had there ever in all experience been anything like the Toscanini performances of *Meistersinger?*

"No," said Claire, smiling, "Except the *Fidelio*. I love that better."

"Ah, well—" Anton spread his square white hands. "If you want to get up on that plane—"

"That's all right, then," Claire said. "We agree."

"How about some coffee, Mama?" Anton asked, peering into the porcelain stove. He added some coal briquettes to the fire.

"Sure." Julka opened the door to the kitchen. "Would you try a fresh *koláč,* too?"

"Ooops," Claire gulped. "Would I!"

Julka laughed. She was careful to emphasize her status as a guest in this house. She wanted nobody to think that she lived with her son in a dependent relationship or that the reverse was true. Anton had a comfortable spare room which he liked his mother to use when she wanted to be in Prague, but Julka carried her passion for independence into individual relationships. She respected Anton's privacy minutely. And he treated her with a combination of camaraderie and grave, rather formal deference which Claire found charming.

She looked about the comfortable room. It was unusually pleasant for the parlor of a typical Prague flat. Claire had no illusions that Czechs were æsthetically as cultivated as in matters political, intellectual, and musical.

Most of their furniture and decoration was pretty awful unless it sprang directly from the sound lines and spontaneous beauty of peasant origin. High-glazed factory furniture with spongy plush upholstery and too much plate glass was what you found when they set out to furnish something. But then everything must be modern. A startling note in the midst of so much mysterious, dreamy mediæval beauty.

Anton apparently did not fall in with the brusque contemporary taste for modern decoration. His flat was furnished with good pieces of Biedermeier, a legacy. he admitted freely when charged with it by his violently nationalist friends, of the Empire. Many Czechs scorned such reminders of the centuries of Austrian hegemony. Yet Anton noticed the comfortable exclamations with which his friends dropped into his padded chairs, put their elbows on his polished round table, and warmed their backs at his antique yellow porcelain stove. The stove was a beauty, a rare piece made in the first decade of the nineteenth century. This flat had central heating but Anton preferred to use the stove as the focal point of conversation and decoration in his parlor. There was a fine Steinway in the window, piled with bound scores and stacks of loose music in folders, and sheaves of music manuscript-paper.

Claire kept prodding herself with the thought: how could Anton be Jerry's brother? There had never been any physical resemblance between them. Now all the other differences had crystallized and shaped two men as different as day and night. Jerry was all hardness and darkness and angles; it lay in the grim set of his jaw, in his thin, high cheekbones, his sleek black hair, the tough Pittsburgh twang of his voice, emphasized by abrupt gestures of his horny blackened hands.

Claire smiled up at Anton as he stood by her elbow lighting her cigarette. How fantastically different he was! He was Julka's son in looks, his face broad and gentle and kindly, with the flattened planes and rather broad nose of his pure Slavic blood. His eyes were perhaps the most startling of all the contrasts to Jerry; wide, soft, turtle-lidded, a rich liquid brown instead of the glittering black which made Jerry's eyes so disturbing. Anton had blond hair, very curly and crisp, thickly covering his broad skull and rising to a jolly-looking tuft above the centre of his forehead. Claire stared so hard at him that he laughed a little and said, "Have you forgotten me entirely that you must study so hard to refresh your memory?"

Claire started and laughed too. "I didn't mean to be rude," she said, "but it must have looked that way."

"Not at all. I'm flattered."

She could not say "I never really noticed you before. I never was curious enough about you to notice what color your hair was, or whether you like Beethoven better than Wagner." She could not say that all Julka's children, to her, had been grouped together in a pleasant collective affection completely secondary to her feeling for their mother, until . . . until . . . She swerved from that with adroit mental dexterity. Then she found herself looking back, as it were, over the shoulder of her own memory and at last feeling perfectly calm and undisturbed. Julka came in with a big tray of coffee and cake and Claire got up to help her arrange the things on the round table. Claire asked about all the Dvořák cousins and what they were doing.

They were all fine, Julka said, Dora was doing brilliantly at the Medical Faculty; yes, here in Praha at the University. Otakar and Tomáš had both graduated with honors. Tomáš was nearing the end of his term of service in the Army and Otakar was working for the Government at present. They were extending the Sudeten fortifications and were employing the best of the young engineers as they graduated from technical school. Claire sighed.

"Julka, tell me the truth," she said, "do you—I mean the ones who really know—do you honestly expect trouble?"

Julka's broad mouth hardened into a sober line. "You've just been telling us about Germany," she said. "Answer your own question. What does this garbage about the master race and tomorrow the whole world is ours and Lebensraum for the German people—what does all that mean if not that we've got to be ready for trouble?"

"Austria will go first," Anton said. "Then they'll start on us. Of course we have our Allies—"

Julka's face was still sombre. "—and three million traitors in the Sudety," she said bitterly.

Claire began to tell them about her Gregory cousins and their Nazi enthusiasms. "Those are your so-called Allies," she said. "The British ruling class. Look at them. Oh my God, I'm so tired of talking about this mess and yet it's all we do. Every night, day in, day out, we sit and chew this thing over till I gag. But how the devil can you think of anything else?"

As if to answer her question Anton got up and strolled over to the piano and began to play in a rambling easy way, a loose melody in mournful Slavic mood, with odd open harmonies. Claire sat back, smoking, feeling relaxed and well fed and content and let her eyes droop in the comfortable warmth. She listened closely to the music.

"What is that?" she asked when Anton paused.

"Part of my concerto," he said casually. "The Romanza."

"Yours?" Claire sat up suddenly. "Why, I didn't know you were composing." She looked at Julka as if for confirmation.

"It's to be published next month," Anton said. "Zimbalist is playing it with the Philadelphia Orchestra in January."

"The world première," Julka said. Her voice quavered with pride.

Claire sprang up and went over to the piano. "Have you got it there? Is this it?" She seized the thick binder of manuscript, minutely scrawled with illegible notes and crossed and recrossed with corrections.

"Concerto for Violin in D minor," she read aloud, translating from the Czech writing on the title page. "By Antonín Hrdlička. Why—why it's wonderful!" Impulsively she threw her arms around his neck and kissed him. He turned a deep scarlet and made a deprecating gesture.

"It's nothing," he said, stammering. "I mean—it's just—*ach*, it's my work, that's all." He shrugged and went to look for a cigar. Claire sat down and began slowly to sight-read the opening bars. They were difficult.

She had not touched a piano in years. She played hesitatingly and scowled at the complicated tempi, the strange modern harmonies worked out cunningly to display the limpid simplicity of the folk themes. Anton was standing behind her looking over her shoulder when she stopped suddenly and said, "My God, I ought not to be butchering this! You play it."

"You're doing fine," he said kindly. "Reminds me of the time you played the Beethoven Concerto with me. Remember?"

Julka wagged her head. *"Bože můj!* That was a long time ago!"

"What I'd really like would be if you'd play it on your fiddle," Claire said.

Anton smiled. "Then you would have to practise. To play the orchestra parts in time."

"Isn't your own orchestra going to do it here?"

"Oh, sure. Some time this year. But I'd rather Zimbalist played it first than—"

"You?"

"A concertmaster hasn't much time to practise," Anton said. "Especially if he spends hours at this." He motioned toward the piles of manuscript strewn on the piano.

Claire had a sudden realization of the inner happiness of which this quiet son of Julka's had found the secret. He had not only not eaten out his heart in futile protest that he could not be a virtuoso. He had made the very best of his talent and in doing so had opened up the far richer, deeper well of creative genius. She could see that he had a good, full, satisfying life; enough activity with his responsible job to keep him stimulated and give his life direction and routine; enough leisure and freedom for his composing. She found herself envying him somehow, in spite of her own new contentment in her work.

"Come on," he was saying. "I didn't realize how late it is. Let's all go out to Barrandov and have a swell dinner. I'm starving."

"You two go," Julka said, looking up from her knitting. She was making a baby sweater for one of the married Dvořák girls who was expecting. "I have a committee meeting at nine and I won't have time to eat dinner first. It's after eight now."

"But you must eat dinner!" Claire said. "Come on, at least you'll have time for a plate of soup."

Julka shook her head, counting stitches. "No, I want to go over some tables before the meeting and I'll make myself a sandwich here. Later we can meet for a glass of beer if you like."

They both kissed her as they went out; Claire, she felt, with peculiar warmth. That was natural of course. She herself was brimming with happiness at seeing Claire again after such a long time. She heard the car snort and sputter in the street as the two drove away. They had laughed till the tears came when Claire described some of her experiences with the puddlejumper in place of her Cadillac. Julka did not laugh now. She sat and knitted in the lamplight, her broad face wise and serious and tender.

CHAPTER LXXX

[*January 1937*]

CLAIRE WAS FLYING from Rome to Prague. She had always felt a little doubtful about Italian planes. The pilots were usually more interested in the passengers than in their work, and if a beautiful woman was aboard, the pilot was sure to be among the passengers instead of in his cockpit. This one had left the plane to the radio operator, who sat at the controls with his neck craned to see how his captain was doing with the ladies. The captain was assuring the ladies that the ship was being flown by automatic radio-direction anyhow; the man was only at the controls for appearances. But somehow Claire thought this funny today instead of frightening.

Since her holiday she had been working in Rome, and on a sudden impulse she had decided to go back to Prague for a week-end. Anton's letters had been begging her to. It still seemed queer that she and Anton should be exchanging letters and telegrams and keeping in constant touch, after those years of casual impersonal friendliness. Since leaving Prague over a month ago she had had a sensation of missing something agreeable; and when she tried to put her finger on it, she decided it must be the music to which she had been listening with Anton. She had not heard so much music in years, not since long before Evan had died. In childhood, though, he had crammed her full of it. He had taken her to Vienna and Leipzig and Dresden and Milan more times than she could count. She could not remember a time when she had not been intimate with operas and symphonies and the world of German Lieder which Evan had made one of her most passionately treasured memories. Yet somehow since his death she had hardly gone to music at all. It was almost as if she had deliberately increased her spiritual vagrancy by abandoning one of the richest resources she knew.

And in Prague she had fallen into the way of hearing music every day. The discovery of Anton's composing—that is, she analyzed to herself, of his *successful* composing—had been a great thrill. It had given him sudden importance and stature in her eyes where previously there had seemed something faintly pathetic and secondary about him. Claire had always thought of orchestra players, those massed anonymous benders to the whips of other men's genius, as failures in the cruel struggle to be virtuosi. This would be their sad compromise with necessity. She knew that the idea was still correct in a large number of instances. But it was incorrect in Anton's case. She had asked curiously to be let into a rehearsal one afternoon and there she realized that Anton had as much outlet for the exercise of authority as his mild nature could possibly demand. She had never realized how much of the responsibility for the orchestra's performance lay directly on the concertmaster. She had thought of it, if at all, as a kind of honorary title.

She looked out as the plane hung in almost imperceptible motion over the Alps. The sight below and around her was enough to freeze one's blood if one took to panic easily. This flight in winter was perhaps no more dangerous than at other times of the year, but it looked infinitely grimmer. They were flying below the ceiling and seeming barely to skim the tops of the highest snow-covered peaks. As far as she could see the earth below them was a wild, threatening stretch of bottomless gulfs and jagged summits cruelly stroked in slashes of hard black and harder white. There was no water to be seen, no lake remained unfrozen; only tiny dots of glittering ice at the bottoms of abysses. She had never liked the Alps, always hated the scenery of Switzerland. The black cast of the landscape was intensely depressing to her, the sense of being locked in by towering death-dealing peaks unbearable.

Danger itself had never appalled her; the fear of death had almost entirely passed her by. Time and again she had found herself in great danger, in motor encounters on wild remote roads, in plane flights when she had been warned not to go, in swift currents of water where the strongest swimmers had drowned. She had always said she would not care if faced with certain death. This flight in a commercial plane should be among the more commonplace of everyday risks. But just now, opening her drowsing eyes to gaze at the threatening sights below, the thought rushed into her mind that this was exceedingly dangerous, that motors did fail and pilots did lose their bearings; that many a plane had crashed in this very pass, and many a passenger been killed. She sat up suddenly twisting her hands in a queer flash of panic. *That must not happen!* she thought in a wild, uncharacteristic way. *Whatever got me thinking of this?* She did not know. She only knew, forcing herself to lie back quietly again and relax in her chair, that she had a completely new sensation, a will not to die, a nebulous feeling that there was something—she could not then have said what—for which she wanted to stay alive.

When she stepped out of the plane at Ruzýň airport she was astonished to see Anton's stocky figure detach itself from the little group by the gate and start toward her. How dear of him! she thought quickly. How funny and kind and European! She was not accustomed to being met on her arrivals. She got around too fast, her comings and goings were too sudden and unpredictable, especially since she had been travelling for her job. She had not said what time she would arrive. But somehow he had found out. He took her small dressing-case and tucked his hand under her elbow as they went into the passenger station to wait for her luggage to be unloaded.

"I've missed you," he said.

"And I've missed you! I got spoiled, just visiting and enjoying myself with Julka and you."

"How is Rome?"

She made a face. "It beats me. You'd think the Italians just out of sheer cynicism would be onto that windbag by now."

"Well, of course they are. But—"

"Poor devils. Anyway I'm slipping some good stories past their noses. How's Julka?"

"Fine. She's gone down to the country on some business or other. She promised to stay with me three full months, but you know Mama—always up to something. She'll be back in a few days."

"I'm so glad you came today," Anton said in the taxi. It was Sunday, and a pleasant quiet had cleared the wide streets of their weekday bustle of traffic. A pale noonday sun shone on the honeycombed tiled roofs and glittering spires as they drove down the Bělská ulice. "I told you I wanted to take you to *Prodaná Nevěsta* and I have good seats for this afternoon."

"Grand!"

It had happened that in all her visits to Prague Claire had never been present at this one particular occasion which had become a national rite—the Sunday afternoon performance of *Prodaná Nevěsta*—the Bartered Bride—at the Národní Divadlo. The public revered the work almost religiously, regarding it as their national opera. It was mounted with all the care and perfection that love could lavish on it. The people never tired of it; year in and year out the house was sold out weeks in advance and it was almost impossible to obtain seats on short notice.

The packed house was a striking sight. There was nothing unusual to Claire about an opera house crammed with men and women in evening dress and decorations and jewels, but this crowd of four thousand plain people dressed in their Sunday best and respectfully assembled in plenty of time for the overture was very different. Whole families sat together in orderly arrangement, little children sandwiched between their elders. Anton had bought two seats in a centre box and Claire had a perfect view of the auditorium and the packed galleries. She was turning around to look up at the crowds in the top gallery when the sweeping red velvet curtains of their own box caught her eye. Seated inside them she had not realized that they were there, framing the box apart from the rest of the tier. She craned her neck up at the parting of the curtains, with an inquiring look, and Anton laughed and said, "That's right, this used to be the Imperial Box. If the Emperor condescended to come to Prague he sat here. Or the provincial governor did. The royal arms used to be up there."

"And now—" They both smiled as a sturdy-looking family of four came in to occupy the remaining seats, the mother carrying what was obviously a package of refreshments for the intermission. Claire and Anton returned their friendly bows.

The first notes of the overture caught her, as she said later, in the small of her back and brought her to the edge of her chair. She had heard this music before, but never in anything approximating this thrilling spirit. Three months ago, at Salzburg, she had said during a Toscanini performance of *Die Meistersinger* that no music could ever grip and excite her to such a degree again. Yet this held her spellbound before the overture was finished. It had no such perfection or polish as the great master's superhuman playing, but it had wonderful qualities of its own; vigor and virility and a glorious, unslackening richness of melody and a performance that tingled with gusto and devotion and sincerity. The voices were not strikingly beautiful; the women's were too meaty and heavy, the men's too hard; but the singers blended into an ensemble of extraordinary excellence, balanced by a clean and hard-drilled orchestra and crowned by the incomparable chorus and ballet. The opening chorus brought stinging tears of excitement to Claire's eyes, but when the act closed with the polka, punched off with magnificent vigor by handsome girls in red boots and gorgeous peasant costumes and strapping young men in richly embroidered blouses and waistcoats, she found herself clutching Anton's hand. "*Look* at them!" she breathed. "They're unbelievable."

"Why not?" he whispered. "They've been doing that all their lives in the villages they come from."

That was the secret of the whole thing, she saw. Authenticity made this work, teeming with life and beauty and humor and rich, inexhaustible melody, the profoundly moving experience that it was. Most of the audience knew every note and every word by heart. They roared at the bluff jokes, they listened raptly to the tender love-lyrics, they hung on every syllable of poor stammering Vašek's aria, "*Má-má-má-matička,*" sung with wistful and dignified pathos.

"He doesn't horse it," Claire whispered to Anton. "He makes it *mean* so much this way. He's a character instead of a clown."

Anton nodded quietly. It did his heart good to feel Claire's response. She was so enthralled by the music that she was not aware just how much of his afternoon Anton had passed in a state of dumb and incredulous happiness. He had been sitting there stealing long, satisfying glances at her, his eyes going back again and again as if to reassure himself that this really was true. It was less than two months ago that this old childhood friend—his mother's friend, which had always put Claire apart from his contemporaries—had walked in to meet his mother at his house and somehow turned a page in his life.

He could not understand why Claire seemed different, and he had been thinking about that through innumerable days and nights. Always before there had been a barrier (gracefully ignored by her, to be sure) of wealth and privilege and high birth; and this time that was changed. He told himself it was because of her job, she really was working now, she really needed the money she earned, and she could no longer have the moon by reaching for it. That should make a change in anybody. But Anton would not fool himself by rationalizing when one simple fact had emerged from the first amazed commotion in his mind. Claire in some way had changed her identity for him. She was no longer his mother's friend. She was a woman of whom he had become intensely and personally and constantly aware. He had been astonished to find how much he missed her when she went off to Rome. He was not used to being dependent on any woman's companionship. He was very self-sufficient.

When the curtain fell on the last heart-filling chords of the final chorus, and the audience was bursting into rapturous applause, Claire sat back limply as the lights went up, and looked at Anton and said, "I can't tell you how moved I am. It's—" her eyes filled with tears. "Why, I'm all stirred up. It's—like looking into these people's souls." She motioned at the demonstrating crowd above them.

He nodded solemnly. "That's exactly what it is. That's why this is such noble music." He was holding her coat, looking intently into her rapt face. "Let's get out ahead of the crowd," he said. His voice was husky.

The winter dusk had fallen when they emerged onto the street and they stood for a moment filling their lungs with cold, damp, smoky air. Anton said, "Where shall we go for coffee?"

Claire turned toward the embankment behind them and said, "What I'd really like to do is walk over to your house. I want to walk across the Karlův Most and see the river in this light."

"Wonderful." He pulled his overcoat collar high around his neck and they started off. They did not talk for a time, until they had passed under the ancient arch of the legend-hallowed bridge and were pacing slowly across. Claire stopped near the middle and leaned on the stone railing with her chin in her hands. Lights twinkled gently up and down the banks of the river and a tugboat hooted softly in the distance. There was a heavy, a tangible sadness in the air, the deep contemplative melancholy of extreme age which lay all about them, inundating their senses, even to the stones and mortar under their feet. Side by side they stood watching the dark stream flow slowly under the bridge, as it had done for seven centuries.

"This is a very beautiful place," Claire said at last, softly. "A place where people's brains and spirits have dignity."

"One must be wise and sensitive to see that," Anton said.

"You've transplanted yourself entirely, haven't you?"

"I think so," he answered slowly. "If it hadn't been for Mama I might not have left America. I'd probably have gone to New York to study."

"How different your life would have been."

"Yes. That's why I am so contented here. I'm not a very good fiddler, you know." He smiled. "Papa always talked that big way and if it hadn't been for Mama he'd have sent me to New York to study with Professor Auer. But Mama was so bent on this Czech passion of hers—"

"Aren't you glad she was?"

"Oh, enormously. Some people might not be happy here if they had been born in America but it suits me through and through. You see—in the things that really matter, their point of view here is almost identical with the American. In fact, when it comes to political and individual liberty the Czechs are even more fanatical, because they fought for their freedom so recently. And they are so proud of this country, Claire!"

He stood gazing across at the spired Gothic glory of the Cathedral soaring into the winter gloom from the bulk of the Hradčany. All about them the heavy weight of centuries closed in; one could sense it, Anton said, placing his hand illustratively on the span of his shoulders, "here. As if each person living here has his share of the weight to carry. People say Czechs are heavy and dour. They are not, but they are serious. Why wouldn't they be? Look what their past has been!" He laid his gloved hands on the massive gray coping of the bridge wall, pitted and polished

with age, and looked at Claire with a grave smile. "I don't know why I've
suddenly begun to orate about my country."

"I do," she said softly.

He arched his thick blond eyebrows and looked at her quizzically. "Are
you a mind reader?"

"Perhaps."

They were silent, leaning close together on the wall with their chins
resting in their hands. It was a fine silence, a silence full of eloquent,
deepening feeling. Little by little they had drawn closer together until their
shoulders and elbows were touching. They sought each other's eyes with a
warm confident gaze.

"You are," Claire said at last, very softly, "trying to tell me why you
are happy. Why your life is good. But I really don't need to have it explained, Anton. I only"—she smiled sadly—"envy you. Am I right?" she
asked.

He did not answer at once. He stood close beside her, his head turned
to let him look full into her face.

"I am very happy," he said after a time. His voice was low.

Claire sighed. She felt so full, in a strange way; the emotions which
had poured into her heart during the hours of music had not drained away.
She could feel the echoes reverberating there. She felt heavy with a strange
mingling of sadness and an unfamiliar sense of peace. And she felt close to
tears. She turned away from the bridge railing finally and they started to
walk slowly the rest of the way to Smíchov. It was growing colder. Before
they reached Anton's door a penetrating wind came up and they linked
arms and walked faster, stirred by the sharp winter evening.

It was warm and welcoming in the flat. The cleaning-woman had been
there and built a good fire of briquettes in the yellow stove. The coffee pot
stood ready for the boiling water. On a plate covered with a fringed napkin
were buttered slices of Sunday bread, sweet yeast bread dotted with white
raisins and lightly sugared. Anton took Claire's coat and she stood by the
stove warming her hands while he made the coffee.

"That beautiful music," she murmured, shaking her head. "I didn't
realize before what there is in it. Every note is perfect poetry."

"And it is all built on folk themes," he said. "That's the whole key to
Slavic art. Anything that blooms true from peasant seed must live—like
this—" he went to the piano and began to play the melody of *Vltava*, the
glorious, sorrowful epic of the river, moving, flowing, carrying its burden
of centuries and history. Claire stood with her head bent, listening intently
as the poignant theme developed under Anton's hands. Its sincerity went
straight to the heart. When he came to the polka he played looking up at
her and smiling.

"You see?" he said. "What we said at the opera. You can't have great
work without tenderness—and humor. Remember what you said about
poor Vašek. Here it is again. A great artist like Smetana expresses nobility
through being human. Saying simple things."

Claire made a mental comparison with the dreary pomposity of Wagner. She had a momentary remembrance of Hitler stalking through the halls at Bayreuth on his way to hear *Siegfried*. She shuddered. Anton noticed it and jumped up from the piano and came over and took her hands.

"What is it?" he asked softly. "What is it—dear?"

Claire raised her eyes and looked full into his. She thought she had never seen such intense kindness in any face. His eyes were like two brown bottomless wells of tenderness and warmth. He was only a little taller than Claire and he stood holding her two hands in his and looking straight into her eyes. The tears she had been feeling all day welled up suddenly and gushed over her cheeks.

"What is it?" he said again. *"Co je Ti, drahoušku?"* His hands were warm and very smooth, with fine strong muscles and bones. Claire tried to say something. She knew she had some answer to the pressing questions in his husky voice, in his searchingly eloquent eyes. But no words came. Her head fell forward. Anton took her slowly in his arms. Her head touched his chest, and rested against it. He held her closer and she felt his lips on her eyelids.

"Drahoušku," he whispered, with his lips on her face. She made a sound, an odd small gasping sob. "My poor, strange, lonely darling." He murmured softly in Czech. She raised her head again and let him look wonderingly at the revelation in her face.

She felt very weak, as if she would fall but for his arms clasped around her. He stood looking into her eyes, his own growing wider and more awe-struck as dawning realization turned into certainty. Claire bent her head against his chest finally as if she were blinded by sudden brilliant sunlight.

"Is it possible?" she heard Anton whisper. "Is it true—what I see?" His arms tightened and drew her hard against him. She did not know her own voice when she tried to answer. She only knew that everything outside the circle of these arms was a wilderness and a desert. His kiss was all strength and peace.

CHAPTER LXXXI

[May 1937]

FRANTIŠEK DVOŘÁK INSISTED on decorating the big farm wagon in the traditional way, with ribbons and garlands, for use as the ceremonial conveyance at the wedding. Julka protested weakly that it would be less comfortable than Claire's automobile for the bridal procession from the Town Hall in Hluboká, where the ceremony was to take place, to the wedding feast at the Dvořák homestead in Suchomel, seven kilometers away. But there was no arguing with František. No, Claire wanted her wedding according to family traditions, and he was going to see that she had it. Julka shrugged, smiling and absently putting on an apron wrong side to, and went away about her business, a hundred different details that she was supervising.

She had been overjoyed when Claire said that she wanted to be married at the Dvořák homestead. At first Julka had hardly been able to believe her. *Claire*—Paul Scott's grandniece—to be married at Suchomel! But then it was so astounding anyway, and so wonderful, and withal, so simple —Claire and Anton. One of those tremendous things at once too great and too simple to have been foreseen. Julka had laughed tearfully and said, *"What!* You don't know what you're talking about, darling. Suchomel! So funny and old-fashioned, nobody but farmers down there—"

"That's exactly why I want it," Claire had said firmly. She had looked at Anton in the way she did. He joined in her insistence.

"She really means it, Mama," he said. "We both do. That's just what we want."

Claire had given him another of the looks that made Julka's heart warm every time she saw it—that long, level glance profound with understanding and heavy with perfectly requited love. It was still too wonderful to believe, Julka thought again, that the goal of all Claire's wanderings and torments of spirit was her fine and gentle Anton. Julka sensed more of the shattering experience through which Claire had struggled to this journey's end than she would ever intimate. She would always remember the striking intuition with which she had watched Claire taking notice of Anton that day last winter when they met at his flat. There had been two or three occasions recently when she had felt Claire almost on the verge of some impulsive disclosure which would be the key to complete understanding of a half-sensed mystery.

But each time Claire only sighed and shook her head and said something about how incredibly blind and confused a person could be. Once she murmured something about the semblance and the reality, and when Julka asked of what, she only looked at Anton working at his desk and embraced him with her eyes. Another time when they came in together from a rehearsal of his concerto which—he laughingly said—he would have to find time to learn in spite of his new distraction, Claire dropped down on the floor and put her head in Julka's lap and said, "Why didn't you show me the way home sooner?"

It did amaze Julka that not even she had ever perceived the utter community of mind and spirit which lay latent between Claire and Anton. Nobody—least of all Claire herself—had looked back through the confused years to the only real happiness she had ever known, the sharing of music with her father. That was one completely sound seed which had lain hidden beneath decades of frippery and empty boredom. It lay ready for Anton to fertilize and bring to fruition quite as much as the womb itself of the woman he loved; and it held for him the same nourishment. He was full of ideas and music now, hard at work on a tone-poem which, he said, was his thank-offering for Claire. And she too was full of new purpose and energy and—Julka saw with deep gratification—of wisdom. She was working harder than ever, beginning to win important international notice with her dispatches and some of her daring feats of newsgathering in hostile and heavily censored places. Her name was becoming a notable by-line. She did not, as a younger and more bedazzled woman would have done, stay moon-eyed in Prague to be with Anton. She went about her business, which took her to the four corners of Europe, and when she had a week or a few days clear, would fly back to him to stay as long as she could. Julka would never forget the clutch at her heart the first time she saw Claire, on return-ing from a journey, go into Anton's arms. That warm and gentle spirit, that vigorous mind, and that strong, stocky body were literally what Claire had called them—her home.

There was only one flaw in the wedding plans, and that was that Mary had written both Julka and Claire that she could not possibly come. They were bitterly disappointed. If, as Julka had said, this marriage and having the wedding here were to bring together all the threads that Mary herself had begun years ago to spin, certainly she ought to be here. It grieved Julka to think Mary was so old and frail that she could not face the journey, though she had not said that in her letter. But Claire quickly put Julka right about that.

"Oh, no," she said, when she and Anton reached the homestead the day before the wedding. "It's not that at all. She couldn't be kept from coming—except by trouble at the mill."

Julka raised her eyebrows. "Trouble" at the mill meant to her either bad times with shutdowns and misery for Jerry, or labor trouble, of which there seemed to be plenty in the United States now. Jerry himself was all wrapped up in this Steel Workers' Organizing Committee. In fact, it was all Julka ever heard from Jerry or about him. But Claire explained that Mary's "trouble" was that threatened by Ben Nicholas. Claire had ex-plained to Anton too that she would have to go back in the early fall for the stockholders' meeting. Mary had written her, "I would love to come for the wedding, dear; you know nothing else in the world would keep me. But I don't dare. The exact status of Ben's stock purchases, which you asked me to send you, is this:

"Since you were last here, he has approached every member of the family except you and me. He bought Willy's share more than a year ago, and tried to buy Angelica's at the same time, but she would not sell. I understand she thinks that 'vulgar.' I do know, though, that she has prom-ised to vote with him in any issue he may make. Then he sounded out Tom and Ruth and Ted. But, as I wrote you, Ruth had already sold her stock to Ted."

Mary had reported that last fall. Ted had bought Ruth's stock when most of the remaining preferred was retired in November, and Ted had had cash for the first time in nearly six years. Ruth had had a dreadful time during the years when no dividends were paid, putting Pauline through college and helping Ruthie's husband who had lost his job. It was really Ted's duty to liquidate her frozen Scott holding for her, and he had done so.

"But," this most recent letter of Mary's went on, "Ben has been press-ing both Tom and Ted to sell him their stock. This is dreadfully serious, dear. So far, Ted assures me that he will not sell his stock to Ben or any-body else, ever; he says it is the one absolute obligation he feels to the mill for his father's sake. But that is not to say he will not vote with Ben if there is any split among the stockholders. And the reason I dare not leave here and go to Europe for your wedding now is that I learned only yesterday that Ben has finally bought Tom's stock. This means that he now owns or controls forty-five per cent of all the stock, just as you and I do. If Ted should vote with Ben in a showdown they will have a majority over us. If we are to keep control, we must see that Ted votes with us. Oh dear, it is just as bad as the deadlock in 1901, and I feel almost afraid to shut my eyes at night for fear I will wake up and find the mill gone in the morning. Of course I don't have to tell you you must come for the meeting in October, you know that yourself. But don't be too upset about leaving Anton if I cable you to come sooner. I shan't do it unless it is absolutely necessary and I feel I can't cope with all this by myself. Or perhaps Anton might come with you?"

That would be impossible, Claire knew already. She would be leaving just at the time when Anton was beginning rehearsals for the winter season. But she would not be gone long, and they must always expect to be separated from time to time on account of her work. They would get used to that; they were not children, thank God, Claire had said.

Julka felt better about Mary's absence when Claire explained the reason for it, and that night they all sat in the big, low-ceilinged room with the carved woodwork, the huge tile stove, the heavy peasant furniture and the embroidered tablecovers, composing a long cablegram to Mary which was to be signed with the names of all the Dvořáks. It would cost Claire a fortune and give the Pittsburgh cable operator a terrible half hour, but they did not care. They laughed and sang and shouted and clinked beer glasses. They had talked a mile a minute all through supper, Jan especially, asking Claire an insistent stream of questions about the planes in which she so often flew across Europe. Jan was seventeen now, and obsessed with aviation. He had got his father's reluctant permission to go straight from the Gymnasium into flight training, instead of to the University like his brothers. He was going to join the Air Force. There was a military field near České Budějovice, and for a year past he had been slipping off on his bicycle to watch the pilots training there.

"He is nuts about aeroplanes," Libuše, his youngest sister, said suddenly.

Julka gasped and said, "Who taught you that? Nuts?"

Claire laughed. "Who do you think? They get a lesson every time I come."

"What kind of lesson? I suppose you teach them to swear, too?"

"Sure," Jan said, looking up from his plate. "I can cuss to beat hell."

Anton exploded into his napkin at that, with Anička bewilderedly slapping him on the back, and his mother saying crossly to Jan, "It's a good thing your *tatínek* doesn't understand English! He'd strap you for being fresh."

After supper, when the men were settled with their pipes and their beer, and the girls had finished washing the dishes, they came and took Claire by her hands and led her over to a corner of the room where a large table stood, covered with a white cloth. Dora and her sister Milada made a little speech, welcoming Claire to the family and wishing her and Anton happiness. Then they took the cover off the table and Claire saw there the piles of linen that all the girls had been making for her. The table was stacked with handwoven and embroidered bed linen and table linen and towels. Claire felt a lump rising in her throat, and though there was no reason why, if she felt like it, she should not weep among these people she loved, she stood struggling with a wave of emotion. She had had to pretend to be surprised; anyone half so observant as she would have noticed the excited quick motions of hiding something, the delighted squeals of laughter from the girls during the past months while Claire and Anton were engaged.

She stood before the piled table, with the girls chattering excitedly around her, incoherently trying to thank them and show them what this meant to her; and Julka stood and watched her and thought how unbelievable life could be. Here was this woman dressed like a fashion-plate in a Paris dress and handmade shoes from Vienna and her grandmother's legendary pearls, the gift of Royalty, while on her left hand shone the old-fashioned cluster of rose-diamonds set in heavy gold which Julka's peasant son had put there. The ring had no monetary value compared with Constance's jewels which Claire kept in bank vaults, but no emerald, no pigeon-blood ruby had ever brought such a look to her face as the odd old jewel of ancient Bohemian workmanship. I ought to have known, Julka was telling herself, I should have understood what she was so hungry for. Why she always loved to come to our house. Why I always loved her.

Claire turned slowly at that moment and saw the look in Julka's plain, worn, passionate face; and thought quickly of what this rock of a woman had given her—everything, Claire said to herself—everything I've learned, even—even— She burst into tears, and threw her arms around Julka. The chattering girls drifted tactfully away. "How," Claire choked and whispered to Julka in English, "how can I ever—"

Julka pressed Claire's face to her breast and said something very softly in her own language.

They were married next day in the Town Hall in Hluboká with all the Dvořák cousins and relatives about them. The mayor performed the ceremony. Julka stood with Claire, Thomáš Dvořák with Anton. Everybody except the bride and groom was dressed in full ceremonial national costume, the women in layers of starched, lacy petticoats, magnificently embroidered blouses and aprons, red boots, and huge bow headdresses; the men in black trousers, full-sleeved white lawn shirts, and waistcoats encrusted with embroidery in silk and gold. Anton had chosen not to wear such clothes. He was, after all, American born, and he wanted to recognize that in the midst of this ancestral setting. He wore a plain dark gray suit, which beside Claire's simple pale blue crepe dress made them look like two modest sparrows amid all the gorgeous plumage.

Some of the relatives had been quite shocked at the idea of a civil ceremony and no church celebration. Even when Julka pointed out all the obvious reasons—Claire was not even a Catholic, she was divorced, Anton was not a devout churchman—they were still puzzled and disappointed. But they listened approvingly as Claire spoke her brief responses to the Mayor's questions in good clear Czech, and they nodded and smiled and beamed when the Mayor pronounced the couple man and wife and Anton took Claire in his arms and kissed her so tenderly and reverently that there was not a dry eye in the room.

Then they all trooped out into the brilliant May sunshine, where František's magnificent red wagon stood waiting, garlanded from stem to stern with fresh flowers, fluttering with streamers, the gray horses in caparisoned harness. Anton lifted Claire up to the front seat and climbed up beside her, while František proudly picked up the whip and reins and the procession started to Suchomel to the homestead. Ahead of the bridal conveyance marched the village band, a dozen glittering brasses played by stout farmers and their sons, the instruments dressed with ribbon streamers, the players red-faced with pride and exertion.

Every passer-by waved and wished them luck as they rounded the gentle curves of the highway and came upon view after view of entrancing loveliness. Farm carts, flocks of snow-white geese, bicycles, and farm machinery towed by teams and tractors dotted the stretches of the road. The landscape was not so lushly beautiful now as at midsummer when it was a dream of waving grain and brilliant field flowers alternating with the funny Indian-tents of the hop-poles with their coverings of vines. But it was beautiful; the freshly planted rich black earth worked this way and that in carefully measured strips, the pale tender green of the winter-wheat fields, the clouds of bloom on all the fruit trees. Plum and pear and cherry orchards were planted at intervals between the worked fields, giving off heavenly perfume as they rumbled slowly by.

At the homestead the high courtyard doors stood open and the procession moved inside, where the riders descended and the bride and groom were motioned to lead the way to the feast. There was a stretch of meadow behind the Dvořák house, separated from the court by a plaster wall and high board doors. These were open wide, and the sight beyond in the smooth meadow, green with fresh young grass, drew shouts of delight from the wedding party. Long tables were ranged in rows under the trees, with benches alongside. The tables were spread with embroidered cloths and set with plates and cutlery assembled from all the branches of the Dvořák tribe. And down the length of the tables was spread such a profusion of food that Claire stopped suddenly, her hand pressing Anton's arm, and gulped down a rush of tears. These people were not rich, certainly not in money; and when she had made her plan to be married here she had never thought with what lavishness they would prepare and serve this feast.

It went without saying that the whole village was invited, and it was clear too that all the guests had made some contribution, of help or of part of the wonderful repast before them. But the Dvořáks, and František's household especially, had done most of the work; the men had raised the food and the women had slaved to prepare it. Claire felt almost stunned by the sudden weight of obligation she had incurred. She would never, she whispered to Anton, never be able to do anything remotely adequate to prove her appreciation.

"You love them, *miláčku*," he said, smiling at her. "That's all the thanks they want."

They were all clustering round the two flower-decked high-backed chairs at the head of the main table, and after the bride and groom were seated amid a clamor of cheers, everybody else took his place and the seven Dvořák girls, František's daughters and nieces, assisted by half a dozen volunteers among their friends, began to serve the meal. Dora, home from her medical studies and looking comically tiny inside her unaccustomed petticoats, was the general supervisor.

"Look at her," Claire said to Anton, "would you think she had just won the highest honors in her class? She looks as if she'd never been away from here."

"She's not the only one," Julka said, leaning across Anton. "That tall girl over there—with the glasses—she's got a doctorate in political economy."

"And she's cutting bread like all the mamas!" The girl was indeed slicing a huge round loaf, holding it against her breast and wielding the knife vigorously.

Claire sighed as a plate was put before her. "If only it wasn't my wedding!" she said ruefully. "I'm too excited to eat. And I want to so badly!"

They all laughed at her. Nobody else seemed to be too full of emotion to have a good appetite. Platter after platter of irresistible food disappeared and was quickly replaced. There were hams, of course, raised and cured by František, great pompous-looking mounds of sweet white fat and delicate pink meat, moist and perfumed with their juice. There were rich crusty roasts of pork. There was goose—Claire could not imagine how many of the famous white inhabitants of the village had made the supreme sacrifice for her, but the platters were heaped with luscious chunks of roast goose, dark tender meat under crisp fat skin, generously salted and specked with caraway seed. There were sausages, and smoking tureens of creamy sauerkraut. There were bowls of mushrooms, cooked in a wonderful, subtle sauce of sour cream and herbs. There was a goose-liver pâté, finer than anything Claire had ever eaten in France. There were whole enormous goose-livers coddled in their own fat, bristling like porcupines with slivered almonds. There were three magnificent carp caught in the nearby lake and cooked in three traditional ways. There were fruit compotes in glass bowls spaced the lengths of the tables, their mingled colors like bright jewels. When everyone had eaten his way through the main mountain of the meal the tables were cleared and the girls emerged in a long single-file procession from the courtyard, carrying the sweets on trays and platters. Cakes and pastry; coffee cakes, cheese cakes, fruit cakes, tarts filled with glittering slices of apple, apricot, and plum; chocolate and mocha tarts rich with butter and cream, delicate pastry pockets stuffed with nuts, cheese, jam, or poppyseed.

And all the time the good local white wine and the delectable pale beer from Plzeň had been flowing from barrels and kegs ranged against the courtyard wall. Now that appetites were satisfied everybody wanted to sit with a full glass before him and join in the toasts and cheers as the speeches began. František led off with a stentorious toast to the bride and groom; then Anton leaped to his feet and toasted his bride, his mother, his uncle, and all the old friends who had given such pledges of loyalty today.

When he sat down Claire turned and looked at him and tried for the thousandth time to feel that it was queer for this man, this musician, this foreigner, this son of poverty whose early home had been a hovel in the shadow of her great-grandfather's steel mill to be her husband now. And she could not feel that it was strange, she could not feel it unrelated to the long courses of all the lives with which hers had been entwined. She felt the forces that had moulded all those lives, and one strange, gentle, irresistible force more than all, one frail tiny woman alone in that house on the other side of the world.

CHAPTER LXXXII

[*June 1937*]

THE BURNING SUN beat on their oiled naked bodies as they lay on the rocks below the garden with the sea lapping at their feet. Close about them it was dramatically quiet; the cry of a bird was startling. But distant everyday noises echoed in the clear hot air. The put-put of a motorboat, a fisherman shouting. Behind his dark spectacles Anton opened one eye and peered at Claire. Her long legs and broad, flat hips and shoulders, her tapering back were smoothly bronzed. Her fingers twined in Anton's strong short ones were deep brown. He pressed them gently and said, "You're a jungle cat, *miláčku*. Haven't you had enough for today?"

She rolled over and rested on her elbows and looked down into his face. His fair skin had turned a ruddy tan. His crest of hair was straw-colored from the sun. The thick blond hair on his chest was bleached to pale gold. She sighed and said, "I'd forgotten how nice it is here."

"Only in the proper company."

"Oh, don't be such an old puritan. You've had fun."

"God knows! I don't understand what I'm doing here or how I got here, but it has certainly been fun. In fact I never had any fun before."

He kissed her lingeringly, rubbing his chin gently on her cheeks.

"Don't string me along with that," she murmured. "What do you expect me to think you did all those years? Enjoy deep thoughts and solitude?"

"Did you?"

"I wasn't an appetizing bachelor."

"You were appetizing, though." He took her brown fingers in his mouth and bit them softly. "*Rozkošná!*"

"Darling," she said suddenly, "did you have lots of different girls?"

"Lots!"

"Pig! Bull!"

"Why did you ask?"

"Why wouldn't I? I hate them all! I'd like to hunt them all down and kill them one by one."

"By all means."

"*Don't* tease me!"

"But I'm not." He put one arm around her and drew her head into the curve of his shoulder. "I always answer your questions truthfully."

"Then who were they?"

"*Ach*, suppose I tell you? Will it make you happier? Will you answer if I ask you such questions?"

"Certainly not." She shut her teeth with a snap. She hoped her tone was as light as his. "Your case is different."

"I see. So a poor little dancer at the *Divadlo*, one of those girls you admire so much, must die to placate your vanity. I said you are a jungle cat."

"Anton! Do you mean to tell me one of those ballet girls was your mistress?" She reared up on her elbow and glared at him.

"But my beautiful brown *lvice*, that's what ballet girls are for. So I would be free and unencumbered until you came to me." His brown eyes glowed, deep and eloquent with tenderness.

"Oh, darling."

"*Drahoušku!*" He swallowed and made a helpless gesture. They stared at each other as if for the first time.

"I can't find words . . ." he spoke thickly.

She shook her head. Sometimes they felt suffocated with the weight of their feelings, the urge to tell each other of their love, the longing of each to hear the other's endearments, the infinite wonder of discovery that had lain at the end of the strange years. Sometimes they woke in the middle of the night, to find themselves locked in desperate embrace, Claire on the verge of tears, crying, "Is it you, darling? Is it really you?" Her hands would run over his face and head, down his stocky, hairy body. "Stay here, Anton. Stay here and never leave me."

"Leave you! After I've found you. After you're mine!" His arms were like steel around her. His head between her breasts was a great warm rock to which she clung. Often when they lay so they felt their pulses beating in unison. It was something they noticed and knew and did not mention until a time when she heard his bass voice muffled almost to silence, a throb, rather than a hum, marking the perfect beat of their joined pulses with an almost inaudible melody. She tightened her clasp about him and listened raptly. Later she whispered, "Have you got it? Our music?"

"Yes. But only for us. Nobody else will ever hear it." They exchanged a look that turned her face a deep scarlet. His too was suffused. They reached out speechless to touch one another. It was if they were on the brink again of their very first discovery.

They had come to the Villa Bellevue on an impulse of Claire's, another

sudden choice as decisive as her wish to be married at Suchomel. And with
quite as much deep-seated reason. Anton hesitated when she suggested it.
She knew he had one great mental obstacle to surmount, the thought of the
wealth and ostentation, the luxury, the aristocratic presumption of her
background which took every kind of privilege for granted. It was very
much harder for Anton to accept and adapt himself to that than for Claire
to make any adjustment to his world, his people, and his past. Claire loved
to reminisce about their childhood in Pittsburgh, the good suppers cooked
by Míla and eaten around the oilcloth table in the kitchen; Charlie
and Jerry tired after their day at the mill; Anton—"you were such
a funny, quiet little boy, darling. I thought you were years younger
than I."

"That's because you were such a worldly little brat." Actually he was
six months older than Claire. "You scared me to death."

"Rot."

But she saw that he was still apprehensive of the background which
had made her seem so arrogant. He was profoundly sure of himself on the
grounds of accomplishment and hard work, but he was reluctant to be
confronted by the tangible magnificences of Claire's childhood. He only
consented to go to Cannes in the end when she told him that it was because
"—I can't put it into words without seeming mawkish—but it's the only
way I have of introducing you to Daddy—and Mère Constance. I want—
to tie everything up."

And when they wandered hand in hand through the vast ghostly house,
lighted only by glimmers filtering through the locked *jalousies;* through
the long elegant salons with their fragile precious furniture draped in sheets,
their Aubussons rolled in mothproofing, their tapestries and draperies gone
from the bare walls and windows, Anton found himself in deep harmony
with Claire's nostalgic quiet.

"She would have loved you, darling," she said.

"I find that so hard to believe, *miláčku.* I think of her as being dreadfully angry at your—what would such people call it—mésalliance?"

"You don't realize what she was like. She used to sit out there on that
terrace under an Indian silk canopy and raise hell with everybody. But
she never raised hell about anything real. She was as tough and clear-
minded as—well"—Claire swallowed—"your brother Jerry."

"But she would never have understood—us."

"That's the only wrong idea you've ever had. She'd have been thrilled.
Quite aside from the novelty—you overlook what a kick she'd have got
from that. But she didn't give a damn who people were or where they came
from, so long as they amused her or were accomplished or powerful or
famous. She couldn't endure nonentities or stuffed shirts. How I wish you'd
known her!"

They were standing in the dining-room, looking at the long sheeted
table where thirty had often sat down to Gonneau's works of gastronomic
art. Claire licked her lips reminiscently.

"I really prefer the food we eat at home," she said, "but you ought to
have tasted his *dindonneau truffé.* And his *petite marmite*—his *poularde*

Louise d'Orleans, his *sauce diable*—" she sighed. "Poor chap, he was a great artist."

"What became of him?"

"Blown to smithereens in his field kitchen. Somebody"—she shuddered —"found his right hand beside a soup ladle."

They talked endlessly about the war. The first hour after their arrival, as soon as they could shake Jeannot, tremulous with joy and tearfully effusive about *"ma p'tite et son joli nouveau M'sieu'"* they walked down to the olive grove and sat with their backs against the very tree where Claire had sat with Evan the day he left for the war. Anton drew her head against his shoulder and listened intently as she talked about her father. He soon perceived that she had never been so close to anyone else until she found him. The lone survivor of her last three cats came slowly down the walk, made his grave acknowledgments to Anton, put a tentative paw on Claire's face as she picked him up, and finally settled down to purr in her lap. She scratched him softly under the chin.

"Poor old Brioche," she said sadly. "He thinks I've come back to stay." The cat was the color of a perfectly baked brioche, the center streak down his back shiny like glazed crust.

"Are you sure you're not sorry? That this is—all over?"

Claire looked at Anton with worship.

"I wasn't even sorry before I found you. This world has ended. And now—you're—you're *life,* darling. This is death. I love the place. I love my memories here. But it's all haunted with death. I've seen so much death here." She told him of tragic scenes during the war when gallant men supposedly on their way to recovery had gone to pieces and died—"just like that." She snapped her fingers. "Once when I was reading to an eye case, a youngster about eighteen—" she broke off and shuddered. Anton held her closer.

"Don't think about those things, *miláčku.*"

She was silent for a time but then she looked up and said in a low, very serious tone, "If we don't think, we're putting our heads in the sand. We've got to think. The whole fearful thing is going to happen all over again, God help us."

"It can't. It mustn't."

"Don't fool yourself, dearest. Don't ever let me fool myself. Think about Spain—just a few hours over there." She waved toward the west. "The war's begun there again. *The* war—not just a war."

His hands tightened on her. "I don't want you to go there."

"I may be sent."

He opened his mouth to protest further and then shut it suddenly. Claire watched him. When she saw what had passed through his mind she drew a long breath and said, "I'd rather die this minute, here in your arms, than be away from you without reason. But—"

"I know."

She told him about the last talk she had had with her father, seated in this very spot. "The things he talked about that day," she said slowly, "are clearer now. Much." Anton waited for her to explain.

"I can hear him," she said, closing her eyes and speaking raptly, "as if it were today. He was British, of course—his speech was so beautiful and polished. He said, 'There are certain things a man has to be willing to die for.'" She paused. Anton said softly, "Of course. Of course there are. Every man knows that."

She turned to him with a sudden motion, scattering the cat off her lap. Flinging herself into his arms she cried, "I don't want it to happen again! Oh darling, I can't bear it to happen all over again!" She burst into tears and sobbed against his breast. He held her tightly and crooned to her.

"Don't cry, *miláčku*. My heart, my dear heart. It has upset you to come here." He pressed his strong hand hard under her breast, tight against her heart. "You're safe now. We've got each other—we're strong together—" They kissed with desperate intensity. "Don't cry." He lifted her over into his lap and sat holding her in his arms, her head buried against him, for a long time, while the blazing June sun sank slowly in a pool of fiery light and the blue water in the distance turned blood-color in the reflection.

CHAPTER LXXXIII

[*September 1937*]

AT THE END OF THE FLIGHT from New York to Pittsburgh Claire sat enthralled as the plane circled over the County Airport for its landing. Her nose was pressed to the window, her eyes strained to catch every part of the panorama below. She had never made this flight before and she thought, "I shall never come any other way again. This is one of the great sights of America." It was late dusk, the time of all times to behold this scene. The juncture of rivers lay spread below, narrow, twisting, brown, oily serpents with a thousand fiery mouths and tentacles belching flames and smoke upward at the thick sky through which the plane was cautiously banking downwards. Long worms of freight trains crawled along their banks. Clusters of blast stoves and chimneys and the snouts of Bessemers strung on mile upon mile of black sheds, spotted the landscape through rolling billows of yellow and red and brown and black smoke. It was terrible, it was beautiful; it was like no other sight on earth; and when Claire stepped from the plane onto the wild, windy elevation of the airport, she lifted her head and drew in great breaths of the heavy, smoke-laden air with its smell of coke, metal, and the penetrating damp of the rivers.

Mary stood waiting at the gate; such a tiny, fragile figure! She was as erect and as light-footed as ever, but she moved quite slowly and her small body seemed half the size and weight Claire remembered. Her hair gleamed snow white and her delicate face was framed in a white cloud. She was dressed in soft dark blue—how like her, Claire thought, hurrying toward her, not to wear the black or gray that made old ladies such a dull, redundant picture!

Claire took Mary in her arms and kissed her papery old cheeks, exclaiming and hugging her. Mary turned her head upwards and looked hard and eagerly at Claire, as if to see whether she looked any different for being Anton's wife now. But Claire only shook her head and laughed and said, "same old *Gesicht,* darling!" and then, instead of going into the terminal, stood for another moment gazing at the fantastic, gripping scene. The great silver plane stood lumbering against a wild, smoky sky. The men moving about it were busy dwarfs tending the wants of a monster poised on this theatrical crag before soaring into its habitat again.

"It's wonderful!" Claire kept exclaiming, craning her neck and deeply breathing the acrid air. "It's the most exciting place in the world. Oh— *look!*" she cried suddenly, seizing Mary's thin arm. She pointed to the ridge along the lowering horizon, just beyond the sharp artificial plateau of the airport. Silhouetted against the yellow evening sky with its streaks and swirls of billowing smoke, a train of dump-cars chuffed busily along, each car a squat box on wheels like a child's drawing, heaping full of flame.

"What is it?" Claire asked. "What's going on?" She was quite unconscious of the stir she was making; everyone around here was so used to the sight that nobody mentioned it. Claire stood still at the gate, staring openmouthed as the train halted in the center of the ridge, its engine spewing out a trail of black smoke. The train jerked a little, the cars shuddered, and with one motion rolled over in unison. From each a charge of fire slid down the slope. The engine chuffed again and pulled the train away, leaving the whole side of the hill a mass of molten flame. Claire still held Mary's arm tight in an excited grip.

"What is it?" she insisted. "What's going on?"

The colored porter told her. "Slag," he explained prosaically. "De bigges' slag heap in de worl'. Dey fillin' some mo' groun' to make de airpote bigger. Dey takes de slag offen de mills roun' hyah an' runs it out an' dumps it while it bunnin'."

"They had to make the whole airport that way," Mary said as they stood waiting for their taxi. "There wasn't enough level ground in Allegheny County to make an airport. So they took a big hill and sliced off the top and filled up the sides."

Mary thought of the excited child whom she had first brought to Paul's house twenty—no, twenty-two—years ago exactly. Claire sat in the taxi craning her neck at the stark landscape. All about lay the ruins of a once lovely countryside, the steep, jutting hills and swooping valleys now a dejected spread of stripped black ground, horribly gloomy in the dark twilight. Abandoned coal tipples leaned crazily from the sides of bare hills. Small wretched trees struggled for survival amid the slag-heaps, and nothing grew on the pitted, riddled earth. Everywhere there were tracks; train tracks and trolley tracks and the gloomy bastion of the PV & C's main right-of-way, elevated on miles of solid masonry high enough to clear the slum streets of Munhall and Homestead. The very names of the boroughs stirred awful memories in Claire's mind. She had heard Uncle Paul tell of the violence and remorseless brutality which had shaped these places and the lives toiled out in them. She shuddered as they drove past row on row of millworkers' houses; crumbling brick and clapboard dwellings shoulder to shoulder, all touched by the same enormous brush of dilapidation, dirt, and poverty. Grimy children and flea-bitten mongrel dogs tumbled on the broken stoops and in the littered gutters. A saloon on every corner sent a beacon of dim yellow light into the cavern-like street.

She thought poignantly of Anton. But for his mother's energy and tenacity he might have been a child exactly like these. He would have been —she was startled as the thought drove in upon her—a millworker like his father, like Jerry. She sat up stiffly in the bumping taxi. Her face set in a peculiar expression of amazement. For the first time the whole concept of identity and position stood out sharp and ominous with promises of trouble. She turned to Mary and said in a breathless tone, "My God, I never thought of it before. *My name is Mrs. Liska.*"

"Rather a strange time to find it out," Mary said. "I thought it had been your name for four months."

"Yes, but—" Claire made a motion of consternation. "It means one thing in Prague and something else entirely here. Jerry—and Bella—and the girls. And the mill," she said breathlessly. "What kind of a spot am I going to be in about that?"

"Difficult, I should say," Mary said. "Ben is going to make all the trouble he possibly can. That's why I cabled finally. Between Jerry's union and Ben's machinations—"

"Good God! And I've never given a thought to Ted and Lauchlan either. What'll they say?"

"I'll be more interested to see what they do. They're not likely to welcome Jerry Liska's sister-in-law with open arms."

Claire burst out laughing. "I've hardly seen them anyway when I was here."

"Well," Mary said, "you'd better be planning to see them now. And Ben too. If you mean to keep the mill, that is."

"What actually precipitated your cable?" Claire asked curiously.

"Lauchlan's telling me that Ted and Ben were just like that"—Mary held up two fingers pressed together, in imitation of Lauchlan—"about the mill, and we might as well save them what she called the 'bore' of a showdown about it."

"And," Claire asked slowly, "you wouldn't know what put Ted in Ben's pants pocket, would you, darling?"

"Lauchlan," said Mary quietly.

"I see." Claire stroked her chin slowly, a queer masculine gesture which of itself said that nothing people did could be particularly shocking to her. "So Ben and Lauchlan—"

Mary's pale, wrinkled skin turned a delicate pink. "Ted has no idea," she said. "If it could be handled without—without—"

"—smashing his life to pieces, poor chap—"

"I thought perhaps you, dear—"

"This isn't a pushover by any means," Claire said. "I'm a Hunky now, you know—at least to Ben and Ted and Lauchlan. I've got quite a situation on my hands."

"I know," Mary said. "You'd have one—even without bumping into some old-fashioned Pittsburgh prejudices."

Claire did not miss the acid note in Mary's thin voice. She thought swiftly of Uncle Paul. Of his bad humor that day years ago when he took her and Ted to call on Lauchlan's family, and Mary stayed at home. She looked intently at Mary and said, "I see what you mean. I've tangled up the dividing lines so nobody knows where I stand. Well"—she lit a cigarette and cheerfully blew out a lungful of smoke—"maybe I've been smart."

"And maybe," Mary said dryly, "both the Liskas and the Scotts will keep their distances."

"I wonder what Uncle Paul would say," Claire mused.

"He'd say you're as bad as your grandmother."

The first hurdle was easier than Claire had hoped. Jerry and Bella came around that very evening. Claire herself let them in at the side door. Jerry's greeting was easy and natural. Bella was a little constrained; she was uncertain how to deal with Claire in her astonishing position as sister-in-law. Claire kissed her warmly and asked about the baby and the other children and ran upstairs to get the presents she had brought them, and did all she could to create a pleasant bustle. She studied Bella narrowly when she had the chance. The set, bitter look was gone from her face. But she had never been pretty, and the years of hardship had etched anxious lines in her forehead and run them sharply from her nose to the corners of her mouth. Looking from Bella to Jerry, and catching a glimpse of herself in the mantel mirror, Claire felt again the startling sensation of unreality that had come over her in the taxi; the curious disbelief that she had the same name as these two, that she was related to them now, that her Anton, the thought of whom flooded her with warm longing, was Jerry's brother. Beyond all that she was bewildered and surprised and incredulously relieved to find that seeing Jerry, and talking to him, knowing he must be thinking the same thoughts as she, did not disturb her in the least. There was nothing in his face to indicate that his attitude toward her had ever been different by a hair's breadth from now. The most surprising part of it all, Claire thought, pouring out beer in the pantry, was that he acted like a shrewd man of the world. In Mère Constance's circles she would have taken this for granted. Here it was unexpected and amazing.

Jerry came through the swing door to carry in the tray of glasses to the parlor. For a moment they stood there together by the sink, silently watching the foam from the last bottle of beer curl up to the top of the glass and cling there without overflowing to form a rich white crest. Then Jerry picked up the tray and stood there a moment looking over it at Claire. She gazed back, a flutter of trepidation giving way to calm reassurance as his dark eyes searched her face.

"You—you okay, Claire?" he asked in a low voice. "You and Tony?"

"We're wonderful," she answered softly.

Jerry smiled a little. "That's swell. Say—I—" he broke off awkwardly. Claire laid her hand on his arm and nodded. "I understand," she said. "I've got a lot to thank you for."

He turned to push open the door. "You're a hell of a swell woman," he said over his shoulder.

"Thanks." Claire's voice was shaky. She followed him into the back parlor carrying a plate of crackers. Mary was busy talking to Bella. She did not look up as they crossed the room.

Over the beer and crackers Claire listened intently to Jerry's account of the union situation at the mill. He prefaced most of his story with the point that he really had no business telling Claire about the S.W.O.C.'s progress in organizing the men, "but if I start trying to decide which side you're on I'll go nuts," he said. It was another way of saying that he trusted her and Claire warmed with pride.

"On the outside," Jerry said, "Scott's looks like all the other shops. Tough and ugly. They never had SOB's like the men at Little Steel running the place but one little independent is as bad as another. Scott's record has been about the same as the rest."

"I wish I'd been here when the big breaks came," Claire said. "I've read every word I could lay my hands on about the U. S. Steel contract and of course the Jones and Laughlin one. But I still feel pretty ignorant about it all."

"Well," Jerry said, "you don't need to know so much. Just that Scott's is the kind of a tough little independent we want to get cleaned up before we move on some more of the bigger ones. In one way the shop's so goddam small it don't really matter—only it fits in the picture the way they've drawn it—" He gulped a draught of beer and wiped his mouth with the back of his hand. "Scott's is gonna sign, that's all. Or else."

"We couldn't afford a strike," Claire said thoughtfully.

"We're not interested in what you can afford," Jerry said, reversing his first placing of Claire and adding, "you stockholders. Strikes are tougher on us. We're not afraid of 'em, though."

"I don't see why there should be one. U. S. Steel didn't have one."

"No," said Jerry, with a hard grin, "but J and L did."

"We don't need to," Claire said slowly. "Not for my money."

"Oh, no? Ask some of your directors. That bastard Rogers—for one."

"Joe Rogers' son," Mary put in.

"Rogers Coke," Jerry snorted. "Dirtiest outfit in the district. Lousy with finks and police. They stink to heaven."

"Are you organizing them too?"

"We can't do everything at once. But you ought to get shed of that crummy hand-me-down on your board. And a few others too."

"I'd be delighted. Only don't expect me to barge in and make a spectacle of my ignorance, Jerry. I don't know most of the directors, in fact I don't even know Gray Simcox except to say hello. What about him?"

"I guess maybe he'll play ball. He oughta be a tough bastard in his spot but he's not. He's kind of gone along because steel men hang together. It's Ted Scott you'll have trouble with—"

Claire smoked thoughtfully. "Ted has nothing to gain by opposing the contract," she said.

"Ted hasn't got a gut of his own," Jerry said.

Mary opened her mouth to say something but changed her mind and stayed silent. Claire finished her beer and sat back, staring at the ceiling. It was as well that nobody had mentioned Ben Nicholas in all this. Jerry was not telling everything he knew and Claire saw it would be smarter if she held back some things too. Bella spoke unexpectedly; she had not joined the conversation at all. She asked, using Claire's first name diffidently, "Why are you so anxious for the company to sign with the union? I'd think—"

Claire smiled. "—I might be a reactionary like most stockholders? Well, but for Mr. Adolf Schicklgruber I probably would be. But I've spent most of the past year working in Germany, Bella. You learn fast on that spot." She turned to Jerry. "There are plenty of potential Thyssens right here," she added.

"You're telling me."

"You certainly have changed," Bella murmured. She was thinking, Claire saw, of the times not so many years ago when Claire had stopped by her house bringing messages or presents for the children from Julka, and Bella had been openly resentful of the lady-bountiful with the glittering car and the fur coat and the graciousness that made Bella feel her own shabbiness like a hair shirt.

The telephone rang. Mary went to the pantry to answer it and came back and said, "That was Ted."

"Oh," said Jerry, "does he keep track of your doings? How polite."

"That'll do for you," Mary said sharply. "Ted's as good as the rest of you—in lots of ways—"

"You've got a nerve," Bella told him. "Come on, we've got to go home."

"Okay, Mama." He paused in the hall and said to Claire, "For God's sake watch your step when you start butting in around the shop. Everybody'll suspect everything about you."

"And mostly they'll be right," she said, laughing. "Good night."

CHAPTER LXXXIV

[September 1937—Continued]

LAUCHLAN SCOTT put down the telephone and turned irritably to Ted. "There," she said. "I hope you're satisfied. She's coming and I'm damned if I see what for."

"I thought we had that all out. You know as well as I do—you told Ben you'd go ahead and ask her. After all it's his idea."

She reached across her breakfast tray for her address book.

"I don't know what I'll do with her," she said. "Nobody'll like her. People always hate a freak."

"Never mind," Ted said. "This isn't the kind of party where it matters. Now you be nice."

He leaned over and kissed his wife lingeringly. After twenty years of marriage he clung to the daily small rituals of affection with constant dependence. Lauchlan absent-mindedly held up her lean, firm jaw for him to kiss. She was ruffling through the pages of her address book, thoroughly annoyed at this business of having Ted's crazy cousin for the week-end. Claire had been queer enough before, the few times Lauchlan had seen her, but now this awful marriage on top of everything else. Married to a Hunky —Lauchlan shuddered. Ted went out to start for the office and promptly ten minutes later the private telephone on the farther side of Lauchlan's bed buzzed softly. She answered at once, saying "Hello, darling," without questioning the caller. This was understood to be a telephone for outgoing calls only.

"Oh, you can't let me down like that!" she cried, after listening a moment.

"Can't tell you how bad this may be," Ben said. He was calling from New York. "Of course I'll come if I can."

"But you let me in for it. I'm not going to sit and be palsy-walsy with her. And Ted—well, you know—"

"I know," Ben said, "but can't you understand English? I tell you the market's broken wide open." Even Ben's imperturbable flat voice was sharp.

"What a hell of a nuisance."

"You may find it more than a nuisance," Ben said. "I sold your Douglas last Thursday. If I hadn't you'd have dropped twenty thousand since yesterday noon."

"God." She paused. "You're marvellous, Benjie."

"We'll see about that. Miss me?"

"Terribly." She wriggled lower in her pillows, holding the telephone in both hands. Her thin nostrils fluttered. Her voice was dark. "You too?"

She listened intently, her tongue caught between her perfect teeth. She said, "I know. I know. Look. You've got to come. I'll meet you—"

"Same place. Two o'clock."

"Friday. Two o'clock."

The talk ended abruptly. Lauchlan dropped the telephone in place and sat up briskly. She had a lot of things to do. She had to invite people for Friday dinner and Sunday lunch—Saturday they were going to Rolling Rock—and make menus and do the housekeeping and see what Peggy had planned for the week-end. Peggy was twelve now; thin and lanky like Lauchlan, and mad about horses. Her room was full of cups and ribbons which she had won jumping hunters in the children's classes all over the horse show circuit. Lauchlan was proud of her but always at a loss if she found herself alone with Peggy. They never had a word to say to each other except about horses. Lauchlan got on better with Paul, but he was away at school now. He was sixteen and as big as Ted, which Lauchlan found completely unbelievable. She could not feel like the mother of that big, deep-voiced blond hulk. She did not feel like anybody's mother; least of all when she stood naked in her silver-walled bathroom and stretched and twisted before the tall triple mirrors to get every possible view of her lean body. She was thirty-nine. And there was not one sign, for she watched with the minutest care, to prove it. Not a gray hair in the smooth black cap shaped to her small skull. Not a bump, a sag, or a telltale stria on the taut surfaces of her thighs, her lanky hips, or her flat stomach. Her breasts were as hard and small, the nipples as tiny and rigid as before she had ever had a child. Sometimes when looking at her own admirable body Lauchlan thought of the soft, spreading hips, the drooping breasts, the curving bellies of the girls she knew; girls her age with three or four children who paid seventy-five dollars for French elastic corsets to mould their squashy shapes into something resembling figures. She gagged at the thought. Something inside her rose in thick repulsion if she glimpsed a female body, soft and fattening and marked with stigmata of childbearing. She hated the sight of women's bodies.

Well, she thought, going in to take her bath, thank God that nutty Claire didn't bring her husband with her. Nobody could take that. The son of a Hunky mill foreman. Ted's mill—that made it all the worse. Ted had explained that this Anton was no ordinary Hunky, he was a celebrated Czech musician and anybody—particularly a musician—might rise from such an origin. But not to our house for the week-end, Lauchlan had answered coldly. Their friends, she reminded Ted, wouldn't care if he was the greatest composer or whatever in the world. They'd only remember that his brother still worked on the open-hearths at Scott's and lived in a slum row and—why on earth had Claire stirred this all up by coming back at all? Why didn't she stay in Europe where she belonged?

"I've told you ten times, already," Ted explained patiently, "she came for the stockholders' meeting next month and if you'll just hold everything and manage not to insult her—"

Those of Lauchlan's friends at the dinner-party handpicked by Ted and Ben who expected to meet a freak on Friday evening were set sharply back by the woman who came slowly down the stairs and into the drawing-room after all the other guests were assembled drinking cocktails. Claire wore a dull white silk jersey dress from Alix draped like sculpture across her square frame and supple hips, deeply cut to bare her bronzed breast and long, graceful back. At the décolletage was a pair of massive clips set with diamonds and two enormous emeralds, prompting the women to exchange eloquent glances. Round her throat was a triple string of fat, perfect pearls; on her right hand a marquise emerald, on her left the cluster of antique rose-diamonds covering the gold wedding-ring. Her short chestnut curls were brushed high off her ears, to accent pearl earrings set in petals of diamonds. She carried her head high and if Anton had been there he would have told her that she had never so well deserved his pet name of *lvice*—lioness. There was amusement in the corners of her broad mouth and a glitter in her eyes as she moved across the room to Lauchlan. Before joining her Lauchlan managed to shoot a startled look at Ted and Ben standing together behind her.

"I told you," an older woman murmured to the man beside her, "she'd look like that. Those jewels—her grandmother—"

"But I thought she was a newspaper reporter." The man stared. "Married to a Hunky."

Lauchlan was piloting Claire around the room.

"Mrs. Randall. Madame Hrdlička. Our cousin, Madame Hrdlička, Mr. MacNaughton." They moved on.

"You pronounce that well, Lauchlan," Claire said. "It's quite a twister."

"Isn't it," Lauchlan agreed.

Claire said, "It's really worse. Hrdličková, for a woman. But Liska is a lot easier."

Lauchlan gave a nervous laugh and said, "Oh, let's give it the works."

Ben brought Claire a Martini.

"My, you're looking handsome tonight," he said. "Marriage seems to agree with you."

"Or hard work."

Ben smiled deprecatingly. "Well, now, you really don't have to work so hard, Claire. That is—we could easily fix that up."

"I like to work," Claire said. "I'm having a wonderful time."

They went in to dinner; a long magnificent table for twenty-two, lace-covered and set with gadrooned Georgian silver and Royal Crown Derby plates. Claire on Ted's right found Roy Rogers on her other hand. She had already guessed that he would be there. All eight directors of Scott's were present. Old John Purcell, a fine-looking erect man who must be nearly seventy, was seated at Lauchlan's right. Gray Simcox, pale and intellectual-looking, round-shouldered almost to deformity, was on her left. Charles MacNaughton, whom Claire identified now as the president of the bank represented on the mill's board, sat opposite her, and each time she looked his way she found his eyes fixed on her in a quizzical mixture of curiosity and frank male admiration.

Claire had never met all the directors, nor seen them together, and now she was very glad that she had come. Ted's—or was it Ben's—plan was perfectly clear; they meant her to see for herself the minds and personalities of all the men concerned in the management of the mill. Perhaps they wanted—but she felt increasingly that the planning was Ben's—to show up the quiet and apparently pacific Simcox against the vigorous wills and known hard-headedness of most of the directors. But one thing she did not yet understand. If Ted had already made up his mind to vote with Ben on a question of eliminating Simcox and such directors (Claire was already trying to spot them) as would obstruct Ben's plans, then why go through all this rigmarole? Between them they could muster enough votes to do as they liked, regardless of Claire.

But here they all were, Ted dividing his attention, as he always did, between his duties as host and his continuous awareness of Lauchlan at the other end of the room. He resembled his father quite strikingly now. He was past forty-five, Claire realized, and the thickening of his bulk, the fading of his blond hair, made him recall Paul Scott vividly as Claire had first known him. But there could hardly be less similarity in the natures of the two men. The dinner was barely under way before Claire saw that

Lauchlan's declaration to Mary was no *fait accompli* at all. It had been thrown out as a warning, or as a feeler; perhaps as an attempt to intimidate. And certainly at Ben's direction. But Ted's mind was not finally made up on any such radical question as giving Ben control of the mill. He was almost as much the object of Ben's carefully staged mis-en-scène as Claire herself. The whole setting, the plan, the atmosphere, had been developed well outside his hands. Claire did not need to intercept a fleeting glance from Ben to Lauchlan to understand precisely how all this had come about. She looked at Ted, although seemingly listening to Roy Rogers, and she was conscious of a sudden surge of feeling; of kindliness, affection; reluctantly, of pity, for this big helpless man. He did not know where he stood, and he would never know until someone—perhaps brutally—told him.

"You know," said Roy Rogers as the salad course was being served, "you had me stumped there for a while." He narrowed his eyes and gave her as warm a smile as his thin red sportsman's face would render. He was one of the hardest men she had ever seen. His dry, rough, sparsely hirsute hands made her shudder inwardly. "I expected something very different."

"You did?"

"Yep. After we heard you'd married—well—"

"—a long-haired violinist, no doubt."

"That's about it." He cackled boldly. "We kind of expected a—well anyway, not a—you know what I mean."

Claire marvelled at such ingenuous stupidity. If—she said to herself—a rag and a bone and a hank of hair and a few diamonds could deceive a man who was supposed to be razor-sharp! Could it be some play on his part that he appeared to forget (if he had ever realized) that she had married into Hunkytown? Was it by design or mere arrogance that he had sat there pouring out verbal vitriol on the C.I.O. and Lewis and Murray and a man named Clint Golden, and on Myron Taylor for "betraying" the steel industry, and on Tom Moses of Frick Coke for being his leg man? And on Ben Fairless for knuckling under to him? He ought to have— Rogers made a fist on the point de Venise tablecloth.

"Fairless had to do as he was told, didn't he?" Claire asked softly. "Isn't he—a hired man, after all?" She bent for the light he was holding to her cigarette.

"Well—yes. But you can't tell me Taylor didn't shove that contract down his board's throat. By God, they'll never get one down ours."

"No?"

He looked around the table, his glance singling out the Scott directors. "Would you say so?" he asked Claire.

"Why, I really wouldn't know. I suppose I ought to. I wish you'd tell me." She stared innocently. "I've always had such confidence in the way the mill was run, I've really never questioned anything the directors did."

"I'm glad to hear it. Because you're going to have to prove you mean that at the stockholders' meeting."

"Really?" asked Claire. "How?"

Rogers glanced down the table at Simcox and Purcell with Lauchlan between them. "This union thing will have to come to a showdown pretty soon and you'll want to straighten out your management before it does."

"Oh."

"It's a bad situation," said Rogers in a muffled tone, "when your board is split on such a question."

"I heard something too about the sales policy," Claire said vaguely.

"That's right. You did. Well—" his eye moved around the table singling out Clarence Randall, Henry Knox, and Craig McCreery. Claire had seen already that these were the men whose opinions agreed exactly with Roy Rogers'. About Charles MacNaughton she was not yet sure. "Tell you what," said Rogers almost in a whisper, as Lauchlan was about to rise and take the ladies away. "If you want to be really smart at that meeting you'll vote your cousin there"—he flicked an eyebrow at Ben Nicholas—"onto the board. That'll fix those—"

Claire winked at him to supply the missing epithet.

When the men came strolling out of the library Claire saw Charles MacNaughton looking for her. Her face felt as if it had been poured into a mould and left to set in an expression of deliberate vapidity. Her ears were buzzing with an echo of gabble about clothes, horses, Palm Beach, servants, Penelope somebody who had just left for her third trip to Reno, and endless reiterations of envy for Lauchlan's fleshless frame. Claire felt that if she relaxed and cracked the mould her mouth would let forth a swoosh of relieving profanity. Like a good—she almost snickered aloud at the thought. She looked up and smiled at MacNaughton, standing beside her chair.

"I'd love a Scotch and soda," she said. He grasped the implication of her twitching lips. Instead of turning to take a drink from a passing servant he steered Claire down the room to a glass and chromium bar-wagon where the butler was pouring drinks.

"Have you learned anything useful?" he asked, as they carried their glasses to a small room—the sort of room called a den in houses like this—and sat down on a leather couch by the fire. Two of Ted's spaniels were sprawled on the hearth, their soft, sensuous muzzles pillowed on feathered front paws. Claire reached down and fondled one, stroking and gently pulling the dangling taffy-colored ears.

"You're charming," she said to the lovely dog. "Almost as charming as a cat."

"What," said MacNaughton, "can you say that after the kind of hour you just appear to have spent?"

"Good God! You wouldn't insult cats by comparing human upper-class females to them! Cats are civilized, Mr. MacNaughton."

"Well, now—"

"Give a cat as much luxury and security as these women and it will have the most exquisite poise and taste. It will never do a vulgar or a commonplace thing. And if it could speak—"

"—it would probably be worthy of your companionship."

She inclined her head in a bantering bow. "That was very gracious of you."

She sat smiling at him, letting him look at her as long and appreciatively as he liked. He was enjoying thoroughly the untypical beauty of her face and figure, the amplitude of her lips, her strong eyebrows and wide hazel eyes, the play of bronze and tawny coloring from her short curly hair to the warm throat and breast made dramatic by thick folds of white silk and the bold majesty of emeralds. Her hands had repose; even with a cigarette in her firm fingers she made no unnecessary motions, but sat quietly following his glance at the massive old ring which contrasted so tellingly with her grandmother's jewels. She saw him eyeing her short, rounded, dark red nails and her bluntly cushioned fingers.

"You know," he said presently, "I cannot believe you're any of the things you're said to be. You don't look it, or act it—"

"Look or act what? Like my Pittsburgh relatives or—my husband's wife?"

They laughed. "Neither. Like yourself."

"Oh," said Claire. "You mean you expected me to bustle, and be short and dumpy and wear a beaded chiffon dress with cap sleeves and a pince-nez?"

"So you have seen some American professional women. Once," he said, with an air of somebody telling a ghost story, "I saw hundreds of them all together. In Washington at a shindig. It was terrifying."

"Have you ever seen a League of Nations Assembly?" Claire asked dryly.

"No," he answered, surprisingly serious, "but I wish I had."

"That's a strange thing for a Pittsburgh banker to say. I should have thought—"

"I know. But some of us do think about the rest of the world even though we seem to be wrapped up in our own concerns. With me it's mostly a question of time. If I only had the time to read and stir around and get out of the treadmill. But I'm lucky if I can squeeze in a round of golf once in a while. That kind of pressure is not very conducive to thinking about the state of the world." He smiled. "And once in a great while if such a pleasure as this comes along—"

"Why have I never met you before?" Claire asked. "You weren't at the last meeting I came to—"

"I wasn't on the Scott board then. I inherited the directorship along with a lot of others when John Rea died two years ago and I moved up to his place in the bank. But I'd much rather talk about you than myself. Tell me"—there was almost a naïve freshness of interest in his manner— "some more about yourself. Where do you live, actually?"

"In Prague." Claire was startled at the proud decisiveness of her own voice. She thought with amazement what a fine experience this was, to have a home and a place where one belonged, to have this answer ready instead of the shrug and the cynical "nowhere" that would have been her reply a year ago. She moved her fingers unconsciously in a spreading, tender gesture as the tactile memory of Anton's firm cheeks and springy hair ran warm through her veins and carried a glow into her eyes.

"Now that seems remarkable to me," MacNaughton was saying. "I don't believe I ever met anybody who lived in Prague." He reflected for a moment and asked, "Is that from choice—or what?"

"To me," she said with sudden artless joy, "it's a combination of everything wonderful in the world. It's my husband's home, of course, and I have always loved it, and it's a very central place for me to work from. I'm not there all the time; I have to go all over Europe on assignments. But that is my home."

"I read your articles whenever they appear," he said. "Maybe that's why I was so amazed when I saw you."

"The point is whether you find the articles any good."

"Too good, sometimes," he said slowly. "You can be uncomfortably convincing about what's going on over there."

"Can I? Then—" she sat up with a quick motion and put her hand on his arm. "Then—will you help me fight it here? Right here—in our mill?"

"Oh, now—" she watched with a sinking of the heart as some of the warm cordiality faded from his face and a look of doubt and deprecation came into it. "I wouldn't rush at things like that. Don't you think you may be—exaggerating—"

"No," she said breathlessly. "Not at all. I've got to talk to you about it, Mr. MacNaughton. I've got to have help. Because I tell you frankly, I am absolutely determined to—to keep that mill out of the—my God," she broke off—"you understand!"

"Well—yes. But I couldn't make any snap decisions about it. I have a responsibility to the stockholders, Madame Hr—"

"—Claire."

He smiled delightedly. "—Claire. You see—we can't allow ourselves to be swayed by personal convictions of right and wrong. We have to regard a company as a business to be run for profit. Our decisions are all made impersonally and unemotionally on that basis. Or they should be. That's why they put business men on boards of directors."

Claire smoked silently, narrowing her eyes. Then she looked up and asked, "Charles, are all business men reactionaries—Tories?"

"Why?"

"Because that's the real basis on which this decision about control of the mill will be based. Some of you directors wouldn't understand what I'm talking about—"

"The thoughtful Rogers, for instance—" They laughed.

"You know," she said, "I could argue this on a business basis really better than on any other. You gamble in business, don't you?—take risks? —bet—?"

"We—ah—find other ways of stating the method, as a rule."

"Yes. But all I'm trying to say now is that there is one stupendous, horrible game being played on the face of the earth, and everybody has got to take sides in it or at least put up some chips. It's not the first time," she said quickly. "Think of the very beginnings of this country. The world was in just as much of a turmoil then. The French Revolution was about to explode. The American Revolutionaries here seemed like Bolsheviks to the Tories—to loyalists here as well as in England. And there were three big groups into which all the colonists found themselves divided, by conviction and instinct."

MacNaughton was listening intently, watching her face.

"All of them weren't at the boiling point. But some were. They were the real Revolutionaries—the teaparty boys. And dead against them were the Tories, loyalists, rich men who wanted to keep everything the way it was. And then in the middle there was a big third who just didn't know. But they had to put their chips somewhere. And then the pot boiled and they all fought the Revolution and what I am asking you to tell me now is—what happened to the Tories after that?"

"Why—" he made a blank gesture.

"Yes," Claire said with force. "That's it. I'm not talking about the morals or merits of the Revolution. We were talking about business, about how to run a business and make money. Well, after the Revolution when the country settled down to business—do you realize that nobody who had ever been identified with the Tory side could make a living? It was the little fellows, obscure little tradesmen from the left and center—excuse the Europeanism—who stepped out and inherited the earth."

She paused but he did not say anything and so she went on.

"The Tories were finished. Through. They'd bet on the wrong number, Charles. They hadn't sensed the current in the world. They hadn't known how to ride it. Or play it. They were stupid. And they couldn't see over the walls of their own amassed property. So they lost it. But lots of the Revolutionaries and the middle chaps had property too, and they staked it on the gamble and look what they won!"

"You seem very sure," he said slowly, "that this ferment in Europe is comparable to the rise of the eighteenth-century libertarian revolution."

"I'm more than sure. But this is a counter-revolution. The revolution to undo the work of the first one. And it isn't just in Europe, that's the stupid error those devils want you to fall into. All the time they're playing a desperate and terrible game and the Tories are betting on them just the way Tories always have put their chips on the reactionary cards. But they can't win now any more than they did in 1776. When this whole thing has finally shaken down, the Tories won't be able to keep their property or do business any more than they could after the American Revolution." She took a long breath and said, "*That's* how to regard the company as a business to be run for profit."

He did not speak at once and Claire sat looking at him, trying to read in the clear gaze of his gray eyes whether she had won him to any degree at all. She was still a little breathless from the pressure of her own eloquence, her pulse ticked sharply in her throat, and far in the back of her mind the knowledge pressed insistently that all she had said was very well, and quite true, but it was only an earnest and daring piece of ratiocination. Unchecked, she would have begged and pleaded her cause—the cause that should need no explaining—with every emotion in her power. She still smiled beguilingly at Charles MacNaughton and he could not penetrate to the part of her brain where she was wondering feverishly whether she had convinced him. He said, "You make me think, Claire. I will think by myself, and also I'd like to think some more with you. Will you come and lunch with me next week?"

"I'd love to. Any day you say."

While he was saying this, Roy Rogers and Ben and Craig McCreery appeared in the doorway behind them.

"Hey!" said Rogers. "No fair. You can't monopolize the beauty all night."

CHAPTER LXXXV

[*September 1937*]

NEXT MORNING CLAIRE ROSE EARLY. Instead of ringing for breakfast in her room she dressed and went downstairs where, as she had hoped, Ted was breakfasting alone in the glassed-in sunporch. He rose as she came in and said, "Well, this is a nice surprise. I'm not used to such beautiful company in the morning."

She dropped into the chair he held for her and murmured, "Orange juice and coffee," to the butler.

Ted had strewn the morning papers all around his chair. He kicked them aside as he sat down again and asked, "Have you been caught in this mess?" He pointed to the financial page at his feet, scowling at the long columns. "It's almost too damned much to have to take."

Claire smiled wryly. "I haven't got much left to worry about except what's in the mill. And since that isn't traded—"

Ted made a nervous motion.

"That's about all there is to say for the damn stock."

"Oh, I wouldn't slam the poor old mill," Claire said. "When it's been doing so nicely the past year."

"Well it won't do nicely any more." Ted's voice was sharp with tension. "They started cancelling orders the day after the market broke last week. Another couple of weeks like this and we'll be right back where we were three years ago."

There was a long silence while Claire took her time choosing between orange marmalade and strawberry jam. She buttered a piece of toast (why, she thought to herself, is the toast always tough and the coffee slops in big houses with a dozen servants?), spread it with jam, and chewed the first bite slowly. Ted sat watching her in a kind of blank fascination as if he had never seen anyone eat breakfast before. At last she said, "I suppose Ben told you his idea for beating depressions long ago."

"Oh," said Ted. "You mean getting orders from—er—abroad."

"Yes."

Ted filled his pipe and lighted it with deliberate motions reminiscent of his father. How like Uncle Paul he was! Claire thought—except in the ways that really mattered.

"Sometimes I think Ben has the right idea," Ted said slowly after the pipe was going.

"Then what's stopped you from taking his advice?"

"Well, for one thing, business got so much better for a while there that we didn't need to worry about sales. We were doing fine right up to a couple of weeks ago. Now with all these cancellations I guess Ben will start talking about foreign business again."

"And you'll shove the contracts through."

Ted raised his eyebrows. "I haven't the authority, Claire. You know that."

"You're the head of the sales department."

"But foreign contracts above a certain amount have to go to Gray and old man Purcell for ratification."

Claire finished her coffee and lit a cigarette. Ted raised his head, hearing voices in the library, and said, "Walk down to the stable with me, will you?"

They started slowly down the walk, thickly bordered with syringa and rhododendron bushes. It was a cool fall morning, the sunlight hazy with the dust of fallen leaves. Ted walked with his head bent, scuffing the gravel with the toe of his riding-boot.

"You know," he said, "it's kind of hard to talk to you because you're not like other girls. I mean—you're smart. You get around. You always give me the notion you know more about everything than you let on."

"I don't mean to. Not with you, anyway. Of course, sometimes—"

"Well, ever since the thing about the old house I've had the feeling you're playing some game of your own. Now that you've married Jerry Liska's brother I feel it all the more. You and Mary," he added abruptly.

"I'm not playing any game," Claire said quietly. "I've got certain ideas that seem important to me and when they tie up to things like the mill and what becomes of my interest in it, I get ready to fight for them. That's about the straightest way to put it."

"Do you mean—like the S.W.O.C. trying to organize the mill?"

"Yes. I wasn't going to slap it down on the table just yet, but since you ask me I'll tell you."

"That makes you," Ted said bitterly, "practically a traitor."

"To whom? Against what?"

"Well—well, my God, Claire, you either own a business or you don't. You've gone and got yourself mixed up with these Hu—" he swallowed— "Liskas and all—and your emotions are running away with your judgment."

"Nothing of the sort. I'd never be able to convince any of you, probably, but being connected with Jerry Liska hasn't got a thing to do with it. I don't think the whole C.I.O. is entirely right by any means. Some of those sitdown strikes last year were outrageous."

"Then in God's name why do you want us to sign with them now?"

They had reached the wide red brick stable, turreted and weather-vaned; a vivid reminder of the nineties. They paused at the doorway, its weathered sandstone pilasters hidden under sheaves of scarlet Virginia creeper. Claire pulled off a leaf and began slowly to tear it to pieces, stripping the red foliage away from the veins. Ted stood watching her. Presently she looked at him intently and said, "Ted, do you know there is a revolution going on in the world?"

"Well—in Europe."

"In the world, I said."

"That's rather dramatizing things, isn't it? Strikes me you always did."

"All right, I always did. But if I could invent half the things that are going on right now I'd be worth a million dollars to Hollywood."

"Even if that's true I don't see why we should give in to the C.I.O. If we sign a contract with them we'll never own our own business again."

"I don't agree with you. But that doesn't matter. All I know is that organized labor is the single strongest force opposed to Fascism in the world and that's the best reason for supporting organized labor. Anybody who doesn't is just a fool—or potentially a Fascist . . . maybe actually, for all I know—"

"—But damn it," Ted interrupted, "this is America. Why do you come butting in over here with your European ideas? All that talk about Fascism. You've never lived in this country, Claire. You don't know the conditions. Why should you horn in on us with a lot of notions you've picked up in the mess over there? It's got nothing to do with us."

"That's where you're wrong," Claire said. "I tell you this Nazi thing is a world revolution. You can't have the nerve to tell me I'm talking through my hat when all I've done for the past two years is learn the facts right on the spot. They talk to me. They're perfectly frank about it. Ideas, they say, that's their first weapon for conquering the world. And economics. And when they're ready, the most stupendous military machine the world has ever seen. 'Today Germany is ours, tomorrow the whole world.' What do you think they mean by that, Ted? Just what in hell do you think they mean?"

He shrugged dubiously.

"You still think I'm half crazy," Claire answered herself. "But I wish you'd remember what I'm saying even if you don't believe it."

She turned away and stood watching Peggy practising jumps down in the paddock. Ted called out approvingly as the little girl took the last of the fences in perfect form.

"She's just like Lauchlan," he said fondly.

Claire shut her mouth on the impulse to say, "My God, I hope not." Instead she moved off toward the long cedar arbor beyond the stable and Ted walked along.

"Even if you can't believe a word I say, Ted," she said, "try to give me credit for something besides being in love with my husband. He hasn't seen his relatives here for nearly twenty years—why should I come over and cook up a stew of sentiment about them? They're swell people—you must know that from way back. Your father knew it. But that has nothing to do with why I came here. I came," she said suddenly, stopping on the path and fixing him hard with her flecked eyes, "to prevent Ben Nicholas from getting control of the company."

He was shocked at her frankness. And she gave him no time to recover. She looked at him earnestly and said, "Will you help me do it?"

He moistened his lips with the tip of his tongue.

"Why—" his eyes moved uneasily. "What makes you think he's trying to?"

"Let's not talk in circles, Ted. You know why he's been buying up all the stock he could. You know exactly how much he's got. Don't you?"

Ted seemed almost surprised at himself for answering as he muttered, "Yes."

"It's only by the grace of God he hasn't bought yours too," Claire said quickly. "How come you didn't sell it to him?"

"Why—why—" Ted's broad face began to darken with embarrassment. Claire stopped looking at him and said in a low tone, "I'm sorry. I oughtn't to butt in like that. It's none of my business."

"That's all right," Ted murmured. "It was just—well, Dad, if you want to know. Something he said to me—awhile before he died. He wouldn't have wanted my stock to go to Ben."

"How about the vote that goes with the stock?" Claire asked sharply. Ted started. Claire looked into his face and said, "Are you going to go along with Ben and vote him on the board of directors and get a gang together who'll do as he says about running the mill?"

Ted moved his head uncomfortably. "I don't know. I haven't made up my mind."

Claire put her hand on his arm. "Well, when are you going to?"

He looked away. "I don't know."

Claire stood still for a time and then said bitterly, "Oh, Ted, for Christ's sake don't go with him. Your vote will decide everything."

A cold look crossed his face. It shocked him to hear a woman swear. Claire lit another cigarette and thought for a while and then asked, in a gentler tone, "If you did vote with Ben to change the directors, what would make you do it? Why would you want—what Ben wants?"

They started strolling again, moving back towards the house by the long path leading from the arch of cedars.

"It would make a difference to me financially," Ted said slowly. "And —and there are other considerations. Ben is—well, we've grown pretty close to him, you know."

Claire locked her teeth to hold back Lauchlan's name, which sprang to her lips. She did not let herself speak until she could say casually, "Don't you ever wonder about his motives in all this?" The question took Ted by surprise.

"Well—I—why—he's an awfully smart operator, Claire. He knows how to make money. I think he'd know how to keep the mill making it if he had some say around there."

"Even," Claire asked, "even if he made it by selling steel to Goering for his airplanes?"

"Well," Ted said lamely, "if you were really right about that I might say—" he broke off and exclaimed with a sudden tense ring in his voice, "Lord, I don't know what to do."

Claire said, in an undertone, "What do you think Uncle Paul would do?"

Ted ran his hand nervously through his hair. "That's one of the things I've been trying to figure out. One of them."

"Well, I think that's fairly simple," Claire said. "Uncle Paul might not want to sign with the C.I.O. but I'd stake my eyesight on his telling Ben Nicholas to go to hell and take his Nazi steel contracts with him."

Ted filled his pipe once more, sighing heavily. They were almost at the house now, and they saw Lauchlan and Ben waiting on the front steps to join them and get into the car to start for Rolling Rock. Claire summoned all her nerve and said softly to Ted, "*She* wants you to vote with Ben, doesn't she?"

He nodded slowly; Claire had never seen a face so racked with bewilderment and doubt.

She came back from Sewickley on Sunday night, tired and depressed. She was worn out from the effort of pretending interest in all the doings over the week-end, tired of making talk and listening to talk and keeping her wits and ears sharpened for the things she wanted to know. She had learned a lot, she told Mary, some of it pretty strong stuff. She saw that Mary wanted her to talk and bring her up to date on everything, but Claire found an expected letter from Anton on the hall table and she could not wait to get upstairs by herself to read it. She missed him desperately. She had been working just as hard these past two days as on any job in any tricky spot in Europe, and all she wanted now was to crawl into Anton's arms and rest and lie there, warm and melting and heavy with happiness under his kisses and his deep murmured endearments. His letter was very long, full of tender and passionate repetitions of how he missed her. But there was news too; a long account of the funeral of Professor Masaryk who had died three days before.

"Everyone is plunged in mourning," he wrote. "It hardly seems possible that each individual among thousands and even millions feels this bereavement so personally. Mama is crushed, as you can imagine. She is staying here with me, she came for the funeral where she was an official representative of the Alliance. I have persuaded her to stay until you come home. She is horribly depressed. She keeps saying this is the beginning of tragic times for the nation. Even though it is two years since Professor Masaryk retired from the Presidency, people are all saying that they felt safe while he was alive but now they dread the future. He was so identified with the Republic—he *was* the Republic in many ways and President Beneš cannot possibly mend the broken thread even though he is a fine man.

"There is growing tenseness everywhere, even since you sailed. We are used to the German Jews, poor devils, with that sick, haunted look on their faces, but how do you suppose I felt when Otto Hallgartner came to my office at the hall yesterday and asked me to give him a job? He was one of the best men in the Wiener Philharmoniker and when I asked him for God's sake why he was here looking for a job, he began to cry and tell me the most disturbing stories of what's going on in Austria. Since August, apparently, when they signed that 'trade' agreement with the Nazis—he says the thing is coming out from underground like a plague of vermin. Hakenkreuz flags all over Salzburg, and open threats from Nazis inside the opera and Philharmoniker. I said I couldn't believe it and then he got hysterical and stood up and screamed, 'That's what they all say. That's why it's happening. Because everybody goes around with a *Rotweissrot* button in his coat saying *"Es kommt nie her"* and patting each other on the back.' The other Jews in the orchestra tap their foreheads when they look at him, he says. When he finally told them he was leaving while there was still time they all told him he was crazy and advised him to stay so he wouldn't forfeit his pension.

"Poor soul, we have no vacancy for him or anybody. I sent him around to Hufnagel at the central refugee hostel and they're going to try to find teaching for him or something. But it's hopeless. Half the first-class musicians in Europe are wandering around starving with their hearts and spirits broken, trying to get affidavits to go to America. He'll have to go too—this small country hasn't room for all the exiles—and God knows what would happen if the Nazis really made a Putsch in Austria.

"I think of you there in Pittsburgh and try to imagine what it would be like to be there with you. I can't make a picture of it. It is all so strange—you and I alone, *miláčku*, in the world we have made for ourselves, that is the only reality there is. But when I try to connect it with Liverpool Street and Papa and Jerry in the mill and you coming there from that palace in Cannes—and Mama running her Alliance and haranguing those poor Slováks and making me practice—it's a dream, that's all. I can't believe any of it ever happened.

"But I'm using your idea for the symphony, my darling. I thought you were a little mad when you said, 'Write me a piece about a steel mill.' I've always felt you were too romantic in your ravings about the mill but after you went away and I really began to think about it (having no more appetizing outlet for my creative urges!) I suddenly saw one night what you meant. It is a good idea. In my own mind I call it 'Symphony for my Father.' The themes are mostly folk melodies and I will build them up against your idea for the orchestration—big brasses and percussion and heavy rhythms suggested by the noises of papa's rolling-mill. I will try my best to do what you said—put in music the epic of the Slavs in American industry. But for God's sake come back to me soon. I will run out of inspiration before long and I must go deep—deep into my treasure house for more. Ach!—my beloved heart and soul, even to think of holding you in my arms makes me wild with longing. I kiss you—every bit of you—every inch of you—I send my love to cover you and hold you and keep you warm and close to your

"Anton"

Claire went to Mary's room to read her the part of the letter about Julka. Then she smoked a cigarette and drank a highball and took Flam and went, deep in a troubled mood, to bed.

CHAPTER LXXXVI

[*October 1937*]

IN THE NEXT TWO WEEKS she travelled as much and as far as if she had been working on a major story in Europe. She flew to New York, to Washington, to Louisiana and Texas, and back to Pittsburgh. She made several shorter trips in a small hired car. Only Mary knew where she was and what she was doing. The last of her jaunts was a trip to Latrobe to look up something in the office of the Recorder of Deeds there. The inner workings of bribery were minute and wonderful, she was finding. She was fitting a strange and shocking jigsaw puzzle together and the smallest, least noticeable pieces came last of all. It was dark when she left Latrobe and started back to Pittsburgh in the noisy coupé with the slipping clutch and the stalling motor. The damned thing—the God damned thing, she said finally and furiously, broke down a few miles west of Latrobe, in the wildest and least familiar curves of the Ligonier Mountain region. Claire had to get out and walk nearly two miles to a filling station to tell them to send a tow-wagon for the coupé; and then she stood wondering what to do. This was indeed a jumping-off place. She thought swiftly of mountain villages in Yugoslavia which in retrospect seemed no wilder. The proprietor of the filling station told her that there was a very nice Tourist Home and Cabins about four miles east of here on the road to Ligonier. If she wanted to spend the night he would be glad to drive her there in his car and he would have hers repaired by ten in the morning. Claire thanked him and got into his car.

Well, she thought, facing a piece of rubbery apple pie and the tentative coffee that went with it, I am seeing something more of America anyway. The small stuffy dining-room had not been aired, she guessed, for weeks. The slice of leathery roast lamb, the pasty gravy, the sodden potato, the swimming canned peas, lay uneasily—what she had downed of it all— on her stomach. She thought of Anton and Julka eating Růžena's barley soup and stuffed breast of veal at home and almost groaned aloud. She lit a cigarette and the lady of the Tourist Home gave her a fishy eye and Claire pushed back her chair and went out into the dark hall and up the narrow gritty-carpeted stairs and toward the bedroom in which she would gingerly attempt to sleep. And then downstairs in the front entry she heard voices. Absolutely unmistakable voices. The lady of the Tourist Home was saying, "Well, hello there," in her twang, and Lauchlan's drawl was answering, "Good evening, Mrs. Green."

"Good evening, Mrs. North. How've you been, Mr. North?"

Noiselessly Claire slipped off her alligator pumps, noiselessly moved to the head of the dark stairs—there were some benefits of stinting electric light anyway—and holding her breath peered carefully over the top of the banister. There they were, big as life. Both of them. Perfectly familiar with their surroundings.

"You can have your same Cabin," Mrs. Green was saying. "Thought it was about time Mr. North got out this way again. Want to go right out to your Cabin?"

"You might bring us—" and Claire did not hear what, because her swift stockinged feet had moved back to her door and into the nasty little bedroom and over to the bed. She flung herself down on the cheap, swaying spring and wrapped her arms around herself and chortled silently with glee. "Oh, Tourist Home," she carolled soundlessly, her wide mouth stretched in an ecstatic grin, "Oh, Little Gray Tourist Home in the West, I Love You. Do I love you! Oh, Home, do I!"

Mary listened open-mouthed to the last details of the jigsaw puzzle as Claire reported them late the next night. It was the eighth of October and the stockholders' meeting was scheduled for the eleventh. There was not another minute to lose. Claire told Mary the last of her discoveries, and Mary was so enthralled that for once in her life she forgot to sew or knit. She simply sat in her high-backed chair, staring, with Flam sleeping and purring in her lap. Mary had succumbed entirely to Flam, but Claire took care never to remark about it.

"It's—it's a melodrama," Mary kept saying, squinting with amazement and disbelief. "You *must* have made it up, Claire. It's unbelievable."

"I'd say that myself if I wasn't used to melodrama," Claire said. "That's all there is where I work, you know—that and epic tragedy."

"But—*Ben*—he's so quiet and unobtrusive—"

Claire laughed. "That's how he works, my dear. Well—did you talk to Ted?"

"Yes. He's absolutely under Lauchlan's thumb. I tried to find out what reasons she gives for pressing him but he isn't clear about it."

"It's too simple to put it down to her lech for Ben," Claire said.

Mary frowned.

"You know perfectly well," Claire shrugged, "if it wasn't him it would be somebody else. In fact—"

Again Mary scowled. "I don't want to know about such things," she said irritably. "At my age."

Claire bent down and kissed her cheek.

"Come on, don't go stuffy on me. You love to hear about such things. Everybody does. Human nature."

"You go to bed," Mary snapped. "You look tired out."

"I miss my man," Claire said, making a rueful face. "I don't want to go to bed without him."

"*Claire!*" Mary's lips twitched. "You haven't any more shame than your grandmother!"

It was cold and rainy when Claire—in a different hired car—drew up under the scowling porte-cochère at Sewickley the following afternoon.

The butler said, "Mrs. Scott is in the den, Madam," and once again Claire experienced the mild sense of triumph with which she had told Lauchlan on the telephone to be alone at home that afternoon. Lauchlan had asked why, and Claire's cryptic answer had aroused enough curiosity in Lauchlan to assure her doing what Claire said. Lauchlan was playing solitaire on a small inlaid backgammon table by the fire; she looked up, with a cigarette drooping from her mouth and said, "What's on your mind, Claire? What's all the big mystery?"

Claire dropped her gloves and hat on a table and ran her fingers through her hair. Lauchlan's as always lay close and sleek against her skull; she was as tightly and perfectly put together as a precision instrument. Claire said abruptly, "I came down to tell you I've got the goods on you, Lauchlan."

One swift flash of expression—fear, panic?—was obliterated from Lauchlan's dark eyes by a scornful stare. "I've no idea what you mean," she said. Her voice was contemptuous and cold.

"No? Would you know what I meant if I described Mrs. Green's Tourist Home and Cabins?"

Lauchlan's red tongue appeared between her gleaming teeth. "Bitch," she muttered, ruffling the cards she had been playing with. "You bitch." Her thin brown fingers twitched.

"I'd say so myself, in your place," Claire said. She lit a cigarette. "But I had very serious reasons for doing this, or I wouldn't be here. You can't think I care what you and Ben do. I couldn't be shocked—even if I were surprised."

"Then what are you doing here?" Lauchlan's voice was hoarse and she kept edging along the leather couch away from Claire as if she expected to make some kind of an escape. She moved in profile, the sleek dark cap of her hair springing away from her temples with the live look which Claire could not help admiring.

"I have plenty to say," Claire said, "but not necessarily in answer to your questions. I have only one thing in mind," she said, "and that is Ted. I know what your game has been all these years, and I know Ben's game—and now I'm playing a hand of my own. I didn't like coming here to confront you—it was cheap and theatrical. But I'm not taking any chances. I want you to know, in case I ever have to swear to it, that I have actually seen you and Ben Nicholas—" Lauchlan made a gargling sound of rage and Claire ignored it—"—together—doing what I know you have been doing for years. What everybody's known, for years," she said, her nostrils dilating with scorn. "Except Ted."

Lauchlan drew a long breath and said, "You're a liar."

"Not," said Claire, crushing out her cigarette, "in this particular case. I don't want to sit here and trade insults, Lauchlan. I came to strike a bargain with you. I've got most of the chips but you can still play—if you will."

She bent her head and studied the rings on her left hand, turning and examining them as if she had never seen them before. She could hear Lauchlan breathing loudly through her nose. Neither spoke for as long as it took to smoke a fresh pair of cigarettes almost to butts. Then Lauchlan cleared her throat and said in a muffled voice, "What do you want?"

Claire looked up. Her large hazel eyes met and stared hard into Lauchlan's frightened brown ones. Then she said, "I want your assurance that Ted will vote with me at the stockholders' meeting on Monday."

Lauchlan made a sound in her throat and said, "For God's sake, what has this to do with the stockholders' meeting on Monday?"

"Everything," Claire said quietly. "Everything, that's all. How Ted votes will decide the whole future of the mill and how Ted votes is the way you make him vote. You had his vote sewed up for Ben. Now you'll either promise that he votes with me—or I'll go to him with this whole story."

"You wouldn't dare," Lauchlan said defiantly. "Why didn't you go to him long ago? You hate me. You wouldn't have cared what happened."

"That's not true," Claire answered. "I don't hate you, and I do care what happens. I hate Ben Nicholas, the bastard, but I don't hate you and Ted. If I did I would have gone to him with this— But he's so damned decent I didn't have the heart. You've been rotten to him, Lauchlan, you've made him weaker year by year. I don't care about your habits— it's not that—everybody in Pittsburgh has known about them since you used to paw the boys in parked cars when you were fifteen."

Lauchlan gasped but Claire hurried on. "Only Ted has no idea," she said. "Everybody in town knows about you. You and Ben. God knows why nobody ever spilled the beans to Ted. I suppose for the same reason I'm here now—because it would almost kill him. He's so horribly helpless. I'm not even sure he'd believe it yet—" she paused and looked hard at Lauchlan and lowered her voice to a throb—"unless I tell him." Lauchlan swallowed. "He'd believe it then."

Lauchlan made one more stab at bravado. "Suppose I tell you I don't give a damn what Ted does? Whether he left me—or anything."

"I wouldn't believe you," Claire said quietly. "You know damn well Ben Nicholas would never marry you. And you don't want Ted to leave you. Ted's stuffy Presbyterian sedateness and all that old Northside family stuff—you've got to have them to cloak you or you couldn't be yourself and still queen it in town and down here. And you love this house and your position and all the rest of it so desperately you'd never give them up. What good would they be if nobody'd speak to you, Lauchlan? You've always known what you had to have—that's why it's been necessary to let Ben chip in, hasn't it?"

A stare of terror came into Lauchlan's eyes. She put her hand to her mouth. Claire watched her and waited a moment and said, "I think that's the vilest part of it all. Apparently you know how Ted would feel if he knew he'd been living in all this swash on money you got from Ben Nicholas. Poor chap, he's never had much self-respect and that would finish him. It hurts to find out what a fool he is. I don't know how he can be such a fool. He ought to know you wouldn't be any more immune to the depression than the rest of us."

Lauchlan began tearing at the hem of her handkerchief. It made a soft, ripping noise.

"When I saw," Claire went on, "how much money Ben was putting up for the privilege of sharing your—" Lauchlan shuddered and Claire hurried on—"your favors, I began to do some serious research. You are, Lauchlan, a very good lay," she leaned forward and spoke as coarsely as she knew how, "but there are lots younger and fresher ones. Especially for a rich chooser like Ben. You *couldn't* be worth all that money to him unless there was something in it for"—she spoke with brittle emphasis—"the Transoceanic Development Corporation."

Lauchlan gave her a stupefied stare. "What the hell is that?" She was really astonished and mystified.

"I'll tell you. Our cousin, my girl, is a much bigger operator than you have any idea. I never really realized how big myself until last week when I was down in Texas. The things that are going on in this world are beyond belief, Lauchlan, and when you expect to be believed about them you get the brush-off. I've been going around getting myself pooh-poohed for talking about the state of the world and trying to warn people what this destruction is that's creeping up on them—but they'd rather stay comfortable with their nice property and their heads in the sand and wait till it rolls right over them. I'm used to being told I'm crazy, but I'm not the only one who knows what's going on. Ben is no fool either. Only, being Ben, he's riding on the steam-roller."

Lauchlan still looked bewildered.

"Among other things," Claire went on after lighting another cigarette, "Ben owns—or the Transoceanic Development Corporation owns—seven of the largest independent oil fields in Texas. Nine in Louisiana. And," she paused for a moment—"the largest and most modern oil refinery in Hamburg."

"Hamburg?" Lauchlan's dark eyes were still blank.

"Germany. Transoceanic, Lauchlan, is another name for Benjamin Nicholas, junior—just the way the phony rent you get from a phony business building in Latrobe, Pennsylvania, is part of two thousand dollars a month that Parkway Syndicate has been depositing in your personal account for the past three years. Parkway Syndicate is the Chicago office of Benjamin Nicholas, junior, Lauchlan. Transoceanic Development Corporation also owns a fleet of tankers operating in both the Atlantic and the Pacific, and is now getting together a small fleet of fast freighters to carry scrap to Japan and—" her voice turned husky and Lauchlan saw tears spring amazingly to her eyes—"all the lightweight alloys Scott's can produce to Germany."

"But what difference does all that make?" Lauchlan asked slowly. "I can't see what difference that makes to anybody."

"You can't? Well, let me tell you it's made a bloody difference to the people who were bombed in Tientsin. It's made hell's own difference to Barcelona and Madrid. Ask some of those butchered women and children if they care where the German and Italian planes get their gasoline—or the metal to make more planes. This is a world revolution, I tell you!" Claire's voice broke in a sudden shocking gasp and a wild, uncharacteristic flash of panic crossed her face. Then she leaned tautly toward Lauchlan, her hand clutching the arm of the couch, and repeated, "A world revolu-

tion. Don't believe me, if you're content to be that stupid. Oh, Christ—"
her fist unconsciously pounded the sofa—"how can I ever make anybody
believe anything? A world plot to destroy civilization! With the dress
rehearsal going on right under your nose! And you sit there blinking and
looking at me as if I were a raving lunatic!"

Lauchlan said finally, "You know, maybe Ben is right about you. He
says you're a sentimental, excitable fool with a lot of notions you've picked
up from the Reds and Jews you run around with—and that Hunky husband—"

"—from Hunkytown!" Claire cried, springing to her feet. "That's
right! A Bohunk, a son of an immigrant millhand. With more heart and
brains than the whole wretched lot of you. Aristocrats! My eye!"

"You should talk," Lauchlan laughed sourly, "with that grandmother—"

"All right!" Claire shouted. "Maybe she *was* the mistress of a Prince.
At least she did a clean job of it!"

"Ben also said the other night," Lauchlan said when the echoes of their
outbursts had died away, "that you're probably having pressure brought
on *you* in this mill situation—"

"My brother-in-law," Claire interrupted, moving close to Lauchlan
and looking her in the eyes, "has nothing whatever to do with this. Somebody's probably told Ben I'm working for the S.W.O.C. but frankly, I don't
have to bother. They don't need me. They can run their own show all by
themselves. They can strike when they run up against Fascists like Ben
and I have no doubt they will. My only interest is to keep our mill out
of his snake's nest of deals with Nazis and Japs."

"My God," said Lauchlan with sarcasm, "what idealism! I suppose
you think a steel mill runs on sweetness and Jesus and light. Do you think
the directors are going to march in your crusade waving white banners
and losing money hand over fist?"

"The directors that are left after we get Ben's crew cleaned out will
find a way to run that mill decently or not run it at all." Claire sat down
abruptly again and leaned toward Lauchlan. "Now look here. I give you
until eight o'clock tomorrow night. Sunday. If by that time I have not
had Ted's promise *in person* to vote with me at the meeting on Monday,
I will not only tell him this whole story, but I will give him the names of
at least ten other men with whom you have—"

"Claire!" Lauchlan's voice was a thin, terrified scream. She sprang
from her chair, twisting her fingers together wildly, stood for a moment
trembling by the couch, and to Claire's horror dropped on her knees and
began beating the floor with her clenched fists. "You mustn't!" she
shrieked. "You can't. Please. Please." She sobbed and gibbered. Then she
turned and flung herself toward Claire's knees. Her mouth and chin were
wet. "Don't do that. You won't do that . . . Claire . . ."

Claire's hand went out and gripped Lauchlan's shoulder in a rigid
squeeze. She had never known such a hideously mortifying sensation. She
had a strong feeling of wanting to protect this travesty of a woman from
herself, and from making a further debased exhibition of herself. She said
quietly, "Sit down. I'm not sitting in judgment on you, Lauchlan. Nobody

could. There isn't a woman with any spunk or blood in her who hasn't
done something—sometime—in her life. You—well—" Claire was suddenly unable to speak any more. There was a lump in her throat. She did
not know why. She only sensed that her contempt and revulsion toward
Lauchlan were being overridden by a deep surge of feeling that carried as
on a flowing stream impulses and instincts which, in that moment, Claire
knew to be those of her mother-in-law and of Mary Rafferty. She drew
Lauchlan onto the couch beside her.

"You want to keep your hold over Ted," she said quietly. "He's absolutely dependent on you. You know that."

Lauchlan sat listening, dabbing at her face with the torn handkerchief.

"That"—Claire's gesture indicated Lauchlan's affair with Ben—"that's
all over, no matter what else happens. You need Ted. You'd go completely
to hell without him and you know that yourself." Lauchlan gulped. Claire
went on. "If I had to go to Ted with all this, you know he'd be through
with you, don't you?"

Lauchlan's dark head nodded slowly.

Claire said, "He'd vote with me automatically. Only I don't want to get
him to do it that way—busting his life to pieces—what there is of it—"

Claire flexed her fingers nervously. This was the most awful ordeal she
had ever faced. She felt pontifical, pharisaical; she hated the thing she
had decided she must do. She said, "You've always realized the only thing
that's cloaked your reputation is Ted's innocence and devotion to you.
And everybody's affection for him. You'd be overwhelmed by scandal if
he left you now."

Lauchlan looked up, her dark eyes rimmed with purple circles.

"Claire," she whispered, licking her lips, "do you really mean—everybody—in town—knows—"

Claire nodded her head slowly, looking straight into Lauchlan's eyes.

"You poor kid," she said softly. "Of course. They always have. Even
your dowdy forgotten sister-in-law. She knew—"

"*Ruth?*" Lauchlan's mouth silently formed the name.

Lauchlan shuddered and buried her face in her hands.

"You can count on me for anything," Claire said slowly. "Especially
to keep my mouth shut. And one thing more I want of you. I'll have to
have your promise not to mention this to Ben."

Lauchlan shuddered again. Claire said after a time, "I'm going back to
town now, Lauchlan. It's getting awfully late."

CHAPTER LXXXVII

[*October 1937*]

THE FIRST SENSATION of the stockholders' meeting was the arrival
of Angelica Scott. Of *Miss* Angelica Scott, Claire whispered to Mary
and Charles MacNaughton, between whom she was sitting. It was as
unthinkable to mention this formidable woman without her title of spinster-

hood as mentally to picture her without the clothes that proclaimed Boston in every seam. Claire said that too.

"You knew she had to come," MacNaughton said behind a paper that he held near his face. "There have been almost no proxies signed—on account of all this snarl." Proxy forms had been sent out a month ago with the notices of the stockholders' meeting, but Ben had warned Angelica not to sign hers and thus place her vote in the hands of the management. She must come in person. He had met her the night before and escorted her, disdainfully curious about this city of her birth, to a suite in the Schenley Hotel. There, over an ascetic meal of chops and fine China tea which Miss Angelica carried with her when she travelled, Ben told her the probable procedure of tomorrow's business and explained exactly how she should vote. The high gastronomic tradition of Miss Angelica's parents had come to an abrupt stop in Beacon Street after their deaths. Julia Scott had died enormously fat, a woman who lived for gossip and gormandizing. Her daughter had turned a relieved and positive back upon the ritual of menus, wines, and cordon-bleu cookery. Miss Angelica's time went wholly into her lifelong genealogical researches and the activities of certain cultural clubs; her money, except for a prudent living allowance and some traditional good works, back into capital investments.

"I must say she belongs in a museum," MacNaughton continued whispering to Claire. "Where can a woman *find* such clothes?" They exchanged another conspiratorial smile. They had become very good friends in the course of their three or four meetings.

MacNaughton had reached his decision to be Claire's man on the board and at this meeting only after long, careful consideration of her pleas and of his own motives. At first the problem in his mind had been somewhat a matter of steeling himself against her eloquence and her charm and her impassioned idealism, not very well informed about the intricacies of realistic business. These were risky props on which to pin decisions so momentous as she was asking him to make. He knew Ben Nicholas for the shrewd and ruthless operator he was; he knew that Claire was naïve in her hope of defeating him in this showdown. MacNaughton had only made up his mind late last night, when Claire had appeared at his house, looking strained and exhausted, and had told him that she had just obtained Ted's promise to vote with her at the meeting. But instead of seeming jubilant at what she had accomplished, she looked, and said she was, very worried. She had said, "Charles, I don't have enough to see this thing through. I don't know what I'm doing. I'm afraid." She had told him the whole tale of Nicholas's operations, and MacNaughton had not needed to point out to her the danger of pitting oneself against such a man. He had only said, "You've gone pretty far, to get cold feet now."

"I know." She had looked at him and said solemnly, "I hoped I'd convinced you by now, Charles. I hoped you'd help me."

"Well," he had asked slowly, "what shall I do?"

"Just—" she had been intensely quiet "—help me. Be with me."

In her simplicity, he thought, she did not really know what she meant by that. She did not know to what she might be asking him to commit himself. And suddenly, looking at her fine, square face and the strong hands on the arms of her chair, he had turned hard in a decision to stake her to her beliefs. They were good beliefs. He held them too. He was sure then that it was better to gamble on them than to see Nicholas, or anything he stood for, in control of the mill. He had said, "All right, Claire. But don't be surprised if it turns out to be tough going." She had squeezed his hand and given a long sigh of relief and thanks, and got into her car and gone home.

So here they were already seated at the scarred yellow oak table in old William Scott's outer office, MacNaughton on Claire's left hand and Mary on her right, when Ben and Miss Angelica arrived. There was a stir of scraping chairs and murmured greetings and many curious sidelong looks at the tall, dry-lipped woman in the execrable gray hat. Mary was staring at her with the calmly assumed privilege of her years. She was looking from her to Ben Nicholas and back again with a succession of expressions in which Claire read utter incredulity that Mary could have known these two from the moments of their births.

They took their seats with stiff greetings to Mary and Claire. They were accompanied by a hard-looking man with shiny black hair, carrying a heavy briefcase; this was Ben's personal attorney. Places were given them on the opposite side of the table from Claire. Also present in the barren, dun-walled room with the dirty windows overlooking the tracks in the gully outside were John Purcell, in the chairman's seat at the head of the table; Gray Simcox on his right, who limped in from his private office with his usual self-effacing mousiness; Ted on his left, accompanied by a secretary with armfuls of minute-books and documents; two strange young men at the foot of the table who, MacNaughton explained, were clerks from his bank and Purcell's law office, here to act as inspectors of election; Roy Rogers on Ben's side of the table; a notary public; and a stenographer to take minutes of the meeting.

"A quorum, you see," MacNaughton said, "of the directors and"—with a surprised glance around the table, "all the stockholders."

It was then ten o'clock in the morning, and it was long past dark when the meeting adjourned. All day the heavy air in the room thickened and staled with tobacco smoke. Every person there except Mary and Angelica Scott and the stenographer smoked almost continuously. At first Claire was worried about Mary; pouring icewater for her, urging her now and then to stroll out to the bridge for a breath of air; but her solicitude soon gave way to admiration. An old woman of seventy-nine should be a meaningless encumbrance to these proceedings. She should be too frail to endure the strain of sitting in this bad air through these long hours, listening to talk; to redundant, excited, argumentative, bitter, technical, complicated talk. She should weary, her deepset eyes should drowse under thin drooping blue lids. She should start occasionally from her doze to nudge a neighbor and whisper a question as to what was going on. But she did none of these things. She sat quietly, hour after hour, upright and prim in her chair, her bony ridged hands folded on the table, her small head cocked a little to the left, for that was her better ear now though she would have choked sooner than confess a lessening of the sharp hearing that had been the early terror of the boys.

Claire could guess what Mary was thinking as she sat there so quiet and shrewdly attentive. She must be thinking of Paul. Every brick and beam and pane of glass and stick of ugly furniture in this gloomy place must bring him back to her. The distant noises of the rolling-mill, discernible through the puffs and roars of the freight engines outside, would bring his face and voice vividly to her mind.

Claire smiled at Mary, whose wrinkled face was inscrutable as she listened to Ted, standing in his place, presenting the minute books of the Corporation. It was too much to expect, Mary was thinking, that any of the best of the Scott qualities would stand the attenuation of three generations. Paul had been less powerful, but more tender, than the Old Man; Ted was without any power and his tenderness had become a terrible weakness, consumed in the hectic appetites of his greedy wife. Yet— he did have one final bolt of potency in his hands, and that a concrete one put there by his father. He did hold the balance and the future of the company.

Claire was careful not to look at him and catch his eye while he was standing there. Never, not to Mary or even, she thought, to Anton, would she repeat the brief talk she had had last night with Ted. Never would she herself know what had transpired between him and Lauchlan, what pleading or fear or desperation had brought him finally to bury his head in his big hands, and groan, "Oh, Lord, Claire, go ahead and tell me what you want me to do. I don't ever want to decide anything again."

She watched Ben narrowly when he was looking the other way. He sat there clothed in his usual calm, very well tailored in his usual indefinable grays and blues, his light hair and cool expressionless eyes part of a personality at once attractive and sinister. If, Claire thought, he were not so completely the master of his own moods and expressions he would be contemplating Ted with a visible air of domination. In his imperturbability Claire thought she could discern satisfaction and the arrogant certainty of knowing that things were as he had arranged and paid for them to be. He was looking at Ted; she could not trust herself to do so. She would not see the quiet blond giant performing a routine duty, but a man who had shown her last night the innermost dismal reaches of his weak soul. Ted sat down and Purcell went rapidly through the formalities of having the minutes approved and of appointing the two inspectors of election. He then made the routine inquiry as to the number of shares of stock present or represented by proxy, to which Ted replied: "There are present one hundred twenty thousand and sixty-two shares of the common stock of the Corporation, and seventy-five shares represented by proxy, out of a total of one hundred twenty thousand, two hundred and fifty shares of common stock originally issued, of which one hundred and thirteen shares remain in the Treasury of the Corporation."

MacNaughton was scribbling on a pad as Ted reported. He pushed the pad along to Claire. He had explained the sixty-two odd shares present: twenty-five belonged to Purcell, twenty-five to Simcox, and six to himself and Roy Rogers. The seventy-five proxy shares were twenty-five each belonging to the three absent directors.

"Most of us had a lot of preferred stock originally," he murmured in answer to Claire's surprise at the small holdings of the officers and directors. "Your uncle wanted it that way—so the voting stock would stay in the family."

"Brr-r-r-r," said Claire with a mock shiver.

At this point John Purcell paused in the proceedings and looked slowly about the long table, moving his handsome white head deliberately as he transferred his gaze from each person to the next. He said, in the polished, mellifluous voice which had been revered in the councils of Western Pennsylvania for fifty years, "The Secretary's report from the minute books of the Corporation having been read and approved, we may now proceed to the discussion of other business. I believe the next order of business might properly be the annual election of directors."

There was a moment of silence; exactly the same silence, Claire thought, as that engendered at weddings by the chilling inquiry, even if an empty form, as to impediments to the lawful marriage of the parties. This time she expected the routine silence to be ended by the resumption of the set procedure of the meeting. And she drew a sharp breath of surprise as Ben Nicholas got to his feet. I should have expected that, she told herself.

Having been given the floor, Ben said, "Mr. Chairman, I wish to introduce certain serious objections to the conduct of this Corporation, which would properly come under the head of new business to be placed before the meeting. And I believe this business would precede that of the annual election of directors."

Entire silence was the reaction to that. Claire saw Mary stiffen slightly in her chair. Purcell stared at Ben and waited for him to continue. Ben's glance circled the table and came back to Purcell. "I should like," he said, "to ask for the floor for my attorney, Mr. Morris."

Ben sat down and his lawyer rose. Claire saw the appraising and scornful glance with which Charles MacNaughton was narrowly watching Morris. The lawyer had a coarse, didactic voice and a truculent manner. He took a folder of papers bound in blue legal bond from his briefcase and said, "In behalf of my clients, Miss Angelica Scott of 147 Beacon Street, Boston, Massachusetts, and Benjamin Nicholas, junior, of 15 Broad Street, New York City, I have a statement to present to the meeting, to be followed by motions. Have I the floor, Mr. Chairman?" Purcell nodded.

The lawyer then put on a pair of spectacles, opened his folder, and began to read. The statement was long but bluntly and clearly couched.

His clients questioned, objected to and challenged everything about the management of the mill, not only during the past year, but retroactively for the past eight years. They objected to the present management, both officers and directors of the company. They objected to the present financial condition of the company as presented in the evasive and misleading profit and loss statements rendered to the stockholders. They objected to the decision of the directors during the previous year to retire the outstanding preferred stock instead of paying dividends on the common stock. They went so far as to imply chicanery and collusion on the part of the directors (who had held the preferred stock) at the expense of the common stockholders. They objected violently, in a long list of specific accu-

sations of incompetence and incapability, to Gray Simcox as President of
the company; recommending that if he be employed by the company at all,
it be solely in the capacity of production superintendent and metallurgist,
without any authority whatsoever in matters relating to finance, sales, or
general policy.

At this point every eye in the room went involuntarily to the silent,
inconsiderable man sunk in the chair on John Purcell's right. Simcox's
sensitive, sickly face, usually very pale, had flushed a painful dark red.
His narrow lips characteristic of a cripple who had made his way by rising
above slights and insults and poverty were tightly compressed. His wiry
hand on the arm of the chair was clenched into a rock. He stared straight
at Ben Nicholas who returned the glance with the insolent blankness of
gazing into space. And both stirred with surprise when Ted's voice broke
in: "This is a damned outrage. I move this unjust and scurrilous personal
attack be stricken from the minutes."

Claire saw for the first time sheer unguarded amazement on Ben's face,
and then an effort, quickly checked, to catch Ted's eye and administer a
protest and a rebuke. But Ted was not looking at Ben. The lawyer laughed
at Ted. He made no sound and the expression of his face could not be
called hilarious, but he laughed nonetheless.

"If the interruption of my statement is ruled out of order," he said,
"I shall continue. I presume relevant motions will be introduced at the
proper time."

Claire flashed a glance of indignant sympathy at Gray Simcox, who
smiled wryly and shrugged. Ben's lawyer was reading again. Now he had
come to the crux of his whole case. His clients, he stated, were totally and
unconditionally dissatisfied with every phase and aspect of the company's
management, and unalterably opposed to any continuation of tenure for
the present officers and directors, wherefore, he read, "my clients present
the following motions to the present meeting. One. My clients move that
profit and loss statements of the company from the date of incorporation
to the present date be rendered them, together with full reasons for any
and all losses incurred,

"Two. My clients move that a detailed breakdown of costs and expenses
be rendered them,

"Three. My clients move that they be rendered copies of the minutes
of the most recent meeting of the board of directors,

"Four. My clients move that they be rendered minutes of the most
recent meeting of the Executive Committee,

"Five. My clients move that they be rendered minutes of the most
recent meeting of the Finance Committee,

"Six. My clients move that the present management of the Scott Steel
Company, Limited, a Pennsylvania Corporation, be censured and con-
demned for incompetence, carelessness, wilful refusal to administer the
affairs of the company for the maximum advantage and profit of the
stockholders, and collusion in the financial administration of the company
for the benefit of the officers and the board of directors,

"Seven. My clients move that the foregoing statement in its entirety
be included in the minutes of the present stockholders' meeting."

The lawyer sat down in a vacuum of appalled silence and Roy Rogers sprang instantly from his chair.

"I second all the above motions," he said sharply.

Purcell, MacNaughton, and Ted—at whom Ben now frankly gaped in incredulous shock—were all on their feet at once, claiming the motions out of order. Claire could hardly sit still. She burned to jump up and add her voice to the angry ones beginning to shout back and forth across the table. Mary sat with her hands folded, sharply watching and listening. Angelica looked as if she had stepped into something disgusting. Ben's lawyer wiped his forehead with a bold-patterned handkerchief, and the stenographer scribbled furiously, covering page after page of her notebook as the minutes rushed by. John Purcell banged futilely with his gavel and when the others paused for breath Ben stood up and said, his voice icy and level as always, "I have a further motion to present. I move that there has been a deliberate policy on the part of this management of restricting sales to the domestic market exclusively. This policy is part and parcel of the incompetence and ineptitude recorded in our statement. Wherefore I hereby move that a new management be installed and that the policy of the company in this as in all other respects be radically changed and that the company undertake to market its products in foreign fields and that the directors appoint a vice-president in charge of sales for that purpose."

"Second the motion," snapped Rogers.

Purcell banged. "That motion," he said, "is out of order. It concerns a matter of policy which properly resides in the hands of the duly elected directors and the officers appointed by them. Such being matters for consideration by the board of directors and not by the stockholders, the motion is getting us nowhere. The motions previously presented are similarly out of order. We cannot effectively transact any other business that may come before this meeting until we have proceeded to the election of the board of directors that is to serve for the coming year. Therefore, in accordance with the bylaws of the Corporation I now call for nominations for eight members of the board of directors of the Scott Steel Company, Limited, to hold office until the next annual meeting of stockholders of the Corporation. Nominations are now in order."

While Purcell was speaking Ben Nicholas had sat with his eyes narrowed and fixed on Ted. Once Ted turned his head and looked straight at Ben, and Claire who was watching them both like a hunting cat, felt a thrill of excitement in the small of her back as she saw Ted's eyes communicate the full shock of his intentions to Ben.

Ben was wasting no time. He had nudged his lawyer and muttered something to him and the lawyer was on his feet again.

"Gentlemen," he said, "before proceeding to the business of nominations for the board of directors I want to place in the record the following notice: that if my statements on behalf of my clients, the motions attached thereto, and the votes of my clients for the board of directors prove to be minority votes and motions and are treated as such, an immediate court action will be involved."

"Wow!" breathed MacNaughton.

"I repeat," the Chairman intoned, "that nominations for the board of directors are now in order."

"Just a moment," said Ben's lawyer. "Before the nominations are made I want a consultation with my clients."

"I move," Roy Rogers said immediately, "that the meeting recess."

"Second the motion," said Ben.

"Very well," said Purcell. "The motion has been made and seconded. All in favor—" He looked around the table. "The meeting will recess for one hour."

CHAPTER LXXXVIII

[October 1937—Continued]

ALLEGHENY BEING ALLEGHENY, with no suitable eating-place accessible, Gray Simcox had ordered in sandwiches and coffee which were spread on a table in his office. He had expected the entire meeting to eat there when the luncheon recess was called, but Ben's lawyer had asked for the use of a room where he might consult with his clients, and Simcox gave him the head bookkeeper's office.

Some lunch was spread on the cleared desk in the office, but Ben and Miss Angelica and Roy Rogers ignored it. They began immediately to talk. The lawyer listened.

"I can't understand Ted," Rogers said several times in succession. "What the hell goes on, Ben? Why don't you go and bring him in here and put the fear of God in him? He's not really going to vote with those—" Rogers realized suddenly that he would have to curb his expressions for the benefit of Miss Angelica. "That Hunky cousin of yours had me fooled the other night," he said disgustedly, "but I was a sucker. I ought to have known."

"Who," asked Miss Angelica, "is this MacNaughton who appears to be so beguiled by her?"

Ben waved impatiently. "We have no time for that kind of thing now," he said. "We might as well tackle the situation straight. I think it looks serious. I think Ted is going to vote with them straight down the line."

"But—why?"

Ben bit his lips angrily. "I'm not bothering with motives now."

"Aren't you going to talk to Ted?"

"No."

"Why?"

Ben was rapidly becoming irritated with Rogers. "Because," he said cuttingly, "I can recognize a skin game when I find myself in one."

"Well, what are you going to do?" the lawyer asked. He was rocking on his heels in the corner, looking out the window and eating a ham sandwich.

"Slap it down to them," Ben said. "That's what you're here for. I don't have to talk to any of them. You get up and say that if they carry through a majority vote for the board of directors you'll bring a minority stockholders' suit so damn fast they'll never know what hit them. That'll set them back. They'll start feeling around and asking what we'll listen to, and you tell them we want representation on the board of directors by just allocation. We'll have to finagle around for a while and if you play it right you'll fix up a compromise board which will give us about what we want."

"Suppose they won't trade?"

"They'll trade. Do you think they want a minority suit on their hands?"

The lawyer was looking thoughtful. He had eaten several of the ham sandwiches by now. He said, wiping his mouth, "I get your idea all right, Ben, but maybe it won't iron out just like that." He scratched his head.

"Well, obviously it's got to be a deal of some kind," Ben said. "That damned Claire—"

"Say," said the lawyer slowly. His voice was a sliding nasal twang. "Has that Mrs. Whatsis—that cousin of yours—has she got any dough?"

There was total silence for a moment. Miss Angelica looked at Rogers and Rogers looked at Ben and Ben looked at the lawyer. Then Ben slammed one fist into the palm of the other hand and smiled diabolically.

"By God!" he said, "I've got it. Morris—you're a genius."

The meeting reconvened. The room had been aired and everybody should have felt more comfortable, but nerves were tense and eyes sharp as they all took their places and warily waited for the nomination proceedings to begin. The usual procedure of such meetings was followed. The management had prepared its own ballot, which was already printed, and which the inspectors of election passed out to each stockholder present. Ben took one look at it and flung it toward the centre of the table.

"This is utterly preposterous," he said. He slammed the back of his hand down on the printed list of eight names. Contemptuously, he read them off aloud. "John H. Purcell. We have already entered a motion of censure for him as chairman. Gray Simcox. We have made ourselves clear about that. Theodore C. Scott." He threw Ted a scornful glance but said, "Under certain circumstances we might vote for at least one member of the original management on this board. Charles Starr MacNaughton. Out of the question." He paused, scanning the next four names with cold disdain. These were the management's substitutions for Rogers, Randall, Knox, and McCreery. "Walter Wilcox," Ben read. "Andrew Morewood." He pronounced the names with increasing contempt. "Huntington D. Tait. McKinley Lane. Why—gentlemen, you must think Miss Scott and I are mental incompetents if you believe we would allow you to elect this board of directors without protesting action from us."

He looked about the table, at the men and women with pencils in their hands poised over the ballots. Then he said, "I request the floor for our attorney who will explain the consequences if you proceed to elect this board as presented on the management's ballot."

He sat down and Morris rose. In terse words he warned the majority that if they elected their ballot he would have an open and shut minority stockholders' suit which the management must inevitably lose since their ballot provided not one representative of the minority stock on the proposed new board. He painted a gloomy picture of the future of the company if it were to be tied up in lawsuits for years to come. He spoke skilfully and persuasively and finally reached the crux of his argument which was that the only hope of avoiding such a suit was a compromise as to the board of directors. He hinted that a satisfactory compromise could be effected with perhaps a fifty-fifty choice of directors; he said something which Claire construed as a suggestion that even fewer directors of their choice would be acceptable to the minority if Benjamin Nicholas himself were to be nominated for the board. He talked for half an hour and all the time the meeting sat with poised pencils, one or two people scribbling and doodling on scratch pads and on the margins of their ballots.

When Morris sat down there was a long silence while Purcell looked about the table and made up his mind as to the next step. Finally he invited Ben's lawyer to present his nominations on behalf of his clients. This was done and an uproar of controversy ensued. For more than an hour the arguments grew bitterer and more acrimonious, while Mary and Miss Angelica sat glaring across the table at each other, Claire smoked and tugged at her disordered hair, and the men sloughed and struggled in the morass of bad temper and frustrated decisions. Names were proposed and before anyone could second them, shouts of protest would drown out the banging of the chairman's gavel. Purcell and MacNaughton and Simcox were all agreed that a compromise ballot must be reached. They would not feel justified for Claire's sake or their own or for any other reason in throwing the company into court. Ben's side fought every inch of the way. Mid-afternoon was past, and the gloomy room was thicker and staler with smoke than ever, when Purcell took his gavel in the midst of a pause for breath, banged thunderously on the table and said, "Gentlemen, I ask that somebody move for the appointment of a nominating committee to confer and work out an acceptable agreement for nominations for the board of directors."

He circled the table with a heavy look which said more plainly than any words that this deadlock had reached the point of no further recourse but private horse-trading. The men looked relieved; they had seen this coming for some time. Most of the angry talk had been elliptic. The time had come for plain words and inducements of the kind that only private negotiators could exchange.

Charles MacNaughton rose in his place. "Mr. Chairman," he said. He had been so silent during the hours of wrangling that his voice now sounded peculiarly impressive. "I move that the two parties holding the two largest numbers of shares of stock should constitute the nominating committee for the board of directors."

"Second the motion," said five or six voices together.

"Motion carried," said Purcell. "The two parties holding the largest numbers of shares of stock being respectively Benjamin Nicholas, junior, and Mrs. Claire Gregory Hrdlička, the same are hereby appointed a committee of two, to confer privately and present the meeting with their joint ballot for the board of directors. Mrs. Hrdlička, Mr. Nicholas, will you kindly withdraw to an office which the secretary will place at your disposal for the purpose of drawing up a compromise ballot."

Claire's knees felt rubbery as she rose slowly from her chair and turned to follow Ted to the bookkeeper's office. Ben walked behind her. Neither stopped to speak to anyone. Each carried the printed ballot and the sheets of paper on which all the alternative names had been scribbled. Ted held open the door for them and they both walked past him into the room. Neither looked him in the eye. He closed the door behind them.

Claire went over and sat down on the window sill where she could see out into the yard. It was nearing the end of the day, and outside she saw a short train of flats being loaded with ingots. She tried hard not to think emotionally as she knew Ben believed she always thought. The presence of her adversary was very sobering. But she felt mortally glad nevertheless that those ingots were not going to Germany. She realized that her mind was recklessly far away when she heard Ben speaking and she had to counsel herself sharply to pay attention to him.

"You've certainly messed up a situation you know nothing about," he was saying. "In God's name why did you want to butt in here and make such a display of your ignorance?"

"If you want to be abusive," said Claire with a shrug, "I can talk dirtier than you. I thought we came in here to make a deal."

"Well—we did."

"All right. I would like to say, though, that if it weren't for the rest of them out there I wouldn't be here. If nobody else was concerned I'd tell you to go ahead and sue and keep on suing till hell freezes over. But since there are others to consider I'll try to be as reasonable and impartial as I can. What do you want?"

Ben smiled in a strange way, a way at once sardonic and nasty and yet intimate. "Exactly the same thing you want. Control of the board of directors."

"You'll never get it."

Ben walked slowly across the room with his hands in his trousers pockets and stood before Claire. She was still looking out at the work in the yard. He was silent for some time, but finally he said, "This is such a stupid performance of yours. Business is no place for emotion, Claire— nobody'd ever get anything done if businesses were what you think they are."

"I don't care about other businesses. I'm only concerned with this one."

"Wherefore you are hell-bent on ruining it. Why don't you leave things to men who know what it's all about?"

"Because I happen to know what you're all about and," she looked up and stared subbornly, "I'm going to block you in the only way I can."

"So a nice little company gets ruined," he said with a shrug. "Either way. Either you ruin it with your damnfool stupidity and sentimentality and unfair female tricks—"

"That'll do!"

"—or I ruin it. You may as well understand that. If you start the ruining here in this meeting I'll finish it in court. I can make mincemeat of you and your crowd in a minority suit."

Claire sighed.

"You believe me, don't you? This is no empty talk, Claire. I'd urge you to take some time and think it over, but I have no more time myself. I've had about all I want of this ten-cent mess. I'll be perfectly frank with you. You seem to know I have reasons—damned good ones—for wanting to control the output of this company. But it could be some other company. There are others. I'm a busy man. Most of my other interests make this one ridiculous by comparison. I can't waste any more time over a one-horse outfit."

Claire was scowling with disgust.

"If it wasn't for the personal angle on this," Ben said, "inheriting my mother's stock and all that, I'd never have wasted a minute on this picayune so-called steel mill. I got involved in it though—"

Claire made a sound very like a snort.

"—and if it weren't for you I could fix the damn thing up into a very smart little business. In fact I still can. You've manœuvred yourself into a spot and I haven't got any more time. So let's cut across the rough and get to the point. I'll give you two choices. You'll take one or the other and that'll be the end of it."

Claire shoved her hair back and leaned forward with her elbows on her knees. She knew now that defiance would be useless. She was on a spot. She had been, she cursed herself, infantile and naïve in thinking that the mere assembling of a majority vote could defeat this man. She had been insane to think she could defeat him. He was super-skilled in the technique of unscrupulous business warfare. That was how men became like Ben, and amassed interests like Ben's. She marvelled now that John Purcell and Charles MacNaughton had stood by her as they had, and allowed her to interfere as she had done. With their backing she could still keep Ben and his crowd off the board of directors, but there was not the slightest doubt that he would and could shatter the company with interminable, remorseless litigation. Not even for reasons as desperately vital as she felt hers to be could she dare precipitate that. She looked up at Ben and said, with her chin propped in her hands, "What are your two choices?"

"Either," said Ben abruptly and in the impersonal hard tone he used with men, "you give me control of the board of directors. With five to three representation." Claire was pale and tense; her pulse thudded sickeningly in her ears. She watched Ben closely and waited. She saw a change of expression flicker across his face, some different set of the mouth, something almost lewdly suggestive of amusement. "Or," he said, in the same tone of voice, "you get rid of me by buying my stock. Immediately. For cash."

Claire was dully astonished to find cold sweat in the palms of her hands. She had never been more completely amazed, never so horribly nonplussed. Forty-two thousand shares, he had. Six thousand more than she. *For cash.* And she had no cash beyond a few thousand dollars in her bank accounts. She thought wildly of her jewels, and knew that they could not bring half enough to buy his stock. But she looked up coldly and said, "If I agree to buy your stock will you give me a signed proxy for it here and now—while this meeting is in session?"

"Certainly," said Ben with a shrug. He had turned away but was looking at her from the tail of his eye. This must be bravado, he thought. He knew she had no cash in any amount remotely approaching the value of his stock. And she must have used up most of her other liquid resources in the years when Scott stock paid no dividends.

Claire had risen to her feet. "Will you give me five minutes?" she asked. She was furious with herself for a tremor in her voice. "You'll have my answer in five minutes."

She went out, Ben holding the door for her with sardonic courtesy. She went to Gray Simcox's office and asked the secretary there to call Charles MacNaughton and Mary Rafferty out of the meeting. They came in a moment, both looking very serious, MacNaughton adjusting his steps to Mary's slow, small ones.

They found Claire alone in the office, standing up and leaning on Simcox's littered desk. MacNaughton held a chair for Mary, but she shook her white head slowly and did not take her eyes from Claire. She stood with her bony hands clasped before her. MacNaughton shut the door and waited for Claire to speak. She looked up and said in a dull voice, "Mary. Charles. Will you help me buy Ben's stock?"

A most extraordinary expression began to appear on Mary's wrinkled white face. If, Claire thought, watching her, if a little old lady of nearly eighty could be said to be itching for a fight, this was surely the way she must look. Mary's thin cameo nose went up in the air, the delicate nostrils dilating. A crinkle about her eyes, a movement of her lips, turned into a slow, delighted smile. Claire could not know that here in this room, here with some of the very same things in the room, Paul had said and Mary at this moment was still hearing him say, "Say, Mary, have you an idea what this mill *is?*" His voice was as clear and live as that of Claire herself, tautly watching Mary's amazing old face. "You have to believe in something," Paul had said, too. And he had talked about the mill's place, its real place. "Any time this country gets in a scrap . . ."

MacNaughton's face was tense and questioning too, but he was not as surprised as Claire thought. This, he was telling himself, is a typical Nicholas play. This is just what he would do. Nicholas had thought to frighten Claire off. He had flung down what he believed an impossible card to beat. There was well upwards of two million involved. Nicholas knew that Claire had no such cash, and he must be damned sure that she had no way of raising it. She hasn't, eh? MacNaughton thought. Is that so! Maybe, he thought, while he stared at Claire in a moment that seemed very long and was actually only a flash, maybe I'm going to do a rash thing. I certainly wouldn't advise anybody else to do it. Nicholas never dreamed I would.

His eyebrows moved and he looked from Claire to that amazing old lady and back to Claire again. He studied in deliberate succession her hair, which was draggled and disordered, her pale, tense face, in which lines had somehow appeared, the dry set of her mouth. She had not powdered her nose nor used her lipstick all afternoon. Her hands gripping the edge of the desk were gray with the inevitable dirt of a day in any part of the mill, and the dark lacquer on her two forefingers was chipped. She looked dishevelled and, he realized with a pang of sudden intense warmth toward her, homely and plain. She stared at him with her queer, prominent eyes, the glare from the white overhead light flattening the odd broad planes of her face. He was startled then to notice gray threads on the crown of her head.

Mary spoke first. "Of course," she said. Her old voice was reedy and thin but very firm. "That's what my stock is for."

MacNaughton said, quietly matter-of-fact, "Certainly. I will buy up to half of Nicholas's stock myself. And our bank—or other banks—will buy the rest for you and Miss Rafferty—with your own shares as security."

He still stared, almost enthralled, as the tenseness began to break in Claire's face; the big eyes began to swim, and the broad mouth to go down like a child's at the corners. She stood holding onto the desk and shaking her head a little. Then she went over and put her arms around Mary and said, "Darling—" She turned to MacNaughton and moved her arms to his neck and began to cry and said, "I don't know why it matters so terribly, Charles. I don't know."

"I do," said Mary, looking at the oak-framed photographs on the grimy wall. William Scott and Paul Scott. Mary's eyes behind her spectacles were deep and steady.

"I do," Charles MacNaughton said also. "You did the explaining, Claire."

He patted her shoulder and offered his clean handkerchief. Hers was a sight. Mary stood there looking straight past them, years and years away. Claire touched her tenderly, then turned to MacNaughton. She was drying her eyes, and holding his right hand in her own begrimed one like a child. They exchanged the delicious secret glances of conspirators again. Claire looked at the clock on the wall.

"Four and a half minutes gone!" she gasped. "Quick! Go and send in the papers and lawyers and clerks and all the rigmarole—oh, and a proxy form—to us in the bookkeeper's office!" She kissed him and opened the door and ran.

CHAPTER LXXXIX

[*1938*]

EVERY MORNING Claire and Anton had their breakfast on the small table in the window embrasure. Their flat on the Hořejší Nábřeží, the southern end of the Smíchov Embankment, had a bay of casement windows overlooking the broad solemn stream of the Vltava. They could sit and look out at the endlessly moving surface of the lead-gray water, flowing majestically down from its necklace of bridges. Just above them the Palacký Bridge spanned the flow. They looked northward past the Jirásek and the

Legion Bridges to fill their eyes with the infinite timeless magic of the Charles Bridge, the Karlův Most, stretched between its spired towers. There was beauty so absolute, compulsion to the eyes and the heart and the mind so irresistible in this daily contemplation of ancient treasure, that the river and its hallowed attributes became integral to their intimate hours. Always the sight of the Charles Bridge renewed the moment when they had stood there together realizing, they knew now, their destiny. Anton said that the bridge had known it first and told it to them. He made a symbol of each tower; one was Claire, the other himself; the span between was their joined selves, solid as the stones and fixedly wrought as the masonry which had stood for seven hundred years. "Smetana was not the only composer the river inspired," Claire said smiling. "The river's capacity for inspiration is infinite," Anton replied.

In the dour gray of late winter mornings, the view blurred by mist and the peculiar smoky air of Prague, the room lamplit and warm from the fire in the yellow porcelain stove, breakfast was particularly delicious. They kept the odd hours of their professions. They rose late and breakfasted late and did not eat again until the relaxing luxury of afternoon coffee with its seductions of sandwiches and pastries. They ate their late-evening dinner after Anton was all through work, after the concert if there was one, after he had finished at his desk if there was no performance. He liked to compose in the hours between dusk and ten or eleven o'clock, and he liked to have Claire in the room while he sat at his writing-table covering page after page of manuscript with minutely scribbled notes. When she was away working, or when she was shut up in her own room writing a story, he worked much more slowly, pacing up and down the room, trying ideas on the piano (a practice on which he sternly frowned, saying it was a lazy amateurish trick), playing and wasting time with Fiddle, the cat. Naturally there was a cat, a chunky square-cut kitten, coal black with great round topazes of eyes and a fantastic chrysanthemum coat and three-inch whiskers. Anton brought him to surprise Claire on her return from Pittsburgh, and the cat immediately preempted a violin-case for his personal quarters, thereby inviting his name.

Fiddle loved breakfast as much as his mistress and master did. He always sat on the side of the table, neatly poised within half an inch of the edge, his front paws decorously tucked away beneath his vest frill, his haunches bunched. He purred loudly the entire time, even if the pleasure of eating and drinking was almost entirely vicarious. There was a theory that Fiddle was not to have his manners spoiled by being fed at table. He understood this with the full intelligence of his breeding. The only weak spot in the discipline was Claire. Sometimes she could not resist the glow in his yellow eyes, the rebuke in his generous purring to celebrate her good appetite. She slipped bits of things he dearly loved—a crumb of chicken liver, a sliver of ham—from her fork to her fingers and invited him to enjoy himself. Not until the transfer from fork to fingers was complete would he relax his decorous restraint and daintily champ the titbit in his black velvet jaws. Claire had never had a black cat before. She was enchanted. "It's a completely different personality," she exclaimed. "A totally different kind of cathood. Something particularly *catty* and very special."

Life had a total, round, complete, absorbed quality which she had never known; which indeed she had not dreamed there could be. It had purpose. Each thing Anton did and each thing she did was in itself important and perhaps still more important as a single chip in a mosaic whose pattern they well understood and worked upon, though it might be too broad to contemplate in one panoramic glance. Anton told her that she was probably more conscious of this sense of purpose and pattern as a consequence of years of aimlessness and formlessness; and she said, "Do you think I could tell so precisely what you mean to me if I had not floundered and shadow-boxed half my life away?" They were not always so serious. But even when they sat with friends convulsed at the particular kind of low humor that their favorite music-hall purveyed, or when Claire's journalist friends, passing through town from Germany, interlarded their horrible reports with the bitter, outrageous jokes that grew in the diseased country like fungi on a dungheap, the roars of belly-laughter sometimes clanged in the back of Claire's mind, sinister as distant alarm bells.

People were no longer so inclined to scoff at anyone who dared to watch for and worry about the quickening landslide. Prague was too appallingly central. Prague was too literally the crossroads of catastrophe. Prague was too full of white, frightened, staring faces; of busy, worried workers in hostels and refugee relief organizations; of furtive dealers in contraband money and contraband identities and documents and passports. One thing was held by everybody in common, everybody from the flower-seller on the street corner and the gruff driver of a rattling hack to the artists at the opera and the sober officials up in the Hradčany: a knowledge that every day of the good life now was a day gained from an ominous and impenetrable future. They would make and listen to their music and cook and eat their delectable food and promulgate and live by their wise laws intently aware that the rim of security and sanity was shrinking, shrinking visibly about them every day. Julka knew it. Julka was too old to waste time by closing her eyes to it. Julka lived down in the country where the army functioned so that one saw it. One knew by sight on the roads the different kinds of tanks and armored trucks and machine guns and heavy artillery as they rolled out from Škoda and Zbrojovka to be manned by the hard, level-eyed boys in the olive brown uniforms. She heard the planes overhead, more and more as the months went by. Jan began his training at the air-force barracks in February. And everybody watched, sickened, while the wretched fanatic, Henlein, prostituted his undeserved rights of free speech and free assemblage to the loathsome purposes of the Sudeten traitors, and his puppets in the Parliament made mockery of the constitution that had put them there.

No, said Anton, you could not ignore portents like Claire's stories written toward the end of February in Vienna; of Schuschnigg's hideous interview at Berchtesgaden; of the criminals forced into his government; of his negotiating desperately and too late for the support of the decent, betrayed workers; of boldening bands of ruffians parading and chanting in the frightened streets; of the roars of the maniac in the Reichstag, heard by radio in every hamlet in Austria. Claire's specialty was people. It was individuals from whom she often drew her news, little men and little women caught for a last quick word or two before the tidal waves of history swept them down. Stories like this etched their fine awful meaning even on the most unwilling minds. But there were still those who shrugged and said, "But that's Austria, why bother about that?" Anton and Claire had to know better, or they must have been fools. And Julka knew better too. So it was the infinite personal perfections of life that glowed warm and treasurable against the thickening miasmas of the wilderness outside. Each homecoming now was not merely the delight of coming home, but the tense appreciation of this home to come to, this perfection balanced so delicately on the brink of the volcano.

"Why don't you get out?" one newspaper friend from Berlin asked Claire and Anton late on a night when they had eaten and drunk and smoked and talked as he had not been free to do for months. There had been no dissembling about the conversation there. "Why do you stay, the two of you?" he asked. "Sooner or later the whole abscess will burst. War is absolutely inevitable. You know that, Claire."

She shrugged in acquiescence with the obvious. "I know more than that," she said. "I know where it'll begin. Right here, for my money."

"Then in God's name—"

"Look," she said, "do you run away from your job?"

"No. But after all, that's not my home. You—" he motioned to include Anton and all he signified.

"But this *is* our home," Anton said. "You don't run out on your home when you see trouble ahead. You owe it something."

"I see. So you think the Czechs will fight, Claire?"

The most extraordinary and arresting thing about her life was the double channelling into which its stream had been directed. There was Anton and her work and all they were and had together. But also there was Pittsburgh and the mill, which had changed on that October afternoon from an idea she had fought for to a tangible, absorbing entity to which she now had the gravest obligations. Charles MacNaughton had told her so. She now owned so much of its stock that no major step or decision could be taken without her approval. It had been only the work of an instant to endow her with something that made her know for the first time what Paul Scott had lived for, and, in a sense, died for: the administration of that mill according to certain principles which in Claire's mind were synonymous with America. When the battle smoke of that stockholders' meeting had cleared, and Claire sat in the littered room with Mary and MacNaughton and Purcell and Simcox and Ted, the others all having left, and when the actual questions had arisen of policy and general procedure now that the changes had been made, Claire had said, "I want you all to know one thing. I think you're magnificent. I've got to go back to Europe because that's where my job is and where my home is. The most constructive thing I can possibly do for all of you is go about my own business and do a good job of it. We've all got confidence in one another here."

She paused then and nobody spoke, and she sat looking at them, seeing how intently they were listening, realizing suddenly that the few words she had uttered in a quick impulse of sincerity were something they all wanted to hear. God knew there had been enough talk that day. Everybody must be exhausted and restless and anxious to go home. But they all sat still, looking at Claire, and Claire sat in her place between Mary and Charles MacNaughton, tired and dishevelled and stripped of every exterior attribute of charm. Her grimy hands were clasped tight on the table before her. She waited for somebody else to speak, but no one did, and also no one made a move to break up the gathering then and there. So she knew that there was something they were still waiting for her to say. She felt a strong desire to lay her head down on that gritty table and cry. All sorts of deep and tangible emotions swept through her mind. She could feel almost through her skin the weight of Mary's thoughts, Mary who must also be full to overflowing with memories of Paul. This was Paul's victory today. If Claire had not first known the mill through Paul, if she had not first seen it at the white peak of its war effort, spurred on by Paul, who in that way was fighting with his sons, if she had not with Paul and Mary loved and revered the Liskas long ago, she would never have brought such adamantine determination to this crisis in the mill's affairs. She looked around the table and smiled faintly and said, "I wouldn't have the impudence to tell any of you what I thought about running the mill. You've run it mostly as Paul Scott would have done. My hope is that you can keep that up. This year is the centennial of our mill, and what we have done today is all the celebration Paul Scott would ask. I can't speak for the earlier Scotts, because I didn't know them . . . but we all knew Paul." She looked at Ted then and gave him a smile of peculiar tenderness, and the color came into Ted's face and he turned his head. Claire paused, thinking that perhaps somebody else had something to say, especially about the centennial, but they were still all quiet, all closely attentive, listening to her. She sighed and said slowly, "This is not Paul Scott's world any more. It's a horrible world, a wilderness. But there are some things to go by. We all know, for instance, that the new board will sign the S.W.O.C. contract when it comes up. That's one of the things we were fighting for—because we believe in our mill and its place in the American future. We all know"—she leaned forward and circled the table with a solemn glance and lowered her voice a little—"that the world is heading into the most appalling catastrophe since the dawn of history." She paused. She had never found herself speaking in this way and for a moment she weakened with embarrassment and would have stayed silent, but five faces were turned intently toward her and waiting for her to finish. "Every steel mill on the face of the earth will be involved. Every steel mill will have a stake—and be a stake—in the future of civilization." She thought carefully for a moment and finally said, "Mary Rafferty and I will never want any dividend badly enough to doubt where we ought to stand." She broke off and stood up and said, "Don't you want someone to move the meeting be adjourned, Mr. Chairman?"

When she sailed for home she carried with her a long canvas carryall which she had had made to hold a certain box. She kept it with her constantly, allowed nobody else to carry it, and on the flight from Paris to Prague held it in her lap in the plane. Even in the taxi on the way home

from the airport, weak with joy to be in Anton's arms again, she watched
to see that nothing jarred the bag. And later, when they could talk and
laugh and think again—for Anton could only motion at first to show that
he was helpless with happiness—she brought the bag in from the vestibule
and told him to open it. Inside the canvas was a brown alligator case, and
Anton opened that with almost a frightened expression. His hands moved
more and more slowly as he realized what he was about to find. There was
a worn purple velvet pad inside over the instrument; he took that away.
Very slowly he picked up the violin from the case and stood holding it in
both hands, looking at it while tears rose in his brown eyes and rolled over
down his cheeks. At last he laid it down again and took Claire in his arms
and buried his wet face in her breast.

"*Miláčku*, you have bought me the Lamoureux Strad." He was crying
like a boy. "I am not worth it, my dearest, my darling, you should not
have done such a thing for me. Oh, my God, I am so ashamed."

"Ashamed? Of what?"

"I'm not worthy of such an instrument. I'm only a—"

She put her hand over his mouth and stopped his talking. Her eyes
never moved from his. She looked at him with worship. Such love suffused
them that they could only gaze dumbly and cling together. He shook his
head again bewilderedly. Finally he took her hand from his mouth and
held it against his cheek and said thickly, "It isn't the Strad, *miláčku*, it's
your loving me so much you think I'm worth it. It fills me all up, it fills
me here—" he drew her closer to his heart, his hand feeling for her breast.
"Here."

They turned and stood clinging together looking down at the beautiful
thing lying in its case.

It was not until two or three days later when he was tuning the Strad
that he looked up with a sudden appalled expression and said, "*Miláčku*,
nobody has money enough to buy a Strad. How did you? What have you
done? What haven't you told me?"

She smiled. "I don't tell everything. I'm that nasty rich woman you
were afraid to marry, remember?"

"*Ach!*"

She kissed the end of his nose and went away to talk to Růžena in the
kitchen. Bless him, she thought, bless every hair of his head. Bless him
because he doesn't know, because he'll never have any idea. Because he'll
never notice anything about the pearls.

Anton's symphony was to be played for the first time on the fifth of
March, and all the musical people in town were making a great occasion
of it. The conductor of the orchestra invited Anton to conduct the work
himself but he refused.

"My God, no," he said to Claire when she tried to urge him. "I hope
you have sense enough not to want me to make a fool of myself. I'm no
conductor. Neither are all the other odd-job men who leave their pianos
and cellos and hope to wake up in the morning finding themselves called
young Toscaninis. I fry too many fish as it is."

"But how can Talich know how you want it played?"

"It's all down there in black and white, isn't it? All I ask is he should do what it says. I'll take care of the players."

"I bet you will. But it seems so queer, darling, to have you sitting there playing—"

"Nonsense. I want to. The chief reason is so I can look up and see you in your box."

She made a face. "Liar. You don't know I'm alive when you're playing."

"I *shouldn't* know, you mean."

To Claire the performance of his concerto a year ago, when he played the solo himself, had been one of the great experiences of her life. Never had she known a sensation like the pride which had kept her breathless while the audience roared and shouted for Anton, and his colleagues sat beaming and beating the backs of their bows on their music stands, and the conductor stood aside applauding, and Anton in the centre of the stage, holding his violin by the neck, made embarrassed, smiling gestures of deprecation.

Claire was not the only one who had marvelled at the strange workings of the creative mind. The critics had all commented on it. Friends in America sent cuttings from the music sections of the principal newspapers, in which American critics undertook also to analyze the development of Antonín Hrdlička. It struck them as remarkable that he had plodded along for years doing his job in the orchestra and composing charming and desultory small pieces, only to produce his first major work at the age of thirty-five and to follow it so quickly with a symphony of true magnitude. The symphony minimized the concerto by comparison. The concerto was a fine and substantial work and was now being played by half a dozen great orchestras, but the symphony had much more stature and profundity.

Anton said so himself; "the concerto is all right," he said to Claire, "but I wrote it before I had you."

And they were not married when the concerto was first performed. Claire had not felt the right to a personal share in the success and had stood carefully aside to place Julka in line for the excited congratulations and compliments. But now it was different. Now it seemed to give everyone pleasure to put Claire at the pinnacle of their attentions to Anton, and he was supremely proud to have it so. In her box she had Julka on her right in the place of honor; also two of the principal ministers of the government, one with his wife; and for the other, a bachelor, Anton's cousin Dora Dvořáková. Dora was so dainty and feminine in her black velvet gown with her curls bunched on top of her head that it was quite impossible to picture her in a starched white coat working over brains and lungs at the Medical Faculty. But her record there was brilliant. She took honors and prizes at every examination period, and her interneship was soon to begin.

The conductor arranged the program together with Anton, and Anton naturally consulted Claire, and Claire demanded that the whole program round out a certain concept which Anton agreed was richly sentimental but perhaps, he suggested doubtfully, too much so? Claire refused to be swerved. No, this program must mean and say exactly what she had in mind. Every soul in the audience would understand and agree. First they should play the overture to *Don Giovanni*. It was unnecessary to explain that to Prague. Then Anton's Symphony number One, in A minor, whose title-page read: *Symphony for my Father*. And, to conclude, Claire insisted, *Vltava*.

"But *miláčku*, that's so—you know."

"Don't you dare tell me it's hackneyed."

"God forbid. Nobody minds how much it's played. No, I mean—" he broke off and looked embarrassed. "Don't you think it's—cheeky—to put me on a program with Mozart and Smetana? Wouldn't it be better to—"

Claire shook her head.

"First you teach me not to be afraid to feel these things and express them, and then you say it's cheeky to—oh, you imbecile." She kissed him and ran her fingers into the thick brush of his hair. "You know why I want *Vltava*. Don't you?"

· She had heard every rehearsal of the symphony and Julka had heard many, but nothing had prepared them for the emotion they would feel when they actually sat there in the gala crowded hall, their eyes fixed on Anton in his place at the head of the fiddles, their ears straining for the first murmured rumble of the tympani with which the symphony opened: *Pianissimo,* a blending of percussion and the bass voices, marked from the first bar with the ponderous four-fourths beat that would continue throughout the movement. The construction was deceptively simple, the muffled opening spreading into a broader and broader background against which the sudden entrance of all the fiddles, first and second, in furious unison, was like an electric flash. Anton had made a curious success of the plan he so succinctly described to Claire. What he called folk themes were brilliantly developed against this steady, thudding, dark rhythm which echoed startlingly the strident clack of a rolling-mill. Yet the music was not pictorial in a circumscribed or obvious sense. It unfolded from its own core of original inspiration in a tremendously dramatic concept. And the "folk themes" were no borrowings from the village lyrics of the Dvořák countryside. The truth was that Anton had a melodic fertility and a realistic equipment for using it which seemed almost anachronistic in comparison with his contemporaries. Modern composers, Claire had always said disgustedly, were barren of melody. That was why they turned to such abortive harmonic monstrosities. But Anton's mind teemed with melodies. Most of them were purely Slav in mood and color, but some, especially in the Scherzo of the symphony, were a startling echo of America. In two places in the Scherzo he quoted "Alexander's Ragtime Band" and "Stairway to Paradise." Claire looked at Julka when that passage occurred. Julka had always protested it. She sat now, shocked and scowling; what kind of fool thing had he done, sticking this trash into his symphony!

But when the audience burst into shouts and roars of enthusiasm at the conclusion, Julka forgot all about her disapproval. The critics themselves stood up in the aisles applauding and shouting *"báječné!"* and asking one another who could remember when there had last been such a triumph for a new work?

Could there be, Claire thought, a more glorious experience than this? Would anything ever again fill her with such a complete knowledge of joy and pride? Could it possibly be the same anywhere else? In a dream she realized that in the whole vast hall, crowded with clamoring people, rimmed in the boxes with the highest officials of the government, there was not a soul who kept his seat except herself and Anton's mother. While the conductor kept Anton standing in the centre of the stage, and the orchestra and audience stood applauding and shouting and thousands of eyes kept turning from the stage to her box, she and Julka sat silently smiling, poised and controlled though their eyes stung with restrained tears and for a time they dared not exchange a glance lest they falter in their composure. But Claire murmured under her breath, "Oh, if Charlie could only be here tonight!" and Julka answered, "Papa always expected this of Anton."

Many a man and woman looking at the two women in the box and then at Anton on the stage, nodded and smiled and said, "No wonder!" Julka looked magnificent. She looked and bore herself like precisely what she was, her gray hair flatly combed back from her broad-boned face, her heavy hands folded in her lap, her severe dark velvet dress, made under Claire's supervision, following the solid outlines of her peasant figure. Beside her, Claire in the same white dress that she had worn last fall at Lauchlan's dinner—what worlds distant that was—was the picture of radiance and grace. Julka was a national figure in her own right, but it must be a woman of towering stature, people observed, who was not in the least eclipsed by such a son and such a daughter-in-law.

There was a great reception after the concert, which kept them very late in a clamor of ecstatic greetings and earnest compliments and endless healths and toasts and a wonderful gala supper. It was three o'clock in the morning when they finally drew up at home and stood deliciously exhausted in the entry while Anton unlocked the door of the flat. There was a cable under the door. Anton picked it up and handed it to Claire. She read it with Anton and Julka looking over her shoulders.

GO VIENNA IMMEDIATELY COVER PLEBISCITE EXPECT
TROUBLE REGARDS MONROE

CHAPTER XC

[Summer 1938]

NOW THE WHITE and frightened faces crowded thicker and more ghost-like into the streets and hostels and coffee houses of Prague. Lines stood silent or fearfully whispering, all day long and all night too, in the railway stations, at the counters of airlines and steamship offices, at consulates and banks and government bureaux. Dazed men and women with bewildered children appeared at the refugee hostels, waiting the clock around to be told what to do next. Nobody needed to ask their stories; they were all written in their faces.

No matter what the proof from horrified eye-witnesses and shattered

victims, nobody could believe the tales of bestiality in the conquest of
Vienna. Over and over wild-eyed men and shuddering women dressed in
unrelated remnants of beautiful wardrobes would say, "Worse. Much worse
than anything in Germany. And *Austrians*, they were. Austrian boys. Our
baker's boy—the one whose mother was my nurse—I saw him with a
horsewhip standing over Professor Mittenberg while he scrubbed—" "And
my Tante Sophie could not leave the house for seven weeks—they were
rounding up the whole Bezirk and taking the Jewish women to clean the
public toilets—" "—her daughter in the clinic with cancer and they made
her get up and—" "He cut his throat with a razor in the Seitenstätten-
gasse—" "Tortured in the Metropole—his own chauffeur—" "Shot himself" "Hanged himself" "Drowned herself" "Gas—"

Claire had seen it all, and stayed until the Gestapo shut down on news
dispatches and there was no further work to be done. She came home with
one fixed idea, that this thing was a projectile, that it had been packed
with the explosive of seventy million compressed, perverted wills and fired
by a fuse in the hands of a hideously lucid, bestially ruthless maniacal
genius. It would not stop now that it had been set in motion. This was only
the beginning. It was reassuring to find how many responsible people in
Prague understood that. But it was infuriating, it was calamitous that
nobody could see how to take steps in time to block the course that this
hell's engineer had plotted for the accomplishment of his next objective.

"We cannot outlaw the Sudeten party," sober, conscientious government officials said when she buttonholed them in the halls of the Hradčany
and made herself, she felt, obnoxious with her insistence and her questions
and her intensity. "We cannot arrest Henlein or deprive him of his con-
stitutional rights. We must not fight the enemies of democracy by suspend-
ing democracy here. Don't you see?"

"No," she said, "I don't see. You are going to be attacked. This is a
war, only nobody knows how to play this kind of game except the man
who invented it. He calls it bloodless conquest. You can't sit and let him
get away with that!"

"We are not. Go and look at the army. Pay a visit to Škoda. Go over
the Sudeten fortifications. We are ready, more nearly ready than anybody
in Europe, probably. Let him attack and you will see whether he makes a
bloodless conquest. And we have our guarantees. From France and Russia
—he wouldn't dare, *milostivá paní!*"

"Oh God," she said wretchedly. "How long is it since you've been to
France? You should go there and look around, instead of telling me to look
at Škoda. I know all about that. But he's too clever to prod you into that
kind of war. He'll find another way to get what he wants. If he wages political warfare with treachery from the inside you should use his tactics too!"

They only shook their heads anxiously, the honest and patient men,
when she talked to them that way. And meanwhile the German press and
the German radio boiled and screamed with manufactured lies about the
persecuted Germans in the Sudetenland, and Hitler made a speech at Rome,
a speech at Breslau, a speech at Fallersleben, speeches at Nuremberg.
Fantastic, incredible excesses of abuse and lies, solemnly commented upon
by the *Times* of London in thoughtful estimation of the advice that "the

advantages to Czechoslovakia of becoming a homogeneous State might conceivably outweigh the obvious disadvantages of losing the Sudeten German districts of the borderland." Claire ground her teeth when she read that and flung the paper on the floor. "What can you do with that sort of mentality?" she said to Anton. "They actually think, those stupid decent British, that any of this can be settled by talk or compromise or giving Hitler any of what he wants. The fools, how will they ever learn he'll take exactly what he wants! Until somebody calls his bluff."

"Mama says we will do that," Anton said. "She's been on that secret committee for six months now—for domestic defense. They've got the whole country ready to rise up the minute he takes a step. Even the old men and women have their orders. And weapons."

Claire only shook her head. Anton himself, in spite of all he learned from Claire at first hand, partook of the same sublime faith as the government ministers in the pledged word of the nation's allies. The enormity of Claire's report—that Chamberlain had told some of her colleagues in London last May tenth that he had no intention of upholding the Czechs— was simply too nightmarish to be believed. Against that, one had to place, she was told, the repeated and more recent promises of the French to stand by their treaty obligations, and the concurrent assurances of the British to stand by the French; and since nobody believed Hitler would dare to precipitate a general war over the Sudeten question, one had only to stand firm and the Teppichfresser would find he had been frustrated.

In August Claire no longer needed to report the British attitude at second hand. Lord Runciman and his sinister mission arrived in Prague and Monroe ordered Claire to cover the developments minutely. She was appalled to discover that a first cousin of hers, the very David Gregory who had so ardently declared his admiration of Hitler two years ago in Salzburg, was on Runciman's secretarial staff. She ran into him in the foyer of the Alcron and in sheer amazement asked, "What are you doing here?" before she could believe that he was attached to the mission. They spoke only a moment together. Clearly he thought her beyond the pale. "Rum place, this Pragg, what?" he remarked, and Claire was too revolted to prolong the encounter. She went home and telephoned Julka in the country. "Mama," she said, "you'd better come up and stay here awhile."

"As if I could do anything!" Julka snorted.

"You can do a lot for us, just being here." So Julka came.

But Claire had hardly any time to see her. The clock lost all relation to everyday existence. Claire was where she had to be when there was a possibility of learning anything, and that was often at queer hours. She still had the puddle-jumper, the second-hand German Ford she had bought in 1936, and now it stood day and night in the street outside the flat. Originally registered in Germany, it still carried the D-plate and the German license numbers. This had proved convenient before and would, Claire suspected, again, though the young Dvořáks and their friends from the University, who always flocked around Julka when she was staying at the flat, reproved Claire and derided her about the car. "A fine Czech you turned out to be!" Jindřich Dvořák taunted her. He was the son of a younger brother of František, a tall, heavy lad of about twenty trying to crowd two years' university work into one. He wanted to take his degree before going into the Army.

"Leave her alone," Dora said.

"She's too Czech for her own good," somebody remarked. "Our impartial American journalist!"

"Shut up!" Claire said. She was trying to put through a call to Paris. That was a major operation these days. The trunk lines were always busy.

The tension tightened day by day. Claire wrote a piece which, she would not know until months later, stirred her American editors to bitter eloquence about the disgusting purpose of the Runciman mission. Yet, as always, the article had to be guarded and phrased in such oblique terms that she would not be put on the Nazi newspaper blacklist. She was scheduled to go to Nuremberg for the party congress opening on the sixth of September and she could not risk being banned at the last minute. The night before she was to leave in the puddle-jumper, she and Anton and Julka had a late supper alone, and Anton's usual warm good humor was obliterated by a fit of most unwonted moodiness and depression. Julka asked him, finally, what was on his mind. He shook his head and pushed his uneaten food away.

"I don't want her to go to Germany tomorrow," he said, looking at Claire. "I'm worried. I'm sick about it. How do I know——"

"But darling, nothing can happen to me. What are you afraid of?"

"Oh, nothing, I suppose," he said impatiently. "But I want you here—where you're safe. Those Germans can't be such fools that they don't know what you think about them."

"Sweetheart, they don't care," Claire said. "They don't give a damn what anybody thinks—so long as they can censor the copy."

"What makes you think she'd be safe here?" Julka asked suddenly, in a bitter tone.

"Why, Mama——"

"Anton, come to your senses!" Julka spoke as if he were a boy. "Claire has her work to do, let her alone. We all have too much to do now to waste time with personal feelings. By the way, did you attend to your papers when I reminded you about it?"

Claire looked up and laid down her fork. That had been months ago. Now she looked narrowly at Julka, counting back—April, March, February—as long ago as that Julka had been in this frame of mind. Telling Anton to check up on his papers. His citizenship was a complicated matter. He was an American citizen but his eighteen years' residence in Prague carried optional Czechoslovak nationality also. Julka had told him to apply for an American passport.

"Mama," Claire said, almost whispering. "Why?"

"You ask me a thing like that?" Julka said.

"You mean?" Claire said very slowly. "You mean you think . . ."

As if they had not moved for eight days, Anton and Julka were sitting, it happened, in precisely the same chairs when they heard Claire's key in the lock at four o'clock in the morning of September fourteenth. Anton sprang up and rushed to the door. He was gray with anxiety, unshaven since yesterday morning. No telephone call had come through for two days. He flung open the door and wrapped Claire in his arms with a groan of relief. Julka sat still, watching the two clinging silently together. Her face was grim and lined with tension. Claire moved from Anton presently and came over and kissed Julka and dropped into a chair and put her head in her elbows on the table. She was sallow and her eyes were sunk in dark circles and her fingers stained with nicotine. Růžena hurried in from the kitchen with a plate of hot soup. She had ignored Anton's repeated orders during the night to go to bed. She stood waiting with her hands folded. She wanted to see Claire eat the soup and she wanted to hear what was happening in the Sudetenland. Claire picked up a spoon but laid it down again and said, "I'm sorry, Růžena. I'm too tired to eat. Let me rest a while, will you?"

The servant nodded silently and took the soup back to the kitchen, but appeared presently in the doorway again. Anton motioned her to stay in the room. She was as racked with suspense as any of them. Julka asked in a strange peremptory tone, "Did you come through Cheb?" That was where the fighting was; martial law had been declared early the previous morning.

Claire nodded slowly. "Of course. I was coming back the direct way through Bor but when I got to the fork at Wernberg there was such a hullabaloo I asked what was up. They told me the fighting had started so I went on up to Cheb."

Anton put his hand on her as if to make sure again that she was there. "Where were you when"—Julka's mouth twisted as if spitting—"Henlein's ultimatum was delivered?"

"Still in Cheb. They were fighting in the streets and gangs of ruffians were rushing up and down heaving paving-blocks through the shop windows. And looting. There are mobs all over the town screaming *Sieg Heil!* and watching the roads for the German Army to march in."

"You mean you drove through that?" Anton said. "Alone?"

"I wasn't alone. I had Bill Lanning with me, a U. P. man I know. He asked to come back with me from Nürnberg. He's downtown now at the Ambassador."

"How is it in town now?" Julka asked. "I haven't been out since this afternoon."

"Perfectly quiet," Claire said. "It's a madhouse in the station, though. A lot of Jews trying to get out. And the boys are in a feaz at the Ambassador. Ever since midnight they've been waiting for the bombing to begin."

"*Ježíš,*" muttered Růžena in the corner.

"But there's no panic of any kind in town. As soon as they heard the ultimatum was rejected at midnight people simply finished their beer and went home."

"What did you expect them to do?" Julka asked scornfully. "Run around wringing their hands and acting like Austrians?"

"Mama," Claire said thoughtfully, "I'm not at all sure he will invade this country tomorrow."

"Why?"

"He didn't sound like that at Nürnberg. There's something dirty going on. You don't think that Runciman mission was just a lot of hot air, do you? They've been in contact with Henlein all the time. And what were those cabinet meetings in Paris and London all day Monday? Do you think Daladier and Bonnet were deciding to go to war—on account of us? Honestly—do you? And telling Chamberlain he'd have to kick through?"

"They must fight," Julka said in a terrible tone. "They are pledged."

Claire looked at her closely, first with anxiety and then with an expression of tragic pity.

"And Russia too," Julka said. "That's a pledge."

"Mama," Claire said quietly, "the Russians have been sounding out the French on this all the past week. I saw Tabouis and all the others at Nürnberg. One thing you must realize is that the Russians are not going to get left holding the bag. Either the collective agreement holds or it doesn't."

Anton stood up. *"Miláčku,* I want you to stop talking and eat your supper and go to bed."

"All right, darling."

"They must fight," Julka repeated to nobody in particular. "They will fight."

It was to be quoted and repeated and kept alive for years to come, the shout of the Prague newsboys when they ran out on the streets with their extras that night. "All about how the head of the mighty British Empire goes begging to Hitler!" Such was the bitter realistic humor of Prague, such the comment for the blundering artisan of peace in our time. Nobody in Prague could indubiously know, but nobody was too dull to suspect the truth. Yet it was too obscenely fantastic to believe. Could the old hawk be preparing a betrayal, egged on by the yellow worms who were likewise eating away at the rotten core of France? Claire's colleagues at their tables and telephones said yes. Stupefied patriots and idealists still capable of indignation said no. The moments crawled by in distorted terrible isolated Prague, blacked out, jammed out on the radio. This was the first blackout of the war. With Julka between them Claire and Anton walked across the Legion Bridge and up the Národní třída and the Václavské náměstí in the total portentous dark to the Ambassador from which they could not keep away. It was easier to wait there with the others for word from Berchtesgaden. Claire wondered later why she had not been assigned to Berchtesgaden herself and was told, "Because we thought you'd better cover the beginning of the war in Prague—"

Julka could see no other possibility. She sat in a corner, with the tide of scurrying, excited, arguing journalists and specialists and editors and messenger boys rising and falling around the table, for everybody knew her, and even those who thought her only symbolic of a vanishing dream felt the compulsion to interpret some of this cataclysm through her eyes. "We will fight," she said, scarcely more than muttering. "You will see. We will fight."

Never again could any nightmare approach that week in the refinement of its horrors. No other suspense in all their lives could torture them again, they thought. Appalled incredulity, horrendous silence, was the typical reaction to the news when it finally came from London, the news of the request *by their allies* that the Czechs consent to cede the Sudetenland to Hitler. And the news that they were deserted. Of the two facts it was impossible to decide which was the more hideous—as if it mattered, Julka said. They would fight, she kept on swearing, they would fight, now they would fight alone, but they would fight.

Claire found herself in Godesberg, working with her able and generous friends upon, she said later, the cadaver of happiness. She had to drive herself to report anything in a coherent way at all. The whole experience receded into a segment of her memory at which it would be impossible to look ever again without flinching. She had no recollection of actually writing anything in Godesberg or a week later at Munich, no memory of getting her dispatches on the wires, no memory of anything but standing in a hall outside a closed door with two ministers of the Czech government and staring sickly at their faces when they said, "We were told to stay out here and wait." "Where are the Russians?" she asked one of them, and received the unbelievable answer that was the truth.

She did not go to bed all that night after the signed outrage was handed out in the hall as a perpetrated finality. She saw them all, the monstrosities strutting with victory and the ghouls making their shameful getaways; the faces of her two Czech friends when they emerged from the room into which they had been peremptorily summoned to perform the filthiest enforced abortion on the body of decency. She was told by somebody to wait for a copy of another agreement to be issued jointly by Hitler and Chamberlain in the morning, and she remembered only the surge of nausea that swept her into some washroom where an old Bavarian hen clucked around her and fetched smelling salts and a blanket to cover her on the lounge where she lay in the place smelling of disinfectant. She was hysterical when she told about that at home—"disinfectant," she shuddered, "in that charnel house."

But Julka only sat in a chair like a stone staring out the window at the river flowing by.

Her silence was terrible. Anton said she had sat in that chair the entire time, listening if there was news on the radio, apparently insensible if there was not. Sometimes he could not believe she realized what was going on, and at other times he knew well that nobody in the entire land could be feeling every pulse-beat of this agony more tellingly than she. Claire dropped beside her chair and buried her sobbing face in Julka's lap when she came home but even then the old woman did not speak. She closed her heavy gnarled fingers on Claire's smooth forearm and said nothing.

When Claire went to her room to take off her clothes for the first time in two days, she found Růžena standing by her bed. The servant's face was gray and drawn, though Claire had expected it to be swollen with weeping; and she was looking at a picture which always stood on the night-table, a small faded photograph of Evan Gregory in his uniform as Claire had seen him last.

"That one," said Růžena in a bitter croak. "That one. He had a chance to fight."

CHAPTER XCI

[*March 1939*]

"IF ONLY THEY wouldn't go out in the streets. If they'd only stay indoors where they didn't have to see it."

Claire had come in from the ordeal on the Václavské náměstí and flung herself face down on the couch. Though her ears were muffled in the cushions, she heard still the clank and thump of the tanks and armored trooptrucks, the ring of marching boots, the groans and hisses and vicious spitting of the desperate people ranked along the sidewalks. Though her eyes were closed she could see still the rows of gray-clad animals with metal skulls sitting like obscene prehistoric gods with their arms rigidly folded on the trucks that drews the big guns. Surely, she told herself, standing with others in a dumbstruck group on the sidewalk, this isn't the *invasion of Prague*. The Nazis are not here. This isn't the German Army invading Prague. This is the invasion of Vienna. This is what I saw on the Kärntnerstrasse. I've never stopped seeing it. Those red-faced degenerates screaming *Sieg Heil!* aren't Sudeten Nazis. They're Austrians. This is Vienna. Everything stopped making sense then. Nothing has made sense since then.

It was not at all like her deliberately to fling her mind into such a distortion. She should not take such a cowardly, cock-eyed refuge. Look at Růžena, she told herself. Take a lesson from her. The servant was standing at the front window, holding the curtain aside and staring out at the Legion Bridge, which she could plainly see. They were coming down the Národní třída in a rumbling thick gray column, machines and beasts, beasts and machines, they were advancing across the bridge to make their way up to desecrate the Hrad. Hitler would be there tonight; obscenity and barbarism in person would be there sleeping in the palace of the Bohemian Kings, in the shrine of Masaryk.

Růžena stood there for a long time, her dumpy body in its black dress and white apron clumsy and rigid, her red hands clenched in eloquent fists. Claire sobbed on the couch, Anton sat on the edge of a chair clutching his head between his hands. They heard Růžena turn from the window finally and they looked up. Her face was gray and tearless as it had been on the night of Munich. She was standing awkwardly at attention like a child about to recite. Presently she opened her mouth mechanically and said in her croaking voice the words of Comenius which every Czech child learns in school. "I believe that after the tempest of God's wrath shall have passed, the rule of thy country will return again unto thee, O Czech people."

Late in the evening they went back to town because Claire wanted to see who was at the Ambassador and what they knew. There was absolute censorship already, no use to try to send anything out, but the correspondents would still be about. The place was a madhouse as it had been during Munich, and now the city was afflicted with a new degeneracy. At the termination of the march the invaders had broken rank and the soldiers were turned free. They fell upon the city, a horde of gluttonous locusts. Storekeepers were ordered to keep their shops open. In every street there were wrangles and riots as the Germans lined up at the counters of shops and the tables of restaurants, buying (with phony money), gormandizing, stuffing their maws with goose and pork and pastry and chocolate and hunks of delicate pink ham and fistfuls of whipped cream and quarts of Plzeň beer and rivers of good honest coffee the like of which some of them had never smelled, slapping together bars of candy, slabs of butter, whole sausages, layers of cheese, ramming the stuff down their throats and swilling everything good to drink after it. Claire was green with disgust, clinging silently to Anton's arm, as they made their way through the mobs on the streets and finally by inches, trampled and shoved, into the lobby of the Ambassador. And there they ran straight into Jack Thomas.

"Claire!" He grabbed both her hands and kissed her and shook hands with Anton and talked all at the same time. He did not give her a chance to ask how he had come there, or when. He had come in with the German Army today. He had been transferred from the Moscow office three months ago and sent to Berlin. Russian censorship was such that he had wasted his time there for over a year.

"Oh, Jack, it's good to see you."

"Good? Jeez!" He grinned at them both. "Listen. I've got to talk to you. I was on my way to try to phone when you walked in."

He looked about uneasily. They were swamped by German officers and gaudy women (whores from Sudety, Claire supposed) and newspaper people fighting to get at useless telephones and sweating waiters staggering under loaded trays of beer.

"Over at our house," Anton said quietly. "We'd better walk, we can never get a taxi tonight."

So they went back. The flat was so peaceful; warm and orderly and welcoming, with all the signs of Růžena's careful housekeeping even on this day of calamity and confusion. Fiddle lay asleep in his violin case, curled round on himself like a coffee cake, with one paw across his eyes. He stretched and miaowed a greeting to them and curled up and went to sleep again.

"Lord, how I envy him!" Claire sighed.

She poured drinks for them and brought cigarettes and pulled the chairs closer together and Anton went to make sure the blinds were drawn on all the windows, though he need not have bothered, knowing that Růžena had closed them.

Claire thought for a moment how very queer it was to have Jack Thomas sitting here talking to Anton as if they were old friends, without the slightest sign of constraint. She did not know whether Anton knew that Jack had once been her lover, but she supposed he must; anyway, nothing in the world could seem less important now. Under other circumstances, and given time to consider the question, Anton would probably have been upset or resentful about it. But now he was paying the closest attention to what Jack was saying, and thinking of nothing else.

"The point is," Jack said in the unnaturally low tone that he had used ever since they met him, "you have all got to get out of here like bats out of hell, the whole kit and caboodle of you."

Anton raised his eyebrows and looked at Jack with a good deal of doubt. Claire said, "Why?"

Jack took a long gulp of his whisky and soda, remarking, "That's the last whisky and the last soda this town'll see for many a long day," and resumed his warnings.

"I'm not talking through my hat. I've been with the Nazis every minute this last couple of months and I know what they're planning to do here. You don't need to believe me, but you'd better because you know"—he nodded at Claire—"I'm no windbag. I tell you they mean the absolute decimation and ruination of this country. With all the trimmings."

"For—for the Jews, yes," Anton said, still with the puzzled look. "But the Czechs—"

"They are going to reduce Czecho to a Belgian Congo—a reservoir of slave labor. They've had it planned for years. There will be sixty thousand Gestapo here by tomorrow night. Hundreds of regiments of S.S. and S.A. Your gold reserve and all the foreign currency in your national bank *are in Berlin already*. Your armaments, your rolling stock, all the textiles and food and clothes and shoes and coal and gasoline and building material and even tobacco and face powder and stockings and toothbrushes in the country are already moving to Germany in stolen trucks and freight cars. The Jews are doomed anyway of course, there's no use wasting time over them. The aryanization is worked out so thoroughly on paper it'll almost run itself. But their real idea goes way beyond that."

"Yes?" Anton was leaning forward tensely.

"They're going to expropriate land. They're going to clean the Czechs out of whole districts and settle their own slobs on their farms. They'll do it with documents—signed at pistol point—and threats and torture and all their different refinements of persuasion—there'll be deeds and bills of sale to make everything nice and regular—"

"You don't know the Czechs," Anton interrupted quietly.

"As a matter of fact, I do. Your gal here introduced me to a few down where you come from and that's why I'm trying to make you believe me—you've got to get your mother out of here—*now*."

"Mama?" said Claire. "Particularly? Do you mean they know—"

"I'm trying to tell you they know," Jack said, with almost irritable desperation. "They've got the names and dossiers of every public employee, national and municipal, down to the scrubwomen in the postoffices. They've got the names of all the old soldiers from the Legions too—so I guess that settles your uncle's hash, didn't you tell me he was one of them? But your mother is a marked number. On account of all she did with Masaryk in the old days, and all that—but mostly on account of the Land Reform Office. That's how they're going to engineer their robbery—by arresting every official and clerk in the entire land administration department and destroying all the records so nobody will ever be able to prove title to anything or straighten out the mess for the rest of time."

"Oh Jack," Claire's face was clay-colored and Anton had covered his with his strong white hands.

"Well, you do believe me. I don't need to be sensational about it, Claire—nothing I could invent would be half as beastly as the truth. And I'm putting you two in danger by being here telling you this. If they thought I was warning you they'd kick me out and make some obscene reprisal on you. I've got to go." He stood up and finished his second drink. "I'd better be seen over where the crowds are or they'll be calling my number. But this is straight—there will be mass arrests and a terror that'll make Vienna look like a picnic—the way Vienna made Germany look like a baby's birthday party."

He put on his hat and took it off again. He kissed Claire and wrung Anton's hand.

"God love you both," he said, "and for Christ's sake take your mother and get the hell out."

They did not try to telephone down to the country because Jack warned them not to; and when Claire said they would start at once in the car he warned against that too. "Wait until morning. They'll be rounding up everything on the roads all night. There are troops moving in on every highway. I don't even know if you can get away with it tomorrow—but you'll have to try."

They started as soon as it was light, and a drive which normally required three hours took almost the whole day. They were stopped repeatedly; always, Claire was relieved to find, by the Army. The Gestapo was evidently not in the saddle yet. Claire had had experience before in the difference between the German Army, which preserved some semblance of law, if not provoked, and the Gestapo whose methods were always bullying and terroristic. Their way was enormously facilitated by the German licenses on the car, by Claire's studiedly polite replies in her perfect German to all inquiries, and above all, by their American passports which worked magic. Anton had a curious reluctance to rely on his, as if he could not feel justifiably entitled to this security in the face of disaster for everybody else.

The road was in such a turmoil that in places it was impossible to proceed and Claire had to pull off onto the shoulder and sit there, her hand clutching Anton's in an agony of silent rage, as columns of troops and tanks and roaring trucks full of grinning young soldiers clanked and clattered by. Staff cars and motorcycles whizzed up and down the outsides of the ranks. The road was a mess of melting slush and the gutters sloughs of mud and manure, and this was spattered back over their car in a continuous shower of filth. But worst of all, they met, coming from the opposite direction, an endless procession of loaded trucks and lorries—Czech trucks with Czech licenses and the names of Czech merchants and forwarding companies, all loaded to bursting and driven by German soldiers. Trucks, hundreds of them, systematically stolen in every town and village along the route and stuffed to overflowing with looted goods of every imaginable kind, foodstuffs, textiles, machinery, thousands of cases of boots and shoes, tons of assorted merchandise swept from the shelves of helpless village storekeepers. All on their way to Germany.

"Banditry," Anton muttered furiously through his clenched teeth.

"God damn the thieving bloodsucking sons of bitches, damn them, damn them . . ."

Claire was too racked to speak at all. Her face had frozen to a stricken pinched mask shuttered like the façades of the houses they passed in the looted villages. There was not an ordinary man or woman to be seen along the way, no Czech farmer or schoolboy or housewife or dairy maid. They were all shut up inside the houses which had become their tombs.

They did not leave the puddle-jumper in the street outside the Dvořák house, but drove it into the courtyard through the gates which František locked and barred inside. They went through the kitchen into the main room, where a dozen people were sitting frozen-faced and silent, as if each were alone. Julka rose from her chair and kissed them on their foreheads with gravity as if they had arrived for a funeral. It was almost suppertime and Anička and Libuše were in the kitchen putting a meal together. Anton looked around the big room, counting noses and remarking those who were absent and asked Julka quietly where they were. Her face broke into a smile at that, a smile of unmistakable triumph, and she said, lifting her head proudly, "Jan got away Tuesday. The whole squadron did. Fifteen planes."

"Oh Mama, how wonderful." Claire's eyes filled with tears. "Where?"

Julka shrugged. "Who knows for sure? Some to Poland. Some to France."

František asked, "Is Jindřich still in Praha?"

"We saw him three days ago. I suppose so."

"He has his work to do there. He should go later."

"How about the others?" Anton meant František's sons; Otakar and Tomáš, next older than Jan, and Jaromír and Václav, the two eldest who were both married, with families and land of their own.

"All gone," said František. Claire was astounded at his calm tone. "All except Otakar. He is to stay."

She knew what that meant. Otakar was the engineer. He had been working for the past two years at the Zbrojovka munitions works in Brno.

"He is to stay," František said firmly, and left unsaid the reason—that Otakar and the men like him were to be the brains of the sabotage, which would start the moment the works reopened.

"But how can you manage without Tomáš, strýčku? How will you get the plowing done next month and the crops in?"

František looked indifferent.

"You want me to raise good crops for those *šváby* to gorge on?" he said contemptuously. "What crops we need the girls can work."

Teta Anička came into the room quietly, with almost a timid air. She was so different from her husband, and so total a contrast to Julka. She would never lack nerve when extremes of courage were demanded of her, but of all the people in the room, her sisters-in-law, her nieces, everybody, only she had red-rimmed eyes and a stricken stare on her face. Only she, Claire saw with an aching heart, was thinking first of the deadly danger to her husband and children and secondly of the nation's tragedy. Of her five sons there was not one who had not already committed himself to mortal danger; she knew perfectly well that sooner or later the Gestapo would be here to take her husband; and the mother of daughters in a land under barbarian invasion must be fated to a crucifixion of anxiety.

"Let us eat supper," she said. Her voice was so low from the exhaustion of weeping, and the gesture of her hands as she raised them to motion the family to the table so embracing that it seemed as if she were praying

Long past midnight they were still arguing and pleading in low, strained voices, the three of them in Julka's bedroom after the whole house was asleep. None of Anton's words, none of Claire's entreaties had moved Julka from her utterly quiet, unwavering resolution. She would not go. She had never thought of going. Nothing they might say could induce her to go. At first they had been evasive about the actual danger of which Jack Thomas had told them, but a point came when Julka herself looked at them severely and said, "I suppose you think I don't know what they'll do to me? You babies!"

"But Mama." Claire's broad cheeks were sallow and streaked. She had not made up or changed her clothes or done her hair for twenty-four hours. "But Mama. Tell me one thing—if you know they're going to do something like that and keep you from doing any more work here, why won't you go? You don't *want* to—to be—" she shuddered and paused.

"Go ahead, darling, say it. Arrested. No, I don't want to be arrested for the adventure of it. But my life is no dearer to me than the life of my country. If they murder the country they can murder me too." She shrugged and folded her big hands on her stomach.

"Mama, it isn't fair," Anton said wretchedly. "It isn't fair to Jerry or the girls. Or—or us."

"I disagree with you, Anton. Jerry and you and the girls have your own lives. I have given you all there is in me to give. You are grown men and women, you have no right to ask me for any more. What is left is for my country."

"But—"

"Don't say it again. 'If they lock me up I can't do anything for the country.' That's what you think. If you're so dumb that's your misfortune."

"*Ach,* Mama . . ."

"My son, I understand why you are putting yourself and Claire and me through this ordeal. You're doing what you think right. But I disagree with you, and I am right. Let that be the end of it."

"Mama!" Anton said hoarsely and passionately, "how can you do this to us? Why did you make all that fuss about me getting an American passport when you never intended to use your own?"

Julka's face spread into a solemn, sardonic smile.

"I have no American passport."

"*What?*"

Claire clapped her hand across her gaping mouth.

"No. Why would I?" Julka shrugged. "I am not an American citizen."

"You—are not what—?"

"How can you be so surprised?" Julka said impatiently. "Why should I be an American citizen? I love America, I am glad for it and grateful for it but I am a Čechoslovák."

Anton's brow puckered grotesquely. "But Papa—Papa was naturalized long ago."

"Okay," said Julka, lapsing characteristically into one of her Americanisms at just such a moment. "Okay. We were naturalized. But what should I come home for and work for the government for if I belong to another country? What kind of politics is that?"

"You mean you renounced your American citizenship entirely?" Claire asked.

"Sure. What's more," said Julka, turning her gray head suddenly to hide a rush of tears to her eyes, "President Masaryk himself handed me my certificate of Čechoslovák citizenship—in 1924. Himself. In the Hrad." Her voice cracked.

Claire wept, huddled on the foot of Julka's bed. Anton said, suddenly, "Why did you let us argue with you like that, Mama?"

"I didn't want to say I *could* not go until you made me say it. It's truer that I *will* not go."

"But you could—even—"

"Oh, I suppose one could get out on a Czech passport. But not with my name on it." She stood up and leaned over Claire and stroked her tangled hair back from her forehead. "Go to bed now, darling. Anton, take her to bed. You are good children, wonderful children." She drew Claire off the bed and walked across the room with them, an arm around each. "Good night, my darlings." They both stared at her with strained wet eyes. She kissed them again and stroked their cheeks and murmured *"Dobrou noc."*

In the morning Julka made an opportunity to get Claire away by herself. It was a dark March day, the ground muddy and thawing, the sky lowering overhead. Out in the courtyard the geese were honking an unholy cacophony. The stable echoed to the nervous stamping of the big gray team—the same team, Claire thought with a poignant stab—that had drawn their bridal wagon. She stood in the muddy courtyard, looking about at the sturdy old plaster buildings, the sheds ranged with farm machinery which Tomáš had been putting in order for the spring work when he received the signal to flee. Claire was standing there staring at these things and shaking her head slowly at the hideous realization that all this, multiplied a thousandfold, all this hard-earned and prudently assembled peasant wealth was to disappear down the sewer of greed and corruption, when Julka came plodding across the muddy court, wrapped in an old gray sweater with a pair of galoshes on her feet. She drew Claire's hand through her arm and walked with her to the rear gates of the walled court.

"Let's slip outside and take a little walk," she said. "Are you warm?"

Claire nodded. Julka unbarred the high gate and they stepped out into the meadow beyond, the meadow where the wedding feast had been celebrated. It was naked and barren now. The land rolled away, brown and streaked with rivulets of thawing ice, sloping gently toward the broad valley of the beloved Vltava. Overhead the linden trees were naked too. Drops of water trembled on the brown twigs and fell like tears on the ground below. They stood a moment gazing down the valley and Julka said softly, "Even the trees are weeping with us."

"Oh Mama—"

Julka put her arm around Claire's shoulder and held her close and they stood there clinging together. Presently Julka drew herself up and wiped her eyes on her apron and said, "That's the first time I've let go that way." She sighed heavily.

They began to stroll slowly down the gentle slope of the hill, arm in arm. They were silent for quite a time, but when Julka felt sure she could control her own voice, and Claire would not cry, she began to talk.

"Darling," she said. "Some things I have to say to you alone like this." Claire nodded. "Anton is good and strong and brave but—" she spread her hands expressively. "Sometimes we must make the decisions for our men. Lots of times. You understand me." Claire nodded again.

"After last night," Julka went on, "he'll tell you he'll never leave the country so long as I am here. He'll think he can protect me by staying here. Of course he can't. He must get out. Both of you must go."

"I knew you'd tell me that today," Claire said slowly. "But don't you see, Mama—we *couldn't* go—and leave you here—to go through God knows what—"

Julka stopped walking and stood looking solemnly at the horizon.

"Listen, Claire," she said. She put her hand under Claire's chin and raised her face to look deep into her flecked tawny eyes. "When I first knew you you were a spoiled child. You never had any discipline all your life. If you hadn't had good blood you'd have been a mess."

'That's true," Claire whispered.

"But it is different now. You are a real woman. You've learned what a real woman is. You've learned from working and from living with Anton. But some tests you haven't met yet."

Claire stared at her mother-in-law, marking the grim lines of the haggard face, the sweep of straight gray hair from the strong brow, the piercing strength of the brown eyes.

"What are they, Mama?"

"Obedience. Not the rotten cringing of German degenerates, but knowing how to obey a cruel command when the reason for it is a good reason. Courage. The kind of courage to make decisions against everything you want. Those kinds of things, I mean. Mary Rafferty knows about that. More than anybody you know."

'Mary," Claire said. "What a wonderful soul!"

"Yes," Julka said, "and a real friend. A real woman. What a life!" She wagged her head sadly. "Now I am telling you, darling. I am commanding you. If it makes it easier to pretend I am an officer and you are a soldier, go ahead and pretend. This is war anyhow. I can't know how long I can fight here back of the lines, but that's what I'm going to do. Sure, they'll arrest me any time now. But you think I didn't expect that? You think we haven't got plans made long ago—plans to resist—plans to spy—sabotage—help the men escape—keep the people informed—work—resist—always resist?" She laughed forcefully. "Those vermin. We've been through this plenty times before."

They started strolling again. A high wind was blowing up; it bucked against their legs and whistled in their faces. They bent their heads and moved forward against it. It gave them a good strong feeling.

"What is it you want me to do, Mama?"

Julka smiled at her. "I want you and Anton to leave the country. I want you to get outside and find the best place and the best way to fight this fight—not for us only—but for the whole world. Believe me, darling child, this crime here is only the beginning. You will see. Crimes against civilization and decency will be committed beyond all the barbarian atrocities of history."

Claire thought then in a fleeting deflection of attention how magnificently Julka could speak when she was moved to do so.

"Each to his own place," Julka said firmly. "Mine is here. Here I will stay and here I will fight until they kill me."

"Mama!"

Julka shook her head gently. "What a child you are," she said, kissing Claire's forehead. "They will kill me in the end. Do you think I care? Is there a better way to die? I am sixty-two years old. So what could be better?"

Claire stared at her.

"When they do kill me," Julka said, "they will be planting a crop of vengeance that will hound them for a thousand years. From me and every other Czech they touch." Her hard hands went into fists.

"I can't bear it," Claire said wretchedly. "This is the second time in my life this happened."

Julka nodded heavily. "Your father, hanh?" She turned and put her hands on Claire's shoulders and looked into her eyes and said, "Well, you've got plenty to go by. So now you'll be a good girl. A soldier. Don't nag Anton to go. Just promise me you both will. I command you to go. And I want you and Anton to have a child."

"I'm so old, Mama. I'm nearly forty."

"You must try."

"But Mama." Claire looked at Julka anxiously. "A child—in a world like this?"

"Do you," asked Julka, "want the world to be populated with monsters? Beasts? Degenerates? Bastards from the—" she used a foul word—"of brownshirts and sluts?"

Claire shook her head.

"Then go and do as I say. Go as soon as possible. If you can go without coming here again to say goodbye it would be better."

Claire stood staring. Julka took Claire's face and raised it between her palms and kissed the forehead and the eyes and the lips.

"This is our goodbye," she said quietly. The wind blew hard and wild and wrapped their skirts around them both as they stood together on the hill. "This is our goodbye. When you start back to Praha with Anton there will be no tears, no scenes. You promise."

"I promise."

"Goodbye, my darling girl. Be strong and brave and keep on fighting wherever you are. And I will fight here. Even when I am dead, I will be fighting with all of you—with our boys and the Legions who won our freedom before and will win it back again."

They kissed solemnly.

"*Sbohem, má drahá. . . .*"

"*Sbohem, maminko.*"

CHAPTER XCII

[*November 1940*]

MARY DID NOT REMEMBER, now that she tried to, exactly when the land at the very back of the place, the river-bottom land beyond Reedsdale Street, had been sold off. The B and O tracks ran along there and had for a great many years; perhaps—yes, probably—Clarissa Scott and Paul had sold that land in the years after William's death. Or perhaps William Scott himself had sold it when the Clarks built their big place on Ridge Avenue and ran the broad sweep of their back lawn up to join his. Anyway, Mary said to herself, standing on the back stoop, she distinctly remembered a time when there had been no house and no other property between the back of the Scott place and the open precipice which dropped down to the river. Now there was a factory right below the rear boundary of the back yard. It must have been there for a long time, and Mary was surprised at her own lack of curiosity as to what was made in it. Could she really be so old, she asked herself, that she lived most vividly in the past? Could it be that at eighty-two one looked at a concrete, existing object and saw, not it, but the clustered elm trees and the grassy bluffs that it had long since obliterated?

She sighed, standing there in the damp November chill with her old seal coat pulled around her and a light woollen scarf tied over her head. She seldom went out walking any more, not that she felt feeble, but she rationed her energy cautiously and had none to spare for exercise. This breath of air on the back stoop had taken the place of her daily walk. She heard Claire come out the side door and walk down the porch and stand beside her. Claire slipped her arm through Mary's and stood silent for a while and then said, "What do you suppose they make in that factory?"

"I don't know. We must ask Ted the next time he comes." Mary looked up at her and asked, "How do you feel, dear?"

"Fine." Claire smiled brightly and Mary knew that she was lying. She felt ill much oftener than she said.

"I thought you promised the doctor you'd lie down all afternoon."

"Well, I did. But I get restless. I can't get used to having nothing to do."

"You have something very important to do," Mary said severely.

"That's right," Claire said.

They walked back along the porch and went into the house for tea. Mrs. Tschuda brought in the tray and set it on the table by the fire in the back parlor. Flam had to be displaced to make room for the tray. He rose indignantly, arching his back and moving with offended deliberation. Claire picked him up and squeezed him, burying her face in his fragrant red fur. To her it was still fantastic, unbelievable, that anything could remain as it had ever been. When she arrived here a week ago she had stood in the middle of this room, eyeing Mary in her armchair and Flam on his table and everything precisely as it had been more than three years before, even to the color of the clean blotting-paper on Mary's desk, and she had said, "Do you realize that every other place that means anything to me has been *destroyed?*"

Mary sat watching her now as she drank her tea, holding her cup in both hands as she had done when she was a child, and drinking the scalding tea in big gulps. She looked badly. Her hair had lost much of its springy vitality and the few gray threads on the crown of her head had widened to a broad spray which feathered out into the short curls above her forehead. Her skin was sallow; that was the trouble, she said disgustedly, with her famous café-au-lait complexion. When she was tired or ill she turned not merely pale but "yellow like old manila wrapping-paper. Thank God Anton doesn't have to look at me every day."

"Oh, don't say that."

"Sorry."

"I know, dear. But if you'd only try to relax more—"

That was harder for Claire than anything. Normally her immediate reaction to the burden of calamity and violence and heartbreak was action and more action, work and still harder work. That had swept her through nineteen months of tortured, catapulting history, and brought her stunned back to Mary in Pittsburgh. She had been here a week and she had hardly talked at all. She had sat or stood blank-faced and homely, her thoughts impenetrable; or through the hollow stretches of the night Mary heard her bare feet padding, padding like a lioness in a cage, back and forth across her room. Everyone knew the outlines of what had happened, everyone knew where Claire had been, everyone had read her gripping and horrifyingly vivid dispatches, right up until last week when the Clipper had landed her in New York. But she was too tense to fill in those gruesome outlines yet. She would, Mary knew. It would all come out, probably in jumbled fragments, not much of it in sequence. But even off here in her quiet seclusion, her utter remoteness from this stupendous death agony of the world, Mary sensed that the mass convulsions of humanity would dwarf for Claire, as they must for all the shattered individuals, the remembrance of daily details and daily torments and daily death and heartbreak. Anton was alive, that much Mary had insisted on knowing; alive and working with the Czechoslovak government in London. And Julka was in prison. That was all Claire had said of them so far; and Mary shrank at her tragic brevity. Mary could not know that some shocks, actually less personal than the fates of Anton and Julka, were at this time the most grinding, the most vivid, to Claire.

Mary did not know yet the mental fever, the dull, dogged fury of work, in which Claire had been swept through the Blitz of last spring, along Belgian roads under dive-bombing and machine-gunning, through the unbelievable disintegration of France, through weeks of ignorance about Anton's fate, through the terrible confusion of housing and feeding and nursing the refugees who poured into the Villa Bellevue which she had turned over to the French Red Cross, only to find herself trapped there incommunicado. She had never meant to go there at all. Following her orders she was moving with the stream of crazed humanity with its wrecked vehicles and bleeding feet and screaming women and crying children and encounters with stunned, demoralized remnants of the French Army. Swamped among the clotted mobs on the broad southward roads she had changed tires and stolen food for derelict children and huddled them into ditches while the Stukas screamed overhead, and fought to get at telephones in infernos of village post-offices, and helped deliver a baby in the back of a smashed truck. They were all headed south, they did not know or care where, and before she got into communication with the authorities in Cannes she saw what she ought to do. Her actual arrival there was a fragment of nightmare; something to do with a motorcycle sidecar and, after it broke down, a day-long walk in the naked fire of the tropical June sun. And when she reeled into the grounds of the place she was confronted by a sight which, curiously, roused only one association in her shattered wits: an old print that she had seen as a child in the attic in Pittsburgh, the wrecked remnants of some Confederate regiment being cared for on a plantation lawn. This was without similarity. These were civilians, old men, and women and children of all ages, still gibbering with terror and confusion, who had been rounded up by the Red Cross and herded to the villa. They were swarming over the grounds and through the house. Every room and hallway was crammed with them. Nobody questioned their right to be there and nobody seeing the stunned, exhausted woman, scarlet and fevered from sunburn, with broken shoes and filthy hands and indescribable clothes, wandering about among them, could have guessed that this was the owner of the invaded palace.

Down in the kitchen old foul-tongued Lizette superintended a force of her neighbors whom she had brought in to man the great range and keep the vats of soup and coffee boiling and slice the bread and distribute the food as long as it held out. She was too pressed and too furiously angry and bitter to say an unnecessary word. When she saw Claire she stood for a moment scowling with horrified disbelief, then gave her one fat smack of a kiss and said, "I let them in, *petite*," and went on with her work. "You did right," Claire said. She found herself after a while in the centre hall where two nuns from the Cannes hospital were clutching their veiled heads and staring at the mob of injured people around them and making empty desperate gestures which showed that they had no more supplies for first aid and bandages.

"Nothing, Madame, *pas rien*," they explained when Claire tried to help. "There is not a thread of cotton or linen or a swab or a bandage left in the town."

Claire went upstairs and stood in the hall looking at the locked doors of the linen-room, a great shelved place twenty feet long. Where, she thought, were the keys? If her life had depended then and there on the answer she could not have said. She called a man from a room nearby and told him to smash the locks. And when she dragged herself up to a servant's room under the roof to try to find a place to sleep, the nuns were tearing Mère Constance's coroneted linen sheets into strips to bandage the torn feet of the people.

Mary had waited all of a week for Claire to tell some of this, and she had said very little. One person's experience of catastrophe, Claire had learned in the past two years, was really no greater and no less than another's. When it all sprang from the same source and all worked toward the same end, the extinction of humanity, it mattered little who described this massacre, who that holocaust. And it was characteristic of those who had been through the grinders that individually they did not want to tell about their experiences. But on that afternoon, when Claire was looking so ill, and Mary knew that the sleep and rest she should have were beyond the power of her will to attain, she tried at last to draw Claire into talk. Perhaps she would talk about Anton, and perhaps that would loosen the tight-wire tension of her nerves.

"Anton," Claire answered Mary's murmured question, "was in the Czech Dunkirk. I suppose you hadn't heard much about it—the real one was so much vaster and the newsboys were there. It came first, too, a month sooner than the other. But there were several Dunkirks—lots of them. Ours were at Bayonne and St. Jean de Luz."

She settled more comfortably in her chair and Flam dug himself into the hollow of her lap and began a long nap with loud purring. Claire's fingers played in his heavy ruff.

"The Czech Army fought at both the Marne and the Loire. They were under the supreme Allied Command—which was Gamelin and later Weygand—and they did what they were told. Only after a while nobody remembered to tell them anything, there were no orders, nothing but total demoralization, and finally it was clear that the French had fallen to pieces and weren't even trying to defend the country. So then the boys saw they'd have to save their skins if they were ever to fight again. Anton's regiment was ordered to defend a certain bridge on the Loire and hold it until the next orders came from G H Q at midnight. The French forces were supposed to be ahead of them making contact with the Germans. But midnight came and went and nothing happened and Anton's colonel sent up a man to find out what was up, and he never found any French at all. They'd simply crumbled up and disappeared. So he got back to the regiment and found them still holding the bridge, but the Germans by that time had quit bothering about the bridge and their tanks were streaming down both banks of the river. So our boys just blew up the bridge and started out for cover. They had a couple of weeks of running hell. By that time the whole region was overrun with Germans and the boys would hide all day and crawl all night, foraging if they could, or just plain starving. They were trying to get to the coast and by bits and pieces they did."

Mary knitted quietly and did not prompt Claire when she paused to assemble her thoughts.

"By the end of June the British were in touch with them and were sending small ships to the Bay of Biscay to get them out. All the seacoast was occupied by that time so you can see it was just like Dunkirk. The British ships had to lie off the coast at anchor while the people converged on the two ports and waited for rowboats and dinghies in which to get away The confusion—" Claire shuddered and put her face in her hands. In a while she began to speak again. "There were Czech and Polish soldiers, and fliers who'd had their planes shot up—all the planes that weren't disabled were in Morocco or England by that time—but there were civilians too. Women and children and old people, Free French and Czechs and Poles and English who'd got stuck in the summer resorts, all milling around in the mud off St. Jean de Luz and Bayonne waiting for their turn to get into the boats. The most they could take at a time was thirty people in a boat and there were thousands waiting to go. It took five days to get them all off. And every once in a while a Stuka would come along and dive-bomb or machine-gun them, and all the time the boys had to hold off the Germans at their backs. But practically all of them got away and got to England."

She stopped speaking abruptly and Mary waited a long time before she asked, "How did you get there?"

"Through Lisbon," Claire said indifferently. "I bribed my way with Mère Constance's flat silver."

She fell into another silence and lay back in the chair with her eyes closed. Mary hoped she was asleep. She got up slowly and took a knitted afghan from the foot of the couch and spread it over Claire and Flam too asleep in her lap. Then she sat down again and went on with her knitting, her tired old eyes fixed on Claire's strained face. Mary was far more worried than she would admit. In all her lifetime full of surprises and shocks she had never known anything so peculiarly startling as the appearance of Claire last week straight from the bombing of London. First there was a cable and then she was there, taking Mary in her arms with a hug, flinging her hat on the floor by her chair and running her fingers through her graying hair and saying, "I've come back to have a baby."

Mary had responded as Claire had known and rather dreaded she would, with tremulous happiness and an infinity of tender solicitude. But she was pained to see that Claire was not as happy as she should be about it. In fact, she was not happy at all.

"I don't know," she kept saying, shaking her head. "I don't think it makes any sense. I cannot feel that anybody has the right to bring a human being into this new dark age. I ought to be full of courage and hope and all the other proper sentiments, Mary, but I'm not. I'm sick at heart and"—she looked up with a shockingly frank stare—"scared. Scared to death. I've never been scared of anything before."

Mary tried to console her and reassure her, and certainly it was wonderful that she had come straight home to Pittsburgh, for there was no better place to have a baby. She would go to the Magee Hospital, where there was such a marvellous doctor and where her own sister-in-law, Jenny Liska, would take care of her—the best nurse in the world—

"I know," Claire said. "I know all that That's why Anton made me come. But that doesn't alter the fact that I'll be thirty-nine years old when the child is born, and well—I just think I'll funk it, Mary. I don't know anything about this business, I've never wanted to know. I've never had a thing to do with a child, I've never thought once in my life about being a mother. I don't feel like it now. Maybe I'm awful, but something's probably been left out of me. Like being born with four fingers."

"Your grandmother was exactly like you," Mary said slowly. "You'll be all right."

Claire shuddered. "I wish to God I hadn't had to see that French woman have that baby," she said grimly.

Mary looked at her with a sharp, severe expression and said, "Claire, you'll have to stop that kind of thing. You've got a job to do and that's not the way to do it."

Claire smiled. "You're right. I'll try to behave."

But when she lay upstairs at night in the white bed which was such an unearthly reminder of those other years, of that other war, of the tears she had wept in this bed when the wound of Evan's death was still fresh and raw, when she thought now of Anton in London with the bombs coming every night, it was impossible to put up a phony show of courage. She did not want to be doing this. It was not her idea of the way to see the war through. She had leaned more and more heavily on the drug, the anæsthetic of her job since leaving Prague. She had worked frantically, fiendishly. When the countries where she worked began to crumble one by one under the Nazi steam roller she had dodged ahead of it, always working, always driving herself, keeping the fire of resistance and indignation at white heat in her mind. The more incredible the facts, the more fanatical her passion. Yet, she said to herself in moments of black discouragement, what use was such passion, what use was decency and bravery and the common cause of good men when the roller crunched on and on and nothing, nobody, had found the means to stop it?

She knew the means. Everybody in England knew. From the moment she had stepped on English soil last July, from the first contact with the earth and the air which tingled with heroic defiance she knew, as every other soul did, whence the means of victory would finally come. It would have to come from America. But the way to this end was hideously obscure. And the interval must be so stringent, it must be the single greatest ordeal to which human fortitude had ever been subjected. There was no soul in England not dedicated to this ordeal. The whole stigma of Munich was burned off now in a terrible trial by fire. If one had English blood like Claire's, even such blood as that of her pitiable grandfather and her foolish cousins, one could count on it now to stand and deliver its charge of courage. So she felt, and so she thought, together again with Anton under the bombs that fell on London.

He was no longer in the Army. He had had a wound—not a bad one, thank God—in his left foot, much aggravated by the hardship and the exposure of the escape from Bayonne, and after recovering, when he wanted to go back to the Army which was re-forming in England, the newly established Provisional Government in London had assigned him other work to do. Like everything connected with the extraordinary secret organization of resistance at home, it was blanked behind a wall of silence. Claire knew what Anton was doing, of course. She knew that his work, which might require him to fly back and forth to Canada and the United States in bombers and air ferries, was extremely dangerous; but that was never discussed between them. Nobody was safe anyway. Claire expected to stay in England, where she was up to her eyes in her own work and half a dozen different war undertakings, until she should be sent to the Near East or the Far East or some other possible theatre of activity. But Anton, on a September night shortly after the terrible attack of the fifteenth, came over to her when she was getting ready for bed. They had a two-room flat in a modern block, considered fairly safe as safety went, and they had given up sleeping in the basement shelter. He took her in his arms and turned her away from the mirror where she was brushing her hair and said, "*Miláčku*, I want you to do something for me."

There was no mistaking the solemn tone of his voice. Holding her in his arms he told her what he wanted and his words were the inexorable reminder of her last goodbye with Julka. Claire did not want to do it. She had never wanted to. But she could not say no. She had only to think of Julka in prison, a thought which was never more than momentarily veiled from the terrible forefront of reality, and she knew that this was something she must do if she could. They lay in bed joined in the only perfection they could attain amid death and blood and fire and destruction, and through the opened window with the blackout curtain drawn to the dark night, they saw the sky go blood-colored in a fresh hail of death, and heard the long familiar wails of warning.

She tried by every subterfuge to hide how ill she was only a few weeks later. But Anton knew. She was a foolish, reckless child to think she could deceive him, or should. He talked to the doctors and then to her and then to the doctors again, and finally he told her summarily that she would have to go to Pittsburgh. She protested bitterly. Anything, bombs, fainting-fits, twenty attacks of nausea a day, was preferable to being away from him now. He was puzzled and baffled and upset. It seemed to him that with her reckless courage and all her hard sense she should see without argument why she must go.

"You know all the facts," he said. "Nobody has concealed anything from you. You are not young to be having a child for the first time and these are desperately dangerous conditions here. Please, *miláčku*—don't make it worse for us by—by—losing the child. Please go."

He looked at her so piteously with his brown eyes, his despair was so great, that she could not resist any longer.

"All right," she said, beginning to cry. "I'll go."

"My darling," he whispered, covering her with kisses. "*Drahoušku*. I am so proud of you. I love you so much. It won't be long, it's only about six months. And I'll be there once or twice in the meanwhile. Truly I will."

"Those bomber flights—" she sobbed.

"Nothing will happen to me," he said firmly, holding her cheek against his own. "Nothing at all. I am sure of it. You must be too."

Jesus, she thought, I must be sure of that. That's why he wants this child so desperately. Because nothing will happen to him. . . . But she only looked at him and kissed him and said, "One thing I wish. I wish Mama could know about this—about us."

"Mama knows," he said tenderly. "Right in the Pankrác Prison she knows. Dear heart, did you think Mama didn't know?"

CHAPTER XCIII

[*January 1941*]

THE AWFUL TALE, as Mary had expected it would, unrolled slowly and unrolled backwards. A good many weeks passed in the quiet, empty old house with the two of them alone there as they had been at other times in these strange modern years, these new years, Mary thought once, these years in which she had expected to be utterly alone and silent and dedicated to her memories. And instead, the explosive horror of the whole shattered world had walked right in here in the person of Claire, and taken its place with them. You could not keep such a monster shut up, muzzled and bound. Sooner or later it would begin to stretch, to rear its infested head, and to make its hot abominable breath felt whenever words were spoken. Claire could not be expected to make smalltalk when she sat long hours by the fire with Mary. Mary was busy already with the clothes for the coming child. And almost the only thing that could draw a relaxed smile to Claire's tense face was one of Mary's reminders how right here in this very room, in this very chair, she had made every stitch of the clothes for Claire before she was born.

Claire stretched her hands over her head and gazed at the ceiling. "It's always been an unearthly sensation never to have known my mother," she said slowly. "And maybe—"

Mary looked sharply at her, sidelong. This was bad. Claire simply must not have that idea. It was not an obsession by any means. But she seemed to be showing a strange inability to project herself beyond the birth of the child. She did not seem to think of it as the beginning of something, but rather as the ending. Mary saw finally the reason for this. So much of Claire's own world and life were shattered. And such unimaginable trials must be endured, such ferocious battles won, such gruelling problems solved before life could be reconstituted that it was easier when she was tired and defeated to take refuge in the idea of non-survival. Something must soon lift or propel or startle her out of that. Meanwhile her ominous self-imposed silence was lifting. Now when Mary prodded her with a purposely vague or half-shaped question Claire would answer, desultorily at first, later as the weeks went on with some of her old graphic verbal passion.

One evening Mary looked at Claire over her gold-rimmed spectacles, laying down her work and saying, "You know, I don't really understand yet just where Julka is."

Claire stared. She did not realize that she had never made that clear to Mary. It was too hideously, remorselessly vivid to her.

"Mama," Claire said abruptly, "is in the Pankrác Prison. All we know is, the Gestapo considers her in the first rank of political criminals, so you can be sure she is in hell there."

Mary's old eyes were somewhat puzzled. "But—but just what did she *do?*" she asked.

Claire shrugged. "Just—be herself. There was all that past history. And she and strýc František—that's Anton's uncle, the head of the family —had been running a clearing-house to get our boys out of the country and into France so they could join the Army. They knew they were in mortal danger all the time. They didn't give a damn."

Claire paused. "Mama was hell bent Anton should get out like the other boys where he could fight outside. And Anton wouldn't go and leave her there. For a good many weeks, that was . . . until . . ." Claire's mouth puckered as if she could still taste some horrible bitter dose on her tongue. Mary sewed quietly and Claire got up and made herself a drink and came back and sat down by the fire again. That was a promising sign; evidently she felt in a mood to let down and talk.

"It was a perfectly futile deadlock and I was on a spot because I'd promised Mama I'd do all I could to get Anton to go. And go myself, too. I wasn't doing any good in Prague—muzzled by the Gestapo. So one day about six weeks after the invasion Anton came home from the hall and I found him sitting on a chair looking like a corpse. He'd had a fearful shock. After a while he told me what it was." Claire drew a long breath and lit a cigarette and shrugged with tragic cynicism. "Just the same old story," she said. "He'd opened the door of the men's room at the hall and found his best friend there in a mess of blood—he'd cut his throat. He was a swell guy and a fine artist, first 'cellist in the orchestra."

"A Jew, I suppose—"

"Oh, sure. He'd been kicked out by the Nazis the first week and was trying to get over here . . . that was one of those affidavits I got Ted to sign, I wrote you about that. Oh, what's the use of disinterring all the cadavers, Mary. The result was it made Anton get out. I'll never forget how he looked. Sitting there on the edge of that dining-room chair, digging his fingers into my shoulders . . . they were black and blue the next day." Two tears plopped suddenly on the back of Claire's hand and she smeared it across her cheek like a child and said, "Anton is one of those men who can't stand seeing a bird with its wing broken. He can't even hear about cruelty or beastliness, much less see it. He hadn't done any work for months. I'd put away his last manuscript, the Slavonic Saga, it had knocked around the desk until I shrank at the sight of it. He never even missed it. And that afternoon he sat there looking at his closed violin case and I knew he was never going to touch that fiddle again . . . until this thing is over . . . maybe never. All of a sudden he stood up and shouted '*Miláčku*, I am going.' I almost crumpled up with relief. But I didn't dare let him see that on account of all the agony he'd been through making up his mind to leave Mama there. She hadn't been arrested then, you see. I'd never heard him talk that way before. People are awful fools about these gentle, mild men. I think they're tougher when they get sore than the hard-boiled two-fisted kind."

"But—Anton didn't know anything about being a soldier," Mary said. "And how old is he—your age?—"

"Oh, you chuck all that stuff," Claire said. "He saw some kind of a look in my face that day and he said, 'You're worrying about my hands. Forget them. Suppose I ruin my hands? Suppose I lose them—if I'm lucky enough to fight. So what? I can always compose if there's a world fit to live in— and if not, what's the difference? I don't want to live in a barbarian hell. I don't want to die like a rat either. I want to fight.' So he did."

"He would," Mary murmured. "Julka's son."

There was a long silence. Then Mary said, "What did you do then?"

"I promised him I'd stay in Prague and try to do something about Mama. He had some wild notion I might still persuade her to leave or at least protect her from the Gestapo. It was perfectly futile, but if it was going to relieve his mind, of course . . ." She shrugged. "They arrested her two days after he left. They watched everything we did, you see. They were just waiting for him to clear out. They didn't dare do much while he was there . . . they were afraid because he's an American. I was so damned glad he left, Mary."

Claire lay back in her chair and closed her eyes. Mary thought she was tired and about to drop into the half-doze which was the most relaxation she seemed to find these days. But that was not the case. Claire had had a sudden swift memory of that last afternoon at home with Anton. It was strange, she often told herself bitterly, that she could not summon up memories like that entirely at will, precisely when she needed them most. She had to wait for them to come to life, burning and sweeping, of their own accord. Anton had stood there that day, taking her in his arms, and now she heard again his husky voice, his own voice after the angry shouts of the furious man a little while ago.

"I love you, *drahoušku*," he had murmured. "I did not know there was love like this. I did not know I could find a whole world, a great beautiful place that nobody else could touch, just here." He had bent over her, holding her body moulded against the length of his own. "I know it so well, this world," he had said, smiling at her. "My world. I know every inch and every drop, every hair and every pore, every sound you make, every breath you draw." He had moved with her toward their room, talking softly with his lips against her hair. "Here we had ten perfect months and twenty-four perfect days together. Since you came back from America. See? It was not long—so I counted every day of it—every moment of it— until they began to tear at it from outside. They cannot touch it, they will never touch it, but we have to fight for it now."

He had led her to their bed and laid her on it and knelt beside her, whispering, while his beautiful hands slowly took away her clothes. "See," he said, in his husky whisper, "see how beautiful you are!" He had bent his head and with his lips traced the outline of her broad flat hips, her round breasts, the firm curve of her belly. "See how beautiful you are! Who ever had such a world to live in? So much beauty. So much peace."

He saw the slow tears coursing from her closed eyelids down her cheeks and into the pillow. He took them up in his lips and said, "You are thinking of your father, *drahoušku*. You are thinking what he said. I tell you too.

There are some things a man is willing to die for. I will die, if I get the chance, for you. And for Mama. For our country. For our world which is you, and the world we want to live in. You are not afraid to hear that *drahoušku?*"

"I knew it," she breathed.

"Of course. Three hundred and twenty-eight good and beautiful days," he murmured, "out of all our lives."

"We will have more," she said, clasping him despairingly.

"After we have earned them."

"It was so little. We waited so long."

"They will come again, my darling, my love, my heart's blood. They will come."

They had loved in ecstasy, they had loved in joy and tenderness and laughter and pride and passion and in the delicate pain before momentary partings and in the wild magnificence of reunion; but they had never loved in bitter tears before.

The next time Claire felt like talking she said, "It was Dora who told me about Mama being arrested. They took strýc František too, Dora's father. My God, Mary, you ought to have known that girl! What guts she had!"

"Had? Is she—was she—?"

"Oh, sure." Claire's voice was bitter and hard. "But *her* story—that's another chapter in the new history of civilization." She pushed her hair back in the way she did when she wanted to think hard. "Dora came through the back alley and the kitchen stairs at three o'clock in the morning, two days after Anton left. She told me how the whole thing went by regular Nazi clockwork. They'd arranged everything—even to the German families who were to settle on the Dvořák farms in Suchomel . . . where we were married, where they'd all lived since the year one. They kicked out teta Anička—that's Dora's mother—and the younger kids, and they went to Hluboká to take refuge with some relatives there. And the Gestapo took Julka and František that night. Next day they gave the village the business, seized the school for a barracks for the Nazi garrison and—the usual obscenities. I asked Dora why nobody'd bothered her and her cousin Jindřich in Praha at the University and she wouldn't say a word. She just smiled—she was the brightest, most enchanting little thing, Mary. And simply brilliant. Pretty as a doll, too. She just smiled and put a piece of paper in my hand and went out by a different door from where she'd come in. The paper was a note from Mama and all she'd written was 'Remember your promises.'"

Mary sighed. "So you did leave then."

"I should have. I wasted a couple of weeks plaguing the Gestapo and trying to do something about Mama. I was a fool, I've always been haunted for fear I might have made it harder for her. It was—oh—" she shuddered. "Secret interviews in the Petschek Palace with those monsters—perverts—I tried pleading and threats and bribery. It was useless. All it added up to was their coming to our flat at five o'clock one morning, three of them, and giving me until nine to get out of the country."

Flam, acting on one of the unfathomable impulses of his kind, woke up on his table at that moment, uncurled, stretched, and very deliberately stepped over into Claire's lap. His purring was loud in the silent room. Claire's fingers closed suddenly in the masses of his fur. Mary heard her breath catch in a gasp, and again could not know what memory, with agonizing sharpness, had cut back to torture her. She was remembering the evening when she had come in exhausted after a degrading scene with the ruffians at the Petschek Palace. She had opened the front door of the lonely flat and waited for the delicious *priaow* of Fiddle's welcome, and it had not come. Růžena had not been there in the hall to meet her either. She had gone to the kitchen and asked, "Where is Fiddle?"

Růžena did not look at her.

"Where is Fiddle?"

"Ach, Milostivá paní . . ."

There was a long green silence.

"You mean they took him—Fiddle?"

Růžena's face was buried in her apron. "The Blockwart. Said there was no food for animals—"

Claire was on her way out again. "Where did they take him?"

Růžena ran after her, wringing her hands. "Don't make me tell you. Don't go looking for him. *Prosím,* for the love of God, don't make me tell you . . ."

Claire had sat down slowly by the kitchen table. She had clamped her handkerchief over her mouth and mumbled, "I see. You don't need to explain."

"What did you do after you left Prague?" Mary asked.

Claire shrugged. "Worked." This time she was not moved to go into details. It was already a blur in her tired mind. It was not worth the effort to tell Mary about those long dreadful months of waiting for the world to explode. In planes and trains and taxis and smelly horse-drawn hacks, in de luxe hotels and dingy telegraph offices and the detective-story melodrama of railway stations and the secret openness of airports, in the deceitful elegance of ministries and the tense qui-vive of broadcasting stations, she had moved through the mechanics of her work in a state of total personal coma. Sometimes she had roused to the very strange fact that cables from Monroe crackled with praise for her daring and brilliant work; sometimes she had stood blankly reading such a message and saying aloud, "What the hell *for?* What did I do?"

But when Mary said, "What happened to Dora? The girl you were so fond of?" Claire sat up suddenly straight in her chair and leaned toward Mary and said, "I'm not perfectly sure I can tell you that. I mean you might break down before I got through telling you—and I couldn't stand that, Mary. The only thing I can stand is anger. If you'll promise me to be angry—just boiling, blazing, crazy angry—I'll try to tell you." Claire stared at Mary. Mary looked up and said, "I don't think I'd—break down —show anything you couldn't stand, Claire." Her thin lips were tightly set.

"All right," Claire said in a jerky snap. "But don't say I didn't warn you."

So she told Mary the thing that had opened the year of 1940. Anton was stationed down in the Midi at Agde, a few kilometers from Béziers. The Czech Legion was attached to the French Army there under immediate command of its own officers. They had their own encampment where they drilled and trained and boiled with impatience to get into action. And the phony war was dragging on and on. New Czech soldiers kept arriving all the time, slipping in with hair-raising tales of escapes from home through Poland—where a butchery was going on which would dwarf the whole history of atrocity—from Yugoslavia and Turkey and Syria and Jerusalem and Alexandria and Morocco. Some had been all the way across Siberia and around the world, others had shipped on freighters and tankers around the Cape of Good Hope. Every day brought its trickle of recruits. And each man brought new accounts of the terror at home, so horrible that one was almost afraid to let him begin to talk.

On New Year's Eve Claire went down to Béziers from Paris to spend the holiday with Anton. He came over from camp bringing half a dozen friends for dinner. They had eaten goose, and had drunk Chateauneuf du Pape, and were sitting, eight of them, around the crumby table in the Restaurant du Chapon Fin, waiting to see the New Year in, when the door of their private parlor opened quietly and they looked up at a man who stood on the threshold. There was a moment of silence, the suspicious appraising silence always caused by a stranger, and then Claire and Anton leaped from their chairs and rushed across the room. It was Jindřich, Jindřich Dvořák, a skeleton with awful black holes of eyes and a locked look about the mouth and, strangest of all, a bald forehead instead of the thick brown hair that had been there a few months ago. There was no telling what the effect on a man of torture might be.

Claire hung on Jindřich's neck, and Anton brought him over and sat him down and began ordering food for him, and signalling the others not to swamp him with questions, but Jindřich said, "I can't eat. Not a whole meal. Let me have a little bread and a piece of cheese."

They gave him that and later a bowl of hot soup, and later still, several slugs of cognac. They all sat around the table long after the Reveillon bells had rung themselves to silence and the first day of France's last year was dawning pale violet behind the spire of St. Nazaire. Then Jindřich began to talk. The special miracle of his presence here was that the last any of them had heard of him was a rumor that he had been among the martyrs shot in the massacre of students in Prague six weeks ago. But nobody knew many details of this. They sat now uneasily fingering their wine-glasses, both impatient and reluctant for Jindřich's story. He was clearly in a condition where he would either talk about that or keep his numb, stunned silence altogether.

He scarcely moved his mouth when speaking and Claire saw that he had had an injury to his jaw. He said abruptly, "After they tortured Jan Opletal to death—"

"So it really was he," Claire breathed. "The same one? We didn't dare believe it."

"Of course it was. Dora's friend from the Medical Faculty—"

Claire covered her face with her hands. The boy had been in their house countless times. Anton sat with his fists clenched staring at Jindřich. He said, "We heard what they did to you at his funeral."

"And did you hear the rest? What came afterwards?"

The soldiers around the table were all rigid. Now they were going to get the firsthand account of a tale of horrors which for weeks had been trickling through the ineffectual walls of silence.

"It was planned the way they plan everything," Jindřich said in his strange new timbreless voice. "To the last signal. It was total, cold-blooded massacre—only with Nazi refinements. Plain murder is too dull for them. It furnishes no orgasms." He drank a mouthful of water. "They gave the signal with a rocket, precisely at half past three in the morning of November seventeenth. We were all asleep. They knew exactly where every student in Praha lived, who slept in dormitories, who in boardinghouses and hostels and at home. They had surrounded every building and house with guns and tanks and loaded cannons and platoons of armed troops, and of course the specialists of the SS with their whips and truncheons. When the rocket went off they broke down the doors of every house simultaneously. If anybody tried to keep them out they shot them down. There was resistance at the Švehla Foundation so they opened fire and the place was strewn with corpses in pajamas. Some places they simply stamped in and bayonetted the boys right in bed. Those were lucky."

The cold daylight was creeping up outside now and somebody got up and put out the lights and opened the window a little. There was no sound in the room save the scraping of boots as men moved their feet under the table. Jindřich thought for a minute and continued.

"They had buses parked outside the buildings and they dragged the men and girls out, prodding them with bayonets, and drove them into the busses like cattle. Some had pulled on shirts and pants but many were still in pajamas. None of the girls were dressed."

He looked at Claire sharply then as if to estimate how much of this she could endure to hear, but she was sitting perfectly still, staring at his face with dry, distended eyes. He went on talking.

"There were thirty-one busloads," he said.

One of the men leaned forward with a puzzled frown.

"You?" he murmured. "You were there?" He was already putting the question that they would all want to ask time and again during this account. How could Jindřich have escaped if he was among these students?

"I was there," Jindřich said. "Never mind about me. I was in a bus. We were packed in like peas in a sack. They drove the buses to Ruzyň. You know." They all nodded. Ruzyň was the airport of Prague. Some of its fields were surrounded by hangars and others by the barracks of the air force. There was also a cavalry riding-school there.

"They stopped the buses and kicked and dragged everybody out and got to work without delay. They set up a circus in the riding-academy. SS stood in the middle with horsewhips and made the men run around the track hour after hour after hour, whipping them when they collapsed from exhaustion, until finally there were none left conscious any more. But that was fairly humane. While that was going on they had a special collection outside on the field, a lot of men who were marked for particular punishment because they had pictures of Masaryk and Beneš in their rooms. They ripped the pajamas off those chaps and knocked them down with their gunbutts and fists and truncheons and then told them to stand up. Most of them were too badly injured to get up, so they brought them to by throwing pails of cold water on them. It was freezing that night," he said. "But that was still rather humane. There were some fellows who had actually offered resistance when the dormitories were broken into. They had these rounded up by themselves. They tied them together in threes." His thin hands were twisted tight on the edge of the table in front of him. "They gave the signal for a free-for-all. Indiscriminate mutilation. Ears, eyes, noses, tongues, fingernails, toenails—no holds barred. A lot of them were castrated then and there." He ignored the smothered moans and stifled gasps of anguish around the table. He seemed to feel that he had a duty to perform in going through with this, though he himself was putty-colored and they all understood that he had carried this commitment of hell locked in silence with him through the terrors of his escape.

"There are no words to tell you what it sounded like," he said. "The sight will come back all the rest of my life, the eyes popping out, the blood running down the legs, but the sound . . ." he clasped his ears in his hands and rocked for a shocking moment to and fro in his chair . . . "the sound never leaves at all. I never stop hearing it. Do you understand? It never stops. Never for a moment. Asleep or awake. Not the cries and screams. There were not so many of those. Our fellows were tough. But the laughs. The things those offal roared at one another, the names they had in their stink of a language for the things they did. The crack of whips. The sounds of bones breaking . . . teeth grinding. And the laughs. I tell you, the laughs—" he leaned forward. "They had some of their own dirt there— stenographers and clerks sitting in the upper windows of the barracks. At typewriters. Laughing and watching the whole thing. A glorious gladiatorial show, free, for nothing."

Claire looked up and stared at Jindřich and opened her gray lips and with her eyes asked a silent horrible question. Jindřich answered as if she had spoken every word.

"Yes," he said, "they took the girls too." Claire and Anton exchanged a look. "All the girls." He did not have the courage to mention Dora's name. "They pissed into spittoons from the offices and held them up and made the girls—" Claire's hand went to her mouth and Anton shot Jindřich a look of warning. But in a moment Claire said coldly, "Go on."

"They drove up a lot of tanks and made a ring of them on the landing field and tied some of us to the tanks, so we would have to watch. Then they dragged the girls out into the ring of tanks and stripped them naked and knocked them flat on the ground and lined up and raped them. Systematically, understand. Always they do everything with system. So many to a girl. Standing there in line, telling each other it was a cold night for outdoor sport."

"Christ!" It was a scream from Claire. But Jindřich seemed not to notice the interruption. "When the girls passed out," he said in the same nerveless voice, "of course they gave them the icewater restorative. Only some never came to. The little delicate ones."

He nodded gently to the question in Anton's face. Claire's head was buried in her arms on the table now.

"They made a clean sweep," Jindřich said. "They won't do this particular show again because there are no more students to do it to. There are no more students or places to study. But you know all that. You know about the closing of the schools. And what they've been doing to the professors and teachers and doctors and writers and scientists. I guess you know all that." He laughed in a deathly way. "They think they've destroyed all the brains in the country now, or made them powerless. So they'll only have a pack of beasts of burden to drive." He shrugged. "They didn't kill us all," he said indifferently. "They need forced labor in Germany."

Two questions were asked him at the same moment. One came from an older man, an officer who had been around the world in the Anabasis of 1918.

"How did you get here?" he asked in such compelling admiration that Jindřich answered in spite of himself, "I killed an SS despatch rider and took his clothes and papers and motorcycle. He happened to look like me."

His reluctance to talk about himself was so commanding that nobody else dared ask how on earth he had escaped from prison to a place where he had had access to an SS despatch rider or a means of killing him. And Claire had asked her own question at that moment.

"Teta Anička," she said, choking. "Did anybody tell her?"

"Everybody," Jindřich answered. "News travels faster now than before. The underground communications are marvellous."

"But teta Anička—"

Jindřich swallowed. "When she heard about Dora she went out on the street in Hluboká with a meat cleaver and split the skull of the first German she saw. They cut her to ribbons. And plundered the whole town."

There was dead silence in the stuffy French parlor with the empty wine-bottles and the ashtrays full of yellow butts and the haggard men in their bulky uniforms. After a long time Jindřich looked at Anton and said, "I don't know what became of the kids. I guess they're doing forced labor in Germany. They were carted off, anyway."

"Do you," asked Anton in a low murmur, "know anything—new— about Mama? And strýc František?"

Jindřich shook his head and fell into a long silence. Then he looked up and smiled queerly, as if it hurt him to change the rigid expression of his face.

"There are plenty of us," he said in a strange, quietly pleading way to Anton. "Plenty. Aren't there?" He looked around the table at the circle of grim unshaven faces. All the heads nodded and some of the hands made slow unconscious fists.

That was what Claire told Mary, sitting by the fire in the quiet back parlor in the old house in Pittsburgh. All the time that Claire was talking, her voice had been a cold monotone, and her eyes had been rigidly fixed on a certain twist of pattern on the hearth-rug. When she stopped speaking she raised her head slowly and looked at Mary, who had promised to be angry. The old woman was huddled in her chair, with her face buried in her hands.

CHAPTER XCIV

[*Spring 1941*]

CLAIRE HAD FORGOTTEN that people could have the time to be so kind. She had forgotten how many friends she had in Pittsburgh, or more exactly how many friends Uncle Paul had had; gentle, old-fashioned people who emerged from memories of twenty years ago with invitations to their serene dinner-tables and their tranquil Sunday luncheons ranged with grandchildren. She had forgotten that clannish and prejudiced Pittsburgh, which disliked her marriage and largely disapproved of her, would rally round her in trouble when it had kept its distance before. She spoke of this to Charles MacNaughton one evening when she was dining with him and his wife and a few old friends at his beautiful house on Woodland Road.

"Their minds are constricted," he agreed, "but their hearts are big. Only—"

"That's it. They're asleep practically all the time."

"It was like that in England, wasn't it?"

"Precisely. Until—well, for most of that kind—until Dunkirk."

"A lot of them think I'm their kind too," he said slowly. "It doesn't occur to them—"

"I suppose they expected you to finance America First."

"They know differently now. But this is a bad situation, Claire. People are actually asking to have themselves anaesthetized."

He quoted talks he had had in recent months with prominent industrialists and business men. Practically all of them were directly involved in the rearmament program which went by the euphemism of "defense." Here in Pittsburgh there was not a drugstore that did not feel the impact of the accelerated steel production which was the basis of the whole effort galvanized by the catastrophe of France. Yet nobody—neither the corporation executives nor the financial people nor even labor in the mills—would look the truth in the face. Everybody had some other name for war, offensive or defensive. Now the United States had raised the first peacetime conscript army in its history and people went about telling one another that that had nothing to do with what was going on in Europe. Now Congress was locked in a bullheaded struggle over the passage of an act to supply Britain with the sinews of war and, Claire exclaimed, grimacing in perplexity, "How can they take the *time* to gas about it? There *isn't* any time—how are they going to be made to understand that?"

MacNaughton smiled and looked at her with a sort of mock severity. "I should think that might be your job," he said. "You're a journalist. You're supposed to deal in information and opinion."

"That's true," Claire said slowly. "But when you've seen whole civilizations go down in three weeks—or even three days—it's awfully hard to think in terms of waking people up and shaping their opinions. You feel violent. You'd have to feel that way—or be a—a—"

The butler was passing a fine red mountain of roast beef, surrounded with dripping squares of crisp Yorkshire pudding; the maids were following with sauces and gravy and silver dishes full of fragrant fresh vegetables from Florida and California. Claire helped herself in silence and MacNaughton saw her strange cold stare as she did so. He knew exactly what she was thinking. She was thinking of all the places she had been in the past year where the sight of such food in such abundance would have reduced hitherto reasonable men and women to hysteria.

"Yet," she said turning to him, and speaking an instinctive answer to his thoughts, "only a year ago I was lunching in the Maginot Line. With seven courses and four wines and roses all down the table and armfuls for me when I left."

"How is your husband?" MacNaughton asked after a time.

The tension cleared in Claire's face and she smiled a little, saying, "So far, so good. Sometimes I can't believe he's alive and safe after what happened to so many of the others. I just keep hoping our luck will hold. He may be here soon."

"Flying, I suppose—"

"Oh, of course. In a ferry. And going back in a bomber."

"I imagine he's very valuable to them," MacNaughton said slowly. He knew that Anton's work was categorically secret, that Claire must at least pretend that not even she knew exactly what it was. She nodded and said, "It's a fortunate combination of circumstances. His being an American and coming from here—"

"That brother of his is quite a fellow," MacNaughton said. "Now he's the head of the Shop Committee in the mill—of course you know all about that." Claire nodded again. MacNaughton was Chairman of the Board now, having succeeded John Purcell last year when the old gentleman had asked to retire. "It's quite a thought—that this Jerry Liska is your brother-in-law. He certainly never says anything that would remind us of it."

"Oh, he's a real guy," Claire said. "He introduced me to some of their S.W.O.C. officers a few weeks ago." She smiled. "I'm afraid I think they're grand people, Charles. It would be just too bad if we ever tangled with them."

"I'll take that as a warning." He smiled.

Later, after she had played a couple of rubbers of bridge, with a weird sense of anachronism, of having stepped backward into a previous incarnation peopled by Mère Constance and glittering ghosts, she asked MacNaughton over a nightcap what he had heard recently of Ben Nicholas and his activities. MacNaughton smiled wryly. He said, "Didn't you read anything about the No-Foreign-War-Committee? You were in too much trouble at the time, I expect. You couldn't have noticed it. Anyway"—he described the malodorous undertaking and its quick discrediting.

"Prompted, I hope," Claire interrupted, "by a thing or two we learned together awhile back?"

"Decidedly," replied MacNaughton, smiling. "But that's not the end of Ben, my dear. Don't think he can be squashed by a set-back or two. Sometimes he goes underground and sometimes, like right now, he comes out with his colors flying."

"Ah."

"Right out in front. Very busy around the Senate these days and very patriotic with his contributions and speeches."

"How do we go about cramping that?"

MacNaughton glanced involuntarily at her swelling figure.

"I know," she laughed. "I'm *hors de combat* until summer. But we might as well be making plans anyway."

"There's one thing we can start looking into right now," he said. "I've been wanting to talk to you about it."

"What's that?"

"Stepping up output at the mill."

"I thought we were at capacity now."

"We are. But there's nothing to prevent our increasing our capacity. Of course we'll be all snarled up with the government—alphabetical agencies and administrators and the Emergency Facilities Control Board and God knows what kind of tax complications but—"

"We mustn't wait a day," Claire said. "We ought to call a meeting right away. I must be swollen in my wits too. What are we making mostly now?—aircraft alloys?"

MacNaughton nodded. "And projectiles and stuff for A-A guns for England."

"Damn," Claire said softly.

"What's the matter? Aren't you pleased?"

"Pleased! My God! No, I'm swearing because I promised the doctor I wouldn't go down to the mill. I think Mary put him up to it. Anyway I can't go because they say it's bad for me or some such rot. If I could, I'd stand there and put my special personal curse into every drop of steel they pour."

"Do you think your doctor would let you attend a special meeting to discuss increasing our capacity? We wouldn't have to meet at the mill—it could be downtown."

"We'll meet at the mill," Claire said, with a sharp gleam in her eyes, "and I will be there. So will Mary—with bells on."

They laughed and she rose to say her good nights. MacNaughton's man drove her home. Sitting alone in the car, gazing as she loved to do at the blazing riverbanks while the car crossed the bridge, she realized with sudden renewed amazement that she and Mary and Charles almost outrightly owned the mill. What a break, she said half aloud. We're only a tiny little toy of a steel mill, but we can do a hell of a lot of damage. And nobody to hold us up or interfere. The thought of Ted crossed her mind. He did not own enough stock to oppose them, even if he should want to—which Claire doubted anyway. It worried her suddenly that he owned so little stock. There was something pathetic, even tragic about that. It hurt to think about it when she thought at the same time about Uncle Paul.

She spoke about that to Mary, and Mary only looked at her with a stare of mild surprise and said, "Well really, dear, what did you think would become of my stock?"

"Why—I've never thought."

"Isn't it fairly self-evident that I would leave it to Ted?"

"That's—wonderful of you, Mary."

"Wonderful?" In her thin old voice she gave a snort. "You have a strange idea of what's wonderful. I've never considered the stock my property. It was just a sort of trust."

"Have you told Ted?"

"I suppose I thought he'd take it for granted. I don't believe I have mentioned it, now you ask me."

"Well—I think I will. Would you mind, Mary?"

She shook her head. "Not if you have some reason."

Claire had many reasons. She had never forgotten the tragic and secret half hour that she had had with Ted the night before the stockholders' meeting of 1937. It had haunted her ever since, even through the furious pressure of the greater things that had crowded her life. Most of all she had been burdened with a knowledge that Ted existed without anything to believe in. Lauchlan had been his only prop, and what a rotten one!

Claire hoped now to find him as keen on the mill's war output as Uncle Paul had been in 1917; as determined as Charles MacNaughton, or even— though she could hardly hope that—touched by some of Jerry's furious and fanatical intensity. None of that was the case. Ted was apathetic. He had nothing to say against capacity production of airplane steels and special alloys for anti-aircraft weapons; no opposition to plans to enlarge the mill. But he was the member of the board who brought up the gloomy question of postwar absorption of the additional space and facilities, though he did not make a controversial issue of it. For his sake Claire could almost wish he had. She wished he could care that much about anything.

One June evening when he had dropped in, Claire walked out to the driveway with him as he left, and suggested he take her for a breath of air. She was heavy and slow-footed and encumbered, and as the doctor had not permitted her to drive a car for a good many weeks, she had an excuse for asking Ted to take her. Her baby was due any day now. Her things were packed ready for the hospital and Anton's sister Jenny had arranged for a substitute to take over her supervisor's job so that she would be free to take care of Claire.

"Where do you want to go?" Ted asked her, with his slow, rather sad smile, as he helped her into his car.

"I want to go all the way out this side of the river to Blawnox and cross over there and go around through Wilkinsburg to Rankin and Homestead and Munhall and come back down the Monongahela and home by Point Bridge and I want to look at mills and blast furnaces and ovens and Bessemers and smoke and fire and steel and iron the whole damn way. Maybe—" and she was horrified to find her voice choked. Ted turned his head quickly and looked at her. He saw only a tightening of her lips, whose dark carmine stood out against the sudden sallow pallor of her face.

"You all right, Claire?" he asked.

"Oh—yes." She shook her head quickly and the queer sharp stare began to fade from her eyes. She could not let Ted guess what she had almost said, what had nearly forced its way into words from the inner vault where her will power had so long kept it locked. She was scared, she had said last fall to Mary, scared to death; and then she had promised not to think that way any more. But here it had almost burst out in spite of her. Maybe it would be the last time. Maybe it would. Well, so what? she said furiously to herself. Was she going on this ride because she wanted to talk to Ted, or because she was afraid she'd never see the mills at night again? Ted was smiling and shaking his head as he settled beside her in the car. Claire and her enthusiasms! "Still the romantic child," he said, putting the car in gear.

"Oh, no. I just love this place so. I just think it's so tremendous and glorious. If it weren't for something like this to give us courage we'd have to go down under the rock-crusher too."

"You are so damned oratorical, Claire. Why should anybody go and get dramatic about a lot of smokestacks? Sure, it's a spectacle, but so was the World's Fair."

"Ted." She put her hand on his arm and tried to make him feel how serious she was. "Ted. This city and all it means is the last hope of civilization. You may not believe me now, but you will. This thing we're going through is the supreme convulsion of the mechanical age. Nothing will win for us except more machines and greater machines than anybody else can possibly produce. Don't you believe we've got to win this thing, Ted?"

"Well—" he sat watching a traffic light and waiting for it to change. "I'm not too convinced this is America's fight."

Jesus, she thought to herself. There it is. It isn't possible. It can't be true, that they don't see and won't see and don't care and won't care. Yugoslavia last week. Greece next week. Hungary and Bulgaria down the drain. The whole continent of Europe. Hunks of Africa, chunks of Asia. Rotting and dropping and crumbling before them, and they don't see. South America lousy with spies and agents and traitors. The United States—

She talked for a long time, all the way around the blazing, belching, smoking periphery of Pittsburgh, filling her eyes with the only good sight in the world now, the sight of more fire and more streaming scarlet arteries of steel to strengthen the hearts and hands of the good fighters, more blinding rains of sparks and more spreading blood-colored arcs dyeing the night sky red and promising the only hope in all the blackness. "And think of our mill, Ted," she said, her voice tense, as they crossed the Manchester Bridge and saw their own mill, dwarfed beside the giants they had passed, the Henrietta lifting her black old snout in a ring of red to the sky, the sheds scintillating in the flashes of red and blue and white fire through their slanting roofs. "Try to think of it the way I do. Think what it's always been. When I was a little girl during the war and Uncle Paul used to take me down there, or turn me loose up in the attic with the old books and records—why, Ted, do you realize what our mill has been in the history of *liberty?*"

He was silent still, but with a different silence.

"Do you ever think of its record?" Claire went on. "Scott's in the Civil War. Scott's in the Spanish War. Think of Uncle Paul—your own father—making Admiral Dewey's shells. Doesn't it make you proud, Ted? Scott's in the last war. With everything we had. Blood and men and money and time and brains and hearts and—and—everything. It's got to be that way now, Ted. That's our part now, not only us with our funny little mill, but every place we've seen tonight. That's what built this world where people lived in freedom and dignity—and that's the only way it will go on. Oh—Ted, come on in and give it all you've got!"

There was a silence while she stopped for breath and shifted her clumsy body slowly on the leather seat. She was very uncomfortable. Her back was aching badly. Then Ted spoke in a low, strangely naked voice, the tone of voice she had heard only once before, on that secret Sunday night when he had come to her from Lauchlan.

"What," he asked with bitterness, "have I got to give? Why the hell should I care?"

"Oh—Ted." She laid her hand on his arm and felt agonizingly aware of and sorry for the empty thing that was his life. She drew a long breath and told him about Mary's stock, "which is really yours, Ted. Mary feels it always was yours."

And though he was listening to Claire and following what she said, he was remembering his father talking across the grimy desk in his office, telling him about Mary. Mary *is* the family—Mary—more than wife—that's why I want her to have—Ted turned his head slowly and looked at Claire's strained, ill face, into which a new look of anxiety and question and fear had suddenly come. She was sitting forward, biting her lip. He had a notion that she was not listening when he said, "Sometimes I've been an awful damn fool, Claire. Lord, what a fool. But maybe it's not too late to help now."

"No!" she gasped, turning to him. She said, very fast, "It's not too late, Ted. It mustn't be! But there's no time to lose. We've got to get going—get into this—we have so much to do! So much to do!" She thought of Julka suddenly, and of Anton away from her now, and of the whole tortured tragedy of life; and at that moment there was a grind of pain in the small of her back and she said, "Hurry, Ted," and held her breath and clenched her fists.

CHAPTER XCV

[*December 1941*]

MARY STOOD AGAIN on the back stoop, holding her coat tight against the raw wind with her ridged old hands. Through her spectacles her deep gray eyes gazed steadily and thoughtfully down the bleak, wintry yard, past the shabby summerhouse draped in a tangle of leafless vines, past the bare patches of cindery earth where strawberries and peas and cucumbers used to grow long ago. It was not difficult even now to picture Joel, down on his overalled knees potting plants for Clarissa Scott's window-garden. Mary had stood beside him there on her very first day in this house. She could remember his husky brogued voice, trying to make the strange new 'tweenmaid feel at ease; saying, as he held up a gloxinia, "These is pretty whin they bloom." His knotty fingers stroked the furry leaves as if they had been kittens. "And thim things is odd," Mary could vividly hear him saying. "Herself sets a store by 'em. Cal-cee-laries, thim are. Pocketbook flowers." Mary sighed. He had been dead forty years.

The mystery of her own survival held her awed today. Next month she would be eighty-four years old. Time in the immediate sense, in the personal sense, had lost its meaning for her long ago. Parts of her had vanished with the lives she had made her own. She knew now that some part of her had died with William Scott and her brother James, a part with Clarissa, a part with Constance, a part in recent martyrdom with Julka Liska; the great part with Paul. Yet her fragile body and her stout will went on and on; quite calmly she often wondered when they would stop. It amazed her now that she should be alive today, to see the closing of the great circle, the answer to portentous mysteries whose beginnings reached back to the roots of her life and of all those other lives that had been part of hers.

Today was Sunday. Down at the bottom of the hill the dusk was rent by flashes of blue acetylene light scintillating through the panes of the factory roof. They were making parts for planes, Ted had told her when she asked, and there was no cessation of work on Sundays. Their own mill was working at furious capacity today, and so were all the others, the giants and the lesser ones. The smoky winter sky was beginning to redden now as the glow from the angry mills crept up the dark high heavens. Today, the seventh of December, had been another Sunday which Mary in her way had reverently observed as the day had always been observed in this house. If she probed the channels of memory to the earliest years of her life here, Sundays shone down the passages of time as no other days ever could. For on Sundays the life of the Scott family had asserted and reasserted, in fixed ponderous patterns—church and best clothes and roast beef and afternoon naps and pickup supper—the permanence that still survived here. And on Sundays in her girlhood she had gone down, back to her home on the Flat, to see her father and to meet Paul. All the sixty-two years, and she had counted every one of them, since her first trembling Sunday walk with Paul, her life had been illuminated by its memory. Many, many things about her strange life with Paul had vanished in the sweep of years, but Sundays stayed, vivid and meaningful, even when she had observed them in desolate solitude.

She was not living in solitude now, and that too was another amazement. Claire was upstairs at this moment, watching Jenny give Evan his bath, before starting back to Washington where she was working. Mary was used to Claire's flying trips, but it was startling to have a child in the house again, the first child in a fantasy of years; more amazing and unbelievable still, the great-grandchild of Constance and the grandchild of Julka.

Claire had persuaded her sister-in-law to stay at Mary's and take care of Evan, "at least," she said, "until I know where I'll be from week to week, and I can't tell that now. And though Jenny had been wanting for a long time to leave the hospital and go into the Navy as a nurse, she had agreed to postpone that until Claire should be settled. The arrangement suited Mary perfectly. And privately Claire and Jenny had agreed that Mary had grown so frail, and aged so swiftly that it was really out of the question for her to stay alone in that house any longer. Physically she was like a feather which the least breath of wind would sweep away. Sometimes Claire stood watching her from the head of the stairs or the end of the hall, drifting so slowly and lightly and noiselessly wherever she was going; and Claire would turn to the memory of Mary, quick-footed and decisive and busy about the house, bossing the boys and Uncle Paul in her crisp voice so faintly tinged with the echo of a brogue. All that was gone; but even now her mind was sharp and shrewd in judgment, and precisely clear. What an unbelievable person!

Yes, Mary thought, watching the last of the purple dusk go black and the mills blast redder and higher, today the circle has fully closed. This afternoon when they were sitting together in the back parlor after Mrs. Tschuda's vastly simplified version of the old Sunday dinner, Mary knitting and Jenny smoking and Claire fiddling with the radio; when the symphony program was wrenched off the air by the voice with the news of Pearl Harbor and Manila and Cavite, Mary had stiffened in her chair and turned her white head with an extraordinary, dramatic stare, and looked through the parlor door at the wainscot in the hall outside. The wall was blank, but Mary did not see it so. She saw a map there, which Paul had hung; and Dickie standing with his father as Paul named the American warships in Manila Bay that were firing their guns loaded with his projectiles.

"*Manila Bay,*" Mary was murmuring half aloud. "*Cavite.*" What had this to do with Claire's furious intensity, with her feverish, frantic steps as she paced the end of the room, snapping at each word of news like an animal on the alert? Jenny was moving restlessly in her chair, lovingly damning the baby upstairs which had kept her from being out there where she had meant to be. And Mary was thinking of Paul, of the Philippines, of Admiral Dewey, of an evening in the mill when Paul, pausing over his supper, had said, "I tell you, any time this country gets in a scrap it's my scrap and the mill's scrap . . ." The voice grew warmer and stronger in her memory, obliterating the quick staccato from the box on the table. "This mill makes death for anybody that bothers the U. S. A."

Mary had raised her head then, and looked at Claire pacing tensely, and at Jenny with her fists clenched on her starched white lap, Jenny whose mother had been shot a few months ago by the barbarians on the other side of this agonized world; and Mary's old face had crinkled with amazement and bewilderment. She had heard her own thin voice inquiring, "Japs—Japan?" and Claire, her attention on the radio, breathlessly answering, "Yes, Japs for the moment, just for the touch-off—you'll see—"

So the jagged pieces of the giant tragic kaleidoscope had fallen into place today. And so there was another Evan upstairs with the name of the one who had died in an earlier act of this same cosmic tragedy. So too, Mary thought, looking at the scarlet glare in the sky, would Paul have gone into action tonight, just as he had done twenty-four years ago and forty-three years ago; as his grandfather had done in '61 when another war for freedom had started the mill on its destined way.

They would all need courage for the terrible unknowns ahead, Mary was thinking now; but it was good to see what courage they had shown in the months and years behind. It had taken courage for Claire to tell Anton, when he came on the second of two flying missions, that she could not go back to London with him now. There was too much to be done in America, which was the only hope and the last hope of the world. Some men and women in America were trying to tell the resisting others what they must know and must do if barbarism was not permanently to engulf mankind. And those who were trying to awaken America needed help, all the help that experience and skill and eloquence like Claire's could be.

Mary had sat beside Claire's bed in the hospital after Evan's birth and listened to Claire working toward this difficult decision, telling Mary about Julka talking on that tragic morning on the hill above the Vltava. Mary had watched Claire making up her mind that this was "the best place and the best way to fight this fight"—even though that meant her condemning herself to loneliness again; Claire to whom loneliness had been a hounding fate until the pitifully brief perfection of her life in Prague with Anton.

And it had exacted enormous courage from all of them to live through those days last October, after the evening when Claire had come in unexpectedly by plane from New York. Mary had heard a sound at the side door, and had gone to see what it was. She had not dreamed of seeing Claire there, standing with her latchkey in her hand, but not trying to open the door. Mary had been murmuring some unmeaning words of mild surprise when she was stopped suddenly by the rasp in Claire's voice.

"Mary," Claire had said.

The old woman had turned her white head sharply and fixed her eyes on Claire's stony face. She had not missed the catch in Claire's voice. She held the door open but Claire did not step inside, so Mary turned to the hall rack and took a coat and put it around her shoulders and stepped outside. It was a warm night, it had been very warm all last fall. She had put her arm through Claire's and they had walked slowly down the porch to this same back stoop. Mary was thinking that something had happened to Anton. But Claire had drawn a breath and said abruptly, "It's Mama. Julka."

"Yes."

"They've shot her."

Mary had not known that a certain sound would burst from her frail old body, a sound that made Claire's heart stand still. Claire had stood clutching the matchstick of the old woman's upper arm while the strange, weak wail came again from the wisp of a body. Claire did not know this sound. Mary herself had forgotten it. It was the last vestige of a very ancient instinct, the last echo of the mourning cry called keening. Mary did not know that she was doing it. They had stood there while the weak old sounds died away and neither of them was able to weep. A long time had passed. Claire had said finally, "How in the name of Christ can I tell Jerry and Jenny? We at least know what hell on earth is. They—they don't know—yet—"

"Now," Mary had said, in exactly the voice in which she always prayed, "I have known a saint and a martyr."

When Jerry strode into the room where they were waiting that night, more than half aware of what he was to be told, for there had been no mistaking the note in Claire's voice on the telephone, Mary had watched him stand grim for a moment looking at the three women. Then with deliberation he had gone first to Claire and put his hard arms around her and kissed her and said, *"Pánbůh s námi."* Mary had not understood, but Jenny had crossed herself, so Mary did the same. And Claire clung to Jerry in silence. She had not heard him say a word in Czech for over twenty years, and nothing else could so poignantly have brought back the old days, the kitchen in Liverpool Street, with all of them together around the table and Mama telling about the Legions in Russia, and Anton and Claire plugging through the Beethoven Concerto after supper—

And so today with hammer blows the full circle had been closed. Mary had felt that during all the past hours, but most strongly at a moment when she had come upon Claire in the upstairs hall on her way, astonishingly, to the attic. There was a wild, rapt look on Claire's face, and Mary heard her murmuring to herself in a rhythmical whisper like somebody praying. Mary stood in a corner and watched Claire and wondered why she was going to the attic and what she could be talking to herself about; for that was unlike her. Claire was going up, by some strange impulse, to the shelves in the attic where the old records of the family and the mill were stored. She had spent endless hours of her childhood among them, and she wanted now to touch and open them again, to tie this day into the sweep of history. And she was saying to herself, with the rare, blind, fervent fanaticism of the irreligious, "Oh, God, you did know the way to help us . . . You did find the way . . . a brutal, endless, suffering way, but you knew America would save itself and save us all . . . It will be frightful . . . it will be long . . . we may never see the end . . . but we know what the end will be. Daddy knew. Mama Julka knew . . . Now we are fighting all together, now they haven't died in vain, none of them—anywhere—all the way back to Daddy . . . because it was the same war then, it will be the same war all the time until the last beast is blasted from the earth . . ."

On Thursday of that week Mary switched off the radio. She and Jenny had just listened for the second time to the solemn drama of the United States Congress declaring war on its enemies. Claire was back in Washington, but not even she, in her seat in the press gallery of the Chamber, had been more enthralled than the old woman to whom this weird instrument, the radio, was still an incomprehensible miracle. Jenny went upstairs to Evan in the nursery and Mary put on her coat and walked slowly down the porch again for her daily breath of the metallic air she loved. Once more she stood alone on the back stoop, gazing down the barren slope which could be so green and so crowded in her memory. There in the summerhouse poor tragic Louise used to sit, complaining and whining—with awful justice, Mary sometimes thought. That had been a bitter fate for a woman. There in the stable Jones used to curry the horses and polish the harness. And far off, down at river level where that new factory was crackling with light, there were other factories, and furnaces and forges and mills; and Paul's mill was just around the bend of the Ohio. The purple twilight sky was dyed in splashes and strokes of scarlet light from those mills along the river. And all throughout the region, over in the tar distance where the Monongahela wound its dour way, the biggest mills of all poured their red smoke and fire into the vast darkening sky, the mills where the red steel for war was streaming out in blazing floods, as it had streamed in Pittsburgh for America at war before.

Dear Paul, Mary thought. She thought of him so clearly and tangibly, thought without flinching that it was precisely twenty-three years and one month ago today that he had died in her arms, with the bells and whistles and sirens for the Armistice shrieking outside. How he had fought that first part of this same struggle, how he had loved his country and how freely he had given his sons and himself and all he had and was; and what an heritage he had left! She thought of the mill, now one white-hot, blinding-red weapon for victory, of her brother and of Paul's father, of the hearts and brains and wills that had fused together to make the mill a fighting sinew of America. "This mill makes death," Paul had said; but it had made life too. There was no life without death, as Mary knew so very well. She thought then of Julka and of Charlie and of the work of hands and brains and bodies which these humble magnificent souls had brought to achievement; of the enormous scene over which the fruit of their lives had spread. She thought of Clarissa Scott, the strong and gentle friend whose love had upheld her. She thought of Constance, wild and passionate and loyal, with all her grandeur so strangely transmuted in Claire. She thought of loves and hates, the living and the dead, the strong and the weak, of birth and death and flood and fire and trial and faith and man and God. She thought of the strange great forces which would always in the end stir all good to battle with all evil, and she thought of America today drawing the last grim line in the rallying of the forces. She thought of the child upstairs with its commingled bloods from the roots she had cherished all her life. She thought of a frightened girl in a gray stuff dress knocking at a kitchen door; and presently she turned and opened the door and went inside to put the kettle on for tea.